THE
DRAGONS
OF
DEEPWOOD
FEN

THE DRAGONS OF DEEPWOOD FEN

THE BOOK OF THE HOLT: PART ONE

BRADLEY P. BEAULIEU

DAW BOOKS
New York

Jacket illustration by Kekai Kotaki
Jacket design by Adam Auerbach
Map by Bradley P. Beaulieu
DAW Book Collectors No. 1954

DAW Books
An imprint of Astra Publishing House
dawbooks.com
DAW Books and its logo are registered trademarks of Astra Publishing House

Printed in the United States of America

ISBN 978-0-7564-1812-0 (hardcover) | ISBN 978-0-7564-1813-7 (ebook)

First edition: December 2023
10 9 8 7 6 5 4 3 2 1

dedication TK

The Wanderi

Gulf of Beltayne

Gehrost

The Scarring

⊙Beltayne

The Fire Plains

Yndevaru

Nikkodemes

Tragos

The Devouring Deep

teppes

⊙ *Kataar*

Ilyndra

Olencia

Praecia

Brevin

Andalingr
The Vagabond

Lyros

Deepwood Fens

The Diamondflow

aldoras   ⊙ *Glaeyand*   *Skjalgard*

The Holt

Gorminion

The Cut

Ancris

Hrindegaard

Erimaea

Sea of Olgasus

Olgasus

⊙ *Altrimir*

Syrdonos   *Syrdia*   *Bragga*
⊙

The Lost Emeralds

| 0 | 150 | 300 | 450 | 600 |

Miles

PROLOGUE

Deep in the Holt, Korvus Julianus and his guide, Temerin, strode over the uneven ground of the forest. Korvus's mood was light, the alchemycal survey he and Temerin had begun two weeks earlier nearly complete. If all went well, he would finish his measurements before the day was done and either confirm his suspicions that a rare sinkhole was about to form or prove them false.

Citadel trees soared a thousand feet into the air as far as the eye could see. Their bark was rough, their branches stubby. Bridgeboughs spanned the gaps between them, one tree supporting the next supporting the next. The bright sun had risen and the sky was clear, but it was early yet, and the light in the forest was dim.

Though well into springtime, a cold snap had arrived two days earlier and had yet to recede. Korvus crunched over frost-covered pine needles and the occasional patch of snow. Temerin followed a few paces behind him as they made for a shallow ridge, where they took a moment to catch their breath.

Temerin leaned on his unstrung bow, his breath pluming, and scanned the land around them. "Haven't we come far enough?"

Master Korvus blew into his hands. "Nearly so, Temerin. Nearly so." He adjusted the weight of his oilskin pack and continued on. Temerin fell in beside him.

The guide had curly brown hair, dark skin, broad cheeks, and ivory eyes, which were part and parcel of his profession. He was tall for a Kin, and willowy from all his rangings. A rapier hung from his belt. A quiver was strapped to his opposite leg. "It's only, I'd like to get back to Glaeyand tonight."

"As would I, but there's no rushing these things."

"I know, but we've walked farther than we did from the *last* vyrd."

"That's because the vyrd you just brought us to is stronger. You should know that. You're a ferryman."

Vyrda were henges, circles of standing stones that marked places of power, and there were many throughout the Holt. Ferrymen like Temerin knew how to unlock their power and use it to travel from place to place via the maze, which was why Temerin was accompanying Master Korvus on his survey, and why Korvus was certain the young man knew the vyrd they'd just visited was more powerful than the one before it. He was only being impatient, an affliction men of his age seemed happy to wear as a badge of honor.

They weren't far from the Deepwood Fens, which was Red Knife territory. The Red Knives were the remnants of the people who once controlled the Holt, and a brutal lot. They considered themselves freedom fighters who hoped to liberate the Holt from the empire, its ruling quintarchs, and, above all, the Holt's imperator, who they considered a pawn. This close to the Fens, the likelihood of a Knife flying one of their dragons overhead and spotting them was still remote, but it had risen considerably.

Korvus and Temerin hiked another mile through the forest. The bright sun rose higher and warmed the air. Ahead, midges hovered over a glade of high grasses; swallows swooped down on them, feeding on the wing.

Korvus unslung his alchemyst's pack and leaned it against the twisted root of a citadel tree. "This is far enough, I reckon."

Temerin nodded, strung his bow, and began his scout of the area.

Korvus crouched, tugged his pack open, and carefully retrieved his aurimeter. With a wooden base, an etched steel plate pitted with age, and a needle that rose up from the base's hollow interior, the aurimeter looked vaguely like a metronome, but the alchemycal instrument had a much different purpose. The weight at the needle's bottom was made of brightsteel, a metal infused with ground dragon scales, likely from an iron, but possibly a brass or a silver. The brightsteel weight, calibrated springs, and etched plate formed a gauge that allowed him to measure the flow of aura, one of two primary sources of arcane power.

Korvus set the aurimeter on a patch of level ground and used a compass to ensure it was measuring the flow due north. Then, he drew his leatherbound journal from the pack's front pocket, laid it on the ground before him, and jotted down the aurimeter's measurement with a freshly sharpened pencil. He turned the instrument clockwise one point on the compass rose, noted the new measurement, and repeated the process, turning and measuring, turning and measuring, until he'd completed a full rotation.

He pulled an umbrimeter from his pack. Similar to the aurimeter, it measured the flow of umbra, the second of the two sources of arcane power. Its weight was darksteel, a metal infused with the ground scales of an umbral dragon—a viridian, perhaps, or maybe a cobalt. He repeated the turning and measuring, and recorded the values.

Aura and umbra infused everything, from plants to animals to the earth itself. During the day, the bright sun, Lux, shed aura upon the world. At night, Lux gave way to the dark sun, Nox, to shed umbra. Living things absorbed both, but there was much more aura and umbra than they could fully absorb. While aura tended to rise and collect in places like hills, cliffs, and mountains, umbra tended to sink and pool in places like swamps, lakes, and fens.

It was also true that these foundational principles of alchemy were unpredictable. Aura and umbra eddied like currents in a river delta, which meant Korvus couldn't rely on a single measurement in case the instruments were merely measuring an eddy in the flow. He needed several measurements to ensure he was measuring the predominant flows. So it was that Korvus repeated the process with both instruments an hour later.

Temerin returned shortly thereafter, holding a rabbit he'd struck through with an arrow. He dressed it, built a fire, and roasted it for their lunch. By then it was nearing high sun, and time to check the instruments for the third and final time.

"Time to head back?" Temerin asked when he was done.

"Not just yet."

Satisfied that his measurements were accurate, Korvus flipped through the journal to a map of the Holt, precisely drawn by his own hand. Near the center of the forest was his home, the tree city of Glaeyand. The Whitefell Mountains bordered the forest in a grand arc to the west. The Sea of Olgasus lay east. In between was the vast Holt, broken here and there by prairies, lakes, gullies, and the occasional mountain or ravine. Its most notable feature was the Diamondflow, the largest of the three rivers that cut east through the Holt on their way to the sea.

North and east of Glaeyand, red dots marked the vyrda he and Temerin had traveled to in the past two weeks. Near each were a pair of hand-drawn arrows: white to indicate the direction of the flow of aura, black to indicate the flow of umbra. Taking them all in, it was clear aura was flowing more or less west, toward the mountains, which was as it should be. Umbra, however, was flowing neatly toward a position east of them, a good way into the Deepwood Fens. In contrast, the surveys he'd conducted more than a decade ago showed umbra from those same vyrda being drawn toward the *Diamondflow*. The only reasonable explanation was that a sinkhole was about to form. It happened from time to time when umbra collected in sufficient quantities to attract even more umbra from the surrounding lands until the earth gave way to its power, causing broad swaths of land to sink all at once.

Taking in the magnitude of it, Korvus found himself smiling, then grinning broadly. He'd suspected, even hoped, he might find a sinkhole, but to have it confirmed . . . to be on the cusp of *witnessing* it . . . made the long treks, the weeks away from home, the sick feeling in his gut from traveling by vyrd, and the trail rations in place of his wife's cooking all feel worth it.

Korvus tapped the arrows on the map. "Remember the sinkhole I mentioned?"

Temerin sat cross-legged near the fire, poking the embers with a stick, and took a cursory glance at the journal.

"It's forming to the east of us," Korvus went on. "I suspect it won't be long before it's triggered."

Temerin said nothing.

"I want to go there, take more measurements."

Temerin's grimace might have been amusing were Korvus not so serious. "*More measurements?*"

"It would delay us a day at the most. I'll gladly pay you for it."

"You've extended our trip three time already."

"I *warned* you that might happen." The flows had been unpredictable at three of the vyrda. Korvus had insisted on remaining overnight to ensure his measurements were accurate.

"I want to go *home*, Master Korvus."

"As do I, Temerin, but this discovery could lead to *more* expeditions. I'll ask for you personally. Or if you prefer, I'll ask that you *not* be considered. Just come with me now. Finding a sinkhole could mean a considerable grant from the imperator."

Temerin drew in a deep breath, regarded Korvus with ivory eyes, then let the breath out in a noisy rush. "I don't want to *not* be considered. I'm grateful for the work. Truly. But my wife . . . she's expected to go into labor soon."

"You'll see that pretty wife of yours soon, I promise." Korvus patted Temerin's shin. "And I'll pay for a dinner for the two of you at The Hog's Head. Assuming she hasn't gone into labor yet. Later, if she has."

Temerin paused. With a hint of a smile, he said, "Make it The Twisted Fork and you have a deal."

"Done!"

Temerin laughed, stood, and did a double take at the map in Korvus's journal. His smile faded. "You want to go to the Deepwood Fens . . ."

"I do."

"That's Red Knife territory."

"Yes, but nowhere near their hideouts."

"Word is they were forced to move south."

"Their old hideout was four hundred miles away. Why would they move it so far?"

"I should think to avoid being discovered *again*."

"Come now, Temerin. The chances are infinitesimal they'll be anywhere near where I mean to visit. Besides, it won't take long. If my measurements are correct, the location is a mere stone's throw from the vyrd. We'll be there and gone faster than you can fletch an arrow. I promise."

Temerin pursed his lips and shook his head, but the man was no wilting flower. "We take *one* set of measurements, and we return to Glaeyand as soon as you're done. No complaining about eddies. No writing endless passages in your journal."

"Well, I do need to take *some* notes."

"Of course, but the minor details can be fleshed out *after* we return to Glaeyand."

"Fair enough." Korvus packed his things into his pack. "Thank you, Temerin. You've been a valuable asset this entire journey."

With a verve Korvus hadn't felt earlier, he hiked with Temerin toward the vyrd. To study a sinkhole as it formed would be a wondrous achievement, the capstone of his long and accomplished career. He was all but certain the imperator would authorize an expedition to record it.

As they retraced their steps through the forest, the wind picked up and the citadels groaned. By the time they spotted the vyrd through the trees ahead, the bright sun was lowering in the west, all but hidden by the citadels' thick canopy. The vyrd's standing stones were tall, round-shouldered, weatherbeaten. The runes on their faces were worn by centuries of rain, snow, and wind. The broad slabs set into the ground between them were covered in thick green moss, all but indistinguishable from the land outside the vyrd.

They positioned themselves at the vyrd's center. Temerin opened a small pouch at his belt and pulled out a lucerta, a silvery-blue dragon scale, and placed it on his tongue. Despite all the advancements in alchemy, they still didn't know why using lucertae to navigate the maze leeched color from one's eyes, but it did. And while most ferrymen needed to wait until the bright sun set or rose—the two times when the vyrda were most active—Temerin was gifted. He could enter the maze several hours before or after the normal times. It was half the reason Korvus had pulled in a favor to have him assigned to the survey.

Temerin closed his eyes and spread his arms. A breath passed, then two. Korvus's guts suddenly felt like they were being drawn through his bellybutton and twisted on a spit. A brief whistle sounded, and they entered the maze.

Korvus blinked. Suddenly, they were in another place entirely. The air was markedly warmer and fetid. The standing stones around them were shorter and more ancient, their runes all but lost to the passage of time. Beyond the vyrd, the vegetation was thicker, and the citadels were spaced farther apart, likely due to the alkaline soil.

Korvus took out his compass and scanned the landscape. "This way."

They headed north, and the stench grew stronger. They came across a deer path and followed it, and the noisome odor grew stronger still. The citadels stood farther and farther apart, and the landscape became more open.

"How much longer?" Temerin asked.

"If my measurements are correct, we're nearly there."

They came to a vast fen, with ponds of still water dotting the terrain. It was nearly treeless, but to their right, a series of tall black pillars stood like palisade stakes.

"Faedryn's wicked grin," Temerin breathed, "what is that?"

"Don't blaspheme." Korvus held two fingers up and moved them in a circle, the sign of Alra. "Not here."

Temerin made the prayer to Alra as well. "Well, what *are* they?"

Korvus counted the glittering black pillars as he trudged toward them. There were seventeen in all. "I've no idea."

Temerin followed, stringing his bow as he stepped through the long grass.

Korvus's first thought was that they'd stumbled on an ancient artifact, something left over from the days when Faedryn walked the earth. But an age had passed since the Ruining, and the pillars looked new. Their edges were sharp; there was no lichen on their glittering black surfaces. As they approached the pillars, a faint curtain appeared between them. Squinting, Korvus saw the curtain curve toward a central point above the pillars. A great dome glittered faintly over the fen.

When he reached the closest pillar, Korvus unslung his pack, set it on a tuft of wiry grass, and threw back the flap. He'd no more reached inside than Temerin said, "Master Korvus?"

Korvus looked up to find Temerin staring at the sky. A pair of dragons soared above the citadels and glided down toward them. One was a cobalt, vivid blue with streaks of midnight running through its wings. The other was an amber, its scales the color of honey. They were umbrals, nocturnal creatures that woke when the dark sun rose and hunted through the night. The taming and bonding of such creatures had been outlawed since the end of the Talon Wars. With very few exceptions, only the Red Knives used them now, and both dragons had riders.

The dragons alighted on a nearby hillock and folded their wings. Korvus glanced at Temerin and saw he had an arrow nocked. "Put that *away!* And for the love of the goddess, unstring your bow!"

Temerin looked like he might argue, but he complied.

By then the riders had slid down their dragons' shoulders to the ground. The amber dragon's rider was Raef, one of the highest ranking members of the Red Knives, a Kin man with dark skin, down-turned eyes, and intricately braided red hair. His left arm ended in a stump wrapped in studded leather. The man beside him was surely Llorn, the Red Knives' cruel enforcer, also called "the Butcher." He had dark skin as well and long black hair, bound into a tail. His cheeks and forehead were covered with blotchy sun marks. Sun marks were a common enough thing in the Deepwood. The sheer number on Llorn's face—as if he defied every-*one* and every*thing*, even the dark sun—was not.

Llorn approached Korvus and Temerin. Raef drew his longsword with his good hand and followed. Both men stopped several paces away.

"Who are you?" Llorn asked.

"My name is Korvus Julianus," Korvus said quickly. "I'm a master alchemyst, and this is my ferryman, Temerin. We've come on a surveying mission."

Llorn looked from Korvus to Temerin and back. "A surveying mission."

"Yes. To study the flow of aura and umbra through the forest."

"And who sent you on this survey?"

It wasn't lost on Korvus that the question was a way of asking who might come looking for them if they turned up missing. But it left him an opening. "Marstan Lyndenfell, the imperator himself. He gave us a sizable grant as well."

Llorn spoke slowly, deliberately. "Marstan Lyndenfell . . ."

Korvus nodded. While Marstan, the imperator, was a nominal enemy of the Red Knives, it was said he held some sway with Llorn's brother and liege, Aarik, the man they called King of the Wood. Surely, knowledge of Lyndenfell's involvement would prevent Llorn from doing anything rash. Surely, the punishment for trespassing on Red Knife territory would go no further than their being ransomed back to Glaeyand. The men might even set them free with a mere warning.

Llorn pointed at the pillars. "Does Marstan know about these?"

Korvus paused. If he lied and told Llorn that Marstan knew, it might enrage him. But telling the truth—that Marstan knew nothing about them—felt like a death sentence. "Of course he does. How else would we have known where to go?"

"So, to survey the crucible, your benefactor, Marstan Lyndenfell, sent an alchemyst"—Llorn looked at Temerin again, longer this time—"and a ferryman deep into our lands with no additional protection?"

Korvus's heart was beating so fast it felt like a herd of elk passing through his chest. He knew the lie he'd just told could easily spin out of his control, but what choice did he have now? "That's right."

Llorn's cobalt dragon issued a rolling growl. Beside it, the amber craned its neck, making its barbs rattle like a spill of bones. Korvus knew little of the bonds men like these had with their dragons, but he knew enough to know that the dragons' reactions were likely echoes of their bondmates' feelings.

Llorn smiled. "I think not, Master Korvus." He tilted his head at Raef and unsheathed his longsword.

Raef gripped his sword and stalked toward Temerin.

Temerin stepped back. "No, please! I have a wife! Our child's birth is only days away!"

Knowing what was coming, Korvus focused on Llorn—only Llorn, but from the corner of his eye he saw Temerin try to draw his rapier. Raef swung his sword in a horizontal arc and sliced through Temerin's neck. The guide collapsed to the ground, gurgled, and lay still.

The cobalt dragon crept forward, flicking its massive tongue at Temerin's bloody corpse, but Llorn raised a hand, and it backed away.

Raef wiped his sword on Temerin's cloak, sheathed it, and walked back toward his dragon.

Korvus pointed to the pillars behind him. "Tell me what it is, at least?"

Llorn stared at the gleaming black pillars. "I'll tell you this much. One day, great power will flow from the crucible. When it does, control over my people's destiny will be returned to us, once and for all."

Korvus shook his head. "I don't understand."

Llorn raised his sword. "Then pray your wisp quickens before that day comes, so you can witness it from your second life." He jammed his sword into Korvus's chest, twisted the blade, and jerked it out. Pain speared through Korvus, and he collapsed to the earth. He raked the wiry grass with his fingers; blood bubbled across his chest, warm and slick beneath his shirt. His vision filled with stars, and a high-pitched ringing filled his ears.

Korvus knew he should pray to Alra for mercy, but he couldn't. He was too riveted by the black pillars. He stared at them—at the curtain that flowed between them and the dome they created above the fen—and wondered at their purpose.

ONE: RYLAN

Rylan Holbrooke fit his dragonskin mask over the lower half of his face, pulled his hood down over his forehead, then padded along the gully in a half-crouch, scanning the forest of citadel trees and the occasional oak and poplar for imperial patrolmen. The scent of a campfire was strong and growing stronger.

Though the birdsong and the noise from the camp were loud enough to cover his approach, Rylan took care to make no sound as he climbed the edge of the gully and hid behind a stand of lilac bushes. Through the branches, he spied a contibernium, a tent group of eight legionaries. Three of the soldiers were gathered around the fire. One was a senior officer, a husky centurion in his late thirties. He sat on the ground, back against a fallen yew, legs stretched toward the fire. His helm and chest armor, brightsteel lorica segmentata, lay on the grass beside him. His dark hair was cut so close to the scalp Rylan could see the scar running up his forehead and over the crown of his head. He had a smug look about him—natural for a centurion, Rylan supposed, but it made him all the more eager to take back the jewelry he'd stolen from a hapless caravan.

The officer sitting cross-legged beyond husky centurion was rangy man of a similar age with lank brown hair, deep-set eyes, and a bent nose. The badge on his scale mail, lorica squamatae as they called it, marked him as a surgeon, but he likely doubled as the contibernium's second-in-command. He was stripping bark from a freshly cut sapling with a hunting knife, likely carving a crossbow bolt to add to the quiver leaning against the trunk next to him.

The soldier kneeling beside the fire, roasting a pair of pheasants on a spit, was barely a man at all. He had bright orange hair, freckles, and saucers for ears. Nestled in the fire was a wide-bellied pot. Steam puffed out from under the lid, scenting the air with garlic and rosemary.

The centurion was regaling the other two men with a tale of his winnings at a gambling den in Glaeyand. "The final game of the night, it was down to me, a fat miller, and his son. We reached the last trick. Whoever took it would win the pot. I threw down a tower. The miller, fucked, tossed the river. And what did that beshitted son of the sawdust collector do but throw down the mountain and screw me?" The centurion chuckled and scratched his chin. "I could've sworn it'd been played seven tricks earlier."

"Might your lack of perfect recall"—the surgeon sent a shaving of wood flying through the air—"not be explained by the fact that you were deep into your fifth flagon?"

The centurion barked a laugh. "Fifth? I can still stand on my hands and whistle an ode after five! The kid was cheating."

Rylan shifted to get a better view beyond the fire. Two more soldiers were pounding stakes and righting a large canvas tent. Near the tent were eight saddles and two pack harnesses, any one of which might hold the overly burdensome fines Rylan had come to retrieve. Beyond the tent, the Salt Road, the ancient trading route from Glaeyand to Gorminion, the port city at the mouth of the Diamond-flow, was deeply rutted. On its far side, three more legionaries were tending to the horses in a clearing. With all eight soldiers accounted for, Rylan breathed a bit easier. The last thing he needed was a legionary stumbling upon him before he could make his move.

"Hold on," the surgeon said, "you said you won, but if the miller's son played the mountain . . ."

The centurion leaned toward the young, saucer-eared soldier and said in a hushed tones, "Never let it be said Two Step isn't the sharpest spear in the sheaf, eh, Balish?" The centurion regarded the surgeon. "I never said I won the *game*. I said I won the *pot*."

The surgeon went back to whittling his crossbow bolt. "*Stole* the pot, you mean."

"Stole . . . Won . . ." The centurion shrugged. "Any day I enter a den with forty stags and leave with two hundred is a good day to my mind."

"I merely want it known," the surgeon called over one shoulder, practically shouting to the other legionaries, "that you are a thief, a ruffian, and a no-good liar."

Chuckling, the centurion interlaced his fingers behind his head and shifted against the tree trunk. "Show me a legionary who isn't."

The surgeon pointed his knife at the young legionary. "What about Balish here?"

"Balish is a bloody recruit, barely out of his nappies."

They laughed heartily as Balish's ears turned bright red.

Rylan had known the sort of men he'd be dealing with from the moment Hollis had described their shake down of the caravan. They felt entitled to the things they took, the centurion especially. It would be a pleasure to see the scales of justice righted, even if only for a few stags.

With the tent nearly pitched and the horses staked and blanketed, it was time to send his dragon into the fray, but Rylan paused, feeling watched. He stared through the trees around him, gazed at the bridgeboughs above. High overhead, on a branch near the canopy, he thought he saw a shape, someone squatting among the green needles, perhaps, but he couldn't be sure. He waited for the shape to move. When it didn't, he reckoned it was just his imagination.

Focusing on the forest beyond the camp, he took a deep breath and released it slowly. The bond he shared with his viridian dragon, Vedron, brightened in his mind. She was two miles away, resting on the broken limb of a citadel tree above the pond where Rylan had unsaddled her in preparation for their heist.

Go, Rylan urged her, *now.*

Rylan felt a brief flash of vertigo as Vedron dropped from the limb. He felt her spread her wings and soar through the forest, felt the rush of air over her sleek back, her legs held tight to her body. Vedron's giddiness echoed Rylan's edginess as they prepared to take action.

Three days ago, the same patrol of legionaries had stopped a Kin trading caravan heading toward Glaeyand on the Salt Road. They'd searched the wagons, which was perfectly within their rights, but when they found a tiny bag of contraband— a rheumatism medicine made from ground dragon barbs—the centurion had used it as an excuse to fine every trader in the caravan. The caravan master lost not only his medicine, but his signet ring purchased years ago at great cost, which granted him and all who traveled with him favorable rates at the great auction houses of Gorminion and a discount on tariffs as well. The ring was immensely valuable.

The traders had argued the fines were too steep, but the centurion had taken it in his stride, telling them that if they were so displeased with the fines, they could register a complaint with the trade board in Glaeyand. The centurion and the traders knew that the chances of the board bringing formal charges against the patrol were slim. And even if they did, the traders would need to admit to the contraband. They'd decided the risk of their master being sentenced to months of quarry work in some distant corner of the empire wasn't worth it—he'd likely die before his sentence was up. They'd paid the centurion's fines, but given that all their coins had been leveraged to buy goods in Gorminion, they'd done so in precious jewelry.

On reaching Glaeyand, they'd discussed the incident with Rylan's friend Hollis. Hollis, among other things, traded in antiques, a common item on caravans, and knew the caravan master well. He also acted as a middle man for missions that resulted in, as he put it, "a fairer distribution of wealth in the Holt." Knowing the sorts of capers Rylan liked to take on, Hollis had told him about it the following day: collectively, the caravan were offering a reward for the signet ring's return. Rylan had hardly waited a beat before accepting.

When Saucer-ears signaled that their dinner was ready, the legionaries began to wander back toward the fire. The only other sound besides their conversation was the intermittent rattle of a woodpecker, which ceased when a long, blaring note sounded in the distance. The long blare sounded again, then rose in pitch, ending in five staccato notes.

The horses nickered, a few tugged at their reins, which were tied to iron stakes. Every last legionary, from the centurion down to young Balish, stopped what they were doing and peered into the forest.

Beyond the clearing, Vedron swooped down through the citadels. Her extended wings were teal with a veins of forest green. Her eyes were vivid emerald in the shadows of the trees. Two curving horns swept back from the ridge bones above her eyes. Measuring five horses from nose to tail, Vedron was hardly the largest dragon in the Holt, but the acid she breathed could melt a man's flesh from his bones, and the legionaries knew it. They scrambled for their crossbows, and their horses tugged on their reins, stomped their hooves, reared, and whinnied.

"Secure the horses!" the centurion bellowed, even as a dappled stallion broke free.

A roan mare bolted after the stallion. Three more horses scattered in opposite directions. Black earth sprayed up as the stakes holding them in place were torn free.

Vedron swept across the road, raising needles from the forest floor in her wake, and shrieked, a raucous, high-pitched noise that made Rylan's sternum itch. Worried Vedron would chase the wrong horse, he focused his attention on the dappled stallion heading away from the camp. As they'd practiced, using elk instead of horses, Vedron veered, followed the stallion, and slowed so as not to overtake it too quickly.

By then the legionaries had several crossbows loaded. The tips of the bolts were coated in black coryza, a poison made from the venom of the yellow-backed wyvern. If a bolt managed to pierce Vedron's scales, it could kill her, but they'd practiced for this as well. Before the legionaries could so much as lift their cross-bows to their shoulders, Rylan sent a warning to Vedron, and she bent around the trunk of a citadel and disappeared.

The legionaries stared into the trees until the centurion shouted, "Well, get a fucking move on!" Then he loped toward the nearest horse.

The legionaries left the camp in a loose group. When they were far enough away, Rylan crept from his position and headed for the two pack harnesses. Rifling through one bag, he found dried meat, hardtack, spices. The other was filled with bags of oats for the horses. He eventually found the caravan master's rheumatism medicine and the jewelry box in the bags of the second saddle he searched. Why the centurion hadn't sold them in Glaeyand, Rylan wasn't sure—perhaps to avoid proof surfacing of just how much he'd taken from them. He must have been planning to sell them in Gorminion, far from the watchful eye of the imperial inquisitors.

Still, the caravan master's signet ring was missing. It stood to reason that if the centurion hadn't sold the other effects, he wouldn't have sold the ring, either. The centurion hadn't been wearing it, but he might have had it on his person, perhaps on a necklace or in his pocket. Banishing the thoughts, Rylan kept digging. There were sealed letters, imperial communications destined for Gorminion or beyond, a battered dulcimer, and a bag of dice. At the very bottom of the bag, he found a heavy chest, likely filled with money imperial patrols were allotted for daily needs. He deliberated taking it, but it was simply too heavy and would jangle if he tried to run.

"Find cover!" a legionary called in the distance. "It's swingin' around!"

The legionaries had managed to corral three of the horses, but they were so busy tracking Vedron's movements they paid the camp no mind.

Rylan hefted the chest and set it on the ground before him. He ducked low as the young legionary, Balish, fought with one of the horses, drawing it toward the clearing. From the hollow in his right boot heel, Rylan retrieved his lock picks. He slipped the picks into the lock, worked the tumblers. In the short span it took Balish to calm the mare, Rylan picked the lock and opened the chest lid. There was money inside, but not as much as he'd expected, and no signet ring. He might take the coins in recompense, but the total was well short of what it would cost to replace the ring.

Vedron roared and swept through the trees well beyond the reach of the patrol's crossbows.

Rylan knew the caravan would be grateful for *anything* he brought back, but he hated how the empire preyed upon the weak. He'd sooner lose another finger than let the centurion win if he had any choice in the matter. He was closing the chest when he remembered the centurion's boasting. *Any day I enter a den with forty stags and leave with two hundred is a good day to my mind.*

He crept across the grass to the saddles. The centurion's was easy to spot—it had steel embellishments and a spear design worked into the saddle horn, an indicator he'd once served in the empire's cavalry. Rifling through the smaller leather bags, Rylan found a coin purse.

He tugged it open and found two hundred scepters, or thereabouts, and at the bottom, the caravan master's signet ring. He clutched the ring in his fist and stood . . .

And found Balish standing on the horse path staring straight at him.

"Hey!" Balish said.

Rylan spun and sprinted toward the lilac bushes.

"Hey, you bastard, stop!"

Rylan heard footfalls pounding over the earth behind him as he crashed through the bushes and dropped into the gully. He ran pell-mell down the slope, glanced back and saw Balish bursting through the lilac bushes pointing a loaded crossbow at him.

Rylan bid Vedron to fly away from camp and circle back to a glade he'd spotted earlier. Then, he reached into a pouch at his belt and pulled out two paper packets, each the size and shape of a plum. He tossed one of them onto the ground as he ran, and it struck with a sound like breaking glass. Pounding onward, he heard the packet sizzle behind him and glanced over his shoulder. White smoke billowed into the air, an alchemycal reaction between an acid Rylan had harvested from Vedron's saliva and some powdered mold he'd collected from a dying citadel tree. Largely harmless, the smoke would irritate the eyes and nose of those who came into contact with it. More importantly, the cloud was thick and impenetrable. Rylan threw the second packet down and cut to his right around a citadel tree, hoping to catch Vedron at the glade and fly away.

As the glade came into view, Vedron broke through the trees, circled down, and landed with her back to Rylan. Rylan ran up her tail, and Vedron launched him through the air. He landed on her shoulders with a leg on either side of her neck. He gripped the spines along her neck and urged her to fly to the pond where they'd hidden her saddle.

"Halt!"

Rylan glanced back and saw Balish at the edge of the glade pointing a trembling crossbow at them.

Vedron spun to face Balish and uttered a deep growl.

"A single—" Balish coughed, blinked tears from his eyes. He sniffed loudly and aimed the crossbow at Vedron's chest. The bolt's black-slathered steel head glinted beneath the bright sun. "A single beat of a wing and I let fly!"

Rylan had no time to reason with the man. He told Vedron to fly. The moment she spread her wings, Balish, blinking fiercely, shifted his aim toward Rylan and pulled the trigger.

The bolt streaked through the air and tore through Rylan's left sleeve. A pinch of pain followed. He looked down, certain the bolt had grazed skin—it would take barely a nick for coryza to kill a man. His heart pounding, he inspected his sleeve and found the bolt had caught the leather and frayed his homespun shirt beneath it, but thank the ancient powers of the forest, it hadn't drawn blood.

Vedron drew her head back like an adder, preparing to spray Balish with acid. In that moment, her desire became Rylan's. There was real danger in allowing Balish to live—the stories the legionary would tell could very well lead back to Rylan—but when he realized his thoughts were not wholly his own, he took a deep breath and calmed Vedron through their shared bond.

Vedron cocked her head to one side, peered at Rylan, then gazed down on Balish once more.

I'm fine, Vedron, Rylan told the dragon, *and his friends will be here shortly. We have to head home.*

Vedron snorted and pounded her tail, refusing to budge, but she didn't spray Balish.

Rylan leaned over Vedron's side and hollered to the saucer-eared legionary, "Turn around and go or get an acid bath. Your choice."

Balish stared up at them. For a moment, Rylan thought the idiot was going to try to take another bolt from his quiver, but he spun on his heels and sprinted back toward camp. Only when he was lost behind a citadel did Vedron lumber over the ground, spread her wings, and leap toward the sky.

TWO: RYLAN

A short flight delivered Rylan to the pond where he'd hidden Vedron's tack. Once saddle and bridle were on, they flew low over the treetops toward Vedron's nesting grounds. The wind had picked up by then; the sky turned pewter gray and smelled of imminent rain. Rylan urged Vedron to fly with greater haste.

They detoured around an imperial trading post and flew below the canopy to avoid being spotted by dragon scouts who sometimes took rest at the small fort. Beyond the post, they traversed a valley over elk walking beside a stream, glided along a gorge at the valley's far end that was so narrow Vedron's wings nearly touched the red rock walls, and entered a broad sheet of land dominated by citadels, idyllic glades, and little else. As was true in many parts of the Holt, smaller ironbarks, bristlecones, and the occasional oak fought for the cavernous space between the citadels and formed a second canopy far below the tops of the citadels trees.

A leonine yowl cut through the thrum of Vedron's wings. Peering through the trees, Rylan spotted a flying lynx at the mouth of its burrow in the trunk of a citadel. When Vedron veered toward it, Rylan tugged on the reins and forced her back on track. "I'm sorry, girl. I can't go chasing today." He patted the saddlebag, where the ring, the bag of medicine, and the jewelry were hidden. "I have to get these back to their rightful owners, remember?"

Vedron huffed. The lynx, perhaps hearing it, swung its head toward them. A moment later, it dropped from the citadel, spread its limbs wide, and soared on the currents down into the forest. Vedron released a yowl eerily similar to the lynx's.

Thunder sounded in the distance; Vedron swooped down and landed on a knoll near the mounded and hollowed-out collection of gnarled bark scrapings of her nest. Rylan slipped down to the soft ground, flipped open the saddlebag, and pulled out the oilskin sack he used for foraging and slung it over his shoulder. Then he retrieved the coin purse, the bag of medicine, and the jewelry box and stuffed them inside. When he tried to unstrap Vedron's saddle, the dragon reared up and beat her wings, propelling herself several paces back. She snapped her frills open, closed them again, ducked her head and shook it, rattling the barbs along her neck.

"Vedron, I *can't* . . ." As much as Rylan wanted to stay and play, he had business to take care of.

He strode toward her, and she beat her wings again, retreating farther. Then, she lowered her cream-colored belly to the ground and thumped her spade-shaped tail against the needle bed in a thudding rhythm. Rylan wasn't sure how a massive beast with horns, barbs, and rows of sharp teeth could look adorable, but Vedron somehow managed it.

"Should I leave your saddle on? Is that what you want?"

Vedron snorted, and her long narrow pupils contracted around the keyhole shape in their center.

"Fine, have it your way." When he started to leave, she cooed like a mourning dove and shuffled toward him. Rylan hid a smile and unstrapped her saddle and bridle and removed them. "I promise, I'll be back soon. Then we'll find that lynx and scare it half to death."

She craned her neck and trumpeted a loud blast.

"All right, all right," he said with a laugh, "no sense alerting the entire Holt."

Vedron lumbered down the far side of the knoll and launched herself into the air, off to drink from a nearby creek and then rest.

A drizzle began to fall as Rylan hid the tack in the hollow of a fallen oak. He pulled the hood of his coat up and set out toward home. On the way, he cut enough stalks of golden calendula to fill his foraging sack. It was the cover he used to be away from Glaeyand for a few days, one of the many alibis he was always careful to set up before beginning a caper.

The rain began to fall harder, hissing on the leafy canopy and pattering on the forest floor, but Rylan didn't mind a bit of rain. It reminded him of the rangings he used to go on with Uncle Beckett. Beckett was dead now, but his memory lingered in the rhythm of the rain and the smell of the loam.

Miles into his journey, his bond with Vedron dimmed, then vanished altogether. It didn't bother him most times—he liked the solitude—but other times he missed the simple pleasure of her company. Not for the first time, he wished Vedron could live in Glaeyand's eyrie as the radiant dragons did.

Hours later and drenched, he reached Tallow, the village below the tree city of Glaeyand. A bare handful of people were dashing here and there along Tallow's dirt roads in the normally busy village. He trekked beyond the village to the corkscrew stairs below his burrow. He passed them and took the dragonbone list instead. It had been a long journey.

The lift's attendant, the young man everyone called Mouse, emerged from his cozy burrow in an adjacent citadel tree, wearing a heavy oilskin cloak and a bucket hat. "Master Holbrooke!" He splashed through the puddles and opened the lift door for him. "Back from your ranging, I see."

Rylan stepped inside the cage, which was three yards to a side. "I am at that."

Mouse closed the door and pulled on the cord. The bell rang high overhead, barely audible over the pattering rain. "What for this time?"

"An acute case of scaleworm."

The lift juddered and began to rise, and Rylan peered down at Glaeyand's vyrd, a circle of standing stones that was part of the vast maze spread throughout the Holt and the mountains beyond. In the dim light of the raincloud-covered dark sun, the tall stones looked like a ring of draugr freshly risen from their graves.

"Scaleworm?" Mouse asked. "You use calendula decoction for that, don't you?"

Rylan nodded. "A salve made from the decoction, yes. I keep telling you, you should speak to Jorrik. Get a job as an eyrie hand instead of minding the bones."

"And I keep telling you, Master Holbrooke, that dragons scare me half to death, and they can smell fear. You know they can. I'd enter the eyrie in the morning and be etten before the bright sun was on high."

It was true. Dragons had a knack for sensing moods, and fear could cause them to become skittish or even aggressive.

"Anyway," Mouse went on as the counterweight dragonbone cage lowered past them, "I thought the eyrie hands checked for things like scaleworm."

"They do," Rylan said, "but Magnor was away for a fortnight on an extended scouting mission. He likely caught it then."

"Shouldn't Andros have checked him, then?"

Andros was Rylan's half brother on his father's side. "He should have, yes."

Mouse said no more. Andros was famous for taking every slight, large or small, to heart. Mouse nattered on instead about Fèill Buinne, the equinox festival he'd been to the day before. Rylan pretended to listen. After the day he'd had, he wanted only to get home and fall into bed.

When they arrived at the broad deck that marked the halfway point to the uppermost reaches of Glaeyand, Rylan offered his thanks and trekked along a suspended bridge to an adjacent tree. Above him, lanterns glimmered through burrow windows and from hooks on the walkways and bridges. In the evening rain, Glaeyand looked like a city of glass.

Rylan wished he could deliver the medicine and jewelry immediately—they felt like a thief's scar, drawing everyone's attention toward him—but Hollis had gone to an auction in Ancris to buy antiques for his shop and wouldn't be back until the following afternoon. So Rylan headed to his burrow instead, one of the lowermost in all of Glaeyand. He still had a room in Valdavyn, the imperator's residence, along with his father and half-siblings, which he used after the occasional formal celebration, but having hailed from Thicket, he liked being closer to the ground, near solid earth.

At last he arrived at the deck before his burrow. He unlocked the door and entered the modest foyer, cut from the outermost wood of the citadel itself. As he closed the door, the faint, cut-wood scent all burrows had entered his consciousness. He took a deep breath of it and felt calmer. He hung his coat and foraging sack on the hooks beside the door, lit the lamp sitting on the nearby table, then stripped out of his sopping wet clothes and hung them on the remaining hooks to dry.

Shivering, he grabbed the lamp and high-stepped it down a curving hall. He passed the kitchen, the library, and finally reached his bedroom. After changing into warm clothes, he took the goods he'd liberated from the imperial patrol to his modest library. The shelves built into the walls were largely filled with history texts, plus a few books of poetry and tales from distant lands. He crouched and pulled his collection of pipes and his box of tabbaq from the lowermost shelf, opened the shelf's false back, hid the stolen goods in the compartment beyond, and put everything back as it was.

Finally, he went to his bedroom, snuffed the lantern, and collapsed into bed. A pair windows in the bedroom's outer wall gave view of the night. The rain hissing against the windowpanes was so lulling he fell asleep moments after pulling up the covers.

A horn blowing a fire signal woke Rylan from a dead sleep.

Bleary-eyed, he rose and threw on fresh clothes, grabbed his foraging sack and rushed from the burrow. It was late morning, the sun bright above the canopy. Beyond the decks, the suspended walkways, and railed bridgeboughs, a column of smoke rose through the trees.

He headed toward it, moving from tree to tree on the walkways and occasionally climbing the corkscrew stairs. Eventually, he came to a ringwalk—a cantilevered deck that connected various walkways; in this case, three suspended bridges. A crowd had gathered along the railing to witness the fire. One tree over, smoke billowed from the broken windows of a storefront—an apothecary, it seemed. Bottles on soot-covered shelves could be seen through the smoke. Thankfully, the fire brigade had already arrived and were controlling the blaze, taking buckets of water from nearby cisterns and passing them to a pair of burly men at the front of the apothecary, who tossed it through the open doorway onto the flames.

"What happened?" Rylan asked a plump woman in an apron and wimple.

She dabbed tears from her reddened eyes. "A bloody shame is what happened."

"What do you mean?"

"That's Korvus Julianus's shop," she said, pointing. "First Korvus goes missing, now poor Tishana."

A body, covered by a gray blanket, lay on the deck outside the burning shop. All he could see of the woman beneath the blanket was her black shoes.

"It's the Knives, you ask me," the woman said. "First they take Korvus, maybe kill him, then they burn his shop."

"But Korvus was an alchemyst, and Tisha was lovely. Why would they harm either of them?"

The woman spat over the railing. "What does it take for the Knives to do *anything* these days? Master Korvus probably looked at one of 'em wrong. Felt like they had to make an example of him. It's not right. It's bloody well not right."

Another woman, quite a bit younger but dressed similarly, was glaring at Rylan like she was angry at *him*. Both women had the fair skin of mountain folk. They'd likely been born in the empire proper, or their parents had. For people like them—people who associated more with the empire than the Holt—it didn't take much to move from hatred of the Knives to hatred of the Kin, and Rylan was half Kin.

With the blaze under control, Rylan offered them a polite nod and left.

The elder woman hadn't been entirely wrong about the Knives. There had been years of relative peace in the Holt, but lately, old tensions were being rekindled. Many blamed Aarik, the one they called the King of the Wood, but Rylan had heard rumors of a split between Aarik and his brother, Llorn. They said Llorn was responsible for the recent violence.

A few trees over, Rylan took a set of stairs up to a triangular staging deck. Beyond it loomed Glaeyand's famed eyrie. Between six citadels was a great well devoid of branches and bridgeboughs, allowing dragons easy entry and egress through a hole in the canopy above. Throughout the well were a hundred nests made of steel and wooden beams, each built on the stubby remains of a cut bough. There were numerous eyries in the Holt and the mountains beyond, many owned and commanded by the reeves charged with the protection of various cities and villages, others built by wealthy landowners or patricians. None were as large or impressive as Glaeyand's, which dwarfed even the imperial eyries in the empire's capitals.

The Holt was not a province, but a vassal state of the empire, an arrangement the empire had grudgingly agreed to after the devastating, hundred-year Talon Wars ended in a bitter stalemate. The empire might have won outright had they continued to fight, but the war had cost them dearly, and the nations on their borders were beginning to sense weakness. The ensuing negotiations were acrimonious, and neither side was wholly pleased with the outcome, but in the end, a lasting peace was forged through a document known as the Covenant.

Among its many provisions, the Covenant stipulated that the Holt could raise and maintain a dragon legion *large enough to defend its interests*. Although the Covenant didn't say so explicitly, everyone knew the limitation had been added to prevent the Holt from becoming a threat to the empire. So it was that Glaeyand's eyrie and nests were home to some thirty dragons: a few privately owned, the bulk Marstan Lyndenfell's to command. Notably, the dragons were all radiants, dragons that came from the mountains and other highlands. There were irons, silvers, golds and bronzes, ranging in age from kits to fully grown bulls and vixen. As the nearby fire began to splutter out, some of the dragons were eyeing dragons in other nests; others watched the rising smoke with keen interest; some few were ignoring everything and everyone around them, raking their bodies with their teeth to remove old scales.

As usual, no cobalts, ambers, onyxes, viridians, or auburns were in the nests because umbral dragons, which came from the forest and other lowlands, were famously resistant to the magical crops and fetters the empire used to bring dragons to heel. The simple truth had led the empire—and by extension, the imperator— to forbid using umbrals as mounts since the time of the Talon Wars. And because the Red Knives, an enemy of the empire, favored umbrals, they were hunted as well. The campaign to eradicate umbrals was so fierce and persistent, some were nearing extinction. Which was why Rylan took such care to hide his bond with Vedron. Were it discovered, the imperator, Rylan's own father, would have Rylan's hand cut off, or worse. Vedron, meanwhile, would be hunted, killed, and rendered for parts. Fortunately, the towering citadel trees were ubiquitous through-out the Great Basin, making their secret easy to keep, as long as Rylan hid his movements to and from her nesting grounds.

The eyrie's lowermost nests were the easiest to access from the staging deck. As such, the eyrie master, Jorrik, a diminutive but intense man with dirty blond hair in a top knot and blue tattoos on the side of his head, orchestrated the nests carefully for the departure of the imperator, his dragon legion, or important guests. At present, a single nest was occupied by a silvery blue indurium, one of the largest of the radiant breeds.

Standing at the center the staging deck were two of Rylan's half siblings: An-dros, wearing brightsteel armor, and Willow, wearing black boots and leather rid-ing clothes. Andros, tall and strapping, was staring down at Jorrik, who was a full head shorter than Andros, and slightly shorter than Willow, but the eyrie master didn't seem to be giving ground in what was apparently a heated conversation.

"Can I help?" Rylan asked.

Andros looked him up and down. "So you've finally decided to grace the eyrie with your presence . . ."

"I've been gone, Andros"—Rylan lifted his foraging sack—"collecting ingre-dients for *your* dragon."

"For two days?"

"The stands of calendula near Glaeyand were wiped out by frost. I had to go south." A lie, but a necessary one to hide his movements.

"Well, your delay has left Magnor's shoulder worse than when you left."

"There was still plenty of salve left when I departed."

"That's just it, Master Rylan," Jorrik said. "Lord Andros came here yesterday afternoon, saying he needed Magnor ready for a flight to Andalingr. I told him it wasn't wise because, even with the salve, Magnor needed more time to heal, but Lord Andros took the remaining salve anyway."

"How much did you use?" Rylan asked Andros.

"All of it," Jorrik answered, "every uncia we had left."

"That's too much," Rylan said. "It'll irritate his skin."

Jorrik flung a hand toward Andros. "A fact I would have shared if I'd been *asked*. Now Magnor's in a state. He won't let me or anyone else near him to clean the wound."

Andros stabbed a finger at Rylan's chest. "None of this would've happened if you'd come back when you were supposed to. I shouldn't have to do *your* job as well as mine, not when temples and apothecaries are being burned. Not when Knives are flying freely all across the Holt." He pointed to the trails of smoke still pluming from the alchemy shop. "The threats are everywhere, Rylan. We all need to do our part."

Rylan shook his head. "A temple was burned?"

Willow answered, "We received word last night that a temple was put to the torch in Andalingr. The Red Knives are suspected. Father wants us to check into it personally." She turned her gaze on the indurium. "Hence, the need for mounts."

Andros, staring at Rylan, clenched his fists. "And if you'd come—"

"All right, all right," Rylan said, raising his hands, "what's done is done. Let's get you on your way to Andalingr, and I'll see to Magnor. Jorrik, do you have another mount that Andros can use?"

"I was just trying to arrange it when—"

"Bloody arrange it, then!" Andros roared. He stormed toward the indurium. "But I shouldn't *have* to use another mount."

Jorrik clenched his jaw, then turned to Willow and bowed. "I'll see to it."

Rylan and Willow stood alone on the staging deck. Of all his half-siblings, Willow had been the least cruel to him growing up. Now that they were older, she treated him merely like an annoyance, a necessary part of her job as under-study to their father, Marstan.

"I'll grant you, Andros isn't completely in the right here," she said, "but he isn't completely in the wrong, either. We all wear different hats to play our roles. Sometimes I think you wear too many." She gestured at the many nests in the eyrie's well. "The dragons need you *here*."

"I serve at the will of the imperator, Willow."

"I suppose that's true of all of us, but it seems to me you've been given quite a bit of freedom in the commissions you take as a dragon singer. Perhaps too much."

Rylan was still formulating his response when Willow turned and walked away. Her coldness left Rylan with a sinking feeling. The things he did, the capers and heists he ran, depended on his having the cover of a legitimate job in the complex workings of the empire and the Holt. It opened many doors that would otherwise be closed and brought up an age-old question: what would he be without it?

The answer was simple. In the eyes of the empire, he'd be just another stinking Kin.

THREE: RHIANNON

Beyond the outskirts of Thicket, a stone's throw from the Trinustine Abbey, fourteen-year-old Rhiannon Bloodhaven foraged among the citadels. She wore a belt of woven hemp, calf-high boots of stout elk leather, and the brown robe of a druin aspirant. Slung over one shoulder was a woolen foraging sack, half full of pine cones. The air was chilly, but not terribly so. On the way to a fresh cluster of pine cones, she passed over a patch of snow and kicked it, sending a white spray over the bed of needles.

She crouched, gathered a half dozen more pine cones, and dropped them into her sack. Then she scoured the needle bed for nuts and stuffed those into a leather pouch at her belt. It was better to harvest the cones in autumn, but winter had come early and stayed well beyond its welcome. Now spring had come, and the cold had preserved the cones and their nuts well enough for a good harvest.

On hearing a familiar yowl overhead, she smiled and stared up. A flying lynx crouched on a bridgebough. Its coat was mottled brown, the long tufts on the tip of its ears black. She'd spotted the same lynx digging a fresh burrow the previous summer and come this way hoping to see it, and there it was, staring out over the forest, likely searching for hare, voles, groundhogs, or even an unwary fox. She was about to move on when the lynx suddenly perked its ears. It hunkered low, the fur on its shoulders twitched, and it dropped from the bridgebough, plummeted straight down, and spread its legs wide. The skin between them stretched taut, and it caught the air, banked left, and soared around the trunk of a citadel. She didn't see if it caught its prey, but it was exciting just the same.

Rhiannon enjoyed the wandering, the birdsong, and the spying of lynx much more than the foraging. Soon enough she'd have to set of the pine cones by the forge to dry, harvest the nuts, and shell and mill them to make pine milk or flour. It wasn't that she didn't like her life at the abbey. She did. It was just that she preferred being in the forest.

She gathered several more cones, dropped them into the sack, and ran her fingers over the bark of a citadel on the way to a fresh patch. With that touch, her sense of the forest grew. She felt the tree's roots driving into the earth, felt them spread and intermingle with those of other, nearby trees. It made the forest feel like a massive patch of ivy, every tree interconnected with every other.

She was jarred from the spell by a voice calling through the forest. "Rhiannon!" She rounded the citadel and spotted Irik running full tilt through the trees. Irik was same age as Rhiannon and had blond hair and gangly arms and legs. His overlarge, hand-me-down robe flapped between his legs as he ran, but when he got close, Rhiannon could see he was alarmed. "Rhiannon!" he called. "Rhiannon, where are you?"

Rhiannon waved her arms over her head. "Over here, you bloody idiot!"

Irik adjusted course, came to a stop several yards away, bent over, and put his hands on his knees. Between gasps, he said, "Llorn's come."

Rhiannon had only seen her uncle a handful of times, and that suited her just fine. He was always cold to her, and he had a reputation for violence. Some folk even called him the Butcher, and for good reason. Rumor had it he had strung up an entire caravan on trees as a warning to others not to trespass on Red Knife territory. "Why is *he* here?"

"I dunno. He hiked in an hour ago with Sister *Dereka*. They asked to speak to Brother Mayhew. Sister Merida joined them, and they started arguing, and I heard Llorn say your name. So I came to tell you."

Rhiannon's insides felt like curds being wrung of their whey. Sister Dereka's reputation was nearly as bad as her uncle's. She was a powerful archdruin and one of Llorn's closest allies. If the stories were true, she was as responsible for the caravan massacre as Llorn.

"What were they arguing about?" Rhiannon asked.

Irik hesitated and looked around the forest. "They were talking about speaking to the dead."

Root and ruin, that can't be good.

Two years ago Brother Mayhew left the abbey to go on a pilgrimage along the Salt Road. Rhiannon had snuck into his chambers the day he'd left and found his book of secrets. All druin knew the citadels were more than mere trees: They were *observers*. They'd witnessed the acts of man throughout the ages, and they remembered. Rhiannon's grandmother, Rygmora, had had a gift. She'd sung to the trees, coaxed them into revealing the past. The things they told her—rituals and wars from the distant past—she recorded in a tome known as the Book of the Holt.

Brother Mayhew's book was a distillation of that larger tome, the key rituals the transcriber had deemed important. The one that most fascinated Rhiannon was a ritual that allowed one to speak to the dead. Hoping she might one day speak to her dead mother, she committed the ritual to memory and, with Irik, had stolen a pinch of auris from Brother Mayhew's supply. Then they snuck off to the swamp, where wisps often gathered. Standing near the swamp's edge, Rhiannon sniffed the auris, felt its power infuse her, and used it to coax a wisp from the water. She asked it to *gather itself*, in the words of the book, to recall its former life.

And it had. The wisp's light intensified, and a face formed in the air before her, the face of a soul who had been a man once, a trapper. She saw him stumble on a gray wolf stuck in the steel jaws of a beaver trap. For a long moment, she felt his sorrow, his love of wolves. They were majestic beasts, even if they *did* compete for the beavers that filled the trapper's purse. He was just crouching down to free the wolf, when Rhiannon was shaken from the vision.

Brother Mayhew had grasped her arm with his big, hairy hand and shook her. "What are you *doing*?"

Irik stood impotently at the edge of the swamp, gaping at the brother. The wisp floated away.

Brother Mayhew dragged her from the edge of the swamp. "You're *not* to do such things. Not without my permission. Not until I've judged you *ready*. Do you understand me?"

She'd said yes, but Brother Mayhew didn't seem to believe her. She and Irik were switched when they arrived back at the abbey. Her backside was tender for a week. She hadn't dared to perform the ritual since. She was afraid the punishment for a second offense would be much worse than a switching.

She later learned that very few druin could summon wisps. Fewer still could make them remember their past lives. She had inherited some small amount of power from her mother, who had inherited it from Granny Rygmora, but she did not expect anything from it. Now Llorn had come asking about the incident. Surely, he would punish her worse than Brother Mayhew had.

She wanted to hide in the forest, but it was no use. She'd have to go back to the abbey eventually, and a delay would only make Brother Mayhew angry.

"Okay, let's go," she said.

They fell into step, and Irik asked, "What do you think he wants?"

"How would I know?"

"Do you think he learned about you doing the thing with the wisp?"

"I don't *know*."

"Do you think he's angry? Will he be angry with *me*?"

"Briar and bramble, Irik, I don't bloody know, all right? Now will you let me *think*?"

Irik lapsed into silence as the grounds of the Trinustine Abbey came into view. The abbey was built in and around four citadels. The house of worship was built into the base of one citadel, the refectory and dormitories in another, the clergy residences dominated the third, and the fourth was dedicated to the famed Trinustine Brewery. There was a smithy and a small stables beyond the brewery, plus bee hives for honey and wax, and a garden where they grew their own vegetables. Normally a bustle of activity, the abbey's yard had come to a standstill. Two dozen clergy and a score of aspirants in brown robes stood gawping at Brother Mayhew as he led Llorn and Sister Dereka toward Irik and Rhiannon.

Brother Mayhew was a burly man of forty-five winters, a ripe old age among the Deepwood druins. He wore the clothes of a woodsman: tough leggings, a belted tunic, a green cloak pinned in place with a beaten bronze clasp. His sturdy frame, striped black beard, and perpetual frown lent him a riled-badger look, which was only accentuated by his bald pate and the blue, runic tattoo that curled around his left eye.

Llorn's weathered cloak, threadbare clothes, and beaten leather boots marked him as a man who spent much time in the wild. His long black hair was pulled into a tail. The dark marks on his cheeks and forehead came from too much time in the dark sun and would likely lead to cancer of the skin.

Beside Llorn strode Sister Dereka. She was tall for a woman and had a long, loping stride. Brother Mayhew had quite a few tattoos, but Sister Dereka had more. The blue runes and pictographs not only covered the whole of the left side of her face and head, they'd crept over the crown of her head and were halfway to her opposite ear. The scowl she wore deepened the many lines around her eyes and mouth, and looked as permanent as the sun marks on Llorn's face.

In the yard, Old Mother Constance used her staff to pull herself tall. "Mighty Alra shines her blessings on the *industrious!*"

In dribs and drabs, everyone went back to work—all except plump, rosy-cheeked, Sister Merida, who stood near the garden in her brown habit and white wimple and fiddled her hands nervously as she watched Rhiannon. She was related to Rhiannon, albeit distantly, through Rhiannon's mother, which made her a cousin of some sort, or maybe an aunt—Rhiannon could never keep it straight. She seemed intent on Brother Mayhew, but when she saw Rhiannon staring at her, she smiled. It was strained, though. Rhiannon could tell she was worried.

Brother Mayhew glowered at Irik as he, Llorn, and Sister Dereka came to a stop nearby. "Go. Start making the milk."

Irik took the foraging sack, sent a worried glance at Rhiannon, and left.

Brother Mayhew continued, "Rhiannon, you know Llorn and Sister Dereka."

Rhiannon bowed to them. "I bid you welcome to the abbey."

Llorn nodded stiffly. Sister Dereka merely stared.

"You're to accompany us to the swamp," Brother Mayhew told Rhiannon.

"May I ask why?"

"You may not." Llorn and Sister Dereka turned and headed toward the path to the swamp, and Brother Mayhew took Rhiannon by the shoulder and propelled her after them. "Listen, don't speak," he grumbled. "No acting like a flighty sparrow today, understand?"

The hike to the swamp was awkward and mostly silent. Brother Mayhew was tense. Llorn, meanwhile, kept glancing back, looking for something, but Rhiannon couldn't imagine what. Sister Dereka ignored her.

Brother Mayhew tugged on Rhiannon's sleeve to slow her pace. When they were well behind Llorn and Sister Dereka, he said, "They want to see you speak to the dead."

Rhiannon wasn't sure if she should act surprised, or if she did, whether it would look rehearsed, so said nothing.

"You'll do as you did before. Summon a wisp, force it to remember a bit of its life."

"I'll try my best, but why would Uncle care about some random wisp?"

Brother Mayhew pinched her ear. "Never you mind, Rhiannon." He glanced toward Llorn, then Sister Dereka, and for a moment, Rhiannon saw fear in his eyes. "Just do it."

Pinch or no pinch, she would normally press him for answers, but the fear she'd seen in his eyes was making *her* scared. What would happen if she failed? And who would be the one to suffer?

At last, they came to a stop the edge of the shallow, stinking water. Lux shone brightly, but the shadows beneath the cypress trees were deep. Rhiannon could see faint blue lights floating in the air like dandelion seeds. They were the souls of the dead, wisps risen from their graves years, decades, even centuries after their deaths.

Brother Mayhew had large golden rings on both of his middle fingers. He opened the left one to reveal a cavity filled with white powder, auris. "One pinch," he said to Rhiannon, and held the ring out to her.

She took a bit of the powder between her thumb and forefinger. It smelled like rosemary and was silky smooth, finer than twice-milled flour. As Brother Mayhew had taught her, she raised the powder to her nose, sniffed sharply, then rubbed the remains on her gums. As her nose burned and the aura in the powder leeched into her body, her awareness of the forest expanded. It was similar to touching the bark of the citadel tree, but it went much, much further. She felt the tall citadels, but also the cypress, the blood maple, the cottonwood. She felt the earth, the water, the grass. A low susurrus rose, as if the trees were passing secrets to one another, or were *trying* to pass them to Rhiannon.

As she crouched near the water's edge, a thought occurred to her. She might only *pretend* to speak to the dead. Or make like she was trying then simply fail.

Brother Mayhew glowered. "Before nightfall, girl, please."

Rhiannon glanced up at him, then returned her gaze to the wisps. Her deception wouldn't work, she decided. Sister Dereka and Brother Mayhew were watching her like hawks. One of them would surely know if she was giving the ritual anything less than her full effort.

She took a deep breath, spread her arms wide, and opened herself to the swamp. Ahead, a wisp hovered above a clump of sawgrass just beyond the edge of the water. Rhiannon held one hand toward it, and it showed her a gnarled hand holding a smith's hammer striking a piece of glowing iron. Another showed a woodswoman slicing elephant-ear mushrooms from the bark of a dying tree. A third showed a woman breaking honeycomb from a beehive. Rhiannon summoned that wisp near. It disappeared into a patch of sunlight, then brightened as it entered the shadow of a leaning cottonwood.

"Why that one?" Llorn asked. He sounded displeased.

"She was a beekeeper," Rhiannon said nervously. "I saw her tending her hives." She paused, wondering if she should say more. "And I like honey."

Sister Dereka snorted.

Llorn merely nodded. "Go on."

Rhiannon beckoned the wisp nearer. It approached but moved in fits and starts, and at one point sidled to one side like a fish on a hook trying to get away. But Rhiannon was patient and persistent. Eventually, it was close enough to touch. That close, it looked like a glowing puff of smoke.

The hint of a nose formed in the air before her, then a woman's eyes, round cheeks, sensuous lips. Rhiannon was just about to say hello when the eyes went wide and the woman shrieked. The image of a man flashed through Rhiannon's mind. He had his hands to the woman's throat. The woman beat him with her fists.

Rhiannon raised her hands and backed away from the wisp, but the shrieking continued.

"Enough!" Llorn bellowed. "Enough!"

Rhiannon knelt down in the sedge and gripped her hands into fists to try to stop it. It had no effect that she could discern, but the image and the shriek soon faded on their own. The wisp remained, glimmering brighter than before above the nearby lily pads.

"I'm sorry," Rhiannon whispered to it.

Sister Dereka watched the wisp float back across the green water with a stunned look on her face. Focusing on Rhiannon, she said, "You can do this with *any* wisp?"

Rhiannon had only done it the two times, but she didn't see any reason why she couldn't do it with others. "I think so."

The sister was silent for a time, then she swung her gaze to Llorn and nodded. The creases along Llorn's brow faded, his shoulders relaxed, and he nodded back. Rhiannon wanted desperately to ask why she'd been asked to do this for them, but she knew no one would answer her. Her only real chance at gaining answers was to wait and press Brother Mayhew when they were alone.

Llorn stared down at Rhiannon. "You'll speak of this to no one."

"Yes, Uncle."

"Not even Irik."

She nodded.

Llorn's eyes narrowed. "I want to hear you say it, Rhiannon."

"I won't speak of this to anyone. Not even Irik."

"Good. Now go back to the abbey."

Rhiannon nodded and began the trek back. She glanced back only once and saw the three of them conversing in low voices. She thought about doubling back to try to learn more but rejected the idea out of hand. It wasn't over fear of the switching she'd receive should Brother Mayhew catch her, nor the fact that Sister Dereka, an archdruin, had seemed awed by what she'd done. It was the sheer amount of relief on Llorn's face. If the man they called the Butcher was that pleased, what could it mean but trouble—for the abbey, for Thicket, for the Holt?

FOUR: RYLAN

As Willow and Andros made ready to depart from the eyrie, Rylan retrieved the stalks of golden calendula from his foraging sack and offered them to Quinn, the eyrie hand with the lazy eye. "You remember how to make the decoction?"

"I remember, Master Holbrooke." Quinn accepted the stalks with a quick bow and ran off to boil them.

Rylan prepared a bucket of soapy water and took it up toward Magnor's nest.

Magnor poked his silver head over the edge of his nest and watched as Rylan circled up the corkscrew stairs. The dragon began to snake his head like an eel, gurgle and squeal, and slap his tail against the side of the nest.

"It's all right, boy," Rylan said while lifting the bucket. "This will make you feel better."

As he reached the walkway to his nest, Magnor reared and flapped his wings. In the morning light, his bright silver scales glimmered like mother of pearl. Rylan waited for Magnor to settle, then stepped closer to the nest. Magnor spread the frills behind his jaws and raised the one between his twisting horns. When Rylan dared another step, Magnor whipped his head so fast it was like a silver blur. Like all silvers, Magnor could use the aura he collected from the bright sun to become wickedly fast in short bursts.

"I know, Magnor. The salve is irritating your shoulder. Let me help you. It might burn a little. Please try not to bite my head off." Rylan had no bond with Magnor, but it couldn't hurt to ask.

Rylan set the bucket down carefully, stood tall, and hid his left hand, the one with the missing pinky, behind his back. He focused on Magnor's eyes—sapphire struck through with white with tall, narrow pupils and a diamond shape at the center. He raised his right hand, spread his fingers, and began to sing a wordless melody. It was made in the moment, as all his songs were, and acted as an introduction of sorts, a way to draw Magnor's attention and begin forging a mental link. He altered the song each time to suit his purpose while taking the dragon's mood and general inclinations into account, if known. In this case, the song was slow and calming, like the Diamondflow in late summer.

Magnor's third eyelids nictated and his tail twitched. He uttered a low growl Rylan felt in his chest, then huffed through his nostrils. He tilted his head this way and that as if trying to size Rylan up. But then he stilled, his sapphire eyes closed languidly, and his tail began to sway in time.

A tentative connection to Magnor made, Rylan sang louder and quickened the song's pace ever so slightly. Rylan's shoulder began to ache, an echo of Magnor's pain. He felt a directionless worry as well.

"It's all right," Rylan said in a sing-song voice. "Tiny worms have snuck under your scales. They're multiplying, but we can stop them if you let us."

Magnor craned his neck back and let out a contented gurgle, and when Rylan stepped closer along the planks, he lowered his chest and spread his right wing wide. Along Magnor's ribs, below the joint where the wing's humerus met the shoulder joint, was a patch of pink the size of a dinner plate. The area was coated with a thick, cream-colored salve, which Rylan proceeded to gently wipe away with the soapy water and rag. Humming softly, he rinsed the rag, wrung it out, and wiped away more of the salve. After a third pass, he inspected the area closely and saw tiny, white worms wriggling beneath his translucent scales. Lifting one scale carefully, he saw the worms' eggs, hardly larger than grains of sand.

"It's better than before," Rylan said. "Another few applications should do the trick." He stepped back. "Rest now. Or fly if you want. We'll put more salve on later, yes?"

Magnor arched his neck and trilled like a whippoorwill.

Rylan smiled. "Feels better, doesn't it?"

With Magnor settled, Rylan circled back down the stairs to the receiving deck. He worked the rest of the day in the eyrie. As various dragons came and went, he finished making the salve from the calendula decoction Quinn had completed. When enough time had passed, he took it up to Magnor's nest and applied a light coating. The silver calmed right down when he saw Rylan and neither squealed nor thumped his tail. Then Rylan helped Jorrik and Quinn tend to a pair of brasses from distant Praecia that were new to the eyrie and were having trouble settling.

When all was done, he promised Jorrik he'd check on Magnor in the morning and headed toward the center of Glaeyand. The sky was darkening by then, and the cant had arrived, the time when the bright sun set and the dark sun rose. A streak of yellow light flashed across the sky, then a fan of blue that wavered toward green as it spanned. A splash of saffron twisted and turned like a sheet pulled off a drying line, then burst, spreading like the shards of a broken vase. For several minutes, the heavenly bodies clashed, aura and umbra striking in the atmosphere, creating wild displays of vibrant colors. One particular sequence—a vivid, bloody red—was the sort of foreboding omen one didn't ignore lightly, and it went on for so long Rylan nearly decided to postpone his trip to Hollis's antiques shop, but he didn't want to wait to return the medicine, ring, and jewelry to the caravan. It had been weighing on him all day.

When he reached his burrow, he opened the hidden compartment behind the lowermost shelf, retrieved the signet ring from the centurion's purse and placed it in the inlaid box with the rest of the jewelry. He set the bag of medicine beside it, then closed the lid. The centurion's winnings, two hundred stags, he dropped into a coin chest he kept for emergencies. Then he closed the hidden compartment, took the inlaid box, and left.

Glaeyand's market was built on a broad square suspended by great cables from eight nearby citadel trees. By the time Rylan arrived, the sky was dim, the market largely torn down for the night. A few stragglers were making final purchases at stalls here and there, but for the most part, the vendors were placing wares in lockboxes or wheeling them away on hand-pulled carts.

Rylan made his way toward Hollis's Historical Artifacts, one of eight permanent buildings at the center of the broad platform, and entered to the jingle of a bell. The shop contained an eclectic mixture of books, furniture, paintings, statuettes, and more lit by the pleasant glow of two lanterns in opposite corners. A trace of myrrh, Hollis's preferred incense, lingered in the air. Rylan breathed it in and felt suddenly calmer.

Hollis, a bald man of middling years with dark olive skin, sat at a desk at the back of the shop, nursing a cup of tea and reading. He looked up as Rylan entered, wagged a finger at him, and went back to his book. Knowing how much Hollis hated having his reading interrupted, Rylan remained silent as he made his way to the desk, pulled out a chair, and sat.

Apparently having come to a good breakpoint, Hollis regarded Rylan with a handsome smile. "Just the man I was hoping to see."

Rylan set the jewelry box on the desk and slid it toward Hollis.

Hollis opened it and nodded appreciatively. "Any difficulties?"

A vision of a crossbow bolt streaking through the air flashed through Rylan's mind. "No more than usual."

Hollis began pulling some of the jewelry out and made two piles on his desk.

"I took a purse off the centurion," Rylan said. "Two hundred stags. Count that as part of my cut. The rest can go into my account."

Hollis adjusted one of the piles appropriately, slipped both into the bottom drawer of his desk, put the jewelry box in, and shut the drawer with a hollow thump. "I have something for *you* as well . . ." From another drawer, he drew a leatherbound book, set it on the desk and slid it toward Rylan

The title stamped onto the red leather cover read, *From Ancris to Olencia, A Brief History of Early Imperial Architecture*. It was likely part of the haul from the auction Hollis had just attended in Ancris. He knew Rylan's penchant for history books of all sorts, but Rylan was still surprised he'd picked out this particular treatise.

"You mentioned the temples in Caldoras," Hollis said. "I thought you might like to know more about them."

"I would at that." Rylan opened the book to a random page and admired the precise script. "How much do I owe you?"

"Gratis. Call it a bonus for your excellent work."

"Well, thank you for—"

The bell above the door rang. Rylan stopped what he was saying and turned to see two men in long cloaks enter the shop. They threw their hoods back, and Rylan felt a chill run along his arms. They were Llorn and Raef, two of the highest ranking members of the Red Knives. A visit from either was an ill omen; a visit from both felt like a guillotine being raised over Rylan's head.

"Which one of you is Rylan?" Raef asked.

Rylan suddenly felt like he was falling. Hollis's gaze shifted from Raef to Rylan and back again.

"Oy!" Raef said. "Which one?"

"I am," Rylan said.

Raef gave Hollis a hard stare. "Out."

Hollis's hands trembled on the desk, but he made no move to stand. "This is *my* shop. No one tells me—"

Raef put his hand on the hilt of his knife and sidled past Llorn, but Llorn put a hand on his shoulder and stopped him.

"We need to chat, that's all." Llorn said.

Rylan's heart started to pound.

Hollis turned to Rylan. "You want me to—"

"It's fine," Rylan said, nodding. "The man just wants a bit of a chat."

Hollis stood, shuffled carefully past Llorn and Raef, and exited through the front door. The pleasant jingle sounded like the toll of a bell before a burning.

Llorn stepped around Rylan and dropped into Hollis's chair. His gaze passed over the book Hollis had given Rylan, and he did a double take. "Garbage." He kicked his legs onto the desk and crossed his arms over his chest. "Word is you can find things."

Rylan glanced back at Raef, who was leaning against a bookshelf, glowering at him, then back at Llorn. "I'm a dragon singer."

"I heard that as well. We'll come back to it before too long. For now, I've something that needs finding."

Rylan tipped his head back toward Raef. "Then have *him* do it. Are his legs broken or something?"

Without taking his eyes from Rylan, Llorn said, "Are your legs broken, Raef?"

"Yes," Raef snorted. "Can't walk a step. Such a shame. Don't even know how I got up here."

Llorn smiled, dimpling his sun-marked cheeks. "Raef's legs are broken, as you can clearly see."

"You've got plenty of other Knives who could help."

"Maybe, but I need this done well, and I need it done *quietly*."

"Well, I'm afraid I can't help you."

"No?" Llorn leaned toward Rylan. "The man who stole bones from a sepulcher in Lyros so they could be reburied in the Holt where they belong can't help? The man who pinched the Sylvan Tapestry and returned it to the abbey in Skjalgard . . . *That* man can't help?" Llorn peered down at the drawers of the desk. "How about the man who crept up on an imperial patrol and stole jewels, contraband, and a very valuable signet ring from right under their fucking noses? You're telling me *that* man can't help?"

Rylan recalled the shape in the tree above him as he hid behind the lilac bushes. It was just before he sent Vedron to harry the patrol's horses. Had one of Llorn's Knives been watching him?

"If it's true," Llorn continued, "that I really *do* have the wrong man, then surely you'll be able to explain these things to your father. Or maybe to your brother, the one who likes to puff out his chest when the girls walk by . . ." Llorn snapped his fingers. "What's his name?"

"Andros . . ."

"That's the one. He seems the understanding sort. I'm sure he won't mind that you steal from the imperial legionaries he loves so dearly, or that you're bonded to a viridian and have been for many years."

Rylan tried not to show his shock. Why would Llorn, one of the top bastards in the Red Knives, care enough to learn so much about him?

"Understand me, Rylan Holbrooke. I don't fault you for any of those things." He leaned back in the chair. "I *admire* you for them. You do the Holt a service by stealing from those sons of bitches."

There was a reason Hollis refused to work with the Knives. "Doesn't matter if it's something big or something small," he'd told Rylan once. "Start working for them and, sooner or later, they'll consider you theirs. You'll be bound by their rules then, whether you take their blood oath or not."

"I'm not a Knife," Rylan said, "and I won't become one."

"I'm not asking you to. I just want you to accept a new commission"—he scanned the shop—"as you have for your friend here. It's one I'm *certain* you'd accepted if it came from him."

Muted conversation rose from the front of the shop, and a young couple passed by the door, lit briefly by the shop's lanterns. Beyond them, Rylan spotted Hollis and willed him not to interfere.

"Come," Llorn said, "aren't you curious to know what I want?"

Rylan shrugged. "Go on then, if you're so eager."

"Watch your fucking tongue," Raef said from behind him.

Llorn glanced at Raef, then flashed Rylan a brief half smile. "It's a wisp. My *sister's* wisp."

Rylan blinked. "Morraine?"

Everyone in the Holt knew the story of Morraine Bloodhaven. Like Llorn and Aarik, she'd been a member of the Red Knives. Ten years ago, a pair of imperial dragonriders, known as dracorae, had spotted her, tracked her to Glaeyand, and captured her. Their commander, a volarch named Trichan Alevada, was set to return her to the mountains when Marstan Lyndenfell stepped in as imperator and requested that Morraine be hung in Glaeyand and that her body be buried in a nearby barrow mound, arguing it would prevent bloody reprisals from the Red Knives.

Trichan, reluctant at first, had eventually agreed, and Morraine was hung. But afterward, Trichan commanded one of his shepherds to quicken her wisp so he could claim it as a trophy. It was as deep an insult as could be imagined in the Holt because it prevented the wisp from attaining peace and rising to the heavenly lands of Déu. In the years that followed, there were several attempts on Trichan's life. None succeeded, but Trichan decided to hide the wisp away. When Trichan was stricken by pneumonia and died several years ago, most folk assumed Morraine's wisp would never resurface, either because it had been sold or locked away in a place so secure it would be nigh impossible to retrieve.

Rylan had no idea what the Alevadas had done with it, which implied Llorn did. "You know where it is," he said.

"It's hardly a secret anymore," Llorn told him. "It's on display in their family gallery."

Rylan reeled. That the Alevada family would do so implied they felt that, with Trichan's death, the danger to their family had passed. It also gave hint as to Llorn's purpose in Hollis's shop—if all he wanted was his sister's wisp, Llorn could easily break in and get it. But it would advertise to the empire what he'd done. "You don't want anyone to know it was taken . . . ."

Llorn shrugged. "Would you?"

"Speak plainly." Rylan glanced over his shoulder, but Raef apparently wasn't following the conversation. "Why do you want her wisp?"

"Because she's my sister. Are you slow?"

Rylan ignored the insult. "And that's the *only* reason you want it?"

"What other reason could there be? I want her soul returned to the Holt. I want it given to her daughter, Rhiannon, so *she* can decide what to do with it."

On hearing the name of Morraine's only surviving child, Rhiannon, Rylan blew out a long breath he didn't know he'd been holding. After Uncle Beckett's death, Aunt Merida joined the Trinustine Abbey in Thicket and became something of a foster mother to many druin aspirants, Rhiannon among them. Rylan had gone to the abbey to visit *Sister* Merida, as they called her at the abbey. He'd met Rhiannon while he was there. She seemed the quiet sort, perhaps from what had happened to her mother, but attentive and dutiful as well. Her mother would have been proud.

"Even assuming I *wanted* to accept," Rylan said, "I'm not a burglar. I need an excuse to be at the Alevada estate."

Llorn nodded. "That's reasonable enough. As it happens, Trichan's widow is nursing an aging dragon, Rugio, her personal mount since she was eight. Even I will admit it's almost admirable how the old crone dotes on it. I imagine she'd welcome the help of a dragon singer as the old lizard slides toward death."

The approach made sense. The wealthiest courtiers in the empire—be they senators, magnates, landowners—often paid handsomely to ensure their personal mounts died as comfortably as possible. Rylan had performed the service more than a dozen times in the past decade. The reputation he'd built and his status as the son of the imperator opened many doors, even if he *was* half Kin. He was reasonably certain he could arrange for a visit or two to the Alevada estate.

"It'll take time," he said to Llorn.

"Of course."

"And my services aren't free."

Llorn nodded to Raef, and Raef reached into a leather pouch at his belt, pulled out a small coin purse, and tossed it through the air, landing it on the desk with a merry clink.

Rylan opened it. It was filled not with silver stags nor gold thrones but indurium scepters. He managed to hide his surprise, but it wan't easy—a hundred scepters was easily the fattest sum he'd been offered for his work, ever.

Llorn said, "You get another one just like it when you hand the wisp to Raef."

It was a staggering sum for a few weeks' work. Llorn obviously wanted his sister's wisp back badly, which made Rylan nervous. Maybe he wasn't seeing the big picture—but he had no reason to think this was anything more than it seemed: a man with access to gobs of money trying to right a wrong. "How will I reach you?"

Llorn smiled and stood. "Leave word with the owner of the Broken Antler in Tallow."

FIVE: LORELEI

In the quiet neighborhood of Ancris known as Slade, Lorelei Aurelius entered the rear garden of a small brick home. The home was owned by an aging woman named Olga, who'd agreed to let Lorelei and her partner, Creed, use her attic to surveil a suspected drug dealer. Their surveillance had been fruitless so far, and the attic had become something of a prison, but Lorelei didn't care just then. She could hardly wait to tell Creed about the invitation she'd just received.

She knocked on the back door, heard the creaking of floorboards a few moments later. The door opened and Olga stared up at her with crinkly eyes. "Well, well"—Olga shuffled away, leaving the door open—"you're smiling for once."

"I know!" Lorelei stepped inside and closed the door behind her. The air in the little house was humid and thick with the scent of mulberries. "I've been invited to join an expedition!"

"An expedition, is it? Olga shuffled to the stove and stirred a pot of berries she was boiling down for jam. "Care to tell me about it over some tea?"

"Maybe later? I just ate, and Creed's been here all day. I'd better go relieve him."

"Sounds fine, dear."

Lorelei went through the kitchen and up the narrow, old stairs.

"Who goes there?" Creed's deep voice called from the attic. Creed was a fellow inquisitor and Lorelei's partner these past seven years. Though he came from Tragos, far to the southwest, he'd been living in Ancris for nearly thirty years, and his accent was hardly noticeable.

"It's your mother," Lorelei said, entering the small workspace. Once a sculpting studio for a stonemason, the attic room was clean and uncrowded with a slanted ceiling, a worktable, and two weathered stools at its center.

"You don't *sound* like my mother." Creed, long and muscular, lay on several thick woolen blankets, small comfort on the rough wooden planks. He was forty years old but fit as any man half his age. He had a spyglass pressed to one eye and was peering through a louvered vent.

"That's because you've been gone from home for so long," Lorelei whined. "You don't even recognize my voice anymore."

Creed rolled halfway over and flashed a bright smile. "*Now* you sound like my mother." He did a double take, then went back to his watching. "You seem chipper."

"That's because I am." She paused, waiting for him to take the bait.

Creed was a ruggedly handsome man with an impeccably trimmed beard and graying hair. He had slight bags under his sharp, hazel eyes—the sort of eyes women melted over, as did a good number of the men in the parlors Creed liked to frequent—but even so, he had an indomitable quality about him. "And what, pray tell, makes you so chipper when all you have to look forward to is hours of trying to stay awake while staring through this goddessforsaken metal tube?"

"I've received an *invitation* . . ."

Creed sat up and handed her the spyglass. "I'm too tired to play this game."

Like Creed, Lorelei had abandoned her inquisitor's uniform for simpler clothes. She wore a wool cap, a cream-colored shirt, patched linen pants, and worn leather shoes. She took off the cap and set it on the spotless worktable. Creed, obsessed about cleanliness, had insisted on cleaning the attic from top to bottom before their surveillance of the chandlery up the street had begun in earnest.

Lorelei dragged one of the stools out and sat. "Ash invited me to visit a *geoflare.*"

"I seem to recall you having access to an indurium dragon." Creed started to get up, nearly bumped his head on the ceiling and sat back on the floor. He settled for raising his arms and stretching his neck and shoulders. "You could've gone any time you wanted, no?"

"I could have, but this is an expedition with a team of *alchemysts*. I'm going to learn so much!"

"Didn't you already read a stack of books about geoflares?"

"Are you kidding? That's *nothing* compared to going in person."

Creed shrugged. "I suppose . . ."

"Don't you ever want to leave Ancris, see the world?"

"Why leave when anything I ever wanted is here? You can't beat living in a capital city."

"I could name a *thousand* reasons . . . You know what? Never mind. You're tired. You want to get home." She pointed the spyglass at the vent. "Anything from our friend?"

"Nothing out of the ordinary." He bent to touch his toes and groaned. "A woman dropped off a crate of perfume. A few customers. They actually looked like they bought some candles."

It wasn't surprising, but it *was* frustrating. She and Creed were part of a special detail in the Department of Inquisitors intended to curb the flow of illicit drugs from the Holt. Three weeks ago, they'd traced several medium-sized shipments to a chandler named Tomas. They began their surveillance a few days later and saw Tomas letting other Red Knives through the side entrance with several burlap-wrapped bundles. They could have arrested him at any time, but they'd held off in hopes of catching a bigger fish, someone higher up in the chain. Like Blythe, for example, the woman who ferried goods in from the Holt, or Llorn, their cruel enforcer, second only to Aarik Bloodhaven in the Red Knives' hierarchy. At the very least, they'd expected to see dealers coming for their supply. But they'd found nothing since those first few shipments.

"He knows we're watching," Creed said. "He must."

Lorelei shrugged. "Probably."

They heard a knock at Olga's back door, then several loud, metallic clanks—Olga tapping her spoon against the pot—then a muffled conversation. A moment later, the stairs creaked, and Kellen, a one-time imperial inquisitor, now a researcher and historian who spent most days at Ancris's famed library, entered the workroom. He was a tall, broad-shouldered man. His face was square face with a prominent jaw. His gray hair was thin and shorn close to his scalp. His belted tunic and hose might have look quaint on a smaller man, but Kellen's massive frame filled the garment almost to bursting, a reminder of the reputation he'd gained as a brutal interrogator. He took in the tiny attic space, chuckled, than laughed out loud. "I tell you true, I don't miss these days."

"Yes, well, it isn't much," Lorelei said, taking Creed's hand and squeezing it, "but we like the home we've made."

Creed smiled, but he seemed to be gazing yearningly toward the stairs. "What brings you by, Kellen?"

Kellen slid out the other stool from the worktable and sat. "I've come with a bit of information for Lorelei about the one and only case we worked together."

Creed frowned. "The missing chalice?"

"That's the one."

"It went unsolved, yes?" Creed, apparently curious, pulled his knees to his chest. "That was right before you retired."

"Right again. Unfortunately, as the three of us are well aware, not every case reaches a satisfying resolution."

"And, I'm guessing," Lorelei said, "that you have hope *this* one might yet be solved."

Kellen sat in silence, grinning like a boy with his finger in the honey jar.

Creed glared at Lorelei. "Now I see where you get it from."

Smiling, Lorelei slapped his knee.

"The case, you may recall," Kellen continued, "was the murder of an auctioneer."

Creed snapped his fingers. "I remember now. He was found with the sign of the Chosen cut into his forehead."

"That's right," Lorelei said. The Chosen were a group of zealots whose sole purpose was to restore the greatness of the Church in Alra's eyes. They did what, for this reason or that, the Church could not do on its own, often in ruthless fashion. Lorelei remembered how their sign, a scourge with five lashes, had been carved into the auctioneer's skin. There had been little bleeding from the wound, an indication the mutilation had occurred after his death. "We assumed the poor fellow had run afoul of the Chosen somehow."

Kellen nodded. "We never disproved that theory, but we never found a solid motive either."

"And now?" Lorelei asked.

"I may have stumbled onto one. While I was researching my upcoming book, the library's head archivist, Ezraela, became interested in my work. We became friendly . . . more than friendly, if I'm being honest. Naturally, I told her about my time at the Crag, the decades I spent as an inquisitor. When I told her about the case—I can't even recall how it came up anymore—she said she knew the auctioneer. I pressed her a bit further, and she confessed to having had a fling with him."

Lorelei cringed. "Was this going on when the auctioneer was murdered?"

"Unfortunately, yes, and she was afraid she might be targeted as well."

Creed said, "The two of you must have had the same concerns—about your own welfare, I mean."

"We did," Kellen said. "We discussed whether or not to continue, but we felt honor bound. At the time, hundreds of rare antiques from a once-great house were being auctioned off to pay the owner's creditors. We assumed the Chosen had seen something in that lot, something damning to them or to the empire."

"Then we discovered," Lorelei added, "the count of the inventoried items taken into the house was different from the number that were eventually put up for bid—off by one."

"A mistake?" Creed asked.

"We considered that," Lorelei said, "but we came to suspect that a private bid had been arranged by the auctioneer. We never found out who might have bid on the missing piece. When word got out about the mark of the Chosen, everyone stopped talking to us. Eventually, the auction house stopped answering questions, too, and we were forced to let the matter go."

"And what about the librarian?" Creed asked.

"She confirmed our suspicions of a preempt. The item in question, a bronze chalice, was ancient, predating the empire by hundreds of years. She admitted the auctioneer had received a late bid, but he'd already agreed to the original deal and planned to honor it. He was so nervous about the chalice being stolen from the auction house, he gave it to Ezraela for safekeeping until the buyer could arrive in Ancris. He was murdered the following day."

"So where is it?" Creed asked.

"At her mother's house in Erimaea. She promised to bring it back with her when she visits her next month."

Lorelei felt a stir of excitement. She'd thought the case dead and gone. To have a new lead fall into her lap made her eager to reopen it.

Creed, on the other hand, seemed anything but pleased. "After all that, you're going to tell me it's not even here?"

"Well, no one asked you to stay and listen," Kellen said. "I came to tell Lorelei."

Creed snorted, pushed himself off the floor, walked off in the hunched way the attic demanded, and clomped down the stairs. The door at the base of the stair opened and closed, and he said something to Olga that Lorelei couldn't hear.

"Ignore him," Lorelei said to Kellen. "It's a good find."

"A *lucky* find. Anyway, I was hoping you might take a look at it when Ezraela returns. If the chalice is as old as she says it is, the runes are likely Graanthan or Kaeldish."

Lorelei had developed a fascination with the empire's elder tongues in her teenage years. It had consumed her reading for the better part of a year, enough that she could decipher both languages. "Certainly."

"Grand." Kellen stood, as stoop-backed as Creed had. "I'll leave you to it, then." He took in the attic again, chuckled, and clomped down the stairs, calling up as he went, "I'll send word when Ezraela returns."

When the house was silent again, Lorelei lay down on the blanketed floor, picked up the spyglass, and began her watch. Her elation faded as the tedium began. The chandlery was on the ground floor of an old stone, wedge-shaped building at an angled intersection half a block away. Olga's attic was perfectly positioned to view both the glass doors at the front and the side entrance Tomas used to bring in supplies. A few people came and went—normal, everyday citizens from the look of them.

The lanky, towheaded Tomas stepped outside into the long shadows of the bright sun to chat with the wheelwright across the street. *Creed's right,* Lorelei decided. Tomas had gotten wind of them, which made her angry they hadn't arrested them when they'd had the chance. Now it was too late. He'd almost certainly gotten rid of whatever evidence might once have been in the chandlery. And Lorelei had no one to blame over it but herself. She was the one who'd suggested they hold off in hopes of getting someone more important.

Soon enough, the bright sun set and cant exploded across the sky, salmon pink, a splash of crimson, a spray of ochre. Sheets of canary yellow momentarily occluded the early evening stars. Then the sky dimmed, and Nox asserted its dominance.

Lorelei set down her spyglass and picked up a similar device called a nightglass. The nightglass's lenses were made of a special glass that turned hot-blooded creatures into wavering shades of purple. Although a nightglass's range was limited, she could still see the chandlery and the streets around it. A few people came and went, but as usual in the sleepy neighborhood of Slade, traffic soon vanished altogether.

An hour later, Tomas stepped out of the chandlery, locked the door, and disappeared down the street.

Lorelei thought about calling off the surveillance and authorizing a raid to see what they'd find. "Not yet," she told herself. "Just a few more days."

SIX: ORDREN

Hours before the bright sun rose, Inquisitor Ordren roused himself from bed and left his small home on the north side of Ancris. He hated that he had to wake so early to visit the Hissing Man. He hated that he had to walk there along the dirty streets of Kiln. He hated that he had to pass through the stink of the dragonworks and descend into the catacombs just to meet with the man. More than anything, he hated the Hissing Man himself.

He walked through a rough tunnel, shivering from the cold, holding a cracked glass globe with a wisp inside it to light the way. The wisp was bright and lit the tunnel well, but its glacial blue glow made him feel even colder than he already did. Worse, the closer he came to the crypt, the more his hands trembled and his heart raced. When he'd first reached out to the Chosen years ago, he'd asked if he could just send a note, but the Hissing Man had denied him.

"Nothing written," he'd hissed. "Ever. When you have information for me, you'll deliver it in person."

Ordren had nearly walked away from the arrangement, but it was such easy money. All he had to do was pass along a bit of gossip from the Crag here and there. Plenty of people did it. All throughout Ancris, rumors were passed to the palace, powerful senators, the Church, the Chosen, even the Red Knives—anyone who paid. It was illegal of course. Ordren could lose his job over it. But no one asked many questions about whispers, and even if he was caught, the chances of a formal inquiry were slim. And the goddess knew he wasn't getting rich chasing down thieves or raiding drug dens.

No, his making an extra stag or two wasn't hurting anyone, but why, oh why did it have to be underground? The cold made his joints ache, and the tunnels seemed to close in the farther he went. It was even worse in the section where the walls turned square and manmade. It felt unnatural, too perfect, and all the more fragile for it.

Light spilled along the tunnel from a globe in the ceiling of the room ahead. Ordren tucked his wisplight into his coat pocket and passed through an archway adorned with Alra's eight-pointed star. He paused at the octangular crypt to take a deep breath and try to pull himself together. The stone columns were stout, the domed ceiling smooth and free of cracks, yet it all felt like it was about to come crashing down on Ordren's head.

The crypt was part of Alra's Acre, a section of the catacombs set aside for the Church. It had three ornate archways set at right angles that led to more crypts. Between each set of arches was a door that led to a sepulcher that housed the remains of an illustra, a high shepherd, or perhaps even a high priest or priestess.

Gaul, a pudgy-faced eunuch in a black habit, stood at the far end of the crypt. Built like a bloody watchtower, Gaul was a scourge, a member of the Chosen assigned to guard the sepulcher the Hissing Man had claimed as his own. While the common citizen would lose a finger for stepping foot in Alra's Acre without permission, and those found disturbing a sepulcher would lose a hand or a foot, the Hissing Man was the head of the Chosen, and no one, not even the Church, dared challenge him.

"Heard any good jokes lately?" Ordren said to tongueless Gaul. It was a crude joke, but the man always looked at Ordren as if Ordren were a beggar. When Gaul merely stared, Ordren went on, "Well, open the door, you leaving from a lumber mill. The man and I have things to discuss."

After another long stare, Gaul blinked languidly and opened the door beside him. He made a few hand gestures to someone inside. Some murmuring followed—too soft to hear—and Gaul bowed his head and stepped aside, leaving the door open. Then, he crossed his arms and stared at the far wall as if Ordren didn't exist.

Ordren entered the sepulcher and found the Hissing Man sitting at a desk beyond a marble sarcophagus. The area was normally reserved for a plinth with a book that told the tales of the deceased. The plinth and its book were in the corner to make room for the desk, a set of chairs, and a bookshelf.

The Hissing Man wore a black habit like Gaul, but it was curiously threadbare. Its hood was pulled up, making the him look more than a little like a hangman. As always, his eyes were all but hidden behind black, gauzy bandages. Some said he wore them in homage to the illustrae, who wore masks that obscured their eyes. Others said it was mockery. To Ordren it had always seemed desperate, as though the Hissing Man felt himself equal to the Church's leaders. He wasn't. He was a proxy at best, a glorified servant, an old hunched mastiff that barked or bit depending on the Church's needs.

This dog pays well, though, Ordren mused as he made his way past the sarcophagus.

The Hissing Man was writing on a scroll but paused when Ordren reached the far side of his desk. "Well?" he breathed, thin and raspy.

For years, Ordren had been convinced his harsh voice was an act, a way to hide his true identity, but time and repeated meetings had eventually convinced him it was real, perhaps the result of disease or injury. Whatever its origin, his voice was surely why he'd adopted the name of the villain from folk tales meant to scare children into obedience.

"You asked me to keep an eye on the shrine renovations," Ordren told him, "and to tell you anything that might slow its progress."

The Hissing Man finished writing his letter, blotted it, and rolled it up. "And?"

Ordren sat in the empty chair. "Master Renato has apparently made an almighty push to catch up on the work so he can sneak off for a day or two. He's arranged a research expedition to Tortoise Peak."

The Hissing Man looked up at Ordren with his bandaged eyes. "An expedition . . ."

Ordren nodded, shifting in the chair so his piles didn't hurt so much. "They mean to study it. Examine its alchemycal properties."

The Hissing Man pursed his lips. "And how did you learn of it?"

"Ash, one of Master Renato's journeymen, is a friend of Lorelei Aurelius. I overheard him asking her to join him." Ordren didn't know the significance of Tortoise Peak, only that the Hissing Man had told him to keep an ear out for anyone looking too deeply into it. Inquisitor Lorelei was young and more like a skittish hare than a proper inquisitor, but she was also sharp. It would likely prove troublesome if she, Master Renato, or any of his assistants spent too much time there.

"Very well," the Hissing Man said. "Anything else?"

"As a matter of fact, yes. Do you recall Kellen Vesarius?"

"The inquisitor . . . retired inquisitor? Yes. He was assigned to the Mykal Mythros case along with Inquisitor Lorelei, if I remember correctly."

Ordren nodded. "He was poking about the Crag the other day, asking about that very case."

The Hissing Man frowned. "Go on . . ."

"He wanted to know if we'd learned anything more about the chalice that went missing from Mykal's final auction."

"And have you?"

"No. The case was cold when Kellen retired. It's still cold."

"Then why was he asking about it?"

"He didn't say."

"He's nearly a decade into his retirement. Why would he be worried about an old cold case?"

Ordren shrugged. "Kellen always was stubborn."

"Where does he do his research?"

The question implied the Hissing Man was interested, which meant Kellen was in danger, especially if the old inquisitor had stumbled onto something sensitive. But what was Kellen but a grumpy old goat who'd never shown Ordren an uncia of respect? "He works on the third floor of the library in Old Town. You want me to talk to him?"

"That won't be necessary."

Ordren put his hands on the arms of the chair. "Very well. I'll just see your man about my payment, shall I?"

There was never a time Ordren had come to the catacombs that he didn't fear the Hissing Man would kill him and leave him in the sewers to rot. That fear arose as the hooded, bandage-eyed man across the desk from him paused and took a long breath. Then he lifted a bell from his desk, rang it, and Gaul ducked his head inside the sepulcher.

"Ten thrones," the Hissing Man told him.

"Oy," Ordren said. "I brought you two bits of information. *Important* information." His fears hadn't ebbed, but let a thing like that go, and pretty soon he'd be walking out with tin instead of gold.

The Hissing Man regarded Ordren. By the wisplight, Ordren saw his eyes blink twice. "Twenty."

Ordren stood, and Gaul reached into a purse at his leather belt and counted out twenty gold thrones. The sum was considerable, equal to two months of pay for his work as an inquisitor. Even so, as Ordren retraced his steps through the cold tunnel toward the dragonworks, he felt like none of it—the sneaking about, the risks, the cursed underground meetings—was worth it.

SEVEN: THE HISSING MAN

The Hissing Man waited for Ordren's footsteps to fade, then held up the letter he'd written. Gaul, the scourge most often assigned to watch over him in the catacombs, stepped forward and took it.

"Take it to our man in the woods," the Hissing Man rasped.

Gaul bowed his head and left. The sepulcher door closed behind him with an echoing boom.

The letter was a simple message to Llorn Bloodhaven, coded in case it was intercepted, demanding he come to Ancris so the two of them could speak in person. Llorn had reported trouble in the Holt. His brother Aarik had apparently gotten wind of their endeavors in the Deepwood Fens. It was troubling but hardly surprising—Aarik was going to find out sooner or later—but it presented them with problems. They needed to decide what to do about it, and soon.

That meeting would be several days in the making. He had other matters to deal with in the meantime, such as the somewhat alarming information Ordren had just dropped into his lap. The Hissing Man would deal with the old inquisitor and his research on his own. The expedition to Tortoise Peak would require a lighter hand, and that meant reaching out to Illustra Azariah, a long-time ally in the Hissing Man's quest to see the Church rise to its rightful place atop the empire.

From the shelf behind him, he fetched a lacquered wooden case and a brass pedestal with a circle of dragonbones mounted on it and set both on the desk in front of him. He opened the case. It had two compartments: one filled with a fine white powder, the other with black.

Many people thought the Hissing Man's bandages an affectation. They couldn't know he'd gone through the same ceremony the Church's illustrae had, nor could they know he'd been granted second sight, the ability to see in any direction, even things above or below him, which allowed him to see in complete darkness, as well, via the traces of aura and umbra that all things gave off. By and large, second sight was colorless, a canvas of white, black, and shades of gray. There were exceptions, however. The wisplight on his desk glowed silvery blue, much as he remembered them from his youth. The white powder, auris, shimmered chromatically, like the scales of the indurium dragon it had been ground from. The black powder, umbris, had been harvested from an onyx dragon. It shimmered, too, but in a deep violet, dim and brooding as Nox staring down from the heavens.

The Hissing Man took a modest pinch of the rosemary-scented white powder, held it to his nose, and sniffed. His nose burned, and he suddenly felt lighter. His breathing and the rush of blood in his ears sounded louder, and the coldness of the sepulcher deepened ever so slightly. He closed the case, feeling the increase in his potency, and turned his attention to the brass pedestal and its circle of dragon-bones. A translucent membrane was stretched between the bones. Made from the silverskin of the heart of the dragon kit that had provided the mirror's bones, the membrane shimmered in his second sight. And little wonder. It had been ritually treated with blood, the Hissing Man's own and that of the man he needed to speak to.

Drawing upon the power of aura, the Hissing Man reached through the silver-skin. He felt a surge of discomfort, akin to vertigo. The silverskin brightened, and the face of Azariah Andrinus III appeared. He was head of the Alran Church in Ancris, a middle-aged man, square-jawed with full lips, and clouded eyes, a result of the acid that had been dripped onto them when he'd become an illustra.

"This couldn't have waited?" His voice was hoarse, likely from having just awoken.

"It's important," the Hissing Man snapped.

"It better be," Azariah said.

The Hissing Man relayed everything Ordren had told him about the Tortoise Peak expedition. When he was done, the illustra looked even more weary. "Will the complications never cease?"

The Hissing Man laughed a long wheeze. "We're nearing the end of our long road. Our 'complications' will only multiply."

"I'm aware. It's only—"

Speaking through the silverskin was a linking of the minds, which could also allow a troubling memory or pressing concern to pass from one to the other. So it was that the Hissing Man knew why Azariah had stopped talking. He'd had a vision of his son, Cassian, a handsome young man with curly blond hair, and in the vision Cassian was lying motionless on an inlaid marble floor, a knife sticking out of the chest of his black priest's habit, blood pooling beneath him. Azariah's son had vanished more than a decade ago, and the investigation that had followed had found no clues as to where he might have gone or who might have taken him. The questions around his son's death had plagued Azariah for years. They plagued him still.

"Our worst fears have a way of manifesting," the Hissing Man said quickly, "especially in difficult times."

"But it felt so real . . ."

"As do dreams while you're sleeping. You're fatigued, Your Radiance. You've been pushing yourself too hard. What you saw was a nightmare."

Necessary lies, especially at this stage of the game. Their ultimate goal was to free their mighty lord, Faedryn, from the prison he'd been placed in at the end of the last age, and they could only do that if they woke one of Faedryn's most pow-erful servants, Strages, from the spell he was under. The Hissing Man believed Azariah was committed to their cause, but the man became intractable when he focused too much on his lost son. It was precisely why Faedryn had given the Hissing Man the power to manipulate his memories, but Azariah had power of his own, and the manipulations never seemed to last.

So, as he'd done many times since Cassian's disappearance, the Hissing Man used a bit of the aura within him to will away Azariah's worries. "Your son's disappearance was tragic. It haunts you, and justifiably so. The vision was merely your mind trying to make sense of it."

Azariah pinched the bridge of his nose and closed his cloudy white eyes. "I suppose you're right." When he opened them again, he seemed calmer. "Very well. The expedition should be simple enough to deal with. A quick word with the quintarch's wife, and it will be quashed. You'll deal with the inquisitor?"

The Hissing Man had made no mention of Inquisitor Kellen, but just as the Hissing Man could sense Azariah's thoughts, Azariah could sense his. "Of course."

"Then tell me of Llorn. Has the meeting been arranged?"

"Nearly. He'll come to Ancris. I'll speak to him in the dragonworks. Aarik will be dealt with, one way or the other."

"Very well, if there's nothing else . . . ?"

The Hissing Man sneered. "So eager to return to your comfortable bed while I do all the work from the shadows."

"That was our arrangement. That has *always* been our arrangement."

"Because I'm foul to look upon, unpleasant to be near . . ."

"You are feared, and rightfully so. Right now, it's better for our enemies to wonder where you are and when you'll strike next." Azariah paused. "But fear not—"

"I don't *fear*. I grow tired of this hole in the ground."

"Either way, when this is done, you'll walk beneath the bright sun as my equal. And I'll visit the catacombs soon. I have a box of the tea that helps with your gout. And a bottle of syris from the Holt."

The Hissing Man hated asking for such things—it felt too much like weakness—but it pleased him that Azariah had remembered them. "*After* Llorn comes. It would be better to speak of his plans in person in any case."

"Very well," Azariah said.

The vision faded, and the silverskin returned to its normal, translucent form.

Wanting his own tasks to be done as soon as possible so that he, too, could find rest, the Hissing Man dipped his fingers into the wooden case again and took a much healthier pinch of the black powder. He held it to his nose, smelled its lush, fecund scent, and sniffed it, then rubbed the remains over his gums.

In many ways, aura and umbra were two sides of the same coin. The former was of the mind, the latter of the body—*animi, corporis*, in the empire's elder tongue. Instead of vertigo, the umbris made his muscles burn, and his joints ache. It worsened his gout, but he accepted the pain as yet another price to pay to see Faedryn freed from his prison.

The Hissing Man left his office and limped down the stone corridor—*slide THUMP, slide THUMP, slide THUMP*—traversed the catacombs' tunnels and entered the sewers. The stink made the air heavy. It was pitch dark, but his second sight guided him. With the power of umbra, he collected shadows, gathered them around him like a cloak, then crawled through an iron grate like a rat to the street.

Overhead, Nox stared down, a glaring, violet eye as the Hissing Man made his way, silent as a wolf, toward Old Town. Each of the empire's five capital cities had a *quadrata*, a square that marked the center of the original settlement. Ancris's was surrounded by stone buildings bunched shoulder to shoulder. The largest of them was a three-story library with a clock tower.

Masking his movement with the shadows, he stole up the stairs to the front entrance. It was locked, so he continued around the side and tried the delivery entrance, but it, too, was locked. He considered shattering the lock with the aura's power, but quelled the urge. Maintaining the spell of shadows was making his limbs burn, and that in turn was pushing him toward rashness. Keeping his purpose hidden was as important as the mission itself.

Gritting his teeth against the pain, he limped around the rear of the library, found a window ajar, pushed it open, and climbed inside. Then he let the shadows go and took a moment to breathe, to let the pain ebb. When he'd recovered, he climbed the main stairwell to the third floor, the one set aside for research. He shuffled along a hallway to a room with a writing desk and a table laden with scrolls, books, and stone tablets—Kellen's research.

Though words written in mundane ink were often dim in his second sight, the Hissing Man could read them well enough given time. He skimmed Kellen's journal for mention of the chalice. Notes were pinned to a corkboard on the opposite wall. He scanned those as well. He rifled through the books, pausing to read the odd note on a scrap of paper pinched between the pages. Eventually, he came to the conclusion that it was unlikely the missing chalice meant anything more to Kellen than a link to a bygone age. He likely didn't understand its significance to the Hissing Man and his plans.

He returned to the hallway, vowing to have Ordren keep an eye out, even ask Azariah to send a shepherd by to pretend to be interested in Kellen's work—try to learn more that way. But beyond that, it seemed unlikely Kellen would seek out the chalice.

He was just preparing to descend the stairs to the ground floor when he spotted a potbellied man in stained work clothes standing next to the door to the clock tower, wiping his hands with a rag. A lantern hung from the crook of his elbow. He stared wide-eyed at the Hissing Man, his mouth gaping. Likely he'd just come from greasing the gears, perhaps resetting the clock tower's weights. He'd seen where the Hissing Man had been snooping. Word of it would surely reach Kellen. The Hissing Man couldn't allow that.

"Can I help you?" the workman said stupidly.

The Hissing Man rushed him. The man retreated, stumbled and fell hard into the door, knocking it open. The sound of ticking gears grew loud.

The Hissing Man lunged and grabbed him by the throat. "You brought this upon yourself," he hissed. He pulled the clock tender to his feet, pushed him into the clock tower—a maze of clattering gears, ropes, pulleys, and chains hanging over an empty shaft—and pinned him to the landing rail. The clock tender choked and wheezed and flailed desperately as the Hissing Man pressed him against the railing. He used the railing to shove the Hissing Man back, but the umbris-fueled Hissing Man pushed him back harder, bending the man's shoulders over the rail. Arms and shoulders burning with power, the Hissing man bit back a howl of pain and heaved the fat clock keeper over the railing. The man screamed and landed two stories down with a sharp crunch. The Hissing Man staggered down the tower stairs. At the ground floor, he crouched beside the clock tender. The man's mouth worked slowly. His eyes stared up vacantly. Then, his head turned and he went still. The Hissing Man drew his knife and cut a five-tailed scourge, the sign of the Chosen, a mark of unforgivable sins, into the man's forehead.

It was unfortunate business, but a necessary distraction. Whoever discovered the clock tender would be drawn to the sign, would think the man wicked, or at the very least that he'd been *judged* to be wicked, and not that he'd witnessed the Hissing Man prowling in the library. Content that the man's death would receive little scrutiny, the Hissing Man clambered back out the window of the library, gathered shadows around him, and returned to the catacombs below the city.

EIGHT: AZARIAH

Azariah stood on the balcony outside his temple office, gazing out over Ancris as the dark sun glowered over the mountains to the west. Though his eyes were covered by his ivory-and-gold mask, he saw the city clearly. The ritual that had ruined his eyes at the age of twenty-five had granted him his second sight, allowing him to see in all directions at once. Even as he gazed out at the halls of government, the temples, and the market district, he saw the lantern on the desk behind him, the inlaid gold filigree on the wooden door beyond it.

For the most part, his vision was shades of gray, as if the city and the mountains beyond were made of clay. It made Nox's angry violet light appear all the brighter. An iridescent blue curtain hung over the city as well, a gauze so thin he could barely see it. That curtain and the seventeen pillars that powered it were known as the palisade. It was a public work, a monumental feat of engineering and alchemy, one of Azariah's crowning achievements in his time as illustra. Azariah couldn't see all the pillars from his current vantage—Mount Evalarus, on which the temple was built, blocked seven of them from his view—but he could see ten of them. Each was a spear of cerulean light in the gray landscape of his second sight. Above and between them, the palisade's curtain shimmered like oil on water, protecting everything beneath it from the dark sun's harmful rays.

A short while ago, he'd sent a request to Highreach for Tyrinia Solvina to attend him at the temple, and he'd come to his balcony to wait and reflect. He found viewing the palisade calming. It gave him perspective, which he needed after his discussion with the Hissing Man. Something about his son, Cassian, had come up during their talk, but for the life of him he couldn't remember what it was. He remembered the struggles and the joys of raising Cassian after his mother had died in childbirth. He remembered playing with him in their apartments after his priestly duties had been completed. He even remembered Cassian blossoming into a fine young man and becoming a priest himself. But when he tried to recall the circumstances around Cassian's disappearance, the memories were like so much sand in a sieve. He recalled Cassian pacing restlessly in his apartments, but then the memory slipped away, replaced by one of a much-younger Cassian running along the halls of the temple while Azariah chased him.

It made him feel broken. A man who couldn't remember the circumstances around his son's disappearance? Well, he was no father at all then, was he? He often had the urge to ask Japheth to fill in the details, but he was so embarrassed about the gaps in his memory that the only person he confided in was the Hissing

Man. He felt calmer when he did, but also hollow, as if the Hissing Man had merely helped him to paper over a hole instead of fill it in.

Footsteps approached his office door. A knock came, and Azariah returned to his office and sat down at his desk. "Come."

The door swung open, and Japheth, Azariah's most trusted servant, stepped inside. He wore the uniform of a high shepherd: a hooded tabard with Alra's full, eight-pointed starburst, a double-circle at the center, on his chest. His head was shaved, his beard trimmed. From his wide leather belt hung a book of proverbs from which he often recited before rendering judgement on the wicked. He bowed and said, "Your Radiance, the Domina has arrived."

"Very good. Show her in."

"At once, Your Holiness."

Japheth left and returned shortly with the Domina Tyrinia Solvina, a stately woman in a thread-of-silver dress. She was Quintarch Lucran's wife.

Azariah gestured to the upholstered chair across from him. "Please," he said.

Tyrinia nodded and sat. Japheth left.

"Thank you for coming on such short notice," Azariah said.

Tyrinia was well into her fifties—the same age as Azariah, more or less—but looked much older. She had worry lines around her mouth and eyes and pale makeup and rouge that failed to hide them. She might be merely tired and aging, but if Azariah's informants were right, it was more than that. Word was she was once again assuaging her grief by partaking in rapture, a euphoric that, over time, sapped one's vitality. Too much left one a withered husk. From the look of her, she was halfway there.

Tyrinia bowed respectfully. "Your message said it was urgent."

"It is, but before we get to that, please indulge me. There's something I've been meaning to talk to you about for some time. I'm aware of the ceremony you held recently in the catacombs to honor your beloved son."

Tyrinia's son Ransom had died from an overdose of rapture some fifteen years ago. Several days ago, Lucran, Tyrinia, and their daughter, Skylar, had attended a brief ceremony to honor his memory. Mere hours later, Lucran had left Ancris on dragonback to rejoin the effort to quash the rebellion in Syrdia.

As any mother would, Tyrinia had been heartbroken over Ransom's death. She also felt responsible, and Azariah could hardly blame her for it. She'd been taking rapture for rheumatism when Ransom was wounded by a Syrdian gryphon. The wound was slow to heal, so he started taking the drug as well. But rapture was a sly seductress. They both became addicted, each giving the other permission to take more, until Ransom took too much.

Tyrinia readjusted herself in the chair, and her gaze darted around the room. "Why do you mention it?"

"I have an offer to make," Azariah said, "but I hesitate because I'm worried you might take it the wrong way."

"Go on."

"You're aware of how the Kin revere wisps."

"Of course," she said, rolling her eyes. "I always though it vulgar."

Azariah waggled his head, neither agreeing nor disagreeing. "I see no issue with the practice myself. Honoring the dead is a sentiment I think we can all agree on."

"But to treat them like they're holy? It's unnatural . . ."

"You're right. Most souls are undeserving of such praise, and they can hardly know which one is which, can they? But wouldn't you agree there are some wisps who likely *deserve* recognition and praise? Who *deserve* to be honored?"

"Is there a point to all this, Your Holiness?"

"You're likely aware that the Church knows how to quicken a wisp?"

Tyrinia leaned forward in her chair and furrowed her wrinkled brow. "Are you suggesting you quicken my *son's* soul?"

"Only if you'd like. We're in the mountains, not some distant corner of the empire. The power of the Holt will cause it to happen one day anyway, whether any of us likes it or not. That will be decades from now, generations, centuries, perhaps. But you could have his wisp *now*, to honor. To cherish." Tyrinia opened her mouth to protest, but Azariah quickly continued. "There's evidence Alra knew how to quicken wisps." He made a circle with two fingers, Alra's sign. "May her memory abide."

Tyrinia made Alra's sign as well. Then her shoulders slumped and she sighed. "The goddess did?"

"Yes, and she used the ability twice. Once to speak to a paragon who died in the days leading up to the final battle with Faedryn. And another time, many years earlier, to wish peace upon a troubled soul."

The first was true. The second was a lie meant to give Tyrinia the sense that it wasn't a single, desperate act on Alra's part.

Tyrinia was silent for a moment. Then she asked, "Will it prevent his soul from rising to Déu?"

"Far from it. I suspect a quickening will hasten his contemplation and allow him to meet Alra that much sooner." Another lie. Azariah had no idea if that was true or not. And of course he left unsaid that Ransom's soul, weighted by sin, could be drawn down to the seven hells of Kharos. "No one need know. The offer I make is for you and you alone. I'll quicken the wisp myself, in secret. Once it's in your hands, you can do what you wish with it. Share it, or not."

"And what will this cost me?"

"Nothing, Domina."

"You invited me here for a reason, Your Holiness."

"I did, but that's separate from—"

"Just tell me what it is."

Azariah composed himself. "I've been made aware of an expedition that's being organized. It's leaving today, in fact."

"The expedition to Tortoise Peak . . . ?"

"The very one."

"My daughter mentioned it to me." Tyrinia shrugged. "What of it?"

"It needs to be called off, today, and the alchemysts returned to Ancris."

"And why is that?"

"Are you aware of the delays in the renovation of the shrine?"

"To some degree, yes."

"They're unacceptable in the Church's eyes."

Three years ago, Master Renato, Quintarch Lucran's chief alchemyst, conducted a survey of the shrine and found that the white quartzite stones were becoming brittle. Azariah knew why—it was a direct result of the palisade—but he could hardly admit that to Master Renato or anyone else. He'd needed a distraction to keep them from looking too deeply into the matter. The very findings of Renato's survey had been the perfect solution. He demanded funding from the imperial coffers to renovate the shrine before the stones' degradation got any worse.

He might have authorized the project using Church funds, but the Church was forbidden by imperial decree from funding such projects—the failure of the Holy Rebellion decades ago had seen to that. It was far from an insurmountable problem, though. Every year, the shrine drew untold thousands of pilgrims to Ancris, which poured rivers of gold into the empire's coffers. Azariah used it as a lever.

Lucran eventually agreed but had insisted on overseeing the project. At first, Azariah resisted any oversight, but he soon bowed to Lucran's will. The point was not the renovation itself, but to occupy the city's alchemysts to such a degree that they wouldn't look too deeply into the underlying causes of the problem.

Things had been going smoothly ever since, but now came the expedition to Tortoise Peak. It could lead to the alchemysts worrying about the palisade, or worse, heading into the Holt to find more such examples. They might stumble onto the crucible.

"It is merely a one-day expedition, from what I understand," Tyrinia said.

"Yes, but how much planning went into it? What sort of research will occupy the alchemysts' time in the days, weeks, and months ahead? I won't stand for it. I cannot. The shrine must be preserved. *Then* there will be time for such research."

Tyrinia considered, then took a deep breath. "It isn't an unreasonable request, truth be told—the shrine is taking an excessively long time to complete—but *Skylar* is the one who authorized the expedition."

"Then *un*authorize it."

"Yes, well"—Tyrinia twisted her wrinkled mouth into a smile—"you're aware that my husband, our quintarch, granted both Skylar and me certain responsibilities before he left for Syrdia. They don't overlap, I'm afraid, and Skylar is the Consul of Ancris. She has authority over the city's public works and related projects."

Azariah was well aware of the arrangement. He would have summoned Skylar if he'd thought he could convince her, but the young woman was famously intractable, at least toward him. He had a much better chance with Tyrinia.

"As much as it galls me to admit," Tyrinia went on, "I don't have the authority to unauthorize it."

"As you say, Skylar has authority over the city and its internal affairs, but you, as Domina, have authority over the Ancran province."

"Yes. And?"

"If I recall, Tortoise Peak lies well outside the borders of our city. Tell them it's a matter of imperial security. Tell them the peak is under threat of attack. Tell them another quintarch expressed interest in it, and you promised them *they* could study the peak first. Choose whatever excuse you wish. Just send them home so they can get back to work on my shrine."

"This seems rather important to you, Azariah. Why?"

"Is the wellbeing of the shrine not enough?"

"For *me*, yes. I'm asking what it means to *you*."

"Vanity," Azariah said. "Pride. Alra's glory is *my* glory, Domina. I want that shrine made whole."

"Well, that's . . . I'm not really sure what that is," she said as she pushed herself to a stand. "Nevertheless, you'll have your precious alchemysts."

"And what of Ransom's wisp?"

Tyrinia hesitated. For a moment, Azariah thought she might decline. Then she said, "Tell me when it's ready," and left in a rush.

As Tyrinia's footsteps faded, Azariah sighed and wiped a drip of sweat from his brow.

NINE: LORELEI

An imperial coach trundled up Mount Blackthorn, bearing Lorelei toward the palace. The sky was still dark, Nox glowing on the western horizon. On the bench beside Lorelei were a sheepskin coat, a scarf and hat knitted by her mother, and rabbit fur gloves. As the coach passed through the palace walls, she pulled the hat on and tucked her red hair into it to keep it from whipping about as she flew.

The coach trundled to a stop at the palace stairs. In a pleasant surprise, Princess Skylar herself opened the cabin door, holding a steaming mug of tea. A strikingly pretty woman with blond curls and glacier blue eyes, Skylar had seen twenty-eight winters pass, same as Lorelei. She wore an elegant dress made of silver silk that glowed violet in Nox's fitful light.

Lorelei picked up her coat, gloves and scarf and stepped down from the coach. "Early meeting?"

Skylar held the mug out and pretended to be affronted. "Maybe I woke early to wish my best friend luck on her adventure."

"You"—Lorelei slipped her gloves under her belt, folded the coat over one arm, and accepted the mug—"willingly get up early?"

Skylar's adorable frown faded. "Okay, you win. I have a meeting shortly after reckoning. Now let's get a move on or I'm going to be late."

Hiding a smile, Lorelei warmed her hands around the cup and sipped the jasmine tea, her favorite. As she and Skylar headed toward the rear of the palace, she asked, "And who is the meeting with this time?"

"The master mason for the Syrdian arch. We're discussing—" Skylar yawned loudly "—the final touches."

Lorelei laughed. "Try to control your enthusiasm."

"You misjudge me, my dear. I'm enjoying the project. I've decided that one of the final touches will be a dracora holding a lance on a spread-winged dragon."

"Ransom?"

"It's meant to honor *all* dracorae who fought in the campaign, but yes, in my heart, it's Ransom." Skylar had adored her brother, but he died in the Syrdian campaign fifteen years ago, though the campaign itself showed no signs of abating.

Lorelei squeezed her hand. "Then it will be for me, too."

"Your expedition, though . . ." Skylar squeezed Lorelei's hand back. "It's rather exciting, isn't it? Part of me wishes I'd taken Ash up on his offer to join you."

Lorelei sipped the hot tea to quell the anxious tickle in her stomach. As they rounded the palace and headed for the rear gate, she said, "You can still change your mind. Postpone your meeting?"

"No, it's too important. Father will be returning soon. I want the arch ready for the commemoration before he arrives."

The guard at the rear gate bowed his head as they approached. Skylar nodded back, and they passed through the curtain wall.

A footpath led down to a broad shoulder of land between two mountains where the imperial eyrie, a massive structure of stone and wood, stood. It had huge, rolling doors at the front and rear, and a large cupola on the roof that allowed dragons entrance and egress. Near the front, a cohort of seven dragons was being readied. The lone silver dragon was the smallest, about five horses from tip to tail. The two brasses and three golds were noticeably larger—each six, maybe seven horses in length. Bothymus, the enormous indurium, was eight horses easily.

Eyrie master Stromm, a giant man with bright red hair, was directing his eyrie hands in the loading of saddlebags. Beyond the dragons, a dozen men and women, the alchemysts Lorelei was set to join, huddled near the paddock fence. As Lorelei and Skylar crossed a stream bed via a small wooden bridge, Lorelei's agoraphobia intensified, and she began to feel nauseous. She'd always felt uncomfortable around groups, especially strangers, which was rather unfortunate for an imperial inquisitor. She managed well enough when she told herself it was her duty, but this was a day of leisure, and none of her tricks were working.

In a small mercy, Ash Torentada spotted them and broke away from the other alchemysts. He was a stunningly pretty man with dark, expressive eyes, long eyelashes, and full lips, and he'd been friends with Lorelei and Skylar since childhood. He wore a hooded coat and boots lined with ermine and matching kidskin gloves.

Skylar looked him up and down as they neared one another. "You know you're going to get dirty, right?"

"Of course I do," Ash said. "It's an expedition."

"Then why are you dressed for a winter solstice ball?"

"Skylar, my love, these *are* my work clothes. And besides"—he shot a glance toward one of the other alchemysts, a gorgeous man with swarthy skin and a trimmed beard—"there's no need to look like a vole when there are pretty birds about."

The dark-skinned man was one of Ash's fellow alchemysts. He'd traveled all the way from Lyros to help with the renovation at the shrine. He had penetrating eyes and the sort of lopsided smile that could melt glaciers.

In another small mercy, the other alchemysts kept their distance. A few waved or smiled. Master Renato ignored her altogether. It was Ash's doing, she was sure. He'd prepared them for her peculiar needs. Lorelei wished meeting new people wasn't so stressful, but she had always felt that way. That she'd managed to cope with it was due in no small part to her friends' understanding.

Stromm, having finished securing the last of the saddlebags, cupped his hands to his mouth. "Ready, Master Renato!"

Master Renato, a portly fellow with jowls and a broad, straight brow, clapped and urged everyone forward with broad sweeps of his arms. "Let's go, everyone. We've a long day ahead."

Skylar kissed cheeks with Lorelei and took the mug. "May your journey be fruitful." She turned to Ash and winked. "Yours as well."

Ash headed toward Bothymus, the big indurium dragon, and called over his shoulder, "From your lips to the goddess's ears . . ."

Lorelei shrugged into her coat, pulled on her gloves, and followed him.

All dragons were stunning beasts, but induria especially so. The light of the dark sun reflected off Bothymus's scales in wild, chromatic displays, as if he'd rolled in diamond dust before leaving the eyrie. Seeing Lorelei's approach, he reared up, beat his wings, and released a piercing cry, much to the consternation of Betheny, the hapless eyrie hand holding his reins. When he'd settled, Betheny handed Lorelei a glowing yellow gemstone wrapped in leather cord. The stone, roughly the size of a grape, was chrysolite, a rare gem harvested from meteorites that struck the mountains in the dead of winter. It was known as a crop and was one half of a pair. Its mate, called a fetter, was fitted into Bothymus's bridle.

Lorelei wrapped the crop's leather loops around her hand and wrist so the stone rested against her palm. She took the reins and gripped the crop tightly, and the link to Bothymus brightened in her mind. Riders described the link differently, but for Lorelei, it was calming, like spotting a close friend across a busy room.

Bothymus swung his head and stared down at her with moonstone eyes. Commanding a dragon with a crop was simple—like making a silent wish. In this manner, she urged Bothymus to ready himself for mounting. His fetter glowing softly in his bridle, he lay flat on the trampled ground and uttered a low gurgle.

Lorelei scratched the spiky wattle beneath his jaw. "Ready?"

Bothymus's gurgle became rhythmic gulping.

"Good boy," Lorelei told him, caressing his scales, but as she was about to mount, Ruko, the excitable silver vixen, trumpeted a rising note and beat her wings. Bothymus turned, spread the frills on his head, and hissed. Lorelei gripped the crop and tried to calm him again. When he started gurgling again, she climbed into the saddle and fit her legs into the padded leather restraints that would keep her firmly in place. She held a hand down to Ash, and he climbed into the saddle behind her. When he was settled and she released her mental hold, Bothymus pushed himself up on his fore-claws, stalked forward in the ungainly way of all dragons, swept his broad wings, and lifted them into the sky. Skylar waved up from the footpath, and Lorelei and Ash waved back. Then Bothymus wheeled to follow the other dragons.

Reckoning arrived with swaths of gold and citrine spilling like ink across the sky. Rust and ruby followed, then a ruddy orange. The show was brilliant, but soon enough, Nox slipped below the horizon, Lux rose above the mountains to the east, and the play of lights faded. Ancris dwindled behind them as they flew south with their cohort under a clear sky, the steady beat of dragon wings broken only by the occasional warble from Ruko.

Lorelei spoke over her shoulder, "I wanted to ask you about a report from Glaey-and I read last night. It said the alchemyst, Korvus Julianus, has gone missing."

"He has?"

"Apparently so. The report said he went on a survey mission but never returned. The ferryman who went with him is missing as well. Then, a few days ago, Korvus's apothecary in Glaeyand was torched. His wife died in the fire."

"Tishana died in a fire? Faedryn's wicked ways, what a tragedy!"

"I'm sorry to break the news. Did you know them well?"

"Not well, no. I met Master Korvus a few times, but he barely spoke to me."

"Well, it's suspected Korvus ran afoul of the Red Knives. I was just curious if Master Renato mentioned anything about it."

"Master Renato . . . speak to *me* about anything besides how many blocks I've cured . . ." Ash snorted. "That'll be the day. But why do you ask? Is it related to your chandlery in some way?"

"I wish . . ." Realizing how Ash might interpret her reply, Lorelei quickly added, "Not that I want anything *bad* to happen to Master Korvus. It's just, watching that bloody chandlery is so tedious. I'd rather throw myself down on those mountains than spend another night there."

"Please don't."

Lorelei laughed. "You'd hardly miss me."

Ash tightened his grip around her waist and kissed her ear noisily. "I would miss you every single moment of every single day."

She laughed again, then turned in the saddle and kissed his cheek. "Then I'll stay."

"Good. Now, let's have no more talk of arson or chandlers or falls to one's death."

"All right, tell me what we're hoping to find at this magnificent mountain then."

She knew some of the details, of course. The geoflare at Tortoise Peak had been discovered more than a year ago. Geoflares were exceedingly rare events, and studying one that had so recently flared was even rarer. Master Renato had wanted to visit it immediately, Ash had told her a few months back, but the renovation to Alra's shrine had forced him to set his excitement aside. He never gave up on the idea, though. As the months passed, he pushed the work crews and managed to get ahead of schedule so that he could justify leaving Ancris for a day to fly to Tortoise Peak and study it.

"The plan," Ash said, "is to take soil samples from the islands and the exposed earth. We're going to measure the strength of their aura and umbra, plus the spectra they throw off. We'll also measure the islands' rotational speeds—or lack thereof—near the top, middle, and base of the mass. When we're done, we'll compare it to other geoflares and see if there's a difference."

"Sounds like a lot of work." Lorelei just wanted to take in the majesty of it all.

"It will be. And it'll take weeks to sort through once we get back to the city, but you'll not hear me complaining. This is why I *became* an alchemyst."

"I though it was to haul stone all day and night."

"Ha!" He raised his gloved hands in front of her. "These hands, dearest, were made for more delicate work."

Unfortunately for Ash, the work at the shrine was drudgery for the most part. Each quartzite block weighed a hundred libra or more, he'd told her, and had to be removed from the shrine, carted to the workspace in the antechamber, and treated with a special alchemycal solution. Only after the block had been cured could it be carted back and fitted into place exactly where it had been taken from. *About as exciting as watching a chandlery, but with considerably more smashed fingers.*

"And what of your handsome friend from Lyros?" she asked him, referring to Deimas and the raven-haired beauty in front of him on the silver dragon.

"Deimas? He hardly even knows I exist."

"Sorry," Lorelei said with a cringe.

Ash shrugged against her back. "Vita est vita," he said. *Life is life.*

They flew several more hours until Master Renato waved over his shoulders to the group and pointed at a mountain in the distance. "There!"

As they came closer, it became clear that the *mountain* was no mountain at all, but a group of floating islands hovering above a massive crater. Lorelei could hardly believe the scope of it. She'd read about geoflares and often wondered what it would be like to visit one, which was half the reason she'd pestered Ash into getting Master Renato's permission for her to come.

Mountain peaks had especially high concentrations of aura. Normally, aura was shed from them, dissipating as it rose toward the firmament, and the mountain remained unaffected. But sometimes the stone was altered in some way—no one knew why—and its ability to shed aura diminished. Then the aura accumulated, building energy over aeons until, eventually, the mountains blew outward in a geoflare. That was precisely what had happened with Tortoise Peak some dozen years ago. Master Renato and the alchemysts wanted to find out what made this mountain different than the rest. And what had caused it to finally explode.

The dragons and their riders followed Master Renato between the floating islands toward the geoflare, then veered and followed wider channel. It felt strange to be flying among floating islands, like gravity had been forgotten. The rock faces below them were dark and bare, and the ones above were layered in snow. She felt an elation of sorts due to the aura still trapped in the stone.

"You know your assignments!" Master Renato roared from his gold dragon.

"Yes, Master Renato!" came the chorus from Ash and the other the junior alchemysts.

Ash pointed to one of the larger islands near the edge of the massive, floating cluster. "We're there."

Lorelei guided Bothymus to the island and they landed. Ash rummaged through a saddlebag and took out a journal, a trowel, and several glass beakers with strips of white cloth glued to them. He dug up four samples from around the peak, placed them in the beakers, and labeled each using a wooden pencil. Lorelei, meanwhile, crunched across the snow toward the edge of the island and stared down.

On the other islands, alchemysts were collecting similar samples while their dragons rested nearby. She hadn't realized it before, but looking down at the other islands and the landscape below, she could tell her island was moving.

"Do the islands shift over time?"

Ash looked up from his journal. "What's that?"

"Do the islands shift?"

He shrugged and continued to write. "Some people say they can, but the islands have a memory of sorts. They tend to remain near, and facing, the fragments of earth they'd once been attached to, so it takes quite a bit of force to dislodge them, like a winter gale."

Lorelei marveled at the spectacle of it all. Leaving Ash to his work, she wandered the island's peak, then its far side, feeling more than a little like the entire thing was about to crumble and send her plummeting to ground below. She was just getting ready to head back when she spotted a crater. At its center was the exposed face of what looked like a broken column of blue-flecked stone.

"Ash, what's this?"

Ash's head popped up beyond a snow-covered boulder. He came over, stared at the broken column, and frowned. "I've no idea."

The near-perfect silence was suddenly broken by the peal of a dragon on one of the islands below them. Across the snowy peak from Lorelei and Ash, Bothymus reared back, flapped his wings, and roared. Staring south toward Ancris, Lorelei spotted a bronze dragon soaring their way.

Ash was suddenly standing beside her. "What's this now?"

A horn blew for everyone to gather.

"This can't be good," Ash said.

They mounted Bothymus and flew to a low-lying hill well wide of the geoflare. The others were already there, everyone watching the bronze approach and land with a snow-lifting sweep of its broad wings. To Lorelei's shock, the rider was none other than Theron, the chamberlain of Highreach. "Master Renato," he said, "I have a message from the Domina."

The Domina was Quintarch Lucran's wife, Tyrinia.

"Yes?" Master Renato said, stepping forward.

"You're to cease your research," Theron said, "and return to Ancris immediately."

A murmur rose among the other alchemysts. Master Renato's cheeks turned red. "But Chamberlain, I was granted permission for this expedition by Consul Skylar."

"Be that as it may," Theron said, "you are not in Ancris any longer, but in the province of Ancrada, over which the *Domina* has authority."

"Are you saying the Domina is refusing to allow us to continue?"

Theron sneered. "How incisive of you. Yes, Master Renato, that's precisely what I'm saying. The renovations are behind schedule—"

"Forgive me," Master Renato said, "but they're not. We're *ahead* of schedule. I made sure of it before we left."

"If you have time for an excursion like this, Master Alchemyst, what can it mean but that you padded your schedule?"

Master Renato blinked, opened his mouth and closed it again. "Schedules are *always* padded," he said, "to account for the unforeseen."

"You had many such setbacks early on, did you not?"

"Yes, but—"

"And you may have more," Theron bulled on, "things that, by your own admission, you did not and could never have foreseen. Is it not so?"

"Yes, but . . ." Master Renato paused for a deep breath. "We're already here, Chamberlain. Surely the Domina—"

"The Domina wishes to make clear that until the shrine has been repaired, it is your one and *only* priority. You are to cease work immediately and return to Ancris, at which point your alchemysts will report directly the shrine and continue their work. You, in the meantime, will report to the Domina at the palace."

Master Renato looked heartbroken, staring up at the geoflare and its floating islands. But what could he say? He couldn't defy Tyrinia openly. And appealing to Skylar would require he return to Ancris, gain an audience, and have her agree to fight for him. And even if Skylar *did* agree, there was a good chance Tyrinia's authority would still win out. It wouldn't be worth the fight.

"Of course," Master Renato finally said.

In short order, everyone was mounted and flying north. More than one alchemyst gazed back longingly. Lorelei did, too, but not from some lost research opportunity. She was too curious about the glittering column of stone in the ground and what it meant.

TEN: RYLAN

Rylan paced beside the elderly dowager, Soraya Alevada, over the manicured lawn of her family estate. Soraya was the widow of Trichan Alevada, who had once been a volarch, the highest rank in the empire's dragon legion. He was also the officer who'd ordered Morraine Bloodhaven's hanging and the subsequent quickening of her wisp. The sun was bright, but the mountain air was crisp, and their breath plumed as they spoke. They were headed toward the eyrie, a massive structure of white marble, brass-work, and red clay tiles. Beyond the eyrie, the Whitefells dwindling to a row of dragon teeth in the distance. In the valley to their left lay Caldoras, one of the empire's five capitals, a quilt-work of ordered streets, stone buildings, and public squares.

The celebration of Soraya's granddaughter's graduation from Caldoras' famed university was set to commence in a few hours—Soraya wore a sapphire dress and matching gable headdress for the occasion—but first they were off to see her failing iron dragon, Rugio. With Rugio nearing death's door, Soraya was quiet and sorrowful, and who could blame her? Certainly not Rylan. He didn't know what he'd do if he lost Vedron.

"His breathing is more labored than ever," Soraya said in a quavering voice.

"So your letter said." Rylan patted his foraging sack, which was slung over his right shoulder. "I've brought seven full libra of the best woundwort I could find."

"And his eyes are crusting again."

"I've brought a concoction of blood maple bark for that as well."

The eyrie had eight stalls, each of which could house two or three dragons, depending on their size. Rylan and Soraya entered the eyrie and then Rugio's stall, the nearest to the door. It was surprisingly warm inside. Rugio, an ancient iron dragon with scintillant black scales, was alone, lying on the far side of the enclosure. Iron dragons were a bellicose breed, and Rugio was no exception, but as Rylan and Soraya approached, the dragon did no more than shift his forge-fire eyes from Rylan to Soraya and back again. Due to his fever, he was giving off more heat than normal, and his eyes were crusted with rheum. He was easily nine horses from snout to tail, but curled up as he was, he looked much smaller. His ribs, hips, and jaw stood out like an old nag's. His sides expanded when he inhaled and collapsed like a bellows when he released his fetid breath in a long huff.

Rugio had been Soraya's personal mount for seven decades. Now he'd never fly again, never leave the eyrie again, which was why the dowager had agreed to let Rylan come in his capacity as a dragon singer.

Like all dragons, Rugio's wings doubled as his forelimbs. One fluttered momentarily as a bright yellow canary landed on his back, pecked him for scale worms, and flitted away. Rylan set his foraging sack down and stood before the massive iron. He held his right hand out, fingers splayed. His left hand, the one missing the pinky finger, he hid behind his back. He took a deep breath, opened his mind, and began to sing.

As always, the wordless melody was inspired by Rugio's mood, Rylan's mood, and, most of all, Rylan's intent. The song he shared with Rugio was one of simple comfort.

All will be well, Rylan conveyed to Rugio, *I promise.*

When an image of Rugio basking on a mountain shelf high in the Whitefells flashed through Rylan's mind, he knew the song was working. Moments later, the link between them formed.

One day soon, when Rugio passed, the stall would be sealed with white marble, transforming it into a crypt. A brass plaque telling his story would be mounted on the wall. Soraya had penned the tale herself and shown it proudly to Rylan on his previous visit. The very fact Soraya had petitioned for and been granted an exemption for Rugio from being harvested for his scales, bones, and flesh was testament to his contributions to the empire. Rylan's feelings soured every time he thought about it. In his centuries of service, Rugio had fought in many battles in and around the Holt, slaying Kin with his noxious breath.

Rylan caught a brief glimpse of Rugio flying toward a cluster of frightened warriors, and his song faltered. Rugio's lips pulled back, and a low growl emerged from between his blunted, yellow teeth. Cursing himself for allowing his reflections to affect Rugio, Rylan inhaled deeply and sang of tranquility. He'd made his peace with Rugio's past. And it wasn't Rugio's fault. Not really. He'd been raised and trained for war.

When Rugio closed his rheumy eyes and let out a contented gurgle, Rylan extended the notes of the song and sang more fluidly, allowing him to sink deeper into Rugio's experience. He felt the pain in the dragon's joints as if they were his own. His eyes itched and began to water. His breathing grew labored. A bit lost in the sensation, he realized his song was faltering again. He regained his composure and catalogued Rugio's symptoms more impassively. Rugio's left wing, in particular, ached from disuse. He no longer had the energy to stretch it. Merely lifting his head led to a heart-pounding dizziness. He'd deteriorated noticeably since the last time Rylan had come.

The eyrie master, a wiry woman with dark, gray-streaked hair, arrived through the rear door as Rylan was finishing. Rylan told her which medicines were to be used for which symptoms, and how much. It was a terse discussion. The dosages had merely increased from previous visits with little sign that they were helping. The woman bowed cursorily to Soraya and left.

When she was gone, Soraya said, "Our family has seven other dragons, you know. I could use a man who tends to them with such care."

Rylan smiled. "Your eyrie master is more than capable of handling them."

"Yes, but she has much to attend to besides dragons. She cleans and maintains all three eyries, manages the staggering flow of food, liaises with the dragonworks for the harvesting of scales and such. I'd feel better knowing someone was dedicated solely to the health and well being of our mounts."

"My thanks, but my home is in Glaeyand."

"People *do* move, you know." Soraya Alevada was not a woman accustomed to being told no.

"It's a kind and generous offer, truly, but I'm happy in the Holt."

Soraya scoffed. "Cut you and you'll bleed sap, is that it?"

Rylan smiled at the old saying. "Just so."

"Well, if you change your mind, we'll be here." She scratched Rugio's eye ridge, and he thumped the end of his tail on the tile floor. "Please pass along my thanks to your father. It was kind of him to see to the arrangements."

Rylan's father, the Imperator of Glaeyand, not known for his generosity, had paid for Rylan's services and the ingredients he'd gathered. Soraya was very important in the social circles of Caldoras. "He'll be pleased to hear it."

Soraya stroked Rugio's neck, then led Rylan out of the eyrie and back to the estate. On the patio, servants in black uniforms were stacking wood into braziers. Soraya had asked Rylan to arrive several days earlier, but he'd told her he'd had other commitments and that, regrettably, the only day he had available in the next month was the day of the celebration. He had been certain Soraya would invite him to stay—it was the easiest, best way for him to get into the gallery undetected—but the celebration was quickly approaching, and Soraya had still made no mention of it. He was starting to think he'd need to make plans to return under cover of darkness, but he wasn't ready to give up just yet. "I wish your granddaughter a bright future," he said as they stepped up to the patio. "What did she study?"

"Philosophy, if you can believe it." Soraya rolled her eyes. "Perhaps she'll spout lines from Diocenes while serving drinks at some posh new taberna along the Greenway."

Rylan chuckled, then said, "Some say the philosophers are the ones who guide our morality."

Soraya frowned. "*Alra* guides our morality, that we may one day greet her in the blessed fields of Déu."

Rylan nodded, not wishing to ruffle feathers. "Then perhaps your granddaughter can guide us where Alra's teaching fails to illuminate."

"And where might that be?"

Rylan tilted his head back toward the eyrie. "As far as I'm aware, she gave no guidance on when it might be more merciful to allow the suffering to pass on."

"Are you saying I should put Rugio down?"

"I'm saying you'll find no answers in Alra's psalms. No clear ones, anyway."

She glanced sadly toward the eyrie, the wind tugging at her headdress. "Yes, well, I suppose Alra *did* grant us leeway to navigate life's little mysteries, didn't she?" She straightened her headdress. "You'll stay for the celebration, I hope."

Rylan bowed and feigned surprise. "You're too kind, but I wouldn't want to impose."

Soraya waved the concern away. "It's no imposition. Consider it part of your work. Quite a few guests will be arriving on mounts of their own. I dare say you'll be able to drum up a bit of business."

Rylan allowed a diplomatic pause to pass before smiling. "In that case, I gladly accept."

The celebration took place in the grand ballroom just before cant. The room was lit by a massive chandelier hanging from the high, arched ceiling. Long tables were laden with every delicacy imaginable, and servants carrying silver trays of wine navigated the crowd of senators, patricians, and thriving merchants.

Soraya fulfilled her promise. She introduced him to a dozen men and women, always with a kind word about his care for Rugio. Rylan spoke to them easily and affably—eagerly as well. Legitimate business in the empire's largest cities gave him reasons to *be* in them, an essential ingredient in the cover stories for his various capers.

A gaggle of children flocked to the windows as a brass dragon winged in and landed near the eyrie. The rider, a military man with a trimmed beard and a bald head, was the volarch of Caldoras's dragon legion, an old friend of Trichan's who'd come to pay his respects. Several more officers also arrived on dragonback. Then Princess Resada, the daughter of Quintarch Zabrienne, arrived on an indurium that roared as she slipped down from the saddle. Soraya greeted her personally, and the other guests were drawn to her like flies to a corpse.

Knowing his father would never forgive him if he didn't put in a kind word, Rylan approached her when he saw an opening. "Your Highness," he said with a bow. "My father sends his regards."

Resada stared at him. "And you are?"

"Ah, forgive me. I'm Rylan Holbrooke, son of Marstan Lyndenfell, Imperator of Glaeyand."

Her gaze drifted away from him. "The bastard?"

It was no secret Rylan was Marstan's bastard. Even so, her casually cruelty surprised him. "The very one," he said, forcing a smile.

"Tell me, has your father made any strides in taming the threats to our empire?"

"Beg pardon?"

"Tidings from the Holt these days always seem to involve temple burnings and caravan raids. My mother lost two dragons and their dracorae to a surprise attack on Brevin. How long will your father allow it to continue?"

The attack was clearly meant to put Rylan off balance, and it was working. "I couldn't say, Your—"

"It seems your father can't, either. Perhaps that should be addressed at the next council meeting."

The Covenant, the document that governed the Holt, stipulated that every five years, the landowners of the Holt would vote to elect an imperator. But the empire had insisted on some sway over the decision, which led to another stipulation:

the winner needed a vote of confidence from three of the five quintarchs. If the candidate failed, elections would continue until a new imperator was found.

Through no end of political maneuvering, Rylan's father, Marstan Lyndenfell, had held his seat for twenty-five years, longest of any imperator since the seat's creation. But the next election was nearing, and there were rumblings the quintarchs were displeased—enough, perhaps, to vote Marstan out. Assuming he even got that far. The original authors of the Covenant also stipulated that only patricians with Kin ancestry were allowed to vote so the imperator would be sympathetic to the Holt's needs, but the empire had skirted the rule in recent years by bribing patricians to favor the empire. Were a vote taken that very day, Marstan would likely still win, but it would be a near thing, and each year the likelihood increased that the seat would fall to someone else, someone more beholden to the empire.

"I'm confident," Rylan said to Resada, "that my father has the full support of the Holt. I hope he's performed well enough to gain the quintarchs' support as well."

"Yes," the princess replied, smiling coldly, "I guess we'll see soon enough, won't we?"

Beyond Resada, a woman in a golden mask shaped like a sunrise and a glittering sleeveless dress with gold accents reminiscent of the togas of old was speaking with several officers. Her lips, painted in a shade Rylan could only compare to eggplant, were neatly bisected by a strip of gold.

Only illustrae, the highest ranking members of the Alran Church, wore masks of that sort, partly to hide their eyes—which, if rumor were true, were cloudy white from the acid used to burn them during their ascendance ritual—but also to honor the goddess herself. *What are mortals but blind in the face of the goddess's wisdom?* Or so the saying went. To Rylan, the masks had always been more symbolic of the Church's willingness to blind itself to the pain it caused.

Resada followed his gaze. "Illustra Camadaea . . . draws the eye, does she not?" When Rylan said nothing, she went on, "Would you care to meet her?"

Rylan planned each mission with the utmost care, not only to avoid getting caught but to prevent anyone from sensing patterns and connecting him to other crimes, which helped him control his nerves, but the presence of an illustra made this operation much more perilous than usual. Their ability to sniff out danger was legendary. They'd lost their natural sight but some folk said their second sight allowed them to peer into men's souls. It suddenly felt like Camadaea—and by extension, everyone in the room—knew why he had come to the Alevada estate.

Having no need to feign discomfort, Rylan placed a hand on his stomach. "Perhaps another time."

Resada pouted. "The food?"

"I'm afraid so."

"A pity, the food in the capitals is indeed very rich."

Rylan felt his cheeks flushing, so with a bow of his head, he slipped away.

ELEVEN: RYLAN

Rylan navigated the increasingly inebriated crowd and made his way to the family gallery. He knew the estate's floor plan from previous visits. Unlike most galleries, which tended to be filled with paintings and busts of celebrated family members, the Alevadas' was filled with trophies—pitted swords, spears, dragonscale shields. A fan of arrows belonging to various Kin rebels hung along one wall. A massive dragon skull rested on a glittering slab of basalt. A plaque below it read: *Here lies Mellok the Unruly, a fearsome iron who fought alongside Lucian Solvina and Casurax to defeat Wyan One-Hand.* Hundreds of other items hung on walls, and displayed on shelves, pedestals, and plinths.

Many Kin would consider it a vulgar display, another example of the empire not only celebrating but *flaunting* its centuries of dominion over the Holt. And it *was* that, but to Rylan the gallery was like a treatise on the long shadow the Covenant cast over the Holt: granting the empire's inquisitors and dragon legions the right to enter the Holt whenever they felt imperial affairs were at stake and allowing the Church's shepherds to judge whomever they felt were unholy in Alra's eyes. The provisions had led to no end of misery for the Holt's people.

But the empire's overreach had also led to the rise of the Red Knives, whose roots could be traced all the way back to the Holt's last true king, Wyan One-hand. The Knives wanted true independence for the Holt, and they weren't afraid to fight to achieve it. Their bloody methods had given Trichan all the cover he'd needed to wage a dozen incursions deep into Red Knife territory, where he'd hunted and killed hundreds of Kin under the guise of stamping out the Knives. He'd slain dozens of umbral dragons, as well, to preserve the empire, he'd said. And he'd collected what he referred to as *trinkets* from the forest, which Rylan was now surveying in the Alevadas' gallery. To Rylan the various artifacts represented not only strife and bloodshed, but the arrival of the empire in the Great Basin, the centuries of friendship they'd had with the Kin, the souring of that friendship as the empire grew hungry for more territory. In the weapons on the walls, he saw the passing of age; in the armor on the plinths, strong alliances fading and turning to enmity.

In the back corner of the gallery was a pedestal made from the beautifully grained wood of an ironbark on which stood a display case with a bed of black velvet. Nestled on the velvet was a glass globe the size of an apple with a glowing blue wisp inside. A bronze plaque read: *Here lies the soul of Morraine Bloodhaven, darkling witch, daughter of Rygmora the Wicked, hung for her sins in the eyes of our goddess, Alra the All Seeing.*

Rylan glanced down the hallway beyond the gallery entrance and, finding it empty, retrieved his lock picks from the hidden compartment in his boot heel. He picked the case's simple lock with ease and opened the rear pane. As he grasped the cool wisplight, he felt himself dropping, a noose tightening around his neck, Morraine's final moments, and blinked the vision away. The feeling lingered, though. He felt watched. He fumbled inside his coat and drew out a woolen pouch that contained a similar glass sphere with a rather different sort of wisp inside it, the soul of a caribou. It was a fake and wouldn't last long—the wisps of animals never did—but it would last long enough to fool the Alevadas, he was sure. To them, Morraine's wisp was nothing more than a trophy, a trinket; they would think little of its final dimming.

Crisp footsteps clacked down the corridor. Rylan placed the fake wisplight onto the black velvet bed, dropped Morraine's into the woolen pouch, and stuffed the pouch inside his coat. He closed the lid, slipped the lock through the clasp, and squeezed it shut. Then he stepped away and pretended to consider a barbed lance, the sort employed by the empire's dracorae to slay enemy dragons.

A heartbeat later, Illustra Camadaea appeared in the entryway, her golden mask glittering as she entered the gallery. "Rylan Holbrooke."

She knew his name. Rylan hid his surprise and dipped his head. "Your Holiness."

Camadaea gestured to the room around them. "I'll admit, I'm surprised you'd come here. It must be painful."

"It is history, Your Holiness." Rylan searched for an excuse to leave—to be anywhere but cornered by an illustra with the stolen wisp in his coat—but to leave too quickly would be suspicious. "I was looking for a bit of quiet."

Camadaea stepped gracefully toward the dragon skull. "Soraya tells me she offered you a job."

"She did."

"And you declined."

"That's true."

Camadaea's mask scintillated in the lantern light. "She said you loved the Holt too much to leave it, which makes me wonder whether you value your mother's blood more than your father's."

Rylan's father could trace his lineage to the earliest settlers to cross the mountains from the west and settle in the Holt. It gave Marstan a certain standing in the empire *and* the Holt. It was a big part of his having won the seat of imperator and retaining it for two and a half decades. Rylan didn't know the identity of his mother—Marstan had never revealed it to him and had refused to discuss it whenever Rylan brought it up. But Rylan's skin was more cinnamon than ivory. His hair was dark, curly, and thick. His cheeks were broader than was common in the empire, as was his chin.

"Hardly a day goes by I'm not reminded of it, so who can blame me if I *do* embrace my mother's people?"

"Certainly not I, but even so, you said you came here for a bit of quiet. I wonder, what sort of *quiet* can come from the history of dominance over your people?"

"Call it not quiet, then, but perspective." He gestured to fan of arrows on the wall. "It's like a stake in the ground, marking how far we've come."

"Or how little . . ."

Rylan couldn't help smiling. "Just so, Your Holiness."

The illustra strolled around the dragon skull, then turned to face the fan of arrows. "I must confess, if your goal was to convince me you don't find the gallery unpleasant, you've failed."

The wisplight in Rylan's coat began to weight heavily on him. They said an illustra's second sight allowed them to peer into a man's soul. Did it also allow her to peer through fabric? "If it makes you happy, Your Holiness. It *is* painful to me. I've always been saddened by war."

The eyes of Camadaea's golden mask seemed to pierce him. "You've tickled my curiosity. Painful or not, what in the gallery strikes you most?"

My encounter with you, he wanted to say. After making a show of considering, he said, "It's no *physical* thing, but the notion that the past often echoes much farther into the future than we realize."

"*Veritas* . . ."

"Pardon?"

"It's a word from the elder tongue often translated as *truth*, but it goes much deeper than that. Veritas refers to truths so undeniable they are akin to the pillars of life. What you just said is the very definition of the term."

There was some hidden meaning behind the unexpected digression, but what it might be, Rylan had no idea. "I really should be going, Your Holiness. I bid you good day."

"So soon? What a shame. I find you rather entertaining, Rylan Holbrooke. But alas, I must go as well. Illustrae cannot disappear for long before a host of guards are summoned. Good day to you."

TWELVE: RHIANNON

R hiannon crouched beside the burbling waters of Dovetail creek. It was the first day of spring. Tiny flies sparkled in the shafts of sunlight streaking down through the canopy. Rhiannon gripped a cord running from a stake to the water and drew her wicker fish trap out of the creek. The vase-shaped apparatus had a dozen red-streaked sticklebacks inside. They flipped and flopped and gawped as Rhiannon reached a hand into the trap, drew them out, and flicked them into her basket. Despite taking care to avoid their frills, she got stung three times.

Farther down the stream, Irik was pulling sticklebacks from a second trap. "Ach!" he yelled and sucked his finger. "Faedryn's smelly balls, how I hate them, Rhiannon. I *hate them!*"

"Don't blaspheme. And you're too impatient. Go slower."

"And make this take longer than it needs to? No, thank you."

He grabbed a few more fish from the trap, tossed them into his basket like they were on fire, and shook his hand. The sticklebacks were too small for good eating, but they made great fertilizer for the garden. When they finished emptying the traps, they'd grind the fish up and add the pink slurry to the fresh plantings in the garden.

Rhiannon was preparing to toss the trap into the creek when she saw a streak of black downstream. She caught the beat of mighty wings, the lash of a tail, then it was gone.

"Briar and bramble," Irik said. "Did you *see* that?"

"Yes."

They stared at each other. Then, without another word, they put down their baskets and sprinted downstream until the creek flattened at a ford; then they leapt from stone to stone across the ford with practiced ease and bolted toward a meadow, the onyx's likely landing spot. By the time they reached the meadow, Rhiannon's legs were burning and she thought she might throw up.

Irik, breathing just as hard, pointed to a stand of pampas grass. Careful of the sharp leaves, they pushed through it, crouched, and peered through the tall stalks. At the center of the meadow was the largest onyx dragon Rhiannon had ever seen.

Irik whispered, "She's as big as a bloody citadel."

"How do you know it's a vixen?"

"Her size, for one. Plus, bulls have big frills between their horns. Hers is small. And look at her tail. Bull's tails are more rounded, like a water oak."

"How do you know so much?"

"Remember the book on dragons that went missing last year?"

"Yeah."

"It's under my mattress."

Rhiannon had seen only a few dragons in her life, mostly in Andalingr's eyrie, and they'd all been from afar, but this one seemed to dwarf those silvers and brasses. The onyx was nine horses at least, maybe ten. Her scales were jet black with a line of garnet running jaggedly along her sides. Atop her triangular head was a crown of twisted horns. Sharp barbs ran down her neck and back. And her eyes were a sharp, piercing yellow.

She seemed to be growing impatient, fanning the barbed frill at the end of her tail. She spread her wings, arched her head back, and screeched so loud and piercing it made the hair on Rhiannon's arms stand up.

"Ircundus, enough!" Brother Mayhew bellowed from the far side of the meadow, lugging a saddle and bridle toward the dragon. "Do you want to call all the dragons in Andalingr's eyrie down on us?"

Brother Mayhew often left the abbey, sometimes for weeks at a time. Whenever anyone asked, he said he was going on rangings to commune with the forest, but it was a lie. Or at least not the whole truth. Rhiannon had once overheard Mother Constance say he flies to the Holt to speak with the Red Knives.

Ircundus twisted her head, rattling the barbs along her neck, and lashed her tail against the earth.

"I know," Brother Mayhew said, "you're very fearsome. Now be quiet."

Ircundus huffed, then settled and allowed Brother Mayhew to approach. Brother Mayhew threw the leather saddle over Ircundus's back and secured it. He stood in front of the dragon's snout and held up the bridle. Ircundus spread her jaws and allowed Brother Mayhew to insert the bit and fit the bridle over her massive head.

Irik leaned closer. "Do you think he's going to speak with Llorn?"

"I don't know."

"Do you think it's to do with the wisp?"

"I don't *know.* Now shut your gob before that monster hears us."

Ircundus lowered to the ground, and Brother Mayhew mounted. With a snap of the reins, Ircundus got up on her hind legs, beat her wings, and launched into the air. The rhythmic *whump-whump* of her wings faded as she soared through the citadels and disappeared.

Rhiannon and Irik headed back toward the creek. Halfway there, Irik said, "What do you think he does with them, the Red Knives?"

"What do *any* of the Red Knives do? Try to overthrow the imperator."

Irik kicked a pinecone, sending it flying. "Do you think the empire will find out he's a Knife? If they do, they'll call him a heretic, maybe call the whole abbey heretics. They might burn it like the Knives burn the Church temples."

"Irik, how would *I* know?"

"I dunno"—he kicked the same pinecone, and it spun off into the undergrowth—"maybe Sister Merida told you something."

"Sister Merida doesn't tell me anything," Rhiannon said.

"But you listen at her door."

"I don't know where he's going or what he's going to do when he gets there, okay?"

Irik was silent for a time but he was chewing the inside of one cheek, which he only did when he was worried. "I wish Mother Constance would send Brother Mayhew away."

"You know she won't. She's too worried about what Llorn would do to the abbey if she did." Seeing how distraught he looked, Rhiannon stopped. "What's gotten into you?"

Irik stopped, too. "I know I grouse about chores, sometimes, but I don't know what I'd do if the abbey was burned. I've nowhere else to go."

"We'll be fine, Irik."

"How do you know?"

She didn't, but telling Irik that wouldn't help. "We'll be fine."

They returned to the creek to collect their baskets and hiked back to the abbey in silence. They ground up the sticklebacks in the grinder in the garden shed and spread the smelly meal around the chickpea seedlings.

After evening meal, Rhiannon, Irik, and the other twelve aspirants were set to copying stories by candlelight in the refectory. The room was curved, hollowed out from a citadel tree. Four deep-well windows overlooked the garden and the central walks of the abbey. The two youngest aspirants, Mearah and Ashby, were practicing their penmanship—they weren't good enough yet to make salable copies. Rhiannon and the others were making manuscripts that would be bound into books and sold in Andalingr. Or sometimes a merchant caravan would buy a crateful to sell in the capitals.

They heard a voice from outside, and Lexie, one of the older acolytes, a tall girl with honey blonde hair, went to the window. "Come see."

The aspirants shoved their quills into their inkwells and crowded around the windows. Mearah and Ashby squirmed their way to the front and stood on tiptoes. It was dark outside, but below a pair of lanterns at the brewery doors, Sister Merida was speaking with a woman and two men.

"Who are they?" Mearah asked.

"The stocky one is Aarik," Lexie answered. "The woman beside him is his beloved, Blythe."

"You mean his *wife*?"

"No, dummy. The Knives don't *marry* like the empire does. She's his *beloved*. The last one is Maladox—"

"He looks like Brother Mayhew!" Mearah blurted.

"He's his twin brother."

"Why are they talking to Sister Merida?" Ashby squeaked.

"That's the question"—Lexie glanced down at Rhiannon—"isn't it?"

The other aspirants looked at Rhiannon, too, even Irik.

Rhiannon wished she had an umbral ring like Brother Mayhew's. She'd use it to shrink herself until she disappeared. Aarik was Rhiannon's uncle, the leader of the Red Knives. Blythe and Maladox were high up, too, right below Aarik himself and Llorn. Whatever the reason for all three having come to the abbey, it was surely to do with the wisp. Or maybe Brother Mayhew had gone missing.

Aarik, Blythe, and Maladox headed inside the brewery, and Sister Merida marched toward the refectory. The aspirants scattered back to their chairs. A short while later, the door to the entry hall groaned opened.

Sister Merida called, "Rhiannon?"

Rhiannon stood, feeling all eyes on her. "Yes?"

"Come with me."

Ignoring the stares, Rhiannon followed Sister Merida from the room and closed the door behind her. Sister Merida led her out of the refectory and into the chill night air.

"Your uncle wants to speak with you," the sister snapped as they headed toward the brewery. "You'll answer his questions in a forthright manner. No twisting the facts. Understand?"

"What do they want to know?"

"They want to know about your summoning beside the swamp."

"I only did as Brother Mayhew asked . . ."

"I know." She opened the brewery door. "Just tell them the truth, all right?"

Rhiannon nodded and entered. Sister Merida closed the door behind her.

The brewery was a circular room with a high ceiling. Aarik and Blythe were staring into a big copper brew kettle. Maladox was walking along a high shelf of wooden casks.

"Uh . . . hello?" Rhiannon said to no one in particular.

The three of them stopped what they were doing and approached her.

Aarik said, "Rhiannon, you remember Blythe."

"Hello," Rhiannon said.

Blythe, pretty like a kestrel, nodded stiffly. This close, Rhiannon could see scars on her face.

"And this is Maladox," Aarik went on.

Rhiannon nodded to him. "Charmed." She felt like an idiot immediately after she said it. She'd read it in a book once. It had sounded so elegant, but now her ears were burning.

Maladox laughed. "Charmed indeed."

Aarik glared at him for a second, then turned back to Rhiannon. "You're nervous, I can see that. But you needn't be. We only wish to hear what you did for Llorn."

That goddessdamned wisp. *I should've left and hidden in the forest that day until Llorn and Sister Dereka left.* "Am I in trouble?"

Aarik smiled. "No, Rhiannon."

"Is *Llorn* in trouble?"

His smile faded slightly. "Never mind that. What did Llorn want?"

"He wanted me to summon a wisp."

Blythe said, "And do what with it?"

"Make it remember who it used to be."

Maladox looked like he wanted to spit. "Was Sister Dereka was there?"

"Yes."

"Did you teach her how to do it?"

"No."

"Did she ask you to?"

Rhiannon shook her head. "No. None of them did."

Aarik said, "Did my brother tell you *why* he wanted you to do this?"

"No."

"Did he mention your mother?"

The question caught Rhiannon off guard. "No. Why would he have?"

Aarik shook his head. "No reason."

"Tell me all of it," Blythe said, "from the moment Llorn arrived. Come, sit."

Rhiannon followed the other three to a round table near some big sacks with stamps on them. They asked her many questions, and she answered them in *forth-right a manner* as she could. They wanted to know what Llorn's mood was like, and Brother Mayhew's and Sister Merida's too. They asked if Brother Mayhew had given her any indication why Llorn wanted her to awaken a wisp. In the end, Rhiannon felt she hadn't been very useful, but she had been truthful. Still, she didn't know why Maladox looked so angry.

Aarik walked her outside and led her toward the beehives. On the way, he said, "I fear I haven't been a very good uncle to you, Rhiannon. I'm sorry I haven't visited more often."

"It's all right."

"No, it isn't." They arrived at the bee hives, six wooden boxes on stilts. "But I'm working on something that will help. One day soon, I should be able to come to the abbey more freely."

"You don't come because of Uncle Llorn, right?"

"Yes. When your mother died, Llorn became very . . . angry. I think he intends to quench his anger with imperial blood."

"What about you?" Rhiannon asked.

"Me?" Aarik turned from the beehives to look at her. "No. The killing, it has to stop."

"And my mother? What would *she* think?"

"She'd likely have sided with Llorn, but your mother was shrewd. She'd be angry with me. She'd say I'm siding with the empire, approving their bloodshed. But I like to think that, given time, she'd side with peace."

"And what is it you're doing?"

"I can't tell you that."

"But I want to *help*."

Aarik smiled handsomely, and the weight on his shoulders seemed to lift. "One day soon, I may ask you to do just that. Until then, keep your head down. Study hard and listen to your elders."

"Yes, Uncle Aarik."

Aarik, Blythe, and Maladox spoke with Sister Merida for a short while, then left the abbey. Sister Merida sent Rhiannon to the dormitory. The other aspirants pestered her to tell them what Aarik wanted, but she refused to say, and eventually they stopped.

Over the snoring and the crickets, Rhiannon heard someone whispering. She thought it was the other aspirants talking about her but then realized it was the trees. They sensed a storm brewing, and it made her think of Mother Constance's history lectures. They'd bored her at the time, but now she wished she'd paid closer attention. If she had, maybe she'd be able to tell if the coming storm would be like Ransom's War, a decade of killing to appease a quintarch's grief. Or maybe it would be longer and more painful, like the century-long Talon Wars. Or maybe it would be as bad as the Ruining, when gods fought and mortals wept.

Unable to tell, Rhiannon felt like a leaf, to be blown about in the coming gale.

THIRTEEN: RYLAN

I t was early evening by the time Rylan reached Caldoras's vyrd. Travel by vyrd was expensive. He waited with a dozen well-dressed travelers, his empty foraging sack slung over one shoulder. Three ivory-eyed ferrymen collected tokens and bunched the travelers into groups. The air was cool but pleasant, the sky clear save dark clouds sweeping along the southeastern horizon toward the mountains.

Beyond the standing stones was a plaza, and beyond that, Caldoras's *regio annalis,* the district dedicated to various temples, arches, and war memorials. The vyrd was a natural feature for the city to have grown around, Rylan supposed, but it felt like the last vestige of an older age, and that the buildings, people, and civilization itself simply hadn't gotten around to consuming it yet.

"Closer," roared the tallest of the ferryman. "You don't want to get lost now, do you?"

Each ferrymen would take a group of travelers to a different city: one to Andalingr, another to Ancris, the other to the vyrd at Glaeyand, where Rylan was headed with three other travelers: a young couple who couldn't keep their hands off one another and a portly man with a tricorn hat who kept staring and grimacing at them.

A spill of crimson spread across the sky. The woman gaped up at it. Then a line of ochre cut the crimson in two like a pen stroke, and the young couple giggled and kissed, almost missing each other's lips. Rylan doubted they'd ever traveled by vyrd. The portly man rolled his eyes. The tall ferryman stepped close, opened his mouth, and placed a silvery blue scale on his tongue. He'd hardly closed his eyes when Rylan felt a brief wave of vertigo. As he steadied himself, a high-pitched whistle sounded.

It was suddenly dark and rainy, and Rylan, blinking from the raindrops pattering against his face, found himself standing with his group and a score of other travelers in a glade surround by citadel trees. The lights of Glaeyand glittered through the rain. Rylan pulled up his hood. The portly man lowered the brim of his tricorn and walked steadily toward a citadel with corkscrew stairs. The young woman yelped and ran with her companion toward the dragonbone lift. The tall ferryman shook his head, pulled his own hood up, and trailed after them.

Most of the travelers were headed up to Glaeyand and took either the stairs or the lift. Those headed toward Tallow, as Rylan was, followed a well-worn but muddy path through the forest. Rylan had stopped by The Broken Antler two days ago to leave word for Llorn that he'd be coming back tonight with his prize.

He wasn't particularly looking forward to speaking with Llorn, or Raef for that matter, but it sure would feel good to be rid of the wisp.

Ten minutes later, Rylan and the others reached the edge of the village, where a gallows stood. Two men hung from it. Both wore huntsman's clothes and had dark skin and curly hair. Rylan didn't know what they'd done, but it was probably serious. It wasn't common knowledge, but Rylan's father had passed orders down to curb hangings and other public displays of savagery, surely to create a semblance of peace in the lead-up to the upcoming vote. As Rylan passed the hanging men, he couldn't help but wonder if Llorn had gotten wind of his father's order and decided to cause more bloodshed because of it.

The other travelers peeled away toward their destinations, and Rylan continued along the muddy central road, past its few shops. Just beyond the village square was a tavern known as The Broken Antler. Above the door hung a massive rack of deer antlers with several tines missing.

Inside, Rylan found an empty hook among a cluster of drying cloaks and hung his foraging sack on it. The trestle tables in the entry hall were all full, the tavern alive with music and conversation. The lanterns hanging from the ceiling cast a soft, golden light, and the smell of tabbaq was strong in the air. Ahead, where the long entry hall met the shorter rear one at a right angle, was the bar, choked with patrons. A harpist, a woman with auburn braids, played on the stage in the corner. She was a mainstay at the Antler, as was her beloved, who stood beside her, singing in a baritone that filled the room. The song was an old favorite, a ballad that told of the Kin's flight from persecution in the southern archipelagos and arrival in the Holt.

As Rylan wove through the crowd, dozens of voices joined in the refrain and raised their mugs. Rylan's spirits rose just hearing it. When he finally reached the bar, he waved down Krannock, the tavern's owner.

Krannock, who towered over everyone in sight, had hairy black arms, a balding head, and a famously short temper. When he saw Rylan, he lifted a finger, set down the beer stein he was drying, and turned to a keg behind him. Holding a mug beneath the tap, he used his opposite hand, the one with only a thumb and forefinger left, and poured a draught of dark beer. Rylan recognized the seal on the keg—overlapping barley stalks, the sign of the Trinustine Abbey in Thicket. Rylan had grown up a mere stone's throw from it.

Krannock poured a second mug and set both on the bar in front of Rylan. Then he picked up the stein and the towel, and jutted his chin toward the rear entrance, beyond the far side of the bar. "At the back."

He'd expected a wait, but apparently Llorn was already here. Or maybe, Rylan thought with a sinking feeling, it was Raef. With a nod of thanks, he picked up the mugs, sidled through the crowd around the bar, and wove between tables toward the rear entrance. *Please don't let it be Raef. Please don't let it be Raef.*

"Rylan!"

Rylan peered through the dimness and tabbaq smoke. At a table in the corner was Blythe. The two of them had grown up together in Thicket, deeper in Kin territory, closer to the hideouts of the Red Knives. Now she was Aarik's beloved, and rumor had it she'd taken Llorn's place as Aarik's right hand man, causing a growing divide between Aarik and Llorn.

"What are *you* doing here?" Rylan said when he reached the table.

"Well, hello to you, too."

Blythe motioned to an empty chair, but Rylan remained standing. "What's going on? Where's Llorn?"

"We're going to have a talk, you and I. And I'm thirsty. So sit the fuck down."

He sat down, set the mugs down on the table, and slid one to her.

"Better." She picked up the beer, took several swallows. Seeing that Rylan hadn't touched his, she motioned to it. "You can't even have a drink with me now? I said I was sorry a hundred times."

"Twice, Blythe. You apologized twice."

"Well, how many apologies do you need?"

"I got eight stitches. One apology for each might do."

"I'm *sorry*, Rylan."

Four years earlier, shortly before she was to wed Aarik, Blythe and Aarik had gotten into a hellacious fight. It had started over the seizure of one of Blythe's drug shipments and ended with Aarik demanding that she get clean. Blythe had started taking brightlace, a rare and very expensive serum made from the spinal fluid of silver dragons. It induced intense, often euphoric hallucinations on the way up and acute paranoia on the way back down. But Blythe hated ultimatums. She left Aarik, swearing she'd never wed him, and fled to Tallow, where she fell into a three-day binge.

When Rylan learned of it, he told Aarik he'd find her and try to smooth things over. He found her unconscious on a dirty cot in a hovel, a dozen vials of bright-lace strewn on a beaten table in the corner. He'd just begun gathering them up, when she rolled over.

"Put 'em down." She sat up, knife in hand.

"Blythe, I'm here to help." He picked up the last of the vials.

She stood from the creaking cot. "I said, put them *down*."

When he opened the purse at his belt and began dropping them in, she'd rushed him. Never in a thousand years had he thought Blythe would attack him, much less stab him, but she was deeper in the lace than he'd realized. She sunk her knife into his side.

Afterward, she claimed she hadn't recognized him, and he believed her, but it left a sour taste in his mouth for her, the Knives, and everything they did.

Rylan picked up his mug. "You still owe me five."

Blythe hid a smile with a sip of her stout, and Rylan took a taste of his own. Notes of cinnamon, chocolate, and raisin swept him back to the time he and Bly-the had snuck into the only sizable tavern in Thicket, and her older brother had ordered them a round. The beer had tasted awful then, but he'd finished every last drop if only to keep from embarrassing himself in front of Blythe. Now he adored it, not leastwise because it reminded him of simpler days.

"There," Blythe said when they'd both set their mugs down, "that's better, isn't it?"

"Look, I'm not trying to be rude—"

"It seems to require little effort. Anyhow, you retrieved the wisp?"

That she knew about the assignment Llorn had given him wasn't terribly surprising, but it made Rylan nervous. How much did she know? How much did *Aarik* know? And what were they prepared to do about it?

A pair of plump men with wiry gray hair looked their way from an adjacent table. Blythe took her knife from her belt, the same one she'd stabbed Rylan with, and laid it on the table with the tip pointing toward the men. They quickly turned toward the harpist and her beloved, who struck up a new song. A moment later, they got up and moved to the entrance hall.

Rylan reached into his coat, took out the woolen pouch, and passed it to Blythe.

She tugged it open carefully, and a bit of blue light leaked out, illuminating her face from below. Then, she cinched the pouch and tucked the it her coat pocket. "Llorn's been a bad boy, Rylan."

"Has he?"

"He killed an alchemyst and a ferryman who wandered too far from home. He's been doing a lot of . . . stuff without Aarik's permission"—she patted her pocket—"including this."

"He told me he wanted his sister back where she belonged."

"And you believed him?"

"It seemed a good enough reason." Feeling more than a bit foolish, he added, "So what did he want it for?"

"Never mind. I'm just surprised you were convinced so easily. I've asked you a dozen times to do work for us."

"Well, he didn't leave me much of a choice."

"So *that* was the trick all along? I should threaten you?"

Rylan took another swig of his beer. The conversation was going from bad to worse.

"Look, forget about that," Blythe continued. "I came because I *do* want you to do something for us."

"I'll pass, Blythe."

"It's simple."

"That's what Llorn said."

"It's important, too."

Rylan raised his hands. "You *know* I don't want to get involved in Red Knife business. I only took *this* job because Llorn showed up in Hollis's shop with that murdering lunatic Raef."

"This isn't a typical job, Rylan. It's something bigger."

"There you go, sounding like Llorn again."

The song crescendoed; Blythe turned to look at the musicians. Then she turned back to Rylan and said, "I requested leave from Aarik to speak to you myself because

I wanted you to know that his offer is sincere. You've been looking to even the scales since Beckett's death, yes? That's why you take on your little jobs against the empire. But I'm telling you, it's all *nothing* compared to what Aarik's trying to do."

"And what is it Aarik's trying to do, precisely? What is this noble calling of his?"

Blythe leaned back in her chair. "Why don't you go upstairs and find out?"

Rylan almost tipped over his beer. "Aarik is *here?*"

"Upstairs. Last door on the right."

There wasn't a constable, soldier, or inquisitor in the Holt who couldn't recognize Aarik. Wanted posters were tacked all over Tallow. That Aarik had come in person to speak to Rylan meant the job was highly important, but that didn't mean Rylan needed to care about it.

Rylan said nothing, so Blythe went on. "I know I'm in no position to ask a favor of you, but I'm doing it just the same. Go upstairs. Hear him out. I think you'll be grateful you did."

Rylan pushed his mug aside, folded his arms on the table, and leaned toward her. "Promise me on your brother's life that you're telling the truth."

"I swear it, Rylan. Just go. Listen. Please?"

Rylan couldn't remember the last time he'd heard her say *please*. She really *was* desperate. "Fine. I'll hear him out, but no promises."

Blythe slid her knife back into its sheath, then took the pouch containing the wisp, and set it on the table. "Take that with you." Rylan took it and stood. As he wove between the tables stairs, he heard Blythe call out behind him, "And I'm sorry!"

He shouted back over his shoulder. "Only four left!"

FOURTEEN: RYLAN

Rylan strode along the second-floor hallway of Broken Antler and stopped at the last door on the right. He heard the sound of a lute from beyond the door. The song was an old ballad about Wyan One-hand, one of Aarik's forebears, the last proper King of the Wood. A soft humming accompanied the jangle of strings. Rylan paused to listen. It wasn't half bad.

He knocked, and the ballad ceased.

"Come," called a baritone voice.

Rylan opened the door and entered a small room with a pair of lit lanterns on the walls. Aarik was sitting close to the door in a homespun shirt and leather leggings at the far side of a beaten table behind a bottle of golden liquor and two empty glasses. His brown hair was a bit grayer and longer, and he had few more wrinkles, but otherwise, he looked much the same as the last time Rylan saw him, other than the sad braided leather headband he wore. It looked like it was trying to be a king's golden circlet, but failing miserably.

"Rylan, welcome." Aarik set the lute on the bed behind him and motioned to an empty chair. "Please, sit."

Rylan sat and set the wool pouch on the table. "This is for you, apparently. Blythe said you had a job?"

Aarik chuckled. "Slow down, won't you?" He leaned forward, poured some liquor into both glasses, and slid one toward Rylan. "Syris?" It was a pleasant, mead-like alcohol made from the fermented sap of citadel trees. "We only have so many days on this earth. Enjoy them while you can." He raised his glass.

Rylan had all but thumbed his nose at having a drink with Blythe, but he knew better than to do that with Aarik. He lifted his glass and poised it next to Aarik's. "To the women we love and the children they bear."

"To the dragons we ride"—Aarik clinked his glass—"and the bonds we share."

Rylan sipped the liquor—nutmeg, cider, and late summer pear; sweet, certainly, but with enough acidity to keep it from cloying. The finish was a pleasant mingling of copper and cinnamon. "It's quite good."

Aarik set his glass down with a clack. "It's out*standing*." He leaned back in his chair, crossed his arms over his chest, and gazed at the pouch. Then he picked it up, pulled out the wisplight, and set it on the pouch on the table. The way the wisp's blue light combined with the lamplight made the syris shimmer like the scales of an indurium dragon. "Do you know much about my mother?"

Rylan shrugged. "A little. I know she was tried, convicted, and burned by the Church for heresy."

"True, if oversimplified. Do you know why the Church feared her so?"

"She was awakening the old ways. Recording them in the Book of the Holt. The Church was afraid of what she would find, what she *did* find."

"Precisely. She knew how to commune with the citadel trees, how to unlock their secrets. The trees remember. They've witnessed many things. The Ruining. The arrival of the Kin. The first bonding with an umbral. The first use of lucertae. They saw the arrival of the empire, saw them shake hands with the Kin in brotherhood, saw it all fall apart when the empire took our most treasured secret, bonding with dragons, and twisted it, used it against us. They saw the Talon Wars play out. They're watching us now, Rylan. They'll remember this conversation."

"Children's tales," Rylan said. "They can't see *everything* . . ."

"My mother believed they could. She never wanted to wage war like people say, but to learn from the trees. And the empire feared her for it."

"You're glossing over the fact that the knowledge she uncovered led to an assassination."

"It did, but that was never her intent."

History said that when the Church first learned of Rygmora's pursuits, they planned to take her prisoner and put her to the question. She fled to the Deepwood Fens with her three young children: Aarik, Morraine, and Llorn. The Red Knives gave her sanctuary largely to thwart the Church, but they soon realized Rygmora's power could benefit them. The empire's centuries-long campaign to suppress knowledge was so successful that many of the Kin's most cherished rituals were lost. After Rygmora moved to the Deepwood, she recovered many secrets, among them the ability to use the lucertae of onyx dragons to gather darkness, move among shadows, become a shadow oneself, all without being a shepherd or a druin. A Red Knife used it to infiltrate the imperial palace in Ancris and assassinate the quintarch, Lucretio Solvina. It was a pivotal moment in the empire's history and led to years of renewed persecution and killings.

Aarik sipped his syris. "The empire didn't give a shit what my mother wanted, though. They sent a full wing of dracorae to grab her. She was, as you said, tried and burned for heresy. But the last thing she did before they took her away was ensure copies of her book were made. She tried to pass on the knowledge of how to use the trees to unlock *more* secrets—not to bring down the empire, but so that the memories stored in the trees could help people. She wanted *peace* above all."

"Why are you telling me all this?"

"Because I want you to understand. Morraine and Llorn were enraged by her death. As was I. We wanted revenge. I killed dozens of imperial subjects, trying to even the scales, to extract justice from the beast that is the empire. It was never enough. Everything I did as a Knife, then later as King, seemed only to make life worse for the Kin." He spun his glass and stared at the gold liquor. "I tired of it, Rylan, found myself wanting peace, like my mother wanted. I still want it. Which is why I've been working with your father on an amendment to the Covenant."

Rylan sat there, stunned. "What *kind* of amendment?"

"A peace amendment, one that will last. The Red Knives will cease all violence and become an adjunct of the constables, reporting ultimately to your father. We will ensure that trade moves freely and that the empire's dracorae, their inquisitors, and their bloody shepherds are left alone so long as they don't cause trouble."

Rylan could hardly believe his ears. "You're going to report to my father?"

Aarik nodded. "Not all of us, but yes, in spirit, that would be true. In return, the empire will officially recognize our territory and villages as part of the Holt. Some of our people will be named reeves and gain voting rights on the seat of imperator and the tax authority. We'll have a say in new trade agreements as well. A tax increase will lead to higher revenue for the Holt *and* the empire."

"You claim to be a king, Aarik. You expect me to believe you're going to bend the knee to my father?"

Rylan expected Aarik to grow angry. Instead he chuckled. "I can trace my lineage to Wyan One-hand, it's true, but the world has moved on since the Talon Wars. It's time we recognize it."

"And Llorn? What does *he* think of this?"

Aarik drew a deep breath. "Llorn's been lashing out. He strung up a caravan, not for trespassing, but because he heard I'd made an offer to the trade master in Gorminion. Then, he killed an alchemyst who claimed to have been sent on a surveying mission by your father."

"He killed his ferryman, too. Blythe told me."

"Indeed. But what I asked her not to tell you was *why* Llorn killed them. They found a project *he'd* been hiding from *me*."

"And what was that?"

"I'm afraid I can't tell you. Too dangerous. I haven't even told Blythe all of it. And this"—he put a rough hand on the wisp—"was part of it. But I need to put a stop to it. All of it. I've put Llorn in check, but the alchemyst's death may lead to complications. His name was Korvus Julianus. Do you know him?"

"I know *of* him. I saw his shop burning. I saw his wife's burned body."

Aarik nodded. "Raef's handiwork. But here's the wrinkle. A day before Raef torched the place, one of Korvus's fellow alchemysts, Master Renato, came from Ancris. There's more than a reasonable chance he knows what Llorn was up to. I need to know for certain."

"Why, so you can kill him?"

Aarik seemed to calm himself. Then he said, "So I know what I'm up against. It was already going to be difficult to get the quintarchs on board with the amendment to the Covenant. It gets worse every time Llorn kills someone."

"Does Llorn know about this Master Renato?"

"No. The information came directly to me."

"I'll ask again. What was Llorn doing?"

"I can't tell you that, so stop asking."

"Yet you want me to go to Ancris and find out what Master Renato knows? I'll find out what he's planning then if you don't tell me now."

"True, but he might not know anything."

"Then send a Knife to find out. Send Blythe."

"No. You're welcome in the capitals. You can go places Blythe can't. You've a knack for making people trust you. Blythe's told me about it."

Blythe? Speaking nicely about him? "Forgive me, Aarik, but this whole thing stinks. I feel like I'm being set up again."

"It's for the good of the Holt."

"So *you* say . . ."

"If you won't believe me, ask your father about it."

Rylan snorted. "He'd probably have me hung."

"We both know that's not true. Speak to him. Just don't mention anything about Llorn and Master Renato." When Rylan remained silent, Aarik's face grew serious. "We want to heal the Holt, Rylan. It's long past time."

Rylan nearly told him no—it *did* feel as if he were being set up—but the very notion that his father might be working with Aarik Bloodhaven, King of the Wood, was monumental, too intriguing to ignore. "Very well," he said, standing. "I'll speak to him."

Aarik nodded, and started putting the wisp back into the pouch. "I'll be gone for a few days. Leave word with Krannock. He'll get it to me."

Rylan stepped toward the door, wondering, if everything Aarik had told him *was* true, how much it had cost Aarik to draft an amendment that would cede much of his power to a man he'd once considered an enemy. A sacrifice like that spoke of love—for the Kin, for the Holt, and their entwined future—and it made Rylan hope he'd told no lies. "Take care, Aarik."

"You too, Rylan."

FIFTEEN: RYLAN

Two days after his meeting with Aarik, Rylan trekked up to Valdavyn, the imperator's residence, at the highest reaches of Glaeyand. Filled with feasting halls, audience chambers, art galleries, music rooms, and more, the estate sprawled through the forest, its four wings spanning a dozen citadel trees, and was visible from almost any place in the city. One wing was dedicated to the private chambers of the imperator and his family. Another provided rooms for servants and guardsmen. A third welcomed visiting guests. The fourth was set aside for formal events and audiences with the imperator.

On the entrance deck ahead of Rylan, his half-brother Kalden and Kalden's wife were shepherding their seven children into the imperator's wing. The two guardsmen on duty bowed to Kalden and his wife as they passed. They bowed to Rylan as well, but it was so quick he would have missed it if he'd blinked. He recalled the two guards joking when he was young. "What's worse than a Kin in Valdavyn?" the taller one had asked when he thought Rylan was out of hearing, and the other, Henrik, had replied without a beat. "Half a Kin." And they'd both laughed.

Rylan might have requested a private audience—and as he passed the guards and entered the residence, he felt like maybe he should have—but the Lyndenfell family dinners represented a rare opportunity. Marstan's ten other children were all grown. The vast majority of them were married with families of their own. It made the dinners quite chaotic, but it was a longstanding tradition, starting with Marstan's grandfather, that a dinner be held once each fortnight so the family could stay in touch despite the flurry of modern life. The presence of so many children and grandchildren often put Marstan in a good mood. He was much more likely to share information with Rylan after a family dinner than he would be during a private audience.

The sound of conversation filtered into the entrance hall from the feasting hall. As Kalden's wife ushered their children toward it, Kalden glanced back at Rylan with a cold stare, then simply kept walking. Rylan had often dreamed of cutting Kalden's head off and tossing it from the high balcony, but he figured the family dinner was probably not the time.

Deciding he wasn't quite ready to face the family yet, he ducked into a side hallway, sidled past a servant wheeling a cart of bread, and pushed through the swinging doors into the kitchen. It was busy as Rylan ever remembered. Near the door, a steward was shouting orders. At the far end of the kitchen, the two cooks, Briar and her twenty-year-old daughter Lyssa, were basting pans of roast pheasants. To their left, two sous chefs were stirring soup and chopping vegetables. To their right, three women in white aprons were glazing pastries. Dozens of servants bustled in and out, throwing empty trays into a massive sink and picking up fresh trays of delicacies from a long central table. Pans clanked, meat mallets pounded, boiling water hissed. Smells of garlic, leek, and thyme laced the air.

Briar, was a stout, rosy-cheeked woman with auburn hair sticking out of her wimple. She moved to a brick oven and bent over it, her back to Rylan. As Rylan headed toward her, Lyssa rushed to a massive stock pot and began ladling what smelled like potato leek soup into tureens. She had the same auburn hair as her mother and a ragged scar running down her right cheek from a run-in with a dragon when she was ten.

"Well, well, well," Lyssa said, smiling, "look what the wyvern dragged in."

Rylan leaned against a tall cabinet. "And good day to you, too, Lyssa."

A boy with rosy cheeks and a mop of blond hair was loading a cart with glass dishes filled with olives, pickles, cheese, and seeded crackers. As the cart rolled past, Rylan snatched a couple of black olives and tossed them in his mouth.

"Oy!" Briar said, glaring at him. "Those are for the *guests*." It was her usual refrain ever since Rylan was a child and snuck into the kitchen to pinch a bit of food.

"And a hearty good day to you, too, Briar! These days, I am a guest."

Briar swung her gaze at Lyssa. "See how he is now?" She set a pan of freshly baked pastries on a rack to cool. "Thinks he's all high and mighty, he does."

Rylan laughed. "If I were high and mighty, would I be *here*?"

"You hear him, Lyssa?" Briar began filling the pastries. It was one of Rylan's favorites—smoked trout, dill, lemon, and capers. "We're the *riffraff* now."

Lyssa's broad smile twisted the ragged scar on her cheek. "Oh, Mother, settle down."

"On the contrary." Rylan leaned forward and snatched a filled puff and stuffed it in his mouth. "You are the jewels in the imperator's crown."

Briar raised her spoon, threatening to smack his hand if he tried to take another. "Tell that to your father."

Rylan put his hand to his mouth and laughed. "I beg your pardon, did you just say *tell that to my father*?" He chewed, savoring the rich canapé. "Better I told him I detest you. He'd probably offer you a homestead."

Briar smiled and her round cheeks reddened. "You'll see to it, then, will you?"

"I'll be sure to mention it to him next time he invites me to tea."

"In that case"—she lifted her arms and glanced down at the pastries—"you may have another."

Rylan feigned to gaze at a female servant, then snatched another pastry, and yanked his hand back.

Briar's wooden spoon came down with a splat onto a pastry. "Oy! See what ya done now!"

Rylan laughed and popped the pilfered pastry into his mouth. Lyssa picked up the smashed pastry and shoved it in hers.

As two servants rushed in and began placing the filled pastries onto silver platters, Briar glowered at Rylan and Lyssa. "You always were too fast for—" She stopped mid-sentence to stare at something over Rylan's shoulder.

Rylan turned to see Bashira, his father's chamberlain, in the doorway. She was a dour woman with swept-back hair, purple-ringed eyes, and an axe for a nose standing near the kitchen entrance. "Dinner's about to begin," she announced.

"Coming, Bashira," Rylan said. He winked at Briar and Lyssa, who were both hiding smiles.

Rylan exited the kitchen, made his way to the feasting hall, and was grateful to find he was seated at the end of the table. It meant he would have fewer neighbors. In another bit of good fortune, Willow sat to his left. She was one of the middle children, several years older than Rylan, and had inherited Marstan and Kathrynn's good looks. Everyone knew Marstan was grooming her for higher office, and anyone who knew her could see why. She was smart, shrewd, and insightful like her father. She knew when to charm and when to bully. She had an intuitive feel for politics, and knew what could be sacrificed and what protected to get what she wanted. He could at least stomach a conversation with her. On his right, however, was Andros, chief among Rylan's tormentors when he was young. Beyond them, Olivar and Kalden were going on about how much money they'd made in the shipping and messenger business they ran for their father.

Lydia, her honey-blonde hair done up in a hive, stared coldly at Olivar over something he'd just said. "You're cheating them, then."

Olivar shook his head with a mildly offended look. "Cheating is such a foul word. Call them market adjustments."

Kalden nodded. "For those we feel should pay more."

Red-bearded Tamrys, sitting just beyond them, swung his overly large head in their direction. "And who is it, precisely, who should pay more?"

Both Olivar and Kalden glanced toward Rylan. On finding him watching, they said something too low for him to hear. The others glanced at Rylan, too, Tamrys smirked, and the conversation moved on.

As usual, Marstan sat at the head of the table. He was a man of fifty-eight winters, though he didn't look it. His scant meals and daily hikes throughout the city kept him fit as a man ten years younger. His kept his peppery beard and mustache immaculately trimmed. For the occasion, he wore a slashed doublet, ocean-blue trousers accented in ivory, and perfectly polished, high black boots.

To Marstan's left was his wife, Kathrynn; on his right, his eldest son, Cato. His twenty-three grandchildren sat at trestle tables with several of their mothers. Beyond them were two patricians in purple—brothers, if Rylan recalled correctly. Marstan was surely trying to get their support in the coming election.

The dinner was a raucous affair—laughter, shouting, clinking glasses, and servants running to and fro. Rylan didn't mind, but he much preferred a fete around a bonfire, singing and dancing to a lute, to the gamesmanship that dominated dinners like these. Halfway through the meal, Willow, who'd been occupied with Kalden, turned to him. "So what made you decide to come?"

"Willow Lyndenfell, always straight to business."

"Rylan Holbrooke, always hiding things."

Rylan shrugged. "It's been too long is all."

Willow nodded. "Hmm . . . no other reason?"

"No. Now why don't you tell me how the trip to Andalingr went?"

"The Red Knives look to be responsible for the temple burning. Their sign was carved into the front doors. And Raef was apparently spotted in Thicket earlier in the day. The constables suspect he set the blaze."

Kalden chimed in uninvited, "They're like a bloody infestation."

"They're not *insects*, Kalden," Rylan said.

"A disease, then. What else would you call a people who suck the life from the Holt and from the empire?"

Rylan knew if he tried to defend the Red Knives, everyone around him would pile on, call him a sympathizer at the least, an aider and abetter at worst.

"Speaking of infestations," Andros said to Kalden, "did you hear what Rylan did to Magnor?"

"Mmm, yes," Kalden said around a mouthful of stuffed mushroom. "You've seen to the shoulder then? Your precious dragon is better?"

Andros nodded and finished his wine. He raised his glass for a refill and said, "He needed a bit of tending to, but yes."

Rylan feigned curiosity. "Tell me again what you did to help him?"

Kalden barked a laugh. "A dragon singer who doesn't know how to deal with scaleworm?"

"The key," Andros said, staring directly at Rylan, "is to use the right amount of salve. Too much of it will irritate the dragon's skin."

It reminded Rylan of the game Andros used to play, where he'd dare Rylan to call him out in front of others so he had an excuse to pound him later. "Very good," Rylan said. "Perhaps you should write a book on the subject."

"Can't. I'm too busy fixing your mistakes."

"Faedryn's teeth, Andros," Willow said softly, "you're like a rabid mutt sometimes, you know that?"

Andros glared at her and then at Rylan. Then he realized a servant was trying to fill his glass and turned away from them.

When dessert was served, the conversation shifted to business and preparations for the coming election and the council of quintarchs. Rylan wished he'd turned Aarik's offer down and gone to fly for a day or two in the Holt with Vedron. She might not talk much, but she was still better company than anyone in the room.

Finally the talking and drinking wound down, and a few families with younger children left. When the patricians followed, Rylan went to the head of the table and bent by his father's side. "May I have a word?"

Marstan's smile raised the curled tips of his mustache. "I wondered when you'd get to it."

Rylan didn't bother to reply—no sense pretending he hadn't had an ulterior motive in coming to dinner.

"You have your pipe?" Marstan asked.

Rylan patted his coat. "Always."

Marstan nodded. "Let's have a smoke."

With a few parting farewells, they left the feasting hall. They passed Willow on the way. She eyed Marstan, then she rolled her eyes at Rylan and murmured. "*Too long is all* . . . yeah, right."

Rylan followed his father to his study, a cozy wood-paneled chamber with a potbellied fireplace, a broad carpet, and a pair of polished leather chairs. Below the window to Rylan's left was a writing desk and, behind it, a shelf filled with books, legal texts, and various nicknacks, most of them gifts to the imperator from visiting dignitaries. On a low table between the chairs was a wooden box with a lid.

Marstan crouched beside the fireplace, took an iron poker from the stand, and stoked the coals. "Sit."

While Rylan settled himself in the nearest chair, Marstan pulled a few logs from the cradle, placed them on the glowing coals, then stood and dusted his hands. He got up, strode to a shelf, and picked up a bottle of brandy and a pair of snifters. As Marstan poured the brandy, Rylan couldn't help but note the similarities between this meeting and the one with Aarik two days earlier.

Marstan set the bottle down and sat. "Something amusing?"

Rylan shrugged, then lied. "Just thinking about the life I lived here."

Marstan opened the lid of the wooden box between the chairs. Inside were three compartments. One held an ivory pipe on a bed of velvet; one loose-leafed tabbaq; the other matches. "You remember it fondly, then?" Marstan took the ivory pipe and began filling.

Rylan reached into his coat, took out his own mahogany pipe, and did the same. "Bits and pieces, yes."

Marstan lit a match and held it to Rylan's pipe, then lit his own and tossed the match into the fire. "Such as?"

Rylan raised his pipe. "This."

Marstan had taught him the rituals around tabbaq: how to properly fill, tamp, and light a pipe, the distinct notes one could find on the palate and on the nose, the best places to buy it. It was one of the very few things they and only they shared—the rest of his children were casual smokers at best.

Marstan chuckled. "Nothing else?"

Rylan blew a stream of smoke toward the ceiling. "Dinners with the servants."

"But not with us . . ."

"It's not that I didn't appreciate them . . . ." They both knew the sort of reception Rylan had received in the imperator's household.

Marstan pursed his lips. "I gather you didn't mind sitting with Briar's daughter . . . uh . . . what's her name?"

"Lyssa. And no, I didn't . . ."

They smoked in silence for a time. Rylan savored the notes of black pepper and anise in the tabbaq, the leather and apricot on the brandy. When tabbaq and brandy were all but consumed, Marstan puffed a funnel of smoke rings into the air. "You wanted to talk."

"Yes. I've gotten wind of some rumors. I want to find out if they're true."

"They're lies, all lies!" He laughed. "Okay, I see you're serious. What rumors?"

"I heard about a proposed amendment to the Covenant, a joint agreement between none other than the imperator of the Holt and the King of the Wood."

His father took an extraordinarily long time to down the tiny amount of brandy left in his snifter. "Who told you this?"

Rylan shrugged. "Does it matter?" When Marstan said nothing, Rylan continued, "Don't get me wrong. I wouldn't blame you if you *were* working with him. Far from it. Lasting peace benefits everyone—me, you, the family, Glaeyand—and we both know striking a deal with Aarik is probably the only real way to achieve it."

The fire popped and hissed and settled back into a comforting crackle. "You've never inserted yourself in imperator business before. Why now?"

"Because I'm tired of the corpses hanging from trees. I'm tired of seeing homesteads burned to ash. I'm tired of waiting for the day when the Kin can thrive in the land they love."

Marstan stared silently into the flames. Rylan couldn't tell if he was angry or if he was considering telling him something. Finally, he said, "When your uncle, as you call him, was burned, I was contacted to determine whether he'd told the magistrate the truth, that I was in fact your father. Instead of disavowing any knowledge of you, which I could easily have done, I took you into my household. Would you care to know why?"

"Please, enlighten me."

"I was having difficulty getting enough votes to retain my seat. The patricians in the eastern reaches were particularly recalcitrant. They said I had too much imperial blood in my veins, said I was just a mouthpiece for the quintarchs. They stymied me for months. Then came Beckett's sentence, and I thought: What could prove my sympathy toward the Holt better than a son with Kin blood? I placed a bet that you would be worth the embarrassment of having fathered a bastard, worth the coldness I would receive from Kathrynn. And in the end, that bet paid off. The landowners were appeased, and I kept my seat."

Rylan realized his mouth was gaping open and shut it. He wasn't sure what sort of reaction to expect from his father, but it wasn't this.

"I'll be honest," Marstan went on, "I expected little return on my investment beyond that, but the decision has been paying dividends ever since. I'd never have guessed you would be so good with dragons, never guessed I might use it to curry even *more* favor—in the Holt and the empire, both."

Rylan's talent for dragon singing was first noticed when Andros landed a tired and furious Magnor on the deck of the residence during a birthday party for Lyssa. The dragon struck Lyssa and several of her friends with its tail before Rylan could calm it down. Other dragon owners began requesting Rylan come sing to their dragons. Marstan allowed it but insisted on deciding which commissions Rylan could take and using them to gain or return favors.

"The arrangement benefits us both," Marstan said. "Let's keep it that way, shall we?" He stood and headed toward the door but paused by Rylan's chair. "In case it isn't clear, Rylan, I advise you to keep your nose out of imperator affairs"—he clapped Rylan's shoulder—"before you lose it like that little finger of yours."

Marstan left the study and closed the door behind him with a soft click.

Rylan raised his left hand and stared at his pinky nub. He'd felt useless plenty of times while he lived in Valdavyn, but he'd never felt like a pawn. He knew Marstan wouldn't have threatened him if Rylan hadn't touched on the truth. And he was still a bit awed that his father would make a deal with Knives, but his gut told him his father's reasons for doing so were self-serving. Nevertheless, if a peace deal was in the offing, Rylan was determined to help it along.

He left Valdavyn, descended past the market and his home to the forest floor and walked back to Tallow, to The Broken Antler. The main room was only half full, but the conversation was loud and the mood cheerful and uplifting.

He went directly to the bar. Krannock was pouring beer into four mugs gripped in one massive hand. He set the mugs on a tray for a waiting serving girl, and raised his bushy eyebrows at Rylan.

"The man I spoke to the other night upstairs," Rylan said.

Krannock nodded almost imperceptibly.

"Tell him I'll do it."

SIXTEEN: THE HISSING MAN

The Hissing Man sat in his sepulcher, a ledger open on the desk in front of him. He'd just begun the tending to the Chosen's finances, a dreary but necessary task, while waiting for word that Llorn had arrived in Ancris.

He summed the columns and scribbled totals, but his mind was more on the man he was about to meet than the bribes they paid to the senators or the stags that went to keep brutes like Gaul in their employ. He kept wishing there had been another way to achieve his goals without relying on a snake like Llorn. Knowing their deal would give Llorn power was a bitter pill to swallow but, as had been true when they'd first come to terms more than a decade ago, he saw no other path.

The deal was simple on its face. The Hissing Man, Azariah, and the Church would build the palisade, and Llorn, his druins, and his Red Knives would build the crucible. If all went as planned, Ancris would be destroyed, and in the chaos that followed, the Red Knives would gain control over the Holt while the Church rose to its rightful place atop the empire. What Llorn didn't know—indeed, what no one but the illustrae and a select few of their trusted servants knew—was that the ultimate goal was to free Faedryn from his prison below the Umbral Tree. It was a goal worth any price, including ceding the Holt to the hated Red Knives.

But what if things *didn't* go according to plan? What if Aarik did something he hadn't accounted for? What if Llorn betrayed him? What if the quintarchs didn't react to the devastation the way he thought they would?

Realizing he'd written a total in the wrong column, he scribbled it away and wrote it in the proper place, and a knock came at the door. "Come," he hissed.

The door creaked, and Gaul stood in the doorway, holding his knife up in front of his face.

"Very well," the Hissing Man replied. "This is boring me to death anyway."

He dropped his pen into its inkwell, left the sepulcher, and followed Gaul down the hallway. He was stiff from sitting and walking was painful, particularly in his hunched shoulder. Though the Hissing Man had no need for light, Gaul dangled a wisplight on the end of a chain, sending wild shadows over the tunnel's rough walls.

The cold air was relatively fresh at first but turned rank as they approached the sewers. They climbed a set of winding stairs to a storeroom, then moved past barrels of saltpeter and alum and shelves lined with vitriol and climbed another, wider set of stairs to reach the dragonworks proper: a massive, open workshop. Along one wall were rows of vats, some covered, some not. In the corner near them was a kiln and a pile of bones waiting to be fired, ground, and sifted. Along another wall, dragon skins were stretched over large wooden frames, curing before being made into armor, boots, gloves, and the like. Beyond the frames were three tuns filled with dull red dragon scales, waiting to be ground and turned into darksteel. The Hissing Man was jaded to much of imperial life, but the dragonworks had always fascinated him. It was a machine that fed on dragons—umbrals killed in the Holt and brought to the city and radiants that had succumbed to disease, old age, or battle wounds—and produced the very elements the empire needed to survive.

Gaul motioned toward the door to the rear yard, where Llorn stood, then tee-tered back down the stairs. A rugged man with dark hair and sun-marked cheeks, Llorn was staring at the rendering vats like they'd just called his mother a whore. It came as no surprise; Llorn had complained about meeting in the dragonworks from the start. More curious was his face. The bruises around one eye and the cuts on his lips glowed indigo in the Hissing Man's second sight.

"Bough and bloody branch," Llorn said as the Hissing Man limped toward him, "why do you continue to insist on meeting here?"

"It's far from prying eyes," replied the Hissing Man as he came to a stop.

"So are the sewers, and I daresay they smell better."

"I'm in no mood to banter," the Hissing Man said. "Out with it. How much does Aarik know?"

"He knows about the crucible. He's seen it."

"Because you were careless?"

"No. Because word was bound to reach him sooner or later. The Rookery was too close."

Several months ago, an imperial scout had discovered the Red Knives' former hideout, where they made the drugs they sold. In a stroke of bad luck, Aarik had chosen to build a new rookery near the vyrd hardly an arrow's flight from the crucible.

The news was a thorn in the Hissing Man's side. "You should have tried harder to get him to move it."

"I did. My brother dug in his heels."

"That only means you failed to sway him."

Llorn's bruises purpled. "You're confusing me for a politician." He practically spat the last word.

"What happened after he saw it?" the Hissing Man asked.

"What do you *think* happened? He bitched and moaned about his lying, back-stabbing brother, even *after* I told him how it would lead to Lyndenfell's fall."

The Hissing Man pointed a crooked finger at Llorn's face. "I take it he did more than bitch and moan."

Llorn shrugged. "He—"

"Why didn't you tell him to go fuck himself? Why not take the reins for yourself?"

"Because nothing's changed," Llorn said. "Too many Knives are loyal to him.

And there's more. When I told him about the crucible, he told me he's been working with Marstan Lyndenfell."

The Hissing man paused to consider the information but couldn't fathom it. "Working at what?"

"An amendment to the Covenant. Marstan plans to present it at the council of quintarchs. He's been maneuvering for months, currying favor from the quintarchs. He has a good chance of getting the vote."

"What *amendment*?"

Llorn spat on the cracked stones at his feet. "An amendment to cede power to the imperator, to become glorified constables in the name of peace."

"But the burnings . . . the *slaughters* . . ." The Hissing Man had thought surely Marstan would respond to the violence with more violence, as he'd done in the past. "Why by Alra's endless grace would he trust *Aarik*?"

Llorn paced over the dusty floor. "Apparently, Marstan is as weary of the fight as my brother is. No doubt Aarik told him the violence was coming from me, not him. And I never would have guessed it, but I suspect the violence spurred Marstan to agree to Aarik's plans for peace, and sooner rather than later."

The Hissing Man drew his lips back in anger. "Your dragon," he said, "couldn't you use its lucerta to sway Aarik?"

"The influence I gain from Fraoch's scales lasts a day, maybe two. I can't keep using it on Aarik forever. We need a *permanent* solution."

It was then that the Hissing Man understood. Llorn knew what had to be done; he just couldn't bring himself to do it.

"Has Aarik told anyone else?" the Hissing Man asked.

"I don't think so."

"Not even Blythe?"

Llorn shrugged. "I can't say for certain."

The Hissing Man nodded. "Bring Aarik here."

"What, to Ancris?"

"Yes," the Hissing Man said. "Wouldn't you agree it's time someone else led the Red Knives."

They'd broached the subject several times in the past, but Llorn, ruthless in almost every aspect of his life, had demurred. "It isn't time," he'd say. Or, "Let's wait until the crucible is built."

Well, the crucible was built, and Aarik showed no signs of coming around to Llorn's way of thinking. Quite the opposite was true, and Llorn seemed to recognize it. "He'll never agree to come here," he said.

"He'd be a fool not to be suspicious," the Hissing Man said, "but tell him I want to give him a look at what we've done in the city. He'll likely agree if only to see the full extent of the problems he and Marstan will be facing."

Llorn paused and stared down at the ground a moment. Then he nodded. "It may work."

The plan the Hissing Man laid out was straightforward: trick Aarik into coming to an abandoned mine, and he, the Hissing Man, would take care of the rest. That way, Llorn wouldn't be troubled by having to do the deed himself, and the Hissing Man could ensure that Aarik's death would be a public one, which should usher Llorn into becoming King of the Wood that much quicker.

As he described more details about the mine, a vision of a young man with curly blond hair swam before him. A knife drove into the man's chest, and he cried out, but only for a moment. It was Cassian, Illustra Azariah's son. The Hissing Man had told Azariah that his fears over his son's death were unfounded, but it was a lie. Cassian hadn't disappeared. He'd been slain.

It was necessary, the Hissing Man told himself. He blinked hard and shook his head, banishing the image. *He was going to expose everything!*

"Why did you stop talking?" Llorn asked.

The Hissing Man blinked. The way Llorn was staring at him made him want to drive a knife into the man's chest, as he had Cassian's. "I was merely collecting my thoughts. Now who do you know in Ancris that's . . . unnecessary in the grand scheme of things?"

Llorn paused, as if doubtful of the Hissing man's explanation, then said, "There's a chandler in Slade who fits the bill, but before we go any further, there's another small matter we need to discuss. My druins have been having trouble with the ritual that will span the vyrda."

The Hissing Man rasped, "You said the archdruin, Sister Dereka, could manage it."

"I thought she could, but she hasn't so far, and time is running short."

"So what do you propose?"

"I need Morraine."

The words spoke volumes. Morraine, Llorn's dead sister, had been crucial to the early planning of this unholy alliance. She was dead now, hung for crimes against the empire. That Llorn had expressed a need for her implied he hoped to raise her from the dead, a thing his druins might actually know how to do. But *why* did he want her? "You'll need her wisp," he said, if only to gain himself a bit of time.

"Someone has already pinched it for us."

"You'll need her remains as well."

"We have them."

The Hissing Man laughed. "Then why are you telling me this?"

"Because if I didn't, you'd be alarmed when you heard about it. When I raise Morraine, I don't want any interference from the Church."

The Hissing Man had long since reconciled himself with the need to commit sins. He was more worried about Llorn's true purposes. He'd been close to his sister, which might explain, at least in part, his desire to raise her from the dead. They'd been aligned in purpose as well, sometimes *against* Aarik. There was likely more to it than merely gaining an ally, but the risk would be worth it if it brought him closer to freeing Faedryn from his prison.

"Very well," the Hissing Man said. "I'll see to it the Church doesn't interfere."

SEVENTEEN: AZARIAH

Azariah strode along a cold tunnel in the Hallowed Grove, an area of the catacombs set aside for the quintarchs and other members of the high family. He wore his ivory-and-gold mask, his white robe with Alra's eight-pointed star embroidered on the chest, his golden locket necklace with its two compartments. Similar to Alra's Acre, the crypts were arranged in an orderly, grid-like fashion. Each had a wisplight set into the ceiling, four archways that led to tunnels, and four sepulcher doors.

He soon arrived at his destination, a crypt with three empty sepulchers meant for Lucran, Tyrinia, and Skylar Solvina. The fourth had a brass plaque above the door that read: *Ransom Solvina, beloved son of Lucran II and Tyrinia Solvina.* Azariah entered Ransom's crypt. Inside was Ransom's white marble sarcophagus, simple but elegant in design. Its lid had a golden sword mount with a brightsteel gladius, the sword Ransom had used while fighting in Syrdia.

He flipped open the locket to the side with the onyx gemstone and unclasped it, to get at the reservoir of black umbris powder, took a pinch, sniffed it, and squeezed the locket shut. As the powder's loamy fragrance overwhelmed all other smells and the familiar, burning ache grew inside him, he gripped the lid of the sarcophagus by the corners and lifted it. Normally, it would take three or four men to open such a heavy lid, but Azariah shifted it to one side with ease and peered down at the Ransom Solvina's remains, wrapped tightly in a linen shroud.

Azariah flipped his golden locket to the side with the white moonstone, took a much healthier pinch of the white auris, and sniffed the rosemary-scented powder; then he ran his powder-coated fingertips over his gums. Aura and umbra were opposing forces. It was difficult to hold both in the body at the same time—it hurt—but Azariah had learned long ago how to master the pain and keep the powers separate within him.

From the leather pouch on his belt, he drew a pyramid-shaped tourmaline, which shimmered from rose to gold to forest green in his usually gray second sight. He placed the tourmaline on Ransom's sternum and retrieved an alchemically treated, empty glass globe from the same pouch.

With one hand on Ransom's chest and the other on his skull, Azariah concentrated, beckoning Ransom's soul. For a moment he felt nothing; then a glimpse of a man on dragonback flying over a battlefield as a gryphon swooped down next to him flashed behind Azariah's eyes. It was common for souls to remember painful memories, but the ritual required the soul to be calm. He wished peace upon Ransom's soul and tried again. He found himself sprinting along the banks of the

River Wend, five-year-old Skylar chasing behind him. It was a good start, but not enough.

A third vision showed Lucran handing Ransom the very gladius that graced the lid of the sarcophagus. A fourth revealed a dark room in Highreach. Ransom lay on a covered bed with high wooden posts. Red curtains covered the windows. Incense filled the air. Next to the bed, Ransom's mother, Tyrinia, lay on a pile of pillows, her eyes fluttering as she stared at the ceiling.

A feeling of contentment flowed from Ransom, and Azariah felt his heart slow, his hands relax. He sighed deeply.

"Did I ever tell you about the girl I found in Syrdia?" Ransom asked.

With some effort, it seemed, Tyrinia focused on him. "I don't care to hear about your exploits."

"It wasn't like that. She was a singer, and I melted every time I heard her voice. I swear, I could listen to her for days, weeks, years, and never tire of it. They're beautiful singers, the Syrdians."

"Then perhaps we'll have one brought here to sing for you." Tyrinia's smile was fleeting. "Would you like that?"

"I'd like that very much," Ransom said, and his eyes fluttered closed.

Azariah continued coaxing Ransom to remember his former life, inviting him to return to it. Eventually, he felt the soul's desire to live again. He beckoned it, made it clear the soul would find peace. Light glowed below the tourmaline, then permeated it. Azariah touched the empty glass globe to the tip of the tourmaline, and it filled with a bright blue flame. Azariah lifted the globe and peered into it. "Perfect."

Azariah's power was all but spent, but he had just enough umbra to shift the lid of the sarcophagus back into place. He turned to leave the sepulcher and shivered. The Hissing Man was hunched in the doorway.

"What are you doing here?" Azariah asked.

"I live here, remember?" Hissing Man rasped. "You quickened his soul? *Why?*"

"As a favor to Tyrinia. Now tell me why you've come."

Waiting for the Hissing Man to reply, Azariah had vision of Cassian, a knife being driven into his chest, blood pooling beneath his fallen body.

The Hissing Man's lips curled, either in anger or frustration. "Your son was *abducted.*"

As was so often the case, the Hissing Man seemed to know his mind. It was due to their constant talks via the silverskin, Azariah knew, but it was disconcerting just the same. "I see him," Azariah said. "I *know* he wasn't abducted, and I know you know what happened to him. So tell me."

The Hissing Man paced toward him. "You don't want to know, Your Radiance."

"Yes, I do." Azariah sidled around the sarcophagus and retreated. "Don't!" He continued backing up until he felt his back press against the cold sepulcher wall. "Please, I was his *father.* I have a right to know!"

"Enough." The Hissing Man shuffled forward until he was close enough for

Azariah to smell the rot on his breath. "Lord Faedryn wishes you to bend your will on his release from his prison"—grimacing, he lifted his crooked forefinger and touched Azariah's forehead—"and nothing else."

Knowing full well what was coming, Azariah summoned memories of Cassian. He held his son's beautiful face in his mind. For a time it worked, but then the vision dimmed and a new one took its place: a citadel tree made of darkness. It was the Umbral Tree, Faedryn's prison.

"Good," the Hissing Man said, "very good."

Azariah listened without complaint as the Hissing Man told him of his meeting with Llorn. He felt weighted down, slow and malleable as clay, as the Hissing Man detailed Aarik's plan for peace with Marstan Lyndenfell and why Aarik needed to die. By the time the Hissing Man was wrapping up his tale, the feeling of being weighed down faded, and Azariah was working through all of the things that could go wrong with the Hissing Man's plan and what Azariah could do as illustra to ensure they didn't.

"Bringing Aarik here will attract attention," he said.

"Yes." The Hissing Man took two shuffling steps back. "I'm counting on it."

"It runs the risk of drawing the attention of the inquisitors and, by extension, the quintarch. At the moment they know nothing, but when the King of the Wood comes to Ancris? They'll wonder what could possibly have convinced him to leave the safety of the forest."

"You don't get it. Ancris is the *lure*. Aarik will want to see what Llorn's agreement has led to. *That's* how we get him here. It gives us a convincing reason for him falling into your hands. Then, when Aarik is dead, no will question Llorn's claim to the throne."

"There are too many ways for it to go wrong. Llorn should just kill him and be done with it."

The Hissing Man shook his head. "If Aarik's allies think he was killed under mysterious circumstances, they might challenge Llorn for Aarik's crown."

"Then kill him in secret. I could send Japheth if Llorn's not up to the task."

"That could lead to their questioning why he was found so easily after being careful for so many years. Even a hint of betrayal could lead to delays that we cannot afford." The Hissing Man pointed upward. "Any day now, the palisade will be ready. Aarik must die so that Llorn can take his place."

It wasn't killing Azariah was afraid of, but missteps. He'd worked for three decades to see Strages freed from his shrine, and he didn't want it all ruined because he or the Hissing Man had acted rashly.

When too much time had passed in silence, the Hissing Man went on, "Delaying is the *greater* risk. You know it is."

"Very well," Azariah said. "See it done."

The Hissing Man bowed. "At once, Illustra." And he left the sepulcher.

EIGHTEEN: LORELEI

L orelei pulled her cap lower, tugged her winter coat tighter. The streets of
Slade were cold and blustery. When she reached Olga's home, the old woman
let her in with a crinkle-eyed smile. Lorelei returned it briefly, then clomped
up a narrow set of groaning wooden stairs. Another night watching the bloody
chandler.

"That you?" Creed called.

"Who else would it be? The milkman?" She found Creed lying on the blankets, peering through the spyglass between the slats of the louvered vent.

"Surf and foaming sea," he said, "are you still on about that? It was one expedition to a bunch of floating rocks."

"Do you have any idea how much studying those floating rocks can reveal?"

"No, but I'm sure you're about to tell me."

Lorelei dropped down onto one of the weathered stools. "What right does
Tyrinia have to cancel a scientific expedition of monumental proportions?"

Creed rolled over and snorted. "Monumental proportions . . ."

"Aren't you the least bit intrigued?"

"Yes, but in precisely the same amount as I am about fermentation. I care that
beer tastes good, not how long the mash is boiled."

"I was looking forward to it for weeks."

"So you'll go again, *after* the work at the shrine is done."

"Maybe," Lorelei said, "so long as another hornet doesn't crawl up Tyrinia's
wrinkled old cunny."

Creed barked a laugh. "Did you just say wrinkled old cunny?"

"Yes. I've been taking lessons from Ordren." She raked a hand through her
hair and huffed noisily. "Honestly, I'm more sad for Master Renato than anyone
else. This is the second time he's had something canceled because of that stupid
shrine."

"It is?"

Lorelei nodded. "He wanted to study a sinkhole, apparently, before Azariah
tapped him to lead the renovation."

Creed shrugged. "The fruit of patience is great reward, as my grandfather used
to say. What news from the Crag?"

Lorelei had mentioned she was going to stop by the Crag, the home of the inquisitors, to ask about the reported death of the library's clock tender. She wouldn't
have thought much of it—Ancris was a big city and murders happened—but a

five-tailed scourge, the mark of the Church's heinous zealots, had been carved into the man's forehead.

Lorelei said, "As far as anyone can tell, the clock keeper was holy as they come. He was a regular at temple. No history with the Red Knives or drugs of any kind."

Creed pursed his lips. "Maybe he just pissed off the wrong guy."

"Maybe."

"Well, I'm off to catch a few winks." He handed her the spyglass. "Meet me at the Tulip later?"

"Certes," Lorelei said. "I'm definitely going to need a beer by then."

The afternoon and evening went exactly as Lorelei feared. Customers came and went. Tomas eventually left. Everything was quiet after that. She though about breaking into the chandlery and searching for crates of drugs, but if she didn't find anything, it would cock up the whole investigation. She wasn't ready to do that just yet, but she was ready for a beer.

She took the creaking stairs down to the ground floor and heard snoring coming from the bedroom. "Goodnight, Olga," she said softly, and left the house.

Though Nox was still low in the sky, Lorelei took its harmful rays seriously. She tugged on her woolen cap and pulled the specially made cuff from her sleeves—a sewn-in half-glove of sorts—and fit her fingers through the holes. She walked along the winding road to the city center, past the blue-veined pillar on the roundabout, and under the shimmering palisade. Even then, Lorelei kept her cap on and her sleeves extended. She knew the palisade worked but had yet to trust it completely.

A few more turns delivered her to the front entrance of The Bent Tulip. Fiddlehead wasn't the safest neighborhood in the city, but the Tulip had been a favorite haunt of the inquisitors for years. It had become an oasis of sorts for the enforcers of imperial law, and all the busier for it.

The common room was as packed and as loud as she'd feared. Every table was occupied, and the space *between* the tables was so thick patrons had to move belly-to-belly to move past one another. The air smelled of bad breath, tabbaq, and men who'd been in their uniforms too long, and there was a woman with an eye patch sitting at a table in the corner who hadn't taken her one good eye off Lorelei since she'd entered.

"There's my girl!" Eladora, the plump, gray-haired woman who, along with her sister Eustice, owned and ran the Tulip, shouted from behind the bar. "Wait right there. Don't move a muscle." She turned to a cask, one of several dozen lined up behind the bar, and poured a measure of beer. When Lorelei reached for the leather purse at her belt, Eladora waved it away. "Creed already paid. He's waiting for you in the back."

Lorelei accepted the glass with a smile. "Thanks, Dora."

The old woman nodded, then bellowed at a pair of men waving their glasses farther down the bar. "Hold your horses, you bloody heathens! I've only got two hands!"

As Lorelei squeezed through the crowd, a table of card players in the corner roared. Nanda and Vashtok, two fellow inquisitors, stood and waved. Ordren was there as well, a cuss of a man with sharp cheek bones and a jutting chin perpetually covered with stubble. He neither waved nor called, just sat there like a surly basset hound. Lorelei guessed the game wasn't going well for him, but then, who knew? Ordren always looked surly.

Lorelei waved back, but the rowdy conversation, the laughter, even the crackle of the lively fire in the hearth, was making her skin crawl. And that thrice-damned woman with the eye patch was now smiling and tipping her head to the empty seat next to her. Lorelei ducked her head as if she hadn't seen and wove through the crowd down a hallway into a lounge meant for quieter conversation. A small fire flickered in a red brick fireplace to Lorelei's right. A few tables, some padded chairs and footstools were spread about, but Lorelei walked past them to her favorite spot, a row of curtained booths along the far wall.

The curtains of one booth parted and Creed poked his head out. "Oy!"

Lorelei slid onto the seat across from him, and Creed pulled the curtains closed. She took a moment to breathe. Creed waited patiently, then motioned to her beer.

"Try it," he said. "It's good."

She took a deep breath, then raised the glass to her lips. It was creamy and delicious, a strong hoppy bitterness balanced by grassy sweetness. But the sense of peace that began to steal over her had less to do with the beer than this calming ritual she'd fallen into with Creed over the years.

"Anything?" he asked as she took another sip.

She shook her head. "I think we need to move on. I say we take Tomas in tomorrow. See what he's willing to tell us."

Creed nodded. "Not every nibble lands a fish. At least we tried."

"I know, but it isn't just Tomas. We've been at this for years and what have we accomplished? We shut down one drug den or supply route and another takes its place."

"We've landed some dealers, a couple lords."

"*One* lord."

Creed shrugged. "Semantics. One of the dealers was promoted the morning we took him."

Lorelei chuckled. "Half a lord, then. Meanwhile, the flow of drugs is stronger than ever."

"We're doing good work, Lorelei. It's *necessary*."

"I know it is." Lorelei shrugged. "It's just—"

Lorelei realized a man was standing beyond the curtains and started, dribbling beer on the table. Probably a beggar who'd snuck in the rear entrance.

"Bugger off," Creed said.

"I wouldn't turn away this opportunity, I were you," a scratchy voice said, Lorelei recognized Tomas immediately.

She had only heard him speak only once, but she recognized his harsh rasp.

She parted the curtains, and there he was, wearing the same drab clothes he'd had on when he'd left the chandlery.

Creed dropped a hand to his knife, but Tomas raised his hands. "I'm only here to talk."

Creed kept his hand where it was. "So talk."

Tomas's cheeks were red, his eyes bloodshot, as if he'd sniffed too much rapture from his own supply, but his pupils weren't dilated and the beat of his heart, visible along his neck, appeared more or less normal."Fine, but"—he glanced at a group of off-duty constables watching them from across the room—"I'm not sure I want the whole fucking Crag listening in on our conversation."

The muscles along Creed's jaw rippled as he turned to Lorelei. Lorelei nodded, and Creed shifted to her side of the booth and gestured Tomas to sit down on the now-empty bench.

Tomas sat, tugged the curtains closed, then wrung his hands and blew into them. "They say you can protect those who bring you information about the Knives. Hide 'em, even send 'em somewhere else in the empire."

Lorelei's attempt to hide her surprise was, she was certain, a miserable failure. "Is that what you want?"

"It is." Tomas blinked hard. Wrung his hands again. "Ten days ago, or thereabouts . . ." He stopped, pulled the curtain closer together, and drummed his fingers on the table.

Creed said, "Say what you've come to say."

Tomas grimaced and continued. "Ten days ago, one of the urchins I've got watching the neighborhood comes to the shop and tells me there's a man and a woman been sneaking in the back of the old stonemason's place. I says thanks, tells her to keep watching and let me know if they keep coming. They do, day after day, so I decide to have a look. I spots a glint coming from the vent in the attic. A spyglass, I figure. Inquisitors watching my shop, I tells myself. Got to be."

The redness in Tomas's cheeks deepened. He grimaced again and clenched his teeth.

"Are you all right?" Lorelei asked.

He jutted his jaw, and the pained look faded. "I told Blythe, like I's supposed to. She tells me to keep calm, says she'll take care of everything. Tells me to keep selling candles in the meantime. Says that's exactly what the shop is for."

"Let me guess," Creed said, "Blythe didn't take care of everything."

"Faedryn's black teeth, no! I hear *nothing* after that. Leaves me hanging in the wind!" He began to wring his hands again, but stopped. "A few days ago, I hears word of a meeting coming up here in Ancris. Something big. King of the Wood is coming in person for it."

Creed laughed. "Aarik never leaves the Holt."

Tomas goggled at him. "You think I don't know that? It's true, though. He's here in Ancris right now."

"You're sure?" Lorelei pushed a stray lock of red hair behind her ear. "You saw him with your own eyes?"

"Not as such. A friend o' mine did."

"Which friend?" Creed asked.

"Never you mind *which friend*. Here's the important bit. Tonight, after I left the shop, I sees a man standing behind a tree near me house. I thought it were one of you lot. But it weren't. It were Aarik's bloody butcher, Llorn."

Creed sneered. "Maybe he just wanted a bit of a chat."

Tomas laughed. "A chat, my skinny arse. Wanted to fashion me a crimson smile, he did."

"You think Llorn was planning to kill you because we were watching you?"

"He's killed for less. I've become a *complication*, as Blythe says it. After all I've done for them, they're gonna cut me up and feed me to the dragons!"

Creed leaned forward on the table. "You know protection comes with a price, yes?"

Tomas snorted. "You think I'm dumb enough to come empty-handed?"

"Let's hear it, then," Lorelei said. "What're you offering?"

"A lot. But let's start with this. I asked around. I know Aarik and Llorn are meeting in the old indurium mine beneath Faedryn's Widow. Tonight."

"Why?" Lorelei pressed.

Tomas stared at her like she was an idiot. "That's *your* bloody job. Tell you this much, though. That alone should buy me passage out of this shit hole."

"Maybe," Lorelei said, "if it's true."

"Of course it's true. And I've got more besides if you want to know."

Tomas's face was so red, he looked like a beet with eyes. The veins on his forehead and neck bulging so hard Lorelei could see them pulse.

"Pardon me for saying," she said, "but you don't look well."

Tomas rolled his bloodshot eyes. "An' you'd be calm and collected in my shoes?"

Lorelei turned to Creed and raised her eyebrows. He nodded back. "We can't guarantee anything," she said, "until we know what you're offering is real."

Tomas slid toward the end of the bench. "Best get to it, then."

Creed snatched Tomas's wrist. "It'd be safer if you stayed with us."

Tomas stared at Creed's hand. "What're gonna give me?"

"Nothing yet, but—"

Tomas ripped his arm away. "Meet me behind the stonemason's garden tomorrow night at cant. I want assurances, from the Praefectus herself, understand?"

Neither Creed nor Lorelei said a word, and Tomas left. When his footsteps had been lost to the general din coming from the front room, Creed slid back to the other side of the table. "Could be a trap," he said.

"Could be." Lorelei shrugged. "Probably worth checking out, though."

"Damika will be in bed by now."

Lorelei nodded. "Probably best not to bother her." She jutted her chin toward the hallway that led to the front room. "Gather a few more eyes and ears?"

"And swords, Lorelei." Creed stood and made for the hallway. "Don't forget about the swords."

NINETEEN: LORELEI

An hour after Tomas's unexpected visit, Lorelei, Creed, and three of their fellow inquisitors were west of Ancris, heading through a forest on horseback toward the mine entrance. A chill wind howled through the trees. Nox shone down from the heavens, dark and angry. The forest's sugar maples and basswoods slowly gave way to pine and birch as they climbed the rough terrain.

Lorelei and Creed led the way on coursers. Ordren came next. Bringing up the rear were Vashtok and Nanda. Lorelei had been trying to talk to the latter two in private when Ordren had returned from the privy and barged into the conversation like a mad bull. She should be happy to have him, but she detested the man—he was crude and cruel, even to those he should count as friends.

"Let me get this straight," Ordren said, bumping along the trail. "This bloke, the fucking chandler you've been watching for three weeks, just traipses into the Tulip, sits down in your booth, and tells you godsdamned Aarik is in Ancris, and he does it for free?"

"Not for free," Lorelei said. "He seems convinced Llorn wants to kill him. He's asking for protection and a bit of money to help him get out of Ancris."

"And *I'm* hoping Damika will polish my knob, but that's not very likely either, is it? This smells like a fucking trap."

Creed called over his shoulder, "You're free to go any time you want."

"What, and miss all the fun, you big dumb auroch? Not a chance." He paused to guide his horse around a patch of mud. "Just for the sake of argument, let's say it's not a trap. Why meet in a bloody old mine?"

"Why *not* in a bloody old mine?" Vashtok said in his thick Sapphire Coast accent. "It's been abandoned for years. For men like them, it's a convenient place to meet away from prying eyes."

"Pfft! What are they going talk about?"

Nanda laughed. She was a dark-skinned woman who's blade was nearly as sharp as her wit. "This is just a fact-finding mission. So why don't you do us all a favor and shut that gob of yours?"

"Fact-finding . . ." Ordren snorted. "We're a pack of straw-brained idiots. How's that for a fact?"

Ahead, the forest ended. Not wanting to risk being spotted, they headed into the trees and tied their horses to a sapling; then they crept toward the mine and hid behind a clutch of midnight dogwood, which had leaves that dulled a nightglass's magically enhanced sight. From there they could see Faedryn's Widow, a mountain shaped like a hooded crone bent with age. A weed-ridden cart path wended between two of the mountain's arms, leading to the boarded-up mine entrance, barely visible beneath Nox's violet light.

"Two guards." Nanda said, unstrapping her bow from the saddle. Then she pointed with it. "There and there."

Lorelei saw nothing in the darkness, so she pulled out her nightglass and spotted the two men hunkered in the scrub brush above the mine entrance.

A dragonsong warbled like an underwater trumpet, breaking the silence. It came from beyond the ridge above the mine entrance.

"Somebody's not happy," Lorelei said. "Sounds like a cobalt. Might be Llorn's."

Nanda's perfect teeth shone in the unlight. "Maybe the chandler wasn't so full of shit after all, hey, Ordren?"

Just then, a man emerged from the mine. He appeared to have a short conversation with the sentries. As he headed back inside, a golden light flashed three times from above the entrance.

"A signal," Lorelei said.

"Yes," replied Vashtok, "but to whom?"

A horse whinnied to their left. The clop of hooves followed, then a horse and rider broke from the trees beyond the cart path. Lorelei raised her nightglass. The rider wore a hooded black habit.

"Alra's bright smile," Nanda whispered, "the Hissing Man."

She was right, Lorelei realized, spotting what looked to be bandages over the man's eyes. But why, by Alra's sweet grace, would the *Hissing Man* be coming to parley with the leader of the Red Knives, a group the Chosen had deemed unholy and had been trying to eradicate for generations? It could only spell trouble for Ancris and the empire as a whole.

"We should get backup," Creed said.

Ordren blinked at Creed, his mouth agape. "The pit bull with the perpetual scowl is ready to turn tail and run?"

Lorelei ignored him. "If we go for backup now, we'll miss our chance." Trying to capture the Hissing Man and the highest ranking members of the Red Knives with only five inquisitors was definitely risky, but they had to know why the Chosen and the Red Knives had thrown in together.

Creed stared hard at her. "The whelp rushes in where the wolf treads carefully. We could have a century of soldiers and a cohort of dragons here within the hour."

"No way. We'd be lucky to get a single legionary to step foot outside their barracks before morning, much less an imperial mount," Lorelei countered. "Aarik will be gone by then. They all will."

"They could have a small army in there," Creed said, stabbing a finger at the mine entrance.

"With only two guards posted? No, they're keeping this meeting small for a reason. The fewer who know, the better, right? Worst case, things get too hot and we retreat. But maybe we can learn something."

Vashtok said, "Lorelei has a point. Surely, Alra herself has delivered this opportunity to us. She'd be displeased if we walk away from it."

"Nanda?" Creed said.

"Name one thing we do that *doesn't* have risks," she replied.

"Risk is one thing," Creed said. "A meat grinder is another. Plus, how would we even get in?"

"Easy," Lorelei said, "we use the mine's layout to our advantage."

"And how do we do that?"

"Vashtok," Lorelei said, "your father was a miner for forty years, yes? A foreman for half that?"

Vashtok's wide brow furrowed. "How did you know?"

"You mentioned it."

"I did?"

"Five years ago, after we chased those bandits into the Wayward Oxen."

"You *remember* that?"

"I do," Lorelei said evenly. "You said he took you there several times. Do you remember anything about it?"

"Now I do," Vashtok said sheepishly. "There are three entrances. Or there were. They might all be boarded up now, or caved in. The two ventilation shafts are our best bet. They were meant to double as escape routes during cave-ins. They had iron rungs spiked into them. We could use them to climb down."

The Hissing Man reached end of the cart path, dismounted, and headed toward the mine's entrance. Lorelei turned to Creed. "We go to the ventilation shafts, we climb down, and we see what's what."

Lorelei could tell he was afraid. It wasn't from lack of courage—Creed was one of the bravest men she knew—but during their stay at Olga's he'd told her that when he was young, his brothers had dug a hole in the sand beside the sea, thrown him into it, and buried him as a joke. Even after all these years, he still had nightmares about it.

"We'd better bloody hurry," he said, with a long sigh. "Whatever's about to happen will happen soon."

Nanda strung her bow in one fluid motion. "I'll keep an eye on the guards at the entrance."

Lorelei nodded. "Good hunting."

The expression meant good luck, but Nanda only laughed. "Good hunting yourself. Trust me, if they take a single step toward the entrance, they'll regret it."

Vashtok led Lorelei, Creed, and Ordren through the forest. When they were far enough to not be seen by the guards, they left the trees and climbed the slope toward a ridge. By the time they reached it, they were all breathing hard. Vashtok scanned the area while tapping his lips with one forefinger, then headed to their right and eventually came to a square hole in the ground that led into darkness.

Vashtok descended the iron rungs first. Ordren followed. Creed lingered near the hole in front of Lorelei, his hands clenched.

Lorelei grasped his hand and squeezed. "One rung at a time, yes?"

After a deep breath, he squeezed back. "One rung at a time."

Lorelei clambered down into darkness. Creed, breathing heavily, followed behind her. Lorelei leaned left, peered down, past Ordren, and saw Vashtok standing in a tunnel, holding a wisplight. The wisp itself, obviously quite old, shed only a faint blue light, perfect for sneaking about.

Ordren dropped beside Vashtok, dusted his hands off, and drew his old, nicked gladius. Lorelei and Creed joined them and drew their rapiers. They heard faint voices in the tunnel as they started ahead. After a few bends, they spotted a golden light. Vashtok stuffed the wisplight in his coat, and they continued toward the light until they saw the Hissing Man, Llorn, and Aarik standing in a carved-out chamber around a brass lantern. Another man, a druin, judging by his bald head, blue tattoo, and robe, was kneeling on the gouged stone floor with a canvas rucksack, a small leather bag, and two vials. He dropped a pinch of white powder into a vial, and stirred the solution with a glass rod.

"Well, Brother Mayhew?" said Aarik.

"The reaction should begin shortly," the druin said.

Slowly, the solution to glow. It started as dark blue, but soon it was such a bright white it was painful to look at.

"Bough and branch," Brother Mayhew said, "can you *feel* it?"

Neither Aarik nor Llorn said a word. They simply gaped at the vial with their mouths hanging open. The Hissing Man's eyes were hidden, but his face was twisted in a grim smile.

Lorelei felt an energy, a giddiness, but it grew into an ache of sorts, like raw power churning inside her desperate for release.

Aarik held a hand up. "Extinguish it."

"No." Brother Mayhew took a green woolen scarf from the rucksack. "Better to let it go out on its own." He laid the scarf over the vial. The light dimmed, and everything in the chamber tinted green.

Lorelei's chest and hands continued to pulse.

"Now," the Hissing Man rasped, "there's the matter of my sample."

"I didn't bring one." Aarik said. "First, I must understand the full extent of our agreement."

The Hissing Man's jaw worked. "I *need* that sample."

"And you'll have it," Aarik said with a quick shrug, "should I decide to move forward."

The light beneath the scarf finally faded, and with it Lorelei's pulsing giddiness. Brother Mayhew folded the scarf and stuffed it, the small leather bag, and the alchemycal equipment in his rucksack.

"We have an *arrangement*," the Hissing Man sneered.

"You made an agreement with my *brother*," Aarik told him, "but he doesn't speak for the Red Knives. *I* do."

The Hissing Man laughed like a jackal. "All you've ever wanted is being handed to you. Llorn saw to it. Tell him, Llorn."

"I *have* told him," Llorn said, "but the king wishes to discuss it with his council. We've called for one—"

"Silence!" Aarik roared.

A long silence followed, until the Hissing Man said, "Convene your council if you must. I expect an answer in one week's time."

Ordren leaned to Creed and whispered, "We should take them now."

The words were hardly out of his mouth when Llorn swung his head toward them. "Inquisitors!" He snatched up Brother Mayhew's rucksack and sprinted down the tunnel behind him.

"Ordren, you bloody idiot," Creed said.

Aarik backed away, drawing his sword, then raced after Llorn. Brother Mayhew picked up the lantern and ran after them.

The Hissing Man turned and peered down the tunnel toward Lorelei and the others. He held his hands out, and a darkness swept toward Lorelei and her companions. Lorelei lost sight of the Hissing Man, the cavern ahead. She felt dizzy and hot, feverish. "I–into the chamber," she stammered.

With her rapier in front of her, she stumbled past the darkness into the chamber. The light of the druin's lantern swung wildly in the far tunnel and then disappeared. From the dark passageway to her left she heard the thud-and-scrape of the Hissing Man retreating. "You two," she said pointing at Vashtok and Ordren, "head after the Knives. Aarik's most important, but grab any of them if you can."

Ordren scowled, though whether it was from annoyance at Lorelei giving him orders or him screwing up his courage, she couldn't say.

Vashtok pulled out his wisplight and offered it to Lorelei. "We have their lamp to follow."

Lorelei nodded and took it; then she and Creed rushed down the tunnel after the Hissing Man. The rutted tunnel floor slowed them, but it had to slow the Hissing Man too. They passed through a small cavern with a mining skip shaft and barreled toward the tunnel on the far side of the room. Eventually they stopped when a another tunnel cut across it. Lorelei spotted a patch of indigo light coming from the mine's entrance to her right. To the left was pure darkness. She listened for footfalls, but heard nothing.

"He can't have escaped so quickly," Lorelei said, panting.

Creed, breathing nearly as hard, said, "He could if he had umbra."

He was right, of course, but she wasn't willing to give up so soon. With a deep breath, she forced her mind's eye to return to the moment she'd entered the room with the mining skip. She saw the darkened room, the skip's dusty, cobweb-ridden frame. She saw the waving shadows, caused by her own movement, but this time she spotted a smudged area on the wood, perhaps by someone brushing up against it, or holding on to it in order to reach the rope. Slowing the scene further, she saw a cloud of dust above the shaft, the barest swaying of the rope.

"He's in the mine shaft," she said, and bolted back down the tunnel.

Creed followed without argument. As they neared the cavern, they slowed and entered in near silence. Lorelei peered down at the skip cable leading into the darkness below. Creed pulled out a tripflash, small glass globe with black and white powder inside, and whipped it at the far wall next to the skip. The globe smashed and powder splashed and sizzled on the wall, lighting up the far side of the cavern. Even across the cavern, Lorelei felt a wave of dizziness wash over her. It would be *much* worse near the shaft, yet the Hissing Man climbed up from it steadily, stepped away from the skip, and held a palm out toward the sparking powder. The sizzling and the wild light quickly faded.

The Hissing Man grimaced and raised his other hand, sent a wave of darkness toward Lorelei and Creed. Lorelei felt like her flesh was being torn from within.

Creed moaned, crumpled to his knees, and fell against the stone wall.

Lorelei clenched her fists and howled, then fell to her knees.

The darkness suddenly ceased, and the pain faded. The Hissing Man lurched toward her, knife in one hand, clutching his chest with the other. "You inquisitors," he hissed through clenched teeth, "really are a menace."

"The Red Knives," Lorelei grunted, *"why?"*

He started coughing, bent over, and hawked up something, then he staggered closer and placed one booted foot on the blade of Lorelei's rapier. "Give the goddess a kiss from me, won't you?"

He crouched, gripped Lorelei's shoulder, and raised his dagger over her. Then an arrow whistled through the air, clattered against the wall to Lorelei's left and rolled onto the floor.

"Stay where you are!" Nanda called from the tunnel.

The Hissing Man turned, and Lorelei kicked him hard in the side of the knee. He stumbled and fell, clambered to his feet, and ran into the tunnel toward the chamber he'd met with Aarik.

Nanda darted into the skip chamber. "Are you all right?"

"I'm fine," Lorelei moaned. The ache in her chest and limbs had ebbed. She scrabbled over to Creed and shook him.

He opened his eyes and looked around. "Did I get him?"

Lorelei laughed even though it hurt. "Almost, Creed." She stood and pulled him to his feet. "Almost."

"Fuck me three ways." Nanda glared along the dark tunnel the Hissing Man had run down. "Want me to go after him?"

"No." Lorelei slipped one of Creed's arms around her shoulders and helped him limp toward the mine's entrance. "He'd slit your throat in the darkness. Let's just go find the others."

Outside the mine, the two sentries were lying on the stony ground with arrows sticking out of their chests. The Hissing Man's horse was nowhere to be seen. Reckoning they might catch Llorn, Aarik, or Brother Mayhew should they try to escape from the mine's rear entrance, Lorelei, Creed, and Nanda headed toward the far side of the peak. They'd not gone twenty paces when they heard a dragon trumpet beyond the ridge. Lorelei spotted the cobalt beating its wings and rising far to the north.

Nanda scowled up at it. "There's only one rider."

Lorelei couldn't see that far in the dark, but when they reached the ridge ahead, they saw Aarik and Brother Mayhew, wrists tied behind them, being pushed along by Vashtok and Ordren.

Nanda, still fuming, flung a hand toward them. "At least we got those two bastards."

TWENTY: LORELEI

Lorelei headed toward the trees with the others, and they soon reached their horses. Vashtok suggested searching for the Hissing Man on horseback, but everyone agreed they'd pushed their luck far enough. They'd head to the Crag and send a team of constables to scour the area.

They put Aarik and Brother Mayhew on Creed's mare and tied their hands to the saddle horn. Aarik had bruises and cuts on his face. Brother Mayhew had a nasty gash and a goose egg on his forehead. It was hardly surprising. Ordren was a scrappy fighter, and Vashtok was a terror with fists and blade. Creed rode with Lorelei.

As they made their way through the forest, Aarik rode silently, staring straight ahead. Brother Mayhew, sitting behind him, seemed angry at first, but when Ancris came into view, the look of anger faded. The way his eyes darted toward the temple on Evalarus, the domed structures of Golden Meadows, and the palace on Mount Blackthorn made Lorelei wonder if he'd ever been to an imperial city. Most druins hadn't for fear of being persecuted.

Lorelei brought her horse even with Aarik's as they crossed the Wend over an old stone bridge. "Seems a bit strange, the Knives and the Chosen making nice."

Aarik said nothing.

"Aren't they your sworn enemy," Lorelei continued, "and you theirs? What could the Hissing Man offer that would make you betray your own people?"

"I would *never* betray my people," Aarik said.

"Then why meet with the Hissing Man?"

They rounded a low hill and entered the city proper at Slade, not too far from Tomas's chandlery, and Aarik lapsed into stony silence. A bend in the street led to a square with a tall palisade pillar at its center. Practically invisible from a distance, the palisade's shimmering curtain arced over the city and Mount Evalarus.

"Sounds like Llorn went around you to make this deal," Lorelei said to Aarik, "almost as if he didn't trust you to do the right thing."

Again, silence.

"The Hissing Man mentioned a sample. A sample of what?"

When they received no response beyond an angry glare, Creed, bouncing in the saddle behind Lorelei, said, "Silence buys you nothing, Aarik. Tell us what you know and I'll mention your cooperation to the magistrate myself. You might live instead of being burned at the Anvil."

"And live a slave in some treeless corner of the empire?" Aarik snorted. "I'd rather face the fire."

He said no more after that, and soon they were approaching a large hill and the fortress known as the Crag. Its watchtowers, curtain wall, and central keep had all been built with utility in mind. From afar, it looked like it was just another part of the hill. Once the primary defense for an imperial outpost, then a garrison for the city guard, the Crag was now the inquisitors' headquarters. As they approached the stout gates, a horn sounded from the tower.

Vashtok stood in his stirrups. "Vashtok the Mighty has arrived with fellow inquisitors Lorelei, Creed, Ordren, and Nanda. Let all within the fortress know we have found the King of the Wood and are bringing him in for questioning."

Ordren rolled his eyes. "Your head's not going to fit through the bloody gate you keep that up."

Vashtok chuckled as he lowered himself back down.

The doors clanked and groaned open. By the time they rode up the courtyard path to the main door, men were peering out the windows at them and a crowd had gathered around the steps. They dismounted and led Aarik and Brother Mayhew down a long hall; the gaoler, seven inquisitors, and a handful of constables stood before the entrance to the stout iron door that led to the holding cells.

"Now *that's* what justice looks like," said the gaoler, a rail-thin man named Marion.

Inside, Ordren broke away and headed toward the Pit, where the bulk of inquisitors had their desks. "I think you girls can manage things from here."

No one argued. Like manure on the soles of one's boots, Ordren was unpleasant and likely to leave a trail of shit.

In the dungeon, Creed led Brother Mayhew to one cell while Lorelei brought Aarik to another.

"I'd like an audience," Aarik said as she was closing the door.

"Who with," Marion cackled, "the bloody quintarch?"

Aarik ignored him and looked at Lorelei. "I'd like to speak with Imperator Lyndenfell."

For a moment, Lorelei was speechless. "Why?"

Aarik shook his head. "Ask him."

Lorelei blinked, unsure where to take the conversation from there. "I can't promise you anything here and now."

"I am promising *you*. He'll want to speak to me."

The appeal was so unexpected and heartfelt that Lorelei actually found herself wondering if she *should* request that word be sent to the imperator. But then she remembered who she was dealing with. "You can make the request of the magistrate at your hearing."

She left and headed toward Marion's office. She'd no sooner arrived than Praefectus Damika, a stout, bleary-eyed woman, entered the room. Her dark skin and heavy accent marked her as having come from the Fire Plains west of the Whitefells. She wore a swallowtail coat, part of her uniform, but her rumpled civilian clothes beneath it. She was tough as old leather, and had an iron will.

Lorelei, Creed, and Marion followed her back down the hall to the cells. She shone a wisplight into Aarik's cell and stared at him. She did the same with Brother Mayhew, then they returned to Marion's office.

"You two," she said to Lorelei and Creed, "come with me." She pointed to Nanda and Vashtok. "You two go to the Pit. Get writing while everything's fresh."

Vashtok's eyebrows shot up. "Why am *I* supposed to do paperwork?" He wagged a finger at Lorelei and Creed. "It's *their* case."

"Were you or were you not the one bellowing that Vashtok the Mighty had captured the King of the Wood?"

Vashtok shrugged. "A bit of bluster for the lads at the gate!"

"I don't care what it was. Get started. Creed and Lorelei will be by soon enough to finish things up."

Vashtok shook his head and left, mumbling to himself. Nanda gave Lorelei a flat stare for a moment, then she squeezed Lorelei's arm. "Good hunting, indeed." She followed in Vashtok out of the room.

Creed and Lorelei followed Damika to her office. Surprisingly, Ordren was already there.

"Don't look so surprised," he said to Lorelei. "Wouldn't *you* want to hear the details from the man who played the most pivotal role in tonight's little adventure?"

Creed barked a laugh. "Pivotal? You just happened to be around was all."

"Enough," Damika said before Ordren could make some snide reply. "Tell me all of it. Start to finish."

Damika headed around her desk. When her back was to him, Ordren sneered at Lorelei. She ignored him.

Lorelei gave Damika the broad brush strokes of the escapade, from their surveillance of the chandlery to Tomas's sudden arrival at the Tulip to their capture of Aarik and the druin.

"I don't understand," Damika said, leaning back in her leather chair, "why would Tomas give them up like that?"

Slightly irritated, Lorelei cleared her throat. "As I said—"

"I know what you said. You really think he'd be angry enough to betray Aarik?"

"If Aarik really *did* send Llorn to kill him, sure I do. What choice did he have?"

"He could've run."

"True," Ordren chimed in, "but how far would he have gotten on his own?"

"He's right," Lorelei said, shooting a glance at Ordren she hoped would shut him up. "Tomas may have thought we could keep him alive if he talked."

Damika considered, then knocked her knuckles on the edge of her desk and pointed at Lorelei and Creed. "You two go find Tomas. I want to know what he knows."

"And Aarik?" Lorelei said.

"We'll let him stew overnight. Ordren can begin questioning him in the morning."

Lorelei could hardly believe her ears. "*Ordren?*"

Ordren smiled his shit-eating smile. "The Praefectus knows a good interrogator when she sees one, dearie."

"Don't *dearie* me!" Lorelei spat, then turned to Damika. "He's just going to beat Aarik until he gets answers."

"So long as I get them"—Ordren shrugged—"where's the harm?"

"It's torture! Aarik will just tell you what he thinks you want to hear."

Damika raised her hand. "I'm giving the task to Ordren. Concentrate on finding Tomas."

Lorelei was about to press when a ruckus broke out in the anteroom. Virgil, Damika's diminutive assistant, called out. "I'll fetch her immediately, Your Holiness."

Creed and Lorelei exchanged a look. Damika raised her eyebrows. Even Ordren seemed a bit shocked. The honorific *holiness* was reserved for the illustrae, which meant Azariah Andrinus had arrived in person.

Virgil opened the door. "I'm terribly sorry to interrupt, Praefectus. You have a visitor."

"I heard." Damika waved her hand. "Send him in."

Virgil stepped back, and Azariah entered the office, wearing white a robe and an ivory mask. Virgil's hand was trembling as the he closed the door behind him.

Azariah was a tall, imposing man with a regal bearing. His ivory mask covered the upper half of his face. Thin strips of gilded wood fanned out above his forehead like sun rays. Though it had no actual eyeholes—illustrae saw with second sight—the outline of eyes had been etched onto the ivory, giving Azariah a detached, dispassionate air.

He seemed to fix his stare on Damika. "You've taken two men into custody," he said, "Aarik Bloodhaven and a druin of the Deepwood Fens. Deliver them to me, that the Church can make them answer for their crimes."

Of all the things Lorelei thought he might say, that was probably the last. Creed looked shocked as well. How had Azariah found out about them so quickly?

Damika stiffened. "The two men have been detained by *my* inquisitors for crimes against the empire. By law they're ours to deal with."

"That would be true had the leader of the Red Knives not ordered the burning of five Alran temples. Ten of our clergy died in those fires. Dozens more were wounded. I will not abide a blasphemer of the goddess's teachings, much less someone who hopes to erase their very existence, to escape Alra's justice."

"Evidence points to Llorn as having set those fires," Damika said.

Azariah shook his head. "And you think Llorn would have acted without Aarik's blessing?"

"Your Holiness, Aarik is wanted for bringing illicit drugs into our city. I ask that you let us keep him. We'll give the Church all the access it requires."

Were the history between the inquisitors and the Church amicable, Damika might simply have handed Aarik and Brother Mayhew over. But the relationship had been icy for generations, ever since the time of the Holy Rebellion, when the Church had attempted, through force, to replace the empire's quintarchs with men and women more sympathetic to the Church. The Praefectus was assassinated the first night of the rebellion. Other inquisitors had subsequently been murdered. It had led to an acrimonious split between the quintarchs' inquisitors and the Church. Surely the last thing Damika wanted was to appear weak in the eyes of Quintarch Lucran.

"Those burnings were not merely a desecration of the Church," Azariah continued. "They were an insult to Alra herself"—he raised two fingers and moved them in a circle—"may her memory abide. The Church will have them both. See to it."

Damika was no woman to be bullied, but even Lorelei had to admit the request wasn't unreasonable. Aarik *was* likely linked to those burnings. Were Lorelei in Azariah's place, she'd probably demand he be brought to the temple for trial as well. Yet she hoped Damika would stand up to him. The Church's idea of a trial was to torture its victims and cleanse them with dragonfire. If Aarik was taken from the Crag, Lorelei would never see him again . . . unless the Church decided to make his burning public.

Damika likely figured she could explain it well enough to Quintarch Lucran so she wouldn't lose his confidence, but Lorelei felt a golden opportunity slipping away. Something big was happening in Ancris. Why else would the Chosen and the Red Knives be meeting in secret? "Your Holiness," she said in a rush, "the Church may have jurisdiction over Aarik, but not over the druin."

The tall illustra appeared to look down the nose of his mask at her. "He is a Red Knife."

"Forgive me, Your Holiness," Lorelei said, "but we don't know that for certain. And there is no evidence linking him and the fires." Azariah clenched his teeth. Lorelei wasn't sure if that was good or bad, but she continued, "By order of the imperial decree regarding inquisitor affairs, Brother Mayhew must remain with the Office of Inquisitors."

It seemed the best option. She appeased the Church by giving up Aarik, and keeping Brother Mayhew would show Quintarch Lucran that she hadn't caved to Azariah.

"You can have Aarik," Damika said, rapping her knuckles on the desk. "The druin stays."

A moment passed in silence. Then Azariah boomed, "Lorelei Aurelius."

She had no idea he knew her name. "Yes, Your Holiness."

"Daughter of Cain, one of our city's finest inquisitors."

"Correct, Your Holiness."

"Be more like him." Then he turned his painted gaze back on Damika. "Bring Aarik Bloodhaven to me at the gates. Now."

TWENTY-ONE: ORDREN

Ordren rushed along the road on the north foot of Crag Hill to the drag-onworks, where the night watchman let him in. Holding his nose against the stink, he rumbled down the stairs to the cellar, entered the hated catacombs, and hurried toward Alra's Acre. Eventually he came to a crypt lit by a lone wisplight in the domed ceiling. Gaul stood on the far side of the room, near the door to the Hissing Man's sepulcher.

"Don't you have a bloody *home* to go to?" he asked the tall guard.

Gaul rubbed his bulbous nose and sniffed.

"I need to speak to him."

Gaul shook his head. Made the hand sign for *gone*.

"This is important, you bloody oak. When will he be back?"

Gaul shrugged.

Ordren walked toward the door. "I'll wait for him inside."

Gaul stopped him with a raised hand.

"You're joking, right? I'm not going to *steal* anything."

Gaul shook his head.

Ordren backed away and sat down on the stone floor with his back to the wall. "Where do you go, anyway, when you're not trapped down here? Kiln? Fiddle-head? A bloody apartment in the temple?"

Gaul snorted and spat on the floor.

"Or maybe the grove where your tree of a mother and father live . . . ? Sur-prised you don't have roots."

The operation had gone more or less according to plan. The Hissing Man had told him Tomas would find Lorelei and Creed at The Bent Tulip and give them a tip that Aarik would be meeting with the Hissing Man in the abandoned mine. Ordren had made sure to be there, too.

The Hissing Man had told him to make sure Aarik was caught and Llorn and Brother Mayhew escaped, but plans never went perfectly. Fortunately, Illustra Azariah managed to take Aarik to the temple, and Praefectus Damika had given Ordren the interrogation of Brother Mayhew, which made dealing with the druin simpler, but Ordren needed to find out what to do with him.

When sitting too long hurt his piles, Ordren stood. But then his trick knee started to ache, so he sat again. When his arse started to ache more than his knee, he stood and headed toward the door again. "I'm waiting inside."

Gaul put his hand on Ordren's throat and shoved him backward against the wall. Ordren's head crashed so hard his ears rang. He felt a piercing pain on the left side of his chest and looked down. Gaul was pressing the tip of a slim stiletto into his ribs.

"All right, all right!" Ordren choked. "I'll wait over there!"

But the pressure on his neck tightened. Gaul's face was red and his lips were peeled back from his filthy clenched teeth. *Mighty Alra, please don't let my final view of the world be the drool on this goon's lips.*

"That's enough, Gaul," the Hissing Man rasped from an archway. "The inquisitor and I have much to discuss."

Gaul's breath sprayed from his nostrils, but he let Ordren go and backed away. The Hissing Man headed inside his sepulcher. Ordren stumbled away from Gaul, tugged his shirt down, and scurried after him. The Hissing Man was already sitting behind his desk when Ordren entered.

"Do you consider it wise to test a man who kills for a living?"

Ordren closed the door, sat across from him, and stretched his neck. "You think it's wise to a have a rabid dog standing outside your door?"

"I would choose Gaul over a hundred other men. Now, who did the Praefectus assign to interrogate Brother Mayhew?"

"Me."

The Hissing Man nodded. "Good, but it shouldn't have been necessary. Why didn't you let him go?"

"I couldn't! Vashtok flattened him. He was almost unconscious. He couldn't have escaped if I'd untied him and given him a map to the exit. And by the time we'd caught Aarik and met up with the others, it was too late."

The Hissing Man worked his jaw but said nothing.

"Perhaps he finds a bit of poison in his food," Ordren continued. He'd done it before and would again for the right coin.

The Hissing Man considered. "Brother Mayhew is valuable to Llorn."

"Who cares?"

"I do. You receive postings on the night watch now and again, correct?"

"Yes, but I'm not supposed to open his bloody cell door and walk away, am I?"

"No, that wouldn't do. Brother Mayhew is a resourceful man, from what I hear. Talk to him. Give him whatever he needs to get out."

"How about a bit of powder to help things along?"

"No. Brother Mayhew will have been searched. If he got caught with umbris now, it could lead to the Church."

"Very well."

"Don't sound so enthused, Inquisitor."

"It's just more than I bargained for."

"What of it? We do this in Her name, do we not?" He held two fingers up and made a circle. "May her memory abide."

For a moment, Ordren was too surprised to do anything but nod. The Hissing Man had just made the same sign and spoken the same words as Illustra Azariah in the Crag. They'd come as no surprise from the leader of the Church in Ancris, but

Ordren had never seen or heard the Hissing Man do it. It made him wonder whether the Hissing Man had spoken to Azariah before he returned to the crypts.

"Is there anything else?" the Hissing man hissed.

Ordren shook his head and stood. As he passed through the door, Gaul casually held out a coin purse—Ordren's payment—as if he'd already forgotten he'd nearly choked the life out of Ordren.

Ordren snatched the purse and headed down the tunnel. *This ain't bloody worth it.*

TWENTY-TWO: LORELEI

The day after Azariah took Aarik from the Crag, Lorelei sent word to Ash that she wished to speak with him. His reply arrived that evening. After the cancellation of the expedition to Tortoise Peak, the teams of alchemysts were working day and night to finish the renovations to Alra's shrine, but some of the quartzite blocks were more brittle than others and needed a special mixture of the curing agent. Ash said he'd be at the palace all morning getting it ready and could meet with her then.

When she arrived at Highreach the following morning, Skylar was there to receive her, wearing a stunning silk dress with gold wildflowers embroidered on the bodice. Her hair and jewelry were similarly impressive

"Well, *someone* looks gorgeous," Lorelei said as she exited the coach.

Skylar shrugged, "I've got a meeting with the planning committee for the arch ceremony. I wanted to look nice"—she leaned close and spoke in a low voice—"*especially* since Mother's going to be there."

"I thought the arch was *your* project."

"It is." They headed through the entrance to the grand hall beyond. Their footsteps echoing, Skylar said, "We had the row to end all rows after she cancelled the expedition to Tortoise Peak, but after we'd both settled down, she extended an olive branch. She offered to share responsibilities in her provincial work so long as I allowed her to offer guidance on mine here in the city."

"And you accepted?"

"She was trying to mend fences, Lorelei."

"She was trying to insert herself into your affairs."

Skylar shrugged. "My mother is my mother. I might have declined a year ago, but with Father returning to the city soon, I thought it best we show a united front." Halfway down the hall, they took a set of curving stairs toward the second floor. "Ash mentioned your coming, and I'm curious to hear—"

"Skylar?" Below them, Tyrinia strode across the travertine floor of the main hall. Her dress, every bit as extravagant as Skylar's, was silver silk with gold accents and an ornate headdress with golden tassels. "We should discuss the arch before the architects arrive."

Skylar halted on the steps, looking like she was already beginning to regret accepting her mother's olive branch. "Very well, Mother."

"And Lorelei, Ash is not to be disturbed."

"She's on inquisitor business." Skylar squeezed Lorelei's hand. "An active case."

Tyrinia stared up at Lorelei. "Is that so?"

"Yes, Domina. The business at the mine."

Tyrinia frowned. "I thought that was given to Ordren."

Tyrinia's knowledge about the day-to-day operations of the inquisitor's office always amazed Lorelei. As Domina, she was supposed to be focused on provincial affairs, yet her insights into the Department of Inquisitors had only grown in recent months.

"Ordren is questioning the druin," Lorelei said. "Creed and I are looking for Tomas."

"And Ash has some special insight as to where he might be?"

"He might, yes." It wasn't the truth, precisely, but it wasn't a complete lie, either.

Tyrinia sniffed. "Well, see that it doesn't take long."

"Of course, Domina."

Skylar shared a wan smile with Lorelei and followed the Domina back down the hallway. Lorelei continued up the stairs and down a carpeted hallway to the alchemystry, a massive laboratory with a brilliant view of the mountains to the east. She found Ash standing at a worktable, placing several large bottles of thick, clear liquid into a wooden crate. He wore a surprisingly clean woolen shirt and canvas overalls.

Lorelei smiled at him. "Do you wash your clothes every night?"

"Should I traipse around looking like a clay golem, Lorelei Aurelius?" He winked and went back to his work. "Now what might I do for my favorite inquisitor?"

"I know you're busy—"

"Oh, it's fine." He packed one final bottle, then leaned against the table and crossed his arms over his chest. "Master Renato can stew for a bit."

"You've heard about Aarik's capture?" Lorelei asked.

"Yes!" Ash's eyes widened. "Well done, you!"

"Did you *also* hear that the Church took him away?"

Ash's expression collapsed into a cringe. "I wasn't going to mention it unless you did."

Lorelei shrugged. "Not much I can do about it, but when we caught up to them in the mine, the druin, Brother Mayhew, was testing a white powder for aura. It was powerful, Ash. Very powerful. I'm wondering what it could have been."

"You say the powder was white?"

"Yes, but the solution turned gray when he stirred it. Maybe even a bit brown."

Ash nodded. "That could have been from the reagents. You felt the reaction?"

"In my gut, in my limbs. Like a sliver of Lux itself had suddenly appeared in the chamber."

"And have you ever felt the like?"

She waggled her head noncommittally. "Remember the experiment you showed me when you were an apprentice?"

"Using the scales we stole from Bothymus?"

"Yes." Lorelei and Skylar had collected the scales. Ash had ground them, created a solution from the resulting powder, and activated it to burn off the aura as Brother Mayhew had done. "It was like that, but much more powerful."

"All right, but power is a relative term. You could get the same effect if you got enough powdered dragonscale and accelerated the release of its aura."

"The vial was small, though. We're talking about a tiny amount."

Ash shrugged. "The most powerful powder we know of is made from ground lucertae. Do you think it could have been that?"

Lucertae were scales that grew between a dragon's eye ridges. Dragons produced one each season, roughly speaking. For those who knew how to use them, they granted a certain power, different for every breed. The lucertae of bronze dragons granted the ability to wield fire, those from brasses granted the ability to summon lightning from the sky.

"It might've been," Lorelei admitted, "but you know as well as I do how carefully lucertae are inventoried. If any had gone missing, the dragonworks would've reported it." Lucertae were, pound for pound, the most valuable part of a dragon by far. They were light, and they could be spent, if one were careful, anywhere in the empire and beyond. With a single bag of them, Lorelei could live a life of luxury for as long as she wished.

"I'll think on it, but I don't know offhand what else it could've been." Ash picked up the crate, and he and Lorelei left the alchemystry together. "What I don't get is why the bloody *Chosen* would be doing this." The bottles in the crate clinked as they descended the stairs. "What does the Hissing Man hope to gain by dealing with the Red Knives?"

"A very good question," Lorelei said, "maybe the only *real* question, and I wish I had a good answer."

Ash lowered his voice. "Do you think they're planning a second Holy Rebellion?"

"Perhaps," Lorelei said, "but I have no direct evidence of it, which is why I need to figure out what they're up to."

"The druin gave you no clues?"

"He said it was a euphoric of some sort. He says the Chosen developed it themselves but obviously they couldn't sell it, hence the proposed arrangement with the Red Knives."

"Are the Chosen so short on funds they need the *Red Knives* to raise money for them?"

"It's possible. Or maybe it isn't the Chosen as a whole, but the Hissing Man acting on his own, or at the behest of someone tied to the organization—there are no shortage of them. This feels more sinister than just a way of making coin, though."

They exited the palace. Down the steps, a coach awaited. Ash loaded the crate into it.

"Get me some of the powder," he said, "and I'll check it out."

Lorelei nodded, wishing she could snap her fingers and have the small leather bag appear in her hand.

The two of them climbed into the coach. The driver clucked, horse hooves clopped, and the coach trundled beyond the palace walls. As they made their way down the paved road toward Ancris, Ash launched into a tale about his attempts to lure the pretty alchemyst from Lyros into grabbing a bite in the city, but Lorelei listened with only half an ear. She was too worried about Aarik, Brother Mayhew, and the Hissing Man. Soon enough, the coach was trundling to a stop before the Crag's stout gates.

Lorelei leaned over and kissed Ash's cheek. "Good luck with your pretty butterfly."

"Fashion me a bigger net, won't you?"

"Immediately"—she stepped down and headed toward the gates—"with thread of gold and ribbons on the end."

Ash smiled through the window as the coach pulled away. "Perfect."

Within the old fortress, Lorelei headed to the Pit, where several dozen inquisitors were conversing loudly across the open space. Nanda emerged from the mayhem and flagged her down. "Creed's looking for you. Said to meet him at the ford as soon as possible. I believe the word *posthaste* was used." Lorelei had halfway turned around, when Nanda added, "Did you hear the news from the temple?"

"What news?"

"Aarik's been tried for heresy and found guilty."

"Already?"

"The Church's trials aren't like ours, Lorelei. They're burning him at the Anvil today."

"Stone and bloody scree, when?"

Nanda shrugged. "Afternoon sometime."

Lorelei took a deep breath. "I bloody knew this was going to happen."

"Sorry, Lorelei. It's a rough turn."

Lorelei rushed down to the stables and was given a roan mare. It was a market day, and the streets were packed. Traffic was barely moving. It made her skin crawl just to be in it. As the homes began to thin, she saw clear road ahead. She concentrated on it, breathed deeply, and the feeling like she was about to be grabbed and pulled from her horse began to subside.

As Tomas had bade them, she and Creed had gone to Olga's the day before to meet him, but he hadn't shown. They went to chandlery next, only to find it empty. Everyone they spoke to said they hadn't seen him since the day before. Lorelei and Creed went to the room they knew he rented, then the brothel he liked to frequent, but he hadn't been in either of them. Creed vowed to return to Slade in the morning and look for him there. So why was he at the ford?

A mile beyond the city's outskirts, she came to the bridge she and the others had crossed to bring Aarik and Brother Mayhew to the Crag. She stopped short of it and guided her mare right along the riverbank. Beyond a gentle curve, the river widened, and she approached the ford, a scattering of stones poking up from the water, rippling the current.

A flatbed wagon with a bored-looking constable smoking a pipe in the driver's

box was parked near a stand of cattails. The portly fellow wore a drab gray uniform and rounded hat. He nodded to Lorelei, then went back to what appeared to
be deep contemplation of the Wend's gentle flow. Lorelei passed by the wagon and
spotted Creed forty yards from the riverbank, staring down at the wild grass,
likely checking for tracks. He wore a uniform similar to Lorelei's, but his coat was
laid over the saddle of his horse, a chocolate gelding with flaxen mane and tail.

Lorelei put two fingers in her mouth and whistled; Creed straightened and
waved. As she was guiding her mare toward Creed's gelding, she noticed the body
lying in the cattails.

"Oh no . . ."

She was still too far away to see much except Tomas's wiry blond hair. She
dismounted and Creed met her near the body.

"A huntsman spotted him on his way to the pines," Creed said. "He went back
to notify the constables."

Lorelei crouched beside the body, and pointed to the cattails matted down in
a trail from the water. "Who moved him?"

"The huntsman said he dragged him from the water."

Tomas had had a naturally pale complexion. In death he was white as a but-
toncap except for the skin around his eyes. His throat was neatly cut from ear to
ear. The sign of the Red Knives was carved into his forehead.

"A message for traitors," Creed said.

"Or the killer wanted us to think it was the Red Knives."

"Yes, but we have the whole business with Llorn being sent to kill him, remember?"

"We have a *claim* that he was sent to kill him."

Creed snarled. "Stop being pedantic."

"Stop making assumptions."

"Assumptions are a starting place."

She gestured toward where she'd seen him walking. "Any tracks?"

He swept his finger in a line that led back toward the bridge. "Only the
huntsman's."

Lorelei noticed a long abrasion along Tomas's neck. Turning him over, she saw
it continued to his upper back. She unbuttoned his damp shirt and found a similar
mark along his ribcage, more along his hips. Each was roughly the length of her
forearm.

"I don't know about you," Creed said, crouching beside her, "but I'll bet
they're from the talons of the cobalt we heard at the mine."

"Okay," she said with a huff, "evidence is *leaning* toward Llorn having killed him."

Creed chuckled and nudged her with his shoulder. "*Leaning?*"

Lorelei pried Tomas's eyelids open. His eyes were yellow, and the veins so dark
they were almost purple. "Did you notice how red his eyes were at the Tulip?"

"Yes." Creed touched one finger to the side of his nose and sniffed. "I assumed
he'd had a bit before he got there."

"I did, too, but his pupils weren't dilated, and his heart rate, while elevated, wasn't anywhere close to what it would be if he'd sniffed a bunch of rapture."

"So what was it, then?"

Lorelei shrugged and waved the constable over. "Could be he was sick, but he didn't sound stuffed up either. Awfully strange." As the constable shuffled through the grass and approached them, she turned and asked him, "Who's he going to be examined by?"

"Trumble's on duty, I think," the man said, bending to tap his pipe on his boot heel.

Lorelei reached into her purse, pulled out a gold coin, and flipped it to him. "Can you make sure it's Galla instead?"

The constable dropped the coin into his purse. "So long as your partner uses those muscles of his to help me get him into the bed."

Creed made a face—he hated getting dirty nearly as much as Ash—but he nodded and helped get Tomas's corpse onto the wagon.

As it rumbled away, Lorelei told Creed, "There's more bad news, I'm afraid."

"What now?"

"The Church convicted Aarik. They're burning him at the Anvil today."

Creed opened his mouth to say something, but settled for slumping his shoulders instead.

"We've got to do something, Creed."

"Okay. What?"

"Question Brother Mayhew."

Creed frowned. "But Damika said . . ." His eyes narrowed. "You have a plan, don't you?"

"I do."

He headed toward his horse. "Tell me on the way back."

They mounted and rode side-by-side back toward the city, and she began to sweat—not from crowds or traffic, but from the conversation she was about to have with the praefectus. It still burned Lorelei that Damika had given the responsibility of questioning Brother Mayhew to Ordren, of all people. He'd learned practically nothing so far. Nearly every piece of information the druin coughed up was something they already knew, and the new information felt premeditated, like Brother Mayhew had been coached before coming to Ancris. And despite the Church's promises, the Department of Inquisitors received nothing from their interrogation of Aarik.

All of which played in Lorelei's favor. Damika was a strong leader, and strong willed, but she was going to give Lorelei some time with Brother Mayhew.

TWENTY-THREE: RYLAN

Rylan was sitting at his kitchen table, sipping tea and reading a book on the caravan trade that built the Sapphire Coast, when a knock came at his front door. The curtains above the sink let in a bare amount of light; it was early, reckoning having come and gone a short while ago.

The knock came again, louder.

Rylan closed the book and stood, curious who would have come so early. A third knock came as he trudged toward the door. "I'm coming, already!" He opened the door to find Hollis looking worried.

"What's wrong?" Rylan asked.

The morning sunlight glinted off Hollis's earrings. His long olive coat was dotted with rain. "Can I come in?"

Rylan stepped aside. "Of course."

Hollis entered, and Rylan closed the door behind him. "I've just come from visiting my sister in Andalingr. On the way back to the vyrd, Blythe waylaid me."

"*Waylaid* you?"

"Yes. She gave me this." He handed Rylan a folded piece of paper. "Burn it after you memorize it."

Rylan unfolded it. It was a map, roughly the size of his palm, showing several landmarks far east of Glaeyand—the Diamondflow, the Deepwood Fens, a set of gently rolling hills known as the Maundering Downs. Between them was an X near what appeared to be an excessively large citadel tree.

"What is it?"

"The Rookery," he said, rubbing his hands together, though it was not cold in Rylan's burrow. "She wants you to visit her."

Hollis wasn't a Knife, but that would hardly matter to the inquisitors if word got out he'd so much as *touched* a piece of paper with the location of the Rookery on it. He'd be brought in for questioning immediately. He might even be shipped to one of the capitals and handed over to the Church so they could put him to the question.

"And why, pray tell, does she want me to visit her?" Rylan asked.

"She said it has to do with Bellicor. He's in a state."

Bellicor was Aarik's mount, a particularly nasty onyx dragon. Rylan had a fondness for all dragons, even those with terrible tempers—perhaps especially those, because an intemperate dragon was almost never the dragon's fault, but the owner's. Rylan had tended to Bellicor years ago when he'd become sick from an infection.

The onyx had been lashing out at everyone who came near, including Aarik, which had made it all the more satisfying when Rylan had helped cure the infection.

"Aarik's gone to Ancris," Hollis continued. "Bellicor's grown restless, angry. Blythe wants help calming him before he attacks the other dragons." Hollis paused. "She wanted you to know it's important. She said to come straight away if you believe in Aarik's vision."

The note of desperation in Hollis's voice was worrying but hardly surprising. He was a fence for stolen goods; he arranged for the occasional theft; he worked from the shadows, and he was good at it. That he'd managed to maintain a low profile for so long was an achievement in and of itself, but the Knives were like a flaming brand, bringing heat on everyone they touched.

"So?" Hollis asked.

Rylan had already made plans to visit Ancris to look into Master Renato for Aarik, but he had to set those aside. He needed to know why Aarik had gone to Ancris, and that meant going to the Rookery and checking on Bellicor. "I'll go, Hollis."

Looking relieved, Hollis nodded, then pointed at the paper in Rylan's hand. "Burn that."

Hollis opened the door to leave but stopped. Bashira was standing outside, one hand raised about to knock. The axe-nosed chamberlain of Valdavyn and one of Marstan's closest confidants put her hand down.

"Bashira," Rylan said, "please, come in. Hollis was just leaving."

Rylan used Hollis's abrupt exit to stuff the paper into his shirt. Bashira stared at Hollis as he left, then stepped across the threshold.

"Your father wishes to see you," she said as Rylan closed the door.

"What about?"

"The iron dragon you've been tending to, Rugio, is on death's doorstep. He wants you to go to Caldoras to give Rugio what succor you can and to pass along our regrets to Soraya."

"I see," Rylan said, buying time.

Bashira's stared at him for a moment. "He'd like you to go straight away. We have a silver waiting to fly you there."

"Yes, I understand." A trip to Caldoras would delay him a day at least, maybe more. He pulled on his boots and his coat, then grabbed his foraging sack. "Tell my father I'll come as soon as I can."

"You aren't going now?"

"Lady Alevada might want Rugio put down." He ushered Bashira outside, followed her, and locked the door. "I'll need a good supply of black henbane for that."

Bashira opened her mouth and closed it again. "Don't we have some at the eyrie?"

"Not enough, and we don't want the job half done." He left Bashira standing there and headed downtree. "I'll be there as soon as I can."

His father would be wroth with him, but there was nothing for it. Rylan had to learn more about Aarik's sudden trip to Ancris first.

Two hours later, Rylan jogged into Vedron's nesting ground huffing and puffing. He caught a flash in his mind of her lounging on a bridgebough, looked up, and spotted her. She was deliberating whether to chase the deer she'd seen passing through the marsh. When she sensed Rylan, however, all thoughts of chasing deer were forgotten. She thumped her tail, sending bits of bark flying, then dropped from the bridgebough, snapped her wings wide, and soared through the trees. But when Rylan shared with her that they needed to visit Bellicor, she pulled up and clawed hold on the trunk of a citadel.

"Come on, now, it's not his fault," Rylan said through their bond. "If anyone's to blame, it's Aarik. He trained Bellicor to be mean." And though Rylan disliked it, Aarik's reasons for doing so were understandable. Bellicor had been hunted from the moment he'd emerged from his egg.

Vedron dropped from the tree and weaved between the massive citadels toward him. The green marbling of her wings shimmered brilliantly in the bright sunlight. She landed some twenty yards away, huffed, and gouged the earth with her wing talons.

Rylan merely waited. When they had stared at each other for several breaths, Vedron beat her wings, folded them at her sides, and lay on the ground.

Rylan retrieved her tack from the hollow in the oak, saddled her, and secured her bridle. Then she lowered her chest so Rylan could climb on, and they soared up into the sky. Despite the tenseness leading up to their flight, Vedron's relief and joy at being reunited began to melt Rylan's worries away. At one point, he laughed from the sheer joy of flying above the Great Forest on the back of a dragon.

The longer they flew, though, the more Vedron's bright mood faded, and a vague sense of dread began to dominate her thoughts. As often happened, Rylan's mood soured, too, as his thoughts drifted to a vision of Blythe, wide-eyed as she drove a knife into his gut. Vedron suddenly dipped, and the vision faded.

At a bend in the Diamondflow, he adjusted their heading left, toward the Maundering Downs. When he spotted the rolling hills in the distance, he veered right and headed toward the Deepwood Fens and guided Vedron toward a citadel that stuck out from the rest of the forest. Vedron fought him—trying to fly to their left.

"There's nothing there but a stinking fen." When she continued to fight him, Rylan pictured her litter-mate, Velox, a viridian dragon that would likely be at the Rookery. "Don't you want to fly with him awhile?"

Vedron finally swerved toward the high citadel. A man in buckskin clothing was standing on a lookout platform of an adjacent tree. He blew a sequence of notes on a horn, giving Rylan permission to land. Vedron dropped below the canopy and wove through the trees toward a cluster of nests close to the ground. Two were occupied by a pair of narrow-bodied, flame-eyed auburns, who craned their necks and watched Vedron land. Another nest held Kreòs, an amber vixen with canary-yellow scales and mottled brown eyes, but she barely blinked at them and went back to sleep.

When Vedron had settled in the nest, Rylan dismounted, walked over the bridge-bough, and descended along a set of spiraling stairs. A few rough-hewn decks and small burrows stood along the citadel's trunk. The Rookery wasn't meant to be permanent. The Red Knives moved it every few years when it was spotted by the empire's scouts.

The acrid, floral smell of drugs being made permeated the air. The source, a long, wooden workhouse camouflaged with dead branches and citadel bark, lay along the forest floor below. Euphorics, hallucinogens, stimulants, depressants, even palliative drugs were the lifeblood of the Red Knives. Everything from mushrooms to rare flowers to dragon carcasses were rendered to manufacture them.

Raef sat on a stool in front of the workhouse with Ayasha, the Rookery's Master of Dragons, standing behind him, braiding his red hair in tight rows. A group of men and women in homespun clothes leaned against the workhouse wall next to them.

When Raef spotted Rylan he pointed his stump up at him and said, "The fuck you doing here?"

"I asked him to come," called a voice from below. Rylan leaned over the railing and saw Blythe standing on the same set of stairs, one circuit down.

"What the hell for?" Raef called.

"To help Bellicor. Or is the wellbeing of your King's mount not good enough reason for you?"

Raef gazed at Bellicor as if he didn't much care what happened to Aarik's mount one way or the other, then he stood, spat on the ground, and strode into the workhouse.

TWENTY-FOUR: LORELEI

Lorelei, with Creed at her side, headed down a hallway in the Crag with stained glass windows on one side, statues of former praefecta on the other. Creed had long legs and often outstripped Lorelei without even thinking about it. Not that day. They'd just left Damika's office, and Lorelei was eager to get things started.

When they reached Marion's small office, they found the diminutive gaoler sitting behind his desk, squinting at a thick tome. He placed a finger on the page and stared up at Lorelei with a wide grin. "Come to ask me to dine in the city?"

"Another day, perhaps." Lorelei jutted her chin to the locked iron door on the far side of the room. "We're here for Brother Mayhew."

"Under whose authority?"

"The Praefectus's."

She handed him the writ Damika had penned a few minutes earlier. Marion read it, shrugged, grabbed a set of keys hanging from a hook, and tossed them at Lorelei. She snatched them from the air and walked over to the iron door.

Creed lingered beside Marion's desk, craned his neck, and peered down at the book. "Poetry, Marion?"

"What's wrong with a bit of poetry?"

"Nothing," Creed said, "just didn't think it was a particular interest of yours."

Marion sighed. "I'm a cultured man, Creed."

Lorelei pulled open the door to the cell block. "Trying to woo Maudrey again?"

Marion's smiled a gap-toothed smile. "And if I am?"

Lorelei and Creed both chuckled as they headed down the hall. When they reached Brother Mayhew's cell, the druin was sitting on the edge of a canvas cot, staring fixedly at the far wall where a dim light filtered into the cell through a dirty glass window. Lorelei opened the door and handed the keys to Creed.

When she entered the cell, she saw the scrapes and bruises across Brother Mayhew's cheeks, nose, and lips. There was a particularly nasty cut over the blue, runic tattoos that curled around his left eye socket. Blood crusted in his eyebrow, down his cheek, and into his beard. The air smelled sour; hardly surprising after days without a bath.

Lorelei took the three-legged stool from the corner, placed it near the cot, and sat down facing Brother Mayhew. "I've been thinking about you quite a bit these past few days."

Brother Mayhew glanced quickly at Creed leaning against the wall across from the open cell door then back at Lorelei. "Why would a druin of the Holt care what an inquisitor from Ancris thinks of him?"

"Oh, I don't know. Perhaps because he's about to face the flames before the Anvil?"

Brother Mayhew stared at her but said nothing.

"When you were in the mines," Lorelei continued, "Llorn said a council of Knives had been called. I'd like to know where it is."

He glanced at the far wall again, then back at Lorelei. "If Aarik called for a council, I know nothing about it."

"You expect me to believe he didn't tell *you*, the one druin in the Holt he trusts enough to bring to Ancris, about a meeting of his captains?" She wasn't certain the meeting was with his captains, but it made sense, and Brother Mayhew didn't deny it.

"You're mad if you think Aarik Bloodhaven confides in me."

"Let's talk about the white powder, then. You told Ordren it was some new sort of drug, a euphoric."

He shrugged his burly shoulders. "It was."

"Yet you never put it on your tongue or snorted it."

"We didn't get that far, did we?"

"That was your next step, yes?"

Brother Mayhew stared at her in silence.

"It's interesting, don't you think," she continued, "that Llorn escaped with the powder but you and Aarik were caught?"

Brother Mayhew laughed a sudden, pathetic chuckle. "Your brother inquisitor already tried that gambit. It was weak then and it's weak now."

"You don't think Llorn is capable of betraying the Knives?"

"He's the last person who would betray us."

"Before he was taken away, Aarik said he wanted an audience with Marstan Lyndenfell. Any idea why?"

Brother Mayhew only glared at her. Lorelei reckoned he wouldn't tell her anything without more incentive. She looked at Creed, but he just shrugged.

"Right." She slapped her hands on her knees and stood. "Come with me, Brother Mayhew." She stepped into the hall and waited.

Brother Mayhew didn't budge, but he seemed to be breathing more heavily.

Creed stepped away from the wall. "The stubborn lamb's fortune is the jaws of a wolf." When Brother Mayhew still didn't move, Creed said, "We're going to stop asking nicely."

Finally, the druin stood but remained near the cot. "Where are you taking me?"

Lorelei headed back toward Marion's office, calling over her shoulder, "You'll see soon enough. A moment later, Creed and Brother Mayhew followed her.

As they exited the dungeon, Marion looked up from his book of poetry and smiled. "Wait," he said, catching the keys from Creed, "are you going where I think you're going? To watch the bloody burning?"

Brother Mayhew stared fixedly ahead.

"Going to see your friend off, you Deepwood bastard?" Marion called as they left his office. "Blow him a kiss for me, won't you?"

Halfway down of the hallway, they took a set of ancient, uneven stairs up, and Lorelei stared through the loopholes down at the road leading to the Crag's main gate. To one side of it was the Anvil, a massive charred boulder. She glanced back and caught Brother Mayhew staring through the same loopholes. When he realized she was watching, he looked away.

At the top of the stairs, they climbed a ladder to reach the tower's flat, wooden roof, and Creed kicked the trapdoor closed. Lux was lowering in the west. All of Ancris was on display, a sprawling quilt of temples, domes, and massive stone buildings. Below the tower, a team of horses pulled a wagon with an open bed along the curving road that skirted the hill. Aarik, wrapped in chains, was kneeling in the bed of the wagon. In the driver's box were two shepherds in brightsteel armor and starbursts on their tunics. The witnesses lining the roadside threw rotten vegetables at the self-proclaimed King of the Wood as he passed.

A bell tolled, and Aarik raised his head and stared toward the temple on Mount Evalarus. Lorelei could see it from her vantage as well, an elegant structure of white stone, flying buttresses, and stained glass windows.

The wagon stopped near the Anvil. One of the shepherds roughly unchained Aarik from the wagon, dragged him off the bed, and led him to the Anvil. He latched Aarik's manacles to an iron hook spiked into the stone's broad, blackened face. The other shepherd unstrapped a curling dragon horn from around his back, lifted it to his lips, and blew a warbling note. The bellow of a bronze dragon, deep and rumbling, came from the Church's eyrie, just beyond the temple.

The shepherd who chained Aarik to the Anvil stepped away from him and raised his right hand. Lorelei caught a glint of gold crop in his palm, the mate to the fetter that controlled the bronze dragon. The shepherd squeezed the crop, and the bronze rose from the temple's eyrie. Sinuous and graceful, it circled higher, its wings beating a slow, rhythmic *whump-whump*.

"Are you aware," Lorelei said to Brother Mayhew as the dragon approached the Anvil, "that Illustra Azariah came personally to the Crag to demand you and Aarik be handed over to the Church?"

Brother Mayhew's lips were pressed tight, his eyes fixed on the approaching dragon.

"I've no idea how he learned of your capture so quickly," Lorelei went on, "but this much is clear—had we allowed it, you would have been be put to the question right beside Aarik, and you would likely be chained beside him right now."

Brother Mayhew swallowed hard as the bronze landed ten yards from Aarik and lumbered toward him. It shook its head, craned its neck, and screeched, showing a glint of the bridle in its mouth. The dragon stepped again toward Aarik, but the shepherd seemed to be holding it back. The other shepherd, meanwhile, unfurled a scroll and began to read, though his words were lost to the dragon's grumbling.

"I fought for you to stay here in the Crag with us," Lorelei continued.

Brother Mayhew glanced at her and looked away. "If so, you did it for your own purposes."

"Which I readily admit, but it should go without saying that you benefited as well."

"I have been beaten and bloodied for no reason."

"Ordren is a thorough interrogator, but believe me, the Church is far worse."

"Listen to her," Creed added somberly. "I've stood in their questioning chamber. The walls are covered with implements of torture. Spiked collars, thumb screws, pears of anguish, chairs made of nails, vats of burning oil, racks of infernal design. You wouldn't like it."

Brother Mayhew stared at him, then swung his gaze back to the scene below.

Having completed the reading of Aarik's judgment, the shepherd rolled up the scroll and stepped back. The other shepherd lowered the crop, and the bronze reared onto its hind legs and beat its wings, and dropped back down. Its chest expanded; it shot its head forward and released a roar of orange flames that consumed Aarik and spread over the soot-stained rock. Aarik screamed and writhed in his chains. His skin blistered and blackened, and at last, his charred corpse hung from the red-hot chains.

"We need information," Lorelei said.

Brother Mayhew turned and furrowed his brow at her. "I've none to give you."

"Why did Aarik wish to speak to Marstan Lyndenfell?"

Brother Mayhew shook his head. "I told you, I don't know."

"That's unfortunate," Lorelei said, "because I know things about the druins, Brother Mayhew."

"You know nothing about us."

"The Crag, the palace, and our imperial libraries have many ancient texts. Though most people don't bother with them these days, I read, Brother Mayhew. A lot. For instance, some of those ancient texts taught me that you, along with your master, choose the tattoos you get when you entered the order formally. I know they're written in the old tongue, and I know yours honors the Holt and the past, and speaks of preserving both so your people will live to see a brighter day."

Brother Mayhew's brows pinched.

Lorelei continued, "You believe your wisp will live beyond your first life, that it will one day become part of the forest itself, and that, when it does, your knowledge will be added to that of your forebears. In doing so, you will become a part of that which you love most, and you will help to cradle your people until the end of days. Is it not so?"

Brother Mayhew shook his head slowly and turned away.

"I also know," Lorelei said, "what you fear most."

"You lie, highlander," Mayhew said without looking at her.

Lorelei laughed. "You believe that were you to burn here in the mountains, your wisp would still quicken and return to the Holt. But silver dragons are a special breed. Did you know they can consume souls, and often did during the Talon Wars? Were that to happen, your soul would become a part of its. It won't become part of the forest. It won't rise to the fields of Déu. It won't even descend to the hells of Kharos." She paused to see if he would look at her, but he did not. "Tell me what I want to know, Brother Mayhew, or I'll tell Azariah myself to forego the flames and feed your soul to a silver."

Brother Mayhew's nostril's flared. The bronze roared again as the shepherd led it away, and Mayhew flinched and glanced at it.

"Why did Aarik want to meet with Marstan Lyndenfell?"

"I wasn't lying about that. I don't know."

"Then where is the council of Knives being held? The Rookery?"

At last, he stared straight into her eyes.

"Is it in Andalingr? Skjalgard?" She waited. "Glaeyand?"

At this, Brother Mayhew turned away again.

"Tell me about it," Lorelei said, "the meeting in Glaeyand."

"I'm not *certain* it's in Glaeyand."

"But you suspect it."

"I overheard Llorn talking with Aarik." Brother Mayhew shrugged. "They hadn't made a final decision."

Beyond the battlements came the drumbeat of a dragon's wings. The bronze, this time with a shepherd in the saddle, soared toward the temple on the slopes of Evalarus. Watching them go, Lorelei said, "I can't go to the praefectus with a guess, Brother Mayhew. Tell me about the powder. It's not *really* a euphoric, right? You made that up."

"It's no lie. The Hissing Man wanted us to sell it through our network."

Creed snorted. "You expect us to believe the Chosen are so strapped they'd deal with the likes of you?"

"I don't care whether you believe me or not. It's what the Hissing Man wanted, what Llorn agreed to, and what Aarik got so worked up about. Finding out Llorn had gone behind has back was bad enough. Aarik turned practically rabid when Llorn admitted he'd been talking directly with the Hissing Man."

"Damika will laugh in my face if I bring that to her," Lorelei said, "so I'll give you one last chance, Brother Mayhew." She pointed to Aarik's charred remains. "When I brought him to his cell the other day, he asked to speak with Marstan Lyndenfell."

Brother Mayhew's brows pinched. "He did?"

"Yes. Tell me why."

"I wasn't Aarik's *confidant*. I'm just a druin who helps the Knives from time to time."

"If you're not going to give me what I need . . ."

Lorelei reached down and lifted the trapdoor, but stopped when Brother Mayhew gripped her wrist. "Just listen to me," he said with a note of desperation. "I'm not high up enough to *know,* but I've heard rumors. Aarik had a deal with someone high up in Glaeyand."

"What sort of deal?"

"Money for constables looking the other way, for not checking the wagons they use to ship goods to the mountains too closely, to let Knives off easy when they're standing before the magistrate's bench."

"Bribes, you mean."

Brother Maybe stared at her like she was daft. "Yes, *bribes.*"

"Do these bribes pad Marstan *Lyndenfell's* coffers?"

"I can't say for certain, but what do *you* think given Aarik spoke his fucking name? Now that's really all I've got, so either take it or feed me to your bloody silver."

Creed looked as shocked as Lorelei felt. If the imperator really was involved, things had just gotten a lot more complicated.

TWENTY-FIVE: RYLAN

Rylan continued with Blythe down the corkscrew stairs at the Rookery. A dragon trilled from the forest, and Rylan felt the warmth of recognition from Vedron in her nest. She launched and winged excitedly toward Velox soaring between the citadels. The two dragons were nearly identical, except their eyes: Vedron's were a deep emerald; Velox's citrine.

They met mid-air and immediately launched into a game of catch-tail. Velox gave chase first, gurgling happily, and Rylan couldn't help but smile. He and Blythe had spent months together in their youth, flying, learning to bond with their dragons. Vedron and Velox had played often then. It had been a joyous time, not only because he was with Blythe, but because, when they went on those flights, the real world and its troubles seemed so far away.

The memories were soured by a vision of Uncle Beckett chained to an iron frame, bathed in a bronze dragon's flames, screaming as he burned.

Blythe watched the dragons play with a lopsided smile. "Like two peas in a bloody great pod."

"That they are." As they swooped down, Vedron shrieked, and it reminded Rylan of their flight in. "On my way here, Vedron sensed something"—he pointed toward the fen—"over there. Any idea what it could be?"

Blythe hesitated, then shook her head. "None."

"You sure?"

"Of course I'm sure." She pointed at the pen in the clearing below them. "I'm just worried about Bellicor."

The Rookery's dragon pen was enclosed by a simple wooden fence. The massive onyx lay on the gouged earth at its center, the sun shining dully off his black scales. A chain ran from his collar to a tree stump. His tail twitched every now and again, but beyond that, he lay still and silent, breathing in huffs. Rylan whistled to test his attentiveness. Bellicor's blood-orange eyes rolled toward Rylan, then Blythe. A moment later, his third eyelids nictated, and he seemed to go back into a stupor.

Rylan glanced toward the workhouse door to make sure he wouldn't be overheard. "Blythe, why did Aarik go to Ancris?"

Blythe's eyes widened. "You know I can't tell you that."

"Is it to do with the amendment to the Covenant?"

"I didn't bring you here to talk about Aarik."

"I know you didn't, but Bellicor may have picked up on Aarik's mood before he left. He may be picking up on it now.

Bellicor craned his neck and stretched his jaws fearsomely wide, jingling his chain.

"A bond cannot stretch from here to Ancris," Blythe said.

"Not normally, no, but history tells us it's happened in the past. Wyan One-hand's bond with Casurax spanned the entire Holt. Aarik is Wyan's descendant, and I wouldn't be surprised to learn that Bellicor is Casurax's."

"Well, be that as it may, I can't talk about Aarik. You'll just have to do the best you can."

Rylan paused at the foot of the stairs and waited for Blythe to do the same. "Fine. Just tell me this. Was Aarik upset when he left?"

Blythe nodded. "That's safe to say."

"Did Llorn go with him?"

"Yes."

"Why didn't you go? I thought Ancris was *your* territory now."

"Bough and bloody fucking branch, Rylan, I *wanted* to go. I asked to go in Aarik's place, but he wouldn't let me, and Llorn was in a foul mood, going on about how I was making his headache worse. The point is, Aarik left, and his dragon isn't eating. Now can you help him or not?"

Just then, the dragon master Ayasha, holding a dead ferret, turned the far corner of the workhouse and approached them, forcing Rylan to abandon his questioning.

"Tell me about Bellicor's appetite," Rylan asked her.

"Since Aarik left," Ayasha said in her scratchy voice, "Bellicor's hardly been eating. We've brought elk carcasses, deer, even live goats. The only thing he'll have is the occasional ferret. He's not drinking enough either."

Ayasha offered him the dead ferret, but Rylan waved her off and headed to the gate of the pen. As he opened the gate, Bellicor suddenly reared onto his hind legs, spread his wings, and bellowed.

Rylan froze in place. "Has he done this before?"

Ayasha shook her head. She and Blythe stood stiffly watching the massive creature.

With measured movements, Rylan stepped inside the pen. He knew what Bellicor could do to him, but he'd come to the Rookery to help. He was also, he had to admit, intensely curious about what might have provoked such a strong response in a dragon hundreds of miles from his bondmate.

As he stepped toward Bellicor, he whistled two short notes. The dragon turned to face him, fanned his wings, and stared down at Rylan. Rylan took a deep breath and raised his right hand, palm toward Bellicor. His left hand, the one missing the pinky finger, he hid behind his back. Staring into Bellicor's eyes, he envisioned an empty glade and sang. He deepened his voice and pictured Aarik riding Bellicor and landing on a verdant clearing. Bellicor lowered his massive head until his snout was close enough for Rylan to touch and rattled the barbs along his neck.

"Not your thing, boy?" Rylan said. He sang another song, one of curiosity and sharing, asking Bellicor what he'd sensed, what he feared. Bellicor could easily kill

Rylan, Blythe, and Ayasha with hardly a thought, and yet on hearing Rylan's new song, he backed away and tucked his tail between his legs.

Rylan sang a more soothing melody and stepped toward the massive onyx. Rylan's own bond with Vedron was still strong, but he let it fade to give more space to Bellicor, but Bellicor lowered his head again. This time, he extended the frills behind his tympanum, exposing the brilliant gold skin between the ivory-tipped spines.

Bellicor's third eyelids swept over his eyes, and Rylan felt a brief wave of vertigo. He felt a lump forming in his throat, an echo of Bellicor's terror. Both were signs of Bellicor allowing the link between them to deepen, but it wasn't enough.

"Can you help me understand?" Rylan asked. "Can you show me?"

Bellicor gurgled, a low mewling sound that went on and on. Then his third eyelids swept again, and Rylan was transported.

He stood on a paved road in front of an old, imperial fortress. Beyond it, a mountain loomed with a walled white temple near the top. A city of stone sprawled in all directions. Beyond the city stood a range of mountains, tall, proud, and white-peaked. A shepherd clad in white and gold dragged Rylan toward a broad stone, its face blackened with soot. The shepherd clamped the clanking manacles binding his wrists to an iron hook.

Another shepherd blew a sonorous note on a dragon horn into the cool mountain air. A bronze dragon trilled its reply and winged above the walls of the temple. As the dragon flew down the mountain toward Rylan, the shepherd read a list of crimes from a scroll.

The bronze landed and crawled closer. Its tack jingled. Its spines rattled. The fetter on its bridle glowed. The shepherd finished reading and rolled the scroll up with sharp twists of his hands.

The bronze reared its head back, bared its yellow teeth. Its head shot forward, and bright flames roared from its gaping maw. His hair crackled. His skin blistered and bubbled, cracked and charred. He writhed in agony, screamed, and jerked at his chains.

Through the terrible pain, Rylan felt Vedron's sympathy, her lament that he was being forced to live through this. Her compassion drew him back to the Holt.

Rylan stood before Bellicor again, but the vision had left him confused. He stared at his hands, at his pinky stub, tied to another burning years ago.

The ground shook as Bellicor bounded to and fro in a rage. His chain swung violently as he jerked his neck back and forth, struggling to free himself from his collar. Blythe and Ayasha were gone, likely to fetch help from the workhouse,

Rylan hoped. He stepped back quickly to avoid being gouged by the razor-sharp frills at the end of Bellicor's thrashing tail.

"Bellicor!" Rylan shouted, raising his hands. "Bellicor, hear me!"

In all the time Rylan had been a dragon singer, he had never tried to supersede an existing bond—to do so would be a grave insult, both to the dragon and its bondmate—but Aarik was being burned alive near the old fortress. Though Rylan had woken from the dream, Bellicor had not. He was experiencing the burning through his bond with Aarik. Rylan had to draw him from it before he went mad. He had to link to Bellicor so tightly that the suffering creature could see the world through Rylan's eyes.

"Bellicor!" he shouted, stepping forward and braving a swipe from the onyx's tail or wings. Then he opened his heart to the ailing dragon.

Bellicor thrashed his head and neck, rattling the chain attached to his collar, unsettling the stout tree stump and the earth around it. He bellowed so loud Rylan felt it in his bones. Forgetting Aarik and Blythe, forgetting Vedron and Velox, forgetting all the other dragons, the scouts, and the workers in the longhouse, Rylan focused solely on Bellicor. "I'm so sorry, boy."

Bellicor stopped thrashing, settled on his stomach, and moaned like nothing Rylan had ever heard.

Bellicor's desperation was now Rylan's, but he was also himself and knew there was no hope. "I can't save him." Tears welled in his eyes and fell along his cheeks. "I wish I could, but I can't. It's not up to me."

Bellicor swiveled his head. Rylan turned to see Blythe and Ayasha sprinting toward the pen. Ayasha brandished a heavy crossbow, cocked and loaded. The bolt's steel head was coated in a powerful, purple sedative.

"Ayasha, don't shoo—"

The bolt soared through the air.

It might have sunk into the flesh of another dragon, but Bellicor had been trained for war since birth. He twisted and spread his wings. The bolt tore through the thin membrane of his left wing but clattered off his scales.

Bellicor reared, beat his wings mightily. The frills along his tail quavered. A black cloud spread from his mouth like ink in water until everything, including Rylan, Blythe, and Ayasha, was consumed by it. It smelled like mildew, but also sweet. Rylan felt disoriented. He blinked hard, trying to clear his mind. Bellicor's black cloud spread.

Suddenly, Rylan's bond with Vedron sharpened. Through her eyes, Rylan saw her break through the citadels around her glade. Through her eyes, he saw Ayasha stagger free of the cloud, but Blythe was still trapped in the dragon's breath, as was Rylan.

He retreated and slammed into the pen's crude fence. He climbed over it, and kept going. He heard Bellicor struggling against his chain, and at last, it snapped. Bellicor charged through the black cloud.

Rylan envisioned a clear sky, a cool breeze, the bright sun warm on his skin, anything to calm the angry onyx. Vedron shared a vision of Blythe staggering from the cloud. Bellicor hurtled after her, bellowing. Vedron swooped down and fell on Bellicor, screeching and slashing the onyx with her rear talons. Velox dove down behind her and clamped his teeth onto Bellicor's tail. Bellicor swung around, flinging Velox away, and clawed Vedron across her neck. Vedron howled and rolled across the gouged earth. Velox lunged at Bellicor, spraying a cloud of green acid at the onyx's face, but, but Bellicor beat his wings and launched himself up and out of it.

Rylan finally staggered out of the cloud. He wiped his eyes and saw Bellicor thud to the ground and rear up over Blythe. Blythe stared up at Bellicor, utterly defenseless.

Despite their link, Rylan knew he couldn't stop the dragon by force, so he envisioned Aarik and Blythe sitting by a fire, passing a bottle of firewater; Aarik laughed at a joke Blythe made about Llorn. Bellicor paused, rattled his frills. He lowered his head and roared at Blythe as if *she* were to blame for Aarik's misfortune. Then, with a keening that made Rylan's heart ache, he launched himself into the sky, beat his wings, and flew away.

TWENTY-SIX: RYLAN

T he morning after Bellicor's escape, Rylan sat on a stool in the Rookery's infirmary. The door was open, letting in warm light and a cool spring breeze. Lying unconscious on the dragon-leather cot beside him was Blythe. The infirmary had six other cots, all of them empty, plus a medicine chest and a broad wooden table where the sick or injured were tended to, often in crude and brutal fashion.

Blythe had inhaled a good amount of Bellicor's breath and still hadn't awoken. Thankfully she seemed stable enough, but the attack still haunted Rylan, as did the memories of the bronze dragon in Ancris spewing flames over Aarik's blistering body. Hoping to banish them, he took Blythe's hand, but it only reminded him of another burning many years earlier.

He'd been thirteen at the time. He and Uncle Beckett had been walking in the Holt, a half-day's hike from their home in Thicket. All around them, as far as the eye could see, the trunks of massive citadel trees dominated the landscape. Daylight was waning, the forest gloomy.

Uncle Beckett glanced up, beyond the canopy, where the sky was beginning to bruise. "Hood," he said, and pulled his own hood up over his head.

The light over the forest brightened. Lux was setting, but the citadels sensed it and were responding in kind, their needles contracting like pinching fingers, their stubby branches hugging the gnarled bark of their trunks. The forest's canopy was making itself small and unseen to protect its delicate needles from Nox's harmful light. Ferns, bushes, and flowering plants began to fold in their leaves. Plants that fed off Nox's potent, umbral light unfurled. In minutes the very complexion of the forest changed.

In the sky overhead, blues, violets, and indigos clashed. Night mosses, ferns, and fanning mushrooms brightened, each responding to the flashes in their own unique way. It was a wild display, indescribably beautiful, a thing many from the mountains and beyond traveled far to witness.

"Hood," Beckett repeated, his voice now cross.

They were dressed similarly. Both wore homespun shirts, belted trousers, and woodman's cloaks. Beckett, though much older than Rylan, appeared the thinner of the two. He was tall and rangy, with a mop of brown hair kept in check by two long braids that started at his temples and wrapped around the back of his head. His skin was darker than Rylan's, Beckett being a full-blooded Kin.

As they skirted a patch of snakeroot, Rylan pulled his hood up and slipped the folds of his cloak around his shoulders, allowing him to hide his hands. "Clouds to the west," Rylan said. "It'll be dark soon."

"Not *that* soon." Uncle Beckett made his way toward a low hill covered in vibrant green moss and a host of dark ferns. "And I told you, umbrals are calmest right after cant. It's the best time for guiling."

When Beckett was no longer looking, Rylan pretended his cloak could hide him like those of the Wardens in the forest's heart, then imagined himself slinking back to Thicket and finding his bed.

They walked to the top of the hill. Beckett stopped and pointed. "There it is."

Fifty paces ahead, nestled between two snaking citadel roots, was a wiry mound the size of a smoke house. It was a dragon's nest, made from the collected scrapings of bark from nearby trees. It looked like a briar patch in late autumn—bare and leafless before the winter snows fell.

As they treaded down toward the nest, Beckett pointed to the entrance, a round hole that looked too small for a dragon to fit through. "Ready?"

"No."

Beckett smiled and retreated halfway up the hill to give Rylan space. "You'll do fine." He whistled three sharp notes. "Just do as we practiced."

A dragon grumbled in the nest. Rylan's mouth filled with spit. He swallowed hard, hoping to clear it, but more kept coming, especially when Skala's scaly green snout emerged from the hole. Her nostrils flared. Her jaws spread and she rumbled again, like the start of a landslide.

The viridian dragon's head inched forward, revealing curling horns, a row of spines along its crest. Her scales were blueish-green, not so different from the lush ferns in this part of the forest. Like all dragons, her forelimbs were also her wings. In daytime, the membranous skin stretched between her long finger bones was the simple green of tree moss. In the cantlight, it scintillated in wild patterns.

Rylan held his right hand up, as Uncle Beckett had taught him, and whistled a long, trilling note. Skala swung her gaze toward him, flared the frills on her head, and hissed. "Remember me? You gave me a ride near Dovetail creek that one time. I'm here to see your kits, if you'll let me."

Skala hissed again, and the wattle along her lower jaw and neck shook. Rylan was convinced she could hear his pounding heart, smell his fear. She was going to charge at any moment, but then she gurgled, dipped her head, and climbed the hill toward Beckett. It was in that moment, as Beckett and Skala's bond was made whole, that Rylan sensed a connection to the kits in the nest.

"Call them," Beckett said. "One will come."

Rylan tried, but he was terrified, not just of physically being near a kit, but of bonding with one. Some people went mad, they said. Others were weak in some fundamental way and became controlled by the dragons they'd hoped to master.

Beckett gave Skala's wattle an affectionate scratch. "Go on, Ry."

Rylan had only just begun to summon his courage when one of the kits—a female, judging from the pattern of bright frills behind her jaws—poked her head out of the nest. She looked toward Skala with emerald green eyes, then stared at Beckett.

Alra's blinding light, the size of her . . . She was only a year old and already twice the length of a horse. When she swung her wedge-shaped head toward Rylan, her frills fanned, and her head tilted. She swayed her head back and forth.

Rylan staggered backward.

"Rylan!"

He heard the kit take wing with a *whoomp,* heard her flap closer. Then she bowled him over from behind. He rolled away, looked up, and saw sharp teeth, a snaking tongue, and emerald eyes glowing menacingly in the cantlight.

Rylan felt her hunger. She knew he'd been ready to bond, and she'd rejected him. Despite Beckett's training, he'd always known deep down that he would fail, that he'd never, in a thousand years, be able to bond with a dragon.

The kit pinned him to the ground with her fore claws.

Rylan heard Beckett footsteps pounding the soft earth toward him. "Bough and branch, Rylan, *feel* for her!"

The kit's eyes narrowed. A third, transparent eyelid nictated over her dark, elongated pupils. Her lower jaw swung open, and Rylan knew he was done for.

But the kit stopped. She tilted her head, looked into his eyes. Rylan felt her fear—of him, of what he might do to her.

"I'm not here to hurt you," Rylan said.

The kit tilted her head and hissed. The hiss became a gurgle, and the kit backed away. Rylan stood slowly, warily, worried the kit would pounce again. But she didn't. Then she bound forward and nudged his chest with her head. She did so again, then she spread her wings and lashed her tail. A giddiness was born inside of Rylan. It felt like when he and Blythe had taken turns diving from a rope swing to splash in the waters of the Vagabond. The feeling with the kit was like the moment he let go and was brimming with anticipation, excitement, joy, even a bit of fear. The feeling grew and grew until he laughed from it. The kit gurgled in an eerily similar manner. Then she went silent, and the giddy feeling vanished.

The emptiness that replaced it made Rylan go cold. The kit dug her wing's talons into the ground and stared up through the boughs. As she spun and bolted back to her nest, Beckett stared up at the canopy. Rylan did, too, and spotted three radiants, two brass and a glittering bronze, winging downward in lazy circles.

"Run, Rylan!"

The two brasses had dracorae on their backs with crossbows cocked and ready. An inquisitor—Rylan would later find out his name was Kellen—wearing scintillant white armor and an owl-wing helm rode the bronze. His rapier was still in its sheath.

Uncle Beckett whistled a long, shrill note for Skala to retreat. Skala backed toward her nest, but stopped as the bronze thudded onto the needle-strewn ground.

Beckett sprinted toward Skala, waving his arms. "Fly away, damn you! Fly!"

As the brasses circled above, the bronze stomped toward Skala. Skala reared, shot her head forward and sprayed green liquid at the approaching bronze. But the bronze curled its wing in front of itself and its rider. The stream of acid struck it, and noxious smoke rose from the bronze's wing; the outer layer of its scales began to dissolve. As soon as Skala stopped her spray, the bronze flapped its wing, shedding the acid. Smoking lesions formed on Rylan's boots and leggings as they were caught in the spray.

In a blinding move, the bronze lunged forward and clamped its teeth around Skala's neck, just below her head. Skala scratched, clawed, tried but failed to bite the bronze's neck or shoulder. In a move that showed why radiant dragons were so feared, the bronze wrenched Skala's neck back and forth until it snapped with a loud crunch. Skala shivered. Her wings twitched. Her tail curled and writhed in front of the round opening of her nest. Only then did Rylan realize the kits were nowhere to be seen.

Uncle Beckett, his face beet red, charged toward the inquisitor, his hunting knife in hand, but the inquisitor was already on the ground, holding his sword and gripping the crop in his left hand. When the bronze swung its head toward Rylan, Beckett stopped, blinked hard at the dragon's open jaws, and slowly sheathed his knife.

What followed felt like a dream. Rylan was taken with Uncle Beckett to the tree city of Andalingr. They were dragged before the magistrate, where Beckett was sentence to burn while Rylan was spared pending word from the imperator about the truth over Beckett's claims. Shortly after reckoning, they were taken to Andalingr's burning deck. The walkways, decks, and roofs were wet from an early morning downpour; the sun's harsh, early light turned the treetop city into spun glass. It was strangely idyllic, like tales of the land of fae. A noose cinched Rylan's neck. His hands tingled and purpled from the ropes binding his wrists.

A bell tolled. Citizenry gathered on decks, bridgeboughs, and ringwalks to watch the spectacle. Townsfolk stood along the railing of the festival square, a broad platform suspended between four massive citadels. Some were imperial officials, made conspicuous by their uniforms and short hair, but the majority were lowborn: laborers, mostly Kin—mixed blood or otherwise—and the like obeying an official summons. They knew the burning was more than a punishment for a crime: it was a message meant for them.

The gaoler, a fat man in drab clothes, pushed Rylan toward the wooden deck and steel frame in front of the courthouse. Rylan stopped short of it, but the gaoler was having none of it. He shoved Rylan hard, onto the viewing platform. The deck's planking was covered in the glittering scales of an iron dragon. A thick, greasy layer coated everything, especially near the steel frame. It stank like burnt lard.

Two dracorae in brightsteel armor stepped onto the deck from the door of an attached burrow and dragged out Uncle Beckett, his wrists manacled in front of him. Uncle Beckett's face was bruised and bloody. A lock of his long, curly hair was stuck to a fresh wound near his right temple. Blood dripped down the dark skin of his neck and blotted his brown, homespun shirt.

The dracorae forced Beckett under the centermost of the frame's three hooks. He slipped on the deck's greasy coating, and they hauled him roughly upright. One of the dracorae grabbed a rusty iron poker from a metal sleeve at the side of the frame and used it to lift the chain between Beckett's manacles onto the hook above him. Beckett, swallowing and glancing often toward Rylan, remained compliant and silent.

It was just a dragon, Rylan thought. *How can merely being bonded to a dragon be a crime?* But he might as well be asking why the stars shone at night. In the eyes of the empire, it simply was. His vision swam with tears. He blinked them away, trying and failing to think of what to say or do to make things right. It was all his fault. If he hadn't agreed to learn how to bond, they'd never have been caught and Skala would still be alive.

"Rylan, my boy," Uncle Beckett said loudly from the gibbet—he was actually smiling. "Tell Merida it happened quickly, won't you?"

Rylan wanted to say he was sorry. He wanted to say farewell. He wanted to give Beckett some word of hope, but all he managed was a dumb nod. He deeply regretted his silence afterwards. He'd witnessed a burning two years earlier. They were anything but quick. Aunt Merida would know he was lying the moment the words left his mouth. Even so, he hoped the lie would comfort her.

The bell ceased tolling, and Inquisitor Kellen soared on his bronze dragon between the citadels and gracefully landed on the deck. The dragon's scarlet eyes met Rylan's, and it grunted like a warthog. It swung its broad, flat head toward Beckett, and the grunting grew louder.

"Have mercy on him," Rylan pleaded. "Please have mercy—"

The gaoler cinched the rope tight around Rylan's neck, cutting off his words. He could barely breathe, much less speak.

Kellen peered up at crowded decks and bridges and announced, "We come to witness the hand of justice."

Rylan's eyes filled with tears again. Blood rushed in his ears.

"Beckett Holbrooke was found guilty of failing to report the whereabouts of an umbral dragon to the proper authorities, of sheltering it and bonding with it." He stared down at Rylan. "And guilty of teaching others how to bond."

The noose tore into Rylan's throat. He couldn't breathe. Stars filled his vision, and the pain spread to his shoulders, to his chest. The edge of his vision was turning black.

"You'll kill him!" Beckett shouted.

Kellen ignored him. "At this reckoning, as Alra died, so you shall die, never to return."

The gaoler finally loosened the noose, and Rylan gasped for breath.

Kellen raised the golden crop in his left hand. "Efflo!"

The fetter in the dragon's bridle glittered as it reared its head, breathed in.

"Rylan?" a soft voice called.

The bronze roared a gout of amber flame over Beckett. Beckett's shriek rose above the dragon's blast.

"Rylan!"

Finally, blessedly, the dragon's breath ceased and Beckett fell silent. Only the crackling of flames remained. Rylan wanted to look away, but to do so felt cowardly, so he watched Beckett's body burn. Watched his flesh peel away. Watched the only father he'd ever known rendered to charred, smoking ash.

"Rylan!"

Hot tears ran down Rylan's cheeks. He opened his eyes and found himself in the infirmary. Blythe was gripping his hand.

He sniffed, wiped tears with the back of his hand. "I'm here."

Blythe ran her thumb over his knuckles. "Beckett?" When he nodded, she squeezed again, a simple gesture, yet it did much to erase the painful memories.

She gave him a moment, then said, "What happened with Bellicor?"

Rylan struggled to find the right words. Blythe had led a hard life and only found a modicum of peace when she'd married Aarik.

Blythe shoved his hand away and sat up in the cot. "Rylan, tell me what Bellicor showed you!"

He took a deep breath. "Aarik's gone, Blythe. He . ... burned in Ancris. That's why Bellicor was so upset."

She stared at him, tears welling in her eyes. "Burned?"

"Yes. I'm so sorry." He tried to take Blythe's hand, but she pulled it away.

"Faedryn's black teeth, I *told* him not to go." She stared down at the floor, and her tears rained down on her lap. "Was Llorn there?"

"I don't know. Not at the Anvil, if that's what you mean."

Blythe stood shakily and began pacing.

"Talk to me, Blythe."

She paused and stared at him. "You know what this means, don't you?"

Rylan nodded. "Llorn's going to take over, assuming he's alive."

"With my luck, he is, and everything Aarik and I worked for will go up in smoke."

Rylan was thinking the same thing. There wasn't a chance in the world Llorn would try to make peace with the empire. He'd sooner lose his crown to Marstan in a battle that would costs thousands of lives. "Blythe," he said softly, "why did Aarik go to Ancris?"

Blythe wouldn't look at him. She crossed her arms and began chewing her thumbnail.

"Blythe, please."

"You need to leave this alone, Rylan."

"You can't be serious."

"I'm dead serious. You don't know what Llorn is like."

Rylan suddenly realized what Llorn's rise to King of the Wood might mean for Blythe, who'd been fiercely loyal to Aarik. She was in danger, as was anyone who'd aligned with Aarik. "I could find you a place in Glaeyand."

Finally, she turned to glare at him. "Glaeyand? My place is *here*, Rylan, with the Knives." She paused and wiped her cheeks. "Look, I know what Aarik asked you to do at The Broken Antler. He wanted you to look into the alchemyst in Ancris. I also know you accepted. Now I'm telling you to forget about it."

"Because of Llorn?"

"Yes, because of Llorn."

Rylan didn't know what to say. He felt like Blythe had just pulled the rug out from under him. He couldn't say with any certainty that Aarik would have actually made lasting peace in the Holt, but if Blythe was giving up, there was no chance.

"Rylan, I'm serious. Leave it alone."

"I need to get back to Glaeyand."

Blythe stared at him a minute, then nodded. She stepped around the cot and hugged him. "Thank you for saving me from Bellicor. And I'm sorry"—she pressed her fingers to the place along his ribs where she'd stabbed him—"and for this."

"You still owe me three."

A fleeting smile. "I know."

As Rylan and Vedron flew off from the nest above the infirmary, Raef was flying in on his amber, Kreòs, the creature's, bright yellow wings shimmering in the morning sun. They exchanged a look, but neither spoke.

TWENTY-SEVEN: RYLAN

Rylan brought Vedron back to her nesting grounds, and for once, she didn't grouse about his leaving nor play games when he tried to unsaddle her. The fight with Bellicor had left her in an unsociable mood.

"Wait," he said as he hid her saddle and bridle in the hollowed-out oak. "Let me get your lucerta." Viridians were highly resistant to the powers of aura and umbra. Their lucertae could protect those who knew how to use them, but all lucertae lost power over time, so Rylan collected fresh ones from Vedron when he could.

He took the knife from his belt, and Vedron lowered her head as he approached. He slipped the knife point beneath the dark green scale between her eye ridges, then pried it until it released with a soft tearing sound. Vedron ducked her head once, then turned, spread her wings, and flew away.

He lifted the scale high. "Thank you!" he called, but Vedron didn't so much as blare a note before she was lost to the trees.

He tucked the scale away in a small leather pouch on his belt, sheathed his knife, and began the long hike back to Glaeyand. He felt a strong urge to rush back so he could smooth things over with his father, but he couldn't return without black henbane—the excuse he'd given Bashira for leaving so abruptly. In a bit of good fortune, he found a stream choked with the flowers. Even so, it took time to gather several libra of it. It was short of what would be needed to put down a dragon like Rugio, but his father wouldn't know that.

Cant was nearing by the time he reached the forest below Glaeyand. Exhausted, he opted for the dragonbone lift. The attendant, Mouse, held the door open for him, locked it behind him, and tugged on the cord. The bell jingled, as usual, then Mouse pulled on the cord three more times.

"What was that for?" Rylan asked.

Mouse shrugged. "I was told to."

"Every time the lift goes up?"

"No, Master Holbrooke, only when *you* did."

The lift rose, and Rylan heard a horn blow, surely the message Mouse had just sent to the lift station being relayed. Mouse was usually a chatty fellow. Most days Rylan could hardly shut him up, but as the lift rose, he said nothing, just stared out at the passing bridgeboughs. At the midway point, Rylan transferred to the second lift, and everyone on the platform gaped at him.

Rylan thought surely Andros, his burly, intemperate half-brother, would be waiting for him at the upper lift station deck, but as the lift settled at the deck, only his father, resplendent in an azure doublet embroidered in thread-of-gold, was standing there.

"Walk with me."

Ignoring the winch hands' pointed stares, Rylan exited the lift and fell into step alongside his father. As their footfalls thudded on the planks of a wide bridge-bough, Marstan said, "Bashira visited you yesterday morning."

"Yes, I'm sorry I left without—"

"She made a reasonable request of you, it seems to me."

"It was, and I wanted to go, but it was important I have—"

"Enough black henbane, yes . . . Last time it was calendula. Star fennel and bark of the blood maple before that. You seem to spend an inordinate amount of time collecting common ingredients."

Rylan was surprised how much his father knew. "I know I'm gone often," he said, "and I apologize for it, but you must understand, the move to Glaeyand was difficult for me. Uncle Beckett and I used to wander the forest for days. I hated it then. I missed my friends. Now, it's the wandering I miss."

It wasn't a lie, but it was hardly the truth. He couldn't let his father—or anyone in Glaeyand, for that matter—suspect he was bonded to Vedron. They'd use him to capture and kill her, then likely hang Rylan for heresy.

They rounded a citadel via the broad ringwalk and crossed a suspended bridge bedecked in spring flowers.

"You asked me the other night," Marstan said, "about conversations I may or may not have had with the King of the Wood."

"Yes. I'm sor—"

"Yesterday, Aarik Bloodhaven was burned at the Anvil."

Rylan wondered if his father suspected Rylan already knew. "I see . . ."

"Given your interest in my dealings with the King of the Wood—indeed, your very knowledge of them—one has to wonder how closely aligned you are with them."

"Father?"

On a deck below them, a gaggle of children were playing tag. Marstan glanced at them, then turned again to Rylan. "Are you a Knife, Rylan?"

It was not a question Rylan expected. "No! I swear it. I'm not. But I *hear* things. It's how I learned of your discussions with Aarik. I came to you the other night because I want to *help*."

"Then do what I ask of you."

"Of course. I'll go back to the Alevadas and make amends. I can leave in the morning. Or tonight if you wish. And if Rugio hasn't already passed—"

"Rugio passed last night. Your condolences have already been forwarded to Lady Soraya."

A few trees away, the eyrie master, a few eyrie hands, and a number of dracorae were standing and talking on the eyrie's triangular staging deck, likely in preparation of a scouting mission.

"Father," Rylan pressed, "I *know* you were working with Aarik. He's dead now, but surely all is not lost? There must be others Knives who want peace." He meant Blythe, but he could hardly admit that to his father.

In the eyrie's open well, three fledgling brasses curled upward toward the eyrie's entrance. One suddenly dove, and the other two gave chase. Watching them, Marstan said, "Just this once, I'll share a few things with you, Rylan. I *was* having discussions with the King of the Wood. We *did* draft of an amendment to the Covenant. But you know it takes unanimous consent for such an amendment to pass."

"I thought you had the votes," Rylan said.

Marstan nodded. "A near thing, but yes, I think I did."

It was a rare moment of candor from his father, but the knowledge was gutting. Rylan hadn't even been aware of the chance for peace two months ago. Now he felt it slipping through his fingers. "There must be *some* way the deal can be salvaged."

"If you think so, you're much more optimistic than I am. Last night, a few hours after Aarik's death, the messenger Aarik and I were using was found dead. No one will dare defy Llorn when he wears the crown. And when word of the peace amendment leaks, which it surely will, some of our own people will try to paint me as a Red Knife sympathizer. Whatever Llorn does from this day forward—whatever he *has* done—will be used against me. I'll be lucky to keep my seat as Imperator."

Rylan refused to believe it was a lost cause, but how could he make a difference? If he could learn why Llorn had gone to Ancris, why he'd been meeting with the Hissing Man, it might convince Blythe and some of Aarik's allies to return to the negotiating table. Blythe was too scared to share anything with Rylan, but perhaps the alchemyst, Master Renato, might know what Korvus Julianus had stumbled onto, why he'd been killed. That knowledge might help pave a path toward peace. But how could he convince his father to let him go?

"Aarik never left the Holt," Rylan said, "but for some reason he did. Let me go to Ancris and see what I can find."

"Toward what purpose?"

"Knowledge. Leverage over Llorn. Leverage over whomever he's working with."

Marstan shook his head. "No, Rylan. First, I need to survive the coming vote. Then I can try for peace with the Red Knives again. Until then, I must ask you to remain in Glaeyand."

"But I've other visits arranged, business to attend to."

Give Bashira a list. She'll get someone to take your place or make excuses if that's not possible."

"Father, please—"

"Let there be no misunderstandings between us." Marstan's green eyes bored into Rylan with an intensity Rylan had rarely seen. "I make it my business to know all I can of persons who conduct business in my name, including my children. When your disappearances became troublesome, I had you followed. I know you travel quite far on your rangings, and that you often head east, close where the nest of a viridian was found."

Rylan's ears rang. He'd been so careful, always watching for followers, visiting Vedron's nesting grounds only when he knew the forest was clear.

"Remind me, Rylan. The man who raised you, this Beckett, wasn't he burned for bonding with a viridian?" He pointed to Rylan's left hand. "Didn't you lose a finger for trying to bond with one of its kits?"

Yes, and it was one of the greatest experiences of Rylan's life. Vedron was like a sibling to him, a soul mate, a protector who at the same time needed *his* protection. He couldn't lose her.

"In all honesty," Marstan said, "I don't care if you keep a pet. The restriction on umbrals always seemed foolish to me. But I won't hesitate to have your dragon killed should you disobey my orders."

On the staging deck near the eyrie, the group of dragon riders parted. Rylan hadn't noticed earlier, but Andros was among them. He stared at Rylan and Marstan with a broad smile.

"Andros doesn't know," Marstan said, "but I'll give him the honor of leading the chase. I imagine he'll make a suit of armor from your dragon." He paused. "Do we have an understanding?"

Rylan nodded numbly.

"Good." Marstan clapped Rylan's shoulder and left, his boot heels thumping on the planks as he went.

Rylan turned away from him and stared eastward into the forest.

TWENTY-EIGHT: RHIANNON

R hiannon sat in the refectory with Irik. The midday meal was potato soup and a hunk of tangy bread that was so delicious it almost made up for the soup's blandness. The room hummed with conversation. The day before, Mother Constance had declared that Llorn was coming to Thicket with several druins and that the abbey would grant them shelter. While the message was for everyone, she'd glared at Rhiannon while saying it.

Rhiannon sipped her cider, then quietly said, "Do you think Brother Mayhew will be with them?"

"Dunno"—Irik stuffed the last of his bread into his mouth and chased it with pine milk—"but I bet Sister Dereka will."

Rhiannon shivered at the very thought—she could still see the archdruin's piercing, awestruck gaze when Rhiannon had spoken to the wisp—but her mind soon drifted to Brother Mayhew and his fate. The abbey had been alive with all sorts of rumors since he left more than a week ago. Most of the aspirants agreed he'd gone with Aarik and Llorn to Ancris to help with some sort of ritual. Where they disagreed was what happened next. Some of them said Aarik and Llorn had been killed by the empire. Others said only Aarik had died. Others still said Aarik and Llorn escaped after a fierce battle with an indurium dragon. Few cared to venture what had become of Brother Mayhew, perhaps for fear of what Brother Mayhew might do when he learned of their gossip. Rhiannon hoped he wasn't dead. He was prickly sometimes—actually, *most* of the time—but he didn't deserve to die.

The clergy on the far side of the room suddenly turned their heads toward the door. The room went silent as Sister Dereka entered the refectory with two male druins dressed in brown habits and green cloaks. All three had shaved heads, runic tattoos around their left eyes, and gnarled wooden staves. As they leaned their staves against the wall and hung their canvas packs, Llorn strode in.

Llorn's eyes were pinched, and his sun-marked brow was furrowed, as if he were in pain. He had a leather satchel slung over one shoulder, which he hung near the druins' packs. He surveyed the room and stopped on seeing Rhiannon. He spoke something too soft to hear, and Sister Dereka's swung her gaze toward Rhiannon as well. Suddenly, the entire room was focused on Rhiannon. She felt her ears burning red. It was all she could do not to hide beneath the table.

Mother Constance pushed herself to a stand and motioned to the newcomers. "We welcome to our house Sister Dereka, Brothers Freyne and Andar, and Llorn Bloodhaven."

A great weight was lifted as everyone's attention shifted back to the newcomers.

Like everyone else, Rhiannon pressed the fingertips of her right hand to her forehead and said, "Alra's bounty be upon you."

Llorn and the druins sat at Mother Constance's table and ate.

As the sounds of conversation returned to normal, Irik widened his eyes at Rhiannon, but Rhiannon shook her head. She didn't want to talk about Llorn, not with so many people listening. Irik nodded, then nattered on about the trip he'd taken to Andalingr that morning to fetch a box of candle wicks.

They finished their food, and thankfully, Llorn seemed lost in conversation with Mother Constance. Sister Dereka, meanwhile, kept glancing Rhiannon's way while speaking with Sister Merida. As Rhiannon stood, ready to head to the kitchen to help clean up, Sister Dereka sat up straight and spoke loudly, "You're making a mistake if you think you have some claim over her."

All conversation stopped except Sister Merida, who said softly, "She is my cousin's daughter."

"And Llorn is her uncle," Sister Dereka replied. "He has requested to speak with her."

Llorn watched the exchange silently, as if he were perfectly content to have Sister Dereka speak for him.

"He's barely visited her since Morraine's death," Sister Merida went on. "What right does he have to demand anything of her, or us for that matter?"

"Rhiannon is of House Bloodhaven," Dereka nearly shouted. "Her uncle will speak with her. What happens then is between them and them alone."

Sister Merida's cheeks went rosy. She peered over at Rhiannon. "She's just a child . . ."

"Be that as it may," Sister Dereka said.

"Aarik wouldn't have approved."

"Aarik is dead," Dereka spat. "His approval no longer matters."

Mother Constance tugged on Sister Merida's sleeve. Sister Merida's nostrils flared, but then she blinked, stared down at Mother Constance, and sat. A hushed conversation followed. Mother Constance seemed mid-sentence when Sister Merida stood in a rush and fled the refectory through the kitchen.

Llorn, finished with his food, stood from the table and motioned Rhiannon to the front door. Mother Constance caught Rhiannon's eye and nodded, effectively giving her permission. Irik gaped at her, his eyes round as a stickleback's.

"Take my bowl up?" Rhiannon asked as she stood.

Irik nodded, and Rhiannon headed toward the door. Llorn waited for her to join him, then retrieved his satchel and accompanied her outside, into the bright sunlight. They headed past the garden and the beehives. They strode past the brewery. When they'd gained the footpath beyond, Llorn said, "Sister Dereka spoke out of turn. I wanted to tell you about Aarik myself."

"It's true, then?" Rhiannon asked as they rounded a citadel and headed toward the deeper forest. "He's dead?"

"Yes. He was taken by the Church and burned."

"And Brother Mayhew?"

"He's still in Ancris. He may be burned as well. We don't know yet."

"I'm sorry. About Aarik, I mean." Rhiannon had no siblings, but she had Irik, who'd been like a brother to her. She'd be devastated if he was suddenly gone.

"I am, too," Llorn said, "but he went to Ancris for a reason. It's why I've come to speak with you." He reached into the satchel and pulled out a wisplight. Within the glass globe, the blue light shimmered and twisted, and it was brighter than any wisp Rhiannon had ever seen. It meant one of three things: that it was freshly risen, that the soul had been powerful in life, or that it had a deep desire to return to the land of the living.

Rhiannon stopped on the footpath and stared at it. "What is that?"

"Your mother's wisp."

Aarik's words in the brewery returned to her. He'd asked Rhiannon if Llorn had mentioned her mother. He'd been worried about Llorn's purpose in having Rhiannon speak to the dead. He'd known Rhiannon's mother was involved in some way. "What do you want me to do with it?"

"I want you to help raise her."

A keen ringing in Rhiannon's ears drowned out the birdsong around them. "*Raise* her?"

"Yes, Rhiannon. We need her to—"

"You want me to help you create a draugr?"

"Yes—"

"They're abominations. They go against Alra's teachings. Even Brother Mayhew says so."

Llorn frowned. "Your mother had a purpose before she died. She wanted to help us liberate the Holt."

"Aarik didn't want to." She pointed to the brewery behind them. "He told me so."

"I don't doubt it, but Aarik was being naive. We spoke about it, and he came around to my way of thinking. He saw that the empire was leaving us no choice but to fight back."

Rhiannon backed away from him. "You're lying."

"No, I'm not. Why do you think he came with me to Ancris? He wanted to speak to the Hissing Man face to face so we could plan our next steps together." His frown turned into a scowl when Rhiannon said nothing, deepened as she took two steps back. "Rhiannon, your mother needs your help."

"I won't do it."

"You will, or I'll hand you over to Sister Dereka until she beats some sense into you."

Rhiannon turned and sprinted into the forest. "I won't do it!," she shouted over her shoulder. "Ever!"

"Rhiannon, stop!"

"I won't raise my mother!" She ran until her legs burned and her lungs ached. When she reached Dovetail Creek, she pounded along the footpath beside it for about a mile and staggered to a stop at the Vagabond River. There she stepped into a stand of cattails, crouched, and stared over the noisy river at the citadels along the opposite shore. She thought about diving into the water and floating downriver somewhere, *anywhere*, as long as it took her away from Llorn. She could board a ship at Gorminion. Travel to Olgasus or beyond. The world would be hers.

But then should thought of Irik. Goddess, how she'd miss him. Sister Merida, too, and Lexie and the other aspirants. She'd even miss Mother Constance. They were the only family she'd ever known. *Besides my mother, and Aarik and Llorn.* But she barely remembered her mother. And Aarik had visited her only a handful of times at the abbey and barely spoke to her. Llorn was even worse. He'd had always stood apart, like he hated the abbey, Thicket, and every last person in them.

She heard footsteps approaching and spotted Llorn pushing through the cattails, the leather satchel over one shoulder. He barely looked winded.

He crushed down some cattails and sat cross-legged, staring out over the water, just like she was. He grimaced and pressed a hand to his forehead, clenched his teeth and closed his eyes so tight his face wrinkled. She didn't want to talk to him, but he looked so pained she started to worry.

"Are you not well?" she asked.

"It's only a headache," he said, eyes still closed.

"Woundwort helps headaches."

"It will pass." He took a deep breath and opened his eyes. "Tell me, do you know much about your grandmother?"

"I know she was a druin. And that she knew how to tap into the trees and unlock their secrets."

Llorn nodded. "During the Talon Wars, the empire decimated our dragon legions and our soldiers, but that was only *half* the war. They wanted to eradicate the things we knew at least as much as our military, so they targeted our druins. They slew our soothsayers, our wisemen and wisewomen. They slaughtered our dragon singers, our eyrie masters, our herbalists. They burned our books, outlawed our practices, all in hopes of stamping out what we knew, the things that could undo them. The Covenant drafted at the end of the war led to peace of a sort, but by then the damage had been done. We'd all but forgotten how to attract dragons and bond with them. The druins forgot many of their rituals and their spells. The trick of using lucertae all but vanished."

Rhiannon knew where this was headed. "Grandma Rygmora helped them remember."

"That's right. She communed with the trees and retaught some small amount of our heritage to us, but even that was too much for the empire. They came for her, and she fled deep into the Holt. The Red Knives sheltered her. I was only four at the time. Aarik was seven, your mother nine. We stayed with the Knives for many years, but then came Lucretio Solvina."

Rhiannon hadn't heard many stories about Rygmora, but she'd heard the one about Lucretio Solvina, the former quintarch of Ancris. "Grandmother had him killed."

Llorn seemed annoyed by the remark. "No, Rhiannon. Your grandmother was always more dove than hawk. But a few months earlier, she'd taught the Red Knives how to use onyx lucertae to draw shadows around themselves like a cloak. One of the Knives' assassins used the knowledge to enter Highreach and kill Lucretio. Lucran became quintarch and waged a furious reprisal. Hundreds of Knives were hung. They found your grandmother and took her to Ancris." Llorn stared absently out over the churning water. "They chained her to the Anvil and burned her. Your mother, Aarik, and I, stayed in the Deepwood. There was nothing we could do. We were still so young."

A fisherman launched a flat-bottomed boat on the far bank and cast a net into the water. Llorn glanced at him and continued.

"Morraine dedicated herself to learning the ways of the druins, but did so with a purpose. While my mother merely wanted to reawaken the old ways, Morraine wanted to burn the empire to cinders."

Llorn reached into his satchel. Rhiannon expected him to pull out the wisplight, but he drew a long narrow object wrapped in linen. He unfolded the cloth to reveal a crystal shard shaped like knife blade. It shone like the sky at cant.

Llorn held it out to her. "Take it."

The crystal made her fingertips tingle. She squeezed it, and her knuckles vibrated like she was holding a lever on some infernal machine.

"It's part of an ancient artifact," Llorn said, "Alra's Heartstone."

"Like the ones in the shrines?"

"Just so."

"But how did you get it?"

"I didn't. Morraine did. She'd wanted it for many years. She'd only just begun unlocking its secrets when she died."

Realizing her hand was starting to warm, like an infection setting in, Rhiannon handed the crystal back to Llorn. "How did my mother die?"

Llorn wrapped the shard in the linen and put it back in his satchel. "She went to Caldoras to find an old text that might shed light on the crystal and how to use it. She was spotted leaving. She fled for the Holt but two dracorae grabbed her in Glaeyand. Aarik was King of the Wood by then. I told him we should attack Glaeyand, but Aarik had been bribing Marstan Lyndenfell for years and said he could negotiate with them."

"It didn't work?"

"No, it didn't. I tried to rescue her when it became clear they meant to follow through on her execution, but it was too late. The dracorae in Glaeyand cut us off at the lower bank of the Diamondflow. The next morning, they hung her for heresy." Llorn reached into the satchel and, at last, drew out the wisplight, and stared at it. "Their shepherds used a ritual, one they'd twisted from our own, to quicken her wisp. They gave it to the commander of the men who spotted her. I thought it lost forever, but we found out a few months ago that was on display, like a bauble, in a gallery."

A prolonged silence ensued. Rhiannon listened to the lapping of the water along the riverbanks, the call of a distant loon. She felt sad for her mother. She felt angry, too, about what had happened to her family, but the anger was indistinct, directionless—she'd hardly known her mother, and she hadn't known her grandmother at all.

"Why would you speak to the Hissing Man at all? Isn't he our enemy?"

"Yes, but we mean to use him."

She pointed to the wisp. "And you need my mother to do it."

"We do."

He held it out for her to take, but she refused to touch it. She couldn't bear seeing her mother's life, sensing her emotions. "You want to use her like you're using the Hissing Man."

"*Use* her . . . ?" Llorn laughed. "Rhiannon, she *made* the plan. I merely want to give her the chance to see it done."

"Will it lead to war?"

Llorn stared into the wisplight's wavering glass. "Peace with the empire can only be achieved through war."

"But the empire is so powerful. How can we stand against them, even if we learn how to use that relic from Alra's Heartstone?"

"The relic is but a key that will unlock something greater."

"And what is that?"

"I can't reveal that. Not yet."

He offered her the wisplight again, and this time she took it. The glass felt cool to the touch. It seemed to drain the very warmth from her fingertips. There were many nights when she wished her mother hadn't died, when she wished Morraine would come back and they could live their days happily and in peace. With the wisp, Llorn was giving Rhiannon a chance for her to grant her own wish.

Rhiannon was no fool. She knew her mother wouldn't be whole, but that made her realize it wasn't only her decision. It was her mother's, too. "I want to ask her," she said. "I need to."

Llorn nodded, then reached into the satchel again. He took out a golden locket on a long chain and handed it to Rhiannon. "A gift."

She held it in her palm and flipped it over. On one side was a setting of milky quartz; on the other, black agate. Feeling like she was disobeying every rule Brother Mayhew had ever taught her, she pulled the chain over her head and opened the side with the milky quartz, finding, as she expected, a reservoir filled with glittering white auris. She took a small pinch of the rosemary-scented powder—the same amount Brother Mayhew had instructed her to use at the swamp—and inhaled it with a sharp sniff. Then she rubbed her fingers over her gums and squeezed the locket shut.

Her nose burned like she'd inhaled flames, but it faded quickly. Then she felt lightheaded. The feeling passed as she cupped the globe in both hands and bent her will on the soul within. For long moments she felt nothing, then she saw herself as a child stacking painted wooden blocks on a red carpet.

"I need to ask you something," Rhiannon said.

In the vision, her mother said, "Yes, dear, please do."

Rhiannon remembered that day. She'd been eager to go frog hunting by the nearby pond and had asked whether she should put the blocks away, but her mother was using it to speak to her. She took a deep breath and said, "I need to know if you wish to return to the land of the living. I need to know if you want to finish what you began with Uncle Llorn."

The vision of her tossing blocks into a basket faded. Suddenly, she was being slammed onto a hard wooden table in a dim room that stank of piss and shit. Her wrists and ankles were placed in iron cuffs. A man wearing the white uniform of an inquisitor shouted questions at her. Red-hot pokers were pressed against the soles of her feet. Her throat went raw from screaming.

Rhiannon shook her head, hoping to banish the memories of torture, but all it did was shift the scene. She was being led to a gallows in the trees. A noose slipped over her head and cinched tight. Blood pounded in her ears. The hangman yanked the lever. She felt a painful tug on her neck. Felt her limbs flail as her breath was stolen from her. Just when Rhiannon thought she might die, the image evaporated.

She coughed hard and pressed one hand to her stomach, waiting for the intense feelings to pass. When she could think again, she realized the torture her mother had endured might be interpreted as an answer to her question, but it might also be that the memories had been summoned by the mere mention of her desire to destroy the empire.

"Please," Rhiannon said, "I need to know for certain whether you wish to return."

A long pause followed, then she was standing in a forest, holding a knife. Ten yards ahead was a soldier in imperial armor. At his feet was a pretty, middle-aged woman with a cut lip and angry welt over one eye. Her skirt and the white slip beneath were dirty and pulled up around her knees. Rhiannon charged over the forest floor while screaming, and the man spun to face her. Eyes wide, he drew his sword back. Rhiannon's left forearm glowed as she lifted it to deflect the coming blow. The sword blurred and struck her forearm, but clanged like it had struck iron. Rhiannon drove forward. Punched the knife up and into the man's skull. They fell together and struck the ground hard. She felt the man's body twitch as a death rattle escaped his parted lips.

Rhiannon tossed the wisplight onto the matted cattails and the vision vanished. She hugged her chest and rocked back and forth but couldn't shake the soldier's bloodshot eyes and fetid breath, the way his body convulsed beneath her.

Llorn picked up the wisp and stared at her. "I take it she gave you an answer?"

Rhiannon nodded numbly, and Llorn tucked the wisp back into the satchel.

She watched the sun glitter off the Vagabond, listened to the rush of the water. She had her answer but was terrified over what came next, because whatever happened, *she* would be at least partly to blame. Turning away from the river, she looked up at Llorn and found he no longer seemed brutish or scary. He was determined, like her mother. "Very well. I make no promises, but I'll try."

Llorn smiled. "That's all I ask."

TWENTY-NINE: AZARIAH

T hree days after Aarik's burning at the Anvil, Azariah strode along a tunnel in the catacombs. He was supposed to be on his way to the vyrd to speak to the other illustrae, but ever since making the offer to quicken Ransom's wisp for Tyrinia Solvina, the vision of Cassian being stabbed haunted him. He couldn't reconcile it with his memories.

He soon arrived at a crypt with four tunnels, four sepulchers, and a wisplight hanging by a chain from the ceiling. It looked like any other in the catacombs, except the brass plaque above one of the sepulcher doors read:

Cassian Andrinus, beloved of Kalyris Andrinus and Illustra Azariah Andrinus III

When Cassian had gone missing, the Church's shepherds searched for him for weeks, but Cassian was never found. In fact, not a single witnesses to his abduction was identified, and Azariah never received a ransom note. When a year passed, he hadn't completely given up hope, but he'd had a sepulcher set aside for Cassian.

He entered the sepulcher and walked to the foot of the sarcophagus, removed his ivory-and-gold mask and set it on the lid. Visions of his son flashed before him. He saw Cassian's eyes go wide, saw blood pooling beneath his body. Azariah could hardly remember a time when his mind felt at peace. He had to go all the way back to the years leading up to becoming illustra, because everything had changed the day he'd pledged himself to Faedryn.

He'd been twenty-five at the time, a diligent priest, one of dozens working in the temple. Cassian was seven and attended the temple school while Azariah saw to his duties. For the first time in decades, the temple was without a leader. The former illustra had been a proud woman who'd lost a valiant battle against consumption. On her death, two of the Church's four surviving illustrae traveled to Ancris to choose her successor. Their method was mysterious, but it was clear they were starting with the temple's high shepherds and working their way down. Everyone thought it would be a simple affair, but three days passed and the shepherds were all found wanting.

Azariah thought surely an acolyte would be chosen—they would all have demonstrated an aptitude for wielding aura and umbra—but another day passed without a successor. On the fifth day, a shepherdess with a sharp chin and overly large eyes entered the nave. "Azariah, Temerus, Sarina!"

Azariah, in the black habit of an Alran priest, had been polishing the pews when he heard his name. He set aside the rag and tin of beeswax and stood. Temerus and

Sarina did as well. All three of them were priests, destined to spread the gospel, not shepherds who wielded aura and umbra in Alra's name.

"Come with me," the shepherdess called.

Azariah waited for the others to pass to hide how badly his hands were shaking, then trailed behind them. The priests and novitiates who remained gaped at them as they left.

Sarina was an attractive woman with full lips, piercing eyes, and long auburn hair, but Azariah didn't like being around her. She always made him feel insufficient. She slowed her pace and walked side-by-side with him. "Will you *calm* yourself?"

He tried but felt certain it only made him look more miserable.

"It's only a test," Sarina went on. "Fail, and you're back to polishing benches."

But failing wasn't what he was worried about. Quite the opposite. Becoming illustra was the highest honor in the church, yet the very notion petrified him. He wasn't even sure why.

"I'll be fine," he managed.

Sarina huffed and largely ignored him after that. They followed the shepherd to the temple steps, where a coach awaited, and the shepherd ushered them into the cabin. Azariah sat as far from the door as he could to avoid being stared at by the shepherdess and was pleased when the coach finally pulled away.

By the time they reached Henge Hill, reckoning was near; the western sky was a brilliant orange. Azariah and the others exited the coach and hiked up the path to the circle of standing stones at the top, where two illustrae in white robes and ornate masks awaited them. One, Camadaea, was as young as Azariah, maybe younger, and though she was slight of frame, she had a fierceness about her, like a cornered fox. The other was Ignatius, and he was tall and had ebony skin and his mask was made of rough dragonbone. The flaking gray mud over his hands and forearms made him look like he was turning to stone. In the vyrd behind them, the old iron dragon, Vattuo, lay on the stones, slowly fanning his tail.

Ignatius stepped forward. "Temerus," he said in a voice as deep as a gorge.

Temerus, a spare young priest with a cleft chin, followed him into the vyrd and was made to stand before Vattuo. Camadaea gripped a crop stone. The matching fetter on Vattuo's bridle glimmered, and the old iron lowered his head and peered at Temerus. A long moment passed as an unseasonably warm wind blew through the stones on Henge Hill; its hollow whisper made Ancris feel empty and forgotten.

Eventually, Vattuo raised his head and turned away from Temerus. Ignatius pointed Temerus back the way he'd come. As Temerus walked dazedly away, Ignatius called, "Sarina."

Sarina entered the vyrd, and the ritual was repeated. What Vattuo might be looking for, and how it could know in the first place, Azariah had no idea, but Vattuo looked away from her and she was dismissed. As she walked back toward Temerus and Azariah, the wind tugged at her auburn hair. She stared at Azariah but didn't speak.

Azariah paced between the standing stones, waiting to hear his name, quavering like a newborn foal and breathing like a racehorse. At last Ignatius instructed him to stand in front of the old iron. Vattuo lowered his ponderous head and regarded Azariah. His third eyelids nictated, and Azariah felt dizzy. The iron blinked again, and veins of power brightened in Azariah's mind like gossamer.

When Vattuo blinked a third time, Azariah entered the maze, that liminal, in-between place ferrymen navigated in crossings. He felt himself sucked into the wet tree roots, the thick dirt and flinty stone, the stinking insects and blind vermin as his essence traversed the maze. He was drawn along its weblike structure toward the heart of the forest and the ancient Umbral Tree, as old as the Ruining itself, grown by Alra's paragons to trap the fallen god, Faedryn.

He stared at the towering black tree, and his gut ached. The feeling grew, like a wound opening inside him. Faedryn, trapped in Gonsalond and hidden behind the veil, had somehow found a way to reach beyond the bounds of his prison. Azariah couldn't fathom how until he stared up at the branches high above. The tree's roots would go deep. They might touch the veins of indurium that formed the maze. The very thing that bound Faedryn might have allowed him to reach beyond the bounds of his prison, to manipulate, to ensnare, to dominate.

Azariah heard a voice that could only be Feadryn's call out, but he couldn't understand the words. He tried to turn away but was fixed in place, rigid. The pain in his gut worked its way to his chest, his limbs.

Alra, please save me! You are the light that guides me. My life is yours!

But then he saw Alra, resplendent in white, standing before Faedryn with a gleaming spear, demanding his obeisance. Faedryn denied her, and Alra slew those who worshipped him. She tore down their cities and ruined their crops. He would never have believed that Alra had been the aggressor in the years before the Ruining, but it was true. He saw it with his own eyes. It occurred to him that Faedryn might be lying, but the thought was there and gone in a moment, and he found himself filled with sorrow at all that had befallen Faedryn.

As Azariah stared up at the Umbral Tree, he heard two words that echoed over and over. *"Free me . . ."*

"I will, My Lord," Azariah said. "I swear it."

He blinked and found himself lying on the stones of the vyrd. Sarina and Temerus were gone, as was Vattuo. Only Ignatius and Camadaea remained, and they seemed calm, accepting of him.

Ignatius stepped behind Azariah and forced him to his knees. "Welcome, brother."

"Yes"—Camadaea drew a glass vial filled with green-tinted liquid from her robe—"welcome, *brother.*" She said it as if she were offended her lord had chosen the likes of him.

Ignatius stood behind Azariah. "Tilt your head back." When Azariah did, the tall, dark-skinned illustra gripped his neck and head and held him in place.

Camadaea, her mask gleaming, stood before him and pried his left eye open. She perched the vial above it and allowed several drops of the green liquid to fall.

Azariah heard a soft hiss. It felt as though a red hot poker were being driven through his eye. He writhed, screamed, but Ignatius held him in place. When he settled, Camadaea repeated the ritual in his right eye.

The pain continued for days, and Azariah was blinded but gained his second sight. At the time, he felt so certain he'd been shown the truth and that his cause was righteous. Standing in his son's sepulcher, his head bowed over an empty sarcophagus, he was no longer certain. What sort of god would take away his son and hide the truth about it?

"You dare?" said a hissing voice.

Azariah shivered, stood upright, and in his second sight saw the Hissing Man hunched in the doorway behind him.

"He is our *Lord*," the Hissing Man continued.

Azariah wiped away his tears. "A father deserves to know his child's fate."

The Hissing Man slouched into the room. "You've had your time to grieve. You have other responsibilities now."

"Tell me what happened to Cassian. I know you know the truth."

The Hissing Man glared at Azariah from behind the gauze wrapped over his eyes. His breath was noisy, his lips curled, as if he were incensed Azariah would ask such a thing. Azariah stared back, willing the Hissing Man to tell him more, but the more time passed, the more certain he was that he was displeasing Faedryn.

"You have *work* to do," the Hissing Man hissed.

Feeling craven, Azariah retrieved his mask. "There was time."

"No longer. The illustrae await."

Azariah wanted to order the Hissing Man away—he wanted to tell Cassian he loved him and that he was missed—but the will left him as he pulled on his mask. The illustra of Ancris once more, he left the sepulcher, and the Hissing Man closed the door behind him.

A light wind tugged at the hem of Azariah's robes as he trekked up Henge Hill and entered Ancris's vyrd. Much like Nox itself, the menhirs shed a fitful indigo light; the effect was brighter along the sharply carved runes, making them glow like arcane ink.

Azariah stood near the center of the vyrd, feeling lonely and a bit lost. He took a moment to identify the source of his discomfort, but when nothing occurred to him, he spread his arms wide and cast his awareness down through the ancient stone slabs. He felt the veins of power in the earth stretching toward the foothills and the Holt.

What I do this night, My Lord Faedryn, I do for you and your glory.

Faedryn didn't acknowledge him as such, but Azariah saw a brief flash of the fallen god wrapped in the roots of the Umbral Tree. Azariah bent his will on Caldoras, and Camadaea came into his mind, standing in a vyrd of her own. Through the strange workings of the vyrda, it appeared as though she was standing several paces from Azariah in *his* vyrd. Ignatius came next. Though decades older, both he and Camadaea looked not so different from the day they'd stolen Azariah's sight: white robes, a mask fashioned into a golden sunburst for Camadaea, flaking gray mud and a mask of dragonbone for Ignatius.

Together, the three of them reached out to the remaining two illustrae. In stark contrast to Camadaea, Moryndra appeared in white robes that hugged her tall form. In place of a mask, she'd applied black ointment in a band across her eyes, accented with gold. The last to join was Bahrian, a bald man with dusky skin and a pock-marked face. He wore an iron mask with Alra's eight-pointed star etched on the forehead.

"Much has happened since we last spoke," Camadaea said. "There have been comings and goings at the Crag as well as profound changes in the Holt." She motioned to Azariah like she might one of her acolytes. "Begin with Aarik and his burning at the Anvil."

Knowing his annoyance might be sensed by the others if it grew too strong, Azariah took a moment to calm himself. Then he told them of Llorn's plans to raise his dead sister, the arrangements for Aarik to meet with the Hissing Man, the sudden arrival of the inquisitors. He gave special attention to his questioning of Aarik in the temple dungeon and Aarik's burning at the Anvil but made no mention of the chalice or the unfortunate business in the clock tower—he'd become convinced it would amount to nothing, so what need was there to share it with the others?

"All went according to plan with respect to the Red Knives," he said as a finish. "The crown is Llorn's."

"You should have tried harder to convince Aarik to join us," Ignatius intoned.

"His dealings with the Imperator prevented it," Azariah said evenly. "No matter what he might have told his Knives, he was working toward peace in the Holt. Our only way forward was with Llorn."

Bahrian said, "Why not kill him in secret then? Why this business with a public execution?"

"Because time runs short. If we'd killed Aarik in secret, it might have delayed Llorn's plans, or worse, left an opening for one of Aarik's captains to challenge Llorn for leadership of the Knives."

Bahrian seemed unappeased. "Are you not concerned that Aarik learned of our plans for the crucible before his death?"

"No," Azariah said flatly.

"He might have told Blythe or that other Knife, the burly one with the loose lips"—Bahrian snapped his fingers several times—"Maladox . . ."

"He might have," Azariah conceded, "but that's why we made it look like the *Church* was to blame for his death. Anyone Aarik might have told will be too desperate for revenge to worry about a disagreement between two brothers. The Red Knives are a loyal lot. They'll bend knee to Llorn."

Moryndra appeared outwardly calm, but Azariah felt her anxiousness the longer he stared at her. "You say everything went according to plan, yet you failed to get Brother Mayhew from the inquisitors. Why?"

"I didn't have the proper jurisdiction."

"You're a persuasive man," Moryndra said. "You have the Church's resources at your disposal. You should have been able to get him out."

"Had I done so," he said as evenly as he could manage, "Praefectus Damika would have fought me. She's long had Lucran's ear, and Lucran is set to return from Syrdia any day now. I didn't want the first news he hears to be that the Church was making unreasonable demands. He might order Damika to scrutinize the meeting in the mine more than she already is. That's the last thing we need right now. Brother Mayhew will keep quiet."

Moryndra tilted her head. "And if he doesn't?"

"Then he'll be dealt with."

For a time, silence reigned, then Camadaea said, "I don't like this business with Morraine."

"Nor do I," Azariah admitted, "but spanning vyrda is taxing. I don't doubt Llorn was telling the truth when he said the other druins weren't up to the task. And the spanning is absolutely necessary to bridge the crucible and the palisade. We may as well stop now if we can't be assured it will happen."

"But Morraine is powerful. She's a wildcard."

"As is Llorn. We'll manage both."

Camadaea paused, then motioned to the others. "The others and I have spoken. We wish to speak with Llorn."

"Certainly. Tell me what you wish to know—"

"No. We will speak to him directly, that we can better judge him."

"Absolutely not," Azariah said. "Llorn made clear from the start he will only talk with me." In truth, Llorn would only talk with the *Hissing Man*, but admitting so would only raise more questions.

"Circumstances change," Camadaea said. "Llorn needs to change with them, as do you."

"I'm telling you, Llorn will refuse. Worse, he'll grow suspicious."

"We will speak to him—" Camadaea suddenly convulsed and cried out in pain. "Forgive me, My Lord! Please, forgive me!" Her body contorted and she shook for several long second, but then her spasmodic movements slowed. Her lips quavering, she pulled herself upright and faced Azariah. She licked spittle from her lips and said, "If you say Llorn will speak only to you"—she bowed her head to him—"then so be it. Tell us how we can help."

"Allow me to think on it. We must step carefully."

Camadaea seemed to breathe easier, and she stood straighter. "As you say."

They bowed to one another, then Ignatius glanced toward the Holt and faded. Bahrian, his jaw jutting, vanished right after. Moryndra fixed her sightless eyes on Azariah, then she too faded and was gone.

Only Camadaea lingered. "You'll forgive me, I hope. I only wish to see him freed, as you do."

"You're forgiven, of course." And Azariah meant it. He believed she and the others were earnest in their desire to see Faedryn freed. In truth, the person he was *least* confident in was himself. His desire to learn the truth about his son, his questioning of Faedryn and his purpose, could very well lead to his Lord deciding he was no longer worth it and removing *him* from the picture.

Camadaea faded and was gone.

Alone in the vyrd, Azariah turned toward the Holt. For a brief moment, he saw Cassian, six years old, leap onto his bed in the temple. "I want a story." His curly blond hair fell across his eyes as he slipped beneath the blankets. "Tell me of the Hissing Man."

Azariah had shared a story of the Hissing Man some months earlier. The stories were parables, told to make children obey the word of Alra. Azariah had never expected Cassian to enjoy them, but he'd asked for more of them in the weeks that followed. "What shall it be, then?" Azariah brushed a lock of Cassian's hair aside. "The Hissing Man and the Hummingbird? The Hissing Man and the Golden Lamp?"

"The Hissing Man at the Bottom of the Sea."

He pulled up a chair and sat beside Cassian's bed. "Very well," Azariah said in a long hiss, "The Hissing Man at the Bottom of the Sea."

Why the vision had come on so suddenly, and why then, Azariah didn't know, but he blinked it away and felt Faedryn's presence again. "Be at rest, My Lord," Azariah said. "Your liberation is near."

Then he turned and left the vyrd.

THIRTY: LORELEI

Lorelei tugged on Bothymus's reins and guided him toward the circle of standing stones below. The mountain wind was chilly, the darkened sky practically cloudless. Reckoning was near, the vyrd, the hill it stood upon, and the ordered landscape of Ancris still bathed in violet light, but the sky was brightening in the east.

After their interrogation of Brother Mayhew, Creed had mentioned a barrow mound near Glaeyand. Dozens of leaders of the resistance during the Talon Wars were buried under it, and the Red Knives had been known to use it for important gatherings. Lorelei and Creed were headed to Glaeyand along with Praefectus Damika to request permission to check it out.

Bothymus landed in the center of the vyrd with broad sweeps of his wings. As he settled himself, Creed stepped between two of the standing stones. "You sure we need that great bloody lizard along?"

"No"—Lorelei slipped down along Bothymus's lowered shoulder and landed on the stones with a *clomp*—"but that's precisely why I'm bringing him. I'd rather have him in Glaeyand's eyrie doing nothing but munching on ferrets than regret leaving him here."

Lorelei wore loose-fitting, homespun clothes commonly found in the Holt. Creed was dressed similarly in huntsman's garb, a tricorn hat, and a bow and quiver strapped across his back. The only thing that gave him away was his beard. It was too neatly trimmed. As were his eyebrows. Anyone looking closely would peg him as having come from one of the capitals.

Lorelei gripped the crop and guided Bothymus to one side of the vyrd, and Creed joined her. With reckoning near, people had begun to gather beyond the stones, waiting to pass to another vyrd. Some seemed excited, others bored. Lorelei's stomach, meanwhile, was already beginning to sour. "Bloody hell, I hate this part."

"Beats riding a dragon," Creed said.

"You know, I'd be sad if I were wrong as often as you are." She pointed to the menhirs around them. "The maze makes you feel like you're being torn apart and rebuilt, but it's not really *you* who arrives on the other end, is it? It's someone who just *looks* like you."

"So dramatic. A flash of vertigo, a whistle"—he snapped his fingers—"and you're there."

Lorelei rolled her eyes. "Riding on the back of a dragon is freeing. You never think about the views?"

"What"—he pointed to Bothymus—"like the ground rushing up at you after he throws you?"

"Bothymus would never do that, would you boy?"

Bothymus gurgled and gave the barbs along the back of his neck a good long rattle. Creed, his burly arms crossed, chuckled, but then he turned pensive. "Look, that stuff that Brother Mayhew gave up the other day."

"Yeah?"

"Did it feel too easy to you?"

"*Easy?*" Lorelei gawped at him. "You saw him. He was terrified."

"Terrified men can still lie. It felt like something he *wanted* to give up, especially that cock-and-bull story about the powder in the mine being some kind of euphoric."

"Yeah, that one stank like one of Ordren's farts, but we have to start somewhere."

"Creed!," called a deep feminine voice from behind them, "Lorelei!"

It was Praefectus Damika, wearing her swallowtail coat and a tall, wide-brimmed hat. She was halfway up the hill, sipping from a mug as she walked. The brass badge pinned to her coat glowed in the light of pre-reckoning. When she arrived, slightly winded, she handed Lorelei a piece of paper. "This came last night."

It was the results of Galla's autopsy on Tomas's corpse. Halfway down the page, Lorelei paused in her reading. Galla, like all examiners, had alchemycal agents that could test blood for aura or umbra. Given Tomas's bloodshot eyes and the way he'd been acting, Lorelei was certain he'd taken something or been drugged, but . . . "She found no traces of aura *or* umbra in his blood?"

Damika took one last swallow from her mug, tipped the remains of her tea onto the space between two stones, and strapped the mug by its handle to a loop on her belt. "Apparently not." She pointed to the bottom of the report. "See there, though?"

The conclusion read, *Likely proximate cause of death was drowning. However, as noted above, evidence is consistent with cobalt dragon compulsion, which was likely a contributing factor.*

"Galla thinks Fraoch used her breath to subdue Tomas," Damika said.

"It would make some sense," Creed said, peering over Lorelei's shoulder. "Llorn would've wanted Tomas quiet and docile."

Lorelei handed the autopsy report back to Damika. "I don't deny a compulsion might have contributed to Tomas's death, but that wouldn't explain his behavior at the Tulip." The breath of cobalts caused confusion initially, which allowed the dragon who'd exhaled it to lull and control its prey, but it didn't allow for nuance of any sort.

Damika folded the autopsy and stuffed it inside her coat. "When we reach Glaeyand, let me do the talking. Imperator Lyndenfell is particular about interruptions, so speak only when I invite you to, or Lyndenfell does."

"Yes, Praefectus," Lorelei and Creed said in unison.

A small crowd, including four ferrymen, entered the vyrd from the opposite side. The tallest among them was a blue-robed fellow with a narrow jaw, arching eyebrows and, like all seasoned ferrymen, ivory eyes. "In your groups!" he bellowed. "Huddle close. Reckoning's almost upon us!"

As the crowd broke into four groups, each with a ferryman, a flash of goldenrod streaked across the sky. Then the sky came alive with yellows, oranges, and rusty reds.

The tall ferryman, the one assigned to Lorelei's group, opened his leather bag and took out a lucerta, harvested from an indurium—perhaps Bothymus himself. In the light of the reckoning, the scale scintillated a silvery blue. "May Alra's light guide us," he said, then placed the scale on his tongue.

Lorelei was so tense she could hardly move. She felt a tug at her navel, then a high-pitched whistle sounded. Unlike the previous times she'd traveled through the maze, she didn't feel as if she were being torn apart. She felt as if she were caught in a bramble, and that its branches were growing, wrapping around her limbs, chest, and neck, slowly choking the breath from her.

She coughed, blinked, and found herself in another vyrd entirely. The stones were shorter, darker, and weather worn. The air was slightly warmer and more humid. She was surrounded forest full of towering trees that all but occluded the splashes of pale orange in the sky overhead.

"Lorelei?" Creed called out.

She wanted to answer him, but she couldn't shake the feeling of slowly being suffocated. When Bothymus trumpeted, she shivered and looked around. Six ferrymen and nearly thirty travelers were staring at her.

Lorelei shook her head. "Sorry," she said softly, "I'm back."

Creed leaned close and put a hand on her back. "You sure?"

"It was just worse than normal."

"Okay, but—"

"I'm *fine*, Creed."

"Welcome," a voice called from beyond the stones. It was Willow Lyndenfell, the imperator's daughter. She was lithe and pretty, and wore a saffron cloak with its hood pulled up.

Her words seemed to wake everyone up. The ferrymen strode from the vyrd, and their groups of passengers followed. Each person nodded to Willow as they passed her on the flagstone path. While some went to a citadel tree with a winding set of stairs, others continued on toward Tallow, but no one approached the dragonbone lift, which Lorelei realized had been reserved for Willow and her guests.

"Come," Damika said. "We have an appointment to keep."

Creed and Lorelei followed Damika from the vyrd. In a small blessing, the feeling like the breath was being squeezed from her faded and vanished altogether as she passed beyond the standing stones.

"My father bids you welcome," Willow said. "He received your dove and is pleased to meet you in Valdavyn." She turned to Lorelei. "You can send Bothymus up to the eyrie or ride him there yourself, as you wish."

Lorelei wanted to ride Bothymus, but she shook her head. She didn't want to miss what was said on the way up to the imperial residence. She squeezed the crop, urging Bothymus to fly to the eyrie. "I'll join you."

She felt something like indignation from Bothymus, like he'd been hoping to stretch his wings. He bellowed—silencing the birdsong in the trees—and flew into the air, a silhouette in the dawn light, and was lost beyond the leafy canopy.

Willow led them into the dragonbone lift, closed the door behind them.

"The news of Aarik's burning is sending waves through the Holt," Willow said as the lift began to rise.

"I should hope so," Damika said. "It will give the Red Knives pause, no?"

"It will incite them, I'm afraid."

They passed the other travelers, hiking up the corkscrew stairs.

"Are you saying Aarik shouldn't have been killed?" Damika asked.

"I'm saying there are realities we in the Holt face that Ancris does not."

"Such as?"

"Let me propose an arrangement," Willow said. "*I'll* stop pretending that Aarik's death isn't, on the whole, the very end a ruthless enemy like him deserves if *you'll* stop pretending it isn't Glaeyand or Andalingr or Hrindegaard that will pay the price."

Damika frowned. "The price must be borne, whatever it is. Aarik's crimes needed to be punished. A message needs to be sent to Llorn or anyone else who crown themselves King of the Holt that they too will be hunted."

"Hear me, Praefectus. Aarik Bloodhaven deserved what he got. But the Holt must be vigilant. A trade caravan traveling west along the Salt Road was raided. Llorn led it. Several merchants and their company were killed, their throats slit, their bodies hung along the route as a warning to all who would think to steal the treasures of the Holt and deliver them to the empire." Willow paused, allowing the words to sink in. "What I'm saying is this . . . We could have been given a proper warning about Aarik's sentence. We could have used more time to prepare."

Damika looked like she was going to argue, but instead she said, "Your point isn't lost on me. But you must know that the Church forced us to hand Aarik over to them. We only learned he was being taken to the Anvil hours beforehand."

Willow sighed. "I understand you were unable to send us a warning, but anything you can do in the future to forewarn us would be appreciated." After that, she moved on to lighter subjects—news from Ancris, the quintarch's health, and the like.

They reached a platform and entered a second lift, which bore them up to Glaeyand proper. Wooden walkways, wide platforms, and viewing decks were spread all about. Bridgeboughs, fitted with planks and railings formed walkways from one citadel to another. More bridges were supported by elegantly curved cables and rope, and countless ringwalks wrapped around the citadel trunks, leading to burrows and shops. In the places with heavy foot traffic, broad nets were hung as a safety measure.

The lift thudded to a stop in Glaeyand's upper reaches. Willow led them to the entry deck to Valdavyn, the imperial residence, an expansive home with several wings that snaked between and through the trees. She nodded to the armored sentries and led them inside, past a man in his mid-twenties with honey skin and dark, curly hair pulled into a tail. He was strikingly handsome, due in no small part to his gold-flecked green eyes. He stepped to the side, and Willow swept past him with hardly a glance.

He nodded to Lorelei and Creed as they passed. "Welcome to Valdavyn."

Lorelei nodded back, feeling her cheeks flush. He seemed overly familiar. Normally, she would have felt put off by it, but she found herself wondering about him. Creed eyed her with a broad grin and she slapped his arm.

"Shush."

Damika glared at them.

"Pardon me," Creed asked as they rounded a corner, "but who was that man?"

"Rylan Holbrooke," Willow said over her shoulder. "Just ignore him."

Lorelei recalled the name. He was Willow's half-brother, an illegitimate child, if she remembered right. His dark skin meant he had the blood of the Kin running through his veins. How he had ended up in Valdavyn with the imperator's legitimate children, she had no idea.

When they reached the audience chamber, Marstan Lyndenfell was sitting on his wooden throne. He looked like a king of old, complete with pepper gray hair, full mustache and beard, and a gold circlet with a jade spread-winged roc. He and Willow had similar, fair features. All but their eyes, Lorelei noted. Willow's were dark brown; Marstan's were the same striking green as the bastard's.

Willow walked to Marstan's side and spoke into his ear. When she was done, Marstan spread his arms and smiled at them like a wolf baring its teeth. "The Holt welcomes you."

Damika told him first about their purpose in Glaeyand. She told him of the tip they'd receive from Tomas, the meeting in the mine and the chase that followed, and Tomas's death. Lastly, she touched on the council of Knives that Llorn had mentioned and their guesses as to where it might be held. Damika said nothing of Aarik's request to speak to him or the bribes Brother Mayhew had mentioned— that was a conversation that could only be had when she and the imperator were alone.

Marstan remained largely silent, interrupting only to ask pointed, clarifying questions. When it was done, he shifted in his chair. "Let me understand you. Llorn Bloodhaven, a man who'd like nothing more than to set fire to Glaeyand and watch it burn, mentioned that a council of Knives would soon take place. Brother Mayhew, a confessed agent of our enemy, told you under threat of being handed over to the Church and consumed by a bloody dragon that it *might* be held near Glaeyand. And you believe it will be used to discuss the succession of the Red Knives."

"That's correct," Damika said. "We don't know why they are meeting, but with Aarik's death, Llorn will likely use it to exert his authority."

Marstan smiled. "The evidence seems thin, Praefectus."

Damika nodded deferentially. "What we have are leads. We're requesting permission to pursue them."

"My daughter tells me she informed you of the somewhat precarious position we find ourselves in."

Lorelei understood that to mean *Marstan's* position was precarious, what with the coming council vote. Damika surely understood that as well as Lorelei, but, ever the politician, she nodded and said, "If you're concerned about the effect our investigation may have—"

"I'm concerned about inquisitors from Ancris barging in and stepping on toes. I'm concerned about the safety of Glaeyand, the Holt, and even the empire."

"Inquisitors Lorelei and Creed are more than capable—"

"I'm sure they are, but they would be operating in an environment they have little understanding of."

"I trust my inquisitors, Imperator. I beg your permission—"

Marstan leaned forward in his chair. "Your request is denied."

THIRTY-ONE: LORELEI

Damika's jaw dropped. "*Denied?*"

"Denied." Marstan leaned back and crossed his arms. "But fear not. My constables will look into the matter."

"Your constables don't know the first thing about this meeting."

"Which is why Inquisitors Creed and Lorelei will tell them what they need to know."

A pregnant pause followed. Then Damika asked, "How do you suppose Quintarch Lucran will feel when he learns you've interfered in an imperial investigation?"

"Interfered, is it?" Marstan smirked. "I'd watch my words if I were you, Praefectus. I'm merely giving the responsibility to people more capable of handling it."

Damika looked furious. She glanced at Lorelei and Creed. "You may go. The Imperator and I have more to discuss."

Willow accompanied them toward the doors. "I'll take them to the guest wing. You can collect them there when you're ready." She led them from the room and down a wide hall filled with idyllic paintings and bronze statues on plinths. "That went well, I thought." They passed under an archway with a guard posted beside it and entered a hallway of richly appointed rooms. Willow opened a set of double doors and entered a sitting room with two adjoining bedrooms. Beyond the sitting room was a set of glass doors that led to a small deck with a brilliant view of the Holt. "I'll have food brought," she said, and left.

Creed plopped onto a sofa and kicked his legs up on a wooden table in front of it. "Did you hear her? That went *well* . . ." He snorted. "It was like a kick in the mollusks."

Lorelei paced over the room's horsehair carpet. "I'll take your word for it."

He flung a hand toward the door. "A guard posted at the exit? Riptides take me, we're bloody prisoners."

Lorelei remained silent. What was there to say?

"Given to people more capable of handling it," Creed grumbled. "What a steaming pile of dragon shit." He stared at the small viewing deck. "It's like he's covering for them."

"What? For the Knives? He's the imperator . . ."

"So? Aarik suddenly wanted to speak to him. And Brother Mayhew said the corruption in Glaeyand went high up. You don't think he might've meant Marstan?"

"I thought you said Brother Mayhew was lying."

"Yes, well, now I'm not so certain."

"Either way, be careful what you say and how loudly you say it."

Creed huffed and tossed his head back on the sofa. "This is *our* investigation."

A constable in a dark uniform and tall hat arrived a short while later. He sat in the upholstered chair across the table from Creed, asked them a few questions, and took notes in a tiny journal, rubbing his hook nose as he did so. Lorelei gave him the broad brush strokes.

"And when is this meeting to take place?" he asked.

Lorelei rolled her eyes as dramatically as she knew how. "We're not sure, but likely soon. Llorn surely knows of Aarik's death by now. He'll want to establish himself as soon as possible. Wouldn't you agree?"

The constable took one final note and closed the journal. "You have our thanks." He stood up.

"Wait," Lorelei said, "are you going to go?"

"We'll look into it." And then he was gone.

"He's not going to do a thing, Creed."

"And you're surprised?"

"I'm furious!" She resumed her pacing. "How can they just ignore everything we've given them?"

Creed stared at the wall, looking pensive. Angry, but pensive. "We came too heavy," he said after a beat. "Either that or we came too light."

"What do you mean?"

He pointed to the door. "Damika was pretty reasonable in there but she came across as bossy. Plus, there was an audience. It should've been just her and Lyndenfell. Failing that, she should have come bearing a writ from Quintarch Lucran."

"Well, we didn't"—she collapsed into the upholstered chair—"and now we're fucked."

As Willow had promised, a smorgasbord of seeded crackers, soft cheeses, sliced pears, sapwater, and a carafe of golden syris were brought by a servant and set on the table after Creed took his feet off it.

Damika arrived as they were finishing up. She poured herself a healthy draught of syris into a glazed mug and downed half of it in one go.

Creed and Lorelei waited for her to speak. When she didn't, Creed said, "So?"

"Marstan wouldn't budge," she said, staring out a window.

"Do you think he's trying to bury this?"

"In truth, no. I don't envy the Imperator. He has an election coming up." Damika drummed the handle of the mug with the tips of her fingers.

Lorelei stared at her. "But . . ."

Damika finished her drink, set the mug on the table, and turned to face them. "What he fails to understand is that all of this"—she waved about the room—"is owed to the quintarchs. All his power, too, the constables he orders about, the dragons he commands."

Though not precisely true—the Holt was a principality, independent in theory—the quintarchs held incredible power over the Holt.

"What are you suggesting?" Lorelei asked.

For several long breaths, Damika said nothing. "I'm not suggesting anything,

Inquisitor." She walked to the doors and stopped. "This aging body of mine can't withstand two crossings in a single day anymore. I've arranged for us to stay the night. We return to Ancris in the morning." With that, she departed.

Lorelei had expected her to say something else entirely. The Praefectus had been considering defying Marstan's orders—Lorelei was certain of it—and had Lorelei pressed her, she might have done it.

"Lorelei, stop." Creed pushed the plates aside and put his feet up on the table again.

"Stop what?"

"You know very well *what*. We have orders."

"We're *here*, Creed. There's a meeting, quite possibly *tonight*, that could decide the fate of Ancris."

"I hate it when you do that."

"Do what?"

"Add dramatic flourishes for effect."

"It isn't drama. Something crooked is going on here. This isn't normal for the Knives. It isn't normal for the Chosen. They're planning something big, and the more time we waste faffing about, the deeper the danger becomes."

Creed clenched his teeth and hissed. "Fine. *I'll* go to the meeting."

Lorelei laughed. "You?"

"Why *not* me?"

"People have called you many things, Creed Vintario, but never *stealthy*."

Creed glowered at her. "Fine. *You* go, but you're going to need a diversion."

Like many important buildings in Glaeyand, the residence had nets below it in case someone, or even a piece of construction material, fell. Though it was forbidden, she'd heard children often jumped into the nets and ran from the constables in a game called Drop and Dash. But the balcony of their room faced an entry hall where guards were always posted and would certainly see her. However, she remembered seeing a servant's deck on the other side of the residence when she had visited years ago. While Creed busied the guard outside their door with some wyvern talk and led him to the window, Lorelei slipped past them and down the empty hallway to the servant's deck, which was also blessedly empty.

At the edge of the deck, she put on her tricorn hat, lowered the brim against the dark sun's rays, and slipped on her gloves. Then she peered over the edge, looking for a ladder.

"The stairs are easier, you know," called a voice from the darkness. "Or, better yet, the lift."

The cloud cover made the forest especially dark, and her eyes had yet to adjust to it after Valdavyn's lantern-lit hallways, but she blinked a few times and spotted Rylan, Marstan's bastard son, sitting at a small table with his back against the residence.

"I was starting to feel a bit cramped," she said lamely. She'd never been very good at lying.

Rylan put a pipe in his mouth, struck a match, and lit the tabbaq. "So I've heard."

"What do you mean?"

"You were the talk around the dinner table. Word has it you feel uncomfortable in cramped spaces."

Lorelei did her best to hide her surprised the rumors of her were floating around Valdavyn. "Actually, it's not to do with spaces at all, but the people. I feel uncomfortable in crowds."

"Tell me," Rylan said, pausing to draw from his pipe, "would remedying this feeling include a trip beyond the borders of Glaeyand?"

He knew, Lorelei realized. More rumors being spread over dinner, she reckoned. When she said nothing, he took several more puffs, then blew out a long stream of smoke, like a bronze dragon after a satisfying gorge. He pointed the pipe stem at the railing behind her. "The netting's a bit soft there. Were it me," he said, moving the pipe and pointing toward the far end of the deck, "I'd leap from there."

"Well, that's good to know. If I *were* looking to leave."

"Indeed." Rylan stood and opened the door, but paused on the threshold. "Good hunting, Inquisitor Lorelei." And then he was gone.

Lorelei nearly followed him back inside, thinking he might still report her, but there was nothing for it now. She'd likely get in as much trouble for trying to leave as she would for leaving. She went to the spot he'd indicated, took a deep breath, and leapt into the darkness. Her stomach rose into her throat. Suddenly, she thought the netting might be brittle with age, that it would give way when she hit it. But it didn't. She landed, bounced once, landed again, and climbed a rope ladder to a ringwalk.

She rushed down the corkscrew stairs, afraid she'd hear alarm bells any moment. When she was far below the city, she took out Bothymus's crop and wrapped it around her right hand. She was just about to call him—he could meet her below and fly her to the vale—but she paused. The Knives would likely have dragons of their own. If Bothymus alerted them, her mission would be doomed. She took the stone off, put it back in her belt purse, and continued to the ground.

She skirted Tallow but made sure to keep its lanterns in sight and eventually came to the old deer path Creed had told her about. It would likely be watched, though, so she trekked beside the nearby stream, parallel to the path. She crept deeper into the forest, listening for anything beyond the wind through the trees, the burbling brook, the whining insects.

The canopy had made itself small for the night. The clouds overhead thinned, enough that she could see Nox staring down like a bloodshot eye. As she hiked down a gentle slope, she heard distant voices. She came to the edge of the vale and saw a large, bowl-shaped depression. Near the center of it, some forty yards from Lorelei's position, the stream diverted around a massive, grassy barrow. Several hundred men and woman were gathered around it. All were armed and watching the group gathered at the top. To the right of the barrow, beyond the stream, were two saddled dragons: a cobalt and a viridian. The cobalt snapped its jaws, and the viridian screeched and swept its wings in retreat.

At the barrow's summit, torches on tall stakes were set in a circle; a dozen men and women stood in the flickering light. Llorn was easy to recognize with his long black hair and sun-marked skin. Standing behind him were his captains: Blythe, her curly black hair unbound, and Raef, red hair braided in rows and a stump where his left hand had once been. Next to them stood a burly, black-haired Knife. Even as far as she was, Lorelei could see the similarities to Brother Mayhew. A twin, maybe? Around them were seven druins with shaved heads, runic tattoos, and tall staves with eagle talons or dragon horns or crystals on top.

Llorn stood near a stone sarcophagus. Whose sarcophagus it might be, and why it had been brought to this place, Lorelei had no idea, but knowing what she knew about druins, she decided it couldn't be good.

THIRTY-TWO: LORELEI

Lorelei listened as Llorn spoke in a booming voice from the barrow mound. "We come together to mourn the loss of my brother, Aarik, King of the Wood, who was burned by the empire . . ."

A rumble arose from the gathered Knives. Beyond the stream, the cobalt dragon, Fraoch, rose and beat her bright blue wings.

"My brother was taken by the inquisitors in Ancris," Llorn went on, "and delivered to the Church, to Illustra Azariah, himself, who tortured him for days."

The rumble grew louder, drowning out the whine of insects.

"They brought him to the Anvil in chains and read lies from their scrolls. They summoned a bronze and bathed him in flames."

The crowd grew began to raise their fists and roar so loud Lorelei wondered if it could be heard in Tallow.

"That the empire burned him isn't surprising. They hope to prevent us from storming Glaeyand and taking it as our own. They hope to *cow* us. But I ask you here and now, brothers and sisters, are you deterred?"

The crowd shouted, "Nay!"

"Are you cowed?"

"Nay!"

Llorn unsheathed a dagger and raised it over his head. Every man and woman in the crowd drew their own knives, raised them into the air. Torchlight reflect off the many blades, turning them into a crown of glittering gold.

"Your blades are clean, I see, their edges honed, as they should be. But we do not kill without cause, as the empire does. We draw blood for a purpose, to make the empire see that, though they tug on the imperator's strings from their halls of stone and treat the Holt like some simple plaything, the Holt is *ours*. The empire is a beast, blinded by hunger and greed, and beasts only learn when they feel pain. Is it not so?"

The crowd lowered their knives and then thrust them into the air with a collective roar.

"*That* is the purpose of the blood we draw. *That* is why we stain our knives red. We will show the empire that we are tireless—"

The Knives thrust and roared again.

"—that we are indomitable—"

Another roar as torchlight glinted against honed steel.

"—and that, in the end, we will drive them back, over the mountains whence they came, or kill them where they stand."

The Knives hollered so loud Lorelei felt it in her bones. She began to wish she hadn't left Creed behind.

Llorn sheathed his knife, the Knives did the same, and at last the roaring died down. "Alas, my brother didn't live to see us drive the empire from these woods, but I pray *you* will. Aarik and I had long been making preparations to do just that. The first of them is at hand."

The seven druins climbed to the top of the barrow mound and surrounded the sarcophagus. A girl of thirteen or fourteen winters with braided, nutmeg hair trailed behind them. She wore the robe of a druin aspirant and cradled a wisplight in both hands. She seemed to tarry on her way up the mound, and a druiness yanked Rhiannon into place so that she and the druins surrounded the sarcophagus like points on a compass rose.

Llorn gestured to the girl. "My niece, Rhiannon, joins us."

The girl, Rhiannon, glanced up at him, then returned her focus to the wisplight, which glowed brighter than any wisp Lorelei had ever seen. The druiness beside Rhiannon opened a ring, took a pinch of powder, and held it to her nose. She gave some to Rhiannon as well. The other druins opened either a ring or a pendant and prepared themselves in similar ways. Lorelei was no expert on the use of magic, but it didn't take an expert know that a spell requiring seven druins and an aspirant was a powerful spell indeed.

"I've told you little of the meeting where Aarik was taken," Llorn called, "but I share with you now more of what I can. What summoned us to Ancris was a meeting with none other than the Hissing Man, the leader of the Chosen."

The crowd grumbled and a general murmur ensued.

"The Hissing Man thinks us simple folk who are easily duped," Llorn continued. "He intends to use us. He's unaware of the knowledge our forbears handed down to us." He waved to the sarcophagus. "He doesn't understand the power it confers."

The druins closed their eyes and began to chant, a low thrum that rose and fell in pitch. Even as far away as she was, Lorelei's skin itched from it. Rhiannon wasn't chanting, and her eyes were open. She was shaking, Lorelei realized, though whether it was due to fear, excitement, or the power running through her, she had no idea.

"One day, the Holt will be ours again," Llorn projected over the chanting. "I promise you, that day is closer than the quintarchs think. It begins here, now, with the return of my sister, Morraine Bloodhaven."

The druins' chanting grew louder, and Lorelei felt as if an infection had been born inside her and that it was spreading. Rhiannon, still shaking, stepped forward, raised the wisplight over her head, and smashed it on the stone lid of the sarcophagus.

The glass shattered in a burst of azure, and the wisp floated in the air. As the wisp lowered toward the lid, the girl, Rhiannon, cried out, "No!" and lunged for it. Before she could reach it, the druiness grabbed a fistful of Rhiannon's hair and yanked her away, and the wisp disappeared through the stone lid.

Rhiannon elbowed the druiness and broke free. She hurtled down the far side of the barrow mound. Llorn watched her go, then returned his attention to the ritual.

The lid of the sarcophagus shifted. No one moved or spoke. Then a desiccated hand rose from the stone box, and the crowd gasped. The hand gripped the lid and thrust it aside. The druins jumped back as it thudded onto the grass. A woman wearing a white shroud rose from the sarcophagus.

Lorelei's skin went cold. "Alra preserve us."

The draugr Morraine had wispy black hair. Her flesh was drawn tight around her face. Black bruises discolored her neck from the hanging. She stared at the druins, eyes bulging, then at Llorn, Blythe, and Raef, then at the dragons and the gathering of Red Knives. Then, slowly, her gaze drifted toward the tree line where Lorelei was crouched. Morraine raised a skeletal hand and pointed at Lorelei. Llorn peered in that direction. Lorelei crept backward.

When the crowd turned to gaze where Morraine was pointing, Lorelei turned and ran. Her footfalls thudded on the soft, leafy ground. She heard shouting, orders being called. She rounded a citadel, stopped, and peered around it. Red Knives were heading for the forest. She bolted. Fraoch, the massive cobalt, shrieked behind her; she heard the *whump* of her wings.

She leapt over an ironbark and raced between the trees, took out Bothymus's crop and wrapped it around her right hand. She squeezed it tight. "Please, Bothymus, I need you!"

The eyrie was far away, though. She wondered if he could even hear her. Fraoch roared over the thudding feet behind her. She sprinted. Her legs were burning. Fraoch swooped down on the far side of a citadel in front of her.

Lorelei dove behind a boulder near the brook. She felt Bothymus stirring. "To me, Bothymus," she whispered, "to me!" She couldn't tell if it worked or not.

Fraoch landed beyond the brook, and her strained bond with Bothymus vanished.

Llorn sat in Fraoch's saddle. He whistled a low note; Fraoch spread her wings and snaked her head forward and sprayed a stream of gas at Lorelei. Lorelei stumbled back and was caught in the cloud. The dragon's moist breath smelled of myrrh and mold. Lorelei felt an urge to slow down . . . and laugh. She found herself stopping and turning to face Fraoch. The massive dragon crawled toward her, crushing the undergrowth beneath her giant claws.

Lorelei drew her rapier; then wondered why. Staring into Fraoch's eyes, she felt connected to the beast—*she* was the one bound by a fetter, and Fraoch her master.

Llorn jumped down from the saddle and approached her. "Your name."

"Lorelei Aurelius."

"Who sent you? Who knows you're here?"

Lorelei didn't even consider lying. "Only Damika and Creed. Well, them and Rylan."

Llorn paused. "Rylan *Holbrooke?*"

Lorelei nodded. She wasn't sure why he was telling him anything except for the lingering scent of myrrh in her nostrils. "He saw me as I was leaving."

Llorn looked like he was going to say something more, but a bright light shone from Lorelei's left, and he stopped. She looked up and saw Bothymus descending toward Fraoch, his wings spread wide and shimmering hypnotically. As Bothymus approached, a pain sprung up in Lorelei's forehead and grew the closer Bothymus came. She grabbed her head, doubled over, and screamed.

Bothymus fell on Fraoch and snapped at Fraoch's neck, but Fraoch whipped her neck around and threw Bothymus off.

Lorelei staggered away, her head still pounding. She looked around but couldn't see where Llorn had gone. Fraoch's hold on her seemed to be weakening. She realized she was still holding the crop. She squeezed it and called on Bothymus. *We have to get out of here!*

Bothymus raised his head and looked at her. In that same moment, the cobalt spun and whipped her tail, sending a small cloud of barbs through the air. Three sunk deep into Bothymus shoulder. Bothymus roared and beat his wings, lifting himself away from Fraoch. He rumbled toward Lorelei, ducked his head, and scooped Lorelei onto his neck. He wasn't saddled, so Lorelei did the best she could. She grabbed onto the spines along his neck and shuffled backward, straddling his shoulders. Bothymus lifted into the air and flew toward the canopy.

THIRTY-THREE: RYLAN

R ylan was in his night shirt, reading in bed, when he heard a pounding on his door. "Rylan, you're needed at the eyrie!" Again, the knocking. "It's the indurium from Ancris, Bothymus!"

Rylan set the book on the bedside table, headed to his front door, and found the lift attendant, Mouse, holding a lantern on the deck outside. "What *about* Bothymus?"

"He was attacked."

Rylan frowned, if only to cover the surge of fear bubbling up inside him. "Attacked by what?"

"A cobalt. Please, just hurry."

"Okay, hang on." He rushed back to his bedroom to fetch his clothes, calling over his shoulder. "How bad is he?"

"His shoulder is wounded, and he won't let anyone near him. He's thrashing and roaring at everyone. Andros wants him put down, but the eyrie master wants you to try to calm him first."

Rylan threw off his night shirt and pulled on the clothes he'd been wearing earlier. He'd gone to Valdavyn to have dinner with Briar and Lyssa. They'd talked mostly about the new arrivals from Ancris: Praefectus Damika, Inquisitors Lorelei and Creed. Briar had told Rylan about Damika's request to allow Creed and Lorelei to investigate the Red Knives and Marstan's refusal to allow it.

Rylan was keen to learn more about Llorn's plans, especially after Aarik's death, so when he'd gone out for a smoke and Lorelei had shown up, he'd thought, maybe she'd do it for him. If she'd gotten hurt, or if Bothymus had been injured, the ease of her escape might be traced back to him.

His clothes changed, he rushed back through his burrow and out the door.

At the first ringwalk, Mouse went right and Rylan continued toward the eyrie. "I'll let Valdavyn know you've left!"

Rylan hurried up the coiled stairway. The forest was dark, but the main walkways were well lit by lanterns. By the time he arrived at the eyrie's staging deck, his lungs were burning. Bothymus was in one of the lower nests. The nests above and to either side of his were empty.

Jorrik stood on the walkway leading to Bothymus's nest, holding a bright orange gourd, the sort eyrie masters hollowed out to deliver medicines to ailing dragons. "Come now, Bothymus," Jorrik said, "you'd like a treat, wouldn't you? It'll settle you right down. I promise."

Bothymus snaked his head back and forth and snapped his jaws at nothing. He made high-pitched gurgling sounds. Near one shoulder joint were three puncture wounds. From each wound, a trail of dried blood ran down his glittering, silver-blue chest. A splatter of crimson stained his right wing, likely due to his flight back to the eyrie.

Jorrik took a step closer, holding out the gourd. Bothymus hissed and slammed his tail on the walkway in front the eyrie master, splintering the planks and railing. Jorrik stepped back and spotted Rylan. "Thank the goddess you're here." He shot a glance over his shoulder at Bothymus. "He came in an hour ago carrying one of the inquisitors from Ancris."

"Inquisitor Lorelei?"

Jorrik shrugged. "The pretty one with the red hair."

"Where is she? I need to talk to her."

"That'll be difficult. She told us she was attacked by a cobalt then fainted right here on the walk." Jorrik tilted his head toward his office. "She's lying on my couch. As for Bothymus, I managed to get some wolfsbane in him, and he let me remove the barbs, but then he got worse, the poison setting in, I suspect." He held up the gourd. "I was about to try black sage, so I can tend to the wounds, but he won't let me."

If Bothymus had failed to respond to wolfsbane, it meant he'd caught a good dose of the poison.

Something moved to Rylan's left. Quinn, one of the eyrie hands, was exiting the eyrie's lift rolling a barrow with a goat carcass in it. Judging from the pool of blood in the barrow and the pink traces of blood on his hands, Quinn had killed the beast himself only moments ago.

"I was hoping fresh meat would help calm him," Jorrik said "but I'm starting to think it's too late."

"Give me some time alone with him. Quinn?" He snapped his fingers and pointed to the dead goat. "Douse the meat in the valerian decoction. Quickly, now." He headed for Bothymus's nest. "Jorrik, make sure no other dragons come near us, and don't let anyone near Bothymus until I'm done. That includes Andros, understand me?"

Jorrik hesitated but then nodded. Rylan headed toward Bothymus, stopped at the shattered walkway, and stood as close to the dragon he dared. Bothymus raised his tail and stared down at Rylan, but Rylan pushed the worry from the dragon's mind. He raised his right hand, hid his left behind his back, and stared into Bothymus's moonstone eyes. Then he took a deep breath and began to sing.

He sang of peace and comfort, but after several verses, it hardly seemed to be doing any good. Bothymus's thoughts were too chaotic to link to. He was confused, his thoughts moving from place to place. Bothymus shared glimpses of flying over a city, of traveling through the maze, of nesting in an eyrie of stone and wood. Rylan saw the lash of a blue tail, felt bright pain and cringed, but the memory was gone in a moment, replaced by a vision of seven induria, perched on a high cliff. Then he saw a mid-air battle with a fearsome, golden-feathered roc.

Reckoning it was the only way to calm Bothymus, Rylan let the dragon's thoughts lead him. He was a beast in chains, the ever-present fetter in his bridle keeping him in line. He was an inquisitor's mount, flying over white-capped mountains, over green, rolling foothills, over a vast endless forest. Rylan felt helpless, lost in the spell of madness. Over and over, he fought to regain himself, only to be drawn back into the storm of Bothymus's wild, chaotic thoughts.

Then a red-haired woman squeezing his crop, pleading for rescue, flashed across their link. Bothymus sped between the citadels. The woman was being attacked by a cobalt, its wings spread, its tail quivering and ready to strike. He engaged the shimmering cobalt, caught a volley of poisoned barbs in his shoulder, broke from the battle, sped toward the red-haired woman. It was Lorelei, the inquisitor, whom he'd helped sneak away from Valdavyn, which reminded him of who *he* was.

He altered his song. Lorelei's story became a rock in the raging river. He clung to it, anchored himself and Bothymus. He continued, slowing the song's pace, and Bothymus's wild thoughts slowed with it, enough for Rylan to urge him to lie in his nest, to rest. Rylan coaxed him to think about his hunger, and the big indurium began to focus on his empty stomach instead of his wounded shoulder.

"Now, Quinn," Rylan said.

Quinn didn't answer. Andros did. "Step away, Rylan."

He turned to see Andros aiming a crossbow at Bothymus. The bolt's steel broadhead was coated in black coryza.

Rylan raised his hands and stepped toward Andros. "Put it down, Andros. Please."

"It's been stung by a *cobalt*, Rylan." Andros glanced up at the higher nests, where the eyrie's other dragons were clustered. "If you think I'm going to wait for it to go mad and start attacking other dragons—if you think I'm going to jeopardize Magnor's safety—you're mad."

"He's *calm* now." Rylan stepped closer to Andros, stealing a glance at the goat in the wheelbarrow. "We'll get him to sleep. I have a salve that will help him overcome the poison."

"How do you know it will work?"

"It will work. And even if it doesn't"—Rylan pointed to the crossbow—"we'll still have that option."

Rylan felt himself tense, which was making Bothymus nervous. The indurium snapped his jaws at the air with a loud clack and trumpeted so loud Rylan had to cover his ears.

Andros stepped right to aim his crossbow around Rylan, but Rylan stepped back in front of it.

"Get out of the way, Rylan." Andros bared his teeth, just like he used to when they were younger and Rylan defied him.

Rylan was certain Andros was about to pull the trigger, but a woman's voice called out from the citadel to his left.

"Are you aware who owns that dragon?"

Rylan and Andros both turned to find Lorelei standing in the doorway to the eyrie master's burrow.

Andros continued pointing his bolt at Rylan. "It's the inquisitors'," he said.

"A common misconception." Lorelei approached them on the walkway. "Bothymus is the personal mount of Skylar Solvina. You may have heard of her. She's the daughter of Quintarch Lucran."

Andros's eyes narrowed. "*You* brought him to the Holt. You've flown him here a dozen times."

"Skylar allows me to fly him." Lorelei stepped across the broad deck and stopped a few paces from Andros. "How do you suppose Quintarch Lucran will react when he learns you put down his daughter's dragon"—she waved toward Rylan—"without even giving your own dragon singer a chance to heal him?"

"You weren't even supposed to be out. My father forbade you from entering the Holt."

"Be that as it may."

"Alra's bright light," Andros whined, "he was poisoned by a *cobalt*."

"And he may need to be put down, but we will try to save him first." Lorelei stepped up next Rylan in Andros's line of fire. "Now put that weapon down and let Rylan do his work."

Andros stared at Bothymus. He shook his head, and the fire in his eyes dimmed. "I won't be far," he said, then turned and stormed away.

THIRTY-FOUR: RYLAN

Rylan moved quickly. He strengthened his link with Bothymus and convinced him to eat the goat. The valerian took some time to do its work, but soon enough, Bothymus stilled and his eyelids grew heavy. When he lay his head down and fell asleep, Rylan applied a thick salve to his wound to help fight the poison. Then he applied a compress treated with an unguent that helped fight infection. Jorrik, Quinn, and Lorelei assisted him in wrapping a bandage around the base of his wing. They'd keep him under sedation over the next day to prevent him from removing it, and by then they'd know if he was getting better.

Throughout, Lorelei seemed beside herself with worry. At first, Rylan thought it was because her foray into the forest had blown up in her face, but way she kept pacing and staring at Bothymus convinced him she cared deeply for the big indurium.

"We should let him rest," Rylan said to her when he was satisfied they'd done all they could. He motioned to the crop stone, still wrapped around Lorelei's right hand. "If you don't mind, please take that off. The quieter his mind is, the better."

Lorelei stared down at it and shook her head. "Yes. I had forgotten about it." She unwrapped the stone and put it in a leather pouch at her belt. "Sorry."

Jorrik and Quinn left to tend to the other dragons, several of which were still riled by Bothymus's tirade. Rylan, meanwhile, gestured Lorelei toward the eyrie master's burrow. "Can we talk?"

"Of course."

They went inside and sat at a small table near Jorrik's desk, which was laden with towers of papers that looked ready to topple should either of them breathe too hard. The rest of the room was cozy, mostly due to Jorrik's wife, who was a particularly good decorator.

"I don't mean to pry," Rylan began, "but I tied my fortune to yours when I let you leave the residence."

Lorelei picked at the edge of the wooden table with her thumbnail. "No one else saw me."

"You don't know that. My father is a thorough man. He'll have the entire household questioned. It's entirely possible someone saw you drop from the deck, and everyone knows I like to smoke there after a meal." When she said nothing, Rylan pressed. "You came to spy on a meeting of the Red Knives you learned about in Ancris. I take it you found it?"

She dug into a crack in the tabletop and scraped at the bare wood. "Does your

hatred of your father extend so far that you'd let an inquisitor he'd expressly forbidden from leaving his residence to pass? Or was it his seat you were trying to
embarrass, and through it, the empire?"

Rylan was taken aback. She hadn't hit the mark, but she wasn't far from it,
either. "I don't *hate* my father."

"Then why did you let me go?"

He could hardly tell her that he hoped she'd find out what was happening with
the Knives since Aarik's death. Feigning amusement, he said, "You're acting like
you wish I'd stopped you."

The trill of a young brass came through the small window behind Jorrik's
desk, and Lorelei looked toward it. "Yes, I found the meeting. It was at the barrow
mound beyond Tallow. Llorn was there. I thought they'd gathered to anoint him,
but they were there for something entirely."

"And that was . . . ?"

"They raised Llorn's sister from the dead."

Rylan felt his jaw drop. "Morraine? You're sure?"

"Absolutely."

It was all he could do not to slap his own forehead as she described the details:
Llorn addressing the gathering; Rhiannon holding the wisplight; the druins chanting around the sarcophagus; Morraine, black marks around her neck, rising from
within. Rylan knew precisely where Llorn had gotten the wisplight, of course. It
was the one he'd stolen from the gallery in the Alevada estate. He vaguely recalled
Morraine's remains having been placed in the barrow mound after she'd been
sentenced and hung.

How foolish he'd been. He'd actually believed Llorn wanted the wisp because
the empire was treating it like a trinket. Llorn had played into Rylan's desire to see
the wrongs of the empire righted, which meant he knew about Rylan before he
came to Hollis's shop. *Llorn offered the bait and I swallowed it whole.*

He realized he'd lost track of what Lorelei was saying. "And then the cobalt
dropped in front of me," she was saying. "It breathed and caught me in its spell.
I'd be dead or captured by the Knives if Bothymus hadn't swooped in and
saved me."

"Did Llorn say what he mean to do with Morraine?"

"No, he—"

Someone knocked on the door. "Lorelei?"

"Be right there!" She stood. "My partner, no doubt here to give me a dressing
down." She smiled awkwardly. "Thank you for helping Bothymus. I won't forget it."

She turned and left, leaving the door open behind her. Waiting on the deck
beyond was her partner, Creed, the tall cuss with the pepper gray hair and the
impeccable beard. He stared at Rylan as if *he* were the cause of Lorelei's misfor-
tunes, then turned and followed her down the walkway.

Rylan remained in the eyrie while Bothymus slept. The other dragons were
naturally skittish, but over the next several hours, they settled somewhat. Andros

returned after reckoning with four of his fellow dracorae. All five wore a combination of brightsteel and overlapping dragonscale, carried steel-tipped lances, and had a crossbows slung against their backs. Andros strode toward his mount's perch on the far side of the eyrie without once looking at Rylan or Bothymus.

Jorrik, returned from calming an irritable brass fledgling, stopped on the walkway nearby, and jutted his chin toward Andros and the others. "He's a prize, that one, isn't he?"

Rylan grunted. "I take it they're off to hunt the cobalt?"

"They are, indeed."

They're more likely to catch a wisp in their bare hands, Rylan thought. The cobalt was long gone, as were the Knives and the druins. Andros and his Talon would find nothing.

Jorrik went about his business, leaving Rylan alone with Bothymus. The dragon's chest heaved with breath. The frill along the top of his head twitched every so often, likely from a dream.

Rylan was tired. He needed some sleep. But he couldn't shake the part he'd played in Llorn's plans, stealing the wisplight for him. Morraine was a very powerful druin. Llorn was stacking wood, piece by piece, and someday soon he would set it ablaze.

Aarik had wanted Rylan to check on Master Renato in Ancris. A voice inside his head told him to let it be, that he was only asking for trouble. But he couldn't let things rest. He wouldn't. He needed to get to Ancris, and to do *that*, he needed to convince his father to let him leave Valdavyn.

The answer came as he stared at Bothymus's bridle and its golden fetter. He left the eyrie, wended his way to Valdavyn, and requested to speak to his sister, Willow. It took some time, but soon enough, Willow came to the receiving deck. Beneath a stormy sky, the two of them strolled along the walkways of upper Glaeyand.

When Rylan had explained his proposal in full, Willow stopped walking. "Let me understand," she said as a stiff wind whined through the canopy overhead. "You want Father's leave to care for Bothymus in Ancris so that you can curry favor with Quintarch Lucran?"

"In our father's name, yes."

"You have no other reason to go."

"None."

"Then, why didn't you ask Father yourself?"

"Because he's annoyed with me. He wouldn't listen, and this is important. The election is five weeks away, and Father's seat is tenuous." They continued across a suspended bridge. After making sure they were alone, Rylan said, "It'll only get worse for him if news about the amendment leaks."

Willow glanced around as well. "You know about that?"

Rylan nodded. "And even if word doesn't leak, Father's denial of Praefectus Damika's request is going to look all the worse when Quintarch Lucran learns what Lorelei saw at the council of Knives."

A gaggle of children raced along a walkway a few trees over, the farthest behind pelting the others with pine cones.

As Willow watched them, Rylan continued. "We both know Father will probably win the vote of the patricians, but he still needs the quintarchs' vote of confidence. How can tending to the wounded dragon of a quintarch's daughter fail to do anything but help?"

"You've hardly showed an uncia of gratitude to Father for taking you in when your uncle died. How can you expect me to believe you care about his interests?"

"Because I care about the Holt, and I genuinely believe he had the Holt's best interests at heart when he struck that deal with Aarik."

Willow's brows pinched. She stared out over Glaeyand's expanse, then looked at Rylan again. "He might not agree."

"Just speak to him, please."

She strode away, erect, her long black hair tossing in the wind.

Rylan called after her. "Thank you, Willow. I owe you."

THIRTY-FIVE: LORELEI

L orelei and Creed sat in the dim anteroom, lit only by a pair of lanterns, next to the closed doors to Marstan Lyndenfell's audience chamber. It was just before the bright sun's rise. Lorelei's gut churned. Marstan Lyndenfell's voice boomed through the doors. He was chastising Damika for Lorelei's negligence, disregard, and sheer recklessness. He threatened to jail her until a magistrate could decide on a suitable punishment. When Damika pushed back, he threatened to have *her* brought up on charges as well. But Damika was a patient woman and nigh unflappable. Eventually the intensity of the discussion ebbed, and their voices lowered below what Lorelei could hear.

Creed sat on a long bench, legs out, arms crossed over his broad chest, and stared at the wood floor as if he were trying to bore a hole through it. "Llorn said the Chosen are trying to use the Red Knives?"

On the way back from the eyrie, she'd told him about the Knives' ritual. "You're worried about *that*?"

He shrugged and rolled his eyes toward the closed door. "Better than stewing about what's going on in there."

Maybe he was right, but she was afraid she'd lose her badge and could hardly think of anything else. "Llorn's exact words were that the *Hissing Man* was trying to use them," she finally said, "though I suppose it hardly makes a difference. For all intents and purposes, the Hissing Man *is* the Chosen."

"I still don't understand why the Hissing Man would ally himself with the Knives. Seems like he'd be the last man to do that."

"Not if he thinks the ends justify the means."

Creed scratched the gray stubble on his cheek. "Tell me again what Llorn said on the barrow mound?"

"He said the Holt will be theirs again, and that the day was much closer than the quintarchs thought. He said it began with the raising of his sister."

"Implies he's got something big planned. Any clue what it is?"

"No"—Lorelei thought back to her interrogation of the druin—"but Brother Mayhew must know something."

"Probably worth asking when we get back. Once we sort through—"

Damika burst into the anteroom. "Up. Both of you. We're leaving."

They followed her into the hallway, through Valdavyn's foyer and entrance to the broad deck outside. The pre-reckoning air was cool. A stiff wind rustled the canopy. The sky was bright in the east.

"I'm surprised we're leaving so soon," Lorelei said nervously as they followed Damika along a walkway.

"Yes, well, I didn't manage it without giving up a few concessions, did I?"

"What sort of concessions?"

"Your involvement in this investigation, to start with. You are both off the case."

"But this is *important*," Lorelei pleaded, realizing she was whining.

"I'm well aware." The suspended bridge they were crossing bowed slightly as they neared the midway point. "Marstan is, too, which is the only reason you were allowed to leave. He's sending the constable you spoke to yesterday to Ancris tonight, at which point—"

"Shouldn't we speak to him now?"

"Absolutely not. I want you out of here before Marstan changes his mind. When the constable comes, you'll debrief him, then both of you will leave the matter alone, and neither of you are to have any contact with the druin."

"Please don't tell me you're going to let Ordren question him again."

Damika turned her head and glared at Lorelei. "I bloody well am, Lorelei Aurelius. You're lucky you're not in chains."

"Praefectus, please—"

At the end of the bridge, they stepped onto a ringwalk around the citadel. Damika halted, spun about, and pointed a finger at Lorelei's chest. "You don't seem to realize the gravity of the situation, Inquisitor, so let me state it plainly—if Marstan even *thinks* you're still on the case—and make no mistake, he has eyes and ears in Ancris—he'll demand you both stand trial before his magistrates, and I daresay Lucran will grant the request. He'll demand that *I* be brought before a tribunal as well. Stay away. Do you understand me?"

"Yes, Praefectus." Lorelei knew she needed to give her time to cool off.

Damika stomped down a set corkscrew stairs. "You'll give Ordren whatever he needs," she called over her shoulder, "then it's back to your other cases."

"What about Bothymus?" asked Lorelei. "He can't leave until his shoulder heals."

"I've made arrangements."

Lorelei cringed at the thought of traveling through the vyrda again. "I can stay and ride him back once he's—"

"No," Damika said, waggling her hand over her shoulder. "We're going to Ancris. Now."

Lorelei hated leaving Bothymus alone nearly as much as she hated the maze, but Damika wouldn't be swayed. They continued down through the city to the forest floor via the dragonbone lifts. The vyrd lay just ahead, ancient and imposing, threatening in ways Lorelei couldn't even comprehend. A portly ferrywoman with bone-colored eyes awaited with a dozen travelers, ready to take the trip back to Ancris. Two other ferrymen were there as well with groups of their own, heading to other locales.

They huddled in the center of the vyrd. The lights of reckoning were muted.

Faint, cream-colored flashes across the sky. The ferrywoman placed the lucerta on her tongue. Lorelei prepared herself for a return of the suffocating feeling in the maze, but as the standing stones and the forest dimmed, she felt only the gut-twisting sensation of being ripped apart and pressed back together. Then the cityscape of Ancris and the mountains beyond it came into view, and she began to relax.

As the ferrywoman and the other travelers exited the vyrd, Lorelei spotted Ordren standing outside the henge. The light of dawn in the mountains, harsh after the dimness of the forest, deepened the sullen lines of his face. "A bit of bad news, I'm afraid."

"Well, spit it out," Damika snapped.

"It's Brother Mayhew."

Lorelei's heart began to sink.

"What about him?" Damika asked.

"He escaped last night."

Lorelei thought Damika would throw her hands in the air in a fit of anger. Instead, she was completely calm, except for a slight twitching of her left eye.

"How?" she whispered.

"We found crushed bore beetle casings in the corner of his cell."

Lorelei recalled the sour smell in Brother Mayhew's cell. She'd thought it was his body odor, but now realized it was the beetles. She cursed herself for an idiot.

"The alchemysts," Ordren continued, "think he lured them with some food, crushed them up, and formed the acid with his spit. Then ate through one of the window bars, made a rope from torn strips of bedding, and climbed down. We found tracks on the southern slope, but lost them when he entered the city."

Damika's chest expanded and contracted. Her nostrils flared and her breath plumed on the cool mountain air. "Out of my sight. All of you."

Lorelei didn't like being lumped in with Ordren, but even worse, she didn't like losing the case to the wiry bastard. She had to sway Damika, and soon.

"Uh . . . I'm sorry, Praefectus." It was lame but it was all she could think of.

Damika glared at her. "Get lost."

THIRTY-SIX: RHIANNON

Rhiannon stood on the barrow mound near Glaeyand, watching the ritual to awaken her mother unfold. Llorn was there. As were Blythe and Raef and Maladox. There were druins from the Deepwood, many of whom Rhiannon had never met, plus a crowd of Red Knives that was much larger than Rhiannon had expected. It was dangerous for so many Knives to gather in one place. Why would so many of them come to see her mother?

Llorn stepped to the top of the mound and spoke, but Rhiannon was in such a state she barely paid attention. Cupping her mother's cold wisplight in both hands, she stared at the sarcophagus Sister Dereka said contained her mother's remains. The chill in her fingers deepened as she thought about what she and the gathered druins were about to do. They were going to grant her mother a *third* life as a draugr. Rhiannon couldn't predict what would happen when they did, but it felt as if the fate of the forest, the fate of the *world*, was about to change.

Sister Dereka yanked Rhiannon into place so she and the druins were spaced evenly around the sarcophagus. "Prepare yourself. Concentrate on your mother's wisp."

Rhiannon squinted, clenched her teeth, and stared into the glowing ball. Anticipation, righteousness, and profound anger came back at her from her mother's soul, and with them the sense that what they were doing was deeply wrong. Didn't the druins preach about the sanctity of freed souls? How wisps deserved peace in their second lives? Didn't they rail against the empire for disrespecting them?

Rhiannon's fingers were growing numb. "Sister, why is it so cold?"

"Shush child, your mother is unhappy, but she wants to live again. Trust me."

But Rhiannon *didn't* trust her. Not in the least.

Sister Dereka opened the cavity in her ring and tipped white auris onto her tongue. Though Rhiannon had her own reservoir in the locket Llorn gave her, Sister Dereka gave her some as well. The other druins sniffed and swallowed black umbris. The powder tingled on Rhiannon's tongue. She felt lighter, as if she could lift from the ground and shine like the sun.

The druins chanted an ancient song from deep in their throats. The moment was nearly at hand. Rhiannon had promised Llorn she'd help raise her mother, but she hadn't counted on how wrong the ritual felt. She wanted to drop the wisplight and run, but Sister Dereka looked so intense, so angry in that moment, that she didn't. She swallowed hard, raised the wisplight over her head, dashed it against the lid of sarcophagus. The glass shattered. Her mother's soul hovered like a bright blue flame over the shattered glass.

Rhiannon lifted her shaking hands and held them near the wisp. She called upon the aura within her and became like a beacon, summoning her mother's soul. Once again, she felt the hot pokers on her feet, her toenails being ripped out with pincers. Then she was driving a knife into the skull of an imperial soldier. The anger, the sheer amount of rage in her mother's soul, felt so very foul.

You shouldn't come into the world like this. You should return with love in your heart, not hate.

She summoned the memory of playing with the wooden blocks, of walking with her mother toward the pond. The wisp dimmed, and Rhiannon saw herself crouch beside the pond and pick up a crayfish. It wriggled between her pinched fingers.

Her mother laughed. "You've found a pet?"

Sister Dereka was suddenly at her side. She gripped Rhiannon's wrist painfully. "She must have *purpose* in her third life, girl. Let her steep in her fury."

Rhiannon wasn't sure if it was caused by her inattention or the pain of Sister Dereka's grip, but she saw the imperial soldier once more and Morraine straddling his chest. She was using her knife to cut out his tongue. What had spurred her mother to such savagery, Rhiannon had no idea, but the sharp sawing motions she was using, the way she sliced his cheeks open to get more space to work, made her feel as though she was committing a great evil upon the world by allowing things to continue. She felt certain Alra was watching from the land beyond and that the goddess would condemn her to endless torture for her sins.

As the wisp floated down toward the stone lid of the sarcophagus, she yanked her wrist from Sister Dereka's grasp, screamed for them to stop, and lunged toward the spark.

"Fool girl, you'll ruin it!" Sister Dereka grabbed Rhiannon's hair and yanked her backward. "Gather your courage." She pointed to the sarcophagus. "Your mother clearly has."

Rhiannon tried to free herself, but the sister's grip was too tight. She tried to force her mother's soul away, but the wisp continued to fall. At last, it vanished through the lid.

She felt her mother's soul awaken, felt her limbs begin to move. She pressed herself to Sister Dereka, as if she needed physical comfort, then elbowed the woman in the ribs as hard as could. Sister Dereka grunted and let go of her, and Rhiannon raced down the barrow mound. She stumbled, fell face first in the grass, then got up and sprinted for the trees. Behind her, the crowd of Knives gasped. A few of them screamed.

Someone shouted, "Intruder!" But Rhiannon kept running. Minutes into the forest, she came to a hole at the base of a citadel and stopped to catch her breath. The hole led to a tunnel that wound its way to the underroot and a subterranean vyrd—the way they'd traveled to the barrow mound earlier that day. She thought of fleeing deeper into the forest, but she was terrified the alarm meant the empire had learned of the ritual, and that she'd be found by their dracorae, then tortured and hung, as her mother had. She thought of navigating the tunnels and entering the maze to escape, but she'd never been properly taught how to use the vyrda and was afraid she'd muck it up and become lost forever.

Feeling useless as a bent blade, she entered the mouth of the tunnel and waited. Sister Dereka arrived a short while later, glared at her, but didn't say a word. Behind Sister Dereka, a burly druin carried Morraine in his arms. Morraine was silent, unmoving, her eyes open but half-lidded, listless. They descended a stone stairway into the underroot, and Sister Dereka led them to a cavern with runes over the uneven floor. Using no lucertae whatsoever, Sister Dereka called upon the power of the maze. A whistle sounded, and Rhiannon found herself in a proper vyrd with rounded stones, an open sky, and citadel trees all around.

Sister Dereka led them along a well worn path, and they soon arrived at an outpost in the trees. It had a number of dragon nests, a scattering of burrows, a long wooden building on the ground that Rhiannon couldn't begin to guess the purpose of.

"It's the Rookery?" Rhiannon asked.

"Of course it is," Sister Dereka snapped.

The sister led them up one of the citadel trees to a burrow. It was small, with two beds, a night table with a candle between them, and a small, shuttered window. Sister Dereka shoved Rhiannon toward one of the beds. "Rest." She lit the candle, then reached into a pouch at her belt and handed Morraine the crystal shard Llorn had shown to Rhiannon near the waters of the Vagabond. "Take this."

Morraine accepted it without a word, then held it to her chest and lay down on her bed. Rhiannon changed into a night dress she found on the other bed, lay down and covered herself with a thin blanket, occasionally peeking out at the draugr, her mother, and hoping she hadn't moved. The exhaustion of the ritual and her flight back to the citadel eventually caught up to her, and she fell asleep. She woke hours later, shivering beneath her blanket. The candle was out, and the burrow was bitterly cold. She pulled her cover down and peeked out. Her mother was sitting on the edge of Rhiannon's bed, staring down, her eyes glowing like distant wisps. The crystal glittered softly in her trembling hands while Nox's brooding light filtered in through the slats of the room's lone window.

Rhiannon pushed herself up and sat with her back against the headboard. "What are you doing?"

"Wondering, child . . ." Her voice was scratchy, but nothing like the hiss of the dead Rhiannon had expected.

"Wondering about what?" Rhiannon asked.

"At everything's that's happened since I died." She smiled a pale, wrinkled smile. "At our old life together."

"Do you remember what happened to you?"

"Not all of it, but much of it, yes."

"Do you know what's happening now?"

Morraine nodded, shrugged, and shivered violently and so suddenly Rhiannon almost ducked under the covers again.

"Are you well?" Rhiannon asked.

"Of course I'm not, child. Are you daft?"

"I only meant"—Rhiannon fought back tears—"can I help in any way?"

Morraine's face softened. "Not with this." She stared at the crystal in her hands. "Llorn came. He and I spoke for a time, so I understand some of what's changed in the years since—" She shrugged, and Rhiannon thought she heard bones scraping. "It will take time to understand everything. You can help me with that if you'd like."

Rhiannon took a deep breath. "I can try."

Morraine smiled again, slightly less wrinkled, slightly less pale. "Then do so."

Morraine grimaced and closed her eyes. When she opened them again, Rhiannon felt a growing emptiness inside of her, like she was being devoured from within. "I can feel your hunger."

"I know you can," her mother said. "We're bound. We shouldn't be, but we are. A result of the ritual being interrupted, I suspect."

"Briar and bramble, I'm sorry. It's all my fault."

"You didn't know." Rhiannon's stomach rumbled, and Morraine suddenly stood. "I must go."

The child in Rhiannon wanted to stop her mother from leaving, but the young girl in her, the one who'd grown up without a mother, only wanted her to go away. She said nothing as Morraine left and closed the door behind her, and the room began to warm. The emptiness inside her ebbed, too, but only a little.

The following morning, Rhiannon woke to the sound of birdsong. Lux's early morning light shone through the window slats. She swung her legs over the side of the bed, stared at the empty bed on the opposite side of the room, then got up and relieved herself in the chamber pot.

She heard clanking of pots and pans echoing in the hallway. She washed her hands and scrubbed her face in the basin. The smell of oats cooking, a common scent in the abbey in Thicket, wafted into the room. She took off her night clothes, put on her aspirant robe, which had grass stains along the knees and smelled of torch smoke from the night before, and braided her hair. Then she left the bedroom and went to the kitchen. Sister Merida was standing stirring a pot on a small, wood stove.

"You're here," Rhiannon said.

Sister Merida glanced over her shoulder and smiled. "I am . . ." She went back to stirring. "Sit. Drink."

Rhiannon sat at the small table and poured herself a glass of pine milk from a pitcher. It was sourer than she was used to, but it was tasty just the same. "Where's my mother?"

"She went to the fens to think." Sister Merida brought her a bowl of porridge, a pot of honey, and a basket brimming with hackberries. "Tuck in."

Rhiannon was so hungry that she didn't at first notice the bruises over Sister

Merida's eye. Her upper lip was cut and swollen, too, and the bottom of her ear was red and scabby. "What happened?"

"Nothing happened, child."

"Your eye, and—"

"It doesn't matter. Eat."

"Did they hurt you? Did Llorn?"

Sister Merida sat across from her. "Not Llorn."

"Then who?"

Sister Merida took a deep breath and let it out slowly. "Eat and I'll tell you."

Rhiannon shoveled a spoonful of porridge into her mouth. It was bland and pasty. She added some honey and berries. Then she stared at Sister Merida as she chewed.

"When I learned you were being brought here, I asked to join you. Sister Dereka tried to deny me. She and I had words . . ."

Rhiannon took another, much-sweeter mouthful. "Looks like you exchanged more than words."

"That's none of your concern."

Rhiannon didn't know what to say. Though they were blood relations, Rhiannon had never felt particularly close to Sister Merida. She'd thought Sister Merida felt the same, yet she'd fought to be here with her. "Didn't you have a husband once?" Rhiannon shoveled in another mouthful.

"Beckett, yes, but he's been gone for some time now."

Rhiannon spoke around her food. "You had a child."

"Chew, then speak, Rhiannon, and wipe that . . ." She pointed to her own chin. "We raised a foster child, Rylan, but he's grown now and moved away. You met him at the abbey a few years ago."

She vaguely remembered him. He was handsome with green eyes. "You didn't want any of your own?"

"*Someone's* certainly full of questions this morning."

"I'm sorry, I know it's rude—"

"It's all right." Sister Merida spun the bowl of hackberries idly. "I would've liked to have children of my own, but I'm barren, sadly."

Rhiannon felt her cheeks flush and paused her chewing. "I'm sorry."

"Oh, don't be." Merida stood and carried the cooking pot to the basin beside the stove and began cleaning it with a washrag. "It was a blessing in disguise. I've seen plenty of childbirths. All that screaming and pushing and sweating. But I did love *raising* a child. I could never stand the quiet." She looked out the window. "With Rylan all grown up, life in the abbey suits me. Now finish up and head to the nests. Llorn has a surprise for you."

"What kind of—"

"You'll see soon enough." Sister Merida continued washing the pot.

Rhiannon finished her bowl as quickly as her mouth would allow and dashed out of the burrow. A few walkways, stairs, and bridgeboughs later, she arrived at the dragon nests. Llorn stood beside the nearest of them. Inside the nest itself, his massive cobalt, Fraoch, was curled around three dragon kits, each the size of a bloodhound.

Rhiannon walked toward them and realized Irik was standing behind Llorn. "Irik!" she yelled.

The dragon kits twitched and shivered at the sound. Fraoch raised her head, fixed her turquoise gaze on Rhiannon, and uttered a low growl.

Llorn raised his hands. "Quietly, girl."

"I'm sorry," Rhiannon whispered and tiptoed the rest of the way to the walkway on the nest's bough. Fraoch growled a little louder, but Llorn whistled, and she laid her head down next to her kits.

Irik was smiling so hard he looked like he'd grown extra teeth. "Rhiannon, I'm to bond with one of them!"

Llorn chuckled. "You're here to see if one of the kits will take to you."

Irik pointed to the shining blue kit closest to him. "One of them already has."

"We'll see." Llorn stroked the kit's jaw with the back of his fingers. Then his brow furrowed, and he pinched the bridge of his nose. When he caught Rhiannon watching, he lowered his hand.

Irik, apparently oblivious, stepped next to Rhiannon and whispered, "His name is Tiufalli."

Rhiannon smiled. *Tiufalli* was the Old Kin word for *devilish*. She stared at the kits' vibrant scales, which were noticeably lighter blue than their mother's vivid cobalt. "All three will be bonded?"

"*One* will be bonded." Llorn turned and faced Rhiannon. "The other two will be sent east, into the wild, to help rebuild their population. Unless *you* wish to be bonded as well?"

Irik's eyes went wide. Fraoch warbled.

"It's all right, girl," Llorn told the dragon. "Nothing's been decided yet."

Rhiannon tried to ignore Fraoch's stare. There wasn't a child in the Holt who hadn't dreamed of bonding with a dragon. Irik and Rhiannon had played Dragonriders of Gonsalond countless times back in Thicket, but this was real. Dragon kits needed constant care when they were young. They needed to be trained to carry a rider and obey their bondmate's commands. Rhiannon wasn't worried about those things as such—she'd gladly dedicate herself to forming a bond with a dragon—but there was the empty feeling in her gut, her link to her mother. It was a bond of another sort, and she worried it would affect a dragon kit. Like a needle driving into its mind, it could make the kit angry or violent. It wouldn't be fair.

"Thank you," she said to Llorn, "but I can't. I'll be happy to help Irik, though."

Llorn looked like he might argue, but he just shrugged. "Suit yourself, but both of you have work to do today." He touched Irik's shoulder and pointed to a deck a few trees over, where a spindly woman was carving up an elk carcass. "Help Ayasha dress the elk." After Irik nodded and left, Llorn told Rhiannon, "Your mother went to the fens. Go. Speak with her."

"Can't I help Ayasha, too?" She didn't wish to carve up a dead elk, but she didn't particularly wish to talk with her mother, either.

He walked away. "Go talk to your mother, Rhiannon. Now."

She watched Irik bound over a suspended bridge. She wondered if Llorn had brought him to the Rookery just to make her feel more at home. Despite what had happened with Sister Dereka, it was almost certainly why he'd allowed Sister Merida to come. Rhiannon was glad for it, but it made her feel manipulated. It made her feel responsible for them as well.

She wished she could go back to the day she'd snuck off with Irik and summoned the wisp beside the swamp. She would've stayed at the abbey instead and left Brother Mayhew's book alone. Now she'd stepped into a mire she wasn't sure she could get out of.

THIRTY-SEVEN: RHIANNON

Rhiannon wound down along the citadel's corkscrew stairs, and the lower she went, the more the emptiness in her gut yawned. She followed the feeling along plank pathways and found her mother standing on a knoll, staring into the shadowy marsh. The long red cloak she wore stood in stark contrast to her bloodless skin. She had her hood pulled up, and the flaps of cloth at the end of her sleeves, normally used at night to protect from the dark sun's harmful rays, were covering her hands, as if it were *Lux's* ray's that harmed her now, not Nox's. In her hands she held the crystal shard Llorn had shown Rhiannon near the Vagabond.

"Good morning." Rhiannon had meant it to sound cheery, but the words had come out stiff as dragon barbs.

Morraine glanced impassively at her, then turned back to the fens. In the distance, cerulean flames of an arcfire drifted through the trees like a fluttering veil. It was a relatively common sight in the fens, where umbra and aura sometimes reacted with one another in spectacular fashion. Soon enough, the flames burned themselves out and were gone.

Rhiannon came to a stop at the base to the knoll. "Are you feeling better?"

"I'm better able to control the hunger."

It was an answer of sorts, but it made Rhiannon wonder whether her mother would soon return to her second life, and whether it wouldn't be better for everyone if she did.

"I'm sorry," Rhiannon said when the silence had gone on too long.

Morraine leveled her cold gaze on Rhiannon. "For what?"

"For trying to halt the ritual."

For several long breaths, Morraine just stared at her. At last she said, "What's done is done."

"I'm sorry for the time you've lost, as well, and for the pain."

Morraine frowned. "What did you see?"

"You killing an imperial soldier, cutting out his tongue."

"He was a rapist and a liar."

"I saw the inquisitors burning your feet, too. I saw your hanging."

Morraine seemed sanguine about it. "The paths forged for us by the fates are often difficult to reckon with, but they have led me here, and they have led you here." She showed Rhiannon the crystal. "For a purpose, surely."

"With the shard, you mean . . . ?"

Morraine turned the shard slowly in her hands, stared at its colorful facets.

Somewhere in the forest, a fox laughed; ahead, a pair of ibises swooped down and landed on the water. "The legend of this artifact is great among the druinic circles. My mother told me about it before she passed. She dedicated several pages to it in the Book of the Holt as well. Those pages revealed where it was hidden." She paused. "Do you know of Gonsalond?"

Rhiannon nodded. Everyone in the Holt knew of Gonsalond. It was a lost city, hidden deep in the Holt. It was where the wardens and the warrior women known as the Seven lived with their undying leader, Yeriel. It was where Faedryn's prison lay, hidden among the roots of the Umbral Tree.

"Even before the empire killed your grandmother," Morraine continued, "I knew they would never be satisfied until the Kin were gone from the Holt, their memory erased. After Mother's death, the words she'd written about the shard haunted me. She said that every seven years, Yeriel leaves the protection of the veil in secret and travels to Glaeyand, where she takes counsel with the imperator. That knowledge sparked an idea, the beginning of a plan I formed with your father to turn the tables on the empire, one in which Llorn became fully invested."

"But not Aarik?"

Morraine's expression darkened, and the emptiness in Rhiannon's gut yawned wider. "Aarik has no part in this tale. Nor should he." She stopped and looked at the shard. "You never knew your father."

"No, ma'am."

"His name was Dalatharan, though most people called him Dala. When the veil opened, he went with me to Gonsalond"—she tapped the shard against the palm of her hand—"to get this. He was wounded during our escape and died shortly after our return. It pushed me to work harder. Faster. To master the powers of the shard so it could be brought to bear against the empire."

"Llorn said that was why you went to Caldoras."

Morraine nodded, crinkling the blackened skin around her throat. "The memories are dim now, but I remember how excited I was when I left Caldoras. I even remember some of what I read. But it made me careless, and I was spotted by their dracorae."

"Can I tell you why I tried to stop the ritual?" Rhiannon asked nervously.

"Please do."

"It felt like we were flirting with powers we know little about." She pointed to the shard. "That feels like it too."

"The greatest rewards come with the greatest risks, Rhiannon." She held the shard out. "Take it. Tell me what you feel."

Rhiannon took the shard from Morraine's cold hands. Her fingertips tingled. The bones in her hand knocked when she squeezed it. And there was more. "It feels like the cant," she said, "or the reckoning. Or maybe both, like the powers of Lux and Nox at the same time."

"Very good. Legend has it Faedryn stood on the verge of victory near the end of the Ruining. Alra used the remains of her power to craft the crystal and hide in it as the bright sun was setting. She tricked Faedryn, made him think she was doing it because she'd lost hope of winning, but she was luring him. Faedryn came for her at the cant. He delved deep into the crystal to find her soul and destroy it. When he did, her paragons shattered the crystal, thus fracturing Faedryn's soul and binding it to Alra's."

Rhiannon stared in awe of the ancient artifact. What had felt like little more than a magical curiosity now struck her as deeply profound. She was holding something linked to Alra herself, to her paragons, to the trickster god, Faedryn.

A fox somewhere in the fen yipped, then barked.

"Knowing Alra would be weakened," Morraine said, "her paragons dedicated their own souls, their own lives, to ensure Faedryn couldn't escape. Thus, all of their souls were tied to a piece of the Heartstone."

"If Faedryn lost, why was he taken to the Umbral Tree? Why not just destroy him?"

"Because they feared doing so would untether his soul, and that it would allow him to escape from the pieces of the Heartstone. But that isn't the point of my story. Tell me, how many shrines are there?"

"Five," Rhiannon said reflexively.

"How many paragons, and how many shards?"

"Also five."

Morraine nodded. "That is the history we were all taught, and yet in your hands, you hold a piece of the Heartstone.

"This isn't one of the five?"

"No, child. As I told you, I stole it from Gonsalond."

"You're saying there are six pieces, not five."

"Yes."

"That means there were six paragons, too."

"Very good."

Rhiannon was stunned. The number five was part of the empire's very identity. There were five shrines, five paragons, five capital cities and five quintarchs who ruled them. "Why would the empire lie about it?"

"It may not be a lie as such. The sixth paragon was likely freed from her shrine before the formation of the empire, and that somehow shamed the religion that would one day become the Church of Alra. The leaders of that sect, who were more like druins in those days than the priests and shepherds of the Alran Church, managed to erase the history of the sixth shrine over the generations that followed. Newer generations inherited those lies. Now nearly everyone alive thinks the empire derived its power from five shrines, five paragons, five pieces of the Heartstone."

"Yeriel is the sixth paragon?"

"Yes, child."

It made sense. Yeriel was extremely powerful and long lived. She'd created the veil. For centuries, she'd seen to it that no one came near Gonsalond or the Umbral Tree. Who but a paragon could have done so?

Rhiannon's heart galloped. She raised the shard and asked the question she didn't think she'd like the answer to. "If this shard is hers, what do you hope to do with it?"

"What I tell you now, Rhiannon, you mustn't share with anyone. I'm telling you because I fear I can no longer do this alone. Do you understand?"

Rhiannon wanted to take her question back. She was just a girl from Thicket who'd inherited a bit of magic. She shouldn't be toying with such things. "I understand."

Morraine nodded. "Alra's paragons were powerful, all but undying. They're alive to this day because of it, and all but Yeriel are trapped in the Church's shrines. The Hissing Man knows much of what I know. He and his Chosen are hoping to awaken Strages in Ancris. He hopes to use the shard to control him."

"Bough and branch, *why*?"

"Because he thinks the Church is corrupt, or at the very least ineffectual. We suspect he wants to wrest control of it from Illustra Azariah, then seize Ancris from Quintarch Lucran. We believe it's the beginning of a plot to complete what the Holy Rebellion started and take control of the empire. His plan all along has been to manipulate the Red Knives into waging war against the empire. The Hissing Man will use it as a pretext to gain control of Strages, but if you and I can master this shard, *we* can gain control of Strages before he does."

Rhiannon heard a sudden, keen ringing sound. She stared into her mother's softly glowing eyes and said, "You want me to control Yeriel . . . ?"

"Not control, no. Yeriel likely isn't bound to it as she once was. We need to understand its nature. Only then can we hope to control Strages."

Rhiannon turned the crystal over in her hands. "Can't you do it?"

"No, child. I tried to command the crystal's power while you were sleeping. I felt myself being torn in two. The ritual at the barrow mound has left me weak, fragile." She placed a cold hand on Rhiannon's shoulder. "Don't fret. You're gifted, and we share a bond. I'll guide you."

Rhiannon had an urge to drop the crystal and run, but she steeled herself and said, "Aarik wanted peace."

Morraine's nostrils flared, and her eyes turned flinty. "I told you, Aarik has no place in this tale."

"But he *does*. He said the killing had to stop. It sounded like he'd found a way to achieve it."

"Yes, with *Marstan Lyndenfell*. Don't fool yourself as he did, Rhiannon. Peace formed with the imperator will never last."

"You'd rather start a war that will kill a lot of people?"

Morraine's head jerked back. "I want the same thing Aarik wanted. I'm just more clear-eyed about it, as is Llorn. Make no mistake, Rhiannon, you and I can work toward the peace Aarik so desperately wanted, but if the empire wants war, they will have it."

"I hate this," Rhiannon said. "I hate being a part of it."

Morraine's look softened. "I didn't wish for this life, either, but here we are. The best we can do now is guide our people, protect who we can, and forge a path for those who come after us. I won't lie to you. The road Llorn and I have mapped out is dangerous, but it will be worth it in the end."

Rhiannon turned the shard over, stared into its glittering facets. Perhaps her mother was right. Rhiannon didn't have *complete* control over the Holt's fate, but she had some, and some was better than nothing, which was precisely what she'd have if she ran. "How do we start?"

Morraine smiled, revealing blackened teeth. "We start by entering the crystal."

"I don't know how to do that."

"Don't worry, child, I'll show you."

THIRTY-EIGHT: LORELEI

I n her home in Old Town, Lorelei packed a pair of old books into a satchel while her mother, Adelia, busied herself in the kitchen.

"Take these," Adelia said, and handed Lorelei a sheaf of warm sesame breadsticks fresh from the oven. "They're good for munching while he works."

Lorelei, in need of some advice, was off to see her former mentor Kellen at the library. She kissed her mother on the cheek. "I'm sure he'll adore them." She nested the breadsticks carefully in her satchel. "As will I."

"No stealing! We've got plenty here. Those are for Kellen and . . ." Adelia frowned. "What's the name of the woman?"

"Ezraela."

"Yes, her. They're for *both* of them." She handed an extra one to Lorelei. "Make sure to tell him."

"That reminds me." Lorelei bit off the end and crunched loudly, savoring the taste sesame, coriander, and thyme. "Creed wanted me to tell you that you're a treasure."

"I'm well aware." She opened the oven door, then took up a bread peel and scooped up the latest batch of breadsticks. "Any particular reason?"

"Your cooking, I guess."

"You guess . . ." With an expert thrust of the peel, Adelia slid the breadsticks onto the counter to cool. "Well, tell him he's welcome any time for dinner."

Lorelei paused her chewing. "You're aware he doesn't drink from the same watering hole as most men, right?"

"Of *course*, dear, but he's as handsome as they come, and that smile of his . . . Like a wolf's." She pretended to swoon. "Makes me wish I was a lamb all over again."

"Mother!"

Adelia winked.

"We'll have him over, if it pleases you." Lorelei headed down the steps toward the front door, calling over her shoulder, "Just see if you can keep from drooling."

"I make no promises!"

Lorelei laughed, but the humor faded when she entered the quaint, curving street beyond the front door. It was empty, but the proposition of passing through throngs of people in the busiest parts of the city was making her heart race. She headed downhill, then cut through a narrow alley to avoid a plaza that was always filled with people this time of day. She waved at the old flower vendor, Magda, and Magda—crinkly eyes, crooked mouth, and all—waved back.

The small park with the leaning willow was next, then the washing well. From one mostly empty place to another, she wove through Old Town, its tall stone buildings and blue slate roofs. The quadrata, the oldest of Ancris's many public squares, was bustling with trade, hundreds of people milling along rows of carts and stands selling fruits, vegetables, jewelry, even antiques. The buildings standing shoulder to shoulder around the square looked like a moot of sullen dragons.

Hands gripped into fists, she crossed the square to the library. In the foyer, she took a moment to breathe, forced her hands to unclench, then made her way up the stairwell to the third floor. The library had been expanded greatly under Quintarch Lucran, and she desperately wanted to stop and browse its storehouse of books, scrolls, and treatises, which had become a major resource for scholars from all over the empire, but she was eager to speak with Kellen.

She found him sitting at his large oak desk, which was neatly stacked with books, papers, and scrolls. To the left, floor-to-ceiling shelves covered the wall behind his desk. The wall on the right was covered in cork board and pinned with dozens of noted in Kellen's precise script. A web of yarn with threads of various colors connected the notes to one another, part of the method Kellen had developed to organize his research into distinct lines of inquiry.

Lorelei went to the cork board and stared at it. "Like a mad spider."

Kellen straightened in his chair. "Madness is a prerequisite. The empire's arrival in the Alran Basin is complex, the truth hidden beneath centuries of exaggeration, distortion, and outright lies. But the truth will out, as they say, and my forthcoming work will surely find a space on the bookshelf of every good citizen."

"Every good citizen who can read."

Kellen shrugged his broad shoulders. "Eight percent isn't bad. The rest can look at the illustrations."

"Well, it *does* seem *very* important"—she reached into her satchel and pulled out the books she'd packed—"which is why I've brought these."

He took the books and held them up, one in each hand. "And they are?"

"A book of Syrdian poetry and a collection of epitaphs from their most ancient tombs."

"Don't think me ungrateful, but why are you giving them to me?"

"They were part of a cache sent to Highreach after the fight to retake Syrdonos. Skylar let me pick them over, and I thought those two were . . . interesting. They cover the same time period you're researching, and both talk about a threat to the north, which I believe stems from the quintarchies making the compact that led to the formation of the empire."

"Hmm, yes"—Kellen flipped through the poetry book—"it might be useful to see what people *outside* the quintarchies thought of us."

"My thoughts exactly." Lorelei set the sheaf of breadsticks on his desk. "And these are from my mother. You're supposed to share them with Ezraela." She paused, waiting for him to reply. When he merely nodded, she said, "How is that going, by the way?"

Kellen set the breadsticks in a desk drawer, then cleaned up the crumbs and sesame seeds that had fallen onto his impeccably neat desktop. "Well enough."

"Well enough? That's it?"

He shrugged. "She's distressed." He waved to the door, beyond which was the hallway that led to the clocktower. "Bowden's death hit all of us hard, but Ezraela especially so. She knew him since childhood."

"Sorry, I meant to come by and ask about that, but I've been so busy. Are there any leads?"

"Vashtok took the case, but he's found little, I'm afraid. Whoever killed Bowden cut the death mark of the Chosen on his forehead, but there's no evidence so far linking Bowden to the Chosen, to illicit drug use, or *anything* scandalous, really."

"Hmm, yes. Vashtok mentioned he seemed a rather upstanding citizen."

"He most certainly was, which is why his death makes no sense. Ezraela was so shaken by it she left early to visit her mother in Erimaea. She's promised to bring our chalice back so we can have a look."

Lorelei nodded. "Let me know when it arrives." She was still curious about the chalice, but the excitement had worn off since Kellen had first told her about it. So much had happened since then. "And your magnum opus?" She pointed to the sizable stack of paper on his desk. "How goes it?"

"Now that you mention it, I've just complete a second draft." He placed a hand on the stack and paused. When Lorelei didn't take the bait, he goggled his eyes at her. "It's ready for a *read* . . . ?"

She smiled. "Yes, yes, I'll look it over. Seems I'll have plenty of free time in the days ahead, anyway."

"Ah. I wondered when we'd touch on your ill-fated trip to Glaeyand . . . ."

Lorelei wondered at first how he'd learned of it so quickly. "Vashtok told you about it, didn't he?"

Kellen nodded, crossed his arms over his chest, and gave her a paternal stare. "Care to tell me what happened?"

She was still embarrassed about it, but the trip and its consequences were half the reason she'd come. She launched into the tale, starting with her and Creed's surveillance of Tomas. As she often did while worrying a mystery, she paced. She continued through the meeting at the mine, her questioning of Brother Mayhew, the wild events she'd witnessed in the Holt.

"Let me see if I understand," Kellen said. "You believe you've uncovered a plot against our city, and now you're so deep in the shit you're not allowed anywhere near it?"

"That's about the size of it"—she stopped pacing—"but I only did what I thought was right. And I found out valuable information."

"In war, small but costly gains often lead to greater failures."

"This isn't war."

Kellen laughed, and Lorelei checks flushed. "Make no mistake," he said. "The life of an inquisitor is a long, *grinding* war."

"Fine, but we mustn't lose sight of the *real* enemy. It's not supposed to be a war against our own system!"

"It isn't *supposed* to be, but sometimes it is. Letting Damika eat away at the Imperator's resolve might have been the wiser choice, a calculated retreat of sorts. Or you might have appealed to him in private. You know Marstan values excellence and precision in his people, because their actions reflect on him. Perhaps you could have convinced him you were the right inquisitor for the job."

"He was adamant."

"How would you know? You let Damika do all the talking. You should have beseeched him. You should have pressed Damika as well."

"Are we talking about the same woman? If I'd pressed her, she would have suspended me, or worse, sent me down to records."

"Well, now we'll never know, will we?" Kellen held up a hand to forestall a reply. "We are where we are. Let's talk strategy. You know as well as I do that Damika will bend if she thinks what you're offering will burnish her badge." His gave her a flinty-eyed stare. "She's forbidden you from direct investigation, yes? The case is Ordren's now?"

Lorelei nodded.

"And you've been relegated to your original mission: stemming the flow of drugs, rooting out drug dens, cracking dealers' heads?"

Another nod.

"Didn't you say Blythe was at the meeting near Tallow?"

"Yes. So what?"

"So focus on *her*. Get the answers you're looking for, and Damika will have no choice but to let you back onto the other case."

Lorelei chewed on that a moment. "After a meeting like that, *someone's* going to come to Ancris to hand down orders. It'd make sense if it was Blythe."

"Any idea when her next delivery might be?"

"No, not yet, but with Tomas and Aarik both dead, everything is upended. Lips will be looser than normal until things settle. The question is whether I can learn about it in time."

"Have any helpful informants?"

Lorelei didn't, but . . . "Nanda mentioned a small-time thief she picked up a few days ago, a fellow named Davin. As far as we know, he isn't a Red Knife, but he runs with that crowd. We might be able to convince him to ask around if we lighten his sentence."

Kellen's gaze drifted toward the window and the buildings of Old Town. "I'm still friendly with Magistrate Carcarus. He's always open to reducing sentences for compliant witnesses. I could stop by his office, see to it he puts this—Davin, you said?—onto his docket."

"You would do that?"

He picked up his manuscript and held it out to her with both hands. "Would you make time for some light reading?"

She went around the desk and kissed the crown of his head. Then she snatched the manuscript from his hands. "I already said I would."

"Yes, but soon you'll be too busy to read it."

"I'll make time." She put the manuscript in her satchel and rushed toward the door. "Thank you, Kellen!"

THIRTY-NINE: RYLAN

Rain pelted Rylan's face as he flew Vedron over the Holt. He wore a thick fur coat and riding gloves. He'd wrapped his woolen scarf around his face and neck twice. He had the hood of his elkskin cloak cinched and pulled low. Even so, the freezing air stung his cheeks, and ice crystals clung to his eyelashes.

The bright sun had long since set. With the dark sun hidden behind storm clouds, the landscape was left in inky shadow. Rylan bid Vedron fly so low that the downdraft from her wings caused the tips of the citadel trees to sway, but at this low altitude, the imperial lookouts and hunting stands sprinkled throughout this part of the Holt would have a harder time spotting him.

Lightning flashed overhead. Rylan squinted at the rain frozen in place. The light faded, and he returned to the bone-chilling cold, the hiss of rain, and the rhythmic *whoomp-whoomp* of Vedron's broad wings. Thunder rumbled in the near distance.

Vedron was annoyed, both by the rain and because she was being forced to fly beyond the forest, which no umbral wanted to do. When Rylan had arrived at her den a few hours earlier, the rain had just begun and it was still light out. Vedron had wanted to chase elk or frighten wolves or race through the trees like they used to, but Rylan couldn't. He had a date with a dragon, and the conditions—though they promised to be miserable—were perfect.

Vedron huffed and a memory flared: lying on the bank of the Diamondflow, Rylan sitting with his back against her flank, tossing dandelions into the water.

"I know I've been gone too often." Rylan patted the rough scales along her neck. "I'll make it up to you. I promise."

His father's threat against Vedron still worried him, but Willow had convinced Marstan that allowing Rylan to tend to Bothymus was in his best interests. A message had been forwarded to Skylar Solvina three days ago. Her reply had been short and sweet. She thanked him for his offer but told him she saw no need for Rylan's help at the moment. Should the situation change, the missive said, she'd inform Marstan and gratefully accept Rylan's help.

It was precisely the sort of response Rylan had been hoping for. He'd wanted them to think everything was going to be fine with Bothymus. Now he was on his way to Highreach's eyrie to ensure Skylar would write a second letter, inviting him to Ancris.

Vedron carried him beyond the forest, over a swath of grassland, the foothills, and then the Whitefells themselves. As the rain mercifully eased, Rylan adjusted their path to avoid the imperial watchtowers. Ahead, lightning crashed through storm clouds, illuminating Mount Blackthorn. Rylan guided Vedron toward the cluster of lights at Highreach, a walled palace and the seat of the Solvina family, on one of the mountain's broad shoulders.

Not far from Highreach was the imperial eyrie, a structure of wood and stone that housed some seventy radiant dragons. All the adult dragons would be trained for war and would easily be a match for Vedron, especially in the rain, which would dampen the effects of Vedron's breath. But Rylan hadn't come to fight. Far from it. If all went well, he'd be in and out with no one the wiser.

"There, girl," Rylan said, pointing, "at the top of that cliff."

Vedron gracefully arced up and landed on the cliff's rocky lip. Rylan waited patiently as Vedron adjusted the talons along her wingtips and hind legs. Only on hearing Vedron's satisfied gurgle did he scale her neck using the row of long, dorsal barbs and the crown of horns along her head. Soon he was onto the rocks and heading along the expanse of mostly flat land that held the eyrie.

He crept as close to the eyrie as he dared and crouched behind a leaning rock shaped like a broken knife blade. The eyrie, some forty yards ahead, looked like a bloody great stronghold left by the giants when they'd abandoned the mountains. Its stone walls measured thirty yards to a side and were nearly as tall. Jutting from its gabled roof was a cupola with high arches, a convenient path of entrance and egress for the dragons. Beyond the eyrie, reachable by a gravel road, was a cluster of buildings—the imperial barracks, where Ancris's dracorae ate, slept, and trained. Rylan studied the road and what little he could see of the training yard for signs of movement and thankfully found none.

The eyrie's rolling doors were cracked open. Rylan had just pulled off his gloves and untied a leather pouch from his belt when the dim blue light coming from inside brightened. He hunkered low as Stromm, a tall man with a red beard, stepped outside. In one gnarled hand he held a lit pipe; in the other, the leather handle of a wisplight, its bright, silvery-blue light casting the muddy landscape into sharp relief. All around the entrance the earth was deeply gouged from dragons' claws.

Stromm was the imperial Master of Dragons in Ancris. He took another puff on his pipe, breathed out a stream of smoke, and tapped the bowl against his boot heel. Orange embers floated to the muddy ground. He stuffed the pipe into his coat, sniffed loudly, pulled his hood over his bald head, and trudged toward the barracks.

Rylan counted to twenty, then tugged his leather pouch open. A strong odor, like rich, freshly turned soil, mixed with the rain's fresh scent. Inside the pouch was a healthy amount of umbris—a select portion of the dead amber dragon Rylan had found and rendered some months ago. The powder was worth a small fortune. As he headed toward the eyrie, he tipped the bag and spread it randomly on the ground. It was one of the reasons he'd needed to come during a rain—the powder had to soak in by morning so it wouldn't be noticed, but it would leave the ground with a massive amount of magical potential waiting to be unleashed.

Rylan used a light hand so that, by the time he reached the gouged, grassless area in front of the eyrie, he still had a good amount of powder in the bag. It was enough; more, and the effect would be too strong.

He tied the bag back on his belt, faced the eyrie doors, and slowly expanded his awareness. In the same way he could sense Vedron clinging to the cliff face behind him, he sensed the dragons in the eyrie shining like distant campfires, each with its own unique hue. Many of the dragons were asleep, but one brightened, an old female, then more.

"It's all right," Rylan said softly as he entered the eyrie. "Everything's just fine."

A wisplight was hanging from a hook on a support beam. It was quite ancient and dim, but it was enough for Rylan to see by. He spotted the bright yellow canaries in a cage. A few were out and were pecking at a brass dragon's scale worm. They chirped loudly at him, then settled again. Beyond the cage was a cluster of brass dragons, the most social of the radiant breeds. Farther on, a clutch of iron dragons lay curled in their stone nests. The largest of that bellicose breed was eyeing him hungrily. Rylan ignored it, and continued toward the far corner of the eyrie. A dozen golds, perched above him in nests built onto a criss-cross of wooden beams, warbled and chirruped.

Rylan kept an eye on them but only enough to make sure none of them were preparing to pounce on him. He was more worried about Bothymus, who lay like a silvery-blue hump in the corner.

Rylan headed steadily toward Bothymus's nest. When he came within five paces, Bothymus lifted his head and studied Rylan with moonstone eyes.

Sensing the dragon's wariness, Rylan spread his arms, opened his mind, and projected a vision of a grassy meadow, a light breeze swaying the grass, the bright sun high above in a cloudless sky. "Remember me?"

Bothymus extended the frills on his head and broadened them in a threat display. Then he spread his wings and raised his tail.

"Easy now." Rylan held his left hand, the one with the missing pinky, behind his back. The other he extended toward Bothymus, fingers splayed. "I didn't harm you in Glaeyand, and I'm not going to harm you now."

Bothymus's third eyelids nictated. He snapped his frills twice.

Rylan wanted to move fast—the longer he stayed there, the more likely Stromm or a sentry would check on the eyrie—but he couldn't rush this. Bothymus was nervous, and Rylan thought he knew why. He took a deep breath and suppressed his bond with Vedron. He felt Vedron slap her tail against the cliff face in agitation, but then his sense of her faded. Rylan would pay for it later, but it couldn't be helped. Bothymus had likely sensed their bond. A mere whiff of an umbral dragon would be enough to raise the big indurium's scales.

Bothymus's wings slowly settled. Only when his frills retracted did Rylan approach the edge of the stone nest. Once there, he pulled on a pair of supple dragonskin gloves, proof against viridian acid, then reached inside his coat and pulled out a small green bottle. Bothymus tilted his head to get a better look at it. Rylan pulled the cork. He stepped onto the large stones at the nest's border, but Bothymus reared his head back, spread his jaws, and bared his sharp, yellow teeth.

Rylan's heart thudded in his chest. "This isn't for you," he said. "It's for your fetter." He held the bottle up for Bothymus to see, then pointed at the golden stone worked into his bridle.

The fetter was chrysolite that had been harvested from fallen meteorites and had many unique qualities. The most important of them—to the empire, anyway—was its ability to link the mind of a dragon to its rider. More specifically, it made the dragon subservient. Unlike the Kin, who *bonded* with dragons, the empire *bound* them with fetters, which was why it was forbidden, on penalty of death, for anyone but the empire to gather or buy the fallen star stones.

Rylan poured some of the bottle's contents, an acid harvested from Vedron himself, onto a special square of cloth made from the rendered fibers of dragon scales. When he tried to wipe it on the fetter, Bothymus reared back again. The iron dragon behind Rylan growled, low and gurgling. Two of the golds stared down from the nests and hissed.

Rylan stayed perfectly still. "It won't destroy the stone," he said softly. "It just dulls its effect. You'll feel like *you* again."

Rylan was aware that the dragon might have had the fetter its entire life and not even know what it felt like without it. So he waited.

Eventually, Bothymus lay his head back down. Rylan extended the cloth slowly and wiped the acid over the stone, then poured a few more drops of acid on the cloth and wiped it again.

The acid would hamper Bothymus's rider's ability to control him, but it would also make Bothymus irritable, perhaps even become dangerous. By all accounts Stromm was a competent eyrie master and a gifted dragon handler. He'd likely separate Bothymus from the others before too long.

"I promise," Rylan said, stuffing the cork back into the bottle, "if this doesn't work, I'll come back and destroy the stone myself, and they'll get you another."

Rylan took a deep breath and projected calmness as he left the eyrie. He couldn't have Stromm or the empire's dracorae picking up any discontent from the dragons come morning. Outside, the rain had become a drizzle. Nox shone through a gap in the clouds over Mount Blackthorn, deep purple like a full-bodied wine.

Rylan tugged his winter gloves on and pulled the hood of his cloak up to protect his skin. He hadn't judged the rain perfectly—he'd thought it would continue a good while longer—but he hoped it wouldn't matter.

He returned to the drop-off and climbed down Vedron's neck to reach the saddle. Vedron spread her wings and soared away from the mountain. She was surly, indignant even, but cooperative, as always.

Rylan laughed. "What, did you think I'd leave you for Bothymus?" When Vedron huffed, then grunted, Rylan leaned forward and pressed his cheek against her neck. "We're doing this so I have a reason to come back, remember?"

Vedron didn't seem to care much.

"What say we go flying in the Deepwood after the rain clears. Race through the forest a bit?"

Vedron gurgled low and beat her wings.

FORTY: LORELEI

Five miles south of Ancris, in a valley surrounded by steep mountains, lay a particularly large hill known as Shepherd's Crook. From afar, it looked like a giant had decided to take a nap near the River Wend. The Wend wove through a valley with a small village, some fertile farmland, and a few copses of pine toward Ancris, making it a preferred location for the Red Knives to fly in shipments of drugs from the Holt. As such, Shepherd's Crook had a propitious view of the nearby peaks, the valley, and the winding river.

Lorelei lay on her belly at the hill's summit, hiding behind a flowering night gorse. The night was cool and cloudless. She held a nightglass to her eye and scanned the mountains, an imposing row of peaks known as the Wayward Oxen, for dragons. The dark sun cast a deep shade of indigo from the west. She'd been watching the tree-studded slopes for an hour, spotted elk, caribou, even a wolf wandering through the trees, but no men and certainly no dragons.

Creed lay on his belly to her left, nightglass pressed to his eye, scanning the Wend. Because it was night, they'd forgone their white uniforms for dark clothing and long coats of a special cloth with fibers of silver dragon scales worked into them to give them some protection against anyone who might be spying on *them* with nightglasses. They both wore black leather tricorns, Lorelei with all three flaps down against the dark sun, Creed with one side buttoned up, like a lowlands cavalier.

Glittering as it was, the Wend looked like a spill of the dark sun itself. Beyond it, directly ahead of Lorelei and Creed's position, was a dock and a small fishing shack with canoes leaning against it.

"Maybe Davin lied," Creed grumbled.

"Maybe, but I doubt it," Lorelei said, lowering her nightglass. "His deal with Carcarus is contingent on us getting what we want."

More than a week had passed since she'd spoken with Kellen in the library. In that time, Davin had been brought before Magistrate Carcarus and agreed to find out about the Red Knives' next shipment to Ancris. Though she thought it would likely amount to nothing, Davin had delivered a promising rumor: Blythe would be flying in a fresh shipment of drugs shortly before reckoning, which was why Lorelei and Creed had met at Shepherd's Crook in the middle of the night.

Creed had ridden a horse from Ancris; the roan mare was tied to a bush near the base of the hill. Lorelei, meanwhile, had gone to the eyrie at Highreach and taken Bothymus, who lay in a rocky depression ten paces behind them. He'd been uncharacteristically ill-tempered when she'd arrived at the eyrie, wriggling as she tried to mount, fighting the reins on the flight, gouging a circle into the earth with the spiny end of his tail as soon as she'd dismounted. He lay in that circle still, as if it were a ward that would protect him from imperial inquisitors and their irksome ways.

Lorelei reckoned it was a lingering effect from the attack by the cobalt. Though the gash to his shoulder was largely healed, the experience had been traumatic—it would be some time yet before he was fully healed in body *and* spirit.

Apparently not finished grousing, Bothymus began beating the ground with his tail and growling. Lorelei was about to squeeze his fetter and command him to stop, when he suddenly ceased the pounding. She let him be. When dragons became tetchy, often the best thing to do was leave them alone.

Creed shot a glance over his shoulder, then returned to his nightglass. "Davin seems an excitable fellow. He might've spooked the Knives. Blythe might have chosen a different location."

"It's also possible she was delayed. Just be patient."

Creed shifted the aim of his nightglass. "Can we at least agree that if she's not here by reckoning, she's not coming?"

"I suppose."

Bothymus thumped the ground again, harder. He snaked his neck back and forth. Then he trumpeted short and loud, a warning. Lorelei cringed as the sound echoed off the valley walls. Near the goat path at the foot of the hill, Creed's roan tugged at her reins, which were still wrapped around the bush Creed had tied them to. Then suddenly the mare was galloping down the path, away from the hill.

"Faedryn's teeth, Lorelei, will you control that bloody drake? Shut him up!"

A dragon's trumpet was hardly uncommon around Ancris, but Creed was right. The Knives might have lookouts. Lorelei squeezed Bothymus's crop and willed him to silence.

Bothymus lay back down on the ground, but Lorelei could still feel him fighting her.

"What's gotten into him?" Creed asked.

"A cobalt's poison can linger. Plus, he's never been fond of night work."

"Neither am I, but you don't see me pounding the ground and screeching."

"I'll mention it to Stromm when I get back, all right?" She stood and headed back down the hill toward Bothymus, projecting as much calm as she could through the crop. "I know, boy, you're annoyed, but we're almost done. You'll be back in your nest before you know it."

When she reached him, she held her hand near his chin, and he leaned into it. His scales were warm and mostly smooth, except near the edges, where they were sharp as flint. She scratched the wattle beneath his chin, and he shook his massive head and rumbled.

"We've got company," Creed called from the bushes.

Lorelei rushed back to the summit and lay beside him. "Where?"

"The tree line beyond the boat shack."

She peered through her nightglass. Beyond the river was a meadow, then a

pine forest that continued up the slopes of the valley's far side. A reedy fellow, glowing violet in the nightglass, emerged from the tree line, loped across the meadow
to the shack, and untied a canoe. Then, he lifted the canoe over his head and
carried it to the end of the dock, but instead of lowering it into the water, he set it
down on the dock and peered upriver.

Lorelei spotted a wavering purple shape far in that direction. The shape grew
and formed into beating wings, a writhing tail, and a long neck. The dragon was
surely Velox, Blythe's nasty, acid-spitting viridian. As the dragon dipped and followed the Wend, Lorelei could see the outline of a rider.

"I believe you owe Davin an apology," Lorelei said.

Creed pointed his nightglass at the dark peaks of the Wayward Oxen and
grunted.

Velox soared above the Wend, glided silently toward the shack, and landed in
the meadow. Blythe dismounted with what looked to be a rucksack over one
shoulder. She set it down and began untying two dark bundles from the saddle.
The reedy man joined her and helped, then the two of them began lugging the
bundles toward the dock.

The bundles were surely the latest drug shipment from the Holt. The Red
Knives' couriers would often drop them off and leave, but Blythe, much to Lorelei's
relief, stayed. Apparently the other rumor Davin had heard about Blythe, that she
planned to stay in Ancris to set things straight after Aarik's death, was also true.

"Wait until Velox leaves?" Creed asked.

"Agreed. Let the canoe reach the ford. We'll take them there."

Creed stood and brushed the dirt from his coat. "Good hunting." Creed headed
downhill toward his escaped mare.

Lorelei's heart pounded. "Good hunting."

Blythe and the willowy fellow had nearly finished loading the canoe. Velox,
meanwhile, lumbered over the meadow, beat his wings, and launched into the
pre-reckoning sky.

Bright goddess, it was all going precisely as Lorelei had hoped. Blythe and the
man launched the canoe and headed downriver. Velox flew up over the trees.

Lorelei felt a sudden alarm from Bothymus through the crop. She turned to
find him arching his back and pushing himself off the ground. She commanded
him to silence, but he snorted and released a long, loud trumpet.

Velox swung around and hovered over the pine trees, then trilled a long note.

Bothymus reared up and flapped his broad wings. His scales glowed and shimmered so dazzlingly he was hard to look at. It was the sort of mesmerizing display
induria used to disarm their prey, but Bothymus couldn't even *see* Velox from his
position.

"Down, Bothymus!" Lorelei called.

She tried to calm him with the crop, but he continued to brighten and snap his
teeth. "Alra's grace, what's *wrong* with you?"

She had half a mind to call off their ambush and fly Bothymus back to the
eyrie, but this opportunity was too good to pass up. She squeezed the crop again

and commanded Bothymus to heel, and after glaring at her a moment, he did. She climbed his shoulder to the saddle, then quickly exchanged her tricorn for the owl helm in the saddle bag, pulled up the collar of her coat and buttoned it tight to her neck. Lastly, she took the dragonscale shield off the saddle horn. Not perfect gear against the acid spray of a viridian, but it would have to do. "Hup!"

Bothymus launched into the air and flew down along the slopes of Shepherd's Crook.

On the Wend, Blythe dove from the canoe and into the water and swam furiously toward the far bank. The gangly man continued paddling hard.

By the time Lorelei and Bothymus swooped down, Velox had landed in the meadow and Blythe had mounted.

Lorelei gripped the reins and the crop tightly. "We want Blythe alive, understand?"

She felt something like assent from Bothymus, but he was flying so strangely. He veered and ducked and suddenly pulled up.

"Damn it, Bothymus!" She focused on Velox and squeezed the crop as hard as she could.

Bothymus finally abandoned the chaotic movements and flew straight as an arrow toward Velox. Velox lumbered forward and flapped his wings, preparing to take flight. Bothymus sped over the churning river, clamped his teeth on Velox's tail, and dragged him back down.

Velox beat his wings, ripped his tail away from Bothymus, and took to the air. He shot his head toward Lorelei, and she raised her shield. A stream of green liquid splattered off it. She felt a sting on her neck, but let it be. There might be more acid on her gloves, and she didn't want to wipe it on her unprotected skin.

Splashes of acid sizzled on the scales of Bothymus's wing. Noxious white smoke rose from it, and before she noticed, Lorelei had breathed some in. She fell into a terrible coughing fit.

"Stun!" she managed to say between choking breaths.

Bothymus spun around toward Velox, spread his wings, and lit them, brightening, pure white morphed to a brilliant, chromatic display, illuminating the river, the rocky bank, and the grassy field beyond the bank. Blythe threw her forearm over her eyes and yanked on Velox's reins.

Velox snaked his long neck away and turned toward the riverbank. Lorelei urged Bothymus to charge.

Bothymus beat his wings hard, propelling himself forward, lunged with a mighty roar, and barreled into the smaller dragon. Both dragons screeched, snapped their jaws, and battered each other's wings. They twisted so closely together that Lorelei and Blythe suddenly found themselves at arm's length.

Blythe reached for the fighting knife at her belt. Lorelei leaned over her saddle horn and snatched the leather strap Blythe's rucksack. "Go, now, Bothymus," she urged.

Bothymus spun around and beat his wings. Lorelei held tight to her saddle horn and the strap, pulling Blythe sideways on her saddle. Blythe scrabbled for her saddle horn with her free hand and slashed the strap with her knife. Lorelei almost fell backwards from her saddle, swinging the rucksack by its strap.

Velox swung his head down and bashed the side of Bothymus's head above his frilled barbs. Bothymus shook his head, lost altitude, but recovered before he hit the riverbank. Velox sprayed the bank with a mist of green acid. White smoke rose and spread, and Velox ducked into it. Bothymus followed, but the cloud was noxious and impossible to see through. He rose straight up out of the cloud. Velox was already beating his wings over the field to her left.

Lorelei wiped her eyes and watched as Velox flew toward the mountain ridge.

Bothymus wanted to fight, but Lorelei forbade him. "It's enough for one night." Were Bothymus not so intractable, she might have let him, but something was wrong with him. He wasn't himself. She'd probably pushed him farther than she should have already.

They glided down and landed on the riverbank. Lorelei opened the rucksack and found several changes of clothes, a water skin, some honey cakes, and a small wooden case. She took out the case, slid the lid back, and stared. Inside was what looked to be a rectangular clump of moist peat.

FORTY-ONE: LORELEI

Lorelei returned Bothymus to the eyrie and spoke with Stromm about Bothymus's ill temper. Still holding Blythe's rucksack, she trekked up to Highreach and asked to speak with Skylar. A servant led her to the solarium, where Skylar was sharing a carafe of wine with a sultry woman in a fine blue dress and a bodice that looked uncomfortably tight. Her breasts were practically spilling from it.

"Ah, Lorelei." Skylar stood and motioned to the other woman with her wine glass. "I'd like you to meet Princess Resada, daughter of Quintarch Zabrienne, a woman with an eye for art and a nose for wine."

Lorelei bowed politely. "Pleased."

"Lorelei," Skylar said, "is one of our sharpest inquisitors."

Resada glared at Lorelei's dirty clothes and the beaten old rucksack over her shoulder. "The one who got into trouble in Glaeyand, yes?"

Feeling her cheeks flush, Lorelei was glad that the only light in the solarium was a dim wisplight on the table.

"Lorelei didn't get into trouble," Skylar said.

The princess smirked. "That's not what the Domina told my mother."

"Well perhaps a *bit* of trouble," Skylar said, "but she may have uncovered a plot against the empire."

"What else did the Domina say?" Lorelei asked.

The question seemed to irk Resada. "That you embarrassed the Imperator, that you defied his authority, that your lack of judgment nearly got an indurium killed. She said Damika should have taken your badge, and I can't say I disagree."

Lorelei peered over at the veranda where Tyrinia sat with Quintarch Zabrienne at a long granite table. Like her daughter, Zabrienne was an intensely beautiful woman with dark, arching eyebrows. Beside them was none other than Quintarch Lucran.

"Your father's back . . ." Lorelei said it to recompose herself.

"Yes, isn't it grand?" Skylar beamed. "He arrived just before cant."

"The rebellion's been put down, then?" Lorelei asked.

"We certainly hope so." Skylar said. "It would be rather embarrassing if we lost it after building a bloody triumphal arch to commemorate our victory."

Unable to stand the weight of Resada's stare any longer, Lorelei leaned toward Skylar and whispered, "Can I speak to you alone?"

"Of course," Skylar said, just as quietly. She squeezed Resada's hand. "Sit. Drink. I'll be right back."

Lorelei led her away, then stopped and turned when they were out of earshot. "Your mother wants my badge taken?"

"Oh, she didn't mean it."

"Didn't she?"

Skylar waved the complaint away. "She and Marstan have always been close. It struck a nerve is all."

"I'm always striking a nerve with her, it seems. She probably blames me for the Tortoise Peak debacle."

"Not at all. And she barely cared in the first place."

"Oh, really? Then why did she insist on calling it off?"

"Illustra Azariah demanded it."

Lorelei paused. She'd suspected that was the case, but it was good to have it confirmed. And it made sense. Illustra Azariah was under pressure to finally finish the damned renovations. "Well, I won't keep you. I only wanted to mention how bad it's gotten with Bothymus." She told Skylar briefly about the encounter with Velox. "He's acting like he did in Glaeyand."

Skylar chewed on that for a moment. "Perhaps a bit of help can be arranged."

"What do you mean?"

"Shortly after you came back from the Holt, one Rylan Holbrooke sent a nice letter, asking after Bothymus's health. He offered to come help take care of him should I feel it necessary. I declined, thinking Bothymus would get better, but now . . ."

Lorelei shouldn't have been surprised. Rylan had been kind in Glaeyand, and it only made sense that he'd ask after Bothymus's health. "A visit might be in order."

Skylar nodded. "I've met him a few times." She leaned in and spoke in a lower voice. "He can help take care of *me* any time."

"Stop it."

"Or maybe *you* need taking care of . . ."

Lorelei felt her cheeks flush. "I said stop."

Skylar laughed. "I'll speak to Father tonight, see if he won't put his seal on a request."

Despite Skylar's ribbing, it was a relief. She didn't want Bothymus getting any worse.

"Skylar?" called a woman's deep voice behind them. They turned to find Tyrinia standing beside the door to the solarium. "We're to play whist. Come join us."

Skylar gave Lorelei a peck on the cheek and left, but Tyrinia lingered. "Word is you were off to catch a Knife."

Lorelei supposed she shouldn't have been shocked that Tyrinia knew, but she was. She hadn't even told Skylar what she was up to. Creed knew, of course, as did Damika, but like all things in the Crag, secrets didn't stay secret for long.

"Yes, Domina."

"Did you manage it?"

She patted the rucksack. "Not completely, but I've found clues."

"Clues . . ." Tyrinia shrugged. "I guess that's better than your ill-advised foray in Glaeyand, yes?"

Lorelei didn't know what to say, so she didn't say anything.

"You took Bothymus on this little excursion, did you not?"

"I did."

"Risking my daughter's indurium."

"The work of an imperial inquisitor is not without its dangers."

"Yes, well, perhaps we should rethink whether Bothymus should be lent to the Department of Inquisitors at all."

Again Lorelei was caught flat-footed. "I hope not," she said. "He's been invaluable."

Tyrinia made a noncommittal grunt. "Good night, Lorelei."

"Good night, Domina," Lorelei said, but Tyrinia was already lost to the solarium.

Lorelei headed to the palace entrance, requested a coach, and told the driver to bring her to the Crag. She was stilled rattled by Tyrinia's threat, and wanted nothing more than to go home and sleep, but first she needed to check on Creed, who would likely be in the Pit.

As it turned out, he'd managed to wade into a flat on the river and apprehend the lanky Knife, but he'd learned little. "He's a bloody trapper out to earn a few stags," Creed said when she found him at his desk. "He was probably hired just to take the stuff downriver."

"Think he's lying?"

"Could be, but even if he is a Knife, he seemed too scared to have been with them for long." He touched her shoulder and turned her toward the exit. "Get some sleep. I'm going to try one more time before I head home. Barlo must wonder where I am by now." Barlo was Creed's adorable mastiff.

Lorelei felt her pillow calling, too. She headed toward the exit, but stopped when Creed called her name.

"I was a bit harsh at Shepherd's Crook," he said. "It's the business in Glaeyand. I was annoyed, but it's not your fault. You did good."

"Then why doesn't it feel that way?"

"Because we live in a cruel world. Now go home. Tell your mother she can fix everything with cheesy biscuits."

Lorelei chuckled. "I'm eating my share before you get near them."

Creed smiled. "Fair enough."

She trekked home and fairly crashed into bed, slept all the way past high sun. When she finally managed to get up, she bathed, dressed, and headed downstairs. After a quick meal of goat cheese, currants, and honey over crackers, she was preparing to leave when her mother stopped her.

"And where are you off to today?" She was wearing her oversized trousers and a threadbare shirt that she'd kept after her husband died.

"To the shrine to talk to Ash," Lorelei said, "then back to the Crag." She gave her mother the high points of the previous night. Creed sometimes questioned whether it was wise to share so much with her mother, but Lorelei had always shared everything with her, and she wasn't about to stop now.

Adelia wrung a pair of old leather gloves. "You're being careful?"

Lorelei had been young when her father died, but she remembered her mother asking the very same question of him when she was worried about his work. The creases beside her eyes and mouth might have gotten deeper, but the look she gave Lorelei was the same one she'd given him.

"Of course I'm being careful."

Adelia nodded. "It's just this business with Aarik, and now Blythe."

Lorelei took her in her arms and hugged her. "It's nothing to worry about."

"We both know that isn't true." Adelia hugged her back, then stepped away. "This isn't like rounding up ordinary dealers—which is dangerous enough, mind you. It feels bigger, somehow, like ravens have started to circle the city."

Lorelei clutched her mother's hands to stop her wringing her gloves, then showed her the wooden case she'd taken from Blythe and the block of peat. "I need Ash to test a soil sample. That's all. And Damika's taken me off the business in Glaey—and anyway."

It wasn't the whole truth, and the look on her mother's face made clear she knew or at least suspected that, but she squeezed Lorelei's hand anyway and said, "Take extra care, okay? For me?"

"I will. I promise."

With that, Lorelei grabbed her tricorn hat, slipped into her swallowtail coat, and headed outside. After taking a moment to calm herself, she moved from refuge to refuge, those streets and squares with the least amount of traffic, and arrived at the gates to Alra's shrine. Several hundred pilgrims prayed on blankets or mats in the courtyard beyond. One of them, a heavyset man with a scar in the shape of Alra's eight-pointed star on his forehead, was standing and staring at the frieze above the fluted columns. His arms spread wide, he mumbled prayers to Alra. At the top of the broad steps, shepherds in white tabards and gleaming, brightsteel armor controlled the flow of traffic at the entrance. Milling near the doors were a dozen or so workmen in boots and overalls, part of the crews helping to repair the shrine.

Lips pressed tight, Lorelei held the wooden case to her chest and headed toward the stairs. A shepherd with a cleft palate sat at the table by the entrance. She climbed the stairs and stood before him.

He broke from his conversation with a worker in dusty overalls and gave Lorelei a cursory inspection. He paused on seeing her inquisitor's badge. "What business, Inquisitor?"

"She's here to see me." Lorelei and the shepherd both turned their heads to find Ash standing in the entryway. "At least, I *hope* that's the reason." He winked at Lorelei. "I'd be offended if it wasn't."

The shepherd regarded Lorelei. "That so?"

"Yes." She pointed at his journal. "Inquisitor Lorelei Aurelius here to see Ash Torentada."

He made a note in his journal. "Move along . . ."

Lorelei and Ash entered the shrine's broad antechamber. Many alchemysts and laborers were moving about their work. The cavernous space looked much the same as the last time Lorelei had seen it, except a scaffolding had been erected. Above the tunnel that led to the shrine proper, a crew of women were cleaning another frieze that showed Alra's death at the cant, the transference of her power to her five paragons, and the battle they'd waged in her name at the reckoning.

"So," Ash said, "is it *really* inquisitor business?

"I'm afraid so."

Ash sighed. "All they want is the mind, never the—oh, forget it."

"You missed your calling. You should've been an actor."

"What"—he waved to the worktables and carts of white blocks—"and miss all this?"

At the center of the far wall, beneath a runic arch, was the tunnel that led to the inner chamber, the shrine proper. Two guards stood at the entrance, and for good reason, Lorelei supposed. The shrine contained two of the empire's most treasured artifacts: a piece of the Heartstone and the remains of the paragon, Stragés. In all her years, Lorelei had never set foot in it.

"The offer still stands, you know." Ash jutted his chin toward the tunnel. "Come with me one night and I'll give you a tour."

"You said it's busy at all hours."

"It is, but I know everyone who works in the wee hours before reckoning. They don't squawk about a quick visit."

She would have loved to, truth be told, but she already felt guilty for trying to circumvent Damika's orders. She didn't want to get caught making an unauthorized visit. "Some day."

"Let me know."

"Will do."

They arrived at a workbench with a white stone block, a magnifying glass, and some jars and paintbrushes on it. "Welcome to my humble abode."

Lorelei pointed to the white block. "You never told me precisely what you do with them."

"Oh, it's *very* exciting, my love!" He ran a finger along the block's surface. "You see the cracks here?"

Lorelei bent over it and squinted. "No." Ash handed her the magnifying glass, and she peered through it. The cracks were thin as gossamer. "*That's* what all the fuss is about?"

"It's serious stuff. The cracks might be narrow but they weren't there twenty years ago when the shrine was last inspected. They need to be fixed now, before it becomes a real problem."

Lorelei shrugged. "If you say so, but how?"

"With this." He pulled a paintbrush from a large earthenware jug and allowed the thick, clear liquid to drip from it. "It's a distillation of night hazel. It seeps into the cracks and bonds the material and *should* hold it for centuries to come."

Lorelei scanned the room. "Wouldn't it be easier to just use blocks that aren't cracked?"

Ash gawked at her. "You sound like a bloody outlander sometimes, Lorelei. Do you even *know* the Church?" He patted the stone. "This is holy. The people who laid it in the shrine were alive to see Alra walk the earth. The day they toss it aside for stone mined from some nearby quarry is the day they burn their habits and denounce Alra herself."

"It just seems like a lot of trouble."

"It's worth it. The shrine deserves to be protected, now and into the future. But enough about that. I'm busy"—he motioned to the wooden case in her hands—"and you came for a reason."

"I did." She handed him the case. "I need to know what this is."

He slid the top open and stared at the dark block of earth. "It's dirt, Lorelei. You've brought me dirt."

"Not dirt. *Peat.* Smell it."

Ash did. "Very well, you've brought me peat."

Lorelei glanced at a pock-face woman who was using a brush to clean dirt from a piece of cracked white stone. The woman glanced back at her and left. Then Lorelei whispered to Ash. "I need to know what's special about it."

Ash poked a finger into the peat, then smelled his finger with a wrinkled nose.

"Ash!" came a booming voice from the shrine tunnel.

The pock-faced woman was standing beside Master Renato, the portly alchemyst. As he had every other time Lorelei had seen him, Master Renato wore a green smock over yellow shirt and trousers. He looked rather like an oddly shaped gourd.

"Back to work!" he yelled.

"Yes, Master Renato!" Ash placed the wooden case on a shelf under his worktable. "What makes you think there's *anything* special about it?"

She was tempted to tell him about the powder that Brother Mayhew had tested in the mines, the Hissing Man's demand for a sample of his own in return, but there was no time, and she didn't want to predispose Ash to anything. "Just test it, okay?"

Ash shrugged. "Fine. Keep your secrets."

She waved and left, unsure whether to hope Ash wouldn't find anything in the peat or that he would.

FORTY-TWO: LORELEI

The day after Lorelei visited Ash at the shrine, a courier arrived at her door with a note from Skylar. Quintarch Lucran had not only agreed that Rylan should come to Ancris to check on Bothymus, he'd sent a request for Rylan to come immediately. Assuming Marstan agreed, Rylan would arrive that afternoon by dragonflight. *You're to come too,* the note said, *to answer any questions the dragon singer might have.* Around the words *dragon singer,* Skylar had drawn roses.

Butterflies took flight in Lorelei's chest as she folded up the note. She wasn't even sure why. Rylan was handsome, but it was more than that. He was caring and quite gentle with beasts in a world that often treated dragons like mounts and nothing more.

Her day at the Crag flew by as she and Creed followed up on a lead the trapper had finally coughed up in exchange for a glass of whiskey. It was the location of the man who'd paid him, but when they went to the tiny flat in Slade, they found it empty, and none of the neighbors would tell them anything.

Soon enough, it was time to head to Highreach. She rode a coach to the palace, and Chamberlain Theron led her to a manicured lawn beyond the veranda. The day was bright, the weather warm. As soon as she arrived, a horn from the eyrie blew three rising notes—an incoming dragon had been spotted. She scanned the horizon and spotted a gleaming silver dragon in the distance, surely bearing Rylan and the imperial courier from Glaeyand.

"Ready?" called Skylar behind her.

She turned to find Skylar all dressed up in riding clothes—chaps, a sky-blue coat with tails, and polished leather boots. She'd even braided her hair and worn the helmet of a dressage rider. Riding dragons became something of a fad several years ago. Many young nobles had taken it up. But few had earned the name of a dragonrider like Skylar had. She adored riding, and took Bothymus out as often as she could.

They fell into step alongside one another. "You look nice, but Bothymus isn't fit for riding."

Skylar waved dismissively. "Bothymus has often seen me wearing these. Stromm and I thought he would take better to it."

Lorelei shrugged. Perhaps they were right. *Dragons are smart beasts, after all, and Bothymus is smarter than most.*

They headed through the rear gate of the wall and navigated the switchbacks on their way toward the eyrie and barracks. As they went, Skylar kept glancing at the approaching dragon. The sun shone off its silver scales, sometimes blindingly so. A courier held the reins, and Lorelei could just make out Rylan peeking over his shoulder.

Skylar took Lorelei's arm in her elbow. "Tell me more about our young dragon singer."

"You said you met him."

"Only in passing."

Lorelei shrugged. "He's . . . nice. Attentive. Good at his work."

"Did you like him?"

"How do you mean?"

Skylar huffed. "What do you mean, *how do I mean?* Did you *like* him, as people do from time to time?"

"He was attentive and good at his work," Lorelei repeated. "What more do you want?"

Skylar rolled her eyes. "You're insufferable sometimes, you know that?"

Below, the dragon set down on the grass outside the eyrie's rolling front doors.

"And sometimes you pester too much," Lorelei said.

Skylar squeezed Lorelei's arm. "I'm only looking out for you. You can't live with your mother forever, you know."

"I'm too busy for men," Lorelei said, though she wasn't sure she believed it.

Skylar pulled Lorelei closer and said. "I'm *never* too busy for men."

"I know. You're not exactly subtle about it."

Skylar released Lorelei's arm and pretended to look offended. Then they laughed. "Did you know Marstan took him in after he lost his foster father?"

"I'd heard, yes."

"The man had been trying to teach Rylan to bond. Kellen was the one who caught them."

Lorelei immediately halted. "*Kellen* caught them?"

Skylar stopped next to her and nodded. "He was on a two-year rotation in Andalingr. The viridian vixen was killed, and Rylan's foster father was burned. They cut off one of Rylan's finger's before he was taken to Glaeyand and given over to Marstan. A rather cruel way to be introduced to life in Valdavyn, if you ask me."

Lorelei felt suddenly awkward. She'd had nothing to do with the death of Rylan's foster father, of course, but Kellen was her mentor. She felt guilty by association.

As they continued toward the eyrie, Stromm, a former saddler turned eyrie master, took the dragon's reins. A tall man with massive, bulging arms, and a thick red beard, Stromm reminded Lorelei of the giants in the children's stories who'd once ruled the Whitefells' grand arc. The courier slipped down from the saddle and Rylan followed. The courier gripped the silver's bridle and led it into the eyrie while Stromm struck up a conversation with Rylan.

Closer now, Lorelei could see Rylan more clearly. His curly, shoulder-length hair was parted to one side. His light stubble and darker skin was a look that many women in the imperial cities secretly favored.

"I told Resada we were summoning him," Skylar said in a low voice as they reached level ground. "Her eyes lit up. She met him at a celebration in Caldoras. Said she nearly asked him to give her a tour of the eyrie, where, in her words, eyrie hands were known to roll in the hay from time to time."

"Skylar, I love you, but please shut up."

"All I'm saying is, if *you* don't try to catch that very pretty butterfly in your net, someone else will."

"You're mistaking me for someone who even *has* a net. Resada, or anyone else, for that matter, can do what they please with him."

Nevertheless, Lorelei found herself wondering what would happen if she, a woman from the mountains and an inquisitor, came on to him. She was suddenly back in the eyrie master's burrow in Glaeyand, talking to Rylan about Bothymus's wounded shoulder. Though Rylan had brought her there to find out what, precisely, he'd gotten himself into when he'd let her leave Valdavyn, he'd been quite amiable. She found herself wishing they could find some quiet time after the business with Bothymus was done. Whatever she might have said to Skylar, Lorelei realized she might like to talk to him about something other than wounded dragons.

Skylar squeezed her arm.

Lorelei gave her a brief smile. "Sorry. I'm back."

Stromm sent Betheny, a young red-haired eyrie hand, away and turned and bowed to Skylar. "Och, where are my manners? Your Highness, this young man is Master Rylan Holbrooke."

Skylar stepped forward and held out her hand; Rylan bowed and kissed it.

"My sincere thanks for your invitation, Your Highness," he said, "and for the trust you've placed in me."

"You come highly recommended," Skylar said, tipping her head toward Lorelei. "Be aware we have accordingly high expectations."

Rylan smiled a white-toothed grin. "I'll certainly do my best."

"Yes, well, before we get ahead of ourselves"—she waved toward the palace on the hill—"do you need rest? A bite to eat?"

Rylan gazed up at the palace. For a moment his brows pinched. "If it's all the same to you, I'd rather see to Bothymus immediately."

Skylar seemed pleased. "Two marks for you."

Lorelei didn't know if Rylan was familiar with the compliment or was ignoring it, but he said nothing. He turned to her, smiled pleasantly, and bowed. "Inquisitor Lorelei, it's good to see you again."

"You as well." She paused. "If you need of nothing else . . . Stromm?"

"Right," Stromm said, remembering himself, "we're just up the hill."

Stromm led them with long, loping strides past the eyrie and the nesting grounds. An old crimson-eyed iron vixen guarding three kits, each the size of a sheepdog, watched from her rocky nest as they climbed the slope. One of the kits raised its head and hissed as they passed.

Rylan glanced over his shoulder at Skylar. "Can you tell me more about Bothymus's behavior since he left Glaeyand?"

"He seemed fine for a few days." The strong summer breeze blew a wisp of Skylar's ivory hair across her face, she brushed it over her shoulder. "We thought he was on his way to full recovery, but then one morning he started snapping at Ruko, the silver you flew in on."

"Then Andrilor," Stromm added, "the quintarch's own mount."

"Have they scuffled before?"

Stromm shrugged. "Oh, they all get into it from time to time, o'course, but Bothymus disobeyed his fetter. He drew blood. We cleared the eyrie after that"— he pointed a knobby finger up the slope—"and moved him up there once he'd calmed down."

Near the top of the hill, nestled against a stretch of exposed basalt, a lone nest was situated far from the others. Bothymus was inside, curled like a sunbathing lizard. He swayed his head like a snake ready to strike and watched them approach.

"I flew him the other night," Lorelei said. "He fought his fetter constantly."

"Where did you take him?" Rylan asked.

"I'm afraid I can't tell you that, but I *can* tell you he tussled with another dragon."

"You seem to make a habit of that."

He'd said it in jest, but it felt overly familiar. "Our work is dangerous, Master Holbrooke, even when a dragon *isn't* fighting his fetter."

Rylan's look hardened. "And who cares about a dragon or two when there are Kin to catch, is that it?"

Stromm glanced down at Rylan. "You'll watch your tongue, half-breed!"

Skylar's eyes widened. "Stromm!"

Stromm stared at her for a moment. "Forgive me, Your Highness."

"It's all right," Rylan said. "*I'm* the one who should beg forgiveness." He regarded Skylar and Lorelei with a look of regret. "Sometimes I let the care I have for dragons go too far."

"*I* care for Bothymus," Lorelei said, genuinely affronted, "*deeply.*"

"I know"—Rylan raised his hands in an act of contrition—"I saw it with my own eyes in Glaeyand. Please accept my apologies."

Lorelei nodded stiffly and waved him toward Bothymus.

As Rylan approached the nest, Stromm, a stormy look on his long face, reached into a pouch at his belt and took out Bothymus's crop. Stromm was just wrapping it around his hand when Bothymus reared onto his hind legs, spread his wings, and lit them in bright, mesmerizing patterns. Like ripples in a pond, bands of blue, red, and yellow started near the center and rushed outward.

Lorelei stopped and shaded her eyes. Stromm, squinting hard, continued on to the nest. "Enough of that, now!" He raised the golden stone and held it like a talisman.

Bothymus's stretched skin grew brighter. The patterns shifted, came faster. Lorelei felt dizzy and then nauseas. Skylar grabbed her wrist. She was shaking horribly and started to moan.

Bothymus lowered himself onto the first joint of his wings, crept from his nest and charged toward Skylar.

FORTY-THREE: RYLAN

Rylan jumped into Bothymus's path and whistled sharply. Bothymus pulled up and snaked his head toward Rylan. Rylan was nearly drawn into the mesmerizing play of lights along his wings, but Bothymus's wings were partially folded, dulling the display, and Rylan had already formed a tentative link with Bothymus. Fixing his mind on it, he held one hand behind his back, extended the other toward Bothymus, and sang a wordless melody, a playful tune, like one might sing on a walk in the forest.

Bothymus gurgled dangerously, but then his jaws slowly closed and his wings dimmed. Relief flooded through Rylan as the mighty indurium edged back into his nest and fell silent, drew his wings against his body and flopped onto his belly. Rylan remained patient. He continued his song, and Bothymus stared at him, then Skylar. He flicked his tongue, and uttered a high-pitched growl, a sign of forbearance if not contentment.

Stromm faced Skylar. "My deepest apologies, Princess." He glanced back at Bothymus. "He's never done this before."

"It's . . . it's . . ." She swallowed hard. "It's fine, Stromm."

"We should leave," Stromm said, "give him time to cool down."

Feeling his window of opportunity rapidly closing, Rylan ceased his song. "No need, Master Stromm. Bothymus was just confused. Tell me"—he stepped closer to the nest—"did his mood improve after he was moved here?"

Stromm shrugged. "Some, yes, though not as much as I'd hoped. Why do you ask?"

Rylan held his hand near Bothymus's broad snout. Bothymus closed his eyes and leaned into it. "When we arrived and Bothymus spotted the crop, his attention shifted toward the eyrie. He seemed afraid of it, perhaps because he thought we were going to bring him back."

Skylar frowned. "Why would he be afraid of the *eyrie*?"

Rylan scratched Bothymus's spiky wattle, and the dragon warbled happily. "Several years ago I was visiting family in Thicket and was asked to tend to a gold vixen with two young kits. The vixen's home was the eyrie in Andalingr, but she'd built a nest along the banks of the Vagabond to raise her young. She became irritable and refused to eat. We thought perhaps an umbral had found her nest and sent scouts to investigate. They didn't find an umbral, but they did find a *rift*."

"A rift," Skylar said.

With Bothymus settled, Rylan turned toward them. "A rift, yes. The alchemysts came and burned it before it could get worse, and the gold soon recovered."

Rifts were imperfections in the syld, the fabric of the world. The syld separated umbra from aura in all things: plants, animals, mountains, the world itself. When rifts were powerful enough, arcfires could spontaneously ignite. Though typically not dangerous, arcfires were a reckoning of sorts, a rebalancing of the basic forces that made and sustained life. Ephemeral blue flames would appear out of thin air as the two opposing forces, aura and umbra, burned one another out. There was nothing to do about such things in the wild, but near villages or cities it was important to find them before they grew strong and ignited in an uncontrolled manner.

The powder Rylan had laid over the ground when he'd visited Bothymus a week ago would mimic a real rift. If it burned as he hoped, it would give him all the reason he needed to remain in Ancris for a time, and that in turn would allow him to dig into Master Renato and learn how much he knew about Master Korvus's ill-fated journey to the Deepwood Fens. That his discovery of the fake rift would help Rylan ingratiate himself with Quintarch Lucran, hopefully aiding Rylan's father in his campaign to retain the imperator's seat, was a fringe benefit, but an important one.

Lorelei looked out at the eyrie. "You're saying a rift is the cause of Bothymus's ill temper?"

"I'm saying it's possible. Induria are particularly sensitive to them. And they can cause degradation in crops and fetters"—he motioned to the glowing fetter in Bothymus's bridle—"especially if they were imperfect to begin with. Imperfections are rare, but I recommend inspecting every stone in the eyrie just to be safe."

Stromm looked embarrassed. "Yes, I'll . . . uh . . . see to that straight away."

"Clear the eyrie," Skylar ordered. "I'll send for Master Renato."

Rylan's jaw nearly hit the ground. The very man he'd come to spy upon was being called upon to seal the rift?

Over the course of the next hour, the eyrie hands gathered the dragons' crops and directed the beasts into the training paddock and the nesting grounds behind the eyrie. Stromm was careful to keep them moving at an even pace to avoid causing a panic. Several of the dragons groused, especially the golds, who liked to roost in the eyrie's rafters. The bronzes trumpeted. The irons snaked their necks and growled. The induria flapped the frills on the sides of their heads.

As the last of them were being moved out, a young man bearing a heavy alchemyst's pack trundled down the winding path from Highreach. Rylan groaned inwardly. The man was Ash Torentada, one of Master Renato's journeymen; his arrival almost certainly meant that Master Renato had sent him in his stead.

"Rylan Holbrooke," Skylar said when the journeyman arrived, "meet Ash Torentada, one of Ancris's most promising young alchemysts. Ash, this is Master Rylan Holbrook, a dragon singer from Glaeyand."

"Pleased," Ash said, flashing a sidelong glance at Lorelei and Skylar.

"As am I," Rylan said with a composed smile. He'd have to find some other way to meet Master Renato, perhaps through Ash himself, but first things first. He needed to make Skylar trust him, and that meant ensuring the rift burning went as planned.

"Master Holbrooke," Stromm called from the eyrie, "a bit of help?"

Four silver kits were chasing one another over the gouged earth in front of the eyrie. Rylan whistled playfully and beckoned them, and they bounded toward him and followed him toward the cluster of dragons.

Ash remained and chatted with Lorelei and Skylar. Their words were too soft for Rylan to hear over the trills of the silver kits, but he caught them glancing his way several times when they thought he wasn't paying attention. As they continued to talk, Ash set his pack down and unbuckled the front flap, opened a notebook and jotted a few notes. He took out a telescoping rod, a glass globe, and a leather roll of implements and laid them on the grass.

When he reached into the pack and took out a jar filled with a clear liquid, Rylan knew the burning itself was close at hand. With the kits more or less calm, he left them to the eyrie hands and headed back toward Ash, Skylar, and Lorelei. "How does the burning work?" he asked as he came near.

Ash had just retrieved two vials from the pack, one filled with a silver powder, one with gray. "You really wish to know?"

"Absolutely. I've seen it done, but never heard it explained."

"Well"—Ash tried to hide it, but Rylan caught him winking at Skylar and Lorelei—"always happy to teach." He held up the jar with the clear liquid and showed it to Rylan. "This is snowmelt thickened with gelatin." He poured the contents of the jar into the globe, then picked up the vial with silver powder and showed it to Rylan as well. "This is ground indurium scale, some of it harvested from Bothymus himself."

He poured the powder into the globe and stirred the mixture with a wooden spoon. The mixture slurped noisily, and Skylar and Lorelei grimaced.

Ash, glancing at them, chuckled and continued. "Then the woundwort is added."

Rylan nodded. "A source of umbra, then."

Ash poured the gray powder in and stirred the mixture again. "Precisely."

"But woundwort is an inferior source of umbra."

"Very good, Master Holbrooke. And why do you suppose an alchemyst would mix uneven amounts of aura and umbra?"

Rylan gazed toward the eyrie. "Because if there's a rift, there's already some umbra that has yet to break through, and that will act as the fuel."

Ash wrapped the glass globe in a cloth net and hung it from the end of the telescoping rod. "Why, then, use any umbra at all?"

Rylan knew the answer, but Ash seemed so pleased to have someone interested in his work that he lied. "I . . . don't know."

"The aura in the dragon scale must already be burning before it comes in contact with the rift." Ash extended the rod and locked the segments into place. It was more than twelve feet long. "The woundwort powder will burn, but the gelatin keeps it from burning up before we get to the rift."

"Ingenious," Rylan said.

"Indeed." Ash winked. "I developed the technique myself." He pulled a fire striker from his pack and scraped some sparks into the alchemycal mixture. Soon, it began to glow a blue similar to wisplights. Holding the pole in front of him, he paced the well-worn path and waved the pole back and forth. Lorelei, Skylar and Rylan followed some ten paces behind him.

Seeing how close Stromm and the eyrie hands were to the place where he'd stopped laying out the umbris, Rylan pointed to them and said, "Should they be standing there?"

Ash glanced toward them as he approached the gouged earth in front of the eyrie. "They're far enough away. And if you've seen this before, you'll know the burning is actually quite tame."

"Most are," Rylan said, "but I've seen fires spread unchecked. I've seen people die from it."

Ash halted and looked back at Rylan. "We'll have it sealed in no time." A moment later, the air near the glowing glass globe flared to life, a sheet of wavering blue arcfire. It spread until it looked like distant sheets of rain. "You see?" Ash cast the globe back and forth, and the sheets of light brightened, then dimmed at the edge of the rift.

Each time the blue light flared, Rylan felt a twisting in his gut, a wave of vertigo. Beyond the eyrie, dragons roared. The kits keened.

To Rylan's left, Skylar looked like she was going to be sick. Lorelei, looking much the same, had one hand pressed to her stomach.

"Ash?" Lorelei called.

No sooner had she spoken his name than the blue fire raced away from the globe.

"Everyone get back!" Rylan shouted.

Stromm and the eyrie hands backed away, many with hands raised to protect themselves. The blue flames sped to Rylan's right, toward the drop-off, twisting and turning like an unleashed dragon. The surges were accompanied by sharp, piercing sounds like a frozen pond cracking as winter deepened; they were so loud it was hard to think. In a blink, the flames were tall as the eyrie and twice as long, surging, retreating, then billowing out again.

"Sweet Alra's grace," Ash hollered, wide eyes sparkling with flame.

He seemed transfixed, so much so that Rylan yanked him back, away from the flames. Stromm bellowed at the eyrie-hands to move faster. Most sprinted away. A few staggered backward while staring wide-eyed at the towering arcfire.

As Ash continued on toward Lorelei and Skylar, Rylan stopped and stared in horror at the eyrie's open doors. The red-haired eyrie hand, Betheny, stood just beyond them. She stared at the blue flames, one hand clutched over her heart. She was transfixed, unable to flee.

When she took a halting step *toward* the flames, Rylan sprinted toward her, through the flames. His skin turned ice cold. His joints ached. Pain wracked his entire body, but he kept running as Betheny reached one hand out and took another step toward the flames.

Rylan stumbled over a deep rut in the gouged earth. He staggered, leapt through the air, and grabbed Betheny around the waist. He hauled her backward, away from the fire, and they tumbled onto the wood chips inside the eyrie. As Betheny tried to crawl away, back toward the arcfire, he jumped up and heaved her to her feet.

Thankfully, she didn't fight him hard, and he was able to force her toward the back of the eyrie. He headed through the empty eyrie toward the rear entrance. Halfway there, Betheny's eyes rolled up in her head, and she collapsed in Rylan's arms. He lifted her and continued on.

Just beyond the doors, he found Stromm. "Here," the eyrie master said, and took Betheny from Rylan.

As Stromm carried her toward a patch of green grass, Rylan followed him like a staggering drunk. He blinked, trying to clear his suddenly blurry vision, but couldn't.

"Rylan?" Lorelei called from behind him.

He wobbled around to look at her. "Hmm?"

She stepped toward him, hands raised. "Rylan, you need to lie down."

Rylan's vision grew blurrier still until Lorelei was but a pale smudge with a hint of red hair. "You know, you may be—"

Then the ground tilted sideways and struck him like a hammer.

FORTY-FOUR: RYLAN

Rylan walked along a suspended rope bridge high among the trees—in a city, he realized. Andalingr.

No, not again.

He saw Uncle Beckett being led along a soot-stained deck covered in dragonscale, saw the chains between his hands being hung from a hook. Beckett looked up at Rylan and shook his head. "Tell Merida it happened quickly, won't you?"

Rylan wanted to save Uncle Beckett. He screamed at himself to do more, but the dream played out as it always did: a bronze dragon swooped down and landed with a boom; an inquisitor stared down from behind his white owl helm.

The dragon breathed flame over Beckett, and Beckett burned and burned and burned. But this time, the flames were blue. They spread across the deck, and exploded wildly, consuming everything, including Rylan.

Rylan sat up in near darkness, panting, dizzy. His skin was clammy, his throat tight. *A dream. It was only a dream.* They always felt so real, though.

For a moment he thought he was lying in his burrow in Glaeyand, but the ceiling was painted with a mural of Alra striking down the trickster god, Faedryn, and the light was not candlelight but wisplight.

He felt a hollowness inside him—an after-effect of the arcfire. He ran his fingers through his sweat-drenched hair and breathed. In the room around him were two rows of beds, six to a side, simple, fitted with gray blankets and white sheets. The only other occupant was the young eyrie-hand, Betheny, who lay sleeping in the bed closest to the door.

He heard voices through the door and lay back down and pretended to sleep.

A nun in a gray robe and white wimple entered the room. Behind her was Quintarch Lucran, a broad-shouldered man with a blond beard and ivory hair. Rylan had seen him several times in Glaeyand but had met him only once, and even then it had been by mere chance in a hallway in Valdavyn.

Behind them was Illustra Azariah, a tall man in white robes and an ivory mask that covered his brow, eyes, and the bridge of his nose. The striking mask and his graceful gate made him look like a god floating in the wake of the quintarch and the nun. He'd been there on one of Lucran's trips, but he hadn't so much as exchanged nods with Rylan. It was a relief, really. The less the illustrae knew about him, the better.

The nun said something to them in a hushed voice, and Rylan gave up pretending to sleep—he didn't want Azariah to think he was spying. He opened his eyes and rolled to face the front of the room. He felt a fool for having misjudged the arcfire so badly at the eyrie. It had been much more intense than he'd expected. Nevertheless, he'd planned on faking illness from the fire as an excuse to remain in Highreach for a few days. Now he didn't have to.

The nun bowed and left. As her footsteps faded, Azariah leaned close to Lucran and said something Rylan couldn't hear. Then, Lucran walked toward Rylan, his boot heels clacking on the stone floor. "Rylan Holbrooke . . ."

Rylan propped himself up against the headboard, dipped his head, and replied, "Yes, Your Majesty."

"How are you feeling?" Lucran asked from the foot of the bed.

Azariah loomed behind him, silent and still as a statue.

"Better than I expected," Rylan finally managed.

Lucran gestured to Betheny, his rings glittering in the wisplight. "We owe you a debt of gratitude, I hear."

"Not at all," Rylan said, shaking his head. "I did what anyone would have done."

Lucran shrugged. "I do hate false modesty."

"No false modesty, Your Majesty, but *embarrassment*. I knew how dangerous the rift was as anyone, and I know my way around an eyrie. I should have made sure everyone was at a safe distance, but the girl was in the shadows. I thought the eyrie was empty." Rylan could still see her standing there, stock still, her eyes wide as saucers.

"Embarrassed or not"—Lucran tipped his head in a sign of respect—"Ancris thanks you for saving her and uncovering a danger to our dragons. The abbess said it will take a few days for you to feel like yourself again, but stay as long as you wish. We'll give you a ride back to Glaeyand whenever you're ready."

With that he left, but Azariah lingered. "Earlier, you smiled."

"Pardon?"

"The quintarch and the abbess were talking." Azariah seemed to choose his words carefully. "You looked at us and smiled. Why?"

It was true, he realized. Azariah had been facing the abbess, not Rylan himself, but that hardly mattered to an illustra. It was a slip. "I thought it was ironic."

"*What* was ironic?"

"There was a rift in the Holt recently, near Glaeyand. The arcfire spread and caught a small tinker caravan by surprise. One man died outright. His wife died from complications a few days later. We've been on edge lately in the Holt, but I remember thinking that at least in the mountains I'd be safe."

Azariah pursed his lips and nodded. "And the rift itself, how did you know about it?"

"Bothymus sensed it. Otherwise, I probably wouldn't have."

"Dragon singers can feel something like that from the dragons they commune with?"

"Not so precisely as that. I felt his discomfort, his fear. It seemed related to the eyrie, and I'd heard of dragons sensing rifts—"

"From whom?"

"Pardon me?"

"Who told you dragons can sense rifts?"

Rylan paused to gather his wits. He didn't want to talk himself into a corner. "Why do you ask?"

Azariah's smiled, cold and pitiless. "In my experience, people who answer questions with questions are often dissembling."

In truth, Rylan hadn't heard it from anyone. It was part of the story he'd concocted to justify his finding the rift in the first place. Rylan nearly elaborated on the lie but stopped himself and made a show of thinking about Azariah's question. "You know, I don't rightly recall."

"You don't recall."

Rylan shrugged. "I heard it around a bonfire, I think."

Azariah grunted quietly and said, "Rylan Holbrooke?"

"Yes."

"Son of Marstan. Your foster father was burned for bonding with a dragon, but you escaped punishment, correct?" He tilted his face down and seemed to stare at Rylan's left hand through the eyes of his ivory mask. "Save for a finger." When Rylan said nothing, Azariah straightened and said, "Well, rest up. I'm sure your father *eagerly* awaits your return."

Azariah strode away, tall and proud, and Rylan felt blood rush to his face. Despite the embarrassment, the illustra had done him a favor. Lucran had come across so warmly that Rylan had started to relax, but Azariah's treatment was a reminder that he had to play things carefully and quickly, then get the fuck out of Ancris.

Word was the alchemyst, Ash, not only lived in the palace but often stayed up late. Praying that would hold true tonight, Rylan pushed himself off his bed with a groan and headed toward the palace proper. He paused at the foot of Betheny's bed. Her breathing was shallow but steady. "Please forgive me," he whispered. "I was reckless."

He left the infirmary and wandered Highreach for a time, eventually arriving at a large rotunda with gilded pillars and broad plinths holding marble statues of Ancris's former autarchs. At the center of the rotunda was a glass globe large enough to fit a man inside. Dozens of wisps floated within, creating an otherworldly display of light over the floor, ceilings and walls. Rylan wondered who the wisps' souls might have been. Had they witnessed the Talon Wars? Were they alive when the Kin first came to the Holt? When Faedryn fell at the Ruining?

His thoughts were interrupted by a clattering on the far side of the rotunda. A train of servants in black uniforms was pushing dining carts topped with crystal goblets, decanters of wine, and plates covered by silver cloches through an archway. They nodded as they passed.

A long-legged, hollow-cheeked man paused behind the train. "Master Holbrooke, I'm Theron, the chamberlain. Is there anything you require? I hear you need much rest."

"Thank you. I was just stretching my legs."

Theron waited, perhaps hoping Rylan would take the hint. When Rylan merely smiled, Theron bowed. "You have but to ask." He trailed after the others and managed to catch up to them while somehow looking unhurried.

Rylan trailed after them, curious where they were headed. A few turns and several hallways later, they wheeled their carts through a solarium and onto a veranda. Rylan waited for them to leave, then entered the solarium and looked at the many plants. The room's walls and roof, composed of slumped glass, gave a wavering view of the veranda, the curtain wall, the mountains beyond. Overhead, Nox brooded among a scattering of stars.

On the veranda, a dozen well-dressed nobles sat around a granite table under a vine-choked trellis. At the head of the table was Quintarch Lucran. To his left, his wife, Tyrinia. To his right, Illustra Azariah. With a number of brazier's providing warmth, the women wore sheer, sleeveless dresses. The men wore shirts unbuttoned to expose their necks and chests. Despite the danger from the dark sun's rays, none wore hats or head coverings of any kind.

Rylan knew enough of Lucran's advisors to realize that this was a meeting of the privy council. Years ago, holding such a meeting at night would have been extraordinary, but having seen how well the palisade worked in the city, Lucran had ordered another, smaller palisade over the palace. It was a wanton display of excess and power.

Like so much in the bloody capitals.

A voice called from the darkness to Rylan's right, briefly startling him. "If you're thinking of joining them, I warn you, the conversations are dull as a sheep's bleating and every bit as annoying."

Shading the light coming from the veranda, Rylan spotted Ash sitting behind a table in a dark corner with a liquor cart behind him. "I rather think the last person a privy council wants to hear from is a half-blood from the Holt."

"Then join me instead." Ash pulled the hood from a wisplight on the table, lighting the solarium in ghostly blue. Ash was sitting twisted and with a leg thrown over one of his the padded arm of his chair, which would seem overly informal, but there was a familiarity about it Rylan found appealing. He gestured with his glass of what looked to be whisky to the empty chair across from him. "Please, sit." When Rylan shoved the chair with his hip, so that it was no longer in the unlight, Ash pointed to the glass roof above them. "You won't be harmed. The glass is treated, and we're under the palisade."

"Yes, well"—Rylan practically fell into the chair—"old habits die hard."

Ash set his drink down, craned like a contortionist over the back of his chair, and grabbed an empty glass off the liquor cart. He poured a generous helping of amber liquor and handed it to Rylan. "I suspect you could use it."

Rylan nodded. "I could at that."

Ash winked and settled into the cushions. He downed a healthy swig, bared his teeth, and gestured toward the eyrie. "That was quite the scene earlier."

Rylan breathed in the whisky's heady scent and took a sip. The smoke and peat were too heavy for his tastes, but the notes of salt and caramel were welcome, as was the buttery finish. "Like something out of a Diocenes tragedy."

"Ah!" Ash seemed surprised. "You sit the stone benches do you?"

"From time to time."

"Well, if it *is* a tragedy, it's a poorly written one. You don't *start* with a conflagration. You end with it."

Rylan smiled. "Perhaps the worst is yet to come."

"Alra forbid," Ash said with a wan smile. "Have you ever seen an arcfire catch like that?"

"No," Rylan lied. He'd tested it three times before he flew to Ancris. He'd made certain the ingredients would mimic a real arcfire. "You?"

"No," replied Ash, "but Master Renato told me about one he saw in the forest once. Apparently it spread through half a village before it burned itself out."

Normally, Rylan would be worried about pressing too hard, too fast, but the way Ash seemed to hang on his every word told him he could press a bit. "Can I share something with you?"

Ash seemed taken aback. "Please."

"Earlier, when I asked you questions about the rift burnings, I was only pretending to know little about it."

"Is that so?"

"Yes. I know a good deal about the alchemycal agents used, the process."

Ash held his drink in front of his chin and stared at Rylan. "Then why did you ask?"

"Because I didn't want to seem presumptuous. People in the capitals often get offended when someone with my . . . background seems to know too much."

Ash sipped his drink and said, "Well, you don't need to worry about that with me."

"I realize that now. I hope you'll forgive me."

"Already forgiven. But now I'm curious—just how much *do* you know about alchemy?"

"A fair bit, actually. You mentioned Master Renato. I know he's overseeing the renovations to the shrine. I know that the formula he developed to fuse the cracks in the stone uses night hazel, and that its distilled with steam to extract the alcohol."

Ash's mouth dropped open in the affected manner of a stage actor. It was an act, but he seemed genuinely surprised. "Are you going to tell me you own an apothecary next?"

Rylan laughed. "No, but I knew a fellow who owned one. Korvus Julianus? I'm sure you knew him . . . ?" In truth, Rylan had spoken to Korvus only once, and only then to buy a flu remedy, but he'd chatted up a journeyman in Glaeyand to learn more about shrine's renovations so he'd be prepared for a conversation like this one.

"Yes," Ash said. "I met Korvus a few times before he went missing."

"You heard about his wife as well? The apothecary?"

Ash nodded, turning his glass in his hand. "Such a pity."

"Do you know much about his disappearance?"

"Very little. He was off on a survey, apparently."

"Any idea what he was surveying?"

"The flow of aura and umbra through the Holt, as I recall."

"The word around Glaeyand is he ran afoul of the Knives. Do you reckon he stumbled onto something sensitive?"

"I've no idea. Korvus and I barely spoke. He and Master Renato always talked about the old days, which bores me to tears. Are you thinking of becoming an apprentice?"

"That depends. Are you offering to become my master?"

Ash put a hand over his smile, then he laughed so loud one of Quintarch Lucran's guests glared through the window. "Perhaps I am, my dear."

"Then perhaps I'll accept, assuming you ever attain the rank, that is."

"Oh ho ho! You think I won't?"

"Well I hardly know you. For all I know, you're going to retire and open an incense shop in the market square."

"Incense irritates my nose." Ash finished his drink in one swift go. "And I quite enjoy my chosen profession, thank you very much."

"I agree, it's fascinating. And to work on the shrine, to feel the history of that place . . ."

"Don't tell me you're a history buff as well!"

"I am. I've always wondered why things are like they are, and that sort of understanding only comes from history."

Ash looked like he'd been about to pour himself another, but he paused. "Would you like to see it?"

"What? The shrine?"

Ash nodded.

Rylan could hardly believe his ears. He'd planned on pressing Ash for more information while he had the chance but he didn't want to push his luck. An extended visit would give him plenty of time to steer Ash back toward Korvus Julianus and his ill-fated trip. Plus, Rylan had long been fascinated by the Church's shrines. He'd never thought to see any of them, given his heritage, but now . . . "I'd love to, but how?"

Ash set his glass down on the table, then stood and motioned to the archway leading back to the palace. "We go. That's how."

"Now?"

"What better time than the present?"

Rylan peered over at Quintarch Lucran, Azariah, and the privy council. The idea of seeing something His Holiness would most certainly deny him was delicious. "I couldn't be more thrilled."

"Okay, then. Wait here a minute."

Ash left and returned a short while later wearing a purple waistcoat. They left through the palace's front entrance, where Ash summoned a coach. Soon they were rumbling down Palace Road toward Ancris. When the coach's steel-rimmed wheels began clattering along the cobbled streets of Old Town, Ash leaned out the window. "Take the river path."

"Aye," called the driver.

They entered a section of the city dominated by tall, narrow, wattle-and-daub homes, many of which butted up against one another. Ash knocked on the roof. "This is close enough."

"We're nowhere near the shrine," Rylan said.

"I know." Ash opened the door and stepped out. "We're picking someone up."

"Who?"

"You'll see."

They trekked down a narrow alley and came to a home that looked just like all the others. Ash picked up a pebble and threw it at a second-story window. When no one came, he tried again. A moment later, one of the panes swung outward, and a woman stuck her head out. It was none other than Inquisitor Lorelei.

"The dark sun's wicked ways, Ash," she hissed, "what do you want?"

"We're going to the shrine."

"No, we're not."

"Yes, we are. All three of us."

"All three . . . ?" Lorelei started when she saw Rylan. "Give me a minute?"

"Your wish is my command, my sweet, adorable newt."

She rolled her eyes and was gone. The window thudded shut.

"She hates it when I call her that," Ash said.

"I gathered."

A short while later, Lorelei emerged wearing loose trousers, an old woolen coat, and a pair of beaten leather shoes that looked like they were made for men. The outfit was so casual, her manner so unassuming, Rylan felt welcomed in her world. It was an illusion, he knew, but he indulged in it. He hadn't felt this way since before Beckett died.

As they headed down the alley toward the coach, he wondered at the sudden giddiness in his chest. It was Lorelei, he realized. Rylan had always been careful to build walls between him and his marks, but there was something about Lorelei . . . She was unassuming, quaintly charming, and threatening to dismantle those walls. For the life of him, he couldn't decide if that was a good thing or not. He suddenly wished she had declined, or that Ash had not invited her at all.

When they reached the coach, Ash and Lorelei piled, but Rylan lingered on the cobbles.

"Coming, Rylan?" Lorelei asked through the window.

He had half a mind to say he needed rest and would make his way back to the palace alone. But only a fool would do so. No matter how uncomfortable it made him to use Lorelei along with Ash, he needed to make headway on his quest to learn more about Master Renato.

"I wouldn't miss it," he said, and climbed in and sat across from them.

FORTY-FIVE: RYLAN

Rylan sat across from Lorelei and Ash in the coach. As it lurched into motion, he said, "So, a newt . . . ?"

Lorelei cringed.

Ash said, "It's a nickname I gave her when we were children, for the endearing way her mind skitters from topic to topic."

"It doesn't *skitter*," Lorelei said.

"While I'll grant you that, O smartest of inquisitors, I was having too much fun to notice at the time." Ash gave her knee and affectionate squeeze. "She, Skylar, and I were tutored together, and she always seemed to have trouble focusing on any one thing. What I later realized was that, whether it was history, literature, maths, or science, when she seemed unable to concentrate on any one thing, she was actually jumping ahead of us. Far ahead, especially in logic. That's why she's become such an outstanding inquisitor. Isn't that right, my little newt?"

Lorelei didn't seem to be paying attention to Ash, or at least she was feigning not to.

Rylan nudged her foot with the toe of his boot. "You're curious about the shrine, too, I take it?"

"She's never seen it," Ash said.

"I'm perfectly capable of answering for myself," Lorelei spat. "As you're no doubt aware, the shrine is heavily guarded. I've had a few chances to go official functions, but the shrine would have been packed, and, well . . ."

"The crowd," Rylan said, remembering what she'd said in Glaeyand.

"Yes, the crowd. Now, during the repairs, there's hardly anyone there."

A short, bumpy ride over old roads delivered them to the shrine's open gates. They exited the coach and walked into the entryway. Ash told them to wait while he went to speak with the guards.

Lorelei watched him stride across the lantern-lit plaza, then turned toward Rylan. "So why do *you* want to visit the shrine?"

"Doesn't everyone want to see it?"

"Most people do, I guess. But why do you?"

Rylan thought about telling her anything that might appease her, but the unexpected visit felt momentous, like it involved him in some way. To lie about it would be to cheapen the experience. "Long ago, in this very place"—he waved to the facade with its majestic frieze and stout stone columns—"the empire was formed."

"No, the empire existed centuries before it came to the Alran Basin."

"True, but back then, it was just a few provinces, each barely able to defend its own borders. When they came to the basin and conquered the five settlements, they claimed it was their destiny. Until then, the provinces had been trying to impose their own laws and customs onto one another. It would eventually have led to war, but the discovery of the five shrines and the legends surrounding them gave them a common identity to rally around. The quintarchs rewrote history to make it seem as though the shrines, and so, Alra's might, had always been theirs, but that was centuries later, of course."

Lorelei's eyebrows arched. "I'm impressed. But it wasn't the quintarchs who rewrote history. It was the illustra."

Rylan waggled his head. "Granted, but it's a distinction without a difference. In those days, the quintarchs and illustrae were very much in lockstep."

Lorelei gave him a scholar's nod. "You know your history."

"As do you. In any case, I'm a man who stands between two worlds—one foot in the empire, the other in the Holt. I'm borne on the currents created by the empire's formation and the long, storied history of the Holt. To say I'm fascinated by their entwined tales would be to trivialize it. At times, it feels like a burning desire, impossible to ignore."

"Believe me," Lorelei said, smiling, "I understand compulsions."

Ash emerged from the shrine and waved them forward. Lorelei and Rylan headed across the plaza toward the entrance. Rylan was so nervous his fingers were trembling. Getting so close to something so heavily guarded by the empire was almost like a theft in itself.

"Welcome," Ash said as they reached the door.

"Thank you kindly, my good man," Rylan said with a smile, and stepped across the threshold.

The shrine's antechamber was bathed in the soft, golden light of lanterns in sconces on the walls. Near the entrance, a curious mix of men, four imperial guards in red and a pair of bald shepherds in white and gold, played tines on a wooden table. They gave Lorelei and Rylan a cursory glance, then went back to snapping cards. Other than a few alchemysts working at wooden tables, the room was empty.

Ash took a lantern from a sconce and led them into the tunnel in the far wall. A breeze that hadn't been noticeable in the antechamber blew cool dry air on Rylan's face.

They walked toward a pinpoint of light. Rylan's gut felt tight. His hatred of the empire ran deep, but the shrine was different. It predated the empire by hundreds of years. Alra herself may have ordered its creation. Walking that tunnel felt like stepping back in time to the days of the Ruining.

Soon they entered a massive, open space with a natural granite ceiling above, glittering white quartzite below. The quartzite on the walls looked like white flames rising, some of which were behind scaffolding. There were a few carts as well, some with quartzite blocks in them.

Not far from the tunnel was a wide ramp, the famed causeway Rylan had read about, also made of quartzite. It curved gently inward toward the center of the circular space and rose about thirty feet above the floor to a glowing crystal and Strages's body, arms spread wide, head thrown back, wrapped in white bandages and floating in midair on an invisible axis. The pinpoint of light was a piece of the Heartstone, the fabled artifact that had shattered into five pieces when Strages and four other powerful magi used the Heart to destroy Faedryn.

"Goddess of light." Lorelei stared awestruck at the twirling body. "I've seen paintings, but none do it justice."

Ash motioned to the causeway. "Let's go have a look."

Lorelei opened her mouth, then closed it again. "You're sure?"

Ash shrugged his shoulders. "Who's going to know?" He headed for the causeway, leaving Lorelei and Rylan to follow if they wanted.

Lorelei looked at Rylan.

"I *am* a bit curious," he said, knowing perfectly well why she was hesitating—it felt blasphemous. But for him that only deepened the pleasure.

"I am, too, but—" She stared down the dark tunnel. "Oh, why not . . ."

They trailed after Ash. The causeway was wide enough for two chariots at its base but narrowed as they went higher. Having been raised in the Holt, Rylan was no stranger to heights, but something about the steady erosion of walking space and the pathway's steep incline was giving him vertigo.

Eventually they reached a square platform of sorts. The floating, iridescent shard was long and narrow, and shaped like a knife. Strages's body was more gruesome than it had looked from below. The linen bandages wrapping his torso and limbs were yellow and threadbare. Why the Church hadn't changed them Rylan had no idea, but they made the exposed skull seem even grislier. The steel helm was pitted and nicked. The eyeholes were covered, making Rylan wonder if the helm was somehow related to the illustrae's masks. His skin was desiccated, his dried lips drawn back, exposing mottled gums and a travesty of chipped teeth. Where his nose might once have been were two slits.

"Would that I looked so good after a millennia," Ash said, breaking the silence.

"Don't joke," Lorelei said.

"What, you think Strages cares? Or Alra does?"

Lorelei shook her head. "Just don't."

"Fine, no more jokes." Ash looked about. "In truth, even after all this time working on it, I'm still struck by it." He pointed to the border along the walls, where quartzite gave way to granite. "Flames indeed. Flames that have lasted a thousand years. Flames that will last a thousand more. It really is something to behold."

"I wonder what the world would look like now," Rylan said, "if the *Kin* had inherited the shrines instead of the empire."

Rylan wasn't sure why he'd said it. Partly because he abhorred the empire's autocratic ways, certainly. Perhaps partly to provoke a response. Lorelei stiffened, and Ash exchanged a look with her.

"No offense," Rylan said quickly. "I'm just amazed by how something so innocent looking can determine so much, how it can change history." He pointed to the fiery quartzite border. "A spark can ignite a wildfire."

Ash nodded. "I agree, though Alra surely had a hand in guiding the fire's spread."

"Perhaps," Rylan said. "But sometimes we ascribe forethought to what was, at the time, nothing more than desperation."

Ash stared at the glowing crystal. "Are you saying she had no plan for the future?"

It was Lorelei who answered. "She must have, but to pretend she saw all of this?" She waved to the shrine around them. "Ancris, the Holt, all of it? I rather think she was worried more about Faedryn destroying everything than she was about an empire yet to be born."

Rylan was pleasantly surprised. He'd assumed Lorelei would have blinders on, like Inquisitor Kellen and his ilk. He motioned to Strages, "The paragons have been floating like this since the shrine was built?"

"We only know what happened since the empire came to the mountains," replied Ash, "but yes, we believe Strages was bound to the shrine in some way."

"Why so?"

Ash shrugged. "No one knows for certain, not even the Church. Our best guess is that it keeps him alive . . . in a manner of speaking."

Ash decided their time was up, and he and Lorelei headed again for the causeway. As Rylan lingered, Strages' body spun to face him. The eyeless helm and the lipless grin made Rylan shiver. What must it have been like when Alra and Faedryn walked the earth?

He rushed to catch up with the others. Halfway down the causeway, he tapped Ash's shoulder and pointed to the carts, the stacked blocks of quartzite. "The work you're doing . . . you're not worried it will interfere with the spell in some way?"

Ash laughed. "Of course, we are. The project was delayed three times because of it. But we had to do *something*, and we've taken a careful approach—we never remove more than a hundred blocks at a time. We're more than halfway done now. I think we'll be fine."

"And why, precisely, was the project required in the first place?"

At ground level, they headed for the tunnel. Ash said, "Many years ago, the shrine was surveyed every decade or so, but then it was stopped for some reason. Maybe they thought it was no longer necessary. When Master Renato restarted it three years ago, they found cracks in the quartzite. He was adamant about fixing them. It took some time, but the Church finally approved his recommendations, and none to soon. It was getting much worse."

"I seem to recall," Rylan said, hoping the time was right, "Master Renato came to Glaeyand not long ago. Was that related to the renovations?"

"Mmm, I'm not sure," Ash said. Rylan was about to press him, but Ash turned to Lorelei and winced. "*Ach*, that reminds me. I forgot all about your peat."

Lorelei glanced at Rylan. "Not now, Ash."

"What? He's not going to say anything. Are you, Rylan?"

Rylan tried to keep his disappointment from showing. "Say anything about what?"

"Lorelei brought me some peat. I meant to run some tests on it, but it's been so busy around here. Now's the perfect time. Just don't say anything about it, okay?" He leaned toward Rylan and whispered. "There's no one around to see me borrowing ingredients!"

As they entered the antechamber, a guard looked up, but one of the shepherds slapped down a card and the guard, along with the rest of the players, groaned.

Ash led them to a workbench and picked up a small wooden box. Rylan immediately recognized the design of the lid's wooden inlay—a thistle in bloom with two unfurling leaves, like Blythe's mother used to make. Rylan managed to hide his surprise. "I wouldn't dream of it."

Ash led them to a storeroom. The shelves at the back were filled with collection plates and glass vials that, in normal times, would be filled with water that had been exposed to the light of the Heartstone. The nearer shelves were stacked with dozens of pots similar to those Rylan had seen on the workbenches in the main room. Ash went to a shelf containing what appeared to be alchemycal agents and reagents, slid off a small chest, and set it and Blythe's box on a table.

"This is a chromatovellum kit." Ash threw back the chest's lid and pulled out a pewter spoon and three glass bottles, one of which was empty, and set them next to the box. When he took out the empty beaker and a measuring spoon, he accidentally knocked the box off the table, spilling peat everywhere.

"Alra's blinding light." Ash bent down and began scooping the peat back into the box. "Do you have any idea what Master Renato would say if he saw me now?"

"It's the rushing rabbit who stumbles down the mountain," Lorelei said in what Rylan guessed was an imitation of Ash's master, "while the goat, planning each step carefully, makes the journey safely."

Ash collected what peat he could, then he stood and made a face. "Be the goat, Ash."

Lorelei and Ash fell into a fit of laughter. Rylan looked on, amused. His life was filled with so many lies and so much worry he honestly couldn't remember the last time he'd laughed out loud. He was well aware his feeling of friendship with Lorelei and Ash was an illusion, but he made no attempt to dispel it.

Ash placed the box back on the table, used a measuring spoon to scoop one cyathus of peat, and dropped the peat into the empty beaker. To this he added a measure of thick, clear liquid—likely a water and gelatin mixture similar to what he'd used near the eyrie. "By exciting the umbra in the suspension"—Ash picked up the bottle and gave it a vigorous stir—"we can view it through the indurium scales, then compare it to the charts."

Ash took a small book the chest flipped to a particular page, and laid it on the table. The open pages contained a list of locations in the Holt—Brevin, Andalingr, Glaeyand, the Deepwood Fens, and the like. Beside each location was a band of colors. Though many of the bands were similar, Rylan could detect minute differences in each.

Ash ran his finger down the page. "These colored lines are called spectra. A sample was taken from each location and charted using the same experiment we're about to run. It should tell us roughly where Lorelei's sample comes from." Ash took out three dragon scales and handed one each to Lorelei and Rylan. Rylan marveled at it. Though its shape was the normal teardrop of an indurium scale, it contained almost none of the milky color. It was all but transparent. Rylan assumed it had been treated to show the colored lines in the book. It was also light as a feather—much lighter than a typical scale.

"When the solution begins to glow," Ash continued, "hold it up to the light. I warn you, it may make you feel queasy. Step into the main room if you need to."

When Lorelei and Rylan had both nodded, Ash took the last bottle, carefully poured some of the contents into the spoon, and dropped it into the peat suspension. The suspension began to glow, indigo blue like a hunk of Nox. Rylan felt like a pit viper was writhing in his stomach. He doubled over and clutched his gut. He heard Lorelei moan beside him. She looked as sick as he felt and dropped her scale on the floor. Then she doubled over, pressed her hands to her belly, and retched.

"Darkest night, where is it?" Ash was rifling through his chest. Then he rushed to the shelf of reagents, grabbed a vial of blue liquid, and unstoppered it. He raised the vial like he was about to dash the contents into the darkly glowing bottle, but the glow darkened until it was pitch black. Staring at it, Rylan felt like he was stepping into his grave.

The bottle imploded with a bone-jarring crunch. The churning in Rylan's gut suddenly vanished, but he still felt uneasy. As he straightened up, he realized they were no longer alone. A shepherd with a bald head and a long beard stood in the doorway. He wasn't one of the ones who'd been playing cards—his robe was more ornate, and the starburst on his tabard had a full eight points instead of four, a shepherd of the first order who reported directly to Illustra Azariah.

"What, by Alra's unending grace," the man said, "are you doing in here?"

FORTY-SIX: ORDREN

O rdren raised his old, cracked wisplight over his head to guide him as he trudged through the catacombs. He'd just descended from the dragon-works, and the stink of chemicals mixed with the stink of the sewers formed a lip-raising, stomach-punching miasma that burned his nostrils like a lit match. His joints always ached in the cold, but a pain in his left knee, which he'd twisted the day before, flared badly with each step. He'd nearly decided not to go see the Hissing Man. He hated coming down to this shithole, and he'd been coming too often of late, but the particular bit of knowledge he brought this time was one the Hissing Man had specifically asked for. If the Hissing Man found out he'd been in the room when that old goat of an inquisitor-turned-historian, Kellen, told Creed about the stupid chalice and didn't immediately inform the Hissing Man about it, he'd probably end up floating in the Wend with a death mark carved into his forehead.

Ignoring the way the walls kept pressing in on him, Ordren continued and eventually reached the crypt with the wisplight in the ceiling. Gaul stood waiting on the far side of the room. Ordren stood far enough away not to get grabbed by the neck and have his head smashed against the wall again. "I've got news."

Gaul looked Ordren up and down, pointed to his neck, and smirked.

Ordren ignored the jibe. "Well, you stupid oak, are you going to bloody tell him or not?"

Gaul sucked his teeth, opened the door to the Hissing Man's sepulcher, and stepped inside. A moment later he emerged, left the door open, and proceeded to act as if Ordren didn't exist. Ordren blew out a deep breath, entered the sepulcher, and closed the door behind him.

As usual, the Hissing Man was at his desk on the other side of the sarcophagus. He was running his fingers down the page of a ledger, the sort used by money-lenders. As Ordren sat in the chair across from him, the Hissing Man snapped the ledger closed and rasped, "I've little time."

"Then I'll be quick. Your chalice is being delivered to the library tomorrow."

The Hissing Man jerked, somehow making his hunched back look even more malformed. "What time?"

"Kellen didn't say."

"Who's delivering it?"

"The archivist. Ezrel . . . Ezraela . . . Something like that."

The Hissing Man paused a moment, then asked, "Where does she live, this archivist?"

Ordren cursed himself. He should've got that before he came to the cata-combs. "I'll find out."

The Hissing Man glared at him, then snorted. "Anything else?"

"That's it."

The Hissing Man rang the bell, then opened the ledger and returned to his figures. "Gaul will pay you."

Gaul opened the door. Ordren stood and headed toward it. Still smirking, the oak tossed Ordren a pouch and glared at him as he passed through the doorway.

Ordren was so flustered he didn't bother counting the coins, but when he was out of Gaul's sight, he stopped and tugged the purse open. It was all there, ten thrones by way of tin wolves and a smattering of silver stags. "The Chosen have fallen so low they have to pay in fucking tin now?"

As he cinched the pouch, the wisplight slipped from his fingers. The treated glass was thick, but the light was already cracked. It broke in two. Ordren watched in horror as the wisp floated toward the ceiling of the tunnel. "Faedryn's black fucking teeth!"

He picked up the two halves of the glass globe and tried to recapture the wisp, but it was like trying to catch a mote of dust. It entered a narrow crack in the stone high on the wall, and then it was gone, and the tunnel was plunged into darkness.

Ordren's chest tightened. He thought about continuing on, but he'd never been good with directions underground. If he kept going, he might never find his way out, and he was already losing track of the twists and turns he'd taken from the Hissing Man's sepulcher. He couldn't do it. As much as he hated the idea, he'd have to return to the Acre and beg for a wisplight.

Hands pressed to the wall, he retraced his path and eventually saw a cool blue light against a tunnel wall far ahead, and then the old, familiar crypt came into view. Gaul was there, but he wasn't alone. Three other scourges in black habits were there, and they were talking with the Hissing Man, who was standing in the doorway to his sepulcher.

He didn't want to know what they were saying, but as he crept forward, a few words echoed down the tunnel to him. The scourges were apparently worked up about an incident at the shrine. When the Hissing Man spoke and pointed, they all left, even Gaul, and headed down a different tunnel—thankfully not toward Ordren.

Ordren had a terrible dilemma. He might steal a wisplight from the Hissing Man's sepulcher, but the Hissing Man would surely notice, and he didn't know the Acre well enough to find the exit on his own. The Hissing Man himself was likely headed toward the surface now. Ordren decided to follow him, then head up to ground level when it was safe.

He stole into the crypt, peered down the tunnel the Hissing Man had taken, and saw him entering the next crypt over. When the Hissing Man had entered the tunnel to the next crypt, Ordren hugged the tunnel wall and followed him. Five crypts down, the Hissing Man turned right and disappeared. At the same tunnel, Ordren peered around the corner and found the way ahead empty. The urge to quicken his pace was nearly overwhelming, but he forced himself to slow down and move silently.

A few steps in, he heard a click. Then the groan of old hinges. He edged farther along the tunnel, and the open door of a sepulcher came into view. Inside, lit by the pale wisplight in the crypt's high ceiling, the Hissing Man was standing in front of a sarcophagus. He tugged something out from beneath his threadbare habit, a dual-sided locket, Ordren realized, the sort shepherds used to store auris and umbris. The Hissing Man opened one side of the locket, take a pinch of powder and sniffed it up his nose; then he took another pinch and sniffed again. He clicked the locket closed and rubbed his powder-laced fingers over his gums.

Stone and scree, this is no business of yours, Ordren.

He knew he should leave, but the thought of making a sound terrified him. And if he was honest with himself, he'd always had a grim fascination for the Hissing Man. Who was he really? How had he risen to the top of the Chosen? Why had he fashioned himself after an illustra?

The Hissing Man groaned and bent over, clutching his arms and moaning. Something popped, and he howled. His limbs cracked and snapped like muted fireworks. He grew straighter, taller. His hunchback disappeared. He stopped groaning and began to breathe heavily, wheezing at first, then more calmly. Bright goddess of old, he seemed to be transforming into a different man entirely. But who? Ordren couldn't see his face.

The Hissing Man stood up straight and tall and gripped the lifted the lid of sarcophagus, which would normally take four men to budge, and slid it aside with ease. He took of his worn habit, his belt, and his shoes, and put them in the sarcophagus. Then he took out a different set of clothes and donned them—a fine white robe, then a long, white-and-gold tabard with a Alra's eight-pointed star on the chest, and a pair of leather sandals. Last, he drew out a mask of ivory and gold and put it on. Ordren watched in horror as Illustra Azariah slid the lid of the sarcophagus back in place.

Ordren lips quavered. He realized he forgot to breathe. He should've braved the darkness. He should've left the catacombs, light or no light. Now he was trapped. If the illustra saw him, he'd be dragged to the temple and put to the question, chained to the Anvil and burned.

Ordren pressed himself against the tunnel wall as the leader of the Alran Church left the sepulcher. Azariah seemed to stare straight at him—but the illustra merely turned and closed the door, then walked down another tunnel, turned at the next crypt, and was gone.

Ordren stared at his trembling hands, clutched them together, willing them to still. It seemed impossible, but then he remembered the similarities in manner and speech he'd noticed on one of his recent visits. "May her memory abide," the Hissing Man had said, making Alra's sign, eerily reminiscent of what Azariah had said and done earlier in the night.

Ordren crept closer to the crypt and read the brass plaque above the door:

Cassian Andrinus, beloved of Kalyris Andrinus and Illustra Azariah Andrinus III

Cursing himself for a fool, Ordren decided he couldn't follow Azariah. He might be spotted. Nor could he steal a wisplight, not even from some long forgotten sepulcher. He knew he would be found out. As he made his way back toward the dark tunnels, he couldn't decide which would be worse: being put to the question in the temple or what the Hissing Man would do to him in the catacombs.

A different sort of terror consumed him as he reached the pitch-black tunnels beyond the Hissing Man's crypt. He took several wrong turns and nearly lost hope he'd ever find his way out.

In the end, it was the stink of the sewers, then the acrid odor of the dragonworks that helped him find his way. He'd never felt such joy as he did breathing in that noxious stench.

FORTY-SEVEN: LORELEI

Lorelei sat on a stool near Ash's workbench as Illustra Azariah and Praefectus Damika entered the shrine and launched into a hushed discussion with the shepherd who'd found them in the storeroom. "I think I'm going to be sick."

Ash, sitting beside her, rubbed her back.

Rylan was leaning against the workbench, arms crossed over his chest, looking as worried as Lorelei felt. "How could it have been so strong?"

Ash shrugged and shook his head. "I've no idea."

Near the door, the shepherd handed the wooden box to Azariah. Though the eyes of Azariah's ivory mask seemed to be staring elsewhere, he ran his fingertips intently over the inlaid design.

"Did you figure out where it came from?" Rylan asked.

"What's that?" Ash asked, seeming preoccupied.

"The book you showed us . . ." Rylan said. "From the chroma it gave off."

"No," Ash said, "there wasn't time."

"It's from the Deepwood Fens," Lorelei said.

Rylan opened his mouth to speak, then closed it again. "You're sure? You barely glanced at it—"

"I'm sure. The closest match to the peat's chroma was the line next to the Deepwood Fens."

"Trust me," Ash said, "if she says it was a match, it was. The trouble is, the Fens are massive, and the samples in the book are only a small fraction of the chroma in the Holt. There's no guarantee that another place wouldn't have a similar pattern."

Azariah seemed to be wrapping things up. He said a few words to the shepherd and Damika. When both nodded, he strode toward the workbenches. "Ash Torentada, you will return to the palace immediately. Master Renato and I will speak tomorrow about your punishment."

Ash's cheeks turned red. "Yes, Your Holiness."

"Rylan Holbrooke," the illustra continued, "know this. If it were up to me, I'd take you to the temple for a chat that you would not enjoy. However, since you're a guest of Quintarch Lucran, and you've done him a great service, it would be impolite of me to do anything more than insist you return to the palace with Ash."

"As you wish," Rylan said, trying not to sound defensive.

"If I were you," Azariah said, "I wouldn't leave the palace grounds again for any reason. The Church's patience extends only so far."

Rylan nodded but didn't reply.

Azariah flicked his hand toward the door. "The two of you may go."

Ash glanced at Lorelei, shrugged, then left. Rylan stayed, seeming to wait for Lorelei's okay to leave. Why he would do so, Lorelei had no idea. He hardly knew her. She jutted her chin toward the door. Rylan nodded and followed Ash.

When they were out of earshot, Azariah ran his fingers over the lid of the inlaid box and said, "Where did you get this?"

"I took it from an agent of the Red Knives, a woman named Blythe," Lorelei said. "She's one of the dragonriders who ferries drugs—"

"I'm aware of her. Why did she have it? What was its purpose?"

"I've no idea. That's what I've been trying to figure out. It might be a new drug, like the one Brother Mayhew tested in the mines."

"The man you allowed to escape from the Crag . . ."

It wasn't Lorelei who'd let Brother Mayhew escape, but that was hardly a distinction Lorelei could argue with the illustra. "Yes, Your Holiness."

"Do you know who Blythe was supposed to deliver it to?"

"I assume the Hissing Man."

"You're not sure, I take it?"

"No, Your Holiness. But if you allow me to keep—"

Azariah laughed. "You think I'd let you keep this after the ineptitude and incompetence you've shown in your investigation thus far?"

"A bit of the peat, then."

"No, Lorelei Aurelius." He raised the box and shook it. "My shepherds will learn what they can of it, and I will decide what to do with their findings."

Lorelei looked at Damika, who stared back at her with arched eyebrows.

"In way, I should be thanking you," Azariah went on. "Your commander has finally come to see things the way I do. This meeting in the mines, the apparent plot behind it, is a threat to the Church, and the Church will address it."

Kellen's voice whispered inside her head, pushing her to advocate for herself, but every argument she could think of sounded facile and inane. She'd made misstep after misstep, and now she'd been caught inside Azariah's house on an unauthorized visit.

"I understand this is your first visit to the shrine," Azariah said.

"That's right," she said.

"I hope you enjoyed it, because it is also your last. That will be all, Inquisitor."

"Yes, Your Holiness." She bowed and made her way toward Damika.

Damika led Lorelei out of the shrine and across the plaza. Halfway to the gates, she stopped, turned, and looked up the shrine's facade. "I don't blame you for intercepting Blythe," she said. "Were I in your shoes, and my commander put a leash around my neck, I would have strained to see how far it let me go, too. What surprises me is that you would put yourself in a position that gives Azariah power over you." She motioned to the lantern-lit entrance. "I can't shield you from him. Not after this. And now he has leverage over our department, too. He'll use it as a cudgel to get concessions from Lucran. And even if Lucran doesn't budge, this is but one weight on the scale that may tip the balance of power in Ancris toward the Church."

"The Church, the quintarch . . . They're on the same side, Praefectus."

"Come now. The quintarchs view the Church as a means to rule over the world. The Church believes the empire's only purpose is to deliver glory to Alra. Sometimes the two are aligned and sometimes they are very much not. Look to the Holy Rebellion if you don't believe me."

"Are you saying the Chosen are planning another rebellion?"

"The peat was surely meant for the Hissing Man, don't you agree?"

"I do."

Damika nodded. "If the Chosen have thrown their lot in with the Red Knives, as seems likely, it's toward some greater purpose. Brother Mayhew's story about it being merely an arrangement to make money from the drug trade is ridiculous, but if it isn't that, what is it? And is the Church helping in any way?"

"If you think the Church might be involved—"

"You're smart, Lorelei. You have a real knack for separating the wheat from the chaff, which is why I regret that I have to remove you from active duty."

Lorelei couldn't believe her ears. "Praefectus, you can't—"

"Go home. Get some rest. Tomorrow, you report to Maudrey in records."

"Damika, please—"

"That will be all, Inquisitor."

"You can't *do* this."

Damika sneered. "Would you care to test that assertion?"

"The peat. The white powder given to the scourge. You said it yourself. They're linked."

"Which is why the inquisitors assigned to it will continue to investigate it."

Lorelei opened her mouth to speak, but stopped when Damika held up a hand.

"Are you aware Tyrinia ordered me to take your badge after your screwup in Glaeyand?"

Lorelei shook her head. Princess Resada had mentioned Tyrinia's musing's on the subject, but Lorelei had no idea Tyrinia had spoken to Damika about it. The strange thing was, Tyrinia had once showered Lorelei with praise and even invited Lorelei to be tutored alongside her own daughter, for goodness sake, but all that had changed in recent years. For some unfathomable reason, she'd grown cold toward Lorelei.

"She pressed me hard, Lorelei. It's only going to get worse after this. The only way I can protect you from her is to show that you've been brought to heel. So keep your head down. Be patient. Do as I've asked."

Lorelei searched for the right words to convince Damika not to take her off active duty, but she found nothing and merely nodded and left. She was too upset to go home, though, so she went to The Bent Tulip.

She thought it likely Creed would have gone home already, but she found him in the front room, nursing a beer with Nanda and Vashtok. She stood near the entrance, unable to force herself through the crowded room. She was just about to turn around and leave when Creed looked up and smiled at her, but his smile faded immediately, and he tilted his head toward the back room. Lorelei nodded and left through the front entrance, slunk past a pair of lovers rutting in the alley, and entered through the back entrance. Creed joined her at their booth, slid a pale beer toward her, and drew the curtains.

Lorelei took a sip of the bitter ale and licked the froth from her lips.

"Care to tell me what happened?" Creed asked.

"I cocked it all up, again." She told him about Ash throwing a pebble at her window, the trip to the shrine, the peat's alchemycal reaction, and finished with Damika's sending her to records, which felt ten times as bitter as the beer. "I wish I'd just gone back to bed."

"No, you don't."

"Yes, I do."

"No," he said, staring into her eyes, "you don't. You're like a cat, Lorelei. You're too curious for your own good."

She shrugged, knowing he was right. "I thought you liked that about me."

"I *do* like that about you. It's just"—he swigged the last of his beer, slid the mug aside, and leaned forward with his elbows on the table—"you need to know when to rein it in. Sometimes getting to the heart of a case is as much about working the overlords as it is about working your informants."

"That's not how it should be."

"You'll get no argument from me, but face it, those are the currents we swim in."

She took a deep breath, released it slowly. "We're making a mistake if we brush it all aside."

"You know Damika. She won't let it go on forever."

"Maybe not, but days will be wasted, weeks, while she tries to let everything cool down."

Creed shrugged. "She knows how to play the game."

"And I don't?"

Creed laughed. "A subtle manipulator, Lorelei, daughter of Cain, you are not."

"Will you at least tell me if you hear anything about the peat?"

A lively fiddle and drum filtered in from the front room.

"For all her faults, Damika is right. Go home. Get some rest. Come spar with me in the morning, then report to records. Stop fixating on Brother Mayhew, the peat, and the Hissing Man. And when you're done binding records, we'll go see Kellen."

"Kellen? Why?"

"He stopped by the Crag today, looking for you. Ezraela's coming back to Ancris tomorrow. You and I will go take a look at this bloody chalice, yes?" He spread the curtains, slid from the booth, and stood. "Good night, Lorelei." He leaned over and kissed her cheek. The stubble along his cheek scratched.

He left, and the music, the clank of mugs, the hum of conversation washed over her. Lorelei abandoned her beer, slipped out the back, and trudged home to do exactly as Damika and Creed told her to.

FORTY-EIGHT: RYLAN

Rylan sat across from Ash in the imperial coach as it trundled up Palace Road. The wheels changed from clattering to drumming as they traversed a wooden bridge over a creek. The scene at the shrine had been tense, but as worried as Rylan was over it, Ash seemed in a full-on panic.

"I'm terribly sorry about what happened," Rylan said to him. "It makes me wish I'd declined your offer."

"Yes, well"—Ash continued to gaze out the window—"I seem to recall working pretty hard to persuade you."

"Will Renato go hard on you?"

Ash shrugged. "Probably not in the short term. We've fallen behind on the renovation. He can't afford to lose me now. But later, yes. Renato is a proud man, and for good reason. He wants the work done cleanly, efficiently. He hates complications, which I've just delivered to him in spades. So yes, when the work at the shrine is complete, I'll be scrubbing scum from beakers and collecting stinkweed from the gullies for some time. He may even block my bid for my master's clasp next year."

"I'm sorry, Ash. I feel responsible."

Ash smiled half-heartedly. "We can share the blame, if it helps."

"It would at that . . ."

As they rode higher up the mountain, more of Ancris came into view. Golden lights twinkled in windows. The palisade's dome glimmered faintly over the official buildings. It wouldn't be long before they reached the palace. Rylan knew this was his last, best chance to speak to Ash alone. "I need to confess something, Ash."

Ash considered him. "Two in one night."

"Yes, and over the same subject, I'm afraid. The real reason I made that clumsy attempt at getting to know you was to get you to introduce me to Master Renato. The business with Korvus has people in Glaeyand worried. We both know the Red Knives killed him for knowing too much."

Ash shifted on the bench as if he suddenly found it uncomfortable. "There's hardly a mystery here. Korvus went too deep into Red Knife territory."

"Then why torch his apothecary? Why do it when they knew his wife would be there? I know Master Renato visited Korvus the day before he left. I'm trying to find out if Master Renato knows something, because if he does, he may be in danger."

The words seemed to sober Ash. "Do you really think he could be in danger?"

"Absolutely." Rylan meant it, though not for the reasons Ash might suspect.

As they passed over the drawbridge and through the palace wall, Ash seemed to deflate. "I don't wish to share Renato's secrets, but if it's true, about the danger and all . . ."

"What are you getting at?"

"When news of Tishana's death reached Ancris, Master Renato was distraught to the point of distraction. I thought it was because he was worried about Korvus, that he was holding out hope his old colleague was still alive. Now I wonder if he was worried about himself. A few days later, I overheard him talking with a journeymen about a journal Master Korvus had given him, apparently to get his thoughts on the survey. To get a second opinion, as it were."

Rylan felt like the world had just turned upside down. "Master Renato has one of Master Korvus's journals?"

"If he hasn't burned it by now." Ash opened his mouth, closed it, and started again. "Assuming he hasn't, it's likely in a strongbox he keeps in his office. I can't ask him anything right now, after what happened at the shrine, but I know where he keeps the key. Give me a few days, and I'll see if I can take a look at it."

Rylan didn't need Ash to look at the journal—he'd take a look on his own—but he needed to make it seem like he did. "Thank you. I'd be in your debt."

The coach jingled to a stop, and the two men entered the palace. After a brief good night, Ash took the stairs up to his room, and Rylan headed toward the infirmary. The palace was quiet, the privy council having long since concluded. At the infirmary, Betheny was snoring much more heavily than before. Almost too heavily. He squatted beside her and felt her pulse. It was weak and slow. He opened her eyes—she didn't even move—and found them red around the edges. A poison, perhaps. More likely a soporific.

He stood up and looked around. The curtains over the window at the far end of the room billowed in the nighttime breeze. They hadn't been open when he'd left.

"We're alone," he said. "You may as well come out."

After a brief pause, the curtains parted and Raef stepped down from the sill. Why he was here, Rylan had no idea.

Rylan walked slowly toward him while scanning the shadows for other intruders.

"We're alone," Raef said.

Rylan motioned to Betheny. "Was that really necessary?"

Raef smiled. "You think I'm going to let her to eavesdrop on our little talk?"

Rylan stopped in the aisle near the foot of his bed. "She was already unconscious."

"Maybe," Raef said. "Maybe not."

"What are you doing here, Raef?"

"I could ask you the same thing."

"That's none of your business."

"The King of the Wood begs to differ. You were seen speaking to an inquisitor in Glaeyand. Now you're in Ancris by special invitation."

Rylan had to take care. Raef was no longer a mere lackey in the Red Knives. He was Llorn's second in command, his enforcer. "I spoke to the inquisitor in Glaey- and because she got the quintarch's indurium hurt. I'm here for the same reason. Bothymus got cranky after his fight with Fraoch and needed a bit of tending."

"And that's the only reason you're here?"

As far as Rylan knew, Llorn didn't know about the connection between Korvus and Renato. Had that changed? Was Raef trying to catch him in a lie? After considering, Rylan doubted it. The one-handed thug seemed merely distrustful, not angry.

"Quintarch Lucran will be in my debt if I heal Bothymus," Rylan said. "You don't think that's worth coming to Ancris for?"

Raef shrugged. "Perhaps. Since you're here already"—Raef reached inside his waistcoat and pulled out a small, linen-wrapped package—"we've got another assignment for you."

"What kind of assignment?"

"Llorn's grateful for what you did with Morraine's wisp." The package was square, roughly two fingers to a side. Raef tossed it onto Rylan's bed. "He wants to reward you."

Rylan snorted. "And in what way is dumping an assignment on me a reward?"

Raef pointed to the package. "Open it."

Rylan nearly refused, but his curiosity won out. He picked up the package, tugged at the twine, and unfolded the linen. Inside was a small vial of clear liquid and a cube of red, chalky substance. Crainh. It was a deadly poison derived from the lucertae of auburn dragons. When activated properly, it produced a miasma that spread quickly, killing anything caught in it. It was expensive, more than pure indurium, but favored by those who could afford it because, though it smelled noxious while active, the odor dissipated quickly and the powder itself was consumed entirely, leaving no trace. Though auburn dragons were very rare, a number of Red Knives were bonded to them.

Rylan folded the linen over the vial and the crainh and held it out toward Raef. "Like I told Llorn, I'm not a Knife, and I'm certainly no assassin."

"You don't even know who the mark is."

"I don't *care* who the mark is. I'm not doing it."

Raef continued as if Rylan hadn't spoken. "Tomorrow night, you're going to sneak into the imperial library in Ancris and leave that shit in a room set aside for a historian."

"Why would I assassinate a historian?"

"Because you are going to steal a bronze chalice. It's being delivered by an archivist to the aforementioned historian."

"What's so special about it?"

Raef shrugged. "The Hissing Man wants it. Llorn wants it first."

"As what, leverage of some sort?"

"None of your business. Get the bloody chalice. The historian dies. The archivist . . ." Raef shrugged again. "That's up to you."

Rylan shook the package. "I already said no."

"What if you knew the historian hasn't always been a historian?"

Rylan snorted. "I suppose next you're going to tell me he was an inquisitor."

Raef smiled. "Good guess. You're smarter than you look."

Rylan's throat tightened. He knew where this was going. He knew who the historian that Llorn, for whatever reason, wanted dead. Part of him didn't want to confirm it, but he couldn't help asking. "His name?"

"Kellen Vesarius. Or, as he was known when he wore the white shield, Inquisitor Kellen."

The name played in Rylan's mind. He was the inquisitor who'd petitioned for Beckett's burning and wanted Rylan burned with him to set an example. If Beckett hadn't blurted out Rylan's birthright, Rylan would be a scorch mark on a burning deck.

Rylan had dreamed of Kellen's death. It had taken him years to let go of the anger, the hate. He'd vowed not to kill as the empire killed, but to leech power from them instead. To weaken them in order to benefit the Holt, the Kin especially.

Rylan unfolded the cloth and stared at the red, chalky cube. The more he stared at it, the more the old hatred filled him.

"You see, Rylan?" Raef said with something between a smile and a snarl. "We can be friends. We can look out for one another."

"Ancris is Blythe's territory. Why didn't she bring it?"

"Blythe is . . . indisposed."

"If you hurt her . . ."

Raef chuckled. "We're not like the empire, Rylan. We don't throw away our own, not without good reason."

"Then where is she?"

"She's staying above Hollis's shop in Slade. She hasn't taken Aarik's death well. She's on the lace again."

Brightlace, the hallucinogen that had nearly killed her years ago.

Rylan shook his head. "And you're letting her?"

"For now . . . Llorn's giving her time to grieve. Get the chalice for us. Bring it to Hollis's shop. You can talk her then. Help get her back on her feet."

It seemed odd that she would stay at Hollis's. Hollis stayed as far away from Red Knife business as he could, which made Rylan wonder if he'd been coerced. Blythe's relapse was also worrisome, but Rylan couldn't worry about either of those things just then. He stared at the crainh and the vial, trying to decide, but then he remembered the orange flames, Beckett screaming, Aunt Merida wailing . . .

"Tell me about the library . . ."

FORTY-NINE: AZARIAH

zariah sat in his office at the top of the temple tower, waiting for the results of the tests Japheth was performing on the peat that had miraculously fallen into his hands. Nox shone through the balcony doors behind
him, looming above the horizon like a lidless eye. Reckoning was only a few
hours away.

Though accustomed to staying up late, Azariah was bone-tired. After the arcfire at the eyrie, the privy council meeting with Quintarch Lucran, and the business with the peat at the shrine, he could still hardly believe his luck. The peat
Llorn had promised had arrived by a most circuitous route. Faedryn had surely had
a hand in it, which bolstered Azariah's confidence that his plan to awaken Strages
would work.

He should have been more pleased by it, but thoughts of the past kept remind-
ing him of Cassian. After becoming illustra, he'd gone to the vyrd often to receive
guidance from Faedryn. Azariah and his fellow illustrae were to build a palisade
on Tortoise Peak and a crucible in a swamp near Hrindegaard. They were to send
slaves to the two sites so the project could begin in earnest.

At the time, Cassian was blossoming from a promising young acolyte to one
of the youngest priests in decades to earn his habit. Azariah considered sharing his
greatest secret with him, but how could he? Cassian was devoted to Alra. He
would never understand the necessity of freeing Faedryn from his prison. Plus, he
was doing so well, achieving what Azariah had wanted at his age. So Azariah let
him be.

In the years that followed, Azariah urged Cassian to go on pilgrimages to
other temples to help deliver their faith to the unenlightened corners of the empire. In truth it was to keep him away from Ancris as Azariah saw to the palisade's
construction. Cassian resisted at first, but he came to enjoy and even embrace the
pilgrimages. He developed a reputation as a gifted orator, even young as he was.
Azariah glowed with pride. Cassian was well on his way to becoming a Priest of
the Second Order.

Japheth, meanwhile, oversaw the project at Tortoise Peak. Azariah arranged
for the slaves to be sent, and the palisade was built. The same was true of the crucible in the Holt, which Camadaea oversaw. Hardly a day went by that Azariah
didn't worry they would be discovered, but months passed without incident, and
eventually the palisade and the crucible were finished, and the slaves were killed
and thrown in mass graves.

Eventually, Cassian truly came into his own. No one was surprised when he attained the rank of Priest of the Second Order, but even Azariah was amazed when he completed all eight trials and became a Priest of the First Order soon after. And his ambition didn't stop there. Mere days after Azariah laid the First Order's golden stole across his son's shoulders, Cassian shared his latest ambition. Erimaea, the site of one of his pilgrimages, had grown swiftly in recent decades, and its Church's congregation along with it. The local order hoped to build a new temple, and Cassian wanted permission to lead the project. It was with no small amount of pride that Azariah agreed.

Months passed, and the power in the earth below the palisade and the crucible grew. As the time to bridge the two powers via the maze neared, Azariah was often drawn away from Ancris. Cassian seemed to take a greater interest in Azariah's comings and goings and asked why Azariah needed to leave Ancris so often.

"I told you," Azariah said, "the alchemysts in Caldoras have found a way to build a barrier against the dark sun's rays. We might use it in Ancris one day." It was the truth but far from the whole truth. Azariah and Camadaea had concocted the story to deflect concerns about their absences.

Cassian looked crestfallen. "I know what you said, but you're gone so often. You promised we'd talk about the new temple in Erimaea. It needs funding, Father. The project is languishing."

"I know." Azariah squeezed his son's shoulder. "We'll talk about the money soon, I promise."

A month later, the palisade was nearing completion, and the pillars needed dismantling. Fresh slaves were brought in to tear the pillars down and bury them in trenches. Then the slaves were killed and cast into the open trenches after them. Azariah had been there to make sure no evidence was left behind. He flew home to find Japheth waiting for him. "I have ill tidings, Your Radiance. Our spies in Highreach tell us Cassian has befriended the eyrie master, Stromm."

"I'm aware."

"Yes, but this morning, shortly after reckoning, Cassian was seen leaving the eyrie on a silver dragon. He flew it toward Tortoise Peak."

Azariah felt a frisson of fear. He hadn't been careful enough. Cassian had become distrustful of him. Cassian must have followed Azariah to Tortoise Peak, but how much had he seen? The dismantling of the pillars? The killing of the slaves? Had he seen Azariah call upon his magic to cover them with earth?

"Tell no one of this," Azariah said to Japheth.

"Of course, Your Holiness."

Japheth bowed and left, and Azariah headed toward his apartments. His unease grew until he felt sick from it. He opened his locket and inhaled a deep pinch of auris to strengthen his link to the Holt. *Today of all days, My Lord, I need your guidance.*

Azariah received a brief flash of Faedryn's tall form, his limbs bound by gnarled roots. Dark eyes stared into Azariah's, and then the vision was gone.

He entered his apartments, planning to change and find Cassian, but Cassian was already there, sitting at the table where they often shared their morning meals.

He wore his black habit and his golden stole. His long blond hair fell over his shoulders.

"Always looking toward the past," came a venomous rasp.

Azariah found himself in his office in the temple, standing across the desk from the Hissing Man.

"I'm merely waiting," Azariah said.

"You're *remembering.*"

"And what business is it of yours if I wish to spend time with Cassian?"

The Hissing Man laughed, then fell into a coughing fit. "He isn't even here!"

"It doesn't matter. You'd understand that if you'd ever loved someone."

"I love our Lord. I feel his pain. It's why I press you when you become rooted in the past."

Though the details were still hidden, Azariah knew Cassian hadn't been abducted. He hadn't gone missing. He'd been killed. "Cassian didn't have to die . . ."

The Hissing Man snarled. "Of course he did! He would have—"

Footsteps padded in the hallway outside, and a knock came at the door.

"Come," Azariah called.

The door opened, and Japheth stepped inside. He bowed to Azariah. "It's done, Your Holiness."

"And?"

Japheth smiled. "It's as powerful as we'd hoped."

"You're sure?"

"Absolutely."

Azariah paused, unsure if it was good news or not. "Are you saying we're ready?"

Japheth nodded. "To wait longer would be to lose control of the trigger."

"Very good, Japheth."

Japheth bowed and left.

When his footsteps had faded, Azariah turned to the Hissing Man. "Tell me what really happened to Cassian."

"No."

Azariah leaned forward over the desk. "I said *tell* me!"

"I will not." The Hissing Man stared at Azariah, crooked-mouthed, gauzy-eyed, and Azariah's desire to learn the truth began to fade. Azariah tried to fix Cassian's face in his mind, tried to hold onto the anger and frustration, but Cassian's face dimmed, and his anger evaporated like so much rain. "Now," the Hissing Man said, "Inquisitor Ordren . . ."

Azariah felt wooden, a puppet with strings. "What about him?"

"Kellen Vesarius visited the Crag this afternoon. Ordren overheard him talking about the chalice. It arrives in Ancris tomorrow. He invited Inquisitors Lorelei and Creed to join him and have a look." The Hissing Man paused, then growled, "Shall I attend to the matter?"

Lorelei had become problematic. Azariah wasn't pleased about it, either, but it wouldn't do to make bold or bloody statements now. "Attend to it, yes, but do so quietly."

"Why *quietly*? She needs to dealt with."

"She does, but she's in check. I've made sure of it. Better that we avoid drawing attention to ourselves, especially over something so distantly related to our cause."

The Hissing Man looked angry—Azariah thought he might even defy him—but then he bowed. "Your Radiance," he said, and limped from Azariah's office.

Azariah put on his mask and walked to the temple's entrance, took a coach to Henge Hill and climbed the slope to the vyrd. In the light of pre-reckoning, he faced the Holt and reached out through the maze. "Your liberation is imminent, My Lord. I only require your blessing, and it shall begin."

Azariah fell a stirring from the Holt, no more. He worried he'd erred in some way, that Faedryn had sensed the trouble with the chalice and blamed Azariah for it. Then he felt himself being whisked away. He was suddenly standing before a black citadel tree. Other citadels loomed around it, but they were blurry and indistinct. The sky was but a shifting, blue-green haze.

Azariah heard a faint whisper, then words echoed in his mind, *"The palisade is ready?"*

"It is, My Lord." Azariah told him everything that had happened since they'd last spoke. "All I need now is your approval."

The black citadel shimmered, and Azariah felt himself sinking, as if the tree was trying to trap *him* alongside His Lord. Then came more whispers and echoing words: *"Trigger the crucible. Awaken Strages. Come to me when it's done."*

Relief flooded through Azariah. "So I shall, My Lord."

The black citadel vanished, and Azariah, feeling suddenly off-balance, staggered backward. He was back in Ancris's vyrd, alone, His Lord's presence hidden behind his prison walls once more. Beyond the menhirs, people were gathering: ferrymen, couriers, mules bearing letters and packages, and travelers waiting for passage to the Holt. Ignoring them all, Azariah stepped from the vyrd and headed down the footpath.

Ancris was bathed in soft light, but it looked ashen in Azariah's second sight. It made him wish Cassian was there to describe the colors and the beauty of pre-reckoning, but the urge soon faded, and he was glad his son hadn't lived to see the destruction of his home.

FIFTY: RHIANNON

Changed and ready for the day, Rhiannon left her bedroom and headed toward the burrow's entrance.

Sister Merida was waiting in the kitchen. "I understand you'll be gone most of the night." She handed Rhiannon a cloth sack. "This should tide you over."

Rhiannon peeked inside and saw a green apple, a wedge of cheese, and a generous heel of brown bread. "I could have made it myself."

"You want to take away the one task at the Rookery I actually enjoy?" Sister Merida smiled and busied herself at the stove. "I'd never forgive you for it." She began washing some bowls in a basin. "Be careful at the vyrd, all right?"

Feeling a pang of regret that Sister Merida was here for *her* sake, Rhiannon nearly told her she should head back to the abbey. Then she thought better of it and said, "I will."

She left the burrow with a smile—she liked having someone around who wasn't trying to use her—but the smile faded as the gnawing feeling in her gut returned. Two turns lower along the stairs, she found her mother waiting for her.

"Ready?" Morraine asked.

Rhiannon fell into step alongside her. "Would you be mad if I said no?"

"I'd be mad if you refused to try."

The day was unseasonably warm and humid, even for the Deepwood Fens. As they wound lower and came near the workhouse, where dragon scales and other ingredients were rendered into drugs, two women—one heavy, one thin—were standing out front smoking tabbaq cigarettes. On seeing Morraine, they stamped them out and went back inside.

Not far from the base of their tree was a shelter with a fenced-in pen for training dragon kits or sometimes to house ailing dragons. Inside the pen, Irik was playfully chasing Tiufalli, the young cobalt kit, while Llorn looked on. Tiufalli gamboled, flapping his wings and suddenly stopped. Irik ran into him, and the two tousled on the ground. Llorn still hadn't declared whether Irik had formed a true bond with Tiufalli, but he didn't need to. The kit loved Irik.

Irik rose and dusted himself off, and Rhiannon waved. Irik waved back and headed toward Llorn, who growled at him to take the dragon's training more seriously. Morraine, stared at them, her eyes softly glowing, and spat on the dirt.

"Morraine!" Heading along a well-worn footpath toward them was Sister Dereka. She stopped several paces away and bowed her head. "The looking glass is waiting for you at the vyrd."

"Very good," Morraine said.

Sister Dereka regarded Rhiannon sourly and headed up the winding stairs, and Morraine led Rhiannon along the footpath beyond.

"What's a looking glass?" Rhiannon asked, all but certain it wasn't a mirror.

"You'll see soon enough."

Rhiannon was tempted to press for answers but the urge died when she noticed how her mother was favoring her right side. Morraine's hands shook as well, and her lips were quavering. She looked like she was in pain and trying not to show it.

"I don't need your pity," Morraine said with a sideways glance.

"It's not pity, and it's getting worse."

"I'll be fine."

Morraine said their shared bond helped to ground her and prevent her soul from slipping from her body, but the bond alone wasn't going to be enough. Only a few days had passed since her quickening, and she'd already grown weaker. Rhiannon worried that soon, she'd simply collapse and her wisp would float up from her body to begin its second life anew. Rhiannon had overheard Llorn tell Morraine that she could take more from their bond, but refused to.

As they took a bend in the path, the gnawing feeling ebbed. "I'm only tired, child. I'll be fine."

It was a lie, but Rhiannon knew better than to press.

Beyond a violet-covered hill, the vyrd came into view. When they came closer, Rhiannon spotted a brass basin at its center, surely the looking glass Sister Dereka had mentioned. The basin had clawed feet and was roughly the size of a serving platter. Next to it was an earthenware jug, the sort used at mealtimes for sapwater or pine milk.

They passed between two tall menhirs and knelt on opposite sides of the basin. Morraine pulled the jug's stopper and tipped the jug over the basin. Clear sapwater *glugged* out. When the basin was filled almost to the rounded brim, she stopped and set the jug down.

"The basin is magic?" Rhiannon asked.

"No"—Morraine pressed the cork into the mouth and smacked it with the palm of her hand—"but the spell I'm about to cast will allow us to use it to roam the forest and search for Yeriel." The blue glow of her mother's eyes intensified as she whispered words of power. "*Sgàthan cian, sgàthan cian . . .*" Repeating the chant over and over, she leaned forward, dipped a finger into the sapwater, and ran it around the basin's edge. She did so three times, then sat back, and the glow in her eyes dimmed. "Sister Dereka tells me you can sense the forest?"

"A bit, yes."

"Well, that sense is like eyesight, and this"—she tapped the basin's rim—"is like a spyglass. Bend your will on it, as you do the citadel trees, and it will take you far from here. We'll use it to search for the veil."

"As simple as that?"

"No, not simple, but the shard will guide us." Morraine tugged on a leather cord around her neck and brought up the shard from beneath her dress. It was wrapped in leather so she could wear it like a pendant. She took the pendant off and held it out. "Take it."

Rhiannon took the shard and felt its tingle, turned it over and stared at its colorful facets.

"Yeriel's soul is tied to that relic," Morraine continued. "Searching for *her* is a matter of searching for that thread and seeing where it takes you."

"How do you know?" Rhiannon asked.

"Because I saw it once, before I died. I was never able to master following it, though."

"And you think *I* can?"

Morraine tilted her head. "There's only one way to find out, child. But be sure not to go too far. We can't have you getting lost."

"Lost?" Rhiannon felt her panic start to rise. "How would I even know?"

"Because you'll feel thin."

"What does that even mean?"

"That if you go too far, you'll start to lose all sense of your physical self. Pay attention to your heartbeat, the stink of the fens, the feel of the wind on your cheeks. Use them as anchors."

The urge to give the shard back was getting stronger by the moment. "But what if I *do* lose sense of myself entirely?"

"Then you'll go mad, so *don't*."

The crystal was tingling so much her fingertips felt numb. "I don't even know what I'm looking for." The words sounded small and pathetic.

"And you never will unless you try. The thread will be subtle, like a single strand of hair on the surface of a pond. Take your time. Be aware. Don't go too far."

Rhiannon clutched the crystal in both hands and held it close to her chest. The bones in her hands juddering, Rhiannon took a deep breath and expanded her awareness. As she had in the past, she felt the trees, their vastness as they went on and on.

"Look into the water," Morraine said.

Rhiannon did, but all she saw was a reflection of the snail-shaped clouds in the sky overhead. "It isn't working."

Morraine tapped the basin's rim, producing a *ting* that went on and on. The view of the sky wavered and was replaced with a view of Irik and Llorn in the dragon pen with Tiufalli. Rhiannon gasped.

"Good," Morraine said. "Now go farther. Listen to the shard."

She willed herself beyond the Rookery, and the view swept toward the fens with its dragonflies and midges. She felt like a wisp, weightless, going where she would with no one to stop her. She came to a small brook and followed it to a creek. She followed the burbling creek and came to the churning waters of the Diamondflow. She felt the wind blow, felt the heat under the sun and the cool in the shadows of the trees. She smelled the river's fresh scent, the stink of a half-eaten deer carcass near the riverbank. Try as she might, though, she sensed no threads, and bending her will on the crystal seemed no help whatsoever.

She continued for some time, always making sure she could sense her own heartbeat, her breath, the feel the solidity of the stone beneath her folded legs. Cant arrived with a clash of lights. As the sky dimmed and Nox rose, Rhiannon returned her awareness to the vyrd. Morraine let the hood of her cloak fall against her back. Rhiannon pulled her own hood up and hooked the loop of her sleeve flaps around her middle fingers. Then she gripped the shard tight and re-entered the looking glass.

For a time, she was drawn to the underroot, where the citadels' roots dove deep into the earth. It made her sleepy, somehow, so she breathed and drew her attention up toward the forest floor. She passed a pack of wolves on their nightly hunt, saw a clutch of onyx dragons taking flight, found a woman and a boy on a night ranging far to the south. She felt villages on the ground, cities in the trees. But of Yeriel hidden behind the veil of Gonsalond, she sensed nothing.

Her mother had said to search for the thread that connects Yeriel to the crystal, yet try as she might, Rhiannon couldn't find it. In the hours that followed, she grew tired and couldn't maintain the connection any longer. Like rain pooling into a puddle, she returned to herself.

"I'm sorry, I didn't find anything." When Morraine made no reply, Rhiannon stood and looked around. The vyrd and the clearing beyond it were empty. "Mother?"

Rhiannon was tempted to go looking for her, but she was famished. She ate the apple, cheese, and bread Sister Merida had packed for her. She sipped the faintly sweet sapwater from the jug. She listened to the whine of the cicadas and the wind through the trees. Somewhere far away, a panther yowled, prompting Rhiannon to draw the small knife at her belt until she was sure it wasn't coming in her direction.

Wisps floated in the distance, making Rhiannon feel sleepier than she already did. When her eyes drifted shut, she blinked them furiously open. Morraine would yell at her if she found Rhiannon sleeping. She was ready to head back to the Rookery to see if her mother was there, but then her gaze fell on the looking glass, and she wondered if she could use it to find her mother. She returned to the basin, set the crystal aside, and focused on the reflection in the water. When nothing happened, she tapped the rim, as her mother had. As the *tinging* sound faded, her vision was swept away.

She'd had difficulty finding Yeriel's thread, but the one that tied Rhiannon to her mother was easy to follow. It led her to the nearby fen. The ground felt peculiar there—*heavy*, somehow, as if the land all around it were being drawn inward. Hearing voices, she floated toward them and saw her mother speaking to a druin with a long, striped beard. Faedryn's teeth, it was Brother Mayhew. His right hand was wrapped in bloody bandages, he had bloody cuts on his face as well, but otherwise he looked much the same as she remembered.

More surprising than Brother Mayhew's presence was the pillar he and Morraine were standing next to. Made of glittering black stone, the pillar was tall as ten men. Beyond it were more pillars. They formed a massive circle in the fen.

"Well, you're back now," Morraine was saying, "that's all that matters." She put one hand on the pillar. "And the crucible is nearly—"

Morraine stopped speaking. She looked confused, wary, then she snapped her head right and seemed to stare directly at Rhiannon.

Rhiannon tore her gaze from the looking glass. Hands shaking, she stood and backed away while staring in horror toward the fen. Her mother had caught her spying. She was going to be furious. As the insects whined, she wondered how bad her punishment would be. Would her mother switch her? Beat her?

A short while later, she heard footsteps shushing through the tall grass. Morraine appeared, standing outside the henge. "Come. It's time to go home."

Rhiannon stood there, stunned. Was her mother just tired? Was she going to punish her in the morning? She picked up the crystal by its leather cord and slung her cloth sack over one shoulder. "Should I take the looking glass?"

"No. Leave it for tomorrow."

Rhiannon left the vyrd, handed the crystal to her mother, and walked next to her in Nox's purple glow. "Aren't you angry?"

Morraine pulled the crystal over her head. "I knew you'd find it eventually."

"But what is it?" Rhiannon paused to let her mother pass through a narrow gap between two bushes, then rushed to catch up. "What are the pillars for?"

"Let me and Brother Mayhew worry about the crucible. I need you to focus on *Yeriel*. We need to know how to master the shard."

"Because you want to control Strages, I know, but the shard is *related* to the crucible in some way. It must be."

"I said leave it alone."

"How am I supposed to help if you keep—"

Morraine stopped and gripped Rhiannon's arm with an ice-cold hand and spun her around. "If I'd had time to raise you properly, you'd know better than to question your elders. Mind your manners, child." Her grip on Rhiannon's arm tightened until it was painful. "Do what you're told." She shook Rhiannon so violently her sack slipped off her shoulder to the ground. "Do you understand me?"

Rhiannon cringed from the pain. "Yes, mother."

Morraine shoved her away and pointed down the path. "Get your worthless hide back to the Rookery."

Rhiannon snatched up her sack and sprinted away. She stumbled, recovered, and ran on. Her arm felt like it had frostbite. She dared a glance behind her and spotted her mother walking in a different direction. Where she might be going, Rhiannon had no idea. There were only wetlands in that direction, lit by the occasional wisp.

FIFTY-ONE: RHIANNON

The day after her first search for Yeriel, a heavy pounding came at the door to Rhiannon's burrow. The door groaned open, and a hushed conversation followed. One voice was Sister Merida's, the other Brother Mayhew's. The conversation quickly escalated. "She will attend me *now*," Brother Mayhew said.

"She will attend you after she's had her morning meal," Sister Merida replied.

"It's mid-bloody-afternoon!"

"She was up late."

In the ensuing pause, Rhiannon thought she was going to be forced to leave the burrow hungry, but Brother Mayhew relented. "Just have her hurry."

The door thumped closed.

"No time to waste," Sister Merida said, standing in the doorway of her bedroom. "Get dressed."

Rhiannon hurried, as much for Sister Merida's sake as her own, and changed into a fresh robe. She headed to the kitchen, where Sister Merida had set out pine milk, mulberries, and cinnamon biscuits. Rhiannon gobbled it up as fast as she could.

"You heard Brother Mayhew?" Sister Merida asked.

Rhiannon nodded while stuffing a biscuit into her mouth. Most of it ended up on her chin and up her nose.

"You'll be curious about his hand," Sister Merida said, "but I'm warning you, don't ask him about it."

"Why not?" Rhiannon asked. "What happened?"

"Swallow, then talk. He went to Ancris and was captured by their inquisitors along with Aarik. Aarik was burned by their bloodthirsty shepherds, but Brother Mayhew was put in a dungeon and tortured. He . . . told them some things he shouldn't have. He was lucky to escape with his life, but Llorn is wroth with him. I don't think a man can blamed for talking under torture, but Brother Mayhew will no doubt feel ashamed of it. So don't mention it."

Rhiannon nodded, then tossed several tart berries in her mouth. She covered her full mouth with her hand and said, "But why should he lose a finger? It's barbaric."

"You'll get no argument from me, but Llorn must think he needs to make examples to maintain order now that he's King of the Wood." Sister Merida busied herself around the wash basin. "You're to meet your mother at the vyrd, but Brother Mayhew wishes to speak with you first."

Rhiannon wolfed down the last of the berries, chasing them with the pine milk, and left the burrow. It was late. The bright sun was already falling. Cant was only a few hours away. On her way downtree, she found Brother Mayhew talking with the archdruin, Sister Dereka. The bandage on Brother Mayhew's hand had been changed—there was only a tiny spot of blood where his pinky had been. He still had his wyvern-claw staff, which made Rhiannon wonder if he'd somehow got it back before he escaped or if he'd never taken it to Ancris in the first place. Sister Dereka left when she saw Rhiannon approach.

"I hear you mucked up the ritual," Brother Mayhew said.

Rhiannon, feeling her cheeks go hot, said nothing.

Brother Mayhew waved to the stairs, and they began circling their way down. "Was your mind wandering again?"

"It wasn't that."

Brother Mayhew's staff thumped on the steps. "Then what was it?"

"She's my mother."

"So?"

Rhiannon stopped. "She's my mother, and she was dead. That was supposed to mean something in the Holt."

Brother Mayhew turned to toward her, vaguely annoyed. His bald pate reddened. "It *still* means something, but we live in precarious times. Your mother is crucial to our plans to overthrow the imperator, as are you now that she's reliant on you."

"I didn't want to force her to relive her torture. *That's* why I hesitated."

Brother Mayhew shrugged. "What's done is done." As they continued down the stairs, he said softly, "When Llorn first came to me and asked if you were strong enough to help raise your mother, I told him yes. I thought your involvement would end when your mother was returned to us. You should have been back in the abbey by now." He glanced down at her. "I'm sorry you're not."

Rhiannon's mouth nearly fell open. Brother Mayhew *never* apologized.

Below, men and women in drab clothing filed into the workhouse. Near it, the dragon pen was empty, Tiufalli, Llorn, and Irik having gone on some trek to formally begin the process of his bonding.

"You're lucky, in a way," Brother Mayhew said. "My father died when I was very young. My mother made scrimshaw cameos and wanted me and Maladox to follow in her footsteps, but the ones that sold the best were profiles of quintarchs or dominae or illustrae. I refused to pay them homage, so I left home and joined a crew of trappers. My mother was furious."

Rhiannon hid a smile. "Are you saying you *disobeyed* your mother?"

"Don't get smart. I stayed with the trappers for three years, then joined a band of mercenaries. I was never good at fighting, but I was good at stitching flesh, and I knew a thing or two about herbal medicines, so I became their surgeon, tending to their wounds, patching them up after run-ins with the empire, the Red Knives, or even other mercenary bands. Then one day we came across a druin." He pointed uptree. "Sister Dereka. She was wounded and dying from a fight with a juvenile onyx. I made an elixir to help her body fight the infection. It was touch and go for a while, but she eventually recovered."

"*That's* how you became a druin?"

"In a manner of speaking. She offered me a place in her order before we went back to the forest. I declined and spent another two years as a surgeon. But I eventually tired of it. I wanted to make a difference, so I went to the abbey she'd told me about and became her aspirant."

"You're the same age, though."

"True, but a fledgling in the druinic ways. My point is, it took me nearly two decades to find my calling. You learned to speak to the wood when you were barely out of nappies. The lessons of aura and umbra come to you easily when you put your mind to it. Don't take it for granted. Use it. For yourself. For your mother. For all of us."

He seemed to leave out that part that he had had the freedom to make his own choices, but he wanted her to obey Morraine and Llorn. She wasn't sure she wanted to. "Did it hurt, you finger?"

"Of course it bloody hurt."

"Llorn shouldn't have made you do it."

Brother Mayhew stopped. "I *deserved* it, girl."

"For what, getting caught? It wasn't your fault. If anything, it was his."

His eyes went wide. "Never say such things. Do you hear me? Especially where other folk might hear you." He held the hand out for her to look at. "It's a small price to pay to gain independence for the Holt. The way ahead will be difficult. You must be brave."

"I'll try."

Brother Mayhew seemed unconvinced.

When they reached the vyrd, Morraine was inside it, holding the crystal and standing beside the looking glass.

"Go on now," Brother Mayhew said, "attend your mother well."

Rhiannon headed between the standing stones.

Morraine watched her approach. "You don't seem pleased he's come back."

"It's not that. It's what Llorn did to him. It wasn't right."

"Yes, well"—Morraine held the crystal out for Rhiannon to take—"Llorn has always confused suffering with virtue."

"And you don't?"

Morraine shrugged. "Suffering is a currency of sorts, the cost of change." They knelt on opposite sides of the looking glass. "The greater the change, the more one must suffer for it."

"But that's not true. Llorn didn't *have* to cut off his finger. But Brother Mayhew hardly seems bothered by it."

Morraine dumped the old sapwater and poured more from the jug. "Brother Mayhew considers it penance."

"Penance for what?"

"Before I died, I was taken by the inquisitors. Brother Mayhew was there. He tried to save me but failed. When he told Aarik about it, he fully expected Aarik would punish him, but he didn't. He admitted to me how it pained him to pay no price for not saving me, as if Aarik thought him not worthy of the effort. I suspect he's secretly relieved that Llorn *did* demand a price for what happened in Ancris."

"But what did he do that was so terrible that—"

Morraine raised a deathly pale hand. "Enough." She gestured to the basin. "Begin."

As she had the previous afternoon, she took a deep breath, spread her awareness, and entered the looking glass with a flick of a fingernail. For a time, she gripped the shard and searched for the thread that connected it to Yeriel, but the strange crucible and its black pillars were like a lodestone, constantly drawing her toward them each time she cast her consciousness over the Holt.

"Concentrate," Morraine said.

"I am."

"No, you're not."

She was right, but Rhiannon couldn't make herself ignore the black pillars she'd seen the night before.

"Bough and branch, girl," Morraine said. "Will your curiosity be slaked if I show you the bloody thing?"

Rhiannon hoped she wouldn't be punished for it, but she nodded.

Morraine stood and led her toward a gap in the vyrd's ancient stones. "Up. The sooner this is done, the sooner we can get back to our work."

Lux was low in the sky by then, but cant was still a good hour away. A putrid scent filled the air, like rotten eggs, and it strengthened as they walked. The nauseous feeling that accompanied it intensified the cavernous feeling in her gut.

"I can feel your hunger, you know," Rhiannon said.

Morraine guided them around a honeylocust tree. "So?"

"You need sustenance."

"I'll be fine."

"All I mean to say is, you can take it from me if you wish—"

"No. Now hush. We're here."

The path cut through a tangle of meadowsweets. Their fragrant scent somehow made the noxious smell of the fen even worse. Beyond the bushes was the sprawling wetland she'd glimpsed the night before. Brother Mayhew was nowhere to be seen, but the first of the glittering black pillars was only fifty paces ahead. The others curved into the distance, forming a perfect circle. Between and above the pillars was what looked like a soap bubble. She stared up at it, blinking. She stepped closer and peered at the intricate, smoke-like patterns forming and dissipating like oily spots on the soap bubble.

"What's the dome for?" she asked.

"The answer lies *beneath* the pillars."

Rhiannon allowed her awareness to spread. She sensed the aura, the power of the bright sun, being dispersed by the dome. "It's shading the fen from the bright sun."

Morraine nodded. "Good."

"But why?" Rhiannon asked. "What does it do?"

"The earth beneath our feet brims with umbra. You know this, yes?"

"Yes," Rhiannon said, and repeated what Brother Mayhew had taught her. "Aura rises and collects in the mountains, where it slowly floats from Vanu toward the realms of Déu. Umbra sinks and flows like water through the earth. Some of it is carried off by the Diamondflow to the Olgasian Sea, but most is drawn deep into the earth and consumed by the seven hells of Kharos."

"Very good. What about lowlands?"

"Much like water flow, the lowlands around bogs and fens are shaped in such a way that umbra lingers. That's why many of the old rituals are performed in such places."

Morraine pointed to the circle of pillars. "The pillars are driven deep in to the earth to give the crucible its power. Together, they create the curtain, which drives aura *away*, preventing it from weakening the umbra."

"That would make the ground here powerful. Maybe more powerful than any other place in the Holt."

"Precisely."

Rhiannon watched as a fiddlehead shape formed on the oily bubble, unfurled, and scattered into smoke. "And the patterns?"

"They're a byproduct of aura and umbra coming into contact. Each acts like fuel and flame. They burn each another up. But some of the aura slips down along the curtain to the pillars and then down into the earth."

"That answers *what* it does, but not why."

"Has Brother Mayhew taught you about sinkholes?"

Rhiannon shrugged. "Some, yes. They happen when the earth below a fen stops allowing umbra to pass through it. A downward pull is created, and eventually the earth gives and the land sinks, creating ponds or sometimes lakes."

"Very good. That's precisely what's happening here. We're creating a sinkhole."

"But why? Why go through all this trouble?"

"Because in order to gain control of Strages, he must be awakened. And that can only happen if the powerful spell that protects the shrine is destroyed." She pointed to the pillars. "The umbra the crucible is gathering will help us do that."

Rhiannon wanted to know more, but she held her tongue on hearing the sounds of conversation coming from behind her. She turned and saw Brother Mayhew and Sister Dereka walking toward her along the path. They stopped short on seeing Morraine and Rhiannon.

Brother Mayhew gaped at them, his long beard waggling in the light breeze. "Are you certain it's wise to show her?"

"She was going to find out sooner or later," Morraine said.

Brother Mayhew's bushy eyebrows pinched. "Later would have been better."

"I disagree."

He looked ready to argue, but apparently decided not to. "As you say. It's fortunate you're here in any case. The sister and I would like a few words."

Morraine laid a cold hand on Rhiannon's shoulder. "Return to the vyrd, child. Begin your search anew. I'll be along shortly."

When her mother joined nearly an hour later, she seemed vexed and wouldn't answer any of Rhiannon's questions.

FIFTY-TWO: LORELEI

The morning after the debacle at the shrine, Lorelei sparred with Creed in one of the Crag's training circles. They wore padded coats, fencing helmets, and wielded blunted rapiers and poniards. In typical fashion, Creed bested her in their first three bouts, but the score was even in the fourth—three strikes apiece—and Lorelei was determined to take one from him before they headed to the library to see Kellen.

She approached Creed warily and swung her rapier. Creed blocked it with his poniard and thrust his rapier at her belly. She turned it aside but had to skip back from his cheeky follow-up with his poniard. He overextended in doing so, and Lorelei swung wildly at his head. Creed ducked and retreated with liquid ease.

A pair of constables stopped to watch as they circled one another. Lorelei waited for an opening, but Creed was as fast as he was big. She swung hard down at his hip, trying to get under his guard, but Creed smashed her rapier down with his poniard so hard her arm went numb.

She sucked air through clenched teeth and dodged back. Creed smiled at her behind his face guard. She flexed her wrist as if she were trying to make the pins and needles to go away, and Creed thrust straight at her gut. She leaned away, swung her rapier up under his guard, and touched his chest.

Breathing heavy, they separated, raised their swords in salute, and lowered their weapons. The constables smiled and headed toward the Crag's rear entrance.

"Not bad," Creed said as he removed his helmet, "but as I've said, you need more power behind those lunges."

"You're just sore you lost," Lorelei said between breaths.

"I just wanted a workout, Lorelei." He wiped the sweat from his brow with the back of his sleeve. "Remember, this is play. Everything changes in a real fight. That poke you just gave me wouldn't have pierced one of Kellen's dusty old scrolls."

They entered the weapons hall, and Lorelei slipped out of her padded coat. "I know the rules change in a real fight." She hung her practice gear on the wall. "I'll change with them." Creed looked like he was about to launch one of his lectures about muscle memory, so she made for the exit. "I'm off for a bath! You're still coming with me to see Kellen and his dusty old scrolls, yes?"

He nodded, but seemed annoyed. "Accuracy and *power*, Lorelei. It'll save you one day!"

After they'd bathed and changed into their uniforms, they left the Crag and headed into the city. Most days Lorelei would need to slip from place to quiet place, but Creed was more talkative than usual, and it helped calm her nerves. As they entered the quadrata, however, it felt like everyone—from the man walking his wolfhound to the woman at her wine cart to the jongleur and the small crowd of children around him—was watching her. She quickened her pace, and Creed, without a word, quickened with her. They hot-footed it to the library, walked through the doorway, and Lorelei took a moment to calm her pounding heart.

"Good?" Creed said after a moment.

Lorelei blinked, let out a slow breath, and nodded. "Good." They headed up the stairwell to the third level. "Knock, knock," Lorelei said as they entered Kellen's research room.

Kellen was sitting behind his desk, poring over an old clay tablet. As Creed headed toward the cork board at the far end of the room, Kellen leaned back, pulled off his spectacles, and laid them on the desk. "Well, well, a more unrefined pair of scofflaws I've never seen."

Creed crossed his arms and considered the crowded notes and multicolored strings pinned to the cork board. "A mad spider, indeed," he mumbled.

"What's that?" Kellen said.

Creed turned to face him. "Lorelei tells me you're penning a masterpiece."

"Mmm . . . You enjoy history, Creed?"

Creed grinned, but Lorelei recognized it as more of a shrug. "Who doesn't?"

Kellen looked amused. "Would you like to hear about Justinian's victory over the Kin at Blackthorn, then? Or maybe you're more interested in the binding of the empire's first indurium."

Creed made a show of considering Kellen's offer. "I think I'll wait for the book."

Kellen nodded. "Yes, perhaps that would be best."

"So"—Creed slapped his hands and rubbed them—"where's this bloody chalice then?"

"Ah, unfortunate news, I'm afraid," Kellen said. "The trading caravan Ezraela joined has been delayed."

"That *is* unfortunate," Creed said with a sidelong glance at Lorelei. "I rather think your former protégé was hoping to postpone her stint in records."

Kellen's bushy eyebrows rose. "Records, is it?"

"Yes, but it was hardly my fault." She gave him the high points, up to and including the discussion with Illustra Azariah and the punishment Damika had meted out.

Kellen took it all in stride. "You know what they say about inquisitors who haven't done time in records, Lorelei . . ."

"No, what's that?"

"They're like rams with no horns."

"Useless?" Lorelei said.

"*Incomplete*," replied Kellen.

Lorelei rolled her eyes. "I'll try to remember that while I nurse the paper cuts and blisters."

"Well, the good news is the caravan should arrive by late afternoon. Perhaps you could come by after your temporary imprisonment? I really would like to look over the writing on the chalice with you."

Lorelei nodded, then looked to Creed. "You?"

He shrugged. "Fine, but I'm not coming hungry. I know how you two get when you start arguing about history. We'll eat, then we'll come." He turned to Kellen. "Does that suit?"

"That suits fine." Kellen pulled on his spectacles and leaned over his scroll. "Good hunting, inquisitors."

Creed accompanied Lorelei as far as the road leading up to the Crag. "Damika's got me chasing a rumor of a new drug den being set up on a riverboat, if you can believe it. I'll meet you in records this afternoon." With that he trotted off.

Lorelei reported to Maudrey, the spindly woman who tended to the voluminous records in the Crag's basement. "You're late," the old woman said.

Lorelei took off her coat and hung it over a chair. "Had to help quell a riot."

Maudrey snorted. "Inquisitors. Always grousing about records, but ask them to help file? Oh, no, that's too much, isn't it?" She pointed to a loose pile of papers on a wooden table. "Last month's reports. Bind them, label them, and stack them over there." She pointed to a similar wooden table with stacks of leather-bound volumes.

Lorelei got to work. The binding she did was nowhere near the quality of a proper bookbinder. It was quick and dirty. It was also mindless, which gave her time to think about the shrine, the peat, and who Blythe had intended to deliver it to. Her mind kept drifting to Rylan, though, and the pleasant talk they'd had outside the shrine, the protective way he'd looked at her when Azariah dismissed him.

Time and again she tried to clear her mind and focus, but she'd been thinking about those other things for days. With no way to follow up on her questions, she was stuck. And Rylan was like the first warm breeze in spring—pleasant, welcoming, calming. The gentle way he had with dragons was endearing. He'd treated Bothymus with care and patience, even compassion, first in Glaeyand after the attack by the cobalt, then again behind the eyrie on Blackthorn. She saw him in her mind's eye, standing in front of Bothymus, one hand held out, fingers spread wide, the other behind his back, singing with his pinched to avoid becoming spellbound by Bothymus's dazzling wings.

Less than a day had passed since the arcfire at the eyrie. She still hadn't had time to digest it all. As was often the case when something momentous happened, memories of it flashed before her, one after another. Stromm holding up the crop stone. Bothymus raising his head like a threatened viper, then spreading his mesmerizing wings. She'd written off Bothymus's display as a symptom of his proximity to the rift. Rylan said seeing the crop had triggered the big indurium, which seemed reasonable at the time, but it was also the same moment Rylan approached him.

She allowed that moment to play out again. Bothymus's third eyelids swept over his eyes on seeing Rylan. His head jerked back. His jaws spread. All were signs of wariness, even distrust.

She began to question Rylan's sudden appearance on the servants' deck in

Glaeyand, why he was helping Bothymus in the first place, his letter to Skylar about Bothymus's health, his offer to come to Ancris. She had no grounds to question why he was in Ancris, but she couldn't stop thinking about. It was a sixth sense she'd come to trust over the years.

As she finished with a bound volume and placed it on the table Maudrey had indicated, she vowed to set her feelings for Rylan aside and let him prove himself.

Or not.

FIFTY-THREE: RYLAN

Rylan sat high up on the winding stairs of the clock tower. The hood of his coat was up. A small cloth sack, large enough to hold the chalice Raef wanted, hung from his belt. His dragonskin mask covered the lower half of his face. The clock's pendulum and gears clanked overhead, loud but lulling.

He sat beside an embrasure that let bells ring out over the city. Through the vertical slats, Lux cast pillars of golden light on the opposite wall. He had a good view of the quadrata, where people milled, out for early evening strolls or on their way home from work. He was looking for a tall man with a rugged frame and closely shorn hair.

The sky darkened to slate blue. When the bright sun touched the horizon, dull colors splashed against the sky's broad canvas, there and gone in a flash. That the cant was both feeble and quick was an omen, but Rylan wasn't sure how to interpret it.

It's good, he decided. *The murder I'm about to commit will have no witnesses.*

One final burst of green reminded him of Vedron, another good omen, he reckoned.

When the bells began to toll, marking the official end of the cant, Rylan plugged his ears, then pulled out the cloth package Raef had given him, unwrapped it, and stared at the red cube of crainh. It had been years since his anger over Beckett's execution had burned so brightly. He thought he'd put it behind him, but the moment Raef had uttered Kellen's name, his long-buried rage had resurfaced, brighter and hotter than ever.

He saw Skala die all over again. Beckett screamed as the bronze bathed him in flames. Kellen watched impassively, as if Beckett's death meant nothing to him.

Vedron keened in a grove of elm trees outside the city.

"There was nothing you could do," Rylan said, peering out through the embrasure. "You would have died along with her."

Two people walked side by side entered the plaza. Even in the dim light of the cant, Rylan recognized Kellen. He was bony and much taller than the archivist next to him. He'd aged. He had a limp. He no longer wore the armor of an inquisitor or his brightsteel badge, but otherwise he looked much the same as he had that day in the forest. Tall. Hair shorn tight to his skull. Chest out, staring straight ahead as if he owned the quadrata.

In the smallest of mercies, time had made the day that followed Skala's death seem like a dream. Beckett and Rylan were taken to Andalingr, paraded before a magistrate, and sentenced to burn. Only Beckett's sudden revelation of Rylan's heritage had saved Rylan's life, but it made the memory worse. Rylan had felt, sometimes *still* felt, that he should have died beside Beckett.

He raised his left hand and stared at the scarred nub where his pinky had been. He felt the pain of losing it all over again. Kellen had cut it off himself, and seemed to enjoy it.

Kellen and the archivist, Ezraela, entered the library.

Rylan stared at the crainh, feeling like he could ignite it with thought alone. *You don't have to do this,* he told himself. *Raef can do it. He* likes *doing this sort of thing.*

But the very thought of turning his back on Uncle Beckett again made him feel small and cowardly.

"Justice will be done," he told himself, as if it could bring Uncle Beckett back.

He wrapped the crainh in its cloth, stuffed it into his coat, and took the stairs up to the third-floor landing. He listened at the door and heard voices from the other side—one booming, the other subdued. The voices grew louder then softened somewhat. Rylan turned the handle, swung the door open while pressing the handle upward to prevent the hinges groaning. Ten paces ahead on the right, lamplight spilled into the hall from the doorway to Kellen's research room. Rylan padded over the scratched marble floor, passed doors with brass plaques and the musty smell of books.

He pressed against a closed door and peered into the room. Kellen was holding a two-handled bronze chalice in his white-gloved hands. Verdigris coated most of it, but bronze shone through on the well-worn places: the handles, the embossed designs along the base, the lettering around the bowl.

Why are you so important? Rylan wondered. But it was a fleeting thought.

"Ancient," Kellen said.

"Yes." Ezraela was a mousy woman with a high forehead and rosy cheeks. "It predates the empire by at least five centuries."

"I'm surprised you haven't tackled it already," Kellen said.

"Yes, well"—Ezraela seemed suddenly uncomfortable—"it was private years ago, and since then . . . well, it hit too close to home."

Rylan had no idea what she was talking about, but he didn't care. He just wanted this over and done with. He crouched, unwrapped the crainh, and set it on the floor. Then he took out the vial of activator it and pulled the stopper.

He paused, thirteen all over again, listening to the *scritch-scratch* of the magistrate's pen, then Kellen's deep voice petitioning the fat magistrate for Beckett and Rylan to be put to the fire.

He shook his head to clear it.

He tipped the vial until the clear, syrupy liquid was bulging at its lip.

"Tell Merida it happened quickly, won't you?"

With the sun of his life about to set, Beckett had been worried not over his *own* fate, but that of his beloved, a woman he constantly bickered with but whom everyone knew he loved dearly.

When Rylan had been allowed to return to Thicket, he'd told the story to Aunt Merida just as Beckett had asked. She hadn't shed a tear. She hardly seemed to feel anything, as if she'd known and had already done her grieving. Only later, when she thought Rylan was sleeping, had he heard her muffled cries.

Rylan had been powerless then. Now, with a tilt of his hand, he could end Kellen's life. He could make his uncle's killer pay. He forced himself to remember how the flames from the bronze dragon wavered in his vision, forced himself to relive Beckett's screams. But no matter how hard he tried, those bitter memories were replaced by Beckett's heartfelt smile, his final request.

Rylan wiped his tears on his sleeve and put the stopper back into the vial. He wrapped the crainh in the cloth and stuffed it back inside his coat. He felt Vedron, hiding in the elm grove. She was relieved. She'd suffered as well, but she rarely thought of revenge, and didn't like it when Rylan slipped into one of his dark moods.

Thank you, Rylan said. He knew she'd been at least partly responsible for the memory of Beckett's parting words resurfacing.

The feelings of warmth he shared with her were cut suddenly short. A week after Beckett's death, days before Rylan had been taken to Glaeyand and given over to Marstan, Rylan had returned to the forest and completed his bond with Vedron. Since then, he'd developed an acute sense of when he or Vedron were being watched. It was a discomfort of sorts, a tickling at the base of his skull.

He peered into the dimness of a large room at the end of the hallway. It was filled with stacks of books and scrolls. He watched for long moments but saw no one.

"In my office," Ezraela said in the nearby room.

"I can get it," Kellen replied.

"I'll join you." While Rylan made himself small against the door, the two of them stepped into the hall. "I bought a crumb cake for us to share."

Kellen's cheery reply was completely at odds with the vision of the monster Rylan had in his head. "I left a little room for dessert . . ."

Their footsteps slowly receded. When they turned right at a gap in the stacks, and the clay lamp they'd taken dimmed, Rylan stepped into the research room. On the desk, lying in a velvet-lined case, was the chalice.

Rylan picked it up. It was ancient, and its inscription had a certain elegance, but beyond that, it looked simple. Common, even.

He ran his fingertips over the script, wondering if it held some ancient secret. Then he stuffed the chalice into the sack hanging from his belt. He was heading for the door when he heard the sound of breaking glass and a woman's high-pitched scream. He ducked into the hall as another scream was cut short. There was a scuffle, a heavy grunt, and a long groan of that swelled into an angry holler.

Rylan's first instinct was to run—it was no business of his—yet he found himself padding toward the commotion.

He peeked down the aisle Kellen and Ezraela had taken and around the shelves. Ezraela lay writhing in a doorway. Blood was gushing from her throat, pooling on the marble tiles below her head. The lamp was near her elbow, still lit, its glass shroud broken and scattered over the floor.

Kellen was wrestling with someone in a black habit. Though old, Kellen was a burly man, thick and heavy. The other man was considerably shorter and frailer looking than Kellen, but he was somehow managing to lower the stiletto he was holding toward Kellen's chest. He had black strips of cloth over his eyes like the zealot group the Chosen wear.

"Tell me where the chalice is," the man in black man rasped, "and I'll give you a quick death."

It suddenly occurred to Rylan that this was the Hissing Man. He was a legend even in the Holt. He was the leader of the Chosen and a ruthless enemy, particularly to the Kin, whom the Chosen had long ago declared as *lesser* than those born of the blood of the empire. Raef had said the Chosen wanted the chalice. That the Hissing Man himself had come to retrieve it spoke of the artifact's importance. The chalice hanging from Rylan's belt felt suddenly heavy.

The Hissing Man slashed Kellen's forearm. Kellen growled and snatched the Hissing Man's wrist. The Hissing Man shoved Kellen against the door jamb. Kellen grimaced, twisted the Hissing Man's hand; the stiletto clattered across the floor, into the pool of blood.

Then the Hissing Man grabbed Kellen's robe and lifted Kellen off the floor, roared and threw him down. Kellen landed awkwardly on Ezraela's corpse.

As the Hissing Man reached for his stiletto on the floor, Rylan told himself to leave. It was none of his business, but instead of backing away, he found himself moving closer, putting his hand on his dagger.

Kellen scrabbled across the floor, grabbed the burning oil lamp, and flung it at the Hissing Man. The Hissing Man batted it away. It shattered against the corner of a bookshelf. Flaming oil splattered on the Hissing Man's trousers and cloak, then spread along the aisle, creeping up the book spines.

Flames climbing up his black robe, the Hissing Man grabbed Kellen again by the throat and raised his bloody stiletto.

"Stop!" Rylan shouted.

The Hissing Man turned toward Rylan. The gauze over his eyes made him like a dead man brought back to life. Kellen struggled, choked, but couldn't escape.

Rylan flipped his dagger through the air. It bounced off the Hissing Man's deformed shoulder as he drove his stiletto into Kellen's midsection.

The fight seemed to leave Kellen all at once. He clutched his gut and groaned, "Why?"

The Hissing Man pulled out the stiletto and batted out the flames licking his left leg. Then he turned toward Rylan. Behind his bandages, his eyes glowed like hot coals.

Rylan felt suddenly cold. He began to fear for his life. The Hissing Man must be using umbra, like one of the Church's shepherds. Rylan was a lot bigger than him, but Rylan knew *he* couldn't have lifted Kellen from the floor like that.

As the Hissing Man stood, Rylan reached into his belt pouch and drew out the lucerta he'd harvested from Vedron weeks ago. Fingers shaking, he placed the scale on his tongue. The taste of burning pine and purified copper made his mouth water. Like holding one's breath underwater, resisting a spell took constant effort and grew painful over time, but slowly, the fear in him eased and he was able to think clearly again.

As the Hissing Man stalked toward him, Rylan became acutely aware of Vedron in her elm grove. She'd sensed his fear and had risen to her clawed feet.

No! he ordered her. *Stay where you are.*

She roared and took flight from the grove. He felt her wings beat the air as she flew toward Ancris.

Black smoke began to fill the room. The Hissing Man, close now, reached for Rylan's mask. Rylan shoved him away and sprinted toward the clock tower. Over the crackle of flames, he heard the Hissing Man's uneven footfalls pounding after him. Even with his deformity, the Hissing Man was gaining on him.

Rylan barreled past the research room and burst through the door to the clock tower. He tried to slam it closed behind him, but the Hissing Man heaved a shoulder into it, shoved a hand through the opening, and grabbed Rylan's sleeve. Rylan jabbed the fingers of his other hand into the Hissing Man's throat. The Hissing Man coughed and fell back half a step.

Rylan shoved the door closed and leaned his weight against it, but the Hissing Man bashed the door with his full weight, sending Rylan slamming against the railing behind him.

As the door crashed open, Rylan climbed onto the iron railing and leapt toward the bell ropes, grabbed an armful of them, and clung fiercely. The bells clanged cacophonously. The Hissing Man stared at Rylan over the railing. The ropes sizzled between his arms, burned his palms and fingers. Rylan held on as long as he could, then dropped to the stone floor and rolled to blunt the impact. He got up and sprinted toward the service door.

He pulled the door open; bells clanged madly again. He glance up, and saw the Hissing Man sliding down along the ropes.

Rylan slammed the door behind him and sprinted toward the quadrata. He heard the door open behind him. He heard a whistling through the air. Felt something twist around his ankles.

He fell hard on the stone quadrata, turned over and saw the stone weights and leather cords of a bola wrapped around his ankles. He sat up, untangled them, jumped to his feet, and the Hissing Man crashed into him.

They tumbled to the ground. The Hissing Man's threw Rylan over on his back and grabbed his throat with both hands. Rylan fought for breath. His ears rang. He felt like his head was going to burst.

"Release him!" a man's voice bellowed. "Lay on the ground, hands behind your head! Now!"

Rylan felt the pressure on his throat ease. The Hissing Man glanced up. Rylan twisted to look, too.

Faedryn's wicked smile, it was Creed and Lorelei.

FIFTY-FOUR: LORELEI

Lorelei finished her work in records and met Creed, Nanda, and Vashtok for a meal at The Road to Beltayne. She was a bit of a lightweight and almost always limited herself to one glass of wine, but she had three glasses of red and a sweet barrel-aged port over the course of their leisurely dinner. Why not indulge herself for once? All she had to look forward to was binding more bloody books.

After Nanda and Vashtok said their farewells, she found herself strolling with Creed around Old Town to walk off some of the liquor. Creed hummed "The Ballad of Hoarfrost Cliff" about a trapped battalion's glorious victory against barbarian raiders. Much to his amusement, Lorelei joined him at the chorus. Normally Lorelei would have sung softly if at all, but she sang full-throated and swept her arms back and forth theatrically. She closed the song on a particularly long note. Creed clapped and fell into a rare belly laugh.

They were on their way to the library to see Kellen and the mysterious bronze chalice when the clock tower bells began ringing discordantly. Lorelei paused, trying to work out whether it was the right time for the bells to ring, when they clanked oddly again.

She and Creed quickened their pace. When they reached the plaza, Lorelei stopped and stared up at library's third floor windows. "Faedryn's teeth."

An orange glow flickered through the glass. Black smoke poured from an open window at the corner of the building. "Faedryn's bloody teeth," she said again. A fire in the library could burn half of Old Town.

Creed made for the entrance. "I'll make sure everyone's out."

"I'll call the brigade," Lorelei said.

Then a masked, hooded figure burst from the clock tower and sprinted across the quadrata. Moments later, a man with a pronounced limp and hunched back whom Lorelei immediately recognized as the Hissing Man raced after him.

The Hissing Man spun metal balls on a rope over his head and flung them at the other man. The weights caught around the fellow's ankles, and he went down hard on the stones with a *whoof*. The Hissing Man jumped on him, wrestled him onto his back, and choked him.

"Release him!" Creed shouted. "Lay on the ground, hands behind your head! Now!"

The Hissing Man looked up. Then he sprinted down an alley of the plaza. The other man ran toward the clock tower.

"Stop!" Lorelei shouted.

Neither man did, but it left Lorelei and Creed with a dilemma. The library was on fire. They needed to get the fire brigade. Plus, Kellen and Ezraela might still be inside.

Shouting arose from the street behind them, and the fire bell rang from the street of the square.

Creed drew his rapier and pointed to the library. "Check on Kellen and Ezraela. I'm going after the Hissing Man."

Lorelei nodded.

"Use the main doors," Creed said. "No confrontations, understand? You're in no state to fight." He turned and pounded toward the alley the Hissing Man had taken.

Lorelei headed though the library's main entrance and up the stairs. The smoke was thick by the time she reached the top floor.

"Kellen? Ezraela?"

No answer, just the crackling of fire. She saw flames burning up the aisles of books in the room adjacent to Kellen's research room. She entered Kellen's room, but found it empty. Other than a cloth-lined case on his desk, everything looked much the same as the last time she was there.

She left Kellen's office and was about to enter the adjacent room where most of the fire was when she heard a resounding boom overhead. It had to be the roof since she was already on the top floor. Then she heard some scraping like scree skittering down a rocky slope. Out the window, fragments of the library's slate roof rained down, and a viridian dragon dropped into view with a rider on its back.

Even a bit woozy, the dragon looked eerily similar to Blythe's viridian. Was the rider *Blythe*? No, she decided. The rider's physique was too masculine.

Powerless to stop his escape, she took a deep breath and rushed toward the main room. "Kellen? Ezraela?"

Nothing. She headed into the smoke and started coughing. "Kellen!" she hacked. The flames flickered dully ahead; the room was like an oven.

"Lorelei?" Kellen shouted weakly. He staggered from the smoke. His tunic was charred. His arm was burned and blistered. His hair and scalp as well. Then he doubled over, clutched his stomach with his good hand. His tunic and leggings were stained with blood.

Lorelei ran to him, slipped his burned arm over her shoulders, and guided him toward the clock tower. Her eyes stung and watered. She could hardly breathe. Kellen staggered and she stopped and righted him. "C'mon!"

At the stairwell, they got a breath of blessedly fresh air. Knowing the air would feed the fire, Lorelei slammed the door shut. Then she led Kellen down the stairs to the ground level service door. He collapsed just outside of it. Lorelei knelt beside him, took a kerchief from her belt pouch and pressed it to his bleeding gut.

"Kellen, wake up!" A crowd had gathered on the far side of the plaza, and she shouted to them, "Get a nun! He's been stabbed!"

A young man and woman sprinted away and returned in less than a minute with a portly nun in a gray robe and a white wimple, who was likely already headed to the library. The nun put her thick leather bag on the ground and knelt beside Kellen. "Tell me what happened."

Lorelei didn't know what happened, but she told the nun where she'd found Kellen as the old woman set to work.

Time passed quickly after that. Kellen's wound was treated and he was taken away on a horse-drawn wagon to the abbey. Creed returned with a nasty gash to his forehead, but without the Hissing Man. He and Lorelei worked with the fire brigade to control the blaze. Somewhere along the way, Nanda and Vashtok showed up and joined them. What turned the tide was a pair of white-robed shepherds, who used the power of aura to help stifle the blaze. Eventually, the fire was brought under control.

By then, it was the middle of the night. Lorelei wanted to go to the House of the Holy Meadow, where Kellen had been taken, but she couldn't. She needed to check Kellen's office first. "Is it safe to enter?" she asked the fire master.

The fire master, a matter-of-fact man with a jet black beard, stared at the owl badge on her swallowtail coat, then Creed's. "It's safe enough. Just be careful on the top floor."

Lorelei borrowed a bullseye lantern from the fire brigade and entered the library. Creed wetted a fresh bandage and cleaned some of the crusted blood from his forehead, then joined her. They headed up the main stairwell, now scattered with debris, to the third floor. The main room, adjacent to Kellen's research room, was a scattering of rubble, burned books, and charred shelves. The roof looked like the blackened ribcage of a tomb drake.

Near a doorway with hinges but no door to speak of lay a blackened corpse. "Ezraela?" Creed asked.

"Must be."

The broken remnants of a shattered lamp were scattered next her.

Lorelei headed to Kellen's research room. The framework around the doorway was splintered. The notes and string and cork board was just a black stain on the wall. Piles of ash lay on his charred desk. A box-shaped hunk of char sat on the floor in front of the desk.

She motioned to it. "I reckon that was what the chalice was stored in."

Creed touched one corner of it with the toe of his boot, and it crumbled. "So where's the chalice?"

Lorelei took a deep breath and let her vision go distant and unfocused. In her mind's eye, she saw the Hissing Man's victim rise and run toward the clock tower. "The one with the mask took it," she said.

Creed's gaze seemed to wander the burned shelf behind her. "You sure?"

Lorelei nodded. "When he ran into the clock tower, he had a cloth sack hanging from his belt. There was something heavy in it."

"Any idea who he was?"

"No, but he was clearly there for the chalice. Maybe the Hissing Man wanted it, too, and that's why they were fighting."

Creed's frown deepened the lines over his blood-stained brow. "This reeks, Lorelei."

Lorelei agreed, but before she could say so, the crunch of approaching footsteps came from the hallway. Praefectus Damika appeared in the doorway. She took off her hat, raked a few strands of her dark, kinky hair into place. "I heard about Kellen. How is he?"

"Stable, last I heard," Lorelei said. "A nun took him to the House of the Holy Meadow, just across the Wend."

"I'll pay him a visit him when I can." Damika glanced back the way she'd come. "The fire master tells me the body is likely the archivist, Ezraela."

"Probably, yes."

"I'm sorry to hear it. Did you know her well?"

Lorelei shook her head. "I've seen her around the library, spoken to her a few times, but that's as far as it went."

Damika nodded. "I hope you'll forgive my abruptness, but as you can imagine, questions are being asked. I need to know if any of this has to do with the Red Knives and the situation in Glaeyand."

Lorelei's cock up in the Holt was the last thing she wanted to think about. "It's possible," she admitted. "The Hissing Man was here, as was Blythe. But we weren't involved, if that's what you think. We were heading to talk to Kellen about a chalice he'd told us about. Then we saw the library burning."

Damika turned to Creed, and he nodded.

"The chalice," Damika said, "Kellen mentioned it's related to the case you were working on with him?"

"That's right," Lorelei said. "Ezraela had just come back from Erimaea, where she'd apparently hidden it away. When we got here, we saw Blythe running from the clock tower and the Hissing Man chasing her—"

"Hold on." Damika stepped back into the hall and waved toward the main room. "Ordren! Over here!"

Ordren entered the room in that lanky, scarecrow way of his.

Damika motioned for Lorelei to continue. "Start from the beginning. Tell us all of it. And then you're going to leave this to Ordren. Go visit Kellen if you wish, then get some sleep. You two look like a dragon chewed you up and spit you out."

Lorelei wanted to argue, but she was in a deep enough hole already. And Damika was right about her needing sleep. She was so tired she could hardly think, and she was getting a bit of a wine hangover. She and Creed answered a few more questions from both Damika and Ordren before the Praefectus seemed satisfied.

"Good?" Damika asked Ordren.

Ordren answered with a shrug and a sneer. "For now . . ."

Damika dismissed Lorelei and Creed.

Lorelei and Creed walked down the stairs and into the quadrata. She felt defeated, but there was nothing she could do. "I'm off to see Kellen," she said.

Creed squeezed her arm, then probed the skin around the gash to his head. "I need to go home and clean this up."

Lorelei made her way to the House of the Holy Meadow. The same nun who'd helped Kellen led her to a starkly appointed room. Kellen lay in the room's lone bed. His head, shoulders, and arm were bandaged. Most of his visible skin was smeared with a shiny ointment applied that reflected the light of the candle on the side table.

"Best you don't stay long," the nun said.

"Of course. Thank you, Sister."

The nun took her lantern with her, leaving the candle on the small bedside table the only light. Kellen, perhaps roused by their voices, opened his eyes and looked around. "Ezraela?"

"I'm so sorry, Kellen."

Kellen tried to speak, failed, then swallowed hard. "The chalice?" He asked and fell into a short coughing fit.

"The chalice was stolen," Lorelei told him.

"By the Hissing Man . . ."

"No, by a thief, we think."

"A thief . . ." Kellen broke his gaze. "I saw him in the aisles when the Hissing Man attacked me."

"Did you recognize him?"

Kellen took some time to think. "He was wearing a mask, but the fire lit him up. He was Kin, and he looked familiar. Someone I met during my time in Andalingr, maybe?" He coughed several times before speaking again. "No, I can't recall . . . Damn, if only I'd . . ."

"Don't worry about it now. We'll find him. We'll find the Hissing Man as well."

Kellen hardly seemed to hear her. He coughed and closed his eyes.

Lorelei went home took a bath to wash off the smoke. As she sat naked in the small copper tub, Kellen's words haunted her: *Someone I met during my time in Andalingr.*

Her aching body begged her to slip into bed and rest, but she couldn't. Not yet. Something Rylan had said was tickling the back of her mind. At the eyrie, he'd told the story of how he'd tended to a cranky gold vixen near Thicket and discovered a rift. He said he'd been visiting family in Thicket, and Thicket was the village below Andalingr, where Kellen had done a two-year rotation with the local constabulary.

She made her way to the Crag. It was an hour before reckoning and drizzling. When she arrived, Maudrey was already in records.

"Will wonders never cease?" the cranky old woman said. "You're actually early."

"I need to see Kellen's old records."

"Well, aren't *you* the cheeky one—"

"He was caught in the fire last night at the library and burned badly. I *need* to see his records."

Maudrey had been working in records for decades. She knew Kellen. They'd been friendly from what Lorelei remembered. After a pause, she nodded soberly and led Lorelei to the shelves on the far side of the room. She pointed to a set of eighteen thick, bound volumes, each lettered with his full name and a range of dates.

She pulled several from early in his career and scoured them until she found what she was looking for, the investigation of Beckett Holbrooke, a Kin woodsman suspected not only of bonding with a dragon, but passing the knowledge to others, both of which carried the death penalty. Rylan Holbrooke was his foster son and had also been apprehended. A viridian vixen had been killed during their capture.

Lorelei scanned the page and found a more detailed description of the chase into the Holt and the apprehension itself. The vixen had been cornered at her nest, which had allowed Kellen's bronze to dispatch her with relative ease, but the nest had been home to two viridian kits, both of which had escaped.

FIFTY-FIVE: RYLAN

Rylan thought surely some radiant, or maybe a full talon of dragons, would be sent from the imperial eyrie to chase him down. Bough and bloody fucking branch, he'd been seen by a dozen people, Lorelei and Creed included, and that was just at the plaza. He'd been furious with Vedron for defying him, but when they reached the elm grove, he was grateful.

"It was still dangerous," Rylan said to her as he slid down her shoulder.

Vedron merely huffed.

He scratched the wattle beneath her chin. "Don't do it again, okay?"

He untied the cloth bag containing the chalice from his belt and stared at it, thinking about what to do next. He was tempted to head back to the Holt, but doing so would implicate him. If Lorelei hadn't already figured out it was him, she surely would when she found out he'd suddenly disappeared. And he still hadn't found out a thing from Master Renato. He needed to get a look at the journal Ash had mentioned.

Rylan stuffed the chalice and the linen-wrapped cube of crainh into one of Vedron's saddlebags, then took out a grapnel and rope and attached it to his belt. "Go to the foothills and hide. I'll call you if I have need."

Vedron lowered her head and nudged him with her snout.

Rylan was heartbroken. "I can't. I have to stay here for a while. I'll come as soon as I can."

Vedron looked like she didn't believe a word of it. She trilled sadly and launched into the cool night air toward the Holt.

Rylan headed toward Highreach. By the time he reached the palace, several hours had passed and reckoning was nearing. He hid in a small stand of pine and waited for the guards to walk past him. Then he threw his grapnel up and scaled the wall.

He scanned the grounds and the palace windows for onlookers. Finding none, he dropped down, ran across the dew-slick lawn, and entered the infirmary through the same window he'd left ajar earlier.

He was just beginning to change out of his smoky clothes when he heard a creaking sound. The injured eyrie hand, Betheny, sat up in her bed. The pale wisplight at the head of the room made her look sickly.

"It's only me, Rylan Holbrooke."

She glanced at the window. "The palace has doors, you know."

"I didn't want to bother the servants. They have long enough days as it is."

She nodded politely, then said, "I wanted to thank you for helping me."

"It was the least I could do."

Betheny shook her head. "You risked your life. Stromm told me to tell you thanks as well. I adore Bothymus. I was worried they were going to put him down."

She was a very nice girl, but Rylan was tired and needed to think. "Well, you're most welcome, as is Stromm."

"You could tell him yourself. He'll be back in a few days."

"I'll be gone by then, I'm afraid."

Betheny looked crestfallen. "You will?"

Rylan nodded. "I'm leaving for Glaeyand this morning, afternoon at the latest."

Her smile faltered. "I'm sure it will be nice to go home."

"What about you? Did the nuns tell you when you could leave?"

"A few more days. Maybe a week." She lay down and pulled the blanket over her. "I'm sorry, Master Holbrooke. I'm so tired."

"It's all right. And please, call me Rylan."

She smiled at that. "Good night, Rylan."

"Good night, Betheny."

He was exhausted, too—beyond exhausted—but the events at the library kept playing over and over in his mind. The chalice was clearly important to the Hissing Man—he wouldn't have gone himself otherwise—but *why* was it important? Why would he be willing to kill over an old bronze cup? Raef might know, but the chances Rylan would see him before he left were slim.

He napped a short while, but was awoken by reckoning's brilliant light. He ate, giving Master Renato and any other lingering alchemysts time to head down to the shrine, then went to the alchemystry and found its doors locked. He took the lock picks from inside his boot heel and easily clicked it open.

Renato's office was at the far end of the room. The door was unlocked. He went to the wardrobe and found the strongbox but it was locked and its lock was considerably more complex than the one on the alchemystry door. It took a few minutes longer than he'd hoped, but he popped it open and threw back the heavy lid. As he'd hoped, Korvus's journal was inside. He flipped to the last few pages and scanned them, hoping to find out why Korvus disappeared, but found little more than tables and notes about the relative strength and flow of aura and umbra in the Holt.

He stuffed the journal behind his back under his belt, then untucked his shirt to hide it. Then he left the alchemystry. In the palace hall he came across the leggy chamberlain. "Ah, Theron, I was hoping I'd find you."

Theron sniffed. "You were?"

"Yes, I'm feeling much better. I was hoping you might be able to arrange a flight back to Glaeyand for me."

Theron flashed a smile. "As it happens, a courier is leaving within the hour. Does that suffice?"

"It does, thank you."

Rylan headed toward the infirmary barely able to hide his smile. Alra had truly shined on him. He was going to escape Ancris having done everything he'd hope to accomplish and more.

But when he got to the infirmary, Betheny was gone and Lorelei, goddess save him, was rooting through his things. She was holding the shirt he'd worn the previous night, and Faedryn's foul laugh, she was smelling it.

"Lorelei," he said as calmly as he could manage.

"Hello, Rylan."

At the sound of footsteps behind him, Rylan turned to find Creed in the doorway. He crossed his arms over his barrel chest and leaned against the stone door frame.

Lorelei dropped Rylan's shirt onto the bed. "Visit to a bonfire last night?"

"In a manner of speaking."

"Oh?" She stepped into the aisle between the beds and faced him. "And what manner would that be, precisely?"

"I found myself waxing a bit nostalgic yesterday." He gestured toward the rear of the palace. "I lit a fire in the cooking pit to remind myself of the Holt."

"That sounds pleasant. Anyone join you?"

"No, it was just me."

Lorelei nodded calmly, too calmly. "I find the written word soothes a troubled mind best."

Rylan motioned to his bed. "I'd love to chat, but I should be getting ready. I'm heading back to Glaeyand shortly."

"Then please"—Lorelei stepped aside and waved to his bed with a theatrical bow—"don't let me stop you, but I think you might be interested what I've been reading."

Rylan walked past her to the far side of the bed, set his rucksack on the mattress, folded the shirt Lorelei had been sniffing, and stuffed it inside.

"Just this morning," Lorelei continued, "I read about a boy who grew up in Thicket. I read about a man, his foster father, whom the boy called his uncle. I read how the man was caught teaching the boy how to bond with dragons, how the man was sentenced to burn for it. The boy was set to burn as well, until his *uncle* bawled out the boy's true lineage. Turns out the boy was related to none other than the Imperator"—she motioned to his left hand—"so the magistrate merely had the boy's finger cut off."

"You're acting like this is all some revelation," Rylan said. "It's ancient history, recorded in imperial records for well over a decade now."

"Yes, but what most people forgot, or never knew in the first place, is that though the uncle's bondmate, a viridian, was mauled and killed by the inquisitor's bronze, its two kits escaped."

Rylan almost choked on his tongue.

"Last night," Lorelei said, pacing the aisle, "a suspected murderer and arsonist was spotted flying of the roof of the imperial library on a viridian while the fire he'd lit raged"—she glanced at his rucksack—"causing quite a bit of smoke."

"Perhaps you should ask around the city." Rylan placed the last of his personal effects—a bar of soap, a tin of paste to clean his teeth, and his smoking pipe and bag of tabbaq—into the rucksack. "I hear the Red Knives have quite a few arsonists and murderers in their ranks."

Lorelei paused her pacing and smiled. "It's funny you should mention that. Given the variety of drake, I thought it might have been Blythe I saw. But a former inquisitor, Kellen Vesarius, told me he'd seen a man."

Rylan almost winced. Kellen was *alive*. "That would tend to narrow things down a bit, wouldn't it?"

"It would, indeed." Lorelei resumed her pacing. "The two viridian kits got me to wondering where Blythe grew up. Turns out, she was born and raised in Thicket, just like you."

"Yes, we played together frequently near the Vagabond." Rylan crouched and, when Lorelei looked at creed, stuffed Korvus's journal into the rucksack.

"She's a Knife, Rylan."

"So what? Is knowing a Red Knife a crime now? Because if it is, you're going to have to arrest the entire Holt."

"Knowing a Knife isn't a crime, but attempting to kill a former inquisitor is. As is murdering the library's archivist."

"I know nothing about that," Rylan said.

"No? Seems like revenge on the man who had your uncle killed would be a pretty strong motivator to come to Ancris."

"I came here to help Bothymus."

"Ah, yes. Bothymus." From a pouch on her belt, she pulled out a leather ball and unwrapped it. Inside were a dragon's golden chrysolite crop and its matching fetter. "I saw how grateful he was to you for helping heal his wound." She showed him the crop and fetter. "But behind the eyrie, he was unruly and distrustful."

Rylan shrugged. "Dragons can be fickle."

"Not Bothymus. At the time, I thought maybe the supposed rift had caused his intractability. Now I think perhaps you had some other interaction with him that I'm not aware of. Which might have led to the degradation of his fetter."

"You're reaching," Rylan said, cinching his rucksack. "You're *trying* to turn me into the villain."

Lorelei smiled coldly. "I'm rather interested in geology, alchemy, and how the two intersect with dragon husbandry. I've read quite a few volumes on the subjects. I even worked in the eyrie for a time before I decided to become an inquisitor. Crops and fetters are often replaced for various reasons."

"Lorelei, you're getting carried away—"

"Centuries ago," she continued, "eyrie masters, fearing dragons would go mad if their fetters were simply taken away, used viridian acid to weaken them. The acid formed tiny fissures in the chrysolite"—she held the stones up again—"much like the ones now running through Bothymus's fetter."

At the very edge of Rylan's consciousness, Vedron sensed his panic and was growing frantic. She bounded along a stream, raising her wings.

Stay, Rylan willed. *Stay, Vedron!*

If the inquisitors saw her, he was a dead man. He was certainly in a bind—Lorelei's story went deeper than he thought it would—but even so, it was patchy. He might be able to lie his way out of it or draw on his father's name to be allowed to return to Glaeyand. Even without his father's help, Rylan had plenty of his own money. He could get an advocate to represent him if he was brought before a magistrate.

"Did you come here to murder Kellen Vesarius?" Lorelei asked.

"No, I did not." It was only half-true, of course—he had intended to do precisely that.

Creed seemed to clench his teeth.

"You're lying," Lorelei said.

"No, I'm not."

"Then why did you come? And don't tell me it's about Bothymus. I know it has something to do with the peat Blythe brought to Ancris and the meeting with Brother Mayhew at the mines. Tell me, Rylan, and I can make sure this goes easier for you."

Part of him wanted to tell her, but he was looking for the same answer. The Red Knives were up to something big, something dangerous, but he didn't know what, and apparently neither did she. For a moment, he thought about telling her everything. She was a brilliant woman—he was sure she could help him unravel the mystery—but how could she help him if he was dead? Telling her anything would be tantamount to chaining himself to the Anvil.

"I know you want answers," he finally said. "I would too, but I'm telling you, you're looking in the wrong place."

She seemed disappointed but not surprised. She put her hand on the hilt of her rapier and pointed to the archway at end of the hall. "Step away from your things, Rylan. You're coming with us."

FIFTY-SIX: RHIANNON

The day after her visit to the crucible, Rhiannon was sitting on the deck outside her burrow, stitching a needlepoint iris as a gift for Sister Merida, when a high-pitched trumpet came from below. She stood and peered over the railing.

"What's all the noise?" she called down to Irik, who was in the dragon pen with Tiufalli, holding a dead ferret.

Irik shaded his eyes and stared up, then beamed and beckoned her. "Come see!"

Figuring she'd done enough for the day, Rhiannon raised a finger. "Hold on!"

She ducked inside the burrow, set the canvas, thread, and needle on the kitchen table, and grabbed the hunk of blueberry bread Sister Merida had left for her. She gobbled the bread and dusted her hands free of crumbs while winding her way down toward ground level. Smoke rose from the workhouse, and the lower she went, the more she smelled a pungent, floral smell on the warm spring breeze. She reached the base of the tree and skipped over to the pen, where Irik was holding up the ferret. Tiufalli, already twice as long as Irik, was crouched on his hind legs, neck arched, looking like an eager foxhound. The dragon eyed the ferret hungrily but made no move to snatch it from Irik's hand.

"So," Rhiannon said, "what's so special you had to take me away from my important task?"

Irik rolled his eyes. "You probably poked your fingers more than you did the canvas." He faced Tiufalli. "And what's so special is, I've created the greatest trick known to man."

Rhiannon leaned against the fence and sneered. "Go on, then."

Irik faced Tiufalli and lowered the ferret. "Ready, boy?"

Tiufalli lowered his head and spread his wings.

Irik flung the ferret high in the air. Tiufalli trumpeted and launched up after it. He flapped his wings with a loud *whump*, and snatched the ferret in his teeth in midair. The leap looked awkward to Rhiannon. She was sure Tiufalli was going to fall on his head, but as he dropped, he twisted and landed on his back legs with his wings spread wide. Then he craned his neck and shot his head forward like a heron, and swallowed the ferret whole.

Irik grinned and rubbed Tiufalli's shoulder with his knuckles. "You see?"

"What's next?" Rhiannon asked. "You going to make him fly through hoops?"

"I'm not a bloody *jongleur*, and Tiufalli's a hundred times smarter than those dogs." He patted the cobalt kit's head. "Aren't you, boy?"

Tiufalli gurgled and shivered his wings.

Their bond was clearly strong already, and it made Rhiannon wonder about the differences between bonding and binding. "What do you think the dracorae feel with the crops?"

"What do you mean?"

"Is it *anything* like a bond?"

Irik shrugged. "I didn't think so, but Llorn says they're similar."

"Similar how?"

"I thought a fetter *forced* dragons into obeying the one who holds the crop, but Llorn said it requires the dragon and rider being in tune."

"What, like harp strings?"

"Exactly like that. He said if a dracora tries too hard, the dragon can refuse his command or even attack. But if the dracora takes the time to match the dragon's tone, the dragon hardly has any choice."

"Match his tone," Rhiannon said slowly, trying the concept on for size. Then she shrugged. "I don't get it."

"Neither do I."

"And it seems cruel."

"Cruel and *crude*." He smiled while stroking Tiufalli's neck. "It's nothing like bonding." Irik's eyes suddenly went wide. "Hey, did you hear? Llorn took Fraoch and the other kits to the nesting grounds."

"Why?

"Because cobalts raise their kits communally. He's leaving them there, then flying west"—he leaned in conspiratorially—"for a meeting with the Hissing Man."

It reminded Rhiannon of Llorn's speech to the Red Knives. He'd announced that he'd come to an accord with the Chosen. The crowd had rumbled at that, but Llorn had gone on to say that while the Hissing Man planned to use *him*, the reality was precisely the opposite. "It's a dangerous game he's playing."

"What? With the Hissing Man?"

"With him, the Church, the empire. It's going to rile them up like a bloody hornet's nest."

"Maybe they *need* riling." Irik watched Tiufalli gambol over the yard, jumping up and flapping his wings. "They think they're so safe in their mountain hideouts. They don't even fear the dark sun anymore, but Llorn will teach them, and then we'll be free."

Rhiannon frowned. "What do you mean they don't fear the dark sun?"

"It's their bloody palisade, isn't it? It protects them from Nox."

She'd heard rumor of the palisade years ago but had thought little of it since. It reminded her of the crucible and the questions her mother had asked her while they stood near it. Aura and umbra were equal but opposite forces. Everyone knew so. The crucible funneled the power of the bright sun into the earth below. The palisade surely did the same with umbra. It would create two very powerful sources of power, one in the mountains, one in the Holt. But what good would that do? They were so far apart . . .

Irik narrowed his eyes at her. "What's wrong?

She was just about to tell him more when her mother called. "Rhiannon?" She was standing near the path to the vyrd. "Come. It's time."

Rhiannon whispered to Irik, "I'll tell you later," then left.

As Rhiannon walked with her mother through the forest, a blue heron swooped silently across their path. Morraine watched it fly toward the fen, then said, "Brother Mayhew was cross with me for bringing you to the crucible."

"He was?"

"Yes, and for good reason. You need to concentrate on the shard. That's all. Forget about everything else. Can you do that for me?"

For a moment, Rhiannon wasn't sure what to say. She'd expected to be chastised. "I can, yes."

The more they walked, the more Rhiannon noticed other changes in her mother. Morraine blinked often, as if her eyes were irritated. She stumbled on occasion and seemed tired most of the time. And the growing emptiness in Rhiannon's gut felt weaker. Rhiannon was confused, but her mother would not accept her help.

Morraine seemed to notice Rhiannon staring at her. "You need to stop worrying over me. Clear your mind." She pointed to the vyrd, which was just coming into view through the trees ahead. "It's important you make progress tonight."

They entered the vyrd and knelt beside the looking glass, and Rhiannon spent hours trying harder than ever to find the thread that would lead her to the veil and Yeriel, but she came up empty again. When she finally returned to her body, cant had come and gone, and Nox was nearing its zenith. She thought surely her mother would berate her for failing again, but Morraine was nowhere to be seen.

"Mother?"

Rhiannon left the vyrd and wandered toward the Rookery while looking for her mother. She had no luck and thought about heading to the crucible instead when, some distance ahead of her, a wisp flew straight as an arrow and then simply disappeared. Wisps were a common enough sight near the fens, but they usually floated randomly and never disappeared. Thinking it must have passed behind a tree, Rhiannon stepped to one side of the citadel in front of her, hoping to catch sight of it. Another wisp flew from another direction, then it, too, disappeared in the same place. She stared there for a moment, but when nothing happened, she headed toward the place where the wisps had disappeared.

She passed from one low hill to the next until she spotted a silhouette in the darkness. A woman, surely her mother, beckoned to a nearby wisp. The wisp sped toward her and lit Morraine's pale face and white hair. Her features were contorted in a look of deep pain. The wisp landed on Morraine's palm, and the frail woman brought it to her lips. For a brief moment, the inside of her mouth was glowing sky blue—teeth, mottled tongue, and all—then she closed her mouth and the wisp was gone.

Rhiannon's first instinct was to slink back to the vyrd and pretend she hadn't seen anything. Instead she walked down the hill to a grassy glade. "Mother?"

A wisp that was drifting down, dimmed briefly, then floated away.

"They're lost *souls*, mother," Rhiannon said.

"I know perfectly well what they are." Morraine said.

"You can't *eat* them," Rhiannon said. "They aren't *mulberries.*"

Rhiannon thought her mother would rail against her, order her back to the Rookery, or yell at her to be quiet, but she didn't. "I cannot help it, child. You've no idea how the hunger gnaws."

"How long has this been going on?"

Morraine shrugged. "Since the beginning."

Root and ruin, how many souls had been devoured since her mother's raising? Dozens? Hundreds? "Couldn't you eat something else? The souls of animals?"

"I've tried. I've had the hunters capture hare, deer, even wolves alive so that I could eat them. But it's like swallowing air. They give me almost nothing." She waved to the wisps. "These are better, but still not enough."

Rhiannon felt the emptiness grow. She coughed and pressed her hand to her stomach. "Couldn't you take more from me?"

"No!" She said it so forcefully, Rhiannon jumped.

"I don't mind! I give myself willingly."

"You can't. *I* can't. It would go too far."

"We could at least try—"

"I said no." Morraine pointed back toward the vyrd. "Now tell me what you've found."

"Same as the other times," Rhiannon said. "Nothing."

Morraine considered this, then nodded. "Head back to the Rookery."

"You're not coming?"

"Go, Rhiannon." Morraine shuffled toward a cluster of wisps between two citadels. "Now."

"Please leave them alone." Rhiannon wanted to force her somehow, but she had no idea how. She walked to the Rookery and climbed the stairs to the burrow, which was becoming more like home every day.

The next night went much the same, except that when Rhiannon woke from her search, Morraine was there, waiting for her.

"Well?" Morraine asked.

Rhiannon shook her head. She was disappointed in herself, but she was relieved that Morraine hadn't left to devour more wisps.

The next few days followed a similar pattern. Dragons arrived at the Rookery. Their riders, carrying news from the mountains or Glaeyand or elsewhere in the Holt, reported to Ayasha, their master of dragons, and left shortly thereafter. Irik trained and played with Tiufalli. Rhiannon and Morraine continued searching for Yeriel. With her mother seemingly less ravenous, Rhiannon was able to put more effort into her search. As she became more familiar with the lay of the forest, she began to sense disturbances.

"What do you mean, *disturbances*?" Morraine asked when Rhiannon described it to her.

"They're like ripples in a pond."

"What does that mean, child? What ripples?"

"It's like I'm a leaf floating on the water's surface. I can sense that I'm bobbing up and down but that's all. I've no idea where the ripples are coming from."

Morraine considered this, then nodded. "It may come in time."

"Can't we go closer to the veil?" Rhiannon asked.

"We might if we knew precisely where Gonsalond was, but the veil is so powerful and so effective, we can't define its boundaries. Those who've entered it, whether on purpose or by mistake, find themselves waking days or even weeks later in another part of the forest entirely. If we try to go nearer, we might accidentally pass through it, and who knows what would become of us then?"

Rhiannon stared at the crystal in her hands. "Aren't you afraid she'll come for it? I mean, we're searching for her. If she knew about it, wouldn't she try to find us to get it back?"

Morraine waved at the path to the Rookery, and they walked side by side along it.

"I doubt very much she can sense the crystal," Morraine said.

"How can you be so sure?"

"For the simple fact that we still have it. If she could sense it, she would have found it by now."

"Maybe she's not really as powerful as everyone says?"

"You're forgetting it was Alra who made the crystal in hopes of defeating Faedryn. She no doubt worried that *he* might find it. Were I her, I would make sure it couldn't be sensed, by Faedryn or anyone else."

"I suppose." Rhiannon handed the crystal and its leather cord to Morraine. "Did she try to find it, after it was stolen, I mean?"

"She sent wardens around the Holt"—Morraine slipped the leather cord over her head and tucked the crystal beneath her dress—"but your father and I knew the dangers. The only person we told about our plans to steal the shard was Llorn." When they arrived at the Rookery, she stopped short of the stairway that led to their burrow. "Go on. Get your rest."

Rhiannon wasn't sure why, but the divide between them felt greater than ever. She wished they could go up together, that Morraine could tell her a story. She wished she could lay in her mother's arms as she drifted to sleep. More than any of those things, she wished her mother hadn't been taken and hung.

As she climbed up the stairs, she watched her mother head toward the workhouse. She nearly called out, hoping to comfort her in some way, maybe offer herself again so her mother wouldn't go hungry, but Morraine had gotten so upset when Rhiannon had offered the first time, she decided against it and went to bed.

She was awoken by a distant wailing. Though it felt like only a moment had passed, the bright sun was up and shining through the curtains. Morraine lay in her bed on the far side of the room, eyes closed. She was so still Rhiannon wondered if she'd passed away, but when Rhiannon pried one of her eyes open, it glowed faintly blue. Rhiannon figured it must be her version of deep sleep.

She heard the crying again, and this time recognized it as Irik's. She rushed from the burrow and scrambled down the stairs. Irik was in the dragon pen. He was clutching his chest, pacing, and mumbling to himself.

"What's wrong?" Rhiannon said as she pass through the wooden gate. "Irik, what's wrong?"

Tears streamed down his face. "Why would she do it?"

"Who?"

"Your *mother!*"

Rhiannon stared at him a second. "What are you saying?"

He shook his head and pointed at the wooden shelter where Tiufalli usually slept, then walked away.

Rhiannon walked toward it and stopped at the entryway. Inside were four nests of rough-cut boughs. Ayasha, the Rookery's master of dragons, knelt beside one of them. Rhiannon approached silently. Tiufalli was lying still on his straw bed. His usually vivid blue skin and scales were unnaturally dull and pale.

She wanted to believe her mother wouldn't do this, but how could she? She'd seen her mother eat wisps, had felt her mothers extreme hunger, now sated as the frail woman slept.

Oh, Irik, I'm so sorry.

FIFTY-SEVEN: THE HISSING MAN

The Hissing Man rode a dappled mare along a mountain path deep in the range known as the Wayward Oxen. In place of his black habit, he wore drab clothes and a hooded cloak. A cool breeze blew, but it was fitful, and the sun was warm, creating a pendulum of warmth and coolness that somehow exacerbated the ache in his hunched shoulders.

Umbra was an unkind mistress. The events at the library had taxed him greatly. His flesh and bones ached for hours, sometimes days, after using umbra only once. But he'd taken a hefty pinch before he went to the library, then more in preparation for his clandestine meeting in the mountains. The ache was deeper than he ever remembered. Every jolt, every plod of the mare's hooves, set fire to his spine.

He was assuaged somewhat by the knowledge that Faedryn watched over him. Lorelei Aurelius had become a nuisance, but she'd done him a favor in taking Rylan Holbrooke into custody.

Had the Hissing Man been able to stay in the city, he would have dealt with Holbrooke himself, but the meeting was too important to delay. He'd sent word to Ordren to deal with the matter, but the scourge he'd sent with the message had reported Ordren acting curiously.

"Curiously how?" the Hissing Man had asked.

"Jumpy," the scourge replied. "Wary."

The Hissing Man wasn't worried about Ordren. The disaffected inquisitor was too interested in coin and too scared of consequences to do anything but obey the Hissing Man's orders. He was probably just jumpy about being involved in the fire and the business at the mine.

Above the foothills in the distance, the Hissing Man sensed Llorn's cobalt flying low in the otherwise nondescript canvas of his second sight. When the dragon landed some thirty paces away, the Hissing Man pulled his mare to a stop and levered himself down, grunting from the pain. Llorn slid down on the rocky ground.

"I've little time," Llorn said.

"Then I'll get straight to it," the Hissing Man hissed. "I sent word to begin final preparations. Why haven't they?"

Llorn crossed his arms over his chest. "There were complications in Morraine's raising."

"Of what sort?"

"She's weaker than I'd hoped."

It still galled the Hissing Man that he'd agreed to allow Llorn to raise Morraine from the dead. It was a complication, and his quest to awaken Strages was complicated enough already. "My sources tell me Morraine's daughter tried to stop the ritual. Is *that* why she's weak?"

"The reason is of little importance."

The Hissing Man wheezed a laugh. "We're mere days away from activating the palisade and destroying Ancris. *Everything* is important at this stage of the game. Tell me what happened."

Llorn's cobalt dragon raised her head, stared at the Hissing Man, and growled.

"You must be confusing me with one of your lackeys," Llorn said. "You don't command me."

"In this I do," the Hissing Man spat, "or this project of ours stops now."

"I think not." Llorn snarled. "The Chosen have come too far for that, as have the Red Knives."

The Hissing Man leaned closer. "Hear me, Llorn Bloodhaven. Your story stinks of deception. It's true the Chosen have invested much—*I* have invested much—but if you cannot convince me the bridging of the vyrda and the attack on Glaey-and will proceed exactly as I've outlined, I'll go back to Ancris, get Lucran to dismantle the palisade and begin releasing the aura. Make no mistake, the Chosen are patient. We'll wait, if that's what it takes. So tell me what's wrong with your sister and what you plan to do about it."

Llorn's jaw jutted. "Her soul was torn during the ritual."

"Because of her daughter?"

"It doesn't matter how. She can't navigate the maze on her own. She needs time to heal. That's all. We cannot risk her failing. We both know that once she begins, the ferrymen will know she's there."

"How much time does she need?"

"Give me until the council of quintarchs."

The Hissing Man paused. The council was five days away, not long in the grand scheme of things, but a lot could happen in that time. "Rather curious timing," he said.

"Is it?"

"You want to begin the day of the council," the Hissing Man said with certainty.

Llorn glared at him. "What do you care as long as it's done?"

Aside from the danger of his plans being discovered too early, the Hissing Man didn't care much. Llorn wanted to kill the quintarchs, or at least flaunt the might of the Red Knives beneath their noses. It would inflame tensions, widen already wide divides. It played perfectly into the Hissing Man's plans.

"Very well," he said. "You have until the council."

Llorn nodded. He walked back to his cobalt and mounted. "The alchemyst who's heading up the shrine's renovations . . ."

"Master Renato? What of him?"

"He may have learned what Korvus was up to before he stumbled onto the crucible. It'd be safer for all of us if he was gone."

The Hissing Man wondered if he was telling the truth. Llorn might have just had a score to settle with the alchemyst and wanted the Hissing Man to take care of it for him. It hardly mattered, though. What was one death when thousands were about to perish? "I'll see to it."

Llorn nodded and snapped the reins. "Hup!" The cobalt loped forward, flapped her wings, and soared into the sky.

When the dragon was just a speck in the sky, the Hissing Man headed back toward his horse, but stopped on spotting something to the north. Colors swirled and settled into a glittering silver dragon, the swiftest of the draconic breeds. A woman in a mask was riding it. When the dragon landed, Illustra Camadaea climbed down from the saddle. Why she would have come in person he had no idea, but she made him nervous, and he hated being nervous.

As Camadaea approached, he bowed his head to hide his anger and spoke in his hiss, "You're a long way from home, Your Radiance."

"As are you. Word is you never leave the catacombs."

The Hissing Man smiled and waved at the landscape around them. "An exaggeration, clearly. But I hope you'll forgive me, Illustra. I'm confused. His Holiness Azariah told me he'd informed you of this meeting. Why come all this way to speak to his humble servant?"

"Because you've been doing much in our name. Perhaps *too* much. And Azariah has refused all requests to speak with you. I've come to correct his error in judgment." She looked him up and down. "Tell me, how did you come to meet him?"

The Hissing Man hated being subjected to interrogations, but he really had no choice but to answer. Camadaea could destroy him in a variety of ways. "We met through his wife, Kalyris."

Her lips pursed. "Kalyris died thirty years ago."

"Yes. I was an acolyte then, but was excommunicated when Kalyris found me reading a tome of unbinding." It was a lie—he had no memory of his first meeting with Azariah *or* Kalyris—but he'd been telling it for so many years it felt true.

"That's how Azariah found you?"

"Not precisely. When the Chosen learned I'd been expelled for reading spells of torture, they recruited me. I met Azariah shortly thereafter. Over time, he came to recognize my desire to see the Church rise to its rightful place atop the empire. I saw the same in him. It has been a fruitful relationship ever since, wouldn't you agree?"

"And your second sight? Did Azariah arrange it?"

"No, I did."

"But why would you suffer through it? The only reason I can think of is that you fancy yourself Azariah's equal."

He knew she meant *her* equal. The Hissing Man was bold, but he was not so bold that he would challenge Camadaea so directly. "I did so because much of my work is done in the catacombs, in the dark of night, or in the hidden places of the city. I did so because it would be useful to Our Lord."

Her face flushed in his second sight. "You dare?"

Referring to Faedryn aloud, even obliquely, was something Azariah might be allowed do, but certainly not the Hissing Man. "Forgive me, useful to Azariah and his fellow illustrae . . ."

She pointed toward the foothills. "Tell me how your meeting went."

The Hissing Man bowed deferentially. "Azariah's instructions were clear. I'm to speak only to him."

"The head of your church commands you, Hissing Man."

The Hissing Man was growing increasingly irritated at being ordered about, but he didn't want to make trouble for Azariah, especially so close to the end. "Llorn has begun preparations to trigger the sinkhole."

"*Begun* preparations?" Lux shone off Camadaea's golden mask as she turned toward the Holt, then back again. "According to Azariah, the palisade and the crucible are both ready. Why not trigger them now?"

"Because the ritual is arduous, and Morraine is still recovering her strength."

"He has other druins."

"Who aren't up to the task."

"So he says."

The Hissing Man bowed again; she was right. "In this, I believe him. And there's more to consider in any case. I suspect he has something special planned for the quintarchs." Camadaea looked ready to argue, but the Hissing Man went on before she could. "The illustrae always meant to place the blame for Ancris's destruction on the Red Knives. Llorn's attack on Glaeyand will do just that. He's playing into your hands."

Camadaea didn't seem wholly convinced, but she let the subject drop. "One last thing. Azariah said the chalice has resurfaced, and that you failed to obtain it."

"That is unfortunately the case, Your Radiance, but I hope to have it back shortly."

"It holds dangerous secrets. You know this, yes?"

"I do. But fear not. The chalice is a loose thread being tied off as we speak."

"How so?"

"We know it was Rylan Holbrooke who stole it."

"Holbrooke . . ." Camadaea frowned deeply. "Marstan's bastard . . . ?"

"Yes."

"I spoke to him at a fete not long ago." The silver dragon gurgled a high note, distracting Camadaea momentarily. "He was there attending to an ailing dragon, but I found him in the room where Morraine's wisp was on display. He must have been there to steal it."

It was interesting news, a wrinkle the Hissing Man hadn't thought to investigate. "You're likely correct."

"Holbrooke is in custody, then?"

"He's in the Crag as we speak."

"Why isn't he in the questioning chamber?"

"He *will be*." The words had come out sharper than he'd intended. "Or we'll deal with him where he is," he said with less venom. "Either way, we'll learn where he's hidden the chalice."

Camadaea exhaled noisily. "This is getting out of hand. If anyone were to decipher the writing on it . . ."

"They won't."

"You can't be sure of that. Who do you suppose sent him to get the chalice? It must be Llorn. For all we know, it's related to his request for a delay. The druins have scholars who still know the old tongues."

"We have little to fear, Your Holiness. Even deciphered, the chalice would hardly expose—"

"Find the chalice." Camadaea spun and strode toward her dragon. "And make sure Llorn sticks to his schedule before I'm forced to do it for you."

Without so much as a nod or word of parting, she mounted, took up the reins, and flew off. The Hissing Man watched her go, cursing under his breath. Camadaea was no great threat at the moment, but she might become one. He'd consider how to deal with her. In the meantime, he had more pressing concerns. With the chalice being seen to by Ordren, it was time to find Master Renato and make him *gone*, as Llorn had said.

The Hissing Man mounted his horse and guided her along the goat path toward Ancris, thinking about the shrine, its scaffolding, and the sort of accidents that might befall a master alchemyst.

FIFTY-EIGHT: RYLAN

Creed clamped the manacles on Rylan's wrists and led him to the front of the palace. Lorelei walked beside them. They guided him into the rear compartment of a waiting prisoner wagon. The coach lurched to one side as Creed climbed into the driver's box.

Lorelei lingered outside the barred window with Rylan's rucksack slung over her shoulder. She looked more hurt than angry. "If you're innocent, you'll help us, Rylan. You'll tell us everything. Helping us helps you. I hope you see that."

Rylan might have replied had Vedron not been flying about in panic. It was all he could do to prevent her from coming to Ancris and saving him again.

Lorelei joined Creed in the front of the wagon. As it trundled over the gravel in the circular driveway, he heard Lorelei and Creed talking in low voices. He didn't bother trying to follow the conversation. He couldn't. He was too busy calming Vedron. By the time he finally managed to do so, the wagon was rolling through the Crag's heavy gates.

The coach rattled to a stop, and Creed and Lorelei led him into the Crag. Once inside, Creed, carrying Rylan's rucksack, headed down the hallway toward an open room with loud conversation coming from it. Lorelei took Rylan to a much smaller room where a gaoler named Marion, a diminutive man whose head looked too large for his body was waiting for them. The gaoler grabbed a set of keys from behind his desk, unlocked an iron door on the far side of his office, and led Rylan and Lorelei down a hall with cells on both sides.

"Oy," called a big man with a shaved head from one of the cells, "you said you'd let my wife in to see me."

"Durgan, Durgan, Durgan," Marion said, "can't you see I'm busy?"

Marion opened a door near the end of the hall and bowed, at which point Lorelei accompanied Rylan into an empty cell. It had a chamber pot and a bed with a steel frame suspended from the wall by chains. The air smelled of piss and mildew.

"What happens now?" Rylan asked.

Lorelei unlocked his manacles."Are you ready to talk?"

Rylan said nothing.

Marion, standing in the doorway, snorted.

Lorelei said, "An arraignment hearing will be scheduled, pending formal charges."

"And how long will that take?"

"A day, maybe two," Lorelei said. Then she left.

Marion locked the door and smiled through the barred window. "Has some-one been a bad boy?"

"Not at all," Rylan replied with an easy smile. "I was looking for a place to stay, and Inquisitor Lorelei recommended your inn."

The gaoler smiled, revealing stained teeth. "My inn." He strolled away, spin-ning the key ring around his finger. "I'll have my cook send up our finest steak, then." He cackled. "Do you like goose-down pillows?" His fading laughter ended when the door to the gaoler's office boomed shut.

Rylan sat on the hard bed and urged Vedron to fly back to her nest. *I'll be back as soon as I can.*

After an hour, Vedron finally relented, and only because Rylan finally made it clear that she was putting him in danger.

He stared at the iron door. It had dark stains on it, as did the floor. Although the lock was only accessible from the outside, Rylan could reach it through the window. He still had his lock picks in his false boot heel. It would be tricky, but he'd practiced picking locks by feel and was reasonably confident he could defeat it. What then, though? He'd still have the whole of the Crag to navigate.

He detested the notion, but he knew it would be better to wait. Imperial law demanded a reasonably quick arraignment. He'd petition for his advocate then. He was more worried about Vedron. She was safe enough for the time being, but what would his father do when he learned of Rylan's arrest? He might help Rylan to escape punishment, because doing so would help *him* save face, but Vedron was a different story. Rylan was all but certain he'd follow through on his threat and send Andros to hunt her.

He closed his eyes but could not sleep. The cell was cold. The man down the hall kept coughing. Worst of all, he felt utterly alone. It harkened back to the days of Uncle Beckett's death. He'd been rushed away to Glaeyand mere hours after word had come that Marstan had agreed to take him in. In one fell swoop, he'd lost not only his foster father, but Aunt Merida, Blythe, and all his friends in Thicket too. That he was well fed and given a warm bed had been no solace whatsoever. His blood family treated him like a beggar, a vagabond, a thief hoping to cash in on their good reputation.

Rylan found himself hoping Lorelei would come back. He felt like a shit-heel for lying to her. She was kind and thoughtful, and he really did believe she wanted to prevent the pain and anguish that might result from the foul scheme Llorn and the Hissing Man were cooking up. He kept thinking about their talk outside the shrine, where she'd treated him like a friend, a *real* friend. He remembered how she'd laughed. He'd never realized how much he liked dimples before.

In the afternoon, the door creaked open. He hoped it was Lorelei, but it was the gaoler again. Through a rectangular gap at the base of a door, he slid a pewter plate into the cell. It contained a hunk of stale bread, a pile of mashed peas, and a small cup of water. "Your steak, milord," Marion said, and laughed as he walked back down the hallway.

Several hours later, clouds dimmed the faint light filtering in through the hole high on the wall opposite the door. A heavy rain began to hiss on the leaves out-side. Rylan was finally beginning to nod off when he heard the clank of the gaol-er's door opening again. He heard light footsteps and hushed conversation.

"Quiet!" someone bellowed, then started coughing.

He heard more footsteps, two pairs, and then the keys jangled outside his door and it groaned open. Durgan, the huge man with the shaved head, stepped for-ward to fill the doorway. "Like to have a word."

Rylan sat up against the cold wall. "Funny, I didn't think they let us out for strolls." He motioned to the open door. "Mind if I take mine now?"

"Cute." Durgan stepped in and swung the door closed. "Where's the chalice?"

Word seemed to travel fast in Ancris. "What chalice?"

"No need to play it that way." Durgan pressed a fist into the opposite hand and cracked his knuckles. "You were in the library. You stole the chalice from Kellen's office. A friend of mine would like to know where it is. It might be worth opening a few doors for you."

"Might this friend of yours be one of the Chosen?"

"None of your bloody business."

Rylan nodded. "And what do you get out of it? Unlocked doors as well? A bit of coin for you and your wife."

"Keep my wife from that foul tongue of yours, darkling."

Rylan raised his hands. "No offense. I'm sure she's a fine woman, distraught over your . . . absence. I can get her twice as much as you've been promised."

Durgan's teeth shone in the dim light. "I know your type."

"Oh? And what type is that?"

"The type who thinks he can talk himself out of anything. The type who thinks, failing that, his family name will save him. I promise you, neither of those things will protect you if you don't answer my question. Where's the chalice?"

Rylan was hardly looking forward to a beating, nor was he under any illusion Durgan might not simply kill him. But he'd dedicated himself to liberating pieces of the Kin legacy from the empire. The chalice was important to the Hissing Man, which could only mean it helped his cause somehow, and Rylan could not allow that.

"I'm afraid you must be mistaking me for someone else," he said. "I'm just a humble dragon singer."

Durgan snorted. "That's how you want to play it?"

"It's the only way *to* play it." Rylan stood, refusing to take his beating lying down. "I came here to help an ailing dragon. Nothing more."

Durgan lumbered toward him. "Filthy, useless Kin . . ."

Durgan swung a right hook. Rylan ducked it and drove his fist into Durgan's stomach. The big man barely grunted. Then he smashed Rylan's ear with an open-handed left and punched his jaw with a straight right that slammed Rylan back against the wall. Durgan came forward again, and Rylan hit him with two quick jabs to the face. Blood flowed from Durgan's lip.

Rylan swung again, a flailing right, but Durgan grabbed his wrist, shoved him against the wall, and pressed his forearm against Rylan's throat.

"Last chance, dark skin. Where's the bloody chalice?"

Rylan managed to wheeze, "In your wife's fucking cunt."

"Wrong answer." Durgan wrestled Rylan around, slipped an arm across his neck, and squeezed.

Rylan choked and flailed. His vision swirled with purple stars. Then everything went dark.

FIFTY-NINE: LORELEI

Lorelei brought Rylan to the dungeon and then went to the Pit, home to some three dozen inquisitors, constables, and commanders. The mishmash of desks, the people sitting behind them, the ever-present din, all of it made her cringe. As always, she felt exposed, which made thinking difficult. It was why she spent as little time there as possible.

She navigated the chaos to her cluttered desk and sat.

Across from her, Creed was rummaging through Rylan's rucksack, which he'd set on his own impeccably neat desk. "Went by Damika's to report the arrest," he said without looking up, "but she's gone to Highreach."

"Why?"

"Virgil wouldn't say."

Nanda and Vashtok stepped out of one of the questioning rooms with a wizened woman sucking at her lips. Nanda led her toward the exit; Vashtok lingered by their desks. "I hear you caught a fresh fish. Still wriggling on his hook, yes?"

"I suppose so," Lorelei said. She still felt horrible about taking Rylan into custody and wasn't in the mood to talk about it with Vashtok or anyone else.

Vashtok leaned in, and the smell of spices came with him. "Fear not, Lorelei. Damika recognizes achievement when she sees it. She'll loosen the leash soon."

All Lorelei could muster was a tepid, "Maybe."

He patted her shoulder and rushed to catch up with Nanda. "May Alra breathe life into your dreams!"

Ordren, looking irritated as usual, came walking along the main aisle. He sauntered up to Creed's desk and pointed to the rucksack and the journal Creed had taken from it. "By all rights that's mine."

"Pound salt, Ordren," Creed said.

Ordren pointed his bony finger at Lorelei. "She has strict orders, from the Praefectus. She's supposed to be in *records*."

"Good thing it's not her case, then."

"You think it's yours now?"

Still holding the journal, Creed stopped rummaging, stepped closer to Ordren, and stared down at him. "I do."

Ordren snatched the journal from Creed's hand. "What is it?"

Just as fast, Creed snatched it back. "None of your business."

Ordren stared at the rucksack and the spilled clothes beside it, then headed back down the aisle. "We'll see about that."

Creed tossed the journal onto Lorelei's desk, then sat and began filling Rylan's arrest report. "Our friend from the Holt share anything with you?"

"No"—she picked up the journal—"but he might. I can tell he's scared."

She opened the journal and found a name—Korvus Julianus—on the inside cover, and a date roughly five years earlier. The date was followed by a dash, likely for an end date, a common practice among alchemysts. Below was written:

THE CHANGE IN ARCANE FLOWS THROUGHOUT THE WEST-
ERN REACHES OF THE HOLT.

She flipped through the journal. There were extensive notes and tables filled with various locations. It seemed to be a sort of alchemycal census, a measuring of the relative strengths of aura and umbra, how they flowed through the forest, and the like. The tables were repeated but with different dates and different values.

Creed glanced up from his writing. "Anything interesting?"

"Maybe." She flipped a few more pages. "I'll talk to Ash about it."

"We have alchemysts in the Crag, you know."

"Yes, but all the good ones are at the shrine. Plus . . ."

Creed looked up from his paper. "What?"

She glanced over her shoulder and lowered her voice. "This place is a bloody sieve. Mention a secret and it's everywhere in hours."

Leaks from the ranks of the inquisitors—not to mention the alchemysts, records keepers, guards, and other Crag functionaries—were once merely an occasional, if annoying, phenomenon. Lately they were commonplace, causing no end of complications to active cases. She didn't want anything from the journal leaking to the Chosen, the Church, or even the palace until she knew more.

"Mark my words"—Creed glanced sidelong at Ordren as he passed through the exit—"there goes the worst of them."

No doubt he was right, but Lorelei had more to worry about than Ordren. After flipping a few more pages in the journal, she stood and pulled on her coat.

Creed's pen continued scratching. "Going to find Ash?"

"I need to."

"I know. Just let me finish this and we can go together."

Lorelei lowered her voice until it was almost a whisper. "I don't need a chaperone."

"Yes, you do." He held up his report. "This is *my* case, remember?"

"Yes, but *I'm* the one in trouble with Damika. You don't have to be too."

"The guards at the shrine will have standing orders not to let you in, and they're not going to deliver a message from you to Ash, either. I'll go, say it's inquisitor business, and see how soon he can meet us. Yeah?"

She wanted to deny him—she didn't want him getting covered in the steaming pile of shit *she'd* already fallen into—but she had to admit it felt good having her partner back. "Yeah."

Creed finished the report, filed it with records, and they left the Crag. He looked over the journal as they headed toward the shrine. "What the journal does or doesn't say is one thing. What Rylan wants with it is another."

"True, but the former may give us clues to the latter." As they trudged over Barrowdown Bridge, a river loon's mournful call mixed with the sounds of water lapping against the boats tied along the quay. "The journal has measurements of aura and umbra, which may relate to Blythe's peat. And if the peat really *was* meant for the Hissing Man, which seems likely, I'm guessing the Knives were afraid Korvus had stumbled onto something. Why else kill him and burn his workshop?"

"Seems a good guess." Creed tapped a finger on one of the alchemycal tables. "He went to measure these places"—he flipped back to an earlier table—"twice a year, apparently."

"Yes. There's thirty of them, but I'm hoping Ash will be able to help narrow them down."

"Narrow them down to what?"

"Down to the ones I should go to."

Creed nodded, his steely eyes intense. "That could take weeks."

"Not on dragonback."

"Or by vyrd . . ."

"I'd rather gouge out my eyes than cross the Holt by vyrd."

"Well, I'm not riding crossing the whole western Holt on the back of a bloody dragon."

Lorelei grabbed the journal. "I didn't ask you to come with me, did I?"

"You think you can handle yourself in the forest all alone?"

"You think I can't?"

"The fens are miserable, Lorelei. The air is half full of midges, the mosquitos are as big as my thumb, and the frogs spit poison. The water snakes there are the size of sewage pipes."

"Look, I know it's a long shot, but something's going on. We need to figure out what."

"Which is precisely why I'm coming with you."

Lorelei shrugged. They had quite a bit of investigating to do before they reached that crossroad.

When they arrived at the shrine, Lorelei stayed back and watched from the corner of an alley. The guard on duty, a leggy fellow with haggard eyes, met Creed at the base of the steps. At first, the man raised his hands and looked angry, but Creed seemed to settle him, and soon enough, Creed clapped him on the shoulder, and the two of them were headed into the shrine.

When Creed came out a few minutes later, he told Lorelei, "Ash will meet us at the Tulip when he can."

Lorelei shot a glance over her shoulder as they fell into step. "How do you do that?"

"Do what?"

"Convince people to do what you want? I never know what to say."

"Ah, that's the thing. It's not what *I* say. It's what *they* say. Get a man talking about himself, make him believe you care, and he'll eventually do anything you want."

"How is it you're still single, again?"

Creed laughed. "In part, because I don't play those games when I'm looking for companionship."

Lorelei stared. *"Never?"*

"Never." When Lorelei continued to stare, he added. "Okay, *almost* never."

Lorelei laughed, and Creed shoved her gently.

It was early, and there were few patrons in the Tulip. Eustice was behind the bar instead of Eladora. "Help you?"

"Two ciders," Creed said.

Eustice frowned like it was an imposition, but turned to the taps and began filling their glasses. Then they sat at their booth and sipped and waited for Ash.

He arrived as they were finishing their drinks. "I can only spare a few minutes," he said breathlessly. "Renato's in the shrine, overseeing the placement of the north wall blocks, but he'll be back to the antechamber before long."

Lorelei slid the red-leather journal to him. "Take a look at this."

Ash made no move to take it. "Faedryn's dark blood, that's Korvus's journal."

"Yes, it is."

"Where did you get it?"

"From Rylan, who we presume stole it from Renato's office."

Ash was silent for several seconds. "If Renato finds out I saw this and didn't immediately bring it to him . . ."

"I know what I'm asking for and what it means," Lorelei said, "but I'm still asking."

Ash seemed to weigh his options while he sat down next to Lorelei. Then he nodded and opened the cover. "Rylan really *stole* it?"

"Yes."

Ash flipped a few pages. "But he seemed so nice."

Lorelei couldn't help but agree, but it had all been an act. She felt like a complete dolt for falling for it. "He was involved in the fire at the library, but I suspect the journal was one of the main reasons he came to Ancris."

Ash's eyes widened. "Did he start the fire?"

"We don't know yet. The Hissing Man was there, too."

Ash flipped through the journal's pages, looking more and more engrossed. Rain began tapping on the Tulip's stained glass windows and grew into a steady patter. "There's a lot here," Ash said absently. "Can I come by your place tonight? Look at it in more detail?"

Lorelei was about to respond when the pub's front door opened with a loud hiss of rain. The guard Creed had spoken to entered wearing a dripping oilskin coat. When Ash turned and saw him, he grimaced. He apparently thought the guard had been sent to fetch him. But when the guard approached their table, he said, "There's been an accident."

"What kind of accident?" Ash asked.

"Scaffolding on the north wall collapsed. Renato fell from the top onto a stack of blocks. His head was bleeding bad."

The color drained from Ash's face. "What?" Ash shook his head in disbelief. "Is he dead?"

The guard shrugged. "I don't know, but you'd better come with me."

Ash stood numbly from his chair. "I'm sorry," he said to Lorelei, "I have to go."

"Of course."

Creed stood as well. "I'd better join him."

Lorelei nodded. "Me t—oh yeah. I'll stay here."

"Okay, wait for me?"

She nodded again and handed Creed the journal. "In case Ash goes back to the palace. The sooner he can look at it, the better."

Creed rushed to catch up with Ash and the guard, leaving Lorelei to brood over the horrible news. The idea that Korvus had been killed because of his research seemed likely if still a bit tenuous. With the death of the man who'd inherited the journal, it seemed certain.

It got her to thinking about Rylan, the man whole stole the journal. He was locked up in the Crag, but that didn't guarantee his safety. As loath as she was to admit it, there were informants among the inquisitors, some beholden to the Church, others to the Red Knives. She decided she couldn't wait.

She ran out the door and down rain-slicked street toward the Crag. By the time she reached the courtyard, she was drenched.

Marion's office was empty. His ring of keys were hanging from an iron hook behind his desk as usual. She snatched them, opened the door, and bolted down the dark hallway. When she got to Rylan's cell, the door was ajar. Someone, likely Rylan, she figured, was choking inside the cell.

She pushed the door open. By the light of the small hole in the wall, she saw a huge bald man holding Rylan in a tight headlock. Rylan's eyes were closed. She couldn't tell if he was still conscious.

Lorelei drew her rapier. "Let him go, Durgan. Now."

SIXTY: LORELEI

Durgan let Rylan fall to the floor, and Lorelei felt some small amount of relief to hear Rylan draw breath.

"Inquisitor . . ." Durgan stepped across the cell toward Lorelei. "Your man and I were just having a bit of a chat."

Lorelei backed into the hall. "I'm warning you, don't come any closer."

"Sorry you had to see that, love." He lunged at her.

Lorelei stumbled back and stuck out her rapier, hoping to slow him down, slicing his forearm, but he slapped the blade avoiding its tip. She drew her poniard with her free hand, but Durgan charged. He grabbed the basket hilt of her rapier and wrenched it from her hand and tried to grab her wrist but she wriggled it free.

Durgan forced her backwards, slamming her into the door to Marion's office, then he smashed his massive forehead on the crown of her head.

She winced, opened her eyes again, and saw two of Durgan's big ugly mugs in her blurred vision.

He pressed her against the door. "Never should have come sniffing about, girl."

She blinked and blinked again until her vision cleared. Then she stomped on his right foot. He growled and pressed his face so close to hers she could smell the rot in his teeth. "Nice try, bi—"

She stomped on his foot again, with the corner of her heal. He grimaced and looked down at his foot. She pulled her right hand free, spun away, and stuck the point of her poniard into his side.

His eyes went wide. She pushed the blade deeper, and he staggered backward, swinging a backhand to her jaw that snapped her head sideways, then he collapsed onto the stone floor, pressing his hands to the wound in the side of his gut, leaving her standing there holding the bloody poniard.

He coughed, raised a bloody hand, and stared at it in disbelief. "Ahh . . . you fucking bitch!"

The door behind Lorelei started to creaked open and hit her in the back. She stepped around Durgan, and Marion walked into the hall. "Stone and scree, what's going on here?"

"Durgan got tired of his cell and went for a fucking stroll," Lorelei said. "Where were *you*?"

"On evening rounds, as I'm supposed to be." He stared down at Durgan, who was curled up and moaning loudly. "How—"

"Never mind that for now." When Durgan suddenly went quiet, Lorelei looked over and saw his eyes were closed and his body had gone slack. "Go fetch a nun and see if you can save this bloody idiot."

Marion looked ready to argue, but he nodded and rushed away.

Lorelei's thoughts raced. Who'd let Durgan out? More importantly, why? What had they hoped to gain by killing Rylan? If she left Rylan in the Crag now, whoever had let Durgan out would try again.

She ran back to Rylan's cell, crouched beside him, and shook his shoulder. "Rylan?"

When he didn't respond, she tried again, but he was still out. She was just wondering if she should get him to the infirmary—a place just as dangerous as the dungeon, maybe even more so—when lightning flashed through the small window. A deep, rolling thunder followed. Rylan flailed his arms and then opened his eyes and gasped for air. Then he looked around the cell, wild-eyed.

"You're safe." Lorelei held her hand out. "Can you stand?"

He lay his head down on the filthy floor. "Do I have to?"

"Yes, we need to get you out of here."

"Where are we—"

"I'm not sure yet." She helped him to his feet.

She led him from the cell, past Durgan's unmoving form, and into Marion's office. On a hook were Marion's tricorn hat and oilskin coat, still dripping with rain. She made Rylan put them on.

In the hallway toward the exit, they passed Marion and a nun. Marion put out a hand to stop them. "Where are you taking him, and in *my* bloody coat?"

"Never you mind, Marion. That big cretin back there seems to be bleeding all over your hallway. Go check on him. Let *me* worry about Rylan." Durgan was likely a dead man, but she needed Marion to remain occupied for the next few minutes.

Marion hesitated, then let them pass.

Lorelei took Rylan out the front of the Crag into the courtyard. Two guards in mail and red tabards eyed her from the doorway to the stables. Rylan seemed to shrink into the oilskin coat, but they went back to their conversation when Lorelei led him purposefully to the front gates.

They walked down the muddy road toward the city.

"Why are you doing this?" Rylan shouted over the downpour. He was shivering so much his teeth chattered.

"Because I need answers," she shouted back, "and I can't very well get them from you if you're dead."

She thought he might argue, but he didn't. They crossed Barrowdown Bridge and were making their way along a narrow street when Rylan looked up at the buildings and said, "Are we going to your *home*?"

She was surprised he remembered. "We are, and it's my *mother's* home as well, so try to pretend you're not a piece of shit."

"I think I can manage."

"I only meant—"

"I know what you meant. I'll be a good boy. I promise."

Lorelei's mother was in the tiny kitchen peeling potatoes when they walked through the front door soaking wet. "*You're* back early—" To Rylan she said, "Well, hello there."

"Mother, this is Rylan."

Adelia's eyes widened. "Rylan . . ."

The two had never met, but Adelia knew quite a bit about Rylan already. Talking through things had always helped Lorelei to sort things out, and the recent mysteries Rylan was wrapped up in had needed a *lot* of sorting.

"Rylan, this is my mother, Adelia."

"Pleased," Rylan said with a bow. "I apologize for dripping all over your kitchen."

"It's only water." Adelia set her knife and the half-peeled potato down on the counter. "I'll fetch some clothes and make you some tea."

She put a kettle on the stove, then bustled up the stairs. When she came back down, she was holding an overlarge work shirt, overalls, and thick woolen socks. She handed the clothes to Rylan. "These should fit well enough."

Rylan opened his mouth, closed it again, then said, "You're too kind."

"They're dry clothes, not blessings from Alra." She pointed to the nearby bathroom. "Now go change before you catch your death."

While Rylan changed in the bathroom, Lorelei went upstairs to her own room. She thought about putting on her spare inquisitor's uniform to keep things formal, but chose a pair of old trousers and a thick sweater instead. Soon enough, she and Rylan were sitting on couches, facing each other across the sitting room table. Their clothes were drying near the fireplace.

Adelia returned with two mugs of fragrant lavender tea. "I'll leave you to talk."

When she left, Lorelei sipped the tea and asked. "How's your neck?"

"Better," he said, even though it was dark red and even purple in places. "Thanks for that, by the way."

She shrugged. "I could hardly have him killing my key witness, could I?"

Rylan smiled halfheartedly. "Spoken like a true inquisitor."

Lorelei paused and then said, "There's something going on in this city, Rylan, and I need to find out what. You're going to tell me."

Rylan ran his thumb over the lip of his mug, then stared into the steaming tea, as if he was trying to read his fortune.

"Lives are at stake," Lorelei pressed.

The rain lashed against the windows, a dull, monotonous hiss.

"I didn't start the fire," he said at last.

"But you were you in the library. A woman died that night. Kellen was stabbed."

"I'm not a murderer." He raised his cup to his lips, but instead of drinking, said, "I'm no assassin."

Lorelei wasn't sure who he was trying to convince. "I didn't say you were."

He seemed disturbed, almost angry. "Kellen had my uncle killed."

"Your uncle committed a crime."

"A crime in the eyes of the empire only. Uncle Beckett never hurt anyone. He adored dragons and he wanted to share that with me. He was no enemy of the empire."

"Forgive me, Rylan, but none of this is convincing me you're innocent."

"I'm telling you so you'll understand. I was offered a chance for revenge. I accepted, thinking it was what I wanted, but when I got to the library, I couldn't bring myself to do it." He shrugged. "I've never killed anyone."

"This offer . . . *That's* why you came to Ancris?"

Rylan shook his head.

"Then why *did* you come?"

"I doubt you'll believe me about this, either."

"Try me."

"Aarik Bloodhaven wanted me to find out what Master Renato knew about Korvus Julianus's disappearance. Aarik was on to some project of Llorn's, and he wasn't sure who knew what."

"Aarik is dead."

"Yes, and when Llorn took over, I came to Ancris hoping to learn more about what he was doing with the Hissing Man."

"So tell me, what have you learned?"

"Nothing concrete, but enough to be worried about what it means for the Holt and for Ancris." Rylan paused and set his mug on the table. "Maybe we could talk to Master Renato directly. Learn what *he* knows . . ."

Lorelei wasn't sure she should tell him just yet, but she decide it might help. "Master Renato is dead."

"What the—"

"An accident in the shrine. Creed and Ash are there now. Or they were." Rylan lapsed into an uncomfortable silence, so she continued, "Help me with something. If you were here to learn about Renato, how does the chalice fit into it?"

Rylan dropped his gaze to the wooden table between them. "Raef asked me to steal it."

Lorelei tried to keep her composure, but her mouth fell open and she struggled with what to say next. "You know, for a man who says he's not a Knife, you seem to deal with them an awful lot."

"I know how it must seem, but Aarik was trying to make peace. I came here hoping it might still be reached, even after his death. And the chalice . . . Raef played me. He used Kellen's death as bait so I'd steal the chalice for him."

"Okay, but why?"

Rylan shrugged. "He said Llorn wanted it because the Hissing Man wanted it. I'm guessing he was planning to use it as leverage, or to pay back a debt."

"I need to see it, Rylan. Where's the chalice?"

Lorelei knew it wasn't a particularly easy request. Rylan would basically be admitting he'd stolen the chalice, but it was why Lorelei had waited so long to bring it up. She'd wanted soften him up first.

Rylan glanced out the window. The rain was barely a drizzle, and a bit of the setting bright sun shone along the horizon. "I arranged for it to be sent to the Holt."

"You sent it ahead on your dragon . . . ?"

Rylan paused a good long while, then nodded. "Her name's Vedron."

She understood his reticence—she wouldn't want to admit to a bond with an umbral dragon, either—but that was the last thing she was worried about. "Can you summon her?"

He shook his head. "Not from here. I need to be close to do that."

"That presents a few difficulties, as you might imagine."

"Such as?"

"You're wanted for Ezraela's death and Kellen's injuries, not to mention the fire."

"I told you, I didn't start the fire. And it was the Hissing Man who killed Ezraela."

"I believe you, but it isn't up to me."

"Then come with me. You could say I'm in your custody and you're collecting more information. You wouldn't even be lying."

"Yes, well, there's a problem with that as well."

"What?"

"I'm not exactly in a position to be taking you—or anyone, for that matter—to gather information."

Rylan tilted his head. "Why not?"

She told him pretty much everything she could. "Tyrinia Solvina wants my badge, and unless I unscrew things up, she just might get her wish."

Lorelei's gut churned, but Rylan seemed distracted. "The chandler," he said, "you said he seemed confused. 'A bit hazy,' as you put it?"

"That's right. Why?"

Before he could say more, someone knocked on the front door. Lorelei's heart started racing. "Wait here."

She picked up her poniard from her belt near the fire, took the steps down to the entryway, and opened the door. Ash and Creed were standing there only slightly dripping. Behind them was Praefectus Damika.

SIXTY-ONE: RYLAN

Rylan was tempted to slip out the back when Lorelei went to answer the knock at the front door, but the sort of trouble he'd landed himself in would follow him wherever he went. Plus, he seemed to have found an ally in Lorelei. He'd be a fool to throw that away now.

So he was still sitting on Lorelei's couch, rubbing his hands while trying to control his nerves, as Lorelei, Creed, Ash, and Praefectus Damika entered the quaint sitting room. Creed leaned against the wall beside the fireplace with a hangman's stare. Ash and Lorelei sat across from Rylan. Praefectus Damika, the last to enter, sat in the upholstered chair to Rylan's right.

Lorelei proceeded to tell Damika everything, from her initial suspicions to her arrest of Rylan at the palace, her rescue of him in the Crag, and his admission about Raef and the chalice.

When she finished, Damika nodded to Creed. "Tell her what you found."

"*I* didn't find anything," Creed replied. "It was all Ash."

Ash, holding Korvus's red journal, looked small and fragile as an orphan. "By the time Creed and I got to the shrine, Master Renato had been pronounced dead. The shepherds were questioning everyone. I nearly got into trouble for being gone, but Creed vouched for me."

"Do you know what happened?" Rylan asked.

"An accident with the scaffolding, apparently. They wouldn't tell us anything. I'm not sure they knew anything to tell us. They shut down work for the day. When they were done with me"—he opened the journal over his knees—"Creed and I went back to the Tulip and I looked this over." He flipped several pages before landing on one with an ordered table of numbers. "Korvus was studying the flow of aura and umbra around the Holt. He'd chosen high points and low points, hills and valley, some with vegetation and some more barren. He was trying to figure out if the flow rates varied by geography type. He seemed to have stumbled onto . . . something."

"What kind of *something*?" Lorelei asked.

"He noticed a shift in the pattern of umbra, in particular. It was moving in ways he didn't expect . . . over a fairly long time, about fifteen years."

Lorelei shrugged. "What are you saying."

Ash tapped a paragraph below a neatly drawn table. "Here, he says that something—"

Damika rolled her eyes. "Ah . . . *something*, again. How helpful."

"Please, Praefectus," Lorelei said, "Let him continue."

Damika shrugged. Lorelei nodded at Ash.

"Something in the Holt was causing the shift. He suspected a sinkhole was about to form, which apparently is very rare. He seemed quite excited about it, and hoped to observe it if he could. In his last entries he talks about a second journal to record it. He must have taken it with him on his final expedition, the one on which he and the ferryman disappeared."

"The place Korvus was looking for," Rylan said, "is probably where the peat came from, yes?"

Damika glared at Rylan and cleared her throat loudly. "Against my better judgment, I've allowed you to stay because Lorelei believes you can help. So tell me, what do you know about this sinkhole?"

Rylan tried to think of anything he might have heard, mostly to try to mollify the Praefectus, but he came up empty. "I don't really know anything about it."

"Do you know where it might be?"

"I don't. There are literally hundreds of bogs and fens in the eastern Holt. The peat could have come from any of them."

"Then why, by Alra's beneficent smile, should I not take you to the Crag right now?"

Rylan felt his freedom slipping away. "Because I can help you. I know a lot about the Red Knives. Stuff you probably don't."

"Such as?"

Rylan felt a bit like he was betraying his people—he was brought up to think the empire was the enemy. He needed to stop thinking that way. This was too important. "Lorelei told us about Tomas showing up at the Tulip and acting . . . weird."

Damika glanced at Lorelei, who nodded. Then she looked at Rylan again. "So?"

"I think Llorn compelled him."

"You mean magically compelled?"

"Yes, with a cobalt lucerta."

Damika frowned. "That knowledge was lost centuries ago."

"It was, but Llorn's mother could have found it."

Damika paused to think. "The Book of the Holt was burned when Rygmora was executed."

Rylan nodded. "A *copy* was burned. Are you sure it was the only one?"

She paused, then jutted her chin at him. "Go on."

"Tomas would never have gone to an inquisitor on his own. Knives vow not to. It would put his entire family at risk. But Llorn could have compelled him with a lucerta from Fraoch."

Lorelei looked dumbstruck. "Galla's autopsy report said the evidence was consistent with a compulsion by a cobalt dragon."

Creed grunted. "Might also explain why his eyes were so red."

"Okay," Damika said, "but why would Llorn make him admit anything?"

Rylan took a deep breath. He wasn't sure, but it was worth a shot. "Because Aarik was working on a peace deal with my father."

Damika's mouth fell open. "Aarik Bloodhaven and Marstan Lyndenfell were working on a *peace* deal?"

Rylan nodded. "Not just working on it. They were nearly done. They were putting the final touches on an amendment to the Covenant. My father thought patricians in the Holt would vote for it. All that was left was to convince the quintarchs."

Creed glowered. "Llorn wouldn't have liked it."

"Not at all," Rylan said. "I suspect it's why things have been so violent of late. Llorn was acting out. But I don't think even he knew quite how close a deal was. If he did, he probably would have tried to overthrow Aarik."

Creed said, "Llorn was the first one to spot us in the mine."

Lorelei nodded. "Almost like he'd been expecting it. And then, after he escaped from the mine, he killed Tomas to hide what he'd done."

"I don't know," Damika said. "It feels like a stretch."

"There's more," Rylan said. "Blythe admitted to me that Llorn had been in a terrible mood before the meeting in the mine and that he'd been having headaches. I read an ancient account once about an imperial thief from Lyros. He used cobalt lucertae to steal mounds of treasure, but came away with headaches that lasted for days afterward. It's what got him caught. When Lyros's quintarch learned of his headaches, she knew what caused them."

"Fine." Damika shifted in her cushioned chair.. "I'll admit the possibility. Put on your dress uniforms. We're going to the palace to explain this to Quintarch Lucran."

Lorelei swallowed hard. "*We?*"

"Yes, *we*. The sooner we nip this in the bud, the better."

"Yes, Praefectus."

Lorelei left to get her uniform. Damika leaned toward Rylan. "You have a personal relationship with Blythe, as I understand it."

The very mention of Blythe's name made him worry about her relapse. "I do."

"Is she still in Ancris?"

"As far as I know, yes."

Damika nodded. "Tyrinia is angry. She's going to try to sway her husband. I'm going to request leniency for you, but I need a bargaining chip. I'd like to tell Lucran you're willing to get Blythe to corroborate some of this, find out what else she knows. Can I?"

It was no small thing. She wanted him to become an agent of the empire, which would mark him as a traitor in the eyes of the Red Knives. But he'd committed himself when he'd remained to speak with them. Besides, he'd wanted to check on Blythe anyway. "You can."

Damika stared at him a moment, then rapped her knuckles twice on the table. "I'm going to hold you to that promise."

Lorelei returned in short order wearing a fresh inquisitor's uniform. "My mother knows you're staying," she said to Rylan. "Make yourself at home." She gestured to the couch. "Sleep if you like."

Rylan's eyes grew heavy at the very thought. "Thank you," he said. "For everything."

She gave him a brief smile and nodded.

Ash, Lorelei, and Damika soon left. Creed stayed, ostensibly to watch Rylan, but minutes later, his head was lolling, and he sat down in the chair Damika had vacated. Soon, he was snoring softly.

Rylan lay on the couch, hoping to catch at least a little sleep, when Adelia came down the creaking stairs with a pair of blankets. She laid one over Creed and handed the other to Rylan. "You must be hungry after the business at the Crag. I made cranberry muffins. I've got some pine milk as well. Would you like some?"

Rylan dearly wanted sleep, but Adelia gave him the impression she wanted to talk. Besides, his last meal had been the stale bread and mashed peas in the Crag. "That would be lovely, thank you."

Adelia headed toward the kitchen, and Rylan leaned back on the couch. Clanking plates and running water in the kitchen lulled him. When she returned with the platter of food, Rylan blinked his eyes open. He had fallen asleep. She set the platter on the table and sat down across from him.

The muffin was fragrant and sweet, redolent of the kitchen at Valdavyn, and pine milk never failed to remind him of his days with Uncle Beckett and Aunt Merida in Thicket. The simple pleasure he found in both brought a smile to his face.

Adelia blew on her tea and sipped it. "Lorelei tells me you're to help her on her inquisitor business."

"I am."

"She says it's important."

"It is."

"And that she thinks you're sincere."

Rylan paused his chewing. "I am."

"Good, because, hear me well, Rylan Holbrooke, if I find different, the next muffin I give you is going to be laced with nightshade."

He swallowed hard. "I would hardly blame you. You've raised a fine young woman. It's nice that you're so close."

"It is. And you? Are you close with your mother?"

Rylan laughed. "We're about as close as this sitting room is to the Olgasian Sea, though I would hardly call the Holt's First Lady my mother."

"Oh, I wasn't talking about Kathrynn Lyndenfell, but your Aunt Merida."

Rylan squinted, wondering how could she possibly know about Aunt Merida.

"Lorelei and I talk a lot," Adelia said.

"Unfortunately, Aunt Merida and I drifted apart."

He'd worded the statement in a neutral way, but their drifting was all his fault. His memories of Uncle Beckett's death were so painful he gradually stopped visiting Thicket altogether. He hadn't meant it to happen, but the memories were too much to bear.

Creed suddenly shifted in his chair, snorted loudly, and fell to snoring again.

Adelia smiled at him, then returned her gaze to Rylan. "What you went through was very sad. It was bound to affect your relationship with her."

Yes, Rylan mused, *but it should have made us closer.* "Would you mind if I asked *you* a question?"

She shrugged, downed more of her tea, then nodded.

"What does Tyrinia Solvina have against Lorelei?"

Adelia laughed. "That's a rather long story."

"I'm happy to hear the short version."

"It's to do with Lorelei's father, Cain." She jutted her chin. "Those are his clothes you're wearing."

Rylan felt rather like a thief caught in the act.

"He passed more than two decades ago, but I haven't had the heart to get rid of his clothes." She paused. "As you may already know, he was an inquisitor. He was smart, dedicated, persistent. Lucran loved him. He rose through the ranks quickly and was on track to becoming the youngest Praefectus ever. But shortly before Lorelei was born, he was assigned a case. Some statues had been stolen from the palace. He went to Highreach a few times to interview witnesses. One of them was Tyrinia, but the interviews went curiously slowly. She was constantly diverting the discussion, then the interview would be cut short by some interruption or another, forcing Cain to leave and come back later. And then he would have to start all over."

"Hmm," Rylan said, knowing where this was headed.

"Hmm, indeed. During their final interview, Tyrinia propositioned my husband. He declined, but Tyrinia does not take being told no well. She became obsessed with him. I'm convinced it was why he never made Praefectus. I'm also convinced it was why he was given the most dangerous assignments, the last of which got him killed."

"That's horrible," Rylan said. "I'm so sorry."

Adelia's smile was restrained, but she stared stoically into his eyes. "After he died, Tyrinia became obsessed with Lorelei. Lorelei was young then, only five. Tyrinia, perhaps feeling guilty, invited her to the palace to play with Skylar. She even offered to have Lorelei taught by the same scholar who was tutoring Skylar and Ash. Years later, she helped get Lorelei a place in the inquisitors' academy."

"Forgive me for asking, but if she did all you say she did, why accept her help?"

"My husband *died* defending this city and the empire. I had little income of my own, and raising Lorelei was a challenge. She needed attention. Lots of it. Don't misunderstand me. I was I was happy to give it, but it left me little time to do much else. The empire *owed* us that money, that tutoring, that job, and a lot more."

"I agree, but I'm a bit confused. If Tyrinia lavished her with all this attention, why is she now trying to end Lorelei's career?"

"I wish I knew. Things changed when Lorelei got her inquisitor's badge. Sometimes I wonder if she expected Lorelei to fail. Or maybe seeing Lorelei with a badge reminds her of Cain, and has hardened her heart. I don't know why, but she's been keen to make sure Lorelei doesn't get promoted. And now she wants her tossed from the inquisitors altogether."

"A mercurial woman, it seems."

"Mercurial . . ." Adelia flashed a wicked smile. "I had another word in mind entirely." She stood and headed toward the stairs. "Sleep well, Rylan Holbrooke."

SIXTY-TWO: LORELEI

An imperial coach delivered Lorelei, Damika, and Ash to Highreach. At the gravel circle near the palace entrance, Lorelei caught sight of a dragon banking through the air high overhead.

Ash followed her gaze. "Skylar's been taking Bothymus out to help him get accustomed to his new fetter." He accompanied Damika and Lorelei to the palace entrance, then kissed Lorelei's cheek. "Good luck." Then he left for another wing of the palace.

Chamberlain Theron arrived and led Lorelei and Damika to the solarium at the rear of the palace. Outside the solarium's glass walls, Quintarch Lucran was sitting at the head of his somewhat famous granite table, wearing a thread-of-gold tunic and his circlet-of-office, both of which complemented his wheat-colored hair and beard. Tyrinia sat to his right, impressive in a brocaded emerald dress. To Lucran's left, much to Lorelei's dismay, was Illustra Azariah in his golden mask and white robe with the Star of Alra. Three large wisplights, each with a swarm of glowing wisps inside, were spaced along the table, casting a glacier blue light on the veranda, their faces, and the vine-covered trellis above their heads. A smaller version of the palisade glimmered softly above everything.

"Wait here, if you please," Theron said and passed through the glass door.

When the door closed behind him, Lorelei said in a soft voice. "What's Azariah doing here?"

"I don't know," Damika replied just as softly. "He wasn't here when I left."

Outside, Lucran nodded, and Theron returned to the solarium. "The quintarch will see you now."

He led them onto the veranda, indicated two chairs halfway down the table, then walked back into the palace. Lorelei and Damika bowed and sat.

"Your Majesties, Your Holiness," Damika began, "I'd like to begin by thanking you for—"

"Let's dispense with the pleasantries, shall we?" Tyrinia said. "Do we know where the dragon singer is?"

Damika nodded. "I'd like to apprise you of what Lorelei and her partner, Creed, have learned first—"

"And *I* asked *you* where Rylan Holbrook is being kept."

In the coach, Damika had expressed hope that Tyrinia might have cooled since their earlier talk, which would allow them to approach the subject of Rylan's whereabouts in a more diplomatic fashion. She clearly hadn't, which was placing

Damika on her back foot from the start. After taking a moment to compose herself, Damika said, "I'd like not to divulge that right now."

Tyrinia stared. "Not divulge it?"

"Yes."

"Why bloody not?"

Damika leaned her elbows on the table and steepled her fingers. "I think we can all agree that important news in our capital has a tendency to . . . drift. It would only be for a short time, Domina."

Tyrinia looked ready to spit fire. "His Holiness deserves to know where Rylan is. Your quintarch *demands* it."

Quintarch Lucran cast a withering stare at the Praefectus but said nothing. Lorelei would likely have folded like a handkerchief, but Damika merely nodded respectfully to both Lucran and Azariah and continued. "I beg your forbearance. Lorelei has exacted a rather intriguing concession from Holbrooke."

Quintarch Lucran grumbled, "A concession of what kind?"

"Of the kind we should consider carefully before dismissing it out of hand, an opportunity we'll likely lose should he be returned to the Crag."

Lucran's head tilted ever so slightly. "Explain."

"Holbrooke has denied responsibility for the fire at the library. He claims it was started by the Hissing Man. He also claims the Hissing Man killed the archivist and then tried to kill him."

"And you believe him?" Tyrinia scoffed.

"I do. Kellen Vesarius has corroborated much of Holbrooke's testimony. Furthermore, the Hissing Man was seen fleeing the plaza. He was apparently there to steal a bronze chalice Holbrooke managed to abscond with. Holbrooke has admitted to stealing the chalice. He's also admitted to stealing a journal of one Korvus Julianus. He did so because he thought it would reveal a link between the Hissing Man's meeting with Aarik in the mine and the peat Blythe was bringing to Ancris." Damika went on to explain how Ash had tested the peat and found it brimming with umbra. "We believe it's linked to the powder the Hissing Man brought to Aarik and Llorn in the mine."

Azariah stirred. "How so?"

"We're not sure yet, Your Holiness, which is why we need Holbrooke. He knows Blythe. He's pledged to find her and learn what he can. It could be an essential clue to discovering not only what's *been* happening but what's *going* to happen."

"Speak plainly, Praefectus Damika," Lucran said. "What do we *think* is happening?"

"The Red Knives are preparing an assault of some sort. Ancris is in danger. I don't claim to know the exact nature of the threat. I'm requesting leeway to find out."

"Whether an assault is imminent or not," Tyrinia said, "you've failed to address Lorelei and her willingness to do as she sees fit."

Damika nodded. "Lorelei, please explain yourself."

"Everything I've done," Lorelei said, "I did for Ancris. I did it because I fear the Hissing Man and the Chosen could ally themselves with the Red Knives." Doing her best to quell the mad beating of her heart, she went on. "Let me pursue this with Rylan. Let us find out where the peat came from. Let us go to the Holt and investigate it."

Tyrinia looked at Lucran with a dead-eyed gaze. "Do you hear? *Rylan*, she calls him. She's soft on him."

"It's most unusual," Lucran said, "what you're asking for."

"Not really," Lorelei said. "And all I'm offering Holbrooke is leniency, not forgiveness, as long as he helps us find out what Llorn is planning."

"Give him to me, Your Majesties," Azariah said, "and my shepherds will get whatever information you want."

"That won't work," Damika replied. "Holbrooke doesn't *have* the information."

Tyrinia snorted. "You can't really believe that."

"I do. Rylan Holbrooke is but a cog in a machine that churns even now toward some infernal goal. It is in all our best interests to find out what is going on before it's too late."

"And why," Lucran said, "is Lorelei necessary to this operation? Surely you have other inquisitors."

Lorelei nearly winced.

Damika said, "Lorelei has been instrumental in uncovering what we know so far. I have every confidence that trend will continue."

Illustra Azariah turned his head so the eyes of his mask faced Lucran. "She's unstable and untrustworthy. And your Praefectus's plan seems ridiculous. Give Holbrooke to us, or put him back in the Crag and let him stand trial."

"Bold words from a man who'd face no consequences for doing so," Lucran said. "I'm not yet ready burn the son of the Imperator."

"The Imperator serves at the pleasure of the quintarchs," Azariah said, "not the other way around. If you feel it too delicate a matter to look into yourself, let the Church investigate the case."

It was apparently the wrong thing to say. "This is the province of the inquisitors," Lucran said, and then turned to Damika. "Investigate as you see fit."

"Of course, Your Majesty. Thank—"

"—but do so without Lorelei."

Lorelei felt her shoulders slump and tried to straighten up. How had she let herself get into this mess?

Damika shook her head. "Quintarch?"

"This has gone on long enough. Lorelei hands over her badge, permanently, or you hand me yours. Furthermore, you will deliver Holbrooke to the Crag at once."

"I beg you, Your Majesty," Damika stammered. "Holbrooke knows the Holt. He was—"

Lucran stared at her incredulously. "The man *stole* from my home and *lied* to my face. Get what information you can from him, but I'll not suffer him walking free a moment longer. Are we understood?"

Damika hesitated only long enough for Lucran to bare his teeth. "Yes, Quint-arch."

"You're dismissed."

A short while later, Lorelei and Damika were back in the coach heading toward the city. Lorelei had no idea what to say. Everything felt wrong; everything *was* wrong.

Damika held out her hand. "I'm sorry, Lorelei, but I need your badge."

"Of course," Lorelei unpinned it from the breast of her coat and handed it over.

Damika stuffed it into the pocket of her own coat. "What they're doing is wrong, but I've no leverage to oppose it."

Lorelei only nodded. What was there to say? What was she if she wasn't an inquisitor any longer?

Nothing. A skiff lost at sea, soon to be swallowed by the approaching storm.

When they reached the city, the buildings leaned in like waves ready to crash. Lorelei's chest tightened. She could barely breathe. Her hands begin to shake, and she balled them into fists. She clenched her jaw so tightly her teeth hurt. Even after all the tricks she'd learned to soothe herself, she floated on the edge of panic.

"Are you all right?" Damika asked.

Lorelei couldn't answer.

Damika leaned forward and squeezed Lorelei's shoulder. "Breathe, Lorelei."

That Damika was there to witness her weakness made it all the worse. It would only cement her feelings that Lorelei was unfit, and that Lucran had been right in taking her badge. She gripped the edge of the seat until her fingers hurt. She was starting to feel lightheaded. She knew what was coming next. She was going to pass out.

Damika switched seats and began rubbing her back. Lorelei stared out the window. Mount Evalarus and the Church's white temple loomed over the city. She thought about the conversation she'd had with Rylan outside the shrine. He said he was a man between two worlds—the Holt and the empire—and that he was fascinated by their entwined history. He'd lied about a lot of things, but that felt true. The empire's history was a messy one. She wouldn't pretend otherwise. And there were troubles still, especially with the people of the Holt, but she refused to let the situation devolve into war.

By clinging to that thin hope, she was able to slow her breathing and stave off a fainting spell that felt imminent. With that tenuous calm came a realization: she was only powerless in the context of her role as an inquisitor. She wasn't pleased with the idea that occurred to her in that moment—it went against everything she believed in—but if it gave her answers, if it had even the *smallest* chance of getting to the root of the mystery she'd stumbled onto, she would do it.

Damika slowed her back rubbing as the coach turned onto Lorelei's street. "Better?"

Lorelei forced a smile. "Better." The image of an indurium dragon soaring through the night air beyond the palace flashed through her mind, and a harried plan began to fall into place. It started with Rylan, and getting him out of her house without Damika knowing. When the coach pulled to a stop, Lorelei pointed to her nicked front door. "Would you mind if I broke the news to him?"

"Lorelei—"

"Please. I freed him. I gave him hope. I owe it to him to tell him the truth."

Damika hesitated, then nodded. "Just hurry."

"I will."

She went inside and rushed to the sitting room, found Creed snoring in the chair and Rylan sleeping quietly on the couch. Careful not to wake Creed, she stoked the coals in the fireplace, then shook Rylan. She held her finger to her lips as he blinked his eyes open and stared at her.

"Can we get the chalice?" she whispered.

"Huh?"

"The Hissing Man wanted that chalice badly enough to kill for it. I need to know why. Can we get it?"

"I thought Damika wanted me to find Blythe."

"That's no longer in the cards. Damika fought for you, but Lucran ordered you back to the Crag. We have to get out of Ancris, and we have to do it now."

"We?"

"Yes, I'm going with you." She pointed to the clothes drying beside the fireplace. "Get dressed. Quickly."

Rylan began undoing the clasps on the overalls. Lorelei turned away to give him some privacy. She grabbed a piece of paper on her mother's tiny writing desk and scribbled a note, telling her mother and Creed that she was leaving the city and would be back as soon as possible.

Rylan, now wearing his hooded coat, stepped up next to her. "How are we going to escape the city?"

She went to the door to the small garden and quietly unlocked it. "I'll explain on the way."

"The way to *where*?"

"The eyrie. We're going to get Bothymus, fly him to meet your dragon, and get that bloody chalice."

SIXTY-THREE: LORELEI

orelei led Rylan through her little vegetable garden, over the stone wall, and down to an alley. Her mind was racing about how they'd reach the eyrie, who might be there when they arrived, and how they were going to sneak Bothymus out unseen.

Rylan stared nervously at the windows of the homes on either side of the alley. "What are you planning to do, just traipse in and take Bothymus?"

"Maybe. I've done it a hundred times."

"When you weren't a wanted woman, maybe, but the eyrie might be on alert by the time we get there. They could be waiting for us."

"Then I guess we're going to have to be extra careful, aren't we? It'll take us an hour to get to the eyrie. That's how long we have to make a plan."

Rylan caught up to her. "It won't take Damika long to realize we're gone."

"Yes, but she'll think we've gone to Fiddlehead or Slade to hide."

"They'll blame *her*."

"I know they will." Lorelei felt queasy just thinking about it. "They'll blame Creed as well. They might even blame my mother. But it can't be helped. We have to do this."

The streets were all but deserted in Old Town. Lorelei listened for alarm bells or the clatter of horses, but there were none. Soon enough they passed out of the city and entered the light forest of pine and spruce that blanketed Blackthorn's western slopes.

"I need to get Bothymus's crop," Lorelei said as they climbed. "It'll be in a cabinet near the front entrance."

"It won't be locked?"

"It often isn't. I'll deal with it if it is. The bigger problem is getting in without being seen. I need a diversion."

They ascended a rocky ridge in the shadowed darkness. At the top, Rylan said, "Remember the old iron vixen behind the eyrie?"

"Yes."

"Is she still there?"

"I think so. Why?"

Rylan smiled, his teeth purple in Nox's light. "I can do more than calm dragons when I sing to them, Lorelei. I can make them angry."

Lorelei ducked beneath the bough of a hemlock. "It could work, but we don't want her angry enough to attack."

"Of course. I'll just ruffle her frills a bit."

Lorelei took Rylan by the wrist and forced him to stop. "I mean it. I care about those dragons."

He seemed surprised that she doubted him. "So do I," he said, "I'll be careful."

They continued on, and Lorelei began worrying. Diversion or not, it would be tricky sneaking a dragon out of the eyrie unseen.

They pushed themselves after that. By the time they crested the shoulder the eyrie was on, Lorelei was panting and her legs were on fire. They skulked into a clutch of pine trees near a dirt road and hid beneath the tallest of them. On the road to their left was the barracks, five stone buildings where the dracorae slept, ate, and trained. Straight ahead was the paddock where dragons were trained for war. To their right was the eyrie, a colossus of stone and wood.

At the eyrie's front entrance, barely visible from her vantage, the rolling doors were open. Stromm stood near them, talking with three dracorae. Lorelei couldn't tell if they'd just flown in or were preparing to fly out.

"I should get moving," Rylan said. "I need to measure the iron's mood before I do this."

"The dracorae's dragons might be ready and waiting. They could chase us." To wait would be to risk the eyrie being alerted, but to fly off with three dracorae nearby was just as dangerous, maybe even more so.

"You said yourself the eyrie likely wouldn't be empty."

"Yes, but I thought it would just be eyrie hands."

"I understand, but Damika and Creed are no fools. It'll occur to them you might make for the eyrie. If we're going to—"

Rylan stopped as Stromm and the dracorae headed inside the eyrie.

"Stone and bloody scree," Lorelei said. She knew how much Stromm liked to talk. There was no telling how long they'd be in there.

"It's not too late to change your mind," Rylan said. "You could go home, say you heard me leaving and chased after me."

She peered through the branches toward the twinkling lights of Ancris, the faintly glittering dome above it. Rylan's suggestion could work. She might escape punishment if not suspicion. But if she did that, Rylan would face even worse charges than he already was. And giving up felt like giving up on ever learning the Hissing Man's greater purpose.

"No," she said firmly, "we stick to the plan."

Rylan paused. "You're sure? I'll be ok—"

"Yes. Go now, while they're inside."

He nodded and pushed through the pine branches and crossed the road, ducked through the paddock fence and ran silently across the gouged earth. Lorelei tried to calm her pounding heart. She eyed the landscape for signs that Rylan had been spotted. She listened for changes in the murmur of dragons coming from the eyrie. When Rylan reached the far side of the paddock, Lorelei parted the branches, crossed the dirt road, and ducked under the fence. Then she followed it toward the eyrie and hid behind a low bush.

Highreach loomed like an elder iron dragon surveying its territory. Skylar would be hurt when she learned that Lorelei had stolen Bothymus from the eyrie. She'd feel betrayed, justifiably so.

"I'm sorry," Lorelei whispered.

Stromm's laugh boomed from inside the eyrie, and the dracorae chuckled. Lorelei balled her hands into fists, willing her heart to slow down. A dragon rumbled in the nesting grounds. The rumble became a roar, and the conversation inside the eyrie ceased.

The Stromm hollered, "Oy! Play nice, now!"

Lorelei counted the seconds. If things went as she'd hoped, Stromm would go to the crops cabinet.

A dragon hissed loudly. Stromm bellowed, "No! *Stop* it, now! That's *enough!*"

The iron was releasing its breath, which could turn human skin into stone, causing scaling and no small amount of pain. It was dangerous, but it was likely only a warning.

She heard footsteps pound over the dirt floor of the eyrie, then a high-pitched squeak. She hoped it was the door of the crop cabinet being opened. Stromm was likely headed toward the nesting grounds with the iron's crop. If he wasn't, she was in deep trouble.

She slipped through the fence rails, crept silently to the gap in the rolling doors, and waited. The iron's grumbling became a high-pitched keening. Lorelei hoped that meant the dragon was fighting its fetter. She rolled the eyrie door to open a gap wide enough for Bothymus to pass through, then peeked around the edge of the door.

The rear doors of the eyrie were wide open. Stromm was standing in front of a roiling cloud of gray gas between the eyrie and the nesting grounds, holding the crop over his head. *"Accumbo! Accumbo!"* ordering the riled iron to lay still. The three dracorae were standing next to him, exchanging glances. Scores of golds, brasses, bronzes, and silvers were spread throughout the eyrie in stalls on the ground or nests in the rafters. Bothymus was in his nest near the far right corner, head turned toward Stromm. Thankfully, his saddle was still on. Lorelei recalled seeing Skylar flying Bothymus earlier that night—to acclimate him to his new fetter, Ash had said. The dracorae's arrival had likely kept Stromm from removing the saddle.

Lorelei stepped inside and padded left along the interior wall. The crop cabinet doors were open; dozens of golden crops wrapped in leather hung from hooks inside it. Beyond was the door to Stromm's office, such as it was. It was hardly more than a desk, a chair, and stacks of papers.

As she slunk toward the cabinet, two gold kits with garnet eyes stared down from a nest in the rafters and cooed like mourning doves. A vixen in the same nest drew her gaze from Stromm, lowered her head toward Lorelei, and made a long, warbling note. Lorelei glanced quickly at the dracorae and then lurched to the cabinet.

She'd no more than grabbed Bothymus's crop than the gold kits leapt down from their nest and blocked her path. The iron roared so loud Lorelei felt it along her ribs. Stromm bellowed more orders, and the kits swung their sinuous necks around to look at him. Lorelei sidled along the wall, planning to slip past them, but stopped when the closest one snapped its gaze back to her, fanned its frills, and screeched a warning cry.

Feeling like all eyes in the eyrie were on her, Lorelei retreated to the cabinet, grabbed the crop of an excitable silver dragon named Ruko, and ducked into Stromm's office. Through the gap in the door, she saw the kits approach the office. One of the dracorae was headed toward them along the main aisle with a worried look.

Lorelei gripped Ruko's crop, focused on the expanse of wood chips beyond the office door, and whispered, *"Protego, protego."*

The nearest kit craned its head to one side while peering into Stromm's office. The dracorae was approaching the two kits. "What's gotten into—"

He stopped and stared up, then dove away.

Both kits screeched and leapt into the air mere moments before Ruko's gleaming silver form landed near the crop cabinet.

"Venatura," Lorelei whispered, willing Ruko to chase, *"venatura."*

Lorelei felt a thrill run through her, an echo of Ruko's eagerness. The silver leapt to the rafters and bounded from beam to beam, chasing the gold kits.

"Faedryn's teeth," the dracora called while staring up, "will you settle down? It's not like she hasn't thrown tantrums before!" With a sigh, he ran toward the center aisle and the back of the eyrie.

Lorelei ducked out of Stromm's office, tossed Ruko's crop into the cabinet, and snuck out through the front doors. As the chill wind struck her hot cheeks, she wrapped the crop around her left hand and sprinted toward the cliff edge, where Rylan was supposed to meet her, she squeezed the stone and felt the link with Bothymus brighten.

Come, she willed him, *we've more flying to do tonight. But move quietly, Bothymus. Quietly.*

At the cliff edge, she didn't see Rylan anywhere and called his name softly.

His head popped up from beyond a rocky ledge to her left, and he waved. She joined him, ducked low. Bothymus emerged the front doors and lumbered toward them, gurgling. Lorelei held her breath as the sounds in the eyrie began to settle, praying no one would follow. She let the breath out in a whoosh when no one did.

When Bothymus reached the cliff edge, he waited patiently for Lorelei and Rylan to climb up on his back. Then he plodded to the edge of the cliff and tipped over the edge. The cliff face blurred past them. Bothymus spread his wings, caught the air, and soared toward the Holt.

SIXTY-FOUR: RYLAN

R ylan and Lorelei flew for hours, deep into the Holt. When Lux rose, reckoning was hardly more than a glimmer of gold overhead. The sky turned
robin's egg blue, and the green forest canopy sprawled as far as the eye
could see.

Rylan pointed over Lorelei's shoulder ahead to their right. "Watch tower."

Lorelei nodded and adjusted Bothymus's path to avoid it. "Can you sense
her yet?"

"Not yet," Rylan said. "Hopefully soon." Rylan was beginning to worry. He
should feel her by now. Each passing mile made him wonder if she'd been spotted
on the way back to her nesting grounds and been hunted. *She's fine,* he told himself
over and over. *We're just not close enough yet.*

It had been some time since he'd ridden an indurium, and Bothymus, typical
of his breed, was a pleasure to ride. Vedron was constantly weaving and ducking,
but Bothymus flew straight as an arrow and wasn't pushed about by heavy wind as
Vedron was. Perhaps sensing his thoughts, the indurium released a long, blaring
trumpet.

Rylan called above the *whump* of Bothymus's wings, "How much time do you
suppose we bought ourselves?"

Lorelei shrugged. "By now they've probably noticed Bothymus has gone missing. They may or may not have had time to send Glaeyand a warning by vyrd, but
we should assume they did. A talon or two will be sent after us, but even so, I
figure we can reach Vedron and get out of the area before they spot us."

She was likely right, but Rylan was nervous. His father would likely give Andros the honor of hunting for him. Rylan could only imagine his smug smile if he
caught them.

A short while later, Rylan was relieved to sense Vedron waiting. He urged her
to meet him at Thervindal's Tor, a place not far ahead where they'd spent many
lazy afternoons. *Stay low,* he bid her, *fly in the trees.* She grumbled at being told how
to fly undetected; she had been doing so every day of her life.

He pointed Lorelei toward a gap in the trees, where the Diamondflow snaked
through the forest. Near a bend in the river was a large outcropping of black rock.
"Land on the rock," he said. "Vedron will meet us there."

Bothymus landed gracefully on the broad, flat top of the tor above the roaring
Diamondflow, and Rylan and Lorelei slipped down from the saddle. The water
churned and frothed as it slipped over a scattering of boulders below them. Vedron's
bond with Rylan grew stronger, lifting his spirits. He hadn't realized how much

he'd missed her. Little more than a day had passed since the fire at the library and her rescue of him, but it felt like an age, and he realized he missed their days flying alone as much as she did.

Bothymus arched his head back and trumpeted a long note, less warning than a claim on the jutting tor. Vedron rounded the trunk of a citadel and began circling lazily down toward them.

Bothymus trumpeted again, louder, beat his wings and extended the frill atop his head. Vedron stopped descending and soared in a level circle. Rylan felt her confusion. She didn't understand why he'd called her to a place with another dragon—a radiant, no less.

"It's all right." Rylan placed his hand on the rough scales of Bothymus's shoulder. "He won't hurt you. Will you, Bothymus?"

Bothymus gurgled noncommittally.

Rylan stepped away from the indurium and tried to calm Vedron. He beckoned her closer. Eventually, she circled down and swooped to a landing on a patch of soft ground ten paces away.

"There," Rylan said, climbing off the rock. "that wasn't so bad, was it?"

Vedron trilled and Rylan scratched the wattle along her neck, but her emerald gaze never left Bothymus. When she was sufficiently calm, Rylan reached into her saddlebag. "Now," he said, "let's see what we've got."

As he unbuckled the bag, he worried someone had somehow beat him to Vedron and taken the chalice, but when he threw the flap back, it was there in its cloth sack, just as he'd left it. He took it out and showed it to Lorelei.

Lorelei gaped. "May I?"

He handed the chalice to her, and she turned it in her hands.

"They're the same as the runes on the vyrda, yes?" Rylan said.

"Yes."

"Can you read it?"

"I'm a little out of practice, but I think so."

The sun shone off her red hair as she rotated the chalice slowly, tapped on a few of the runes, and *hmm*'d. Finally, she pointed to the top row. "As near as I can tell, it says, 'Here lies a part, or maybe a *piece*, of Alra the Blinding and thus, a part of us all, for it was Alra who struck Faedryn down.'"

"That's odd," Rylan said. "I thought it was Alra's paragons who defeated him."

She pointed to the second line. "That's acknowledged here. Sort of. It says, 'Through her charges was the trickster god lured near, through her charges was the dark sun's child laid low, through her charges was he delivered to his tomb 'neath the Umbral Tree, all as the bright sun's daughter had deemed.'"

Vedron seemed to grow bored. She darted toward Bothymus and stopped just short of clapping her teeth on one of his wings. Bothymus pulled his wing away and huffed.

Lorelei glanced at them and smiled, but Rylan scowled. "Settle, down, Vedron. Can't you see he doesn't want to play?"

Vedron cooed, swung around and nudged Rylan's leg with her head.

"Shush, girl. We have business to take care of first." He turned to Lorelei again. "So it's saying Alra acted through her paragons, and therefore, everything that followed was, in essence, due to her?"

"That's how I interpret it, yes. The last line reads, 'May Faedryn lie in darkness forevermore; may Alra lie in peace until once again made whole.'"

Rylan stood there, stunned. "Made whole?"

Lorelei seemed just as shaken as he was. "That's what it says."

"What does it say on the base?"

She turned it over. "It's a list of names." She pointed to one. "This one says 'Izrahim.'"

Izrahim, as everyone in the empire knew, was one of Alra's five paragons. As Strages was interred in Ancris's holy shrine, so was Izrahim in Olencia's.

Lorelei pointed to the other names in turn. "Rai'al, Strages, Cinder, Ember . . ." She pointed to a sixth name. "And then there's Yeriel."

Rylan shook his head. "Six?" Lorelei handed it to him and he turned it around. Sure enough, there were six names on the chalice, not five. "It can't possibly be the same Yeriel, can it?" Yeriel was the leader of the wardens who guarded Faedryn's prison below the Umbral Tree in Gonsalond.

"She's said to be long-lived," replied Lorelei. "Some say she's undying."

"I know, but it seems preposterous to think she's related to the events of the Ruining."

"I don't think we can rule it out, but you're missing the most important point."

"And that is?"

"If there really were six paragons, why does history tell us there were only five?"

It was a question with staggering implications. "Perhaps the sixth fell into disgrace," Rylan said. "It wouldn't be the first time the empire wrote something out of their histories."

"Maybe, but there was *so much* written about the five. There were the shrines and the quintarchs and the cities as well."

"I don't follow."

"I'm saying that if, at the time of Faedryn's fall, there were six paragons, wouldn't there have been six pieces of the Heartstone as well? Wouldn't a sixth shrine have been built to hold it?"

"I could make any number of arguments for Yeriel having done *something* that displeased Alra, or the other paragons, or the generals in her war against Faedryn. It could easily have led to her being denied a shrine of her own."

"I suppose . . ."

Just then Vedron darted toward Bothymus again, and this time she *did* nip his wing with her teeth. Bothymus roared, reared up, and beat his wings. When Vedron didn't back away, Bothymus spun and lashed his tail at her. Vedron flapped her wings and tumbled back—

—straight into Rylan and Lorelei.

Rylan fell. Lorelei stumbled, and the chalice went clunking down the tor's steep, rocky slope.

"Bloody hells," Rylan grumbled.

He leaned over and spotted the chalice on a ledge, near the base of a gorse bush. It was tricky, but he climbed down to it. The bowl was dented and scratched, and the rim was terribly bent. Then he noticed faint lines where the verdigris had scraped away on the rocks. They were words of some sort, or maybe a drawing. He tried scraping away more, but it was difficult.

"The fuck are you doing?" Lorelei asked.

"There's something here."

"Something *where*?"

"Just give me a moment." He climbed back up the bank but instead of handing the chalice to Lorelei, he carried it to where Vedron was hunkered some distance away, rummaged through a saddlebag, and pulled out a kerchief. Then he held the chalice to Vedron's snout and said, "*Exhalo*. Just a little, understand?"

"Stone and scree, Rylan, what are you—"

"Just wait."

Vedron opened her mouth and breathed a thin stream of acid from beneath her tongue. Rylan caught it in the bowl of the chalice.

"Rylan, don't!"

But it was already done. Rylan swirled the acid around in the bowl, then wiped it away with the kerchief. The shiny bronze surface of the bowl's interior was completely cleaned.

Lorelei snatched it from him. "How *could* you?" Then she stared into the bowl, and her eyes went wide. "Sweet Alra's grace."

Trees and a winding river were etched into the bottom of the bowl. They looked exactly like the Diamondflow from the maps Rylan had loved poring over. Along the edge of the bowl, the Whitefells were arranged in a grand arc.

"It's a map of the Holt," Lorelei said.

"Yes." Rylan pointed to the center of the design—a tree much larger than the others. "There's the Umbral Tree. And here"—he pointed to the designs that looked like caves in the mountains—"are the shrines."

"Six of them."

"Yes."

"There were six shrines."

"*Are* six shrines," Rylan said. "There were six then, and there are six now."

The map was fairly detailed and seemed quite accurate. The five known shrines in the empire's five capitals, were easy to spot, which made the sixth stand out, northwest of Ancris and south of Caldoras, like a wisp in a dark swamp.

"Look at these." Lorelei pointed to several peaks. One had a hook at its peak, another a hole along one side, a third had a wavy lake. "I know these mountains."

As Rylan stared at them, he started to feel giddy. "Are you suggesting what I think you're suggesting?"

Lorelei lowered the chalice, stared Rylan straight in the face. "We have to go there. We have to find the sixth shrine."

Were it not for his worries over what the Red Knives and the Hissing Man had planned for Ancris, he would have agreed to go immediately, but he found himself wondering if they shouldn't return to Ancris to let the others know. "Shouldn't we consider going back to Ancris?"

"Yes, but we can't really go back without more in any case. We *have* to see why the chalice is so important, why the Hissing Man wanted it so desperately."

Vedron, sensing Rylan's mood, flapped his wings, arched his neck back, and trumpeted enthusiastically.

Lorelei smiled. "Is that a yes?"

Rylan couldn't help it. He smiled back. "That's a yes."

SIXTY-FIVE: RHIANNON

Rhiannon stared at Tiufalli's still form, lying still in its nest, its scales pale and dull. Rhiannon's hands shook; tears welled in her eyes. That the kit was dead wasn't in question, nor was the cause. Morraine had killed it and consumed its soul to sustain herself. She'd admitted the souls of deer and wolves hardly helped to stem her hunger, but dragon's souls were more complex, richer than those of common forest animals.

Rhiannon had many questions, but several stood out. If Morraine had come this far only weeks after being raised, what next? How long before she needed to feed again? And would her hunger grow?

She vowed to find answers to these questions, but first things first. "Can you handle Tiufalli?" she said to Ayasha, the dragon handler.

"Aye, girl." She jutted her chin toward the eyrie doors. "I'm more worried about Irik."

"I'll speak to him."

Ayasha nodded. "And there's the matter of the cause of Tiufalli's death."

"I'll speak to her as well."

Ayasha was a hard woman who rarely showed emotion, but she seemed relieved. "She'll take it better coming from you."

Rhiannon left the nest, entered the yard, and trudged across the gouged earth toward Irik, who was hugging himself at the far side of the training pen.

Irik watched her approach, then blinked fiercely, tears trailing down his cheeks. "She didn't have to take him."

Rhiannon's heart wept as she took him into her arms. "I know."

"She could have taken a deer or an elk."

"I know, Irik"—she held him tighter—"and I'm so very sorry."

The words felt insufficient. Meaningless. The sort of bond Irik had made with Tiufalli was for life, and it was deep beyond the understanding of people who'd never experienced it. Irik's bond might have been recently forged, but that hardly mattered. The loss would be devastating.

Rhiannon felt Irik's warm tears against her cheek. He slipped his arms around her, held her tight. His whole body wracked as he wept, and Rhiannon wept with him.

A short while later, Ayasha left the shelter and pointed toward the workhouse, beyond which lay the paddock with their few horses. "I'll go fetch a cart. We should bury him."

Irik pulled away from Rhiannon. "We're not going to render him?"

Everyone in the Holt knew how valuable dragon remains were. They accepted it as a way for their bondmate to provide for those who outlived them.

"His flesh," Ayasha said. "His scales, his bones. I'm sorry, boy, but they might be tainted."

Rhiannon wasn't sure about that, but she knew Ayasha wouldn't to listen to her—the Red Knives were a superstitious lot.

Irik stared at the shelter, wiped his eyes, and said, "I'll help."

"You don't have to," Ayasha said. "I'll take care of it."

"No." Irik walked to the gate and opened it. "I want to."

Rhiannon took the stairs up to her burrow. Morraine was sitting in a chair at a table on the deck out front, staring out over the forest. She made no outward sign that she was aware of Rhiannon, not even when Rhiannon passed in front of her and sat in the chair opposite her.

As a family of swamphens chirped below and insects buzzed overhead, Rhiannon searched for the right words to start what was going to be a hard conversation. An auburn dragon trumpeted one long note from the nest in an adjacent tree. Another answered. Then Bellicor roared and silenced them both. The onyx, whose bond had been severed in sudden and ruthless fashion when Aarik was burned, was still inconsolable, which brought a certain clarity to Rhiannon's thoughts. "Tiufalli's dead," she said.

What sort of response she'd been hoping for, Rhiannon wasn't sure. Certainly more than the momentary gaze Morraine gave her.

"Tiufalli's dead," she repeated, "and Irik is heartbroken."

"He'll find another dragon."

"You think it's so easy?"

"You're making a dragonbond out to be something precious. It isn't."

"You don't know that."

She pointed up at Bellicor. "Did you know Aarik was bonded to another dragon before Bellicor? It died in a raid not far from Thicket. And Bellicor himself is old. He's had seven bondmates that I'm aware of, maybe more."

"You're making it out to be meaningless."

"No. I'm saying life goes on. Irik will find another dragon, perhaps one of the other cobalts that were flown to the nesting grounds. Or maybe he won't, and he'll come to accept the loss of a dragon kit."

"You *killed* Tiufalli."

"If you think I had a choice in the matter, you have little understanding of what's become of me."

Rhiannon stood and leaned over the table, pressing her face close to her mother's "You cannot do it again."

Morraine's eyes softly glowed. She met Rhiannon's hard stare. "If I were you, I'd choose my next words with great care."

On the way up, Rhiannon had been terrified of what her mother might do, but her mother's callousness had vanquished that fear. "You *cannot* do it again. I won't allow it."

"Is that so?" Morraine smiled. "And how will you stop me?"

"I won't help you search for Yeriel. I won't go near the vyrd or the shard."

Morraine's smile vanished, and her wrinkled brow furrowed. She looked angrier than Rhiannon had ever seen her. "You will do as you're *told*, Rhiannon."

"No, I won't, and all Llorn's plans will have been for naught. But there's another choice. You can get what sustenance you need from *me*!"

A sudden chill bit the air. Morraine stood and loomed over Rhiannon, but Rhiannon refused to budge. Her mother raised a gnarled finger, as though she were about to rebuke Rhiannon, but Bellicor warbled long, low, and loud.

Morraine glanced up at the onyx and lowered her finger in increments. The chill in the air faded. "You don't understand, child. I can't always control myself. What happened to Tiufalli could happen to you."

Rhiannon took her mother's cold hands in hers. "I *do* understand, Mother. And I'm willing to try if it will help you."

Morraine closed her eyes and clutched Rhiannon's hands. "Then so we shall."

Late the following afternoon, Rhiannon stood at the base of a citadel, holding the shard, as Morraine, in her red cloak, and Irik, in his woodsman's clothes, approached along the wooden walkways of the fen. Irik didn't look pleased—far from it—but neither did he look as heartbroken as he had that morning. Morraine had requested he accompany her so she could explain what she'd done and why. Rhiannon sincerely hoped she'd apologized as well. Rhiannon knew Irik well enough to know he wouldn't easily forgive Morraine—especially not in the near term, when the sting of Tiufalli's death would still be strong—but he'd never been one to hold a grudge. With a better understanding of the compulsions that drove her, he'd likely forgive her in time.

Llorn, returned from his meeting in the mountains, met them, and spoke with Irik for a time. He patted Irik's shoulder when he was done, and Irik nodded and walked away. Irik glanced at Rhiannon as he went, but didn't so much as wave as he climbed the corkscrew stairway into the trees.

Llorn spoke with Morraine. He seemed serious and somewhat irate. Everyone said he'd flown to the mountains to speak with the Hissing Man. Had that gone poorly? And if so, what would it mean for Morraine and Rhiannon?

Soon they separated, and Morraine approached Rhiannon. "Come," she said, glancing up at the darkening sky. "We've little time to waste."

"What was *that* about?" Rhiannon asked.

"Put it from your mind, child."

"Llorn looked angry."

"I said put it from your mind." They made their way to the vyrd to the growing sound of crickets and bullfrogs. Fireflies sparked among the wisps. "All you need know is that time grows short."

"*How* short?"

"We need progress, soon, or I may as well return to my second life."

Overhead, Bellicor uttered a groan that rose in pitch until it was a long keening. Irik was just passing Bellicor's nest, which made Rhiannon wonder if the onyx dragon's call was in response to Irik's mourning.

Rhiannon pointed up to him. "Irik and I were talking yesterday."

"I've already apologized to Irik."

"No, it's not about that. He reminded me of the palisade in Ancris."

The Rookery was lost as they took a bend in the path. "What of it?"

"That's how you're going to undo the spell around the shrine, isn't it? It will be destroyed when the palisade releases its aura."

Morraine glared at her. "Do you have a point?"

"Yes. I just wonder, is there more to it than that?"

"I told you. We'll take Strages."

"I mean will more happen to *Ancris*? That's a lot of power to unleash in a city packed with people."

"You're worried over over a city a thousand miles from here?"

"Well, yes. I am."

"Fear not, child," she said in a sneering tone, "Ancris will survive. Our purpose is to get Strages and the shard. Nothing more."

"You're *certain*?"

Morraine only glared, and Rhiannon let the subject drop. When the empty space inside Rhiannon yawned wider, she said, "You should feed before I start searching."

"I'll allow our bond to deepen," Morraine said, "but know this. It's the feeding itself that sometimes makes me lose control. My hunger feels insatiable at times."

Rhiannon swallowed involuntarily as she wove her way around a willow sapling. "I'm still willing to risk it."

Morraine stared over at Rhiannon, her eyes softly glowing. Her chin quavered, a common sign of her hunger, but she smiled. "Very well, child."

At the vyrd, Morraine and Rhiannon knelt near the looking glass and clay jug. Morraine, facing Rhiannon, spread her arms wide and made a beckoning motion, as she had with the wisp, and the gnawing feeling inside Rhiannon yawned wider. In moments, it felt as if she were being hollowed out from within. She coughed from it, and the feeling ceased.

Morraine stared at her.

"I'm fine," Rhiannon said. "It just takes a bit of getting used to."

Morraine seemed to size her up, then she nodded and the empty place grew wide again. The discomfort was easy to deal with at first, but the longer it went on, the more exhausted Rhiannon felt. Minutes in, Morraine closed her eyes and threw her head back. Her nostrils flared, and Rhiannon's body ached like it did when she had the flu. She worried her mother's inhibitions might fade or vanish altogether, and Rhiannon would be devoured from within as Tiufalli had been. She pressed her lips tight and steeled herself to go on for as long as her mother needed, but the empty feeling ebbed mere moments later.

"No," Rhiannon said. "Take what you need." She meant it, but was relieved all the same when Morraine shook her head.

"It's enough," her mother said.

Though Rhiannon had eaten just before leading the burrow, she felt suddenly famished, like she hadn't eaten in days, and she had a horrible case of cottonmouth. She took several large gulps of sapwater from the jug, and both the cottonmouth and the hunger ebbed.

Morraine placed the looking glass between their knees and filled it with sapwater, then cast the spell that would allow Rhiannon to search the forest. She struck the basin's rim with a fingernail, and it rang like a gong. As the sound attenuated, Rhiannon held the shard close to her heart, entered the looking glass, and cast herself into the forest like a canoe on a river.

She could immediately tell that the link to her mother was stronger; it felt as if she were helping Rhiannon search instead of merely watching. Even so, hours passed with no success. But then Rhiannon felt the strange ripple in the air, as she had in days past. The link with her mother granted a better sense of her perceptions, and that, in turn, gave Rhiannon a sense of direction and of distance. She could feel where the waves were coming from.

"Good," Morraine whispered. "Now find the thread."

Rhiannon gripped the shard tighter and for the first time in all her searching sensed something like a curtain running along a winding gully.

"That's it," Morraine said in an awed voice. "That's the veil, the border of Gonsalond."

In the gully, a squad of five men and three women suddenly appeared. All wore brown clothes and mottled green cloaks. They had swords at their belts and bows and quivers on their backs.

"Who are they?" Rhiannon said.

"Wardens," Morraine replied, "the keepers of Yeriel's domain, protectors of Faedryn's prison."

The wardens completed their crossing, and the ripples faded. It was then that Rhiannon felt something new: an impossibly thin thread traveling through the veil.

Rhiannon drifted away from the gully, fearful of what pulling on the thread could mean, but Morraine reached across the looking glass and gripped her wrist. "Stop. It's Yeriel. It must be. Follow it, Rhiannon. Pass through the veil."

Rhiannon tried but had no success. She might be *aware* of the veil's boundaries, but it was doing nothing to help her pierce it. She felt Morraine's desperation, felt her join in the effort, felt her *tug* on the thread.

Rhiannon felt suddenly cold, then a pain, like needles being pressed into the corners of her eyes, grew and grew until it felt like spikes were being hammered into her skull.

"Release it!" Rhiannon screamed. "Release the thread!"

When Morraine didn't, Rhiannon drew her awareness back to her body. Her mother was lying on the stones beyond the basin, quaking and staring up at Lux.

It was Yeriel's doing, Rhiannon realized, mere moments before her own body went rigid. Sweet Alra, it felt as if she were turning to stone. She reached for the basin, hoping to tip it over, but her arm seized, her fingers mere inches from the rim. She gritted her teeth and tried again, but it was no good. Her arm wouldn't obey.

The shard, still held in her opposite hand, thrummed loudly. She gripped it harder, hoping to command Yeriel to release her, but doing so only deepened the pain. It reminded her of her conversation with Irik about crop stones. "If a dracora tries too hard," he'd said, "the dragon can refuse his command or even attack. But if the dracora takes the time to match the dragon's tone, the dragon hardly has any choice."

She loosened her grip on the Heartstone shard and opened herself to it, allowing its resonance to become hers. For long moments, she felt nothing but the hammering pain in her skull, but then she sensed someone on the string's opposite end. She felt recognition, like she and Yeriel were staring at one another through a window.

"Release me!" Rhiannon shouted, and *shoved* Yeriel away.

She felt surprise, anger, even fear—

—and was suddenly able to move again.

She flipped the looking glass upward. Water flew in bright arcs, splashed against the vyrd's central stones. The basin clanged loudly, rattled, and came to a rest.

Morraine pushed herself off the stones with shaking arms. Her white hair was mussed. She looked exhausted and confused, then she smiled faintly. "You did it, child."

Finding no comfort in those words, Rhiannon stood and stared into the trees. In the days since her mother's raising, Yeriel and Strages hadn't felt real. They'd been mere concepts, parts of futures that might or might not come to be. Now they loomed large, as did the notion of who they'd once been in life. "This is madness," she said. "We can't hope to control Alra's *paragons*."

Morraine made her way unsteadily to her feet. "They're paragons no longer, child." She looked hungry in ways that were different from the raw need for sustenance, hungry in ways Rhiannon couldn't define. "They are servants now—*our* servants—who will drive the empire from the Holt and beyond the mountains. Soon enough, the empire will be rewritten in *our* image, not Alra's."

Rhiannon was stunned. She saw at last the true purpose of Morraine's raising. It wasn't so the Kin could *defend* the Holt from the empire. It was to become the aggressors.

"Come," Morraine said and headed toward the path to the Rookery. "Llorn will be glad of our tidings."

Rhiannon wanted to run away—she wanted to take the shard with her and rob her mother and Llorn of the ability to hurt—but she couldn't. Her courage had vanished, leaving her terrified of what Llorn and her mother would do to her if she tried.

Morraine glanced over her shoulder, then stopped and turned. "I said come."

"Yes, Mother," Rhiannon said, and trudged after her.

When they got back to the Rookery, Morraine talked with Llorn for a time. Eventually, Llorn nodded and headed toward Rhiannon.

"Prepare yourself, Rhiannon" he said to her. "We'll be traveling soon."

"To where?"

"Glaeyand. There's a council of quintarchs we're inviting ourselves to."

SIXTY-SIX: AZARIAH

Under Nox's dim glare, Azariah trekked up Henge Hill. The time to speak with Camadaea and the other illustrae would soon arrive, but he needed to talk to Faedryn first. Too much was slipping out of control.

Last night, he'd met with Lucran, Tyrinia, and the inquisitors in Highreach. He'd managed to play on Tyrinia's peculiar hatred of Lorelei and seen to it that Lorelei's request to continue her investigations had blown up in her face—instead of getting permission to continue, she'd lost her place as an inquisitor altogether. He'd left the palace feeling like things were well in hand, but mere hours later, an imperial messenger had arrived at the temple with ill tidings. Lorelei had fled Ancris on dragonback along with Rylan Holbrooke.

According to Lucran's message, Damika claimed that, in doing so, Lorelei had disobeyed direct orders, but Azariah wasn't so sure. He suspected Damika had had a hand in their escape, but he had no leverage to move against her openly, and Lucran, fool that he was, had agreed to give the Praefectus time to apprehend them. The fact that they'd taken the indurium, Bothymus, made Azariah wonder if Lucran himself was helping them and lying to him about it. Even if he wasn't, what would happen if Lorelei and Rylan deciphered the chalice, or worse, discovered the source of the peat?

In the vyrd, Azariah faced the Holt and spread his hands wide. "I would speak with you, My Lord."

Long moments passed, the only sound the song of the crickets.

Speaking with Faedryn had always been tricky. Trapped as he was, the fallen god took great care to speak only when Yeriel's attention was focused elsewhere. It sometimes meant delays for hours or even days at a time, but there was no way around it. The moment Yeriel or her wardens discovered that Faedryn had found a way to exert his will upon the world, they would reinforce his prison walls and silence him. And Yeriel was no fool. She'd likely understand that the Alran Church had been subverted centuries ago. It would be a disastrous turn of events; the illustrae were the sole means by which Faedryn exerted his will upon the world.

So Azariah was well aware of the need for caution, but this was important. "Please, My Lord. I have need of your guidance."

More time passed, the cool wind tugging at the hem of Azariah's robe. He was nearly ready to give up and try the following night when Faedryn's presence brightened like a distant bonfire. Closing his ruined eyes, Azariah sent his awareness down below the vyrd. He sped through wet earth and cold stone toward the foothills and beyond. He wove through citadel roots and the glowing caverns of the under-root, making his way ever closer to Gonsalond.

He suddenly stood before the Umbral Tree, glimmering darkly in his second sight. Other citadels with proper brown bark and green-tipped branches stood beyond a clearing, but they wavered, dreamlike in Azariah's perceptions of that place. Feeling sick to his stomach, a sign Faedryn was listening, Azariah told His Lord everything that had happened since last they'd spoke: the fire at the library, Rylan's capture, his escape with Inquisitor Lorelei. When he was done, he said, "Should I have pressed Lucran harder?"

The sourness in his gut intensified.

Azariah pressed a hand to his stomach. "As you say, My Lord, but Lucran is freshly returned. He'll want to exert his authority, especially over the Church, over *me*. But if he were removed—"

The sourness turned to a pain so intense Azariah doubled over from it. "I understand!" he said through gritted teeth. "Lucran will remain!"

The pain ebbed, and Azariah took a moment to breathe.

"You're prepared to assassinate a quintarch?" Camadaea, wearing her golden mask and white robes, stepped from beyond the Umbral Tree and made her way toward him. "Do you understand the risk in killing Lucran *now*?"

It took all Azariah had not to gape. He'd always been able to sense the other illustrae when they met near the Umbral Tree, but he'd felt nothing until Camadaea spoke.

"Don't be so surprised." Camadaea came to a stop several paces away. "You've been given free rein for too long, and Our Lord agrees. Now answer my question."

Despite his lingering discomfort, Azariah pulled himself tall. "Lucran could upend everything if Inquisitor Lorelei learns too much. And removing him wouldn't be as difficult or problematic as you think. With Lucran gone, the quintarch's powers would fall to Tyrinia. She's been in my pocket for years. Lucran's death would give us *more* control over the situation, not less."

"Assuming Tyrinia didn't find out."

"She wouldn't."

"You don't know that." Camadaea shrugged. "And in any case, you don't play your strongest cards early. You save them for the endgame. Lucran will keep, at least until Morraine begins bridging the vyrda." She tilted her head. "You granted her time to gather her strength, did you not?"

For the second time in moments, Azariah was caught flat-footed. He hadn't had time to inform Camadaea and the other illustrae about Llorn's request for a delay, which made him wonder if she'd spoken to him directly about it. Then a much more likely possibility occurred to him: she'd spoken to the Hissing Man. Why the Hissing Man wouldn't have told him about it when he returned from his meeting with Llorn, Azariah wasn't sure, but that was a problem for another time. "Llorn wanted the bridging to coincide with the council of quintarchs," he said easily. "I granted the request."

"You mean the *Hissing Man* granted it."

"With my permission. We always wanted Ancris's destruction to be pinned on the Red Knives. What better way to accomplish it than if Llorn spills imperial blood mere hours before the palisade explodes?"

Camadaea seemed to consider that, then nodded. "Fine. The Red Knives seem well in hand." She crossed her arms over her chest and paced before the Umbral Tree. "I'm more concerned about the bloody chalice. Why did you hide it from us?"

"I wasn't *hiding* it. I thought things were under control."

She stopped her pacing. "And were they?"

"Quibbling over the past helps no one, Your Radiance. You seem keen to help, so help me with *this*." He told her how Rylan Holbrooke had stolen the chalice from the library, how he and Inquisitor Lorelei had fled the city.

Camadaea's lips pursed. "They could decipher it."

"I consider it unlikely, but yes, it's a possibility. Even if they don't, they may have gone to the Holt to search for the crucible. Either way, they must be found, but Lucran has forbidden me from sending shepherds to search for them, and I can't disobey him. Our eyrie is being watched at all hours."

Camadaea nodded. "I'll have two shepherds sent to Glaeyand to ask around subtly. Two more will go to the lost shrine, in case they've found the chalice's secrets. Will that suffice?"

"It will," Azariah said.

"Very well. All that remains is the matter of the Hissing Man."

"What about him?"

"He knows too much."

"He's as dedicated to Our Lord as I am."

"He's unstable."

"He's *useful*."

"You have Japheth."

"Japheth is useful too, just in different ways. Both of them have their parts to play, as do your own High Shepherds."

Camadaea lips were pressed into a thin line, but before she could say anything further, a wave of terror emanated from the Umbral Tree. Judging by the way her head jerked back and the eyes of her golden mask shifted toward the black citadel, Camadaea had felt it too.

"My Lord," Azariah said, "what's happ—"

Azariah's second sight went dark, and he felt himself rushing away from the Umbral Tree, back toward Ancris. He traversed the many miles between Gonsalond and the mountains in a rush and found himself lying face-down on the vyrd's cold stones. His mask was askew. His chin and right cheek ached like he'd woken from a barroom brawl.

His second sight slowly returned, and the world around him filled in. Working his jaw, he stood and righted his mask, then tuned toward Caldoras. "Camadaea?"

He felt nothing from her, nothing at all, nor could he sense Faedryn's presence in the forest. The maze was completely, utterly closed to him. The eastern sky was brightening. Reckoning would soon arrive, and with it, the ferrymen and their passengers.

Hoping his sense of the maze would return as his second sight had, he left the vyrd with a feeling of deep unease. Faedryn's terror had been so strong. Had Yeriel learned of his ability to speak to his servants from afar? Was *she* the reason Azariah was unable to speak to Faedryn or Camadaea?

As he headed toward his waiting coach at the base of the hill, the city sprawled before him. In days past, he'd pictured Ancris breaking apart, pieces of it rising into the sky. Now the city felt immutable, his long-laid plans a foolish dream.

"You worry too much," came a hiss of a voice. The Hissing Man shuffled in his odd gait to Azariah's left.

"You're not the least bit concerned?" Azariah asked.

"Of course I am," the Hissing Man spat, "but there's nothing to do about it now. In all likelihood, Faedryn was merely being cautious in sending you away. And even if Yeriel *did* sense something, she likely knows little enough so far. We have time."

They reached the coach, climbed into the cabin, and sat on opposite benches. As the coach jolted into motion, Azariah's discussion with Camadaea returned to him. "Why didn't you tell me you met Camadaea?"

The Hissing Man stared from behind his strips of gauze. "Camadaea is nothing. Concentrate on Lucran. Concentrate on Llorn. *That* is where real the danger lies."

Azariah supposed he was right, but it felt like he would only be going through the motions. He watched the city though the window, wondering what his son would think of him if he saw him now.

SIXTY-SEVEN: LORELEI

Lorelei was champing at the bit to head to the shrine, but she was dead tired
and Rylan was worse. Bothymus needed rest, too, so they decided to make
camp for the night in a hollow at the base of Thervindal's Tor. Rylan built
a fire. Lorelei lay near it on a patch of soft earth. The snap of the fire and the roar
of the river lulled her. The only thing keeping her awake was worry about being
spotted and Vedron's excited chirping. When Rylan assured her Vedron would
watch over them, and the viridian flew to the top of the citadels, Lorelei fell asleep.

When she woke, it was early, and Rylan was up and packing things into
Vedron's saddlebags. "How can you be up already?" she asked in a croak of a voice.

Rylan tipped his head to Vedron while buckling the saddlebag. "She's excited
we're here." He shrugged. "It's infectious."

Vedron tipped her head back and cooed, and Bothymus, lying nearby, opened
his eyes and rumbled.

They ate a spare meal of seed cakes and river water and soon departed. Hours
later, they reached the western edges of the Holt. Ahead lay the foothills and the
Whitefells, looking like the jagged teeth of a river trout.

Vedron flew in spurts, slowing then sprinting ahead, glancing at Bothymus,
hoping he'd join in the fun. When Bothymus didn't, Vedron flew around him,
annoyingly close. At one point, their wingtips touched, and Bothymus belched at
Vedron. Vedron circled around the big indurium unaffected.

"Can't you control her?" Lorelei called over the thrum of their wings.

"Probably, but why? She hardly ever gets to play with other dragons."

"Bothymus doesn't like to play."

"Oh, I don't know"—Rylan's smiled—"he seems pretty amused to me."

He might be right, Lorelei realized. Rylan had a way with dragons.

Rylan, seeming to guess her mind, said, "Ever thought of bonding with Bothymus instead of binding him them with those stupid stones?"

"They're not stupid. And I can't."

"Why not?"

"I'm not Kin."

"It's not in our blood, Lorelei. Don't forget, the empire used to bond."

"All right," Lorelei said, "but I've read about bonding rituals gone bad, of
dragons eating the person trying to bond with them."

"I didn't say everyone is suited to it, but you are."

For a moment, Lorelei had no idea what to say. "What does it feel like?"

"It's like—" A golden roc swooped down from the distant clouds into a gorge

and was lost from view. He started again. "It's hard to explain. It's love. It's familiarity. It's trust. It's the joy of experiencing something outside of you."

"Pride, you mean?"

"Sort of, but it runs much deeper. The Old Kin word for it is *feorinh*. It means
something like *share* or *experience*, but for man and dragon both, at the same time,
understand?"

"No, not really."

He reached down and stroked Vedron's neck. "Like I said, it's hard to explain."

Lorelei felt a lump in her throat. All the talk about bonds had made her think
about her mother back in Ancris. She'd no doubt been questioned about Lorelei's
departure. She'd be worried sick by now. She pretended to check the sky to their
left and wiped away a tear. Then, she turned to Rylan and said, "Well, radiants
aren't like umbrals. They don't take to bonding."

Rylan snorted. "Did your history books tell you that?"

"As a matter of fact, they did. I read a several books by eyrie masters and
dragon trainers."

"Did the authors ever mention having bonded with a dragon?"

"Well, no, but that's only because they knew what would happen."

"Because they were trained that way . . ."

"Well, yes!"

Rylan paused. "May I tell you a story, Lorelei?"

She narrowed her eyes at him. "I suppose."

"Far to the east lies the island of Olgasus. You know of it?"

"Of course."

"There are monkeys there with golden fur and bright green eyes. The Ol-
gasans revere them, mostly, but one day, a boy thought it would be fun to play a
trick on the monkey colony that lived near his home. Each morning, he brought
them grapes and bananas. When they went to the bananas, he let them eat at their
leisure. When they neared the grapes, however, the boy pelted them with rocks,
whether they were eating grapes or not. The monkeys naturally backed away from
the grapes, but soon their hunger would convince them to try again. Again and
again, the boy let them have the bananas but punished them if any of them tried
to eat the grapes."

"I hope they attacked *him* for being so bloody cruel."

"Quite the opposite. They began attacking their own. Any monkeys that went
anywhere near the bowl of grapes were scratched and bitten by others in the colony. The boy eventually grew tired of his cruel game, but the monkeys never
forgot. They continued to punish any monkeys that tried to eat grapes from the
vines around the island. To this day, the descendants of that colony eat bananas,
cranberries, kumquats, starfruit—anything but grapes."

The wind whipped Lorelei's hair as she considered his story. "I fail to see the
relevance."

"The eyrie masters and dragon trainers likely wrote what they wrote because
the ones who trained them told them so. They reinforced their own thinking

when they used the crops and fetters to bind the dragons in their care. They never *tried* to bond with dragons, or did so only halfheartedly." He paused as Vedron trilled. "There's nothing stopping you from eating a grape, Lorelei."

Lorelei wasn't so sure. Even so, as they flew on, she gripped the golden crop, and her sense of Bothymus strengthened. Ever since she'd learned how to ride, their link had felt special to her, a bond of sorts even if it wasn't the same the Kin's bond with their dragons. Now she felt like she was holding a leash. Bothymus turned his head to look back at her. She felt a mental tug on his fetter, but then the feeling was gone and he was flying straight ahead again.

"Lorelei?"

Seeing Rylan was peering to their right, Lorelei followed his gaze. Beyond the gap in the peaks up ahead, a chunks of rock were floating in midair above a massive crater. "A geoflare," she said.

"Odd, don't you think, that we'd find one in the very place we'd hoped to find a shrine?"

"I guess so," she said. "I visited one not long ago."

"What? A flare?"

"Yes. At Tortoise Peak. Ash invited me on an expedition organized by Master Renato. It was called off unexpectedly, and rather rudely, by Tyrinia Solvina."

Rylan considered that bit of news as Vedron beat his wings. "And now Master Renato is dead."

"Yes . . ." She had no reason to believe there was a connection, but it was strange.

"How do we know this isn't some recent geoflare?"

"See there?" She pointed to the crater below the floating islands. It was covered with yellow lichen and small, flowering bushes. "Lichen grows slowly, but the rocks are covered with it, so the eruption must have happened quite a while ago."

"But how can the islands still be floating now?"

"I'm hardly an expert, but I know geoflares occur when the earth—mostly granite, basalt, and the like—is no longer able to release aura into the atmosphere. The aura becomes trapped—*fixed* is the term alchemyst's use. When that happens, the stone becomes brittle. Eventually the pressure of the aura becomes too much, and the mountain explodes outward. The aura is still trapped, though." She waved to the floating islands. "It's what keeps them afloat like this."

"Okay, but why does the stone become brittle in the first place? And if it happened here, why hasn't it happened to the other peaks as well?"

Lorelei shrugged. "I don't know. Ash might."

Squinting, Rylan pointed at an island the size of a palace. "What's that?"

She hadn't noticed it at first, but near the island's center was a neatly cut stone column. "Let's find out."

They guided their dragons toward the island, then landed and dismounted. As had been true at Tortoise Peak, Lorelei felt an elation building in her chest, like happy nervousness. And it still felt odd to be standing on a bloody great hunk of rock floating in the wind.

The column was three times as tall as Lorelei and half that wide. The dark gray stone looked to be basalt, but was flecked with silver and blue indurium. A terrible chill ran through Lorelei as she stared at it.

Rylan was heading toward the pillar, but stopped when he noticed how pale she looked. "Are you okay?"

She motioned to the column. "Does this remind you of anything in Ancris?"

Rylan paused a moment, and then said, "The palisade stones."

The column was a good deal larger, but it glittered the same shade of blue as the pillars spaced around the city. "Let's see if we can find anything that looks like a shrine."

Rylan nodded. "We should split up, cover more ground."

Rylan flew Vedron toward the geoflare's uppermost reaches while Lorelei guided Bothymus down. She started at the bottom and guided Bothymus methodically upward, examining all the islands through the geoflare. Some were covered with flowering bushes and tufts of mountain grasses. Others had copses of pine trees, some with flocks of birds flitting between them. There was even a small pool of water on one of the larger islands with glittering water spilling over the edge like diamonds. Halfway down, a black wyvern darted through the falling water droplets, playing, it seemed. When it spotted Bothymus, it veered into a fissure in the rock face, and was gone.

She flew Bothymus below a medium-sized island. Vedron whisked past one of the gaps above her. A few more pillars jutted from below a ledge. Then she noticed a rectangular indentation in the rock with a perfectly level, neatly cut shelf protruding horizontally from it. It looked like it might once have been part of a floor. Much of it, both the wall of the indentation and floor, were covered in white quartzite tiles.

She squeezed Bothymus's crop and he trumpeted. A short while later, Vedron came winging around an adjacent isle. They landed and Rylan and Lorelei climbed down onto shattered remains of Yeriel's shrine. It wasn't terribly impressive to the eye, but it gave Lorelei the same sense of awe she'd felt in the shrine in Ancris, the same sense of holiness. They'd come to a place that had once housed a paragon and a piece of the Heartstone. As such, it was like a doorway to another time. She felt the weight of the history: Alra's sacrifice, Faedryn's fall.

The quartzite floor felt strangely soft. She crouched and ran her hands over it. It was rougher and more porous than the blocks Ash had shown her in Ancris. She drew her poniard and pressed the tip into the white stone. It gave way easily, and a piece crumbled off.

"Lorelei?"

Rylan was standing before an inclined section of floor. If the shrine was built in the same style as the others, it was likely the base of the causeway that would have led to Yeriel and the piece of the Heartstone. She stood and walked closer. Rylan pointed to the stones at his feet. There was writing there, written in Graanthan.

"What does it say?" Rylan asked.

It took Lorelei some time to decipher, but eventually she had the gist. "Here lies Yeriel Darksinger," she read, "Umbral Witch, betrayer of Faedryn and his fell servants. May she atone for her sins when Alra rises again."

Rylan's mouth fell open. "Yeriel *Darksinger*? The Umbral Witch?"

"The words could be interpreted in a few different ways, but that's the closest I can get without looking at some older texts."

"Why would it say she's a betrayer of Faedryn? She was a paragon."

"Yes, I was wondering the same thing."

"It flies in the face of everything we've been taught."

"Agreed," Lorelei said, "but right now, I'm more concerned about the bit at the end: *When Alra rises again*. Some Church historians think Alra might be made whole if the pieces of her heart were reunited. I always thought it was the ravings of zealots, but now . . . the builders of the shrine must have believed it would happen." She touched the toe of her boot to the end of the inscription. "This would not be written in faint hope. It's a prophecy."

Rylan's brow creased. "How could we know so little about all this?"

"It wouldn't be the first time history was rewritten," Lorelei said.

"Yes, but this?" He waved at the shattered remains of the ramp and the ruined shrine around them. "Alra *won* the war. Or her paragons did. They were the *victors* in the Ruining. Why would they want to erase any of it?"

Lorelei was about to respond when Bothymus's crop shuddered in her hand. Bothymus rose from his crouch and stared north. Vedron swung his head in same direction and hissed. Two brass dragons winged toward them.

"Bluff and broken bones," she breathed.

Rylan loped toward Vedron and leapt on Vedron's outstretched tail. Vedron vaulted him into the saddle, then swept her wings and rose skyward, away from the approaching dragons.

Lorelei realized she was gawking at Rylan and Vedron's agility. She climbed up on Bothymus, and he teetered to the edge of the island and dropped over the side. Then he spread his wings and flew her toward Vedron.

"We have to go," Rylan called over his shoulder.

Brass dragons were known for their speed and endurance, and Lorelei could see a pair of shepherds in white on them. They would be able to use the power of aura and umbra to subdue or even kill them. "We can't leave the geoflare. They'll chase us down if we do."

"They're war dragons, Lorelei. We can't fight them."

"I don't mean to fight them. Not for long, at least." Her mind raced, playing various scenarios out. "Can Vedron use her breath on command?"

"Yes, but why?"

"Because we need to try to shower them with rocks."

SIXTY-EIGHT: RYLAN

Lorelei's plan was for Bothymus to take a stand on the large island above them and draw the two brasses in. Rylan, meanwhile, would fly to the cloud of rocks above and have Vedron spit her acid over the stones. The umbral acid would work against the aura trapped in the stone and cause them to lose their buoyancy, turning them into deadly weapons.

It could work, but it felt rushed. They'd have only seconds to make the plan work. But they'd both agreed it would be just as mad to fight the brass dragons bearing down on them. And fleeing would merely delay the conflict and put Bothymus and Vedron at a disadvantage. They hadn't even discussed surrender. For Rylan, it was no choice at all—Lorelei might survive incarceration; *he* likely wouldn't.

Rylan squeezed the saddle restraints with his legs, grasped the saddle horn with both hands, and bid Vedron fly straight up through the floating islands. Below and to his left, Lorelei pointed to a large island up ahead, and Bothymus swerved toward it.

"There!" she called. "Fly hard!"

Hanging above the island was another, smaller isle with a field of sharp rocks and boulders floating directly underneath it. "You heard her," Rylan said to Vedron,"let's show them how fast you can fly."

Viridians were wickedly fast in short bursts, and Vedron was no exception. She outstripped Bothymus, but Rylan still felt they weren't moving fast enough. If Lorelei's plan was going to work, Vedron had to be over the lip of that island and out of sight before the brasses approached.

As Vedron swung higher, the view before Rylan began to change. The dark rocks, the bulbous clouds, and the blue sky grew brighter. Soon his entire field of vision was almost perfectly white and painful to look upon. A glance back showed the shepherds on their brasses closing the distance. One of them, his mace raised high, had glowing eyes.

Below him, Lorelei cried out, "Rylan?" She sounded worried. "I can't see!"

"Focus on your crop," he shouted over his shoulder. "Trust Bothymus." Whether she'd be able to do what was needed or not, Rylan wasn't sure, but he couldn't worry about it. He had to concentrate on his part and hope for the best.

Moving carefully but quickly, Rylan reached in the pouch at his belt, retrieved the lucerta he'd used in the library, and placed it on his tongue. By then the shepherd's spell made it feel like needles were being driven through his eyes. The lucerta's familiar, pine-and-copper taste assaulted him as he pressed the scale against the roof of his mouth. The pain slowly ebbed and his vision returned to normal, but it was like fighting for air in a raging river. It was a constant struggle. Any small slip in concentration saw his world turning white once more.

Behind him, the shepherds were close on their gleaming brass dragons. He urged Vedron to fly over the edge if the big island. She did so and, when she was out of sight of the shepherds, burst upward. Below, Bothymus plunged over the same ledge. The brasses were only seconds behind, leaving Rylan very little time to reach the cloud of rocks floating beneath the smaller island above him.

Bothymus landed on a snow-covered stretch of ground. He spun about, reared, and spread his wings. Then he screeched and lit his wings, beautiful and fearsome, blazing blues, purples, and yellows expanding in bright, hypnotic swirls.

Vedron turned her head toward the big indurium and stopped beating her wings. She began falling away from rock cluster toward the big island below.

Rylan bid her, *Don't look at him!*

Vedron whirled back up toward the floating cluster of rocks.

Exhalo, Vedron! Exhalo!

She breathed a spray of acid at the rocks. The acid splattered on the rocks, hissing and bubbling, and white smoke rose in a plume.

Again, girl. Keep going.

Vedron breathed another spray over dozens of rocks.

Below, the brasses landed on the edge of the big island. The shepherds averted their gaze from Bothymus and yanked their dragons' reins to the side.

"Verseo!" bellowed the shepherd closest to Bothymus.

His brass darted at Bothymus, spun, and lashed its tail across Bothymus's neck, leaving a bloody gash across the big indurium's silvery blue scales. Bothymus swept his flashing, flickering wings, propelling himself backward, and the attacking brass froze, tilted its head, and just stared at Bothymus's wings. The other brass spun around and faced away from Bothymus.

Vedron sprayed another stream of green acid, eating through half the cluster of floating rocks. Rylan held his breath against the noxious fumes and urged her to keep going.

The second brass spun toward Bothymus, eyes closed, opened its mouth, and blasted a bolt of lightning at Bothymus. Bothymus roared. His wings ceased flashing an swirling and he dropped to his forelimbs and convulsed.

Once more, girl!

Vedron sent another green spray of umbral acid, noticeably weaker this time, at the stones. The stones began to fall. Stones the size of grapes and plums plummeted down. Rylan had to jerk Vedron's head away to avoid it being hit. Then bigger stones, the size of wine kegs, began dropping down.

The rocks pounded the ground around the brass dragons and their shepherds, sending halos of earth and snow flying up in their faces. The shepherd who'd cast the blinding spell swung his arm to signal the other shepherd, and a rock the size of a mastiff fell on him. He tumbled from his saddle, limp, bloodied, and the pressure of fighting the spell of blinding vanished. The dead shepherd's brass skittered away, and another stone, as big as a horse, crunched down on its back, splattering blood out both sides and crushing the creature.

The other brass flapped backward. A falling stone pierced its left wing as it reached the outer edge of the rain of rocks. Then it dropped off the edge of the island, spread its wings, and disappeared below it.

Lorelei and Bothymus stood on the other edge of the island, well away from the rock storm. Bothymus's chest was still bleeding, but only a trickle. Rylan flew Vedron down to her and bid her follow them. They flew southeast, vaguely toward Ancris. One final look back showed the wounded brass gliding toward a distant isle.

"We should land once we're sure we're not being followed," Lorelei said. "I need to tend to Bothymus's wound."

Rylan nodded, and they flew on until Bothymus bellowed and the beat of his wings became erratic; then they glided down to their right and landed in a steep defile—several hours northwest of Ancris, Rylan guessed. Before Rylan and Lorelei had even dropped from their saddles, Vedron approached Bothymus and began licking his wound. Much to Rylan's surprise, Bothymus stretched his neck and gurgled. When Rylan and Lorelei had dismounted, both dragons lumbered to a stream nestled in the long grass, drank their fill, and curled up to rest.

Rylan gathered branches, built a fire in a clearing between some pine trees, sat beside it, and rested. Lorelei sat across from him and shared some walnuts and dried berries she'd brought in Bothymus's saddlebags. They sat in silence and ate.

When they were done, Rylan threw more branches onto the fire. "Where do we go from here?"

Lorelei stared into the fire. "We need help, Rylan."

"I take it you have an idea?"

She glanced at him, then back at the fire. "I do, but you're not going to like it."

"I got that impression."

"We need help," she repeated, "from Kellen."

"Ah."

"He studied the Ruining and the breaking of the Heartstone for years."

"So go!" Rylan was angry she'd even think of asking him to meet with Kellen. "No one's stopping you . . ."

"I need you there, Rylan. He needs to hear everything about the chalice and the shrine."

"There must be someone else who can help."

"There isn't." The firelight played over Lorelei's face. "I know what Kellen did to you and your family. You have every right to be angry. But we've stumbled onto something that's bigger than either of us. Yeriel figures into this somehow. Maybe the other paragons, too. Alra herself may be involved."

"Lorelei, I—"

"Your uncle was executed unjustly. I know that. But your aunt . . . her very way of life is threatened by the Hissing Man, Llorn, the Red Knives. I feel it in my bones, and I think you do too. We have to figure out what's going on before it's too late, and right now, that means we need Kellen."

Rylan was too angry to speak. The fire crackled and popped, and he stared at the nub on his left hand. He didn't want to see Kellen, much less speak to him, but to refuse Lorelei's request would be to abandon his own people—Aunt Merida, Hollis, Blythe, even the Lyndenfells. He had to go with her, he decided, no matter how he felt about Kellen.

"Fine," he said.

Lorelei smiled a tentative smile. "You'll come with me?"

"Yes."

"Alra's bright light, thank you, Rylan." Her smile deepened, crinkling her dimples. "It means a lot to me."

They laid out blankets, and Lorelei threw a thick branch onto the fire. Bothymus groaned, long and rumbling, and Rylan sang a song of calming for him. He reckoned Vedron needed it as well, and Rylan himself did, too. The very thought of standing in the same room with Kellen was making his scalp tingle and sweat.

A short while later, Bothymus lowered his head to the ground and closed his eyes. Vedron followed, then Lorelei. As Rylan lay on his side, watching the firelight play off Lorelei's sleeping face and her red hair, he wondered at all they'd been through in such a short time. He wished they'd met under different circumstances. They might have become friends. It was impossible now. Lorelei took betrayals seriously, and the lies Rylan had told her were both numerous and of great import.

He'd go with her to Ancris, do what he could to help her, and then go back to life in the Holt, he decided. Then he rolled away from the fire, pulled his blanket tighter over his shoulders, and went to sleep.

SIXTY-NINE: RYLAN

Rylan guided Vedron toward the elm grove. Lorelei followed on Bothymus. It was night and, with a bit of cloud cover, quite dark. They landed; then they watched and listened for any signs they'd been spotted. When they were reasonably certain no one had seen them, they dismounted and prepared to hike to Ancris.

They'd discussed what to do with the dragons and decided there was really no choice. "Go, old friend," Lorelei said to Bothymus, squeezing his crop stone. "I'll see you again one day." She dropped the crop into his saddlebag. Bothymus glanced at Vedron, perhaps wondering if she'd join him, and then launched into the air and away.

Rylan rummaged through Vedron's saddlebag and took out three paper packets, each the size and shape of a plum.

Lorelei frowned at them. "What are those?"

He stuffed the pouches into the leather bag at his belt. "Something I hope we don't have to use."

"Rylan—"

"They're harmless. They just make a lot of noise and smoke. I like to have them if I need to get out fast."

She seemed to relax after that. "You missed your calling, Rylan. You should've been an alchemyst."

He winked at her. "Who says I'm not?" He went to Vedron and ran his knuckles along her neck. "Go on, now. I'll be at the glade soon."

Vedron keened.

"I said *go.*"

She beat her wings and rose into the sky and, much to Rylan's dismay, trailed after Bothymus. Rylan conveyed his alarm through their bond, and finally she veered and headed toward the Holt.

He watched her silhouette dwindle, then he and Lorelei left the elm grove at a steady jog. They arrived in Ancris an hour later. As they entered the city proper, reckoning came and went with a muted display of goldenrod and shimmering pearl. Soon enough they arrived in Old Town and the House of the Holy Meadow, where Kellen was apparently recuperating. As Lorelei spoke quietly with the portly nun in the entryway, Rylan began to feel sick to his stomach. Memories of Beckett's writhing body covered in flames kept flashing before him. Rylan blinked the vision away.

Lorelei took three gold coins from her purse and slid them into an iron lockbox with a slit on the top. The nun limped from her desk and headed down a hallway. Lorelei wrote a note on a small piece of paper, folded it, dripped wax onto it using a candle on a side table, and sealed it with a brass stamp of the House of the Holy Meadow, a bright sunrise over a field of wild grass.

The nun returned with a sixteen-year-old girl in a simple brown robe, sandals, and a rope belt. "Arnesse will deliver your message," the nun said.

Lorelei handed her the sealed paper, gave her Creed's address, and the girl sped through the front entrance. When she was gone, Lorelei glanced at Rylan and did a double take. "Are you all right?"

"Let's just get this over with."

The nun led them to the back of the abbey, opened a door, and waved them in. Lorelei thanked her and she left. Rylan took a deep breath and followed Lorelei into the room. They found Kellen propped in a bed, his back against a stack of pillows. A terrible burn mark covered the left side of his face, his ear, and scalp. In some places the burn was so bad the skin was mottled and bumpy. His hair was thinner and grayer, but still closely shorn. His cheeks sagged, and a wattle had begun to form under his chin.

Nevertheless, his ice blue stare remained unyielding. He looked at Rylan and pushed himself higher against the backboard. "Come to gloat, I suppose."

"He's come to help," Lorelei said before Rylan speak.

"Help?" Kellen snorted. "How could he possibly help?"

Lorelei reached into the bag at her belt, pulled out the chalice, and held it out to him. Kellen's eyes went wide. "You *stole* it."

Lorelei said, "How we got it doesn't matter right now. Ezraela died for this chalice, and you'd be dead, too, if it not for Rylan."

Kellen reached for the chalice but stopped. "This isn't over," he told Rylan, "you're going to tell me what happened."

Lorelei tapped the chalice with her fingernail, producing a soft *ting*. "Just look at the bowl, will you?"

Kellen finally took it and stared at the bowl's bright, shining interior. He frowned deeply. "You've treated it with something, some chem—" Then his eyes widened again. "A map . . ."

"To all six of Alra's shrines," Rylan said.

Kellen looked at Lorelei.

"It's true," she said, "and see along the base? It names Alra's paragons. The five we know, plus Yeriel."

He ran his fingers over the map inside the bowl and the inscription around it. "You'd better start from the beginning."

Over the next hour, Lorelei told him of Rylan's arrest, Durgan's attempt to kill him in the Crag, her rescue of him, what Ash discovered in Korvus's journal, and her trip to the palace with Praefectus Damika.

When she came to the point in the story where Quintarch Lucran refused to let them investigate, Kellen pursed his lips. "Tyrinia's doing, yes?"

"Likely so," Lorelei said, "but whatever the cause—"

"Hold on," Rylan said. "Your mother told me about your father and Tyrinia, but why would she hold that against *you*? And if she *is* holding a grudge, why would she have given you a tutor and sponsored your enrollment into the academy?"

Lorelei turned to look away. "It doesn't matter."

"It does matter," Rylan said. "She had your badge taken. If we're to have any hope of finding out the truth about the shrine and Llorn's plan, we need the freedom to move about the city, question Azariah or even the Hissing Man if we can find him, and that's only going to happen if we get Tyrinia to back off."

Lorelei shrugged. "It's never made much sense to me."

Kellen cleared his throat. "I believe I can shed a bit of light on that."

Lorelei opened her mouth. Closed it again. "You can?"

Kellen picked at a loose thread in his blanket. "You're aware that Tyrinia's labor with Skylar was difficult, yes?"

"Yes. So what?"

"Well, it was worse than most people realize. Tyrinia nearly died. The nuns told her she would if she conceived again. Lucran and Tyrinia were at odds even before then, but it worsened after Skylar's birth. I suspect it was why she made advances toward your father. When Cain refused her, rumors started that she'd demanded our then-Praefectus, Austrus, to give Cain all the worst cases in Kiln, Fiddlehead, and Slade. After he died, well, I think she felt responsible. She reached out to your mother and offered her a stipend as a way for the city to honor his sacrifice."

Lorelei frowned. "Which she made my mother *dance* for."

"I have no doubt." He turned to Rylan. "As you say, Tyrinia was kind to Lorelei. She . . ." He trailed off and looked at Lorelei.

"What?" Rylan asked.

Lorelei said, "I had some . . . problems. Being in public, being around people. Tyrinia knew about them. I'd confided in her, Skylar, too, hoping to get over it. I desperately wanted to follow in my father's footsteps and become an inquisitor. It was a noble calling, and I was well suited to it in many other ways."

Rylan waited for her to continue. When she didn't he said, "But if you couldn't go out in public . . ."

"I couldn't do the job. I still wanted to try, and Tyrinia made sure I got that chance."

"I took Lorelei under my wing," Kellen said. "I gave her books, challenged her with active cases. We debated to sharpen her rhetorical skills. She was great at all of it. But her inability to stay calm in public, to pursue a case . . . well, it stopped her from moving up."

"Then how did you fix it?"

"Kellen gave me a book by a philosopher named Anaghoshta."

"Ana*ghosh*ta," Rylan said, trying the name on for size.

"Anaghoshta III, in fact," Kellen said. "Gehrost had recently been conquered. There wasn't a man, woman, or child in that faraway city who didn't know his name, but his texts had only recently started flowing to Ancris."

"An empire that devours all it surveys," Rylan said, "and still hungers for more." It was an old Kin saying. He knew it was rude, but just then he didn't care.

Kellen glared at him, but Lorelei quickly continued, "Anaghoshta's teachings helped me find peace with myself, helped me control myself enough to become an inquisitor."

"Which was precisely when Tyrinia's attitude toward her changed," Kellen said.

Lorelei pulled a stray lock of hair behind her ear. "Yeah, but why?"

"When she saw you might be as successful as your father, she tried to prevent it. She tried to scuttle your graduation, but Austrus and I stopped her, which led to his firing and Damika getting his position. It's what, in part, led to my own decision to retire."

"Why didn't you tell me any of this?" Lorelei asked.

"Because you were doing so well. I thought Tyrinia might lay off when you became a full-fledged inquisitor. And she seemed to for a while, but this business with the Red Knives. Perhaps some of her old feelings came back when you began making headway on the case."

Rylan said, "Making headway or stepping on toes?" When Kellen and Lorelei gaped at him but said nothing, he went on, "Lorelei said Tyrinia is close with my father."

"She is," Lorelei said. "With Lucran gone so often, she's practically been forced to as Domina. What of it?"

"Maybe she took your disobeying him as a direct affront to *her*."

"It's possible," Lorelei said, "perhaps even likely. Whatever the case, she got the last laugh. I'm no longer an inquisitor, and I'll probably be charged with insubordination, disobeying the quintarch's orders, stealing an imperial mount. I'll be lucky to avoid time in the quarries."

"You're deep in shit, no doubt." Kellen said, holding up the chalice. "But you're onto something with this. Find out what, and Lucran might go easy on you." He turned the chalice around in his hands. "Six shrines . . . Amazing. And *Yeriel* a paragon."

"Did you know about any of this?" Lorelei asked. "Anything from your research?"

Kellen shrugged. "Perhaps. I have come across several mentions of Yeriel, her wardens, and the veil. The Church of Alra had yet to form at that point. Most people thought Yeriel was an oddity, something that could be let alone, at least until the empire gained a more solid foothold in the mountains and the Holt. One account mentions that Yeriel had been thrown in prison, but seven women, all of them wardens, freed her. I assumed some rival of hers had imprisoned her, some powerful but long-forgotten mage. If you're right about what this"—he raised the chalice again—"says, it seems more likely she was trapped in the shrine, like all the paragons were after the Ruining, and that the wardens—the original Seven, I suspect—freed her from it."

"But what would the wardens gain by helping her escape?" Lorelei asked. "And why her in particular? Why not one of the others? Why not *all* of them?"

Kellen rubbed his thumb over Yeriel's name on the base of the chalice. "Not sure. We know very little about the Seven and the wardens, even less about Yeriel herself."

Rylan motioned to the chalice. "The Chosen seem very keen to get that back. How could it have stayed hidden for so long? And how did it suddenly reappear?"

"Let's not forget," Kellen said, "the Chosen are far from ancient history. They formed only eighty years ago, after the failed Holy Rebellion. The Church and the people most loyal to them never forgot how they were treated by the quint-archs. But they couldn't strike back directly, so they decided to play a long game. They worked in secret to place their followers in the senate, in the courts, in the halls of the constables and the inquisitors. Just as importantly, they worked to pro-mote their officers in our armies, fleets, and dragon legions. They haven't been wholly successful—the quintarchs work constantly against them—but even so, the Chosen's reach is now vast. The question isn't how the chalice escaped their notice or how it suddenly reappeared. Both are easily explained by the way the rich and powerful families of the empire grabbed everything they could and hoarded it, and how some of those families fell into misfortune and"—he lifted the bronze chalice—"were forced to sell their property to pay off the moneylenders."

"Then what *is* the question?" Rylan asked.

"It's why it's so important to them to prevent the chalice from falling into the wrong hands. They care very much about maintaining the illusion that the Church is not merely *holy* but perfect and unquestionable. If people start asking questions about them—like why there are five and only five shrines—they might start dig-ging up other questions or doubting the Church's preeminence." Kellen stabbed a hairy finger at Lorelei. "What did the inscription at the shrine say?"

Lorelei put on an official voice. "Here lies Yeriel Darksinger, Umbral Witch, betrayer of Faedryn and all his fell servants. May she atone for her sins when Alra rises again."

"'When Alra rises again . . .' Clearly there's more to the Ruining than we know. Perhaps that's what they're trying to keep secret."

"Or maybe it's to do with the Hissing Man's meeting with Aarik and Llorn," Lorelei said.

Kellen shrugged. "It could be both. The Hissing Man's plans could very well be related to Alra's rising."

"That's mad," Rylan said.

"You think so?" Kellen stared hard at Rylan. "Ill winds gather over Ancris, Rylan Holbrooke. Who's to say what fortune they'll bring?"

They heard footsteps pounding down the hallway. A moment later, Creed's voice bellowed, "Lorelei?"

Lorelei rushed to the door. "We're here!"

Creed appeared in the doorway, breathing hard. He glanced at Rylan, then beckoned Lorelei. "We've got to get out of here, now."

"Why? What's going on?"

"The praetorian guard are on their way here. They're coming for you."

SEVENTY: LORELEI

"Stone and scree," Lorelei said, feeling a panic coming on, "the praetorian guard?"

Creed nodded and wiped sweat from his brow. "I came right here after I got your note and saw eight of them on horseback, headed this way."

"You're sure they're headed *here*?"

"Want to take the chance they're not? They'll be here any moment."

Rylan stood up and headed out the door. Lorelei followed but paused in the doorway and spun to face Kellen. "Thank you."

"Lorelei, wait," he said, reaching a hand out toward her.

"I can't, Kellen—"

"Remember our talk about using all your resources?"

"Yes. So?"

"You seem to be ignoring one the few people who can help you with the Domina. She's Tyrinia's daugh—"

"Skylar?" Lorelei shook her head. "No. I'm not dragging her into this."

"You have to. It's too important, Lorelei."

Creed tugged on her wrist. "Let's *go*!"

The front door of the abbey groaned open; the rapid clack of boots and the clatter of armor echoed down the hallway.

Kellen nodded, and Lorelei bolted after Creed. They caught up with Rylan at the iron-bound door at the end of the hall, slipped through the door and into a portico that overlooked the abbey's rose garden. They hurried between the rows of flowers and into an alley. They were nearing the end of the alley, when two praetorian guardsmen in red feathered crests and gleaming lorica segmentata rounded the corner of the abbey's brick wall. The taller of the two had a spread-winged eagle centurion design on his breastplate.

Rylan extended a hand behind him. "Back up!" Then he whipped something at the ground—one of the plum-shaped packets.

The packet burst at the guards' feet with a sound like breaking glass. White powder hissed and billowed into an impenetrable cloud. The soldiers disappeared inside, coughing, hacking, and cursing. A crossbow twanged; the bolt struck the building with a sharp *crack* next to Lorelei's head.

The cloud wafted and caught Lorelei in it. Her nose burned. Her eyes watered. She staggered into clear air, coughing uncontrollably and followed Creed and Rylan down the an alley. "I thought you said those packets were harmless."

"They are. Just breathe and exhale. It'll wear off soon."

They followed the alley to the bank of the Wend. The burn in her throat became an annoying tingle, and the sting in her eyes was nearly gone. They ducked under a bridge, heard clop of hooves on the cobbled Old Town's streets. Someone was bellowing orders. They stood silently, the water rushing below them, and the sounds of the guards slowly faded.

Creed wiped his eyes and stared at Lorelei. "Mind telling what you had to talk to Kellen about with the praetorian guard after us?"

"I have to talk to Skylar, but I can't go to the palace."

Creed blinked his red eyes and grinned. "You don't need to get into the palace."

"I don't?"

He pointed across the river, toward the temples and arches of Ancris's *regio annalis*. "The Syrdian Arch . . . The dedication ceremony is today. Skylar's going to be there."

Lorelei was just working through how they might do it when Rylan said, "Won't she be surrounded?"

"Yes," Creed said, "but I know a fellow."

An hour later, Lorelei was standing on a wide thoroughfare in Golden Meadows, waiting for the dedication ceremony, where she would hopefully be able to arrange a private meeting with Skylar. Creed and Rylan were with her, hovering around a manure cart, an integral part of their disguises. The cart had a rack of shovels and horsehair brooms and a massive wooden barrel filled halfway with horse shit. They wore drab clothes of the sort worn by Ancris's sanitation workers: sandals and brown robes with the hoods pulled up for the two men; Lorelei in similar sandals, a brown dress, and a beige palla around her head to hide her red hair.

Along the center of the street, a line of chariots, cavalry, and foot soldiers moved steadily forward and under the new Syrdian arch. Both sides of the street were packed, maddeningly so. As far as the eye could see, men, women, and children cheered as the parade passed them by. Many revelers, especially the children, wore willow wreaths entwined with white jasmine, which signified peace and had been used in Ancris for centuries.

Lorelei took a deep breath, huddled with Creed and Rylan, and told herself over and over again that no one could possibly recognize her. She stared at the Syrdian arch, which they would go to when the parade was over. It was a magnificent piece of architecture with a dedication along the top and statues of the men who'd played a part in Syrdia's conquest, including Quintarch Lucran himself. Lorelei spotted a dracora riding a dragon with a lance held high overhead, the design Skylar had included to honor Ransom, and her heartbeat finally slowed. The memory of Skylar sharing that personal touch with her, and the love she had for Ransom, was soothing, but then a man bumped into Lorelei from behind, and the crowd around her came rushing back into her consciousness.

"Make way!" Creed pushed the man aside. "Make way for the procession!"

Lorelei appreciated what Creed was trying to do, but she didn't know how much more she could take. Every moment that passed felt as if the crowd were pressing tighter, but the smell of manure from their barrel in the wagon actually calmed her, took her to quiet pastures, far from Ancris. "Nothing like a bit of shit to remind you how deep in it you are."

Rylan looked down at the muck and laughed deep from the belly. He had a good laugh, she decided.

At last, the procession finally ended, and a talon of dragons flew in formation overhead. Another five dragons swept past, then another—five talons in all. A bright, glittering indurium in the final group trumpeted so loud, it tickled Lorelei's ears. The crowed gasped and cheered.

The crowd followed the parade and began pressing in and around the new arch. Creed heaved the manure cart into motion. Rylan and Lorelei grabbed brushes and shovels and began picking up horse dung from the street. Hardly anyone even looked at them.

A stage had been built under the arch. Quintarch Lucran stood there, staring out over the crowd. In a nod to the empire's elder days, he wore sandals laced to the knee, a toga, and a golden willow crown. Three people stood behind him: a legate in shining armor, a volarch in black dragonscale, and Skylar in a stunning, sleeveless stola made of shimmering white silk. Even with all the madness at the abbey and the rush to reach the parade in time, Lorelei couldn't help but notice how radiant Skylar looked. The golden brooches at her shoulders complemented the dress and her braided blond hair. Her rings and bracelets sparkled in the sun.

When he had everyone's attention, Quintarch Lucran told of the conquest in Syrdia, but Lorelei paid him little mind. She was watching Skylar, willing her to look in their direction. When she finally did, Lorelei pulled her palla down off her bright red hair. Skylar did a double take. Lorelei pulled her palla back up and pointed to the Sanctum of the Eternal Flame at the end of a long promenade. It was a monument to Alra's sacrifice at the close of the Ruining. Skylar and Lorelei had visited the sanctum and the hedge maze behind it many times.

Skylar nodded subtly, and Lorelei turned toward Creed and Rylan. "Let's go."

They pulled the cart away, pushed it through the temple's iron gates, and left it between a pair of quince bushes. Then they walked along the promenade with some of the crowd already making their way home. Inside the temple, beyond the fluted columns, a massive brazier burned. An honor guard of two soldiers holding pila stood to either side of it.

Lorelei led Creed and Rylan beyond the temple into the shadow of the Curia Ancrata, a massive building with an impressive rotunda and a hedge maze. Lorelei motioned to a patch of blossoming cherry trees not far from it. "Wait over there."

As Creed and Rylan headed toward the cherry trees, Lorelei entered the maze, navigated its simple design to an open space with a marble pool, and sat on a bench near the tall hedges. She waited as dozens of people wandered through the maze. Nearby, two girls with flowers in their hair giggled as they tossed bread to the ruby-colored fish in the pool. In the relative calm, Lorelei finally managed to unclench her hands, and her breath slowly returned to something like normal.

She was starting to wonder how long it would take Skylar to break away when she heard footsteps on the gravel behind her. "Don't turn around," called Skylar's voice from beyond the hedge. "Act natural."

Lorelei spoke just loudly enough to be heard over the din of conversation and the girls' laughter. "Thank you for coming."

"Where's Bothymus?" Skylar asked curtly.

"I sent him back to the eyrie. He's probably napping there now."

"You could have bloody told me where you were going."

"There wasn't time."

"Well, you could have—"

"Skylar, please, I can't explain everything now. I need your help."

Skylar paused. "You have no *idea* how much you need my help right now."

"Why? What's happened?"

"It's your mother," Skylar said. "She's been taken for questioning at my mother's insistence."

Lorelei's mouth went dry. "*Who* took her?" she asked, praying it wasn't the Church.

"Vashtok and Nanda," Skylar said. "I tried to convince Mother not to, but she was adamant. She wants you to turn yourself in before she'll even consider freeing her."

"Goddess of light . . ."

"Look, I'll do what I can on that front," Skylar went on, "but there's more. Ash—"

Footsteps crunched on the gravel path from the far side of the hedge. "Good day," someone said, and continued on.

Lorelei waited for the footsteps to fade and then asked, "What *about* Ash?"

"He's hurt. As far as I know, he's still unconscious. He's at The Bent Tulip now."

"The Bent Tulip? Why, by the great white mountains, would he be *there*?"

"Since Master Renato's death, he's been determined to find out about the peat you showed him. He couldn't do that in the alchemystry or the shrine. He needed someplace quiet, someplace discreet. But something went wrong. Eladora sent word a few hours ago. She heard an explosion of some sort and went to the room he'd rented. She found him unconscious and his equipment shattered."

"Did you go see him?"

"I couldn't leave the ceremony. It would've drawn attention to him. Eladora's note said his breathing had stabilized and that she has someone tending to him. Just go, okay? I'll be there as soon as I can, and then we can decide what to do about your mother."

"All right," Lorelei said. She felt numb, like she couldn't even think.

Skylar's footsteps faded, and Lorelei left the maze and walked to Rylan and Creed beneath the cherry trees.

"What's wrong?" they asked in unison.

"My mother's been taken, and Ash is hurt. I'll explain on the way."

SEVENTY-ONE: LORELEI

Lorelei, Rylan, and Creed approached The Bent Tulip from the alley out back. Given that many of Tulip's regulars were a part of law enforcement and would recognize Lorelei and Creed instantly, they sent Rylan in through the tavern's rear door. He ducked his head out shortly thereafter and waved them in. It felt odd to be sneaking in like thieves, but there was nothing for it—they couldn't risk being spotted.

Inside, Eladora led them through the back room, down the hallway, and up the stairs to the third floor, the one with the private rooms. As Eladora keyed the lock of a door on the left, Lorelei noticed sooty smudges on the bottom of the opposite door. The air smelled of brimstone.

Eladora led them through a quaint sitting room through a doorway on the right-hand wall and into a small bedroom with a sloping ceiling where Ash lay in the lone bed. His hair was mussed and looked singed in places. The skin on his face was red, and his neck was wrapped by a bandage with blood stains on the left side. Eustice, Eladora's stone-faced elder sister who normally worked the kitchen, was sitting in a rocking chair beside him.

"Has he woken?" Eladora asked.

Eustice, her iron gray hair tied in a bun, shook her head. "His breathing is steadier. His heart, too." She pointed to Lorelei. "Are they going to tell us what he was doing in our bloody storeroom or not?"

"Not now, Eustice."

"It's ruined! It'll take weeks to repair. And the stink! We're struggling enough as it is, Dora—"

"I said not *now*, Eustice. Go man the bloody bar."

Eustice looked like she was in the mood to fight, but she stared down at Ash, and the look faded. Without another word, she stood up, trudged past them, and left.

"Ash came by yesterday," Eladora said, "asking for a private space. Our rooms were full, what with the dedication and all, but he said he'd be happy in the store room. He even paid extra—for the short notice, he said. Seeing how he'd been with you, I thought why not?"

"Did he say what he was going to do?"

"He wanted a place to work. Said the shrine was too busy and the palace too far." Eladora shrugged. "I didn't ask much beyond that. Last night after reckoning, I heard a loud boom. I came up and found him passed out among his beakers and whatnot."

Lorelei couldn't take her eyes off Ash's red, blistered face. "Did he tell you anything else?"

"No, but I found this." She went to the bedside table, picked up a leatherbound journal very reminiscent of Korvus's, and handed it to Lorelei. "It was on the floor under some broken glass."

Lorelei opened it and flipped to the last written pages. Two of the pages were burned and all but missing. She held the journal close to her face and noticed a distinct tinge of violet on the blackened pages. When she touched the char and rubbed her fingers together, her skin tingled. Only a few words were discernible near the top of one page:

Trial one: 1 sextarius suspension, 1 ligula of peat. Mix and add 1 ligula of . . .

The rest of the two pages were black char.

"I don't understand." Creed said. "You said Azariah took the peat. How could Ash have enough to run an experiment?"

Lorelei had been wondering the same thing. "Maybe it was different peat—"

She paused, remembering the storeroom at the shrine and how excited Ash had been.

"What?" Creed asked.

"At the shrine, Ash dropped the wooden box containing the peat. A bunch of it spilled onto the storeroom floor. He must have collected enough to run another experiment."

"That would have given him enough?"

She pointed to the formula. "One ligula is a tiny amount, and he'd spilled quite a bit."

"A small mass," Rylan said, "yet it caused an immense amount of damage."

She paged backward and read:

A white powder delivered by the Hissing Man, tested by Brother Mayhew, and found to have an abundance of aura. Peat, meant for the Hissing Man, found to have an abundance of umbra. Suspect the two were meant to be used in conjunction, either by the Hissing Man, the Chosen, or perhaps the Red Knives. But why?

Related to Tortoise Peak in some way? Perhaps the lake?

What he might have meant by the lake, Lorelei had no idea, but Tortoise Peak had to be about the geoflare. She closed the journal and handed it to Creed. "Can we see the storeroom?"

Eladora nodded and led them to the room across the hall, unlocked the door, and gave it a light shove. The door groaned open. "Just close it when you're done." With that, she left.

Lorelei, Creed, and Rylan entered the storeroom. It was a complete shambles. On the left wall were mismatched shelves filled with blankets, pillows, sheets, bars of soap, and small bottles of what looked to be fragrance. On the right wall was a warped shelf with hooks under it. Overturned buckets, brushes, and more soap lay on top. Mops, brooms, and feather dusters leaned against the wall. All of it was covered in soot she'd seen on the door.

She touched the singed feather of a sad-looking duster. It crumbled and left the tip of her finger tingling.

On the far side of the room, beyond the shelves, a wooden desk was set in front of a broken window. Shattered pieces of beakers, bottles, and vials were scattered on the desk. Rylan, stepped past Lorelei, crouched, and reached for a thick piece of broken glass.

"Don't touch it," Lorelei told him.

Creed stepped up next to him. "Best we leave her alone." The two men left the storeroom.

Lorelei catalogued the bits of broken glass glinting in the sunlight, noted the sulfurous odor and the stain on the floorboards near a broken flask, which she assumed had held the suspension liquid. But what had he added to it? His journal entry mentioned the white powder from the mine. Had he found its source and brought some of it to the Tulip?

It seemed likely, but if so, where was it? It was possible he'd blown it all up in the experiment, but Ash wouldn't have done that if he'd had a choice—he would have wanted to have more on hand in case something went wrong.

The breeze blew in through the window, and Lorelei peered at the broken window frame. The glass inside the room all seemed to be from Ash's alchemical equipment; the larger pieces were rounded, like parts of a flask or beaker. There were no flat pieces of glass anywhere. The glass in the windows, of course, would have been blown out, which made her wonder what else might have been ejected from the storeroom.

She leaned over the desk, and looked out through the empty broken window. Outside was the slanted, shingle roof of a second floor room. Bits of glass were everywhere, some large, some small. Near the edge of the roof was a marble mortar. The pestle, she suspected, had fallen over the edge. She climbed onto the desk, careful not to cut herself, leaned through the window, and retrieved the mortar. Then she climbed inside and examined the bowl. It contained traces of a white powder.

She touched rubbed it with her finger. It was gritty as expected. Then she smelled it, but it had only a faint mineral scent. She set the mortar down on the desk and retraced her steps, back toward the storeroom door.

"Lorelei?" Rylan called.

"Shhh," Creed hissed.

Lorelei took the stairs down to ground level. She heard Rylan and Creed's footsteps behind her. She went through the rear exit to the alley, then around the corner of the building to the courtyard where the Tulip occasionally hosted beer tastings. At the base of the red brick wall that bordered the property was the pestle. Near it was a hunk of white stone. She walked across the courtyard and picked it up. "Alra preserve us . . ." It had square edges, like cut building material.

Rylan scowled. "Is that . . . ?"

"Yes," she said. "White quartzite."

"Which means it came from the shrine."

"Catch me up," Creed said.

Lorelei walked over to them. "Ash wanted to find out if there was some relationship between the peat and the powder from the mine. Some of the peat was spilled before Azariah came and took the box of it away. Ash must have picked some up off the floor. He must have been comparing it to quartzite."

Creed stared at the chunk of quartzite in her hand. "You're saying *that's* the source of the powder we saw Brother Mayhew testing?"

"That's precisely what I'm saying."

"It's part of the shrine," Creed continued, "which means the rest of the quartzite is likely just as potent."

Lorelei recalled Ash showing her the tiny cracks in the quartzite, explaining how it was becoming more brittle over time, and thus, the renovation project. Then she remembered the quartzite at *Yeriel's* shrine, how soft it had felt under her feet. "I suspect it's not only the quartzite, but the stone around it, the mountain itself."

"Faedryn's broken teeth." Rylan grumbled. "Why didn't I see it before?"

Lorelei shook her head. "See what?"

"Yeriel's shrine, the columns . . ."

Lorelei suddenly understood what he meant. "Alra's unending grace . . ."

Creed looked worried. "What?"

"Rylan and I found stone columns at the shrine. There were signs they contained indurium."

"So?"

"The palisade stones around the city are rich in indurium. It's what protects the city from the umbra shed by Nox." Her thoughts were running wild. She could hardly slow them down enough to speak.

Creed's brows pinched. "I'm still not getting it."

"Whatever the reason, it's clear Yeriel was freed from her shrine centuries ago. It's also clear that a geoflare erupted at that very site. The two can't be coincidental. I think the geoflare was *manufactured* to free Yeriel, and I think another geoflare is being made right here, right now, in Ancris. That's what the palisade stones are truly for. They're trying to blow up Ancris."

Lorelei paced the courtyard. Seemingly random bits of information were taking flight in her mind like a flock of swifts. She felt like she was trying to catch them all in a tiny net.

"Tell us something, Lorelei," Creed said.

"When Ash and I went to Tortoise Peak, we found evidence of similar stone columns. We couldn't quite figure out what they were. We thought it was an ancient altar, perhaps. It wasn't though. Those stone pillars *caused* the geoflare, just like the ones at Yeriel's shrine did at Tortoise Peak. And now they're all around Ancris."

"You're sure?"

"Positive. The eruption at Tortoise Peak happened roughly twelve years ago. The palisade in Ancris was begun about a year later. They wanted to prove it would work first."

"Who did?"

"*Azariah. He's* the one who pressed to build it. *He's* the one who got our expedition to cancelled. He's working with the Hissing Man. He *wants* this to happen. He wants destroy Ancris."

Creed gaped at her, mouth hanging open. "That's *mad*. Why, by Alra's sweet smile, would he want to do that?"

For a moment, Lorelei had no answer. But then she recalled the crystal shard and Strages slowly rotating below it. "Stone and bloody scree, he wants to awaken Strages."

SEVENTY-TWO: LORELEI

orelei heard footsteps approaching the courtyard. She thought surely they'd
been discovered, but a moment later, Skylar came around the corner. Her
jewelry was gone. Her toga had been replaced with a green woolen dress,
the sort more commonly seen in Fiddlehead. It looked somewhat ill-fitting. "What's
happening?"

Creed looked up at the windows of the surrounding buildings. "Not here.
Upstairs."

They went up to Eladora's flat and huddled around her tiny, doily-covered
table, which might have been humorous were the moment not so grave. Lorelei
told Skylar everything that had happened since she'd left Ancris, about the chalice,
Yeriel's shrine, Kellen and, finally, Ash and his experiment in the storeroom.

Skylar's mouth opened and closed, and then she said, "So you think Azariah
and the Hissing Man are trying to awaken Strages?"

"I do," Lorelei said.

"The goddess's grace, why go through so much trouble?"

"The Church maintains that the shrines have spells embedded into their construction that preserve the paragons, but I wonder if there's more to it than that. I
wonder if those same spells actually trap the paragons in the shrines."

Skylar shook her head. "Why trap them there?"

"The inscription at the shrine called Yeriel an *Umbral Witch, betrayer of Faedryn
and all his fell servants.* It says she might atone for her sins when Alra rises again.
Whoever built the shrines clearly thought Alra might be reborn in some way.
Why else write it?"

Skylar considered this. "And Yeriel?"

Lorelei shrugged. "I don't know, but if she *did* betray Faedryn, thus siding with
Alra, perhaps her reward was to be freed from the shrine."

"But that would mean the other paragons couldn't be trusted." Skylar shrugged.
"It turns our ideas of the paragons on its head."

"It does, but don't forget that everything we know about the Ruining comes
from the Church. They definitely lied about the shrines. What else have they lied
about?"

Skylar pursed her lips a moment, then said, "Let's assume you're right about
Yeriel's shrine. What does it have to do with Azariah and Strages?"

"Remember when we went with Master Renato to Tortoise Peak to study the
geoflare?"

"Yes. So?"

"Ash and I found a hole in the ground and a column very similar to ones in the palisade."

"You're saying the columns caused the geoflare at Tortoise Peak?"

"I think so, yes. And I also think may have stumbled onto something. See here?" She opened Ash's journal to the page about Tortoise Peak.

Skylar read it aloud:

"A white powder delivered by the Hissing Man, tested by Brother Mayhew, and found to have an abundance of aura. Peat, meant for the Hissing Man, found to have an abundance of umbra. Suspect the two were meant to be used in conjunction, either by the Hissing Man himself, the Chosen, or perhaps the Red Knives. But why?

Related to Tortoise Peak in some way? Perhaps the lake?"

"I didn't make the connection earlier," Lorelei said, "but years ago, Master Renato planned to study a recent sinkhole. It was called off when the renovation at the shrine began. Sinkholes often form lakes. I'm guessing it was the same lake Ash was referring to. And a sinkhole and a geoflare at the same time? It can't be coincidence. The sinkhole probably formed on the same day Tortoise Peak blew. The fen where the lake formed likely had a massive store of umbra, just as Tortoise Peak did with aura. I think they caused each other. That's what Ash was onto when his experiment blew up. I think Azariah used the renovation project as an excuse to occupy Master Renato, and all other alchemysts in the city, and force Renato to abandon the expedition to Tortoise Peak."

Skylar winced. "My mother called off the expedition at Tortoise Peak. Are you saying she's in league with Azariah?"

"No. I think Azariah manipulated your mother into that."

"But why," Skylar asked, "would Azariah want any of this?"

"I think he's trying to awaken Strages, as Yeriel was. It explains so much. Why the Hissing Man was so desperate to get the chalice. Why Azariah was so interested in the peat we got. It even explains why the palisade was built. What was sold to your father as a way to protect Ancris was in reality a way to destroy the city."

Skylar sat motionless for a long time before speaking. "To be completely honest, Lorelei, it's a lot to take in. I'm not sure what to believe."

"We have to assume the worst," Lorelei said, tapping a finger on the doily-covered table. "If we don't—"

Skylar held up a hand. "I agree it's worth checking out, but I can't tell my father any of this unless I can explain why Azariah would do it."

Rylan, who'd remained quiet throughout, suddenly blurted, "Bough and branch . . ."

Skylar turned to him. "What?"

"Azariah wants the same thing as the Hissing Man. The Chosen make no bones about wanting to install a theocracy, as they attempted to do during the Holy Rebellion. They want the empire beholden to the Church, not the other way around. And, despite protestations to the contrary, we all know there are members of the Chosen spread throughout the Church's hierarchy. Is it so inconceivable

Azariah is one of them? They might not be powerful enough to openly challenge your father, but imagine what they could do if they awakened a paragon?"

Skyler paused a moment. "Who says Strages would obey the likes of Azariah or the Hissing Man?"

"I've no idea," Rylan said, "but they must think they can, or they wouldn't have gone to all this trouble."

Creed blew a long sigh. "What about the Red Knives? Why involve them?"

"If Lorelei's right about how all this is supposed to work," Rylan said, "they need a source of umbra. A massive one. That could only come from the Holt."

Creed, looking pensive, nodded. "They'd have to get it without the quintarch knowing. What better way to do that than by manipulating the Red Knives?"

Lorelei was annoyed she hadn't seen it sooner. "The Church wants a scapegoat."

"Precisely," Rylan said. "If the empire suspects the Church intended to destroy an entire city, it would galvanize the other quintarchs, and even the people, against them. But if everyone thinks the Knives are to blame . . ."

Rylan went silent; Lorelei thought she knew why. The empire might blame the Red Knives, but the Kin as a whole who would pay. The empire would unleash untold violence and misery across the Holt and beyond.

"I'm so sorry," Lorelei whispered.

Rylan smiled briefly.

Skylar took a deep breath. "Whatever danger may or may not exist—"

"The danger *exists*," Lorelei said.

"I believe you, but we're in a difficult position. To start with, your mother's been taken."

Lorelei groaned. "Do you know where?"

"No. Likely a safe house." Skylar said. "Rylan was already destined for a cell in the Crag. You," she said, gesturing at Lorelei, "were asking to be locked up next to him when you stole Bothymus. After what happened with the praetorian guard at the abbey, Creed will be there with you. Even *Ash* will be in trouble when he wakes up, and I have no power to change any of it."

"Aren't you still the Consul?" Rylan asked.

Skylar tilted her head and shrugged. "With my father back in Ancris, I still have the title but little of the power. If Mother didn't have his ear so much, I might be able to . . ."

"What?" Lorelei asked.

"I might be able to help, but it's dangerous."

"Everything's dangerous at this point."

"I know, it's just . . ." Skylar paused, took a deep breath. "Several times a year, an elite gathering, a bacchanal, is held in Ancris. Wine, liquor, all kinds of illicit drugs are available. The drugs from the Holt, as we all know, are the most potent, and so are the most sought after. The guest list is filled with senators, patricians, aristocrats, landowners . . . artists, poets, musicians . . . The wealthiest of the wealthy. The empire's upper crust, as it were."

Lorelei narrowed her eyes. "Are you saying Tyrinia frequents these parties?"

"She *hosts* them, Lorelei. She arranges the invites, the location, even the drugs. They always coincide with official ceremonies or celebrations so guests have reason to come to Ancris. There's one tomorrow, after the Syrdian conquest celebration."

"So what are you proposing?" Rylan asked.

"That we infiltrate it, expose my mother. Use it for leverage."

Rylan laughed. "You expect me to believe you would use your own mother to help us?"

Skylar glared at him. "You, a newcomer to Ancris and a fugitive, doubt me?"

"Forgive me," Rylan said, staring down at the table a moment. "It's only, I don't understand why you would betray your mother."

"I'm not convinced you need to know anything, but for Lorelei's sake, I'll tell you. I had a brother named Ransom who died when I was young."

"I'm well aware of Ransom."

"I thought you might be. What you may not know is that he was wounded by a gryphon during the first Syrdian campaign. He was sent home to Ancris to recuperate, but the wound was slow to heal and very painful. A fellow dracora, also wounded, gave him some rapture. You know it?"

"It's a palliative made from the hearts of umbral dragons," Rylan said, "often used for chronic pain, but at higher doses it's a powerful euphoric."

"It's also quite addictive, and proved so for Ransom."

"It's forbidden for dracorae to take it, isn't it?"

"Outside of abbeys and field hospitals, absolutely," Skylar said, "but Ransom was home and he was the quintarch's son. His compatriot eventually died, but before he did, he put Ransom in contact with his supplier, a Red Knife. Ransom began hosting drug parties. Mother learned of them, but instead of stopping him, she joined in. She had bad gout and began using rapture and other drugs for it." Skylar was silent for a time, then she shrugged her shoulders and continued. "When Ransom overdosed and died, Father was furious . . . with Ransom for having taken the drug in the first place, with Mother for condoning it, with the dead soldier who'd introduced him to it, but especially with the Red Knives. It led to fighting in the Holt."

"I need no lectures on Ransom's War. It's why my uncle was taken." Rylan held up his left hand. "Why I lost a finger."

"I'm sorry for it," Skylar said. "Ransom's death led to a lot of unnecessary bloodshed, and not only in the Holt. It was partly why Father was obsessed with the Syrdian campaign and left to fight in it. With him gone, Mother fell into a dark place, and we couldn't get her out of it. She loved Ransom, and began using rapture to mask her pain. It was a way to remember him, too, I think. She began hosting similar parties, small at first but as more people found out them . . ."

"Lucran *must* know about them, right?" Lorelei asked. "Someone must have told him?"

"He's probably aware, but they barely even talk anymore. He still blames

Mother for Ransom's death." Tears welled in Skylar's eyes. "Some days I think he secretly hopes she'll overdose and die like Ransom did."

Lorelei took her hand and squeezed it.

Skylar squeezed Lorelei's hand back, then wiped away her tears. "I've begged Mother to stop, but she won't. And now she does as she pleases without regard for anyone else, including you, your mother, even Ancris."

Lorelei was confused. "What are you saying?"

"The drugs, Lorelei. She gets them through Marstan. It's why she was so upset when you disobeyed him in Glaeyand. It's why she had you assigned to records. It's why she insisted your badge be taken."

"And you knew?"

Skylar clenched her hands. "I'm so sorry, Lorelei. I thought it would all blow over. But it hasn't, and now it's fucking everything up. It has to stop. I'm going to make it stop."

If Rylan was shocked, he didn't show it. "Forgive me, you know your mother better than I do, but isn't there an easier way? Wouldn't the Domina back down if we tell her everything we've found out, everything *Ash* has found out? Wouldn't she listen to reason?"

"She might," Skylar said, "but I can't guarantee it. She seems angry and miserable most of the time these days. And what proof do we have? An exploded broom closet?"

Rylan shook his head. "It's more than that."

"But she'll require proof, real evidence. Father will listen to her even if we get it." Skylar rolled her eyes. "He'll start an investigation, which will take weeks, months, perhaps. And in the meantime, Mother will demand Lorelei be tried, that you be returned to the Crag, and that Creed be taken off active duty, at least until the investigation is finished. And I think she'll go after Ash, too, make sure he's not allowed near an alchemystry."

"Root and bloody ruin," Rylan blurted, "doesn't the quintarch care what happens to his city?"

"Of course he does," Skylar answered, seemingly without offense, "but we have to consider who we're up against. If we're right, and Azariah is somehow wrapped up in all of this, he'll be pushing my father hard, as will my mother. Father just got back from Syrdia. He's relying on Theron, Mother, and Azariah more than he might otherwise."

"So how do we convince him?" Rylan asked.

Skylar shrugged. "We'll need witnesses. Documents. Confessions. Proof that the peat sample is something more than a lump of mud from the Holt."

"Would it help," Rylan asked, "if I could find out exactly where it came from?"

"Yes, of course."

"Then let me to go, and I'll find it if I can." Rylan paused and looked out the window. Lux was shining between banks of steel-gray clouds. "Right now, if possible."

"Where will you go?" Skylar asked him. "And if it is so easy, why haven't you found it already?"

"I haven't had time. And"—Rylan smiled—"much as the inquisitors prefer to keep their sources secret, so do I."

Skylar seemed to weigh him very much like Lucran might. "All right, then. Go."

Rylan turned to Lorelei. "Leave word with Eladora where I can reach you. I'll be back as soon as I can."

Skylar watched him leave, then huddled with Lorelei and Creed as if they were a newly formed privy council. "The fete . . ."

"Yes. I'd almost forgotten," Lorelei said.

"Here's what we're going to do."

SEVENTY-THREE: RYLAN

R ylan walked through Fiddlehead first and then to Slade. Callum's Way, the large boulevard that bisected the city's poorest neighborhood, was little more than cobblestones overrun with weeds. Some few of the streets that ran off it were paved, but most were packed dirt. The half-timber homes had sagging roofs and leaning walls, their windows dirty as the children who ran along the streets.

Rylan slowed as he approached a small but bustling marketplace. At the center was a palisade column, bright and new save the lower third, which was covered with graffiti. The palisade protected only half of Slade, and it must have been particularly galling to the city planners to bother with even that much, but the pillars had been constructed in a perfect circle around Ancris—Slade was just in the way.

Beyond the outer ring of market stalls was a shop with a sign above it that read: *Hollis's Historical Artifacts*. A bell above the door jingled as Rylan entered. The shop was a narrow room that looked very much like Hollis's shop in Glaeyand. The artifacts were markedly different, though. They were meant to cater to a clientele who wanted a piece of the Holt or Gorminion or Olgasus. Scattered over the shelves were dragon eyes encased in glass, steel helms with antlers, swords and knives with sharp dragon-talon hilts. There were compasses, ivory carvings, and more. Hollis often flitted between the two cities, purchasing various antiques while fencing stolen goods and arranging assignments for thieves like Rylan.

Hollis sat behind a cluttered desk wearing a tan shirt that accented his olive skin. On the desk was a bowl of mushroom stew and a hunk of bread. The savory smells made Rylan's stomach growl.

Hollis slurped tea from a mug and set it down. "Raef said you might stop by."

Rylan glanced down the hallway behind Hollis. "Is he here?"

Hollis shook his head. "He flew back to the Holt last night. Said you'd have something for him?"

"Well, I don't. What are you doing, Hollis? I thought you wanted no part of this."

Hollis shrugged. "I didn't—believe me, I didn't—but I owed Blythe a few favors. I promised to give her a place she could be alone."

"Then how did Raef—"

"He found out—I don't know." Hollis lowered his voice. "I thought he'd come to kill her, Rylan. I thought he was going to kill me, too, but he said just to keep an eye on her. Let her do what she wanted for the time being. Threw a bag of coins on my desk for the trouble. I couldn't say no."

Rylan knew what it felt like to be squeezed, but he had more things to worry about. "Where is she?"

Hollis pointed to the hall behind him, which led to a stairwell and the shop's rear door. "Third floor."

"Thanks, Hollis."

Rylan took the stairwell up to the third floor and a landing with a lone door. The door was unlocked and groaned as he entered. In the small sitting room, swaths of plaster were missing from the red-brick walls. On the far side of the room was a lopsided couch. Above it, a hopelessly dirty, cracked window let in a meager light. A pair of threadbare stools sat along another wall. Between them was a low table laden with liquor bottles, all but one empty.

To Rylan's right was a doorway with no door. It led to a dimly lit bedroom. He moved to the doorway and found Blythe lying on a sweat-stained mattress. She wore a tatty old night shirt, exposing bruises on her bare legs. Her eyes blinked languidly. She seemed to be staring *through* Rylan. Then her eyes suddenly widened, and she snatched a knife from beneath her pillow. She brandished it while propping herself up.

"Oh . . ." Her wild look of terror slowly faded. "It's you . . ." She lay back down and slipped the knife back under her pillow.

Rylan stepped into the room and found it almost stiflingly warm. Traces of cheap liquor laced the air. The lone window on the opposite wall was covered with a thick woolen blanket. The afternoon sun beat against it. Blythe's trousers, shirt, and sword harness hung from hooks on the right-hand wall. Near the mattress was a foot locker and, on its scratched surface, several glass vials of iridescent white brightlace with cork stoppers. The same euphoric she'd been addicted to before.

Rylan wondered just how much she'd taken since Aarik's death. "Blythe . . ."

She followed his gaze and gave him a patronizing smile. "It's under control." She shifted on the mattress and patted the space she'd just made. "Lie down with me."

Years ago, back in Thicket, Blythe had snuck though his bedroom window many times, and they had lain together, whispering deep into the night. It had been innocent when they'd been young, a way to simply be with each another. As they grew older, they explored each other's bodies and made the first clumsy attempts at lovemaking. "That's not why I came, Blythe."

"No, you came to talk." Her eyes drifted shut, and she patted the mattress again. "So come. Tell me how you're not in a cell in the Crag."

He nearly denied her, but the truth was he missed those youthful days. He lay down, felt the warmth coming off her, and stared at the cracks in the plaster ceiling. "I escaped."

"I can see that," she said softly. "How?"

"You heard I was attacked?"

"Mmm . . ." Her eyes still closed, Blythe scrunched the pillow under her cheek. "A bloody great mountain tried to strangle you, and the gaoler saved your ass."

"The mountain was a fellow named Durgan—one of the Chosen, I reckon—but the gaoler wasn't even around. It was Lorelei."

Blythe's eyes opened. "The inquisitor? *That* Lorelei?"

Rylan rolled to face her, slipped one arm under his head, and nodded. "She poked a rather sizable hole in Durgan's belly. Later, after Renato's accident in the shrine . . ." He paused. "That was the Knives, yes?"

The blanket over the window blew inward, and afternoon light spilled into the room. Blythe seemed reluctant to answer, but then she shrugged. "It was the Hissing Man."

Rylan wouldn't have been able to pick Renato out in a crowd. Even so, he regretted the man's death. "Did Llorn ask for it?"

She stared at him, her lips in a thin line. "Why are you here, Rylan?"

He thought about pressing her on Renato's death, but that's wasn't why he was there. "I know what Llorn is planning to do here in Ancris."

"Oh really? Enlighten me."

"He means to destroy the city in a geoflare."

The room was dim, but her cheeks flushed. "How did you find out?"

"Lorelei figured it out. How do *you* know? I thought Aarik kept you in the dark."

"Llorn told me."

"Just like that, Llorn told you?"

"No, not *just like that*. He was testing me. If I'd gone against him . . ."

She didn't have to finish. As with Hollis, Rylan felt badly about her predicament, but in her case, he could do something about it. It meant putting Blythe in danger, but Llorn had to be stopped. "We can't let him do this, Blythe."

"Can't we?"

"No," he said, "we can't, and Aarik wouldn't have wanted it."

"Aarik is dead. Llorn is King of the Wood now, and I owe him my allegiance."

"Aarik wanted peace, Blythe. You can't just abandon that."

Blythe laughed. "Peace died the moment the empire chained Aarik to the Anvil. Llorn would never agree to it, and even if he did, your father would never work with him. You know he wouldn't. And why do you care, anyway? They killed your uncle. Lucran blamed us for his son's overdose and started a war. The empire is a sickness that has plagued the Holt for centuries. It's time they were cleansed."

Rylan shook his head. "Those are Llorn's words."

"Doesn't mean they're not true."

"Look, I'm not saying we don't have grievances. We do. But killing everyone isn't the answer."

"You know so fucking much?" She propped herself up on one elbow. "Well, did you know this was all the Hissing Man's idea? *He's* the one who wants this, and he's one of them. We're merely seizing the opportunity."

"Blythe, somewhere in the fens, there's a device like the palisade collecting umbra. Tell me where it is. That's all I ask. I'll take care of the rest."

Blythe barked a laugh. "No, Rylan. The crucible is the key to everything. It's going to give us power like we never imagined."

"Like *who* never imagined? Llorn or Aarik?"

She turned her head away from him. "Stop saying his name."

"I can't." He paused, hoping to cushion the blow. "Blythe, I need to tell you something that you're not going to like."

Blythe turned back to him, eyebrow raised. "Go on, then . . ."

Rylan had a second thought—maybe he shouldn't tell her. *It's the right thing to do,* he decided finally. *She has a right to know.*

"Rylan, will you bloody spit it out already—"

"Llorn had Aarik killed."

She stared at him, then she fell back on the pillow. "He didn't."

"He used a lucerta from Fraoch to compel Tomas, forced him to go to Lorelei and Creed and snitch about the meeting at the mine, then he killed Tomas."

Blythe shook her head. "Wrong! Tomas was killed for being a traitor."

"He was killed because he knew too much."

Blythe sat up against the wall. "Those are lies, Rylan. They're all fucking lies. The empire killed Aarik."

"You know Llorn, Blythe. You know he would do anything to stop Aarik from making peace."

Blythe grabbed the knife from beneath the pillow and stood. She looked just like she'd looked when she stabbed him in the side years ago. "I know he's a bastard, but he wouldn't *do* that."

Rylan rolled away from her and came to a stand. "Don't fool yourself. Everyone knew Aarik and Llorn didn't see eye to eye on the future of the Red Knives. Everyone knew Llorn was going to rise up against Aarik eventually."

"Shut your mouth, Rylan."

"Why? You know it's true! Llorn thought Aarik was weak. Then Aarik found out about Llorn and the Hissing Man. He demanded that Llorn bend the knee, but Llorn had already come too far."

She gripped the blade tightly, forearm shaking. "I said *shut up!*"

"Llorn arranged Aarik's death so he—"

Blythe leapt over the bed, slashing with her knife. Rylan leaned away from it, and shrugged. He knew it was only a threat. He walked away and stopped in the doorway.

"Blythe, just listen—"

She stalked toward him, and he backed into the sitting room. He grabbed a cushion from the couch and held it like a shield. Blythe swung the knife, but Rylan just pushed it away with the cushion. Some wool stuffing floated to the floor. She roared and charged again, tried to sneak the knife under his guard, managed to nick his right arm, but he grabbed her wrist and twisted it. She grunted, bared her teeth, and dropped the knife.

He kicked it spinning across the floor and wrestled her down. She struggled, but the fight was already leaving her. Her head thumped on the floorboards, and her body went lax. "Get the fuck off me."

He rolled away and lay on the dirty floorboards, felt a trickle of blood on his forearm and used his sleeve to stanch the flow. For a time, they just lay there breathing heavily.

Blythe sat up and raked her fingers through her tousled hair.

"Where is the crucible, Blythe?" Rylan pressed.

She looked at him sadly. "It's too late."

"No, it's not. Just tell me."

"You don't know what Llorn is like. He's already killed a dozen men who refused to bend the knee to him."

"He doesn't have to know."

Blythe laughed and waved a hand around at the room. "He'll know you were here."

Rylan wasn't sure what to say next. Blythe was terrified of Llorn, maybe too terrified to tell him. "Do you believe in the old ways?"

"Of course I do," she spat.

"Then you know Aarik is watching you."

"Fuck you, Rylan. The dead are dead. I need to worry about the living."

"Where's the crucible, Blythe?"

Her eyes reddened. "I loved him, you know. If it weren't for Llorn, we'd have been happy."

"I know you did. And he loved you. I could see it. I was happy for you. Truly."

"It might've worked. We might have finally had peace . . ."

"It would have been great."

She stood up and walked back into her room, threw off her nightshirt—her back was scarred and had bright red marks that would never heal—and put on a stained white shirt, trousers and boots.

"Where are you going?" Rylan asked.

"None of your fucking business."

"Please tell me where the crucible is."

"You already know where it is."

"No, I don't."

She strapped on her belt and grabbed her waistcoat and sword harness from the hook on the wall. Then she headed past him to the door. "Yes, Rylan, you do." She opened the door, walked out, and slammed it behind her.

Rylan stood there, wracking his brain, trying to think what Blythe meant. He went downstairs and found Hollis sitting at his desk, staring at the front door to the shop.

"What, under bright sun or dark, did you do to piss *her* off?" Hollis asked.

"What did she say?"

"Nothing. Just stormed out."

Rylan wondered if he'd made a mistake telling her. In all likelihood, she was headed to the Holt to confront Llorn. Llorn would probably kill her for it, but there was nothing Rylan could do about it now.

Thinking about Llorn made him think about the Red Knives, and that reminded him of his journey to help Bellicor, of Vedron tugging at her reins as they approached the Rookery. "Bough and bloody fucking branch, why didn't I think of it before?" Vedron had sensed the store of umbra in the crucible. She'd been trying to fly toward it to investigate, and Rylan had stopped her.

He headed through the cramped shop to the front door. The door jingled as he opened it. Then he turned toward Hollis. "You need to leave the city."

"What? Why?"

"Trust me, Hollis. Leave Ancris. Do it tonight."

Rylan ran out the door and down the street toward The Bent Tulip.

SEVENTY-FOUR: RHIANNON

Rhiannon strode with Morraine and Brother Mayhew along a path through the forest. The day was idyllic, Lux shone brightly through the canopy, and the temperature was perfect, which only served as a reminder of how life would change—for the entire Holt, not just Rhiannon—if Llorn had his way. They were off to span the first of the vyrda. It would create the first part of a bridge of sorts between the palisade and the crucible, allowing both to unleash their power. When it was done, the spell around the shrine would be destroyed, and Llorn would rob the Hissing Man of Strages.

Brother Mayhew walked on her left, thumping his staff on the soft ground. He seemed worried. And little wonder. He'd been toiling for years to make this day possible. Morraine marched stolidly on Rhiannon's right, her hood up. She had hardly looked at Rhiannon since they left the Rookery. If the bridging of the vyrda came down to sheer determination, Rhiannon had no doubt her mother would succeed.

When they reached the vyrd, the longhouse workers were gathered near the standing stones—all of them, Rhiannon realized, more than thirty in all. Irik and Sister Merida were there as well.

"Is it true the workers are leaving for a new rookery?" she asked no one in particular.

Brother Mayhew stared down at her. "Who told you that?"

Rhiannon said nothing—Irik had told her the night before, but she wasn't about to rat him out.

Brother Mayhew glowered, then shrugged. "The empire will learn of the crucible soon if they haven't already. There's no sense wasting lives."

It was then that Rhiannon noticed his right hand, the one holding his staff. As usual, he wore his golden ring with the reservoir of umbris, but there were cuts along the backs of his knuckles, and his skin was red. "What happened?"

Brother Mayhew shifted his staff to his left hand and flexed his right. "Never mind, girl."

The workers watched in silence, some nodding, others smiling, as Rhiannon, Morraine, and Brother Mayhew approached. Sister Merida smiled at Rhiannon, while Irik gaped at Morraine.

As Rhiannon, Morraine, and Brother Mayhew stepped inside the standing stones, a dragon pealed overhead. Fraoch entered the well above the vyrd with Llorn on her back. The sun shone through her marbled blue wings. When they landed, Rhiannon noticed a dark spot on Fraoch's head—between the ridges above her eyes. Her lucerta was missing.

Llorn slipped down from the saddle. As he led Fraoch into the vyrd, Rhiannon pointed to the bare spot. "Did you harvest it?"

Llorn didn't answer, but Brother Mayhew pinched her ear. "Mind your manners, girl."

Six more dragons followed, all but one bearing a rider wearing armor made of darksteel, boiled leather, or dragonscale. The first four dragons were auburns that looked so similar, down to the canary yellow starburst on their russet wings, that Rhiannon guessed they were litter mates. The other two were nasty looking onyxes. The one with a saddle but no rider was Brother Mayhew's bondmate, Ircundus. The other onyx had a clouded eye and a nasty scar down one brow ridge. Maladox, Brother Mayhew's burly twin, was in the saddle. He looked much the same as he had when he'd come with Aarik to the abbey, except his black beard was now braided and held in check by three tarnished silver bands. He had cuts on his forehead and cheek, and a large, half-healed bruise over one eye.

Rhiannon glanced at the cuts on Brother Mayhew's knuckles. Brother Mayhew scowled at her, then continued to watch Maladox.

Maladox glared at Mayhew. "What are you fucking looking at?" Then he led his onyx into the vyrd.

Brother Mayhew beckoned to Ircundus.

Llorn, Brother Mayhew, and all the other dragonriders formed a rough circle around Morraine and Rhiannon. The dragons gurgled and trumpeted, bumped shoulders and growled at one another. Rhiannon hoped the dragons would ignore her, but Maladox's onyx kept twisting its head to glare down at her with its good eye.

"Careful, girl," Maladox told her, "He hasn't been fed in a week, and nervous girls make him hungry."

Rhiannon knew he was only trying to get a rise out of her. Even so, she found herself watching the onyx from the corner of her eye. Maladox laughed a deep rumble of a laugh. Brother Mayhew frowned at him.

"Begin," Llorn said.

Morraine nodded, closed her eyes, and spread her hands wide. They were beginning their crossing through the maze, but it felt markedly different from other crossings, deeper, more intense, which made Rhiannon worry. Nine humans and seven dragons was near the limit of what the maze could handle. She'd heard stories about people getting lost in crossings gone wrong. She wanted to tell Morraine, but when she looked up and saw the scowl on Brother Mayhew's face, she decided to hold her tongue.

Morraine's lips pulled back in a ghastly grimace. Rhiannon had never before been able to sense other vyrda. She could now, though. There was one due west of them. The first spanning had begun.

As her mother's effort continued, the hollow feeling in Rhiannon's gut yawned wider. She coughed, pressed her hands to her stomach, but it only felt worse, and she doubled over and groaned. She was about to beg Morraine to stop when the clouds overhead changed from white to gray, and the standing stones became fatter and squatter. They were in another vyrd on a low hill.

Finally the gnawing feeling faded, but it made Rhiannon nervous. When all six segments of the bridge were complete, there would be no turning back.

Llorn led Fraoch between two tall stones. "Set watch."

Brother Mayhew, Maladox, and the others led their dragons from the vyrd. Beyond the menhirs, the landscape rolled like waves. The citadels were shorter in this part of the Holt, their trunks thinner.

"They're younger," Rhiannon said, pointing to the citadels.

Brother Mayhew nodded. "A fire burned everything up during in the Talon Wars."

"But that was centuries ago."

"Citadels grow slowly. The forest is still recovering. They still call it the Torchlands, though."

Maladox and the other dragonriders climbed onto their dragons and flew them up near the canopy.

Brother Mayhew left his onyx outside the henge, walked back into the vyrd, and stood next to Morraine. "Are you unwell?"

She waved him off. "See to the ward. We can't have anyone sneaking up on us."

Brother Mayhew opened the reservoir in his ring. He took a pinch of umbris, sniffed the black powder, and rubbed his finger over his gums. Then he closed his eyes, gripped his staff, and spread one palm toward the trees.

As he began to chant, Morraine made to leave the vyrd but stumbled. Rhiannon helped steady her. Morraine blinked and yawned. Her skin was so pale, her eyes so haunted, she looked unnatural, ghostly. Beyond the henge, Llorn stared down at Morraine from Fraoch's saddle.

Morraine glared back at him. "I warned you spannings would take time to recover from."

"Yes, but there are five more before we get to Ancris. If you're this weak after the first—"

"I'll get us there." She headed toward a gap in the stones. "Come, child."

They left the vyrd, hiked down along the hill's easy slope, and found a patch of moss between the roots of a nearby citadel. Seeing her mother shake so, Rhiannon wondered how bad the coming feeding would be. She wished she was running through the forest with Irik instead of heading toward Ancris. She wished she hadn't mucked up the ritual so they wouldn't have needed to drag her along. She wished she hadn't agreed to help Llorn. She wished Llorn had never decided to try to trick the Hissing Man.

She unslung her wool sack, nestled it beside a weathered rock, and knelt on the spongy, moss-covered earth. Morraine sat cross-legged before her. Rhiannon had hardly taken a breath when Morraine's eyes glowed blue and the void in Rhiannon's chest expanded. A prickling pain suffused her, and she felt like her flesh was rotting, her bones becoming brittle.

Rhiannon thought her fear of the feedings would diminish over time but her dread had only grown. Visions of her mother losing her inhibitions and continuing until Rhiannon was a withered husk made her want to reel back, to stop her mother, but she stifled the thought and let her mother feed. Her mother needed this, so Rhiannon would give it. It was as simple as that.

Finally, the intense gnawing in her gut faded. Morraine still looked exhausted, though.

"It's enough," Morraine said. She tugged on the leather cord around her neck and pulled the piece of the Heartstone from beneath her dress. "As we discussed"— she handed the shard to Rhiannon, leaned back against the root, and closed her eyes—"watch for Yeriel. We can't have her sneaking up on us. Not now."

Rhiannon held the crystal but made no move to use it. "I'm worried, Mother."

"What is it now?" Morraine asked without opening her eyes.

"If there's enough power in the crucible to create a sinkhole, what's going to happen to the palisade in Ancris?"

"I told you, it will awaken Strages."

"I know, but it's going to go beyond that, isn't it? It has to."

Morraine opened her eyes. "You're testing my patience."

"I'm a part of this now," Rhiannon said, realizing she was whining. "I deserve to know."

Morraine stared at her. "You'd never have become this impertinent if *I'd* raised you."

Rhiannon held her tongue, willing her mother to tell her something, anything.

One of the auburns trumpeted a long, rising note. Morraine stared up at it. "The empire used us, Rhiannon. Treated us like pawns. They accepted the gifts we gave them and used them in conquest. They took our religion and twisted it. And when the lands they wanted grew too distant, they called us unclean and fought us. When we brought that war to a bitter stalemate, they pretended to grant us the Holt"—she regarded Rhiannon, jaw set, eyes filled with a fire—"and they've been eating away at us ever since. So I ask you, where does it stop?"

"Aarik had a plan for peace."

"I loved my brother, but he was a fool. The empire would never have abided by that agreement. The only way to stop it is through violence. That's what we're doing. We're going to strike a blow against the empire that they'll never forget."

"You're going to destroy Ancris."

"So what?"

A shiver ran through Rhiannon, thinking about the lives it would cost. "It will cause a war."

Morraine seemed pleased. "A war that should have been fought long ago."

"But we can't hope to stand against the empire."

"That's where you're wrong, child. What starts with a blow against Ancris ends with the destruction of the entire empire." Morraine grimaced and pushed herself to a stand. "Now do as I've said. Watch for Yeriel."

As her mother strode away, Rhiannon stared at the vyrd. She was no warrior. This was no life for a girl like her. But she'd felt the tingling sensation of entering the maze a dozen times; she'd felt herself being whisked from one vyrd to another. She was sure she could learn the trick of it. She could find Irik and Sister Merida at the Rookery. They could go back to the abbey, or run away and hide.

The hollow feeling in her gut intensified. Morraine had stopped ten paces away and was staring at her. "What did I just say?"

Rhiannon nodded and gripped the shard tight. *Of course you can't run away, you dumb lamb. They'll stop you as soon as you try.* She stared on the shard's colorful facets. She'd only just begun to concentrate when two sharp whistles came from the tops of the citadels.

"Dragon!" Maladox bellowed.

Llorn pulled a longbow from Fraoch's saddle and strung it. He nocked an arrow, aimed up between the citadels. Rhiannon looked up and spotted the inbound dragon. It was a viridian, difficult to see as it flew toward them. Llorn drew his bow and sighted along the arrow, but then he lowered the weapon. It was Blythe. He'd sent her to Ancris, though. Why had she come back to the Holt?

Velox landed with a thud on the slope of the vyrd. She looked furious. She jumped down from the saddle, drew her rapier and charged Llorn. "You *killed* him?"

Llorn dropped his bow, backed away and drew his sword just in time to block a swing from Blythe. Blythe swung again, and their swords clanged. Velox screeched. Three of the auburns and Maladox's onyx swooped down and landed near the henge. The riders remained in their saddles, awaiting orders from their king, but Llorn hardly seemed to notice them. He gawked at Blythe. "Have you gone completely mad?"

"Mad?" Blythe swiped her sword at his chest, but he backed away again. "Mad is killing your own brother." She swung again, narrowly missing Llorn's neck. "Mad is betraying a king who was guiding us toward peace."

"Peace?" Llorn laughed. "Eating the empire's scraps while they steal the forest from us? Standing by as they outlaw more and more of our religion's beliefs? There's no peace in that, Blythe."

"Aarik had a plan."

"With Syrdia conquered and the other quintarchies at peace, do you really think they wouldn't turn their sights on us again?"

"We could have negotiated trade and taxation," Blythe shouted. "Land ownership. We could have voted in our own elections! Who would have thought he'd be able to get peace from Marstan fucking Lyndenfell? *I* certainly didn't, but he nearly did. Then you killed him!"

"You're making the same mistake Aarik did, Blythe. Signing on to that amendment would be tacit agreement that the Covenant is valid. It isn't, and it never was. Aarik might have realized that if he'd asked me, but he didn't so much talk to me before he went to Lyndenfell."

"Why should the King of the Wood ask for *your* permission? He knew what you'd say. You, on the other hand, broke your oath to him as soon as you spoke to the Hissing Man. You broke it again when you built the crucible without telling him, when you took the shard"—she flung a hand toward Morraine—"when you tricked Rylan into fetching your sister's bloody wisp."

Morraine watched the exchange in silence. Brother Mayhew seemed distraught. Maladox and the other dragonriders, who Rhiannon thought would surely intervene, stood by silently, occasionally exchanging sidelong glances.

"You did all that," Blythe went on, "because you thought you knew better than your king. And when Aarik found out, you arranged for him to speak to the Hissing Man in person. It was a setup, a way for you to have Aarik killed and pin the blame on the empire."

"You're talking nonsense."

"Am I?" With the tip of her sword, Blythe pointed to the dark blue spot on Fraoch's head. "Are we to believe you don't know how to use her lucertae? Are we to believe you didn't harvest one before the two of you left for Ancris? Are we to believe you didn't use it on Tomas to let the bloody inquisitors know *precisely* where and when he'd be meeting the Hissing Man?"

Llorn's nostrils flared. He looked at his dragonriders, then he fixed his angry glare on Blythe again. "Sometimes the end justifies the means."

Rhiannon gasped. She didn't know a fraction of what was going on, but she knew that Llorn had just admitted to killing Aarik.

Blythe began circling Llorn. "You stole Aarik's crown. I mean to have it back."

"I'm a little confused, Blythe. You'll have to speak more plainly."

Blythe lifted her sword and pointed it at Llorn's chest. "I challenge you, Llorn Bloodhaven, for the Holt's crown."

Llorn smiled. "In that case, I accept."

SEVENTY-FIVE: LORELEI

Hours after cantfall, Lorelei stood in the rotunda of the Curia Ancrata, the one-time home of Ancris's senate, now a preferred locale for state functions. The striking fresco on the massive dome overhead depicted Alra at the edge of a cliff, holding a gleaming spear. At her feet lay Faedryn, eyes wide, one hand raised against the impending blow.

The fete in the city's catacombs would follow the celebration, but Lorelei and Creed couldn't enter it without specially marked dragonbone coins. Skylar hadn't had enough time to secure any, which meant Lorelei and Creed needed to find some on their own.

Hundreds of masked men and women—senators, magistrates, landowners, and magnates—milled about the curia's open space. The women wore gowns. The men wore doublets with surcoats or half capes. The masks were an ancient custom, a nod to the conventional wisdom that man was blind compared to the goddess. That celebrations of military conquests used symbology so similar to the illustrae and *their* masks was recognition that it was the goddess, not the quintarchs, who brought victory to the empire's armies.

A few military officers also attended: legates from the army, trierarchs from the navy, volarchs from the dragon legion. They wore crisp uniforms, but no masks—soldiers, the old chestnut went, received glimpses of Alra's wisdom through the blood they spilled, and thus were more clear-eyed than the common man.

The gown Skylar had arranged for Lorelei had a crimson bodice, golden sleeves, and a flared collar. Her mask, fashioned after a vixen fox, was embroidered with tiny pearls to accentuate the eyes, snout, and ears. She'd dyed her hair with black henbane, transforming it from its normal flame red to a muted brown. She'd hardly recognized herself in a mirror, yet worried constantly that someone else would. Her breath was short, and every time someone looked at her, she moved to another part of the rotunda.

When a leggy nobleman seemed to be following her, she moved in front of the stage at the center of the room and pretended to be entranced by the four female Syrdian singers in robes standing on it. They had bone-white hair in tight braids, golden torcs around their necks, and broad bracelets covering their forearms.

Lorelei had her back to the crowd, and suddenly the nobleman was standing next to her. "Would you care for some wine?"

"My husband's already fetching me some."

The nobleman walked away, and she breathed a sigh of relief. Soon, she found herself enthralled by the Syrdian singers. Their soaring harmonies raised goose-bumps along her arms. She didn't imagine the women had come willingly, and even if they had, how could traveling to Ancris and singing for their conquerors be anything but shameful?

As their song ended, a bell rang, and they were led away. The guests turned their attention to Quintarch Lucran, standing on a dais at the other end of the room, holding a goblet. He was striking in his circlet-of-state and shimmering blue-white tunic. Standing side by side behind him were Tyrinia and Skylar in silver gowns embroidered with thread-of-gold. All three wore masks noticeably smaller than those of their guests.

Lucran stepped to the edge of the dais and gave a speech in honor of the sacrifices made by the military, but Lorelei listened with only half an ear. Her fellow inquisitor, Nanda, was standing near the dais in a canary yellow mask and a marigold dress. Lorelei recognized her pert chin, her full lips. It seemed curious that she would be at the ceremony. Though the inquisitors were not enemies of the military, the two organizations had always had a cold relationship, mainly because it was the duty of the special office in the Department of Inquisitors that investigated and charged soldiers for misconduct. Praefectus Damika might be extended an invitation to a celebration such as this, but the rank and file inquisitors most certainly would not.

On the dais, Lucran raised his goblet. "To our glorious victory."

The assemblage echoed, "To our glorious victory!"

"To the might of the empire," Lucran intoned.

"To the might of the empire!"

"To Alra's blinding truth."

With the final pronouncement, the guests closed their eyes and bowed their heads for a respectful moment of silence. Then Lucran continued, "Many preparations must still be made for the coming council in Glaeyand, so I take my leave, but I bid you all enjoy your evening."

The guests applauded, and Lucran bowed and shared a quiet word with Tyrinia. In that moment, Skylar looked at Lorelei and nodded. Then Skylar left the rotunda with her father and several praetorian guardsmen trailed behind them.

Lorelei was just about to head outside to meet up with Creed when she spotted Vashtok approaching the table where Nanda was sitting. She thought there must be some innocent explanation why they were there, but when they left together through the rear entrance that led to the maze and the Sanctum of the Eternal Flame, Lorelei began to strongly doubt it.

Lorelei followed them to the patio. Overhead, Nox was approaching its zenith. The glimmer of the palisade made the stars and the dark sun waver ever so slightly. Beyond the patio, lanterns bordered the promenade to the Sanctum of the Eternal Flame, turning the gravel path into a river of gold. Nanda and Vashtok were strolling along the promenade.

Lorelei rushed down the steps and caught up to them near the entrance to the hedge maze. "Nanda, Vashtok, I would speak with you a moment."

Both inquisitors froze, then turned to face Lorelei.

Nanda's eyes narrowed behind her bright yellow mask. "Lorelei? What are you doing here?"

Lorelei motioned to the hedge maze. "We need to talk. Privately . . ."

Nanda shook her head. "For your own good, Lorelei, turn yourself in. *Now.*"

"Are those *your* words," Lorelei asked, "or Tyrinia's?"

Had Nanda and Vashtok not been headed toward the entrance to the catacombs, Lorelei might have thought they were there just to hear the quintarch speak, but they *were* headed there, which implied they had been invited by Tyrinia.

"We're thinking of *you*, Lorelei," Vashtok said. "And your mother. She's worried about you."

"Where is she?"

"Come to the Crag and we'll sort that all out."

Lorelei wanted desperately to see her mother, but Vashtok's offer was a ruse. He wanted to get Lorelei where he and Nanda could trap her. When a small crowd on the patio burst into laughter, Lorelei glanced back. "We need to talk," she repeated and headed toward the maze. She thought Nanda and Vashtok might refuse, then she heard the crunch of footsteps behind her.

Lorelei led them to the pool at the center of the maze. "How long have you been working for Tyrinia?" Lorelei asked.

Nanda glanced around, then whispered, "The department is in an uproar. You know that, don't you? The quintarch no longer trusts Damika. Vashtok and I reached out to Tyrinia to try to smooth things over. She invited us here so we could start to rebuild the bridges *you* burned. That's all this is."

"Your chat with the Domina," Lorelei said. "Were you planning on having it at the Sanctum?"

Nanda smiled. "We were out for a stroll. The curia was too crowded. Surely you of all people can sympathize."

"Let me check your coats and purses, then. If neither of you has a catacomb token, I'll tell you more."

"Listen to yourself," Nanda said. "We're your friends. We're trying to help you. Come with us to the Crag. We'll help you navigate things. We'll protect you, Lorelei, as much as we can."

"How long have you been feeding Tyrinia information? That's how she learned I was at the fire so quickly, wasn't it? It's how she found out I took Rylan from the Crag."

"Alra's sweet, loving grace," Vashtok said, "do you even remember who you work for?"

"I do, and I remember what our job is. It's to stop drugs from entering our city and, above all, to protect its citizens. It isn't to look the other way so our matriar—"

"Enough." Nanda grabbed her elbow. "You're coming with us, Lorelei."

No sooner had she said it than Creed appeared behind them as planned.

Nanda gaped at him, and Lorelei jerked her elbow away. Then she pulled a cloth soaked with a sleeping agent from the purse at her belt.

Creed rushed forward, ducked a hurried blow from Vashtok, slipped an arm around Vashtok's neck, and clamped a similar cloth over his mouth and nose.

Nanda stepped toward Creed and Vashtok; Lorelei jumped her from behind and pressed the wet cloth to her nose and mouth. Nanda managed a strangled cry. Lorelei looked around, but no one else seemed to be near them. Vashtok went limp, and Creed lowered him gently to the ground. Nanda struggled, but Lorelei held her in a headlock and pressed the cloth harder against Nanda's face. Nanda slumped to the ground.

Creed stood over Vashtok and shook his head. "It just keeps getting worse." They'd planned on luring two random fete-goers into the maze, not a pair of inquisitors. "Never imagined I'd be going to war with the people I work with." He rifled through Vashtok's coat. "Nothing . . ."

"I couldn't let them go." Lorelei took Nanda's purse and upended it. "They would've recognized us." A few personal effects fell out—a kerchief, a lilac sachet, a few imperial coins—but no catacomb tokens. Lorelei worried they'd been telling the truth, but then she squeezed Nanda's purse and in a secret pocket she found two dragonbone coins. She titled one into the light. Etched onto the surface was a dragon's head with long, twisting horns.

She handed one of the coins to Creed, and he grumbled, "I hope this bloody works."

"Me too," Lorelei said, "or the Anvil will have a fresh pair of burn marks come reckoning."

SEVENTY-SIX: LORELEI

orelei and Creed climbed the steps to the Sanctum of the Eternal Flame. Lorelei had been in plenty of dangerous situations before, but there was something about the fete that was making her scalp prickle. Drug dens and dealers she understood. The fete was a different beast entirely. The empire's upper crust would be there. They could make her life a misery. They could send her to the salt mines, her mother, too. They could have them both to be tried and burned as heretics.

They walked past the fluted columns through an open space with a massive glowing brazier and a stairwell leading down. The praetorian guardsman stationed at the stairs held out a hand to stop them. Lorelei steeled herself for questioning, but the guardsman just glanced at their dragonbone coins and waved them on.

The next level down was a modestly sized room with lanterns on iron hooks illuminating a dozen bronze plaques about the Talon Wars. In the center of the room was a spiraling staircase leading down. Beside the staircase were two masked woman with blonde hair and a table with champagne flutes filled with sparkling wine. The two women handed a glass each to Lorelei and Creed.

Lorelei and Creed continued down the stairs. Granite blocks gave way to scarred rock and, eventually, a high tunnel. Wisplights hung from the tunnel's ceiling by chains, their pale blue light chilling the tunnel's already chilly air.

They navigated the tunnel through a misshapen cavern, its walls covered in dragon bones and skulls. Masked guests in fine gowns and suits milled about. Servants wore pearl-white togas, calf-length boots, and willow wreaths made of silver. Some carried platters of sparkling wine, others whisky. A woman approached Lorelei holding a wooden platter of glass vials filled with a bright red liquid—likely seraphim, a hallucinogenic serum made from cobalt dragon blood.

"Care to partake?" another woman purred and held out a bowl of glittering blue scales. "Cobalt scales," she said. "Put it on your tongue, and it will clear your mind of troubles."

Lorelei waved off the offer and caught up with Creed, who was heading toward a red-lit tunnel. As they entered it, the sounds of conversation were replaced with moans and grunts of pleasure.

A handsome man with dark eyes and luscious lips walked up to them with a bowl of red powder and a stack of tiny spoons. "Fireheart?" It was a powerful aphrodisiac made from the dried blood of auburn dragons.

Creed waved him away and moved on. Lorelei rushed to catch up with him. They passed by an alcove full of scantily clad whores, both men and women, well muscled, for the most part, but some with softer, more supple bodies, and all chained loosely to hooks on the walls. Some were bald or had closely shorn hair, and others with long hair, some braided. Most smiled as Creed and Lorelei walked by. Others blew kisses or waved lazily.

Lorelei watched in fascination as a masked woman with stark cheekbones lifted the chains of two muscular men off the hooks and led them to a grotto dug into the wall with pillows on the floor. All three were soon naked and writhing on the pillows.

They pushed through the crowd past several similar grottos with more guests and servants of flesh, rutting and moaning. The backdrop of dragon bones and eyeless skulls made the place feel like a drug-fueled dream.

For the most part, Lorelei avoided Creed's gaze. When she dared a look, he seemed unconcerned, but he was very good at masking his emotions.

In the final grotto were the Syrdian singers. All four were naked and bent over, their heads and wrists clamped in a stockade. Their torcs and bracelets were gone. Their braids had been undone, leaving their hair a mess of tangles and snarls.

Beside the stockade, a young man in a black mask took one of several straight razors from a pedestal and stared at the trapped women. Only then did Lorelei notice the clumps of white hair on the stone floor. The Syrdian women's scalps were patchy. There were small cuts here and there, some of which still bled, staining what remained of their white hair.

The nobleman stepped into the grotto. The young man handed him the razor, and the nobleman grabbed a lock of hair on the woman on the left, pressed the razor against her scalp, and sliced. The woman howled and her knees buckled, but she was held up by the stockade. The nobleman crouched and held out the lock of hair under her face. "My uncle died because of you." He tossed the hair on the floor and left. The crowd in around the grotto entrance applauded.

Lorelei felt sick to her stomach. Blood trailed down the singer's forehead, along her nose, and dripped onto the pile of hair.

"Come on," Creed growled, taking Lorelei by the elbow.

They continued down the main cavern. Several servants in togas entered from a wisp-lit side tunnel. Two guards in scale armor bookended the tunnel's mouth, watching the room with arms over their chests.

At the opposite end of the cavern, people were crowding around the entrance in some sort of commotion. Lorelei spotted Tyrinia among them.

"Now?" Creed asked.

Lorelei nodded. "As good a time as any."

Creed reached into his belt pouch and headed toward a table with plates of half-eaten food. Lorelei, meanwhile, approached a servant with a tray of empty plates headed toward the guarded tunnel. "Pardon me"—she put a hand on his shoulder, leaned in close, and whispered—"no one told me where the privies are."

"Of course." He pointed to a tunnel closer to the entrance. "Just down there."

Lorelei smiled and squeezed his shoulder. Creed swept in, set a small plate among the others already stacked on the platter, and deposited a glass globe filled with powder between the plates while doing so. It was a tripflash, one Creed had modified to start popping and sparking after a minute's delay.

Lorelei thanked the man, and watched the servant walk past the guards and into the tunnel.

Tyrinia and her gaggle drifted toward the center of the cavern, and the closer she came, the more Lorelei worried the sound of the tripflash would draw her attention. They'd needed Tyrinia to be in the catacombs, but they couldn't have her finding them before they reached the cavern where the drugs were kept.

At last, she heard a sizzling sound from the guarded tunnel, then a bunch of people shouting, a scream, the crash of shattering plates. Fortunately, it was far enough down the tunnel, and the crowd was so loud, that few people seemed to hear it except the guards, who rushed into the tunnel.

Lorelei and Creed snuck in behind them. Twenty paces in, they passed a tunnel on their right. At the far end of the tunnel was a natural chamber with several wisplights, tables, and crates. In the entryway, servants were talking to one of the guards. The other guard was crouched, rooting through a pile of broken dishes on the stone floor. Behind them, in the center of the chamber, was a bronze statue of a woman, gladius held high, one foot propped up on the skull of a dragon, a hero from the Talon Wars the servants desecrated with their very presence.

Lorelei and Creed rushed straight ahead into another, much larger cavern, and crouched behind a mound of stone to get their bearings. Like nearly everywhere in the catacombs, the walls and columns were covered with dragon bones, but this one had a limestone crypt some thirty yards from where Lorelei and Creed were hiding. The rectangular crypt had a peaked roof and a frieze supported by fluted columns. Wisplights on iron posts marked a path across the cavern floor toward it. Lorelei recognized this place. Skylar's tutor had brought Skylar, Lorelei, and Ash here for a history lesson. The crypt honored the memory of Sanctus Lucian Solvina, one of Skylar's forebears and the quintarch credited with creating the Covenant and ending the bloody stalemate with the Kin.

The frieze over the crypt depicted a man in armor and helm holding a spear, the rays of Lux shining down on him. Beyond the crypt was the skeleton of Lucian's mount, Fulgor. Its wings were spread, its neck arched, preparing to strike. At its feet, was the skeleton of Casurax, the mount of Wyan One-Hand, the Kin leader whom Lucian slew. Lighting both in ghastly pale blue was a large wisplight, hanging by a chain from the cavern ceiling. It was the soul of Wyan himself, captured and trapped by Lucian's son decades after Wyan's burial. It was dim now, a faint, glimmering star threatening to wink from existence altogether.

"Rather bold to use a sacred crypt to divvy up contraband," Creed said. "An insult to Lucian's memory, I would think."

"This fete has been going on for years in some form or another," Lorelei said. "Tyrinia seems to have lost her capacity for shame somewhere along the way."

A servant carrying a platter exited the crypt with a tall, hollow-cheeked man whom Lorelei immediately recognized as Theron, Lucran's chamberlain. He spoke to the servant tersely and returned to the crypt.

As the servant followed the wisp-lit path toward Lorelei and Creed, Lorelei stood, leaving herself in plain view.

Creed immediately snatched her wrist and tried to pull her back down. "Let him pass!"

"No. Tyrinia needs to be told we're here before she's out of her mind on rapture."

Creed heaved a sigh, then nodded and stood. As they headed side by side toward the servant, he said, "Do you suppose they'll let me choose the urn for my ashes?"

"Yes, and I'm sure Tyrinia will deliver it personally to your mother."

On seeing them, the servant pulled up short. "Y-you're not supposed to be here."

"We have business with Theron," Lorelei told him in passing.

The man looked ready to argue, but he stiffened when Creed pointed to the mouth of the nearby tunnel. "Run along now."

He glanced at the crypt, then turned and hurried away.

SEVENTY-SEVEN: LORELEI

L orelei and Creed climbed the steps and entered the crypt. Stacks of crates and boxes and piles of burlap sacks, all full of drugs, lined the wall on the right. In the center was a roseate marble sarcophagus with a greatspear, the very one Lucian had used to kill Casurax, on a stand on its lid. Next to the spear was a loaded crossbow, a ledger, an inkwell and quill, and an alchemycal scale, on which Theron was measuring an uncia of rapture. Beyond the sarcophagus was an archway that led to a hall containing relics from the Talon Wars—the shield Wyan One-Hand had strapped to his crippled arm during battle, and other similar items.

"So?" Theron tipped the powder into an empty serving bowl beside the scale, then took up the quill and made a note in the ledger. "What are we running low on?"

"Honesty," Lorelei said, "integrity, the least amount of respect for the dead."

Theron lifted his gaze and glared at Lorelei and Creed. Then he lunged for the loaded crossbow. Creed leapt toward him, grabbed Theron's wrist, pressed a stiletto to Theron's throat. "Let's keep this friendly." When Theron didn't let go, Creed pressed the stiletto up and into Theron's chin, forcing his head back. "I'm asking nicely, Chamberlain."

Theron dropped the crossbow and raised his free hand. "I don't know what you think you're doing, but it won't go well for you."

"Oh, I don't know"—Lorelei took off her mask, set it on the sarcophagus, and picked up the ledger—"it seems to be paying handsomely already."

Creed took off his mask as well, then picked up the crossbow, backed away, and leaned against the crypt wall.

"You'll burn for this, Lorelei." Theron spat. "If you even get out of here alive." They heard armor clanking outside the entrance to the crypt "You see? Now put down that crossbow and give me the ledger. It'll go easier on you if you do."

"We'll take our chances," Lorelei said.

Theron opened his mouth to say something more, but stopped when four palace guards in shining dragonscale armor filed into the room, swords in hands. "Put down the crossbow," one of them barked at Creed, "now!"

Creed slowly uncocked the crossbow and set it on the floor. Theron dashed behind the guards.

"Kick it to me," the guard said. "The knife, too."

Creed slid the crossbow across the floor with the toe of his boot, then tossed the stiletto after it.

The guard picked up both weapons, then called over his shoulder. "It's safe, Domina."

Tyrinia entered the crypt and flicked her fingers at Lorelei. "The ledger."

"I'm afraid not. It's evidence of crimes against the empire."

Tyrinia laughed. "I hardly think a party qualifies as a crime against the empire."

Lorelei gestured to the crates. "Do you have any idea how long quarry sentences are for possession of this much umbral contraband?"

"What makes you think you'll ever get it to trial?"

"If I didn't know better," Skylar said, in the doorway to the crypt, "I'd call that a threat."

Tyrinia spun around. "Skylar!"

"Yes, mother."

"This little stunt is *your* doing?"

"It is."

"And just what do you think you'll gain by pulling it? Leniency for Lorelei and the thief from Glaeyand? Freedom for Lorelei's mother?"

Skylar stepped into the crypt, staring at Theron and the four guardsmen. "Do you really want to have this conversation in front of everyone?"

Tyrinia continued to glare at her. "You mean these witnesses to your attempted theft and"—she waved to the ledger in Lorelei's hands—"extortion?"

Skylar smiled. "Will you say the same if we talk about where all this contraband came from? Or the man who allowed it to pass through the Holt unchecked?"

Tyrinia clenched her teeth. "Leave us."

Theron waved toward the doorway. "You heard the Domina."

"You as well, Theron."

"Your Highness—"

"*Out*, Theron!"

Theron paused, then bowed and departed, leaving Tyrinia alone in the crypt with Skylar, Lorelei, and Creed.

When the sound of their footsteps had faded, Tyrinia turned on Skylar. "Let's get this little temper tantrum over with, shall we? What do you want?"

"What I *want* is for you to listen to what we have to say. We have evidence that Ancris is in grave danger."

"Grave danger, is it?" Deep lines gathered along Tyrinia's lips as she pinched them tight. "How convenient that you found this *evidence* only after Lorelei's mother was taken into custody. Perhaps I should have done it sooner."

"For the good of the empire," Skylar said, "I *beg* you to listen. Ash has been hurt."

Tyrinia pointed a finger at Lorelei. "Because of her?"

"He was doing an experiment to prove that the peat Lorelei found would react with the quartzite from the shrine."

Tyrinia rolled her eyes dramatically. "Alra's bright smile, *another* sin added to the pile."

Skylar continued as if her mother hadn't spoken. "He did it because he sensed something dangerous was happening. And he proved that the shrine is the target of a conspiracy, that the Red Knives, the Hissing Man, and even Azariah are trying to awaken Strages."

Tyrinia stared at her daughter, eyes wide. Then she laughed. "Azariah?"

"Yes," Skylar replied.

"That's preposterous."

"Not if you know what we know. All I'm asking you for is the time to prove it."

"Time to manufacture more evidence, you mean."

"No. We want leave to go to the Holt and find the peat's source. We believe—"

"Enough!" Tyrinia roared. "I won't hear another word of this nonsense."

"You will, mother"—Skylar waved to the crates and sacks of drugs—"or I'll tell father about all of this. I'll tell him the Imperator is helping you arrange to get all this stuff."

"Lucran can speak to Marstan all he wishes. His story will be the same as mine, that neither of us made any sort of *arrangement*. And he will say that because it's the truth."

"And the fete?"

"An indiscretion. I'll tell Lucran it won't happen again, should he ever learn of it, but he won't, Skylar."

"He won't?"

"No, because if you tell him, I'll see that Lorelei is chained to the Anvil and treated in the same manner as that filthy darkling, the self-proclaimed King of the Wood. And when the flames die and the Anvil cools, I'll make Adelia gather her bones, then send her to the slave quarries for the offense of having mothered such a traitor. Press me, Skylar, and I'll see to it that Bothymus is put down as well, and that you're forced to watch it."

"Father won't allow it." Skylar fumed. "He won't allow any of it."

Tyrinia scoffed. "Your father has been wrapped around my little finger since Ransom died. What makes you think that's going to change now?"

Footfalls pattered beyond the dimly lit archway at the back of the crypt. All eyes turned toward it as Quintarch Lucran stepped from the shadows. Two praetorian guards holding crossbows appeared behind him. Lucran gazed at the stacks of boxes and crates, the piles of sacks, and rubbed his hand over his head.

Lorelei stepped aside, but he did no more than glance sidelong at her as he walked toward the sarcophagus. "How *dare* you invoke Ransom's name. How *dare* you conduct this sort of business"—he touched the lid of the sarcophagus, just beside the measuring scale—"here."

"I—" Tyrinia stopped and stared at the floor.

Lucran picked up the serving bowl, still filled with an uncia of rapture, raised it to his nose and sniffed. "Our son *died* from this."

Tyrinia's cheeks flushed. "Lucran, it's but a small gathering."

"Yes, well"—he set the bowl down—"we shall see, in the end, precisely how small."

Tyrinia glared at him. "What is that supposed to mean?"

"It means the praetorian guard are arresting everyone in the catacombs. I'll see them all charged, Tyrinia."

Tyrinia stepped closer to him and lowered her voice. "There are *magistrates* out there. *Senators* from all five capitals. You cannot give them over to the inquisitors."

"I'm not giving them to the inquisitors. Their crimes are sins of the heart and soul. The Church will try them. Only through Alra's grace can they find true forgiveness. Is it not so?"

"Lucran, you cannot. I forbid it."

Lucran looked like he might laugh, but he just shook his head. "You'll forbid nothing. I strip the title of Domina from you. Return to the palace. Now."

"Lucran—"

Lucran extended a hand behind him at the two guards. They stepped around him and one gripped Tyrinia's arm. Tyrinia ripped it away and rushed Lucran, but the other guardsman grabbed her and dragged her from the crypt. The other praetorian stood there, crossbow aimed at Theron.

"Lucran, you can't do this!" Tyrinia called from the cavern. "Lucran!"

Theron and the four guards went peaceably. Lorelei, Creed, and Skylar remained in the crypt with Lucran.

"Now," Lucran said evenly, "Inquisitor Lorelei, tell me about this plot."

SEVENTY-EIGHT: RYLAN

Rylan was dead tired by the time he stumbled through the back door of The Bent Tulip and headed up to Eladora's flat. He hadn't slept properly in days. To his surprise and great relief, Ash was awake, his head propped up on pillows.

"You're back!" Ash said.

"You're awake!"

"And thank Alra's unending grace for that." Ash paused. "You look exhausted, if you don't mind my saying." He looked at Rylan's forearm. "And you're bleeding."

Rylan stared down at the cut Blythe had given him. "The bleeding's stopped"— he dropped into a chair next to the side table—"but you're right about the exhaustion. I swear, I could sleep standing up."

"I don't doubt it. But *please* tell me what's been going on first. Eladora won't tell me anything."

"Well, you did blow up her storeroom."

Ash rolled his eyes toward the ceiling. "Yes. I really cocked that one up."

"It helped us, though."

"It did?"

"Yes, your journal and the evidence Lorelei found . . . it's amazing how much she can put together so quickly."

Ash smiled. "She's a marvel, that one."

"She is at that."

Rylan wasn't sure just how much Lorelei or Skylar would want him to share, but he did his best to catch Ash up on his visit with Blythe.

"And the crucible?" Ash asked. "Did she tell you where it is?"

"Not as such—I think she felt she'd be betraying the Red Knives—but she hinted at it. Several weeks go, I was flying toward the Rookery, and Vedron kept tugging at her reins, trying to fly toward something that caught her attention. It was the crucible. I'm sure of it."

"You were flying toward the Rookery?"

Rylan nodded and made a shooing motion. "A story for another day."

"Does Lucran know? About the crucible, I mean."

"Not yet. I just got back." Rylan tried and failed to stifle a yawn. He was so bloody tired his eyes itched. "Lorelei and Skylar are off trying to convince him to help us. I take it you haven't heard from them?"

"They were gone when I woke." He groaned and swung his legs off the bed.

"Ash, don't! You need rest."

He gripped the headboard to steady himself, and shook his head. "I'm too hungry to rest."

"I can get you food from downstairs."

"My back aches from lying in bed for so long. And you look like you're about to fall over." He gestured to the bed. "We've a long day ahead, I suspect. Lie down, sleep while you can."

Rylan couldn't refuse. "Thank you."

He pulled off his boots and lay down as Ash limped out of the tiny bedroom. He heard the clank of plates, the clink of silverware, but it felt dreamlike, and soon he was asleep.

He woke what felt like moments later to Lorelei shaking his shoulder. "Rylan, we need to go!"

"Go where?" he said in a scratchy, tired voice.

"To Glaeyand."

He got up and stared out the window. It was dark out. Reckoning was still some time away. "Where's Ash?"

"Waiting in the coach."

Rylan suddenly remembered what Skylar had said about Lorelei's mother. "Is your mother safe?"

"Yes." Lorelei smiled briefly. "She's back home. I dropped her off before I came here." Before Rylan could say more, she held up a hand. "I'll explain the rest on the way."

Outside the Tulip was a royal coach. Several late-night patrons stood gawking at it. Rylan climbed in beside Ash, and Lorelei followed, closing the door behind her. "A lot's happened," she said as the coach eased into motion. She told them about her visit to the Curia Ancrata, about the catacombs and how Skylar showed Quintarch Lucran everything Tyrinia had been doing in his name. "I told him everything we know about the palisade and the crucible. He's ready to help, but he wants proof before he moves against Azariah. We're headed to the Holt to get it for him."

"*We* are?" Rylan asked.

"Yes. Ash says you know where the crucible is."

"I *think* I do, but it's far into the Holt. It'll take time to get there."

"Lucran is aware."

"It'll be dangerous. I don't know how many Knives will be there."

"There's no way around it. Lucran needs proof. And it may not take as long as you think. The council of quintarchs is today. Lucran is joining us as far as Glaeyand. We're to continue on to the crucible while he speaks with your father."

"My father . . ."

"Yes. Lucran is furious with him."

"Why?"

"Because Marstan didn't merely look away as drugs were funneled through the Holt to Ancris. He helped broker the deal with Aarik."

Rylan was stunned. "My father?"

"Apparently so." Lorelei seemed to study him. "Do you have any idea why?"

"To gain favor with Tyrinia, of course—" Suddenly, it struck Rylan. "In all likelihood, the deal was made years ago."

"It was," Lorelei said. "So?"

"Lucran's campaign in Syrdia had been raging for years. My father had every reason to believe it would continue. He likely bet that Tyrinia would be sent to vote in Lucran's place, or, failing that, that she'd sway Lucran to vote for the deal he and Aarik had been working on." Rylan was gutted that peace was likely a lost cause, but he had no time to worry over it just then. "What sort of proof does the quintarch need?"

"The crucible's precise location and evidence that it's building a store of umbra."

"And he'll accept that evidence from *us*?"

"It won't be just the two of us. Creed is coming, and we'll have a fourth." She turned to Ash. "Lucran wants an alchemyst to bear witness as well."

Ash stared at her as the coach rounded Henge Hill toward Palace Road. "Is that a question, Lorelei Aurelius?"

"I suppose it is. I want someone I trust, but you've been hurt—"

Ash laughed. "Of course I'll come, you bloody stupid auroch."

Lorelei raised her hands defensively. "I didn't want to presume."

Ash leaned forward and kissed her cheek. "And I love you for it, but I wouldn't dream of missing it."

Lorelei squeezed his knee. "Thank you."

"Where would you be without me, anyway?" Ash asked with a smile. "I broke this case wide open!"

"And blew yourself up in the process."

"Well, yes, there is that. Lesson learned."

"I bloody well *hope* so."

At the palace entrance, Ash and Lorelei stepped down from the cabin and were met by two praetorian guards. When Rylan stepped down to the gravel, one of the guardsmen grabbed him by the throat and slammed him against the side of the coach.

"Hey!" Lorelei tried to get between them but the centurion's comrade blocked her with an outstretched arm. "Leave him alone!"

The man holding Rylan, much to Rylan's dismay, was the same centurion he'd used fog packets on to escape from the abbey. The man's eyes were afire. He shoved Rylan again. "The quintarch might have forgiven you, but *I* haven't."

Rylan was finding it rather difficult to breathe. "Forgiven or not," he croaked, "I'm very sorry about that."

The centurion pressed his face closer to Rylan's. "Pull a stunt like that again, and I'll slit your bloody throat."

"Seems fair enough," Rylan wheezed.

He pulled Rylan away from the coach shoved him away. As Rylan massaged the lump on the back of his head, the centurion pointed toward the rear of the palace. "The quintarch awaits."

When Rylan, Lorelei, and Ash began walking across the lawn, the guardsmen followed a few paces behind them.

Lorelei leaned close to Rylan. "You all right?"

Rylan stifled the urge to rub his neck. He didn't want to give the centurion the satisfaction. "I'm fine."

They rounded the palace in silence, headed through the rear gate, and followed the path toward the eyrie. Rylan was paying so much attention to the two guardsmen that, at first, he barely noticed the five talons being readied near the eyrie—a full wing, twenty-five in all, plus three more to carry Lucran, Rylan, Lorelei, Creed, and Ash. The dragons were largely a mixture of golds, bronzes, and brasses. There were also three massive irons, and Rylan spotted Bothymus on the far side, near Andrilor, Lucran's magnificent gold. Creed stood holding the reins of Ruko, the swift silver vixen that had borne Rylan from Glaeyand.

Stromm wove among the dragons, directing his eyrie hands, making sure everything was ready. A column of dracorae in brightsteel armor filed along the road from the barracks. Rylan spotted Quintarch Lucran speaking with Praefectus Damika. Lucran handed her a scroll, clapped her shoulder, and headed toward Rylan, Lorelei, and Ash. As he neared them, he nodded to the praetorians behind Rylan, and both men departed.

Rylan had faced quintarchs before and hardly flinched, but he'd been an imperator's son then, albeit a bastard, and a dragon singer. He'd had the veneer of respectability. Now he'd been exposed as a thief and a liar; he dreaded meeting the quintarch again.

Lucran nodded peremptorily at Lorelei and Ash and then faced Rylan. "Inquisitor Lorelei has vouched for you. My daughter has come to trust you as well. Tell me, Rylan Holbrooke, is their trust misplaced?"

"No, Your Majesty."

Lucran stared hard at him for a long moment. "Good, because I'm relying on you. There's much at stake."

"And I'm here to help, however I can."

Lucran backed away and addressed all three of them."Then prepare yourselves. We leave shortly." He headed toward the dragons. His gold, Andrilor, tilted his head back and roared.

Quintarch Lucran flew first. Rylan and Lorelei followed on Bothymus, then Ash and Creed on Ruko. The draconic wing flew behind them in standard formation: five across, five deep.

Reckoning came and went, and a cool wind gave way to a warm breeze. In the early morning light, the forest canopy undulated like a lumpy carpet. The farther they flew, the more Rylan realized how much danger his father was in.

"You're quiet," Lorelei said over her shoulder.

"Now that we're headed back, I'm worried about the consequences for my father."

"You are?"

"I am, yes. Lucran is angry about the deals he made with Aarik and Tyrinia."

"Lucran isn't just angry. He's furious."

"Exactly. He won't be satisfied even if Marstan loses the imperatorship. He'll want to punish him. He might even demand he stand trial before the Church."

"And you care?"

"I'm not saying my father is a great leader, or even a good father. But he was trying to do the right thing with Aarik."

"I'm inclined to agree, but Marstan made a grave misstep when he worked to funnel drugs to Tyrinia."

"I know. It's just . . . I don't want to give up on their dream just yet."

"Me either, but what is there to do about it?"

"I don't know," Rylan said, but it was a lie.

He had a card to play, a powerful one, but he needed to play it in the presence of all five quintarchs, not just Lucran. The plan was simple enough: he would tell them the truth about Marstan's plans with Aarik. Marstan would try to stop him, but Lucran was the bigger problem. He wouldn't let Rylan speak to the quintarchs if he thought it would benefit Marstan. Rylan could lie to get an audience, but if Lucran found out, he would use that against him, cast him as a liar feigning to tell the truth.

No, he needed to find a way to make Lucran assume the worst.

He spotted the gaping hole in the canopy that marked Glaeyand's eyrie. Behind him, a dracora blew three long notes on a dragon horn. A few moments later, a horn blew from the eyrie, giving them permission to land. They swooped down and found more than half the nests occupied. The other quintarchs and their entourages had already arrived, leaving little room for Lucran's cohort.

In the end, there were just enough perches. Most of the dragons settled in the topmost nests. Andrilor, Bothymus, and Ruko landed on three lower nests. Lucran dismounted and headed to the triangular staging deck. The volarch of the draconic wing and his four talon commanders followed. Rylan, Lorelei, Creed, and Ash came last.

Marstan was there to receive Quintarch Lucran, as were Willow and Andros behind him. Marstan and Willow seemed to be ignoring the newly arrived dragons, but Andros kept glancing up at them. The stiffness of their postures and their forced smiles spoke of nervousness, and little wonder. The patricians' vote for the Imperator's seat would be held in a few hours. The council of quintarchs would convene immediately afterward to hold their vote of confidence. Now Lucran had come with a show of force.

"Be welcomed," Marstan said with a bow.

Lucran merely stared. "To the council," he said tersely. His fury would no doubt be burning brightly now that he and Marstan were face to face, but Lucran was a private man. He'd wait until they were behind closed doors to tell the other quintarchs about Marstan's transgressions.

Marstan paused, perhaps waiting for more. When Lucran said nothing, he bowed and gestured to a bridge between the citadels. "Of course."

Seeing his window of opportunity rapidly closing, Rylan stepped forward. "Pardon me, Your Majesty, but I wonder if I might address the council."

Marstan's face went stony. Willow looked shocked. Andros looked angry and put his hand on his sword hilt.

Before any of them could speak, Lucran said, "The journey to the Deepwood Fens isn't a short one."

"This won't take long, Your Majesty, and the dragons need a bit of rest anyway."

"If it's quick, tell me now."

Rylan lowered his voice. "It's about the Red Knives and the King of the Wood." He tilted his head toward the people watching them from the bridgeboughs and landings. "It might be best to talk behind closed doors."

Rylan had never seen his father look so nervous. No doubt he was regretting having admitted anything to Rylan.

Lucran looked at Marstan, then back at Rylan. Lorelei, Creed, and Ash exchanged nervous glances. Even the volarch and his commanders seemed confused.

"The quintarchs' agenda is quite full, Rylan," Marstan said.

"Yes." Willow floated to Rylan's side. "Let's you and I chat, brother." She tried to lead him away. "I can bring your concerns to the council later."

When Rylan refused to be led away, Andros stepped toward him, but stopped when Lucran spoke.

"You may address the council," the quintarch said. He strode toward the suspended bridge but stopped just short of it and turned to Marstan, who hadn't moved. "Will you be joining us, Imperator?"

Marstan stared at Rylan, then walked stiffly toward Quintarch Lucran. Willow joined him. Andros did not. After the others had departed the staging deck, he rounded on Rylan and poked him in the chest. "What do you think you're doing?"

Rylan shrugged. "Quintarchs' ears only, I'm afraid."

Andros bared his teeth. "Answer me, Rylan." When Rylan didn't, he grabbed Rylan's shirt collar and shook him. "Answer me!"

The tip of Creed's rapier poked up under Andros's chin. "I'd let him go if I were you."

When Andros didn't, Creed pressed the sword's point deeper. A drip of blood coursed the shining blade.

Andros pushed Rylan away and touched his neck. "You'll pay for that, inquisitor."

"One day, perhaps." Creed wiped the tip of the blade on Andros's trousers. "Get out of here."

Andros glared at him, then marched away.

Lorelei watched him go, then asked Rylan, "Are you trying to bury him?"

"No, Lorelei. I'm trying to save him."

SEVENTY-NINE: RHIANNON

Rhiannon watched as Llorn and Blythe prepared to fight. She felt like she should be more shocked, but the Red Knives were a brutal lot. And if Llorn really had killed Aarik, this was bound to happen sooner or later. She was more disturbed by her mother who, since the moment Llorn accepted Blythe's challenge, had watched things unfold with a smile on her face. Morraine, like everyone else standing around the vyrd, knew how it would end. It wouldn't only be Llorn or Blythe who died; the loser's dragon would be put to death as well.

Velox lumbered toward Blythe, and his green scales darkened. He spread his wings, lowered his chest to the ground, snaked his head toward Fraoch and hissed. Blythe climbed into her saddle and grabbed the shield hanging from Velox's left side. After slipping her arm through the shield's straps, she took up the reins and grabbed a spear with her right hand, and Velox spread his wings, launched himself skyward, and flew toward the canopy.

Fraoch watched Velox ascend, then he crouched next to Llorn. Llorn mounted and took up a similar shield and spear. Ircundus, Brother Mayhew's burly onyx, crept forward as if he too wanted to fly, but Brother Mayhew whistled a trilling note, and Ircundus slunk back.

Spear and shield, bow and arrow, sword or dagger—all manner of weapons could be used during the trial. Dragons, on the other hand, could use talon, tooth, and tail, but the use of their breath was forbidden.

Rhiannon looked up to Morraine beside her. "Can't you stop this?"

"It isn't my *business* to stop, nor is it yours."

"But why do they have to fight?"

Morraine stared down at her. "When are you going to learn that some things cannot be solved through words?"

"I know that," Rhiannon said, "but they could at least try." She pointed at Fraoch on a bridgebough high above them. "You could make Llorn see reason. He's your brother."

"Blythe left Ancris on a fool's errand. She abandoned her post to confront the king. She deserves what she gets."

When Rhiannon was young, Mother Constance had told her about how brave her mother was, how much she cared for and protected the Kin. The woman Rhiannon had cobbled together from those stories was akin to a goddess, a sister to Alra herself. She was nothing like the cruel woman who stood next to her. Faedryn had surely kissed her in the grave.

High overhead, Velox roared and dove. Fraoch launched from her bridgebough with a *whoomp*. The dragons streaked past each other. Fraoch raked Velox's neck with her wing talons. Streaks of blood appeared on his green scales. It looked like Fraoch had escaped unharmed, but as both dragons swept up and grabbed onto two different citadel trees, Rhiannon saw blood running down Fraoch's glacier-blue belly.

Both dragons swooped down from the trees, spread their wings, and arced toward each other. Blythe cried out and threw her spear into Fraoch's right wing. It caught like a porcupine quill. The dragon screeched and tumbled through the air. Llorn was nearly thrown from the saddle, but Fraoch spread her wings and grasped a stout branch. Llorn grabbed the spear in Fraoch's wing and yanked it out. Fraoch roared.

Velox swung around a tree and winged hard toward Fraoch, but Fraoch pushed off from the tree, shrilled, flew unsteadily through the trees, and swung back around. As the two dragons neared for a third pass, Llorn flung Blythe's spear at her, but it clattered off a citadel next to her. Then he threw his own spear straight at Blythe's chest. She blocked it with her shield, but the spearhead pierced the metal. She screamed and let go of the shield, and both spear and shield toppled to the ground.

Fraoch lashed her barbed, blue tail at Velox. One barb stuck into the viridian's shoulder. Two more punched into Blythe's chest.

Both dragons swung around again and flew head on. Rhiannon thought they'd surely crash into each other, but both rose up and tangled with talons. One of the leather straps on Blythe's saddle, perhaps weakened by Fraoch tail, snapped, and the saddle slipped down along Velox's chest. Blythe held tight to the saddle horn, but Velox's beating wings caused the saddle to slide farther down the dragon's side and the harness to catch his left wing.

Rhiannon thought surely Blythe was about to plummet to the ground. Blythe must have realize it, too. She whistled two sharp notes, and Velox dipped his head and snaked his body downward. Blythe, holding tight to the slipping saddle, wedged her boots into the spikes along Velox's rump. As Velox tilted, she drew her fighting knife and launched herself through the air at Fraoch and Llorn.

Llorn raised his shield just in time, and Blythe crashed into him with a metallic clang. Her knife spun glinting toward the ground.

Fraoch's wing began to bleed heavily. She circled down and landed hard on her wounded wing. Blythe tumbled away and lay there for several seconds, then got up and faced Llorn. She drew her rapier, but as Llorn climbed down from the saddle, she stared down at the two black barbs sticking out of her chest, just below her collar bone. With her free hand, she ripped the poisoned barbs out and threw them to the ground.

Llorn drew his sword and stomped toward her. "You should've stayed in Ancris."

Blythe fell to her knees and stared up at him with a blank expression. "I . . ." Blythe stared at the rapier in her hand, then Llorn, then blinked hard. "I . . ."

Velox landed a few paces behind Blythe. He clawed furiously at the ground with his wing talons. Snapped his teeth at the air and swung his head madly.

Llorn eyed Velox. When Velox didn't charge him, he walked over to Blythe.

"Please," Rhiannon cried, "can't you let her go?"

Llorn glanced at her, then raised his sword.

Rhiannon lurched toward them, but Morraine snatched the collar of Rhiannon's robe and yanked her back. "Quiet, child!"

"Let her go!" Rhiannon screamed.

Rhiannon couldn't tell if Llorn was disappointed in her or merely surprised at her outburst. "It's the way of the wood, girl. The sooner you learn it, the better."

Beside Rhiannon, Morraine was looking on eagerly. Rhiannon wondered if she would consume Blythe's soul, maybe Velox's, too.

Rhiannon was about to scream again, but a white arrow blurred down in from above and sunk into Llorn's right shoulder. Llorn spun away, grunting, and looked up into the trees.

Another white arrow streaked down and stuck into Brother Mayhew's leg. Then another caught a dracora in the chest.

"The vyrd!" Llorn bellowed. "Run!"

As they tromped up the hill toward the vyrd, two more dragonriders howled and fell, one with an arrow jutting from his neck. Rhiannon couldn't see where the other had been hit. Then one of the auburn dragons roared behind her, and she turned to look. An ivory dragon that seemed to appear out of nowhere had its teeth clamped on the auburn's neck. Ivories never appeared outside the veil. They were bred and trained in Gonsalond by Yeriel's wardens, and were reserved for her personal guard, the warrior women known as the Seven.

Rhiannon ran up the slope to the vyrd and hid behind one of the stones. A woman was kneeling on the thick, broken branch of a citadel just down the hill. She wore a green cloak that blended with the bark and the canopy. She had blond hair and scars across her forehead and cheeks. Then another woman in green leaned out from behind the trunk of a citadel. And another jumped down from a branch.

Another ivory dragon appeared high above the vyrd. It streaked down, landed hard on Maladox's nasty onyx, and blew a white fog on the dragon's head. Frost coated the onyx's head, and there was a crackling sound, like ice breaking. The onyx writhed, its wings raking the forest undergrowth, then it ceased its struggles and lay still. The ivory dragon shrieked so loud Rhiannon had to block her ears, then it launched itself into the air.

"No!" War axe in hand, Maladox lumbered toward his dragon.

A dragonrider named Gwilyn with rare ruby eyes and copper hair dragged Brother Mayhew into the vyrd and sat him against a standing stone. Blood was dripping from his thigh. Morraine climbed up after them.

"Use the vyrd," Morraine said.

Rhiannon was staring at Brother Mayhew. He was clutching his leg with both hands. He turned to look at her and hook his head.

"Rhiannon!" Morraine shouted again. "Use the gods-damned vyrd!"

Rhiannon backed away. "I don't know how."

Brother Mayhew sucked air and said, "I've seen you stand at the very edge of the maze a dozen times! Step into it!"

Rhiannon stare at the moss-covered stones. "But where will we go?"

"It doesn't matter!" Morraine screamed. "Just go, fool girl."

Two of Llorn's dragonriders flew over the vyrd, chased by cloaked wardens on swift ivories. Gwilyn's auburn dragon and Fraoch entered the vyrd. Arrows clattered against the stones, their steel heads sparking.

Rhiannon tried to calm herself and concentrate on the vyrd, but it was impossible.

Halfway down the slope, Blythe lay her head back, staring at the sky, mouthing something Rhiannon couldn't hear. Velox slumped next to her, staring at the ivory dragons and the women in the trees. Then he got up, clamped his jaws around Blythe, lifted her into the air, and flew away.

Rhiannon thought about Irik, how much she missed him, and she wanted to cry. Then she closed her eyes and allowed her awareness to spread to the citadels around the vyrd, then to their roots winding deep into the earth. Like a glittering web, the maze and its many tendrils became known to her. Where various threads met were bright points, the vyrda, doors through which she could travel to other parts of the forest. The maze seemed to beckon to her; all she need do is enter.

Down among the trees, Brother Mayhew's onyx, Ircundus, roared. At the foot of slope, the scarred blond woman raised her bow, and aimed her arrow at Rhiannon, and loosed the string.

As the arrow sped toward her, Rhiannon stepped into the maze.

EIGHTY: RYLAN

Rylan sat alone in the anteroom of Valdavyn's audience chamber, listening to the murmur of conversation coming through doors to the adjacent room. It had been going on for some time. Lucran had done most of the talking, but Marstan's voice had risen up several times.

Eventually the doors swung open, and Willow appeared. "The quintarchs will see you."

Willow headed back to her seat beside Marstan, and Rylan entered the audience chamber and closed the doors behind him. The dais at the far end of the room had been reconfigured for the council. In place of Marstan's throne was a curving table with five high-backed chairs in which the empire's quintarchs, three men and two women in full regalia, were sitting. Marstan and Willow, sitting on the left side of the room, looked like supplicants waiting for their grievance to be heard.

Drynon Osongeli, a tall man with olive skin, aquiline nose, long black hair, and a curling scowl, sat in the rightmost seat. Quintarch Zabrienne of Caldoras sat to his left. Though well beyond her fiftieth year, she'd aged well, and the resemblance to her daughter Resada, who Rylan had met at the Alevada estate, was striking. Lucran, in the center seat, studied Rylan's approach, but more than once glanced Marstan's way. Next to Lucran was Marle Erenhardt of Olencia, who wore a golden crown over his slate-gray hair and had think pink scars over his ruined left eye. And in the last chair was Yarina Allesandro, the lone quintarch Rylan had never seen before. She looked to be thirty, and had long black hair held in check with a garnet-studded circlet. Her steely gaze, coupled with her straight back and erect head, gave the air of an impatient school mistress.

Rylan strode up to the dais and bowed. "Your Majesties."

Drynon gestured to his fellow quintarchs. "Lucran has told us what happened in Ancris as he understands it. We know about the crucible. We know about the palisade as well, and the threat it poses should the Red Knives unleash its power."

Lucran crossed his arms over his chest. "I've also shared your suspicions that Illustra Azariah is involved and that I've authorized you to travel to the Deepwood to find the crucible. Time is of the utmost importance, but you requested an audience. Given all you've done, here you are."

"And I thank you for it. I thought it important that you know the truth about how we got into the mess, but before we come to that, I beg your indulgence as I ask a few questions." He turned to Lucran. "Have you told the other quintarchs that my father helped the Red Knives ship rapture and other illicit drugs to Ancris?"

"I have."

"Have you also told them who the drugs were for?"

At this, Lucran stiffened. "That seems of little import."

"It's important if you want to understand what motivated my father—"

"Get to your point," Lucran growled.

"I can't without the proper context."

Zabrienne's gold and diamond headdress jingled as she turned from Rylan to Lucran. "I'd like to hear this."

"As would I," said Drynon.

Marstan looked bored, but raised his eyebrows, twisting the scars over his bad eye, and nodded.

Lucran gave them a withering look, paused and said, "The drug shipments were for my wife."

Marle, Zabrienne, Drynon seemed unfazed, making Rylan wonder if they'd been guests at one of Tyrinia's fetes. Yarina seemed completely caught off guard. She was a staunch teetotaler, and seemed not only surprised but offended. Her eyebrows arched and she sniffed noisily.

Rylan bowed to Lucran, then turned to Zabrienne. "I'm also aware my father performed a number of favors for you, among them my trip to help the dowager, Soraya Alevada, with her ailing dragon Rugio."

Zabrienne nodded. "So?"

Rylan looked at the other three quintarchs. "Is it safe for me to assume he's been currying favor with the rest of you?"

Marle shrugged and said, "The Imperator needs our votes. He always *curries favor* with us. What of it?"

"My father wanted more than his seat this time. He wanted an amendment—"

"Rylan," Marstan said, with a brisk shake of his head.

Drynon scowled. "You were asked to remain silent, Imperator. Rylan, what sort of amendment?"

"He and Aarik Bloodhaven—"

Marstan jumped to his feet. "Rylan, don't you—"

Lucran pounded the table. "Silence!"

Marstan glared at him

"Sit," Lucran spat.

Marstan lowered himself slowly back into his chair.

Lucran nodded to Rylan. "Continue."

"My father and the King of the Wood were trying to negotiate a lasting peace in the Holt."

Drynon raised a bent finger. "And how do you know this?"

"Aarik told me before he flew to Ancris to meet with the Hissing Man."

Marle sneered and spoke in a ruined croak of a voice. "Do you expect us to believe Aarik wasn't involved in the building of the crucible? That he wasn't involved in Llorn's conspiracy with the Hissing Man?"

"I do. Aarik is dead because Llorn hated the idea of peace with the empire. More importantly, Llorn knew Aarik would stop them from using the crucible. So he arranged for Aarik's death at the hands of the Church, leaving himself above suspicion."

Yarina said softly, "I've heard rumor that you and your father are not on good terms. I have to wonder, why you are telling us all this?"

"I'm telling you because I'm tired of the strife and the bloodshed. Since the Talon Wars, we've been living with the constant threat of violence. My father saw peace would only be possible if he gave the Holt more independence. That was the future they were working toward, and I believe the amendment could have worked. Could *still* work."

Lucran laughed. "Are you actually asking us to consider it?"

Rylan looked at Lucran straight-faced. "What my father did, he did for honorable reasons and in the best interests of the empire *and* the Holt."

Drynon threw his head back and burst into laughter. "I swear to you all, I thought he came here to burn his father's house down, but he actually wants his father to retain his seat!"

The wrinkles around Zabrienne's eyes deepened. "Does Drynon have the right of it?"

"He does," Rylan said. "There was no hiding what my father was doing. You were going to find out soon enough, but you needed to hear all of it to make sense of it."

"It's a dangerous game you play," Zabrienne continued. "You could be brought before a magistrate for treason and be burned at the Anvil."

"I'm aware, but to weigh my father's actions without his intent would be a dishonor to him, to you, and to the Holt. If my father is chosen by the patricians today, I beg you to ratify their choice. I beg you to listen to my father and the provisions of the amendment. If enacted, in whole or in part, we might finally have peace."

Lucran seemed displeased with Rylan, but not nearly as much as Rylan thought he would be. "Are you done?"

"Yes," Rylan said.

"Then go find the crucible before it's too late. Succeed, and you may very well affect our attitudes toward your father and your appeal."

Rylan was relieved he'd said what he came to say, but he was still worried about Marstan. He bowed, and when he turned to leave, his father didn't so much as look at him. Willow stared at him but said nothing. Rylan wished he had time to talk to them, but he didn't know what'd he'd say, or if they'd even listen. He left the room, closed the doors behind him, and rushed through Valdavyn toward the front doors.

He thought he'd have to walk to the eyrie, but when he reached the entrance deck, Lorelei was already there on Bothymus, and Creed and Ash on silvery Ruko. He jumped up on the saddle behind Lorelei, and the dragons flew up toward the canopy.

EIGHTY-ONE: RHIANNON

Rhiannon found herself standing in a place that beggared description. It was a vyrd, but the stones were pure white. Ahead of her, beyond the menhirs, was a footpath and a burbling waterfall that fed a pool. All of it was white. The vyrd and the pool were surrounded by citadels, but they were dead, ashen, like the leavings of a flash fire. The sky was granite gray with stars that shone like diamonds. The air smelled of jasmine.

"Who are you?" called a voice behind her.

Rhiannon spun around. Beside a broken standing stone stood a woman with pale skin. Her eyes were lilac, as were her lips. Her black hair, long and thick, writhed like snakes. Rhiannon had never seen this woman before, but she had a feeling like she knew her. "You're . . . Yeriel."

"And you're but a child," Yeriel said, stepping into the vyrd.

Rhiannon had no idea what to say to that, so she pressed her lips tight. Yeriel walked a circle around her.

"You couldn't have pierced the veil alone," Yeriel continued, hair writhing, "so who helped you?"

"Please, my lady. I mean you no harm. I only wish to leave."

"You mean me no harm"—Yeriel smiled, teeth like polished ivory—"and yet you waited for my wardens to slip through the veil before you pierced it. You searched for me . . . Why?"

Morraine had been right about the shard—Yeriel was all but blind to it or she likely would have been more angry than curious.

"I wanted to know more about the veil. About Gonsalond. I had no ill intent."

"You wanted to know more about Gonsalond?"

"And you," Rhiannon replied. "I've heard many stories about you. Surely there's some truth to them, but there must be lies as well, or truths twisted by time. I wanted to see you, but I overstepped my bounds. And for that you have my sincerest apologies." She didn't feel good about lying, but she had no choice. She wanted to get out of this place as soon as possible.

Yeriel replied in a singsong voice, "Were I to pin your limbs to the ground and draw out your entrails, would you tell me the same story?"

Rhiannon's pulse quickened. "Of course, my lady."

As she had in the vyrd after the sudden, intense battle, Rhiannon sensed the maze. She was still *inside* of it, she realized. As was Yeriel. They were in an in-between place, a place that existed everywhere in the forest and, at the same time, nowhere.

"Well, well, well," Yeriel cooed, "if it isn't a true child of the Holt who stands before me." She paused and stared at Rhiannon a moment. "You don't even know it, do you?"

Rhiannon had no idea what to say to that; she just wanted to run.

Yeriel's pupils glowed like Morraine's. "Where are you taking them, child?"

"To Ancris." She realized she'd answered without thinking, but it seemed harmless to tell her that much.

"And *why* are you taking them there?"

"To complete the bridge."

Yeriel frowned. Her hair writhed. "What bridge?"

"The one that will link the crucible to the palisade and trigger them both." Rhiannon had no idea why she was telling Yeriel so much, but she suddenly noticed that the world around her was gaining color. The grass had turned mint green, the water in the pool a faint shade of brown. The sky was now the milky blue of a winter sapphire.

"Tell me, child," Yeriel said, "what do you hope to accomplish in Ancris?"

"Llorn wants to take Strages from the Hissing Man."

Yeriel gasped. "Strages?"

Rhiannon knew she was saying too much, yet she found herself saying, "Yes, and you can't stop it. We have your shard."

Yeriel's nostrils flared. Her hair twisted, then settled on her shoulders. "Come to the mere, child. Let me show you what will come if you awaken Strages."

Rhiannon knew she should leave—the maze was feeling farther away each time she opened her mouth—but she followed Yeriel down to the edge of the mere.

Yeriel pointed at the rippling water. "Look."

Rhiannon stared into the water, and a vision appeared—a citadel tree, but it was much larger than any she'd ever seen. Its bark was almost pure black with hints of violet that shimmered like heat off a summer stone.

"It's the Umbral Tree," Rhiannon said in awe.

Yeriel crouched. "Look closer."

Rhiannon crouched beside her, and saw a man in dark armor limping toward a walled city. Men, women, even children stood atop the wall holding bows. Some looked to be proper archers; others had tattered clothes and dirty faces. It looked like the final stand of a people who'd already lost hope.

The man in the dark armor had drawn flesh and an eyeless helm.

"Is that Strages?" Rhiannon asked?

"Indeed, child," Yeriel answered.

Where his nose might once have been were mottled scars and two gaping holes. Behind him stood a host of men and women with rotted gray skin. Rain fell in large drops, plastering hair to pale skulls. Their eyes were dull, lifeless, yet on they marched, through the mud, shambling and stumbling ever closer to the city walls.

Strages drew a pitted greatsword and held it before him, tip down. He drove it into the ground, and the earth split. A fissure sped toward the wall, widening, dirt and stone tumbling into it. When it reached the wall, the stone blocks buckled and collapsed into the chasm, screaming men, women, and children falling with them. Through the gap, Strages' host swarmed like insects into city streets.

Strages entered the city with his ragged host, and a woman, a shepherd in golden armor with the eight-pointed star of Alra on her breastplate, met him. They traded blows. Each time their swords clashed, sparks flew and a burst of golden light lit the battered buildings and fallen rubble around them, and the undead shaded their faces from the light. But with each blow, the light dimmed. Soon the shepherd was breathing hard and the sparks from her sword barely illuminated her shining armor.

With an almighty blow, Strages smashed the sword from the shepherd's hands, and it clattered away on the stone street. She fell to her knees, and Strages beheaded her with a terrible, two-handed blow. The people of the city wailed as Strages limped into the city.

Then the vision faded. Rhiannon found herself breathing fast and ragged. Her hands were balled into fists. "That can't be Strages."

"It can, and he is."

Rhiannon turned to face Yeriel. "How would you know?"

"Because Strages was my lover, before Faedryn turned him"—she gestured toward the water again. It brightened into a vision of Strages shooting streaks of violet fire toward a phalanx of soldiers—"into that."

Rhiannon looked up from the pool and noticed that the grass around her was greener, the trees browner and lusher, and she suddenly understood why. Yeriel had been drawing her closer to Gonsalond the entire time. She was taking her beyond the veil, where Rhiannon be all but powerless.

Rhiannon wanted to return to the maze, to leave this place, but she couldn't. Not yet. She had to know the truth. "You're lying," she said to Yeriel. "*You* made that vision in the water. It's not real."

"Tell me your name, child."

Rhiannon thought of defying her. She thought of lying, too, but she thought Yeriel was about to reveal deep truths, and a lie felt wrong. "My name is Rhiannon of House Bloodhaven."

Yeriel tipped her head. "The stories you've been told, Rhiannon of House Bloodhaven, are riddled with lies."

"If there are lies, it's the empire's fault. They lie about everything, all the time."

"They lie about much, it's true, but don't deceive yourself. The Kin tell their own lies. The source of the lies no longer matters. The lies I speak of were told for myriad reasons, but their effect is the same: they hide the truth about Faedryn, about Alra, about me, Strages, and the other so-called paragons."

"Tell me the truth, then."

Yeriel held out her hand. "Join me and I will."

She meant join her in Gonsalond. Rhiannon was tempted. If she was going to be a part of Llorn and Morraine's war, she wanted to know the truth. She wanted to know the consequences: what would become of Ancris, of the Kin, of the Holt, even the world. She still wondered if Yeriel was lying, but the vision she'd shared in the pond had *felt* true. And what would be the harm in going to Gonsalond? She could listen to Yeriel's story, and if she felt Yeriel was being insincere—if she felt Llorn's plan was truly the right choice for her people—she could go back into the maze and finish what she'd started.

She reached out to take Yeriel's hand, but Yeriel screamed and fell to the ground, writhing and thrashing. Her legs splashed into the pond as she clawed the mossy bank.

The world went white again, so bright she closed her eyes. When the brightness behind her eyelids dimmed and stopped stinging, she opened them and found herself in a vyrd with tall citadels and a ring of oak trees around it. Morraine was standing over her, holding the shard. She was saying something, but the ringing in Rhiannon's ears was so loud Rhiannon couldn't hear it. The ringing faded, and Morraine clutched Rhiannon's shoulder in her cold hand and shook her. "Are you *well*, child?"

"Y-yes," Rhiannon stammered.

"Yeriel was trying to take you."

When Rhiannon said nothing, Morraine's eyes narrowed. "Were you even aware? Did she try to speak to you."

Rhiannon shook her head. "No . . . she didn't."

Morraine glared at her. Rhiannon stared up at her wizened face. Then Morraine slipped the shard's leather cord over her head and beneath her dress. "Come, Rhiannon!"

They hurried through the standing stones to a clearing blanketed with pine needles. Llorn was there. His shirt was off and he had a bandage on his left shoulder. Brother Mayhew was there as well, leaning against a citadel root. His robe was pulled up, and the bandage around his thigh was stained with blood.

An auburn and Fraoch lay at the edge of the clearing; Gwilyn, standing near them, stared at Rhiannon with his ruby eyes.

"Is . . . this all that's left?" Rhiannon asked.

Morraine snapped her fingers in front of Rhiannon's eyes. "Stop acting like a sparrow and sit. We have work to do."

Rhiannon knelt. Morraine sat across from her. Her eyes glowed blue as she prepared to feed off Rhiannon's soul, but she paused. "Tell me what happened."

Rhiannon said she'd been trapped by Yeriel, but Yeriel hadn't spoken to her. She said she thought Yeriel was drawing her toward Gonsalond, which was probably why Morraine had been able to find her. She told her mother just enough truth for the story to be believable, and by the time she was done telling the tale, Morraine shrugged like she'd heard more than enough.

In the hour that followed, Morraine fed. When it was done, she stopped so quickly Rhiannon reeled from it. By then cant had arrived with a splash of color.

"Rest," her mother said, and went to speak with Llorn.

They spoke too quietly for Rhiannon to hear, but Rhiannon didn't care. Her mind was elsewhere. She closed her eyes and pictured the mere in Gonsalond, thinking how woefully unprepared for the coming day she was, and that she'd made a terrible mistake by not acting faster on Yeriel's offer.

EIGHTY-TWO: ORDREN

Ordren waited on a wooden bench in the temple atop Mount Evalarus as High Shepherd Japheth left to notify the illustra he'd arrived. He wondered if he was making a mistake. Antagonizing street thugs was one thing. Poking an illustra squarely in the eye was quite another.

Then again, although Azariah was powerful, he was also vain. He wouldn't risk the truth about his relationship to the Hissing Man going beyond the walls of the temple. Ordren was certain that, when all was said and done, Azariah would cave to Ordren's demands. Then he'd leave this city, its chemical stink, and its bloody catacombs behind and never look back.

You have a plan, Ordren told himself over and over. *It's a good one.*

And yet, as he continued to wait, his resolve seemed to fade. He was nearly ready to leave when he heard the crisp sound of Japheth's footsteps in the hallway.

"The Illustra will see you now."

Ordren followed Japheth up several sets of stairs to a richly appointed office. Azariah sat behind a broad desk in his white robe and an ivory-and-gold mask. To the right of the desk was a bookcase with items arranged in a fashion curiously similar to the shelf in the Hissing Man's sepulcher: books on the top and bottom shelves, a wooden case and a silverskin frame in the middle one.

Japheth departed, and Azariah motioned to the empty chair across from him. "Sit."

Ordren bowed and sat, wishing he were somewhere else. "Your Holiness."

"Tell me, what brings an inquisitor to the temple on a day like today?"

The blood rushing through Ordren's ears was so loud he could barely think. "I . . ." He swallowed hard. *You have a plan, you bloody fool. Take what you can get and leave.* "I normally come to the Hissing Man with information . . ."

Azariah's head tilted, making the golden rays on his mask shimmer. "The Hissing Man?"

"That's right."

Azariah nodded slowly. "If, as you say, you normally deal with him, then why are you here?"

Ordren couldn't tell if Azariah was playing dumb or not. "I have news about Quintarch Lucran."

Azariah smiled crookedly. "And?"

"He knows what you're trying to do."

"And what, precisely, does Lucran think he knows?"

"He knows about the crucible. He knows it's linked to the palisade. He knows that the end goal is a geoflare, right here in fucking Ancris. He knows it's linked to Strages and the Heartstone shard. He knows Llorn has likely begun the final stages of triggering the damn thing. He left for Glaeyand an hour ago to tell the other quintarchs and get more evidence."

Azariah seemed to ponder that for a while. When he finished, his crooked smile had vanished. "He's gone to the council of quintarchs. It's entirely normal."

"He took a full wing of dragons. He's sending Lorelei and Creed and the bastard, Rylan, to the Holt for more evidence."

"And who's acting in his stead while he's gone, the Domina or the Consul?"

"Neither," Ordren said. "He had some sort of row with Tyrinia last night, stripped her of the title and gave Praefectus fucking Damika authority to act on his behalf. She'll be here within the hour with veterans from the Syrdian campaign. They plan to seize the shrine and search the temple."

Azariah lapsed into silence. The last bit of news seemed to stun him, but it was hard to tell with the bloody mask on.

When the silence had gone on for too long, Ordren asked, "Is it true?"

"Is *what* true?"

"About Ancris. Are you planning to destroy the city?"

"How is that your business, inquisitor?"

"It's my business, Your Holiness, because my livelihood is tied to Ancris. There's not much coin if there's no bloody city to work in."

"If the city is under threat, that would hardly be the fault of the Church."

"The Church pushed for the palisade."

"And the quintarch approved and funded it."

Ordren paused. He'd reached the point of no return. Utter his next words, and there was no turning back. *Will you bloody get on with it?* "I need more money."

Azariah paused. "If you have some sort of arrangement with the Hissing Man—"

"You're well aware of that arrangement. You're the one who made it."

Azariah scoffed. "I did nothing of the sort—"

"I know you're the Hissing Man . . ."

Azariah laughed. "Are you on drugs, Inquis—"

"In the catacombs," Ordren said, "I saw the Hissing Man enter your son's sepulcher. I saw him take umbris, change . . . himself, put on different clothes. Then I saw you, Your Holiness, leave that sepulcher. You and the Hissing Man are one and the same."

Azariah stared at Ordren, and Ordren stared back, determined to force Azariah to make the next move.

"Have you told anyone of this?" the illustra growled.

"Not as such, but I've left messages that will be delivered to the Crag and Highreach if I don't come back from our little chat. I'll remind you I came here with useful information. I've been giving you useful information all along, while you and your allies plotted to destroy Ancris. The information has been worth a lot more than what I've been paid, I'll wager. All I'm looking for is just compensation."

Azariah started to laugh but stopped. "Are we to give you a chest of gold? Perhaps a palace in—"

"Lucertae, Your Radiance. I want lucertae, and the temple has plenty of it tucked away in its vaults. Give me a libra of them. Iron, indurium, or bloody viridian, I don't care. Give them to me, and you'll never see me again."

"It's true," Azariah said, "I could easily give you some . . ."

Ordren leaned his elbows on Azariah's desk. "Then stop faffing about—"

"But how can I reward a man who deals with the likes of the Hissing Man?"

Ordren clenched his teeth. "Your Holiness, I'm not playing games. People know I'm here. If I suddenly disappear—"

"I don't know what you saw in the catacombs"—Azariah pushed his chair back from the desk, its legs screeching across the floor—"but it wasn't what you think. How could it be?" Azariah cracked the knuckles of his right hand. "I am Alra's highest servant, her voice in Ancris, and what you say is an insult to the goddess herself."

When Azariah took off his mask, revealing his ruined, white eyes, Ordren realized he'd made a terrible mistake. He scrambled out of his chair and tried to make for the door, but Azariah leapt over the desk, grabbed Ordren's arm, spun him around, and drove his fist into Ordren jaw. Ordren's head spun, and he fell to the carpet. Azariah pounced on him, wrestled him onto his back, and punched him again, crushing his nose.

Ordren tasted blood. He couldn't breath through his nose. "Please!" he yelled. "Stop! I won't tell anyone!"

"You're right about that," Azariah snarled. He raised his fist again.

EIGHTY-THREE: AZARIAH

D*amn* . . . Azariah lowered his fist and stared at the unconscious inquisitor beneath him. He still needed information about the notes the man had supposedly written.

His right hand began to throb, and he stared at his cut-up knuckles. His sleeve and the front of his robe were splattered with blood.

A knock came at the door. "Your Radiance!" It was Japheth. "Forgive me, I come with urgent news."

Azariah picked up his mask, put it on, and stood. "Come."

The door swung open, and Japheth stepped inside. He pulled up short on seeing Ordren lying on the floor all bloody, but quickly composed himself. "It's Praefectus Damika. She's marching at the head of a column of soldiers. They'll be at the gates in minutes."

Ordren hadn't lied about that, at least. "Send word to the eyrie. I want three dragons circling Evalarus. Send anyone who can wield a weapon to the shrine. Arm the shepherds with powder, white and black. Stand them on the wall in plain sight. I want the Praefectus and her soldiers to see who they're dealing with."

"And the gates?"

"Keep them closed until I arrive. No one is allowed in. Not even the Praefectus."

Japheth motioned to Ordren. "And him?"

"Bring him to the questioning room."

"At once, Your Radiance."

Japheth left and returned a short while later with a pair of black-robed priests and a litter. A moment later, the Hissing Man stepped into the doorway, hood pulled up. As the priests flopped Ordren onto the litter, the Hissing Man limped into the room, stared down at the hapless inquisitor, and merely grunted. Neither of the priests looked at the Hissing Man as they carried Ordren from the room.

Japheth lingered. "One last thing, Your Radiance. The shepherdess I assigned to watch the vyrd came to the temple a short while ago. She said the link to the maze is noticeably stronger."

Azariah had ordered him to have the vyrd measured twice a day. If the link was stronger, it meant Llorn had begun spanning the vyrda. Azariah should have been be pleased by it, but Ordren's accusations haunted him. "Very good, Japheth."

Japheth opened his mouth, seemed to decide better of speaking further, then bowed and left, closing the door behind him.

"What the inquisitor told you is a lie," the Hissing Man rasped.

Azariah suddenly felt too scared to speak, but he had to know. "He said he saw you transforming. He said we are one and the same."

The Hissing Man laughed, a sickening wheeze. "Do I not stand before you?"

"But why fabricate such a wild story? Why try to extort me if he knew it was a lie?"

"Trust me," the Hissing Man said with a cold, gauzy stare, "you don't want to know."

"Yes, I do."

"No, you don't. And you never have."

"It's to do with Cassian, isn't it?"

The Hissing Man seemed to glare at him from behind his bandages.

Azariah felt almost commanded to remain silent, but he couldn't. "Tell me!" he roared.

"What good would it do? I've shown you a dozen times, and you always regret it. When will you learn that we cannot escape Faedryn?"

"Why would I want to?"

"Because that is always the result of these revelations. Our bond is unbreakable. We serve him, and we will free him. Find comfort in that."

A vision of a brightsteel knife being driven between Cassian's ribs flashed before Azariah. "No . . ." He ran from the room, darted down the hall, staggered into his apartment, and stared at the table where he'd found Cassian waiting for him.

The Hissing Man was suddenly beside him. "Leave it be . . ."

"I will not!"

In his mind's eye, he saw Cassian, looking concerned but determined, stand from the table. Azariah slapped his head, willing himself to remember more, but nothing came. "Seven hells take you, *show me!*"

The Hissing Man stared at him through those damn bandages, breathing noisily. "It won't change anything . . . ."

When Azariah only stared back, the Hissing Man sighed and pressed a palm to Azariah's forehead.

Azariah strode down the temple hall. He'd just come from the temple eyrie, where Japheth informed him that his son had been spotted flying a dragon from the imperial eyrie toward Tortoise Peak. Azariah opened his locket, took a pinch of white powder and inhaled it.

Today of all days, My Lord, I need your guidance.

He saw a glimpse of Faedryn struggling against black tree roots. He blinked his ruined eyes to clear the vision, continued to the sitting room in his apartments, and found Cassian sitting at the small dining table in his black habit and golden stole. He looked so concerned Azariah worried he'd made a mistake in taking the auris—did Faedryn really need to listen to a conversation between father and son?

Faedryn struggled against the roots like an eel caught in a net, and Azariah turned his attention to his son.

On seeing Azariah, Cassian stood from the table. "We must speak, Father."

"Indeed," Azariah replied, "I've just heard some rather disturbing news."

Cassian gestured to the chair across from him. "Please, sit."

Azariah was ready to rail at his son, but he sat patiently, and Cassian joined him.

"I'm guessing you've heard about my flight from the eyrie," Cassian said.

"You would spy on your father, Cassian?"

"You left me no choice. These past months—"

"You spied on your *illustra*, the leader of your faith . . ."

"I spied, yes, but not on my father and certainly not on the leader of my faith."

"Don't lie to me, Cassian. Japheth just told me a dragon was spotted leaving the eyrie—"

"Yes, but—"

"—and that *you* were riding it."

"I was . . ." Cassian clasped his hands on the table before him. "Hear me, father. The shimmering dome I saw at Tortoise Peak, the tearing down of the pillars, the killing of slaves and throwing them in a pit . . . I know *you* couldn't have done those things."

Azariah felt his pulse quicken. He dare not speak for what those words might lead to. He prayed Cassian was saying something *other* than what he feared.

"Hardly a day goes by" Cassian continued, "that I haven't wondered what you saw in Vattuo's eyes the day you became illustra. I knew you changed that day. I felt it."

"All illustrae change when they're chosen. It cannot help but be so."

"Which is why I thought little of it at first, but something always felt wrong about it. And then came the days and weeks you spent away from Ancris. I heard about slaves going missing, about meetings in the catacombs between you and the Chosen. It made me wonder all over again about the changes I saw in you. It made me wonder about the ritual you underwent, the nature of the vyrda, the very nature of the illustrae. It made me wonder if it all relates to the Ruining."

Faedryn pulled against the roots, roared in his prison, and Azariah felt his palms go clammy.

"I've been researching the history of the illustrae," Cassian went on. "I've looked deeper into the Chosen and their birth in the ashes of the Holy Rebellion."

"Cassian, don't . . ."

"What you're doing makes little sense if one believes you and the other illustrae are acting in Alra's name, but it makes perfect sense if one supposes you're acting on behalf of someone else."

Faedryn railed at the roots. He managed to free one arm, but more roots grew and wrapped around his wrist, restraining him. Faedryn bellowed, though whether it was in pain, fear, or both, Azariah wasn't certain. "Cassian, stop, please . . ."

Cassian shook his head. "Don't you see? It isn't your fault. Centuries ago, Faedryn found a chink in the walls of his prison, wide enough for him to touch the maze. Through it, he lured the faithful and poisoned their minds, poisoned *your* mind. It's what he's done to *all* the illustrae."

Faedryn's body shook so violently the earth around him trembled. The roots remained, but Azariah felt His Lord's command. Faedryn was pressing him to draw his knife and run it across his own son's throat.

Azariah blinked hard and shook his head. He wouldn't obey Faedryn. He *couldn't*. Not in this.

"We can gather our most powerful shepherds," Cassian was saying. "We can excise Faedryn from you, return you to the goddess's light. This, I promise you."

Azariah found himself standing through no will of his own. Faedryn's terror felt bottomless. He wouldn't stand by and allow a common priest to ruin centuries of careful planning. Faedryn forced Azariah to grip the ceremonial knife at his belt, and Azariah was stunned. Not once had His Lord used him in this way. Azariah hadn't even known he could.

Please, My Lord, he needn't die. He only needs to be shown that you are the One True God. We can take him, as we did with Japheth.

Faedryn bellowed in his prison, tore at the roots that bound him, breaking one after the other, and Azariah drew his knife. But the roots grew at an astounding rate. They bound Faedryn, tighter than before. One slipped around the god's neck, choking him, and for one brief moment, Azariah felt himself again.

Azariah didn't wish to defy his Lord, but he couldn't stand by and watch his son die. He used the power of aura *against* Faedryn and fought for his own free will. He'd just managed to sheath his knife when Faedryn ripped the root from around his neck. A high-pitched ringing filled Azariah's ears, and a sudden, terrible pain pierced his skull. He fell to the floor and writhed.

When he could think again, he saw, through his second sight, a crooked little man in a worn black habit stalking toward Cassian with a brightsteel knife.

"Father!" Cassian called, his hands raised. "Father, please!"

The pain in Azariah's head ebbed as the crooked man tackled Cassian and climbed on top of him. Azariah felt for his own knife, but it was gone. "Let him go!" he cried.

He clambered up from the carpet and lunged toward Cassian and his assailant.

The bent man punched the knife into Cassian's chest.

"No!" Azariah roared. He shoved the crooked man away and dropped to Cassian's side. The crooked man tossed the knife to the blood-soaked carpet. Cassian stared at the ceiling, his eyes blinking fiercely. "We'll fix you," Azariah said, opening his locket to reveal its well of black umbris.

The crooked man was suddenly by his side. "No," he hissed, and touched Azariah's forehead.

The world tilted, and Azariah felt his head strike the carped. Saw his mask clatter away. Then world went dark. When it filled in again, he blinked, pushed himself off the floor. Cassian lay nearby, his eyes glassy, his body still. Azariah felt for a pulse and found none. Cassian's skin was cold.

Azariah stood and faced the crooked man. "What have you done?"

The crooked man stared back with ruined eyes and rasped, "What you couldn't." He passed a hand before him, and Azariah saw Faedryn, calm as subterranean lake, the roots around him still.

Azariah shook the vision away. He gripped the Hissing Man's habit and shook him. "He was my *son!*"

"I *had* to kill him. He would have exposed everything." The Hissing Man gripped Azariah's wrists, and Azariah, despite his anger, released him. "You and I have work to do. Cassian will be reported as having gone missing. *I'll* take care of the body, and *you* will continue our Lord's work."

"I won't." Azariah shook his head. "I can't."

"You can and you will."

Azariah stared down at Cassian's unmoving form. "I can't," he said, weaker than moments ago.

"You can"—the Hissing Man pressed his palm to Azariah's forehead—"and you will."

Azariah tried to hold on to his anger, but the longer he stared at Cassian, the more he realized the Hissing Man had been right—there really had been no choice in the matter. If Azariah had truly cared, he would have ended his son's life quickly and not left it to the pathetic creature before him.

"Of course," he heard himself say while picking up his mask, "I'll continued our Lord's work."

Azariah felt a wave of dizziness and steadied himself.

He stared at the carpet where the Hissing Man had straddled Cassian and driven Azariah's own knife into the young priest's chest. The carpet was different now, and there was no body, no blood stain. But the pain and the shame of what he'd allowed to happen remained. He ripped off his mask and threw it clattering into the corner. A chunk of ivory broke off and spun across the floor near Azariah's feet.

Behind him, the Hissing Man rasped, "Your son served his purpose."

Azariah spun around and shouted, "His death served no *purpose!*"

The Hissing Man's jaw jutted. "You may not acknowledge how much we've been able to accomplish since that day, but I know you recognize it."

"He didn't have to *die.*"

The Hissing Man stared at Azariah with a pitiless expression. "Of course he did. The will of our Lord will not be defied. Not by you. Not by anyone." He held out a locket, Azariah's locket. "Auris, take it. Renew your bond. Forget."

"I won't forget!"

But then he stared down at his broken mask, and a memory stirred. Cassian, nine years old, kneeling beside Swallowtail Lake. He smiled as he tore off a piece of bread and tossed it onto the water, laughed as the trout gulped at it. Then the lake was full of blood, and Cassian was being drawn into it.

Tears welling, Azariah snatched the locket from the Hissing Man, opened the reservoir of auris, and took a large pinch of the white powder.

"Yes," the Hissing Man hissed. "We must be strong, relentless."

Azariah held the powder to his nose, sniffed deeply, and felt his bond with Faedryn strengthen. The horror of Cassian drowning in blood was replaced with a memory of the two of them casting aside their clothes and swimming in the lake's clear waters. It was a lovely day, the two of them escaping life in the temple to simply be father and son.

That memory faded, too, but it was pleasant, like staring into a slowly dying fire while reminiscing. When that joyful day was lost altogether, Azariah's mind was filled a renewed purpose, myriad plans, and the steps he needed to take to achieve them.

The most pressing was Praefectus Damika, who dared march on the temple with a host of soldiers. He picked up his broken mask, pulled it on, and headed toward his office.

EIGHTY-FOUR: AZARIAH

When he got to his office, Azariah called for a basin of water and a fresh robe. He washed his hands, changed into the clean robe, and sat at his desk. Lucran's show of force was stronger than anticipated, but Azariah was confident he could manage it—he only needed a delay. Plus, Llorn had built plans around the quintarch's council, which could further delay Lucran. Even if it didn't, the end was now less than a day away.

Azariah pulled a sheet of vellum from his desk drawer and laid it on the desk. He took up his pen, dipped it in dragonscale ink, and composed an edict, forbidding the quintarch's forces from stepping foot on holy ground. Then he signed it and set the pen down. He dripped wax on it and pressed his signet ring into it. Then he rolled it up, stood, and left his office.

He left the temple and climbed into a waiting coach. As it jingled into motion, three golden dragons rose into the sky from the temple's eyrie. The coach passed beyond the curtain wall and headed down along Temple Road. One of the dragons let out a piercing cry. They rolled past a column of shepherds and acolytes marching toward the shrine, and Azariah felt a thrill of excitement. He hoped to avoid violence, but if they couldn't, the Praefectus would regret it. The coach was crossing the shrine's plaza toward the outer wall when he caught a glimpse of Faedryn smiling even as black roots bound him. Azariah smiled, too. The bridging of the vyrda continued. Everything was coming together, just as His Lord had willed it.

The coach rolled to a stop behind the gates. Azariah exited and nodded to Japheth. "Open them."

With the help of three other men, Japheth lifted the bar and pulled one of the stout doors open. Azariah exited to the street. Praefectus Damika and a trio of centurions were gathered there with, as Japheth had said, three hundred legionaries with gleaming spears, helms, and lorica segmentata, surely veterans of the war with Syrdia. They stood in ranks along the cobblestone street. Their armor was nicked. They looked grim, battle ready.

Damika stepped forward with a dead-eyed centurion in battered brightsteel and a helm with a red horsehair crest. The praefectus had an imperturbable confidence about her that Azariah grudgingly admired. Her gaze drifted to the rolled vellum in his bruised and cut hand. The centurion, meanwhile, stared at Azariah like he'd just found his next meal.

"So many soldiers," Azariah said with a flick of a hand toward the ordered ranks. "One would think you were preparing for war."

Damika looked up at the wall. Dozens of shepherds and acolytes stood at the ready, and more were emerging from the inner stairs. The acolytes were competent fighters in their own right, but the shepherds were the real power The spells they could summon were devastating.

Damika pointed up to them, then at the three gold dragons circling Evalarus. "I suppose these shepherds and dragons are here for a tea party?"

"You should be happy, Praefectus. The Church is ready to protect Ancris against the dire threats everyone keeps talking about."

"The Church needn't trouble itself." She held out a hand, and the centurion handed her a scroll with the quintarch's seal. Damika unrolled it and held it up for Azariah to read. "We're to safeguard the shrine until Quintarch Lucran returns to Ancris."

The scroll's mundane ink was difficult to read, but Azariah could make it out well enough. It was a terse declaration that Damika was now in charge of the shrine's security. Azariah sniffed. "I can't allow it."

Damika shrugged. "I'm afraid you have no choice."

Azariah held out the edict he'd written and handed it to her. "I beg to differ."

Damika unfurled it. "A declaration of extraordinary powers?"

"Pursuant to the accords between the quintarchs and the Church, it allows us to use necessary force against threats to the Church, be it our clergy, our holy sites, or our most precious artifacts."

"Only if the quintarch is unable to provide protection." She waved to the ranks of soldiers behind her. "That's clearly not the case."

"Come, Praefectus. Three hundred soldiers against the Red Knives? They'll crush them."

"I can bring more."

"That won't be necessary. The Church will protect the shrine."

Damika rolled the sheet of vellum and shook it in the air. "The quintarchs can override this."

"Yes, and my understanding is they're holding a council in Glaeyand as we speak. By all means, ask them to vote on it. Until then, this remains holy ground. Alra's land, not Lucran's."

Damika took a half step closer and lowered her voice. "Put aside your squabble with Lucran, Azariah. The city is in grave danger."

"I hardly see it that way."

"They're planning to use the palisade to destroy Ancris."

Azariah forced a laugh. "A rumor at best, a lie at worst. The Red Knives are trying to gain access to the temple or the shrine."

"And you're willing to risk everything that you're right?"

"Here is what I know, Praefectus. Quintarch Lucran has had his eye on Syrdia for the better part of two decades. He's blinded himself to what's happening in his own capital. Now that he's come back, he worries that he has lost control of Ancris. He sees phantoms in every corner. Mark my words, these rumors about the palisade are only more of the same."

Damika lowered her voice again and whispered, "We have reason to think the Church has been conspiring with the Hissing Man, that the Chosen are controlling the temple, not you. What is Quintarch Lucran to think when he learns you defied common sense?"

"Let's find out when he returns from the council, shall we?"

For a moment, Azariah thought she might order her legion to take the shrine by force. Then shook her head. "This isn't over, Your Holiness."

Edict in hand, she stalked away, and the centurion followed. After a brief discussion with several of his officers, the centurion bellowed orders and the soldiers made way for Damika to pass through, but the soldiers didn't leave. Damika seemed to be preparing a siege.

Azariah walked back to the temple plaza, and the gates were closed. "See to it we're ready to repel any attack," he told Japheth. "Three dragons flying at all times. Rotate them as needed. After cantfall, send scouts into the city. Watch the vyrd especially. I want to know the moment anything changes."

"Yes, Your Radiance."

Azariah climbed back into his coach. As it was pulled back up the mountain, he looked out over the city. He saw stone buildings, leaning hovels, temples, parks and bath houses. He imagined it all rising into the sky like Tortoise Peak had. The destruction of Ancris and the liberation of Strages had seemed impossible then. Now they seemed inevitable. Llorn and Morraine had begun spanning the vyrda. When the tunnel was complete, the rush of power would trigger the eruption of Ancris. More importantly, in the minutes leading up to the eruption, the surge of power would break the spell that kept Strages in permanent slumber. As Yeriel had awoken, so would Strages. With the shard in Azariah's possession, he would command a power greater than any the world had seen since Faedryn.

The coach stopped in front of the temple. Azariah got out, entered the temple, and took the stairs down to the questioning chamber. Ordren was chained to its broad table, spread-eagled and naked. He twisted his head and looked toward the doorway. His chains clanked. "Your Holiness," he wheezed, "it's all a terrible mistake."

Azariah walked past him to a rack of iron implements. He chose a pair of pincers.

"I've changed my mind," Ordren pleaded. "I don't need anything. Just let me go, and you'll never see me again. I swear it. Please, Your Holiness, I beg you!"

Azariah turned to face the table. "Silence."

Ordren's ribs stood out like chair rails as his chest rose and fell, and he closed his gaping mouth.

"Now," Azariah said, "let's talk about these messages you've written."

EIGHTY-FIVE: RYLAN

Rylan sat behind Lorelei in Bothymus's saddle as they flew in silence toward the Rookery. The sky was overcast, the wind calm.

Far to their right, Ruko, the gleaming silver vixen, soared above the treetops with Ash and Creed in the saddle. A short while ago, an elk had bugled in the distance, and Ruko had fought her reins to hunt for it. Ash, inexperienced with crop and fetter, had lost control of her for a time. He'd finally regained it and was guiding Ruko back toward Rylan and Lorelei.

Lorelei glanced over her shoulder. "You're being quiet again."

"I get quiet when I'm worried."

"What are you so worried about?"

"We've been flying for nearly an hour and I still haven't heard from Vedron. We're going to the Deepwood Fens, which could go wrong in a thousand different ways. And even if we get through that alive, we may be too late to do anything about the crucible."

Lorelei tugged on Bothymus's reins to fly closer to Ruko. "I'm surprised you didn't mention your father."

Rylan had told her about his audience with the quintarchs. He still wasn't sure he'd made the right move. "Yes, I'm worried about that as well."

"The audience or Marstan?"

His first instinct was to brush the question off—he liked to keep his life to himself—but Lorelei deserved better. "My relationship with my father is complicated."

"Yet you cared enough to fight for him."

"I cared enough to fight for someone who wouldn't sell the Holt to the highest bidder."

"You think you doomed him by telling them so much . . . ?"

"Wouldn't you feel the same?"

"Perhaps, yes, but in my estimation, you did the right thing. Whatever faults he may have, Marstan seems to care about the Holt and wants peace. I admire him for that much."

"You do?"

"Don't be so surprised. There are people in the empire who sympathize with the Kin, probably more than you realize." She paused, the wind whipping her hair in Rylan's face. "I can't believe I'm saying this, but I wish Aarik was alive."

"So do I."

Ruko swept up next to them, and Rylan found himself wishing the silver had chased the elk farther—he would've liked more time to talk with Lorelei alone. When he caught a brief flash of Vedron, her tail slapping the waters of a burbling stream, he realized it wouldn't have mattered. He tapped Lorelei's shoulder and pointed to a shorn bridgebough on a dying citadel up ahead. "Land there."

Lorelei nodded and guided Bothymus toward it, leaving Ruko circling overhead, and landed gracefully. Vedron streaked upward from below, tucked her wings, and landed lightly beside them. She cooed and stared up at Bothymus, but Bothymus looked away.

Rylan eased himself down on the bridgebough, balanced across to Vedron, and climbed up in her saddle. Then they flew up and met Ruko again, and all three dragons flew hard toward the Rookery and the fen where Rylan desperately hoped they'd find Llorn's crucible.

Vedron seemed to enjoy Ruko's frequent trumpeting. She trumpeted back a few times, but fell silent when Bothymus blew one long blaring note.

"He's right, I'm afraid." Rylan leaned forward and patted Vedron's neck. "We need to be quiet."

The skies darkened to pewter gray. The Diamondflow shone like molten lead as it bent southward. Rylan knew they were getting close. "Fly below the canopy!"

The dragons descended, and as they wove between the towering citadels, Rylan felt Vedron's curiosity about something to their left like she had last time they'd approached the Rookery.

Rylan loosened the reins. "Go ahead and find it, but fly lower."

With Bothymus and Ruko trailing, Vedron descended until her wings brushed the tops of the blood maples and swamp cypresses that dotted the landscape. The smaller trees soon vanished, leaving bare swampy terrain and the occasional citadel. A patchy mist drifted slowly above the mire.

Ash pointed to their right. "There!"

In the distance was a series of black stone pillars, set in a circle. Vedron gurgled wetly and dipped in the air. The discomfort he felt from her was an echo of his own. It felt like his bowels were twisting in knots.

"Powerful," Ash said.

Behind Ash, Creed grimaced and spat.

As they approached the closest pillar, Bothymus and Ruko began circling down.

"Get started," Rylan called to them. "I'll scout the area."

As Bothymus and Ruko glided toward a hillock, Rylan flew Vedron upward, and the whole of the crucible was laid bare. The dimensions looked roughly the same as the palisade at Ancris. He counted seventeen pillars, also the same.

He scanned the horizon and the trees for scouts or dragons, but saw none, so he guided Vedron to the hillock. By then, Ash had unstrapped his case of alchemycal equipment and opened it on the grass. Much as he had in the shrine, he was using a chromatovellum kit to detect the nature and relative amount of umbra trapped in the soil.

Creed crossed his arms over his chest. "You're not going to blow us all up, are you?"

Ash glared up at him. "I was caught off guard in the shrine."

"*And* in the Tulip."

Ash rolled his eyes. "I hadn't made the connection between the peat and the stone." He used a tiny spade to dig a bit of soil. "It won't happen again."

Creed still cringed when Ash dropped the peat into the serum and swirled it.

The sour feeling in Rylan's gut worsened. Ash looked queasy, too. He handed Rylan, Lorelei, and Creed each a nearly transparent indurium scale from the chromatovellum kit. Rylan used his to view the colors of the cloudy liquid in the beaker. "Looks similar to stuff at the shrine."

"Not just similar," Lorelei said. "It's an exact match."

Creed handed his scale to Ash. "Fine." He coughed. "We've confirmed that we have two sources of unimaginable power. If they're getting ready to sink this bloody thing"—he gestured to the empty bog around them—"where is everyone? Why isn't this place being guarded?"

Although Lorelei was staring at the transparent scale pinched between her fingers, her gaze seemed to go beyond it. "They don't need to protect it anymore."

Rylan winced. Of course she was right. "They think the geoflare can no longer be stopped. At least, not from here."

Ash stood and looked around. "Is there a vyrd near here?"

"Yes," Rylan said, "a short flight"—he pointed to a tract of land beyond a bright red blood maple—"that way."

Ash closed his case, locked it, and slung it over his shoulder. "Show me."

They mounted their dragons, and Rylan and Vedron led them into the trees. It took a bit of finding, but eventually he spotted a clearing with a circle of standing stones and led them to it. The menhirs were weathered and considerably older than the ones in Glaeyand and far older than the one in Ancris. Ash slipped down from Ruko's saddle and opened his alchemyst's kit on the mossy ground. He took out an alchemycal device with a heavy wooden base and a needle sticking up from it. Behind the needle was a metal plate with a scale on it.

"What is it?" Rylan asked.

"A wayfinder." Ash set it down in the center of the vyrd. "We use them to find the direction of, and approximate elapsed time since, the most recent crossing at a vyrd." Near the base of the needle was a hook that held it in place, presumably to protect the delicate instrument while being transported. Ash unhooked the needle and rotated the wayfinder, and the needle began to shift along the gauge. "The direction that produces the most movement in the needle indicates the direction of the crossing. The distance the needle travels, generally speaking, tells how recent—"

Ash stopped and gaped at the instrument. The needle tip tilted all the way to the right, beyond all the markings on the scale.

"What does that mean?" Rylan asked.

Ash frowned. "It doesn't make sense." He pulled the needle back and let it go. It swung right and emitted a soft metallic *tink* as the needle met whatever restraint was inside the base. Ash picked up the wayfinder. "Either this thing is broken or the signal coming from this vyrd is stronger than any we've ever measured." He stood and peered into the forest.

"What?" Lorelei asked.

"Stone and scree and bright blue sky, this is how the crucible is going to interact with the palisade.

"Through the vyrda?"

"Through the *maze* . . ."

Lorelei squinted and said, "The maze is a concept, a way for ferrymen to navigate from one vyrda to another."

"That's true, so far as it goes, but the maze is much more than that. We've long believed that what underpins the vyrda and allows crossings is a vast web of indurium. Rich veins of it travel the length and breadth of the Holt as far as the Whitefells, but no farther. It's why the vyrda are found all across the forest and the edges of the Great Basin but nowhere else in the world. We know that the segments between vyrda have a memory of sorts." He held the wayfinder up. "It's how we can determine the direction and elapsed time since the last crossing. The strength of this one indicates that the connection between this vyrd and the next is much more powerful than it used to be. A tunnel of sorts has been created for the umbra in the crucible to flow toward Ancris."

"That's how they are going set off the geoflare," Lorelei said.

Ash nodded. "A sinkhole here, a geoflare in Ancris. The power will equalize, but only after a huge explosion."

Lorelei scratched her head. "There must be some way to stop it."

Ash stared down at the rune-covered stones at their feet. "Someone created this tunnel to the next vyrd. It must go to the next and the next until it hits Ancris. If we can stop the flow before it gets there, we can avoid catastrophe."

"Well, *bravo*," called a scratchy, feminine voice.

Rylan spun and saw Blythe leaning against a standing stone. She was white as a sheet. Her waistcoat and trousers were torn and dirty. Her white shirt was stained with blood. A cut on her shoulder was bright red and still seeping.

"What are you doing here?" Rylan asked.

"You know what I'm doing here."

"I mean, I thought you'd challenge Llorn."

"I did."

"And you won?"

"Sadly, no. Our fight was interrupted rather rudely by the Seven."

"The Seven? *Yeriel's* Seven?"

"Never mind, Rylan. You wanted to find your bloody crucible and now you have. So why don't you all be good little boys and girls and leave?"

"We can't. We need to figure out how to stop Llorn."

Blythe pointed to Ash. "The pretty man just told you how. You need to stop Morraine from making a bridge to Ancris, but by now she and Llorn are likely standing on its fucking doorstep. Say buh-bye to your precious capital."

EIGHTY-SIX: LORELEI

Lorelei stared at Blythe. "It can't be too late."

"Those are a child's words," Blythe said with a laugh.

"But there must be something we can do," Lorelei said. When Blythe merely stared, Lorelei went on. "If you care about the people in Ancris—"

Blythe sneered. "I don't, and you're lucky I'm feeling charitable, or I'd finish what we started in Ancris."

Lorelei knew she had to get something out of Blythe, some kind of help. "Whether or not you care about the people of Ancris, you seem to care an awful lot about stopping Llorn." She looked Blythe up and down. "You're clearly in no shape to do so yourself, so help *us* stop him before it's too late."

Blythe stared dead-eyed at Lorelei, the wind tousling her dirty hair. Lorelei thought surely she was going to say something vicious, but she took a deep breath and said, "The final link in the chain will be made in Glaeyand, where the council of quintarchs is being held. Knowing the city will be well guarded, Llorn sent the dragons from the Rookery ahead to lie in wait. He's called in dragons from outposts all across the Holt. They're going to stage a battle intended to look like a small uprising, but it's a feint, a distraction away from the vyrd to give Morraine the time she needs to span from Glaeyand to Ancris."

It answered a lot questions that had been eating away at Lorelei. "But that's only part of the story, isn't it? They want to destroy Ancris for a reason." Without really meaning to, she began pacing the worn stones. "We have good reason to believe the Hissing Man wants to awaken Strages in his shrine, as Yeriel was awakened in hers, which is understandable, perhaps, from where he sits. The Chosen have long wanted to rule the empire absolutely. Freeing Strages and controlling him with his shard would give them that."

"What Lorelei is getting at," Creed said to Blythe, "is that we still don't know what *Llorn* wants in all this."

"Precisely," Lorelei said. "Llorn would never have agreed to this if he thought it would give the Chosen so much power. It would merely be trading one evil for anoth . . ." Lorelei paused a moment. "He must have found a way to take Strages from the Hissing Man." She turned toward Blythe. "That's why he agreed. That's why he raised Morraine. She's not just there to start the geoflare. She's going to steal Strages right out from under the Hissing Man's nose and deliver him to Llorn."

Blythe half smiled and turned to Rylan. "I see why you're infatuated with the nosy little bitch."

Rylan wasn't having it. "How do we stop them, Blythe?"

"Why would I want them stopped?"

"You do or you wouldn't still be here. Do it for Aarik if no one else."

Blythe tsk-tsked. "You've already played that card, Rylan."

He stepped toward her and took her hands in his so intimately Lorelei felt uncomfortable watching it. "Then do it for me," he said.

Lorelei thought it a ploy. Blythe apparently didn't think so.

"The empire's appetite for cruelty is endless," Rylan went on, "we both know this. But literally blowing it sky high is not the way. Aarik knew that. You do too, or you would never have gone back to the Holt to challenge Llorn."

Blythe's face, so pale until then, flushed, but Lorelei couldn't tell if it was from anger, embarrassment, or something else. Blythe snatched her hands from Rylan's and glared at Lorelei. "I'm surprised you haven't figured it out already."

"Figured what out?"

"You saw Morraine come back to life. You know the ritual was nearly stopped."

"So?"

"Morraine's daughter, Rhiannon, got scared and fouled it up and Morraine came back broken, dependent on the weak little girl, teetering between life and death. Get Rhiannon and you might stop Llorn." She turned and walked away toward the Rookery. "Best hurry, though," she called over her shoulder, "or *kaboom!*"

Cant arrived a moment later. The citadels began drawing their needles in. The mire and the vyrd brightened. A splash of crimson light shone through the cloud cover, like blood spilling from the heavens.

Lorelei turned to Rylan. "How much do you know about Rhiannon?"

Rylan was still staring down the path where Blythe had vanished. "Not much," he said. "She's an aspirant to Brother Mayhew, gifted in the ways of the wood."

Lorelei was going to ask more about her, but Ash broke in, "Um, what's wrong with Bothymus?"

Lorelei turned to find Bothymus tilting his head almost sideways, curling and uncurling his tail. Lorelei gripped his crop and willed him to calm, but it did no good.

The sky continued to blaze. Broad swaths of indigo, violet, and persimmon struck through the clouds.

"Is it my imagination," Creed said, "or does the cant seem particularly strong tonight?"

Rylan nodded. "It might be affecting Bothymus, but so might the crucible, or the vyrd itself."

"Bothymus will be fine." Lorelei squeezed the crop harder. "Just give him time. The key question is whether Rhiannon will help us and, if not, what we do about it."

"I wish I knew her well enough to answer," Rylan said. "She's a kind child from what I know of her. She might help us if we tell her we're saving the city, and the Kin, too, but even if she refuses, merely taking her away from her mother might help."

"Well, we're doing any of that," Creed said, "if we don't get a bloody move on."

"True," Ash said, "but it's going to take half the night to get to Glaeyand."

Lorelei hardly heard him. Bothymus seemed to be getting worse. He uttered a long gurgle and clacked his teeth, spread his wings and briefly lit them.

Ash's eyes widened. "It's the tunnel. It must be. All dragons are sensitive to vyrda, but induria especially so. And Morraine has already cast her spell on this one."

Vedron cooed and twitched her tail. She seemed excited.

"Did you know," Rylan asked, "induria were once the empire's sole source of transport via the vyrda? That was before crops and fetters, before ferrymen learned how to use their lucertae."

"So?" Lorelei asked.

Rylan looked at her as if she were thick. "Bothymus might be able to navigate the maze and bring us to Glaeyand."

"You can't be serious."

"I'm *dead* serious. He seems like he's one foot in it already. A nudge from you might very well do the trick."

Lorelei shook her head. "I'm not bonded with him, Rylan."

"Yes, but the two of you have known each other for what? Twenty years? You've ridden him dozens of times, maybe hundreds. You're linked in ways you're not even aware of." He motioned to the runic stones at their feet. "Try it."

Lorelei's instinct told her to refuse, told her it was impossible. She nearly told the others it would be safer to fly their dragons to Glaeyand, but that would be a lie. The truth was, she was scared of the maze and the peculiar feelings it gave her every time she made a crossing. She always felt like she'd never see the light of day again, like she'd simply cease to be, or worse, be drawn into the forest's awareness and become part of it forever.

But her mother and Skylar and Praefectus Damika were depending on her. Even Quintarch Lucran was depending on her, though she didn't much care for the man. Ancris itself was depending on her. She had to try.

Lorelei stared at the crop wrapped around her right hand, stared at the golden fetter on Bothymus's bridle. She couldn't possibly control Bothymus without them, but of course she would say that, she liked rules—things were supposed work a certain way. *"You could do it too, you know,"* Rylan had told her about bonding instead of binding. She still wasn't convinced, but he was right about induria—they'd once been used to navigate the maze.

Rylan nodded to her encouragingly. She blew out a long breath and unwrapped the crop from her hand; then she unclasped the buckles of Bothymus's fetter and removed it from his bridle. Beneath it was Bothymus's lucerta, a bluish scale standing out among the glittering white. She put the crop and fetter in the purse at her belt.

Bothymus was nearly eighty years old. He'd had many riders. He'd traveled much of the Holt and the length of the Whitefells. He was well trained—by the eyrie master, Stromm, and his father before him. Even so, a voice in her head whispered that what she was doing was foolhardy and would likely get them all killed.

Her doubts vanished, however, when she stared into Bothymus's moonstone eyes. An unexpected calm came over her. Bothymus wouldn't harm her, nor would he harm the others. Quite the opposite. He would do anything to protect them.

On their flight to Yeriel's shrine, Rylan had told her what bonding felt like. He'd said it was love and familiarity and trust. *Feorinh*, he'd called it, the Old Kin word that meant sharing and experiencing at the same time. She was not bonded to Bothymus, yet she felt sympathy from the dragon, felt him reaching out to her, a beckoning of sorts.

When she raised her hand, Bothymus lowered his head. Lorelei put her hand on his snout. "Shall we try?" Bothymus craned his neck and gurgled, like he did when Stromm approached him with a dead ferret, and Lorelei laughed. "Okay, boy."

As Rylan, Ash, and Creed corralled Vedron and Ruko and crowded them near Bothymus, Lorelei considered the moss-covered stones. She'd read about how ferrymen entered the maze. She'd even spoken to one to calm herself before her first crossing. When they placed lucertae on their tongues, the maze and its myriad threads became known to them. Most ferrymen needed to have been to a particular vyrd before they could travel to it—to get the unique signature of the place in their mind so they could propel themselves toward it. Lorelei knew the vyrd at Glaeyand all too well.

Cantlight waned. Time was running short, but Lorelei didn't rush. She placed her palm on Bothymus's glittering blue lucerta, closed her eyes, and felt the forest around her, felt the great citadel trees reaching toward the sky, felt their roots delving deep into the soil, felt the brightness of the vyrd and the gossamer network— the veins below the earth—connecting one vyrd to the next to the next, far and wide, impossibly complex, fearfully powerful.

As she had when she'd traveled to Glaeyand, she suddenly felt as if she were choking, only this time, the cords wrapping her neck didn't feel like branches. They felt like roots. It felt as if she were trapped underground. And she felt angry, wrathful. She would tear the world apart, if only she could free herself.

She blinked and found herself standing in another vyrd, but it wasn't Glaeyand's—the stones were set on a hill, and the nearby citadels were younger and much shorter than those around the tree city. The stones beneath their feet were covered with patches of dried blood, dark and muddy brown. In a clearing at the base of the hill lay an onyx dragon, its head a crushed mass of flesh, bone, and horn. The air was thick with the smell of rot.

Ruko, staring at the dead dragon, shook her neck and rattled her barbs. Vedron uttered a long, mournful note that made the hair on the back of Lorelei's neck stand up.

"This must be where Blythe challenged Llorn," Rylan said. "Where they were attacked by the Seven."

Lorelei was listening, but she felt lightheaded. The trees and the stones around her wouldn't stay in place.

Creed was suddenly next to her, holding her waist to steady her. "You all right?"

"Yes, but . . ." Lorelei took a deep breath and let it out slowly; the dizziness began to fade. "I felt something in the maze." She pointed east, away from Glaey-and, in the direction the feeling had come from. "Something terrible. Something angry and vengeful . . ."

Creed rubbed her back gently. "It's alright. Take it slow."

"Creed, I think . . . I think it was Faedryn."

Creed frowned. Then he kissed his fingertips and pressed them to his forehead. "Faedryn is trapped. He's *been* trapped for an age." He peered into the trees. "You sure it wasn't Yeriel?"

Lorelei though about it. "Not entirely, no."

He squeezed her shoulder. "Whatever the case, you're safe now, yes?"

She smiled. "I hope so."

"I know this place," Ash said, looking around. "Master Renato called it the Torchlands."

"That's right," Rylan said, "though the name hardly fits anymore. It was the site of a terrible battle in the Talon Wars. The forest burned for days."

"How far from Glaeyand does that put us?" Creed asked.

Rylan glanced at Lorelei. "Still quite far, I'm afraid, but we've come a good distance from the Rookery."

"Can you try the maze again?" Ash asked.

Lorelei looked up at the darkening sky, and a sinking feeling settled in her stomach. "I'm sorry, but no. We should fly the rest of the way."

Creed pursed his lips, but nodded at Lorelei. "You did well. At least now we might make it to Glaeyand in time."

They mounted and departed the vyrd immediately, Rylan and Vedron first, then Creed and Ash on Ruko. Lorelei, the last to leave, touched Bothymus's shoulder and whispered, "Thank you."

Bothymus arched his neck back and warbled a long note. Lorelei took out the crop and fetter from her purse. The golden chrysalite glittered in the twilight. The stones felt different to her now—not only unnecessary, but cruel. She stuffed them back into her purse and climbed into the saddle. Bothymus spread his wings and carried her through the forest.

EIGHTY-SEVEN: RHIANNON

Rhiannon knelt in the forest's murky dimness, Nox barely shining through the canopy overhead. They'd reached Lodrik's Vale, which some claimed was the site of the first of the many vyrda Lodrik Runeforger had made in the Holt. Morraine had just finished the fourth spanning, and she was weak. It was time for another feeding.

Rhiannon steeled herself as Morraine knelt across from her. It began as it had the other times, but Rhiannon was tired, too. She felt like she'd only just recovered from the last one. In mere moments, her hands were shaking. Her lips trembled. She felt like a shell with nothing inside her, and that soon she'd simply tip over and die. "Slow down!" she cried. "Please!"

Morraine looked disappointed, even angry, and the feeding went on. When the world started to spin around Rhiannon, Morraine finally stopped, but she did so abruptly, even though she knew it added to Rhiannon's discomfort.

Rhiannon coughed and fell backward.

Morraine stared down at her. "I need more."

"I know," Rhiannon whispered. "I only need some time to rest."

"*You* offered this."

"I know, but you're taking more than you used to. It's too much."

"It takes what it takes."

"Just let me rest. Please."

Morraine looked as though she were going to spit out some biting reply, tell Rhiannon to suck it up or some such, but she looked into the vyrd and said, "We're nearly there, child. Gather yourself. I'll need only one more after our next crossing."

It was no comfort. The next spanning would deliver them to Glaeyand, then came Ancris itself, which would set into motion the destruction of that ancient city. What Yeriel had told Rhiannon continued to haunt her. Their plan to steal Strages from the Hissing Man would not only devastate the empire, but the Kin as well, the very people Morraine claimed she was trying to protect.

Llorn limped toward them. He'd taken a number of wounds in the fight with Blythe and the attack by the Seven, but Brother Mayhew had tended to him as best he could and given him a few pinches of aura and umbra to speed the healing process. Gwilyn, the ruby-eyed dragonrider with the copper hair, had come through the battle miraculously unscathed. They'd been forced to leave Maladox behind when they entered the maze, but he'd rescued a wounded dragonrider and flown

Brother Mayhew's onyx to meet them at the next vyrd. Sadly, the dragonrider had lost too much blood and died shortly after.

Llorn stood with Maladox, Gwilyn, and Morraine, all but ignoring Rhiannon. "We need to leave soon, but only if you can make it to Ancris by reckoning."

Morraine stared up through the trees. Nox hung like a pendant between two citadels. Half the night had already passed. Even if they started crossing now, they'd be lucky to reach Ancris by reckoning.

"We'll make it," Morraine said.

"Are you absolutely sure? I can't begin if—"

"We'll make it," Morraine repeated.

Llorn finally looked at Rhiannon. "Can you give her what she needs?"

Faedryn's dark smile, she wished she'd had time to talk to her mother alone. She wanted them to give up on this horrible plan, but she was afraid of what Llorn might say, what he might do. Not only that, she was still shaking, and no longer even wanted her mother to feed from her.

In the end, she merely nodded. Llorn would leave soon; Rhiannon would try to convince her mother then.

Llorn glared at her. "Can you give your mother what she needs or not?"

"I can," she said. She had no choice.

Llorn nodded. "Morraine, I'll leave Maladox and Brother Mayhew with you. Gwilyn will join me to rally the others. The attack begins shortly before reckoning, so be ready."

"What of Camadaea?" Morraine asked. "Has everything been arranged?"

"I'm off to meet with her now."

Rhiannon wasn't sure who Camadaea was, but just then she didn't care. She only wanted Llorn to go away.

"Very well," Morraine said.

Llorn left on Fraoch, taking Gwilyn and his auburn dragon with him. Maladox was in quite a state. Having lost his bondmate to the sudden attack by the ivory dragon, he wandered around the vyrd, muttering to himself; he wouldn't eat or drink or even rest by the fire. Rhiannon was still haunted by the image of the onyx dragon raking its wings over the ground. Irik had shared a bond with Tiufalli for only a short time, and he'd been devastated when Morraine had consumed his dragon's soul. How deep would the sorrow be for a man who'd shared a bond for decades?

Brother Mayhew limped with his wyvern-claw staff to Ircundus and whispered something in the dragon's ear. Ircundus groaned, then reared up, launched herself into the air, and winged away from camp.

Brother Mayhew watched her go, then set to building a fire. "Gather some brightcaps won't you?" he called to Maladox. The glowing mushrooms, when ground into a poultice, helped fight off infection.

Maladox nodded and walked into the forest.

Fortunately, Morraine didn't much like sitting by fires. She stayed in the dimness at the edge of the vyrd, staring toward Glaeyand, her eyes glowing faintly blue, which gave Rhiannon an opening to speak to her alone. She stood and walked over to her.

"What will happen with Strages?" she asked.

Morraine took out Yeriel's shard and stared at it. "I told you. He will become a weapon, which the Kin will wield against the empire."

Rhiannon picked up a stick. "It seems a great load of trouble to go through." She dug her thumbnail into the stick's soft bark. "And it's dangerous to try and control a paragon, don't you think?"

"Perhaps, but remember what I told you—the greatest rewards come only with the greatest risks."

"Do you really think you can control him?"

"We . . ." Morraine said, indicating the shard beneath her dress. "*We* will control him, or have you already forgotten?"

"Yes. Do you really think *we'll* be able to control him for long?"

Morraine frowned, further wrinkling her ashen face. "Why are you asking questions, child?"

"It's only"—Rhiannon pointed at the vyrd with her stick—"we're closer now. And once we do this, we can't turn back."

"There was no turning back once you raised me from the dead, Rhiannon. I will see this done."

"But you said you were doing it for the Kin."

"I am."

"It's not for revenge over the empire killing you?"

The soft blue glow in Morraine's eyes brightened. Her skin was so pale, she looked like a snow cougar, creeping hungrily down from the mountains in the depths of winter. "Were the men who tortured me in Caldoras here now, I would flay them alive, but our plans were set in motion long before then. We will free the Kin from the yoke the empire has placed on us. The empire is a blight upon the world, Rhiannon. It must be destroyed for our people to prosper."

It all seemed to make sense, except for one part. "Do you know much about Strages?"

"I know enough. And what does it matter? We'll have his shard."

"You don't think he could break free?"

"Break free . . . ?" Morraine glared down at Rhiannon. "Did Yeriel speak to you?"

Rhiannon's first instinct was to lie, but she this was probably the last chance she would have to speak to her mother alone. "She told me how cruel Strages was. She showed it to me in a vision."

"A vision of lies."

"It didn't feel like lies."

"And how would you know? You're foolish little sparrow who got caught up in something far too big for her."

"I'm not a sparrow." Rhiannon felt a lump growing in her throat. "And what she said made sense. We don't know what will happen if we awaken Strages."

"It's a risk I'm willing to take."

"What if I'm not?"

"Say what you mean, child."

"All I'm asking is for you to consider—"

"Hush! You made a veiled threat. I want it spoken plainly."

Rhiannon wished she could take it all back and start over. She could apologize and say she didn't mean anything by it, but she knew if she did, she'd regret it forever. "You need me for the crossing."

Morraine cackled. "Oh, I do, do I?"

"Yes, you do. You're too weak to span the next link in the bridge. I can feel it."

Morraine's eyes widened and glowed like blue fire. "I can take it from you."

"You can try," Rhiannon said, "but you'll use more power than you get."

"Would you care to test that theory?"

Rhiannon stood there, breathing hard. She'd said it. Now she hoped it was true.

Morraine raised her right hand toward Rhiannon, her eyes brightened, and Rhiannon coughed as she felt her essence being drawn from her. Balling her hands into fists, she tightened every muscle in her body and drew on the very same reserves her mother was trying to take from her. Like a swordswoman parrying her enemy's attack, she blocked her mother's attempts to draw power from her.

Morraine's chin quavered. She tried again and again, and Rhiannon's muscles soon ached from her efforts to protect herself. At one point, her knees buckled, but she righted herself and kept fighting. Finally, Morraine lowered her hand, gasped for breath, and roared in anger.

Brother Mayhew, staff in hand, limped closer and stared at them. "Morraine, is all well?"

Morraine glared at him, then at Rhiannon. "Have you forgotten Tiufalli so soon?" And she rushed toward Brother Mayhew, one hand raised.

"Brother Mayhew!" Rhiannon shouted. "Run!"

Brother Mayhew didn't so much as glance at her. He stood straight as a spear, eyes wide, body quavering, as he stared into Morraine's glowing eyes.

Rhiannon ran at her mother. "Stop it!"

Morraine backhanded her so hard she fell to the ground. Blood filled her mouth.

Maladox returned to their camp, cradling an armload of sickly green mushrooms. He still seemed distracted, but when he saw Morraine, hand stretched out toward his brother, he dropped the mushrooms and screamed, "My Lady, stop it. Please! You'll kill him!"

Morraine ignored him and stepped closer to Brother Mayhew. He fell to his knees, and she stared down at him, mouth open. Brother Mayhew, eyes eerily wide, opened his mouth. A soft blue light emanated from it, reflecting off the facets of the shard hanging on Morraine's chest, and drifted toward Morraine's open mouth. Brother Mayhew flung his arms flung wide. He craned his neck back and looked up to the night sky. Then his eyes fluttered closed and he fell face-first onto the ground, his wyvern-claw staff thumping down beside him.

Maladox ran to his brother and dropped to his knees. "Mayhew?" He shook Mayhew hard. "Brother!"

Morraine spun around to Rhiannon. "You see what happens when you defy me?" She pointed to the vyrd. "Now go to the stones."

"I won't," Rhiannon said.

Morraine stalked toward her, and Rhiannon retreated.

"I won't," she repeated. "You're vile, evil, like the creature you're about to unleash upon the world!"

Morraine glanced at Maladox. He was holding Brother Mayhew tight to his chest, rocking him back and forth. She glanced at Rhiannon once more; then she spun around and headed into the vyrd. Filled with the power she'd stolen from Brother Mayhew, she had more than enough to complete the bridging, likely enough to make it to Ancris as well.

A blue light gathered around her, attenuating outward, then drawing back toward her. Then, with a rising whistle like some distant songbird, she was gone.

EIGHTY-EIGHT: RHIANNON

Rhiannon stood by Maladox as he knelt on the ground beside Brother Mayhew. She felt useless. Felt responsible for everything that had just happened. There were times when she'd prayed to Alra that Brother Mayhew wouldn't return from one of his frequent trips to the Deepwood. Now she wished she could bring him back. He'd been harsh with her at times, but she was old enough now to understand why. The power of aura and umbra was nothing to trifle with. He'd been trying to protect her and everyone around her from her foolishness, her impulsiveness—he knew the danger she could cause without proper training. For Brother Mayhew, that was caring.

She wiped the tears from her cheeks and said, "I'm so sorry."

Maladox, mistakenly thinking the apology was meant for him, looked up. "Not your fault."

The *whoomp* of beating wings drifted down from the sky. Rhiannon looked up to see Ircundus, dark violet in Nox's light, gliding down. The onyx landed with great flurry of pine needles. Rhiannon spun away to avoid catching a face full of them. As the needles rained back down, Maladox stood and walked toward Ircundus.

Ircundus clawed the earth with her wing talons and roared. Maladox tried to pat her head, but Ircundus shook him off. Rhiannon had seen Bellicor grieve after Aarik was put to death. The dragon had raged so long and violently that Ayasha had fed him lamb doused in milk of the crown thistle to sedate him.

Rhiannon expected the same from Ircundus. Perhaps Maladox did too, but after a short fit of gouging furrows in the undergrowth, Ircundus quieted and went still. A moment later, she raised her head, approached Brother Mayhew slowly, and stared at him. Then, in a gesture eerily similar to what Maladox had done, she lowered her body to the ground and lay her head on Brother Mayhew's chest. Maladox joined her for a time, leaving Rhiannon to watch in awkward silence, an unwelcome witness to their grieving.

Eventually Maladox stood and took a shovel from a pack near the fire. He went into the woods, chose a spot, and began digging.

"I can help," Rhiannon said. She wasn't sure how, precisely, but she wanted to do *something*.

"Just stay out of the way, girl."

As Maladox dug, Rhiannon cut a branch from a willow tree, twisted it into a wreath, and placed it on Brother Mayhew's head. When Maladox returned to get Brother Mayhew's body, he stared at the wreath and nodded at Rhiannon. Then, he picked up his brother, carried him to the grave, and laid him gently down in it. He walked back for the wyvern-claw staff and carried it to the grave. "May you find peace, brother, but if not"—he crouched and wrapped Brother Mayhew's finger's around the staff—"at least you'll have this."

Ircundus watched the entire affair, silent as a deer mouse. As Maladox began throwing dirt over Mayhew's corpse, she snaked her neck, pounded her tail, and trilled a dragonsong of a sort Rhiannon had never heard before. When it was done, she launched into the air and flew to the upper reaches of the citadel trees, alighted on a bridgebough, and continued singing.

Maladox, half lit in orange light by the campfire to his left, stared at the mounded earth. "He was a miserable cuss sometimes, but he cared about his brother. He cared about our mother. And he cared about the Holt."

Rhiannon, feeling too small for the moment, said, "And he was a good teacher, too."

Maladox looked at her, then ambled toward the fire and sat on a log. "Harsh, though . . ."

Rhiannon sat cross-legged on the ground across from him, still feeling a little like an intruder. "Sometimes he was." She might have left Maladox in peace, but she didn't want to go near the grave or linger in darkness. "I'm sorry she took him."

Maladox stared into the flames. "I told you, it's not your fault."

"I know, it's just . . ." Rhiannon was aware how very short of allies she was at the moment, and she was becoming progressively more uncertain of Maladox. There was a good chance he might give Rhiannon over to Llorn to gain his favor. She needed to know where his loyalties lay. "I mean, I didn't want to provoke her, but it didn't seem right, what she and Llorn are doing."

Maladox threw another log on the fire, sending sparks flying.

"You said Brother Mayhew cared about the Holt," Rhiannon continued hesitantly. "*I* care too, about everyone, not just the Kin. And I think Yeriel cares, too. What she showed me—"

"Briar and bloody fucking bramble, girl, stop your yammering." He looked up and fixed her with his teary, red eyes. "Your mother's to blame, understand? *She* killed my brother. Don't think I don't know it."

Before he could completely shut her up, she blurted, "I won't help them, Llorn *or* Morraine. Not anymore."

"I didn't ask you to." Maladox paused, and his eyes narrowed. "What, you think I'm going hand you over you to them?"

"Would you blame me if I did?"

Maladox looked into the fire and touched the bruise above his right eye. "Would you care to know how I got this?"

"I already know. You fought Brother Mayhew."

"Yes, but why?"

"I don't know."

"I knew Llorn betrayed Aarik, knew it before Blythe came to challenge him. Or I was pretty sure of it, at least. I told Mayhew I was going to leave the Knives.

He didn't take it well, but eventually he convinced me that leaving would be like signing my own death warrant. Fool that I am, I believed him."

Rhiannon couldn't imagine what he must be thinking now that his own brother was dead less than a day later. "You're going to leave now, aren't you?"

He shrugged. "That's not your concern. My point is this. Llorn's a snake who deserves to rot beneath the roots. I won't stop you from leaving."

For a time, all Rhiannon heard was Ircundus's haunted trilling, the buzz of crickets, and the occasional snap of the fire. Far into the woods, a pair of wisps floated gently among the trees. Rhiannon was just beginning to wonder if she should make some food when Ircundus suddenly ceased her singing. She dropped from the bridgebough and arced away, into the forest.

Maladox watched her go, then stood in a rush and peered in the opposite direction. "Get back."

"Why? What's—"

Three dragons approached through the forest. At first, Rhiannon thought they were Llorn's, but two of them were radiants—one a silver, the other a mighty indurium. The third was a viridian, and there were four riders in all, one each on the indurium and the viridian, two on the silver.

Maladox picked up his war axe as they dismounted. "Who are you," he bellowed while striding toward them, "and what business have you in the Holt?"

The shortest of the three men, a Kin, gazed at Rhiannon instead of Maladox. He had curly hair and a comely face. He looked very familiar, but just then, with the orange fire flickering and Nox barely shining down, Rhiannon couldn't place him. Two of the others, a big man with piercing eyes and a slender, timid-looking woman, wore imperial inquisitor's uniforms. The fourth seemed to be a very handsome man, but he hung back out of the firelight.

"Hello, Rhiannon," the curly-haired man said. "I'm Rylan Holbrooke, Sister Merida's son. We met a few years ago at the abbey?"

Rhiannon suddenly remembered their short visit. They'd shared some honey muffins and gone on a short walk around the abbey, though Rhiannon had mostly dawdled while he talked to Sister Merida. "I remember," she said. "You're her foster son."

"That's right." Rylan smiled awkwardly, then stepped closer to the fire.

Maladox took a step toward him, gripping his axe in both hands. "I asked you your business."

Behind Rylan, the male inquisitor drew his rapier. "Friend, I'd put that down if I were you." He had a strange accent Rhiannon had never heard before.

"I'm no friend of yours, farlander," Maladox snarled. "Now, if you know what's good for you—"

"Please," said the woman, "we mean you no harm." She stepped forward and stood next to Rylan. "We're from Ancris, and we only wish to speak to Rhiannon."

Maladox made no move to lower his weapon. "I'm getting more than a little tired of asking why."

"We believe Ancris is threatened, and that Rhiannon may be able to help."

Maladox gaped at Rylan for a second, then lowered his axe and looked back at Rhiannon.

She'd never felt so scrutinized as she did just then. She knew she was partly to blame for everything that was happening.

"Rhiannon, I'm Lorelei," the female inquisitor said. "I was at the barrow mound when your mother was raised. I saw . . . I saw you almost stop the ritual."

She was right, and Rhiannon now wished she really had stopped it. But she wondered if these people just wanted to use her, like Llorn and her own mother had used her.

"We have reason to think you've had second thoughts," Rylan went on, "not only about the ritual, but about everything that's happened since." He stepped closer, stopping just out of range of Maladox's axe. "We have little time, Rhiannon, so I'll speak plainly. We need your help. We're trying to stop Llorn, trying to stop your mother. Me"—he pressed his hand to his chest—"a man from the Holt, a Kin"—he gestured to the others—"and three people from Ancris who I've come to care very much about."

The inquisitor Lorelei arched her eyebrows, but Rylan seemed not to notice.

"We've joined in common cause," he went on, "because what Llorn and Morraine and others are planning is wrong, and I think you know it."

They were saying precisely what Rhiannon had been thinking, but she was starting to feel overwhelmed. She was just a girl from the Holt who'd been swept up in what was looking more and more like a war. "I tried standing up to her"—she pointed to the grave at the edge of the forest—"and all it did was get a man killed."

They turned to the mounded earth and then looked at her again.

"I'm very sorry about that," Lorelei said, "but this time you'll have *us*. We can work together."

A moment passed in silence. Rhiannon didn't know what to do, but she knew she wanted to do *something*.

"Rhiannon, please—" Rylan took another step toward her.

"Oy!" Maladox raised his axe and held it at Rylan's chest. "No closer."

They were all staring at her. She felt cowardly, a betrayer, the worst insult among the Kin. "Let me speak to Maladox alone."

When none of them moved, Maladox lifted his axe and pointed toward the forest. "You bloody heard her! Back off!"

Rylan looked like he wanted to say more. Lorelei too. Then the big man with the penetrating eyes touched their shoulders and nodded to Rhiannon. "Take your time," he said, and led Rylan, Lorelei, and the handsome man away.

A whippoorwill sang in the distance while Rhiannon waited for the four interlopers to move beyond the edge of the firelight where their dragons were huddled.

Rhiannon sat on the log, wishing once again she could run away with Irik to some distant part of the world. Maladox sat beside her, but kept his axe in hand.

The firelight played over the bruises and abrasions on his face and made his braided beard look like it was on fire.

"I don't know what to do," Rhiannon said.

She was sure Maladox would howl at her for even considering helping them, but he just stared into the fire and tapped the haft of his axe.

"Mayhew and I were in a tavern in Tallow once," he said finally, "we were young—it was years before Mayhew joined the druin—and we were drunk. Not falling down drunk, but drunk enough that Mayhew was itching for a fight, didn't really matter who with. The town fool might've sufficed, but he chose a bloody legionary who, for some fucking reason, was drinking alone in a Kin tavern in the Kinnest part of a Kin village. Maybe the legionary was looking for a fight, too. I don't know. I tried to talk Mayhew out of it, told him no good can come of it, but he kept cursing at the man." Maladox nudged the edge of a burning branch with the tip of his boot, sending a curl of embers toward the canopy. "Mayhew threw the first punch. The legionary was strong, well trained. I really had no choice but to step in and help. We beat that fool senseless. Nearly killed him. Even then, even as drunk as I was, I knew, every time I hit him, I was digging the entire village into deeper trouble."

In the darkness of the forest behind them, Ircundus keened.

"What happened?" Rhiannon asked.

"Mayhew and I left for the fens that night. A full bloody imperial cohort arrived in Tallow the next day. They beat the villagers bloody. Cut off fingers, toes, hands, feet. Even hung three men, including the tavern owner, who refused to tell their commander who we were."

Rhiannon felt sick to her stomach. "Why are you telling me this?"

"Mayhew was blinded by drink. Not me, though. I knew better and still didn't stop him. Your mother is blinded, too. Blinded by her rage for what the empire did to her, blinded by vengeance, blinded by the chance to strike back at the empire she hates, which is what Llorn and the Hissing Man are offering her. She'll do anything to make it happen. Doesn't matter what happens to the Kin or anyone else, so long as it hurts the empire."

Rhiannon had felt that same yearning in her mother through their link.

"The story you told about what Yeriel showed you in the pond," Maladox continued. "Did you believe her? Do you think Strages will attack the Holt?"

Rhiannon nodded. "I do."

Maladox pursed his lips. "I do, too. Seems to me that you and I have a choice to make. We can stand by and let it happen"—he looked toward where Lorelei and Rylan were huddled with the others—"or we can try to stop it."

"But my mother's already gone to Glaeyand. She might already be on her way to Ancris." She glanced at the standing stones. "And I don't even know if I can use the vyrd again."

"We'd be fools to go that way, anyway."

"What are you saying?"

"We fly, girl. Glaeyand's not far by dragonflight. Ircundus will take us there."

"But Llorn will be there. There'll be a dozen dragons, maybe more."

"No doubt about it, it's going to be dangerous. Let's say I can get you close, though. Can you stop your mother from completing the last bridge?"

"I can try."

Maladox shook his head. "Not good enough. Can you do it or not?"

"I think so."

Maladox stared at her, eyes glittering in the firelight. "Close enough." He slapped his hands on his knees and stood up. "Oy!"

Maladox waved Rylan, Lorelei, and the two others to join them around the fire.

"I'll help," Rhiannon told them, "but you should know, Llorn's rallied many Red Knives and their dragons. He's planning make some sort of statement at the council of quintarchs."

"He knows Glaeyand will be well protected," Maladox went on. "He's prepared what you might call 'a commensurate response.'"

"Meaning what?" Rylan asked.

Maladox shrugged. "He plans to attack the eyrie at reckoning to give Morraine time to span the final bridge to Ancris."

"We'll do our best to warn them," Lorelei said, "but the most important thing is to stop your mother."

"I think I can," Rhiannon told her, "but I need to get close first."

Lorelei nodded. "I think we can make that happen. We have three"—she stared toward Ircundus—"perhaps four dragons. We can create a distraction of our own."

Maladox frowned. "You're going to need more than that."

Rylan's eyes narrowed. "You have a suggestion, I take it?"

"I do." Maladox stood and, as Rhiannon had heard Brother Mayhew do with Ircundus more than once, whistled a string of trilling notes. Nothing happened.

"You plan to whistle?" Rylan asked.

Rhiannon winced.

"Damn dragon," Maladox said. "It's not mine. It's . . . it was my brother's." He whistled again, this time a little more smoothly. "C'mon, girl."

Rhiannon heard the *whoomp* of Ircundus's wings. She emerged from the forest and landed a few paces from the fire. "Ircundus will get her close." He faced the onyx and spread his arms. "Won't you, girl?"

Ircundus lumbered closer, stared down at Maladox and Rhiannon, then lowered her head. It was far too soon for them to have bonded, but Maladox approached Ircundus slowly, pulled a hunting knife from his belt and slipped the tip beneath Ircundus's lucerta. The scale glittered in the unlight a midnight blue. With a simple twist of his knife, Maladox pulled it off her.

Maladox turned to Rhiannon. "Know how to use one?"

She shook her head.

His smiled, a mouthful of yellow teeth. "Don't worry. I'll teach you."

Ircundus swung her great head until one eye was even with Rhiannon's, and growled.

EIGHTY-NINE: RYLAN

As Rylan and the others flew toward Glaeyand, Vedron's strength began to flag. She could carry him a good distance, but she wasn't known for her endurance like a brass, an amber, or even an auburn. The wind blustered, and the air smelled of rain. Nox hung over the horizon behind a thin layer of clouds, dark as a rotted plum.

Lorelei rode Bothymus to Rylan's right. Behind them were Creed and Ash on Ruko. Rhiannon and the burly cuss of a Knife, Maladox, on the onyx, Ircundus, brought up the rear.

Maladox's low rumbling voice carried over the distance now and again. He was teaching Rhiannon how to use the lucerta he'd harvested from Ircundus. In a short while, Rylan, Lorelei, Creed, and Ash would make for Glaeyand's eyrie while Maladox brought Rhiannon as close to the vyrd as possible. Rhiannon would then use the lucerta to gather darkness around her, sneak to the vyrd, and stop her mother from completing the final segment of the tunnel to the vyrd in Ancris. Ash believed it would prevent the geoflare in Ancris, but their plan felt doomed from the start. Rhiannon was just a girl. She'd never used an onyx lucerta before. She'd never used *any* lucerta, she'd admitted before they left Lodrik's Vale.

"We should *all* go to the vyrd," Rylan had said on hearing the plan.

"Four bloody dragons?" Maladox scowled and shook his head. "They'll tear us apart and eat us for breakfast. Our best bet is to get Rhiannon there *unseen*, and we can only do that if I take her there on Ircundus."

"He's right," Creed said. "And if the rest of us fly hard for the eyrie, there's a chance we can fend off Llorn's attack and send a flight of fucking dragons down to help. We might even gain the upper hand if we're quick enough."

Rylan had grudgingly admitted it wasn't a terrible plan. For all their size, onyxes were silent fliers, and their dark scales absorbed much of Nox's unlight, making them difficult to spot. It still bothered him that so much depended on Rhiannon, but try as he might, he couldn't think of anything better.

A steady drizzle started to fall as they neared Glaeyand. Maladox guided Ircundus below the canopy, planning to head south and sweep toward the vyrd from another angle.

Watching them go, Lorelei said, "I'm worried, Rylan. There are so many unknowns."

Rylan spotted the lights of Glaeyand through the trees. "I'm worried, too. Llorn needs to make sure Morraine has enough time at the vyrd, but he may view the council as a chance to—"

"Hush!" Creed shouted. "Can you hear it?"

Over the steady thrum of their dragons' wings, Rylan heard the faint bleat of a horn.

"That's a warning horn," Creed said.

"Yes," Rylan said, "but it's a fire warning."

As they neared the city, the twinkling lights grew brighter. What he'd assumed were the myriad lanterns of Glaeyand was a massive fire, spread over what looked to be dozens of citadel trees. Dragons were flying above it—silvers, brasses, golds, induria, their flapping wings and shining scales like molten metal in the firelight shining up from below.

"They've torched the eyrie," Rylan said.

Creed called over from Ruko, "We need to go to there, Lorelei. Lend what help we can."

Lorelei swung to face Rylan. "He's right. If we can help turn the tide at the eyrie, we can send some help down to the vyrd."

A silver dragon blinked from one location above the treetops to another, then dove, toward what, Rylan couldn't see. "Go," he called to Lorelei. "The quintarchs and my father are likely well guarded, but just in case, I'll fly to Valdavyn and warn them to be ready for an attack."

Neither of them stated the obvious, that an attack may already have taken place.

"Be safe, Rylan."

"You as well."

Vedron dipped below the canopy. It being night, the needles of the citadel branches were drawn in, giving him less cover, but he kept the broad trunks of the citadels in front of him as much as possible. Lightning crashed overhead, lighting up Valdavyn between the citadel trunks ahead.

Quietly now, Vedron. Silent as a lynx. Vedron slowed the beat of her wings, reducing their *whoomp* to a soft *whooshing.*

As they flew closer, Rylan spotted an auburn dragon on the entry deck of the residence. Several bodies lay near it—guardsmen, likely caught by surprise. An auburn's breath could sap the life from anyone in its cloud. It was a miserable way to die.

Rylan bid Vedron fly wide of the residence so they could approach from another angle. He worried about the servants and even his family, but a reckless approach would only get him killed.

The citadel trees whipped past as Vedron curved and headed toward Valdavyn's rear deck. Another auburn, this one with a dragonrider, was perched on it. More dead guards were strewn at its feet. The only other access was the servant's deck, but Rylan needed to make sure it was clear first. He called to Vedron to land on a citadel a few trees from the deck.

Vedron swooped up and grasped the bark with her talons. Rylan peered around. Kreòs, Raef's amber dragon, was squatting on Valdavyn's roof, craning her neck to stare down at Raef and four Red Knives with longswords on the servant's deck, guarding a dozen kneeling servants, their hands bound with rope. Chamberlain Bashira was among the captives, as were the cook, Briar, and her daughter, Lyssa. The others were chambermaids, cupbearers, and scullions. Raef, also wielding a longsword, stood over them. Bashira looked to be pleading with him.

Raef hauled Bashira to her feet and dragged her to the edge of the deck. Rylan rooted in Vedron's saddlebag for his smoke packets only to remember he'd used the last of them in Ancris. But then his hand felt a cloth bundle. It was the crainh, the poison Raef himself had given Rylan to kill Kellen and Ezraela. Rylan gripped the package, taking care not to shatter the glass vial that contained the activating agent. *Quickly now, fly toward the deck.*

Vedron dropped from the citadel and sped toward Valdavyn. She landed on another tree some thirty feet above the deck. Raef had Bashira pressed against the railing.

Kreòs spread her wings and screeched. The four Knives stared up. Raef glanced up, swore, and pinned his sword to Bashira's chest.

"Let her go, Raef," Rylan shouted.

"I thought we had an arrangement, Rylan," Raef hollered up. "For your sake, for Blythe's sake, you were to keep your nose out of our fucking business."

"They've done nothing to deserve this. They're only servants!"

"I haven't come to debate. The Holt's liberation starts here, tonight. Examples must be made." Raef drew his sword back.

"Don't do—"

The sword flashed, but Bashira ducked and wrapped her arms around Raef's midsection. She grabbed the hunting knife from Raef's thigh sheath and tried to stab Raef with it, but Raef clubbed her wrist with his leather-capped stump, and the knife clattered to the deck.

Now, Vedron!

Vedron dropped and soared toward the deck. Rylan gripped the cloth bundle in his right hand and crushed the glass vial. The crainh began to hiss. Rylan whipped it down at the four Knives. The cube flew out of the cloth and a red mist billowed around it. The Knives shouted.

Kreòs swooped down from the roof, snapping her jaws. Vedron rolled away and swung down over the deck. Rylan leapt from the saddle and skidded to a stop. Vedron slid across the decking toward Raef. Raef clubbed her with the stump of his left arm. Vedron crashed into Raef and Bashira. The railing gave way, and all three plummeted over the edge, Vedron snapping her jaws at Raef.

The Red Knives howled and coughed on the deck. Rylan covered his nose and mouth and rushed toward the servants. "Up!" He helped Briar to her feet. "Away from the cloud!"

The servants clambered to their feet and rushed away from red cloud. Rylan and Briar followed them. The gas was spreading quickly, but Rylan hustled them to the far side of the deck.

One of the Knives staggered out of the cloud, but he was no longer holding a sword. His eyes bulged, and he choked, bent over and retched. Then he fell to the deck and lay still. Rylan drew his dagger and readied himself for another Knife, but the breeze swept the red cloud away and the other three were sprawled on the deck.

Rylan scanned the trees. He'd lost sight of Kréos, and still didn't see the massive amber anywhere. He turned around and cut the ropes from Briar's wrists.

Vedron screeched and then roared from below the deck.

Rylan handed his dagger to Briar. "Free the others." He rushed toward the railing and leaned over.

Kreòs was clinging to the underside of the net, and Raef cutting through the net toward his dragon. Bashira was crawling across the net toward a rope ladder. Vedron clawed toward Raef, but the spongy net bounced her up and down awkwardly. She opened her mouth and spit a green stream at Raef, but Raef hacked through the net and plummeted onto Kreòs's shoulders. Kreòs turned and faced Vedron, spread her jaws, and shot a stream of clear liquid on the net and on Vedron's wings. The sticky serum cracked and began to solidify.

"Don't let it harden!" Rylan shouted. "Breathe on it!"

Vedron was already doing so, breathing on her wings to prevent them from sticking to the net.

Raef struggled to maneuver into the saddle with only one hand. When he finally did, Kreòs dropped and flew away through the forest. It wasn't like Raef to run from a fight; Rylan wondered just how much of the crainh Kreòs had inhaled.

The acid-doused net gave way under Vedron, and she dropped through it, spread her wings, swung around a citadel, and landed on the deck.

Below Vedron, Bashira reached the rope ladder and climbed up to a ringwalk. She stared at Rylan, haggard and bruised but alive. She nodded to Rylan, and Rylan nodded back.

"Drop down," Rylan told the other servants. "Join Bashira, and go to Tallow."

As the first of the others dropped to the net, Lyssa, her cheeks red, her hair wild, stepped across the deck and hugged Rylan. "Thank you."

Rylan hugged her back. "Go on."

Briar handed Rylan his dagger back. "You should go, too."

Rylan tilted his head toward the residence. "I can't. Not yet."

NINETY: RYLAN

R ylan peered warily through the trees for Kreòs, the auburns, or any dragons. He saw none, but that didn't mean they weren't on their way. He
couldn't leave Vedron outside, he decided. She'd be too vulnerable. She
was also cut on her shoulder, likely from Raef's sword, and Rylan could feel she
wanted revenge.

"We're not out to kill," Rylan said, "unless we can't help it. Understand?"

Vedron gurgled noncommittally, lowered her head, and nudged his knife
hand.

"Good idea, girl. Thank you." Rylan slipped the blade under the dark scale at
the center of her forehead and pried it gently. He felt a sting of pain through their
bond, and plucked off the lucerta.

He put the scale on his tongue. It tasted of copper and burnt sap, but it wasn't
wholly unpleasant. His mouth filled with spit, forcing him to swallow repeatedly.
As the flow of saliva eased, he pressed the scale against the roof of his mouth and drew
on its power. A low tone, like a distant bell, rang in his ears. He felt powerful—not
strong, but more like . . . indestructible. He had to be careful, had to remember
he wasn't really invulnerable, had to try not to get killed.

He mounted Vedron, but realized the servant's entrance wasn't wide enough
to accommodate Vedron's girth. He bid her climb onto the roof instead, then
guided her slowly and quietly toward Marstan's audience chamber.

Rylan had Vedron breathe a green spray on the cedar shingles. The acid hissed
and ate through the wood, the planking, and the framing below it, burning a hole
as big as a wagon wheel. Then he tugged on his dragonskin gloves.

Rylan lowered himself though the hole, dropped down, and landed on a
horsehair carpet with hardly a sound. He stepped aside as Vedron lumbered down
almost as quietly. They were in his father's sitting room. He opened both doors
and the body of a dead guardsman toppled into the room. Rylan recognized him.
Henrik. He'd always been gruff toward Rylan but he'd been loyal to the Imperator.

Rylan stepped carefully over the body and onto the long red carpet down the
center of the hall. He and Vedron crept to the end of the hall and though an archway to the main hallway of the wing. The doors to Marstan's audience chamber
and its anteroom were open. Rylan heard voices coming from it and padded toward it. Vedron followed, but Rylan bid her wait for his call. Vedron hissed
softly—she'd sensed a dragon ahead; Rylan guessed it was likely Llorn's cobalt,
Fraoch.

Rylan stepped into the anteroom. The spicy-sweet smell of cobalt breath lingered in the air. The double doors to the audience chamber itself were open wide. Marstan was sitting in the chair on the left side of the dais, clutching its carved wooden arms. He was staring at something in the near-left corner of the room, eyes wide as coins, shaking like he was having a fit.

Llorn stood at the base of the dais, a pair of Red Knives in dragonskin armor to his left, three more to his right. All had longswords at the ready.

Standing to the right of the dais was Quintarch Lucran, his left arm held tenderly against his chest, and the other quintarchs—Zabrienne, Yarina, Marle, and Drynon. All of them seemed a bit dazed, especially Marle, who kept blinking his one good eye, and Zabrienne, who swayed like she was ready to pass out. To the left of the quintarchs, Andros lay near the foot of the table, either unconscious or dead. Willow crouched near him, a cut above her left eye.

A dragon gurgled and a blue tail swung into view. Fraoch was hunkered just beyond the doors.

Lucran, sweating profusely, stepped closer to Willow. "Tell us what you want."

Llorn paced before the dais. "What I *want* is for the empire to leave the Holt forever, and for you to recognize it as sovereign territory."

Rylan slid his cutlass slowly from its sheathe and crept closer to the audience chamber doors.

When no one else said anything, Llorn said, "I thought as much. Failing that, perhaps you can give Morraine her life back, a life you stole."

"She committed crimes against the empire," Lucran said.

"*Crimes?*" Llorn spat. "She was caught in a crusade that *you* began. You lost a son, yes? Your precious Ransom died. We lost *thousands* when you attacked us because your little boy overdosed."

Willow looked at quavering Marstan, and she blurted, "Stop it! My father tried to *help* Morraine."

Llorn laughed. "Is that what you call standing by and as she was hung from a tree?"

"My father wasn't to blame for that."

"He did nothing to stop it."

"He was in no position to!"

Llorn stopped his pacing and fixed his gaze on Willow. "You're proving my point. Had the leader of the Holt had real power, the empire wouldn't have been allowed to kill her. It would have been up to us to see justice was done." Llorn stepped onto the dais and stood directly across from Marstan's chair and raised his sword. "I intend to change that."

Rylan sprinted into the room. "Stop!"

Llorn drove his sword through Marstan's chest with a sickening crunch. His quavering suddenly stopped as a torrent of blood flowed around the blade. Marstan groaned and his face turned red. He turned and looked at Rylan. Then he slumped forward and coughed blood into his lap.

Two Knives stalked toward Rylan, swords raised.

Behind them, Llorn wrenched his sword from Marstan's chest. "Stand back!"

His Knives exchanged glances, but they backed up toward the dais as Llorn stormed forward. Lucran and the other quintarchs were still frozen and staring at Fraoch.

Rylan knew trying to talk to Llorn would be useless. He met him halfway across the room and swung his cutlass at Llorn's neck. Llorn blocked it, quickly twisted his sword around, and swung it backhand at Rylan's stomach. Rylan jumped back, and the tip of Llorn's blade clipped his tunic.

"You're slow, Rylan," Llorn growled. "The empire has made you weak." He lunged forward and swung his sword two-handed down at Rylan's head. Rylan raised his blade just time, but the clash of metal sent a painful shiver up his arm.

Vedron begged to come to his rescue, but Rylan forbade it.

Llorn advanced again and leveled a mighty swing at Rylan's neck, Rylan ducked and staggered back, hit something with his heel, and he toppled backwards on his rear end. Fraoch's damned tail. The dragon gurgled wickedly.

Llorn stood over Rylan and stared down at him. "You should have stuck to thieving."

Rylan crept back a few inches, hand still holding his cutlass, and shrugged. "Maybe so." *Now, Vedron! Now!*

Vedron burst through the doorway. Fraoch snapped her teeth at Vedron's neck, but Vedron ducked, spun, and whipped her tail at Fraoch's head. Her sharp frills gashed Fraoch's neck, cutting scales and ripping flesh. Seeing Llorn distracted, Rylan rolled over one shoulder and gained his feet near the room's corner.

Fraoch, meanwhile, roared and scrabbled away, battering benches across the floor. Then she drew in a breath and opened her mouth wide. As a blue haze roiled at the back of her mouth, Vedron shot her head out like a cobra and streamed green acid into Fraoch's open maw. White smoke billowed up from Fraoch's mouth. She screeched and writhed into a corner, thrashing her tail against the benches, the wood paneling, the ceiling beams.

Llorn backed away from Vedron, fixing his gaze on Fraoch and whispering to her. The two Red Knives closest to him stared at him. Lucran swung a right hook into the jaw of the Red Knife next to him. The stout man fell like a tree. Yarina snatched a stiletto from her boot and drove it into the neck of the Knife standing beside her. A third Knife slashed at Drynon, but Drynon deftly dodged the blow and wrestled the man to the floor.

Willow snatched Andros's saber from the base of the dais and pointed it at the two remaining Red Knives. Quintarch Marle took up a fallen Knife's longsword and leapt beside her. Vedron hissed loudly and skirted along one wall toward the two Knives, and they climbed over the toppled benches toward Llorn.

Somewhere outside, a warning horn blew.

Fraoch slunk through the double doors into the anteroom. Llorn followed and motioned for his men to join him. "Consider this a short reprieve," he said to the quintarchs, then all of them were gone.

Willow stared at her father, slumped in his chair, blood pooled in his lap, then knelt by Andros's side. She checked Andros's pulse and blew a sigh of relief. Then she turned to Rylan. "How did you know they were coming?"

"A fellow in the woods told me." Before she could say more, Rylan held up a hand to her and looked at Lucran and the other quintarchs. "Not now. We need to rally everyone to the vyrd."

"The vyrd? Why?" Lucran asked.

"Because if we don't, Ancris is doomed."

NINETY-ONE: RHIANNON

Ircundus soared through the citadels, light rain pattering on the canopy overhead. Maladox gripped the reins, and Rhiannon held tight to his waist with both arms. In her right hand she held the lucerta Maladox had given her. She could still see Rylan, the inquisitors, and the other man flying to their right toward Glaeyand. Maladox guided Ircundus wide of the city. The blustery wind forced Ircundus to make adjustments as they wove between the citadels.

"Not far now," he said. "Go ahead. Put it on your tongue."

Rhiannon recited a silent prayer to Alra, then put the scale on her tongue. It tasted like burnt garlic and lemon rind. Ircundus hadn't looked back at her since they'd left the vyrd. The onyx did so now and uttered a low growl Rhiannon felt through the saddle.

Maladox leaned forward and patted Ircundus's neck. "Quiet now. We don't want to give them warning, do we?"

On the flight from the vyrd, Maladox had tried to prepare her. He'd told her the lucerta's magic would feel like her innate sense of the forest, but it was completely different. The world around her dimmed. Nox's violet light turned inky black, as did the citadels, their needles, even Maladox himself. They were pools of darkness, sources of power, he'd told her, that she could draw upon.

Rhiannon had sniffed umbris and used the power it gave her to cast spells. It made her feel heavy, as though each spell cast was a thread tying her to the earth and pulling her down. Ircundus being an umbral dragon, using the power around her was likely similar, only instead of drawing on the umbra *inside* her, she was using the lucerta to take it from a well that already existed.

She concentrated on the lucerta and its sour taste, drew upon the shadows, and felt herself becoming dark as the world around her. She heard a rushing sound, like a waterfall, and it grew louder and louder. Soon she could barely concentrate.

"Careful now." Maladox twisted in the saddle to peer at her. He was a shadow with diamond eyes. She could barely hear him over the roaring in her ears. "You're drawing too much from me and Ircundus. Reach all around, lest someone senses it. And believe me, the powerful and those who protect them will."

She tried to do it—to draw from everything, all around—but she felt the color returning to the world even as she did. Nox, especially, turned bright as fresh blood.

"Small steps, girl!" Maladox said. "Start overthinking and you'll lose it altogether. Just be aware of your surroundings. Drawing breath takes air from above and below, ahead and behind. Do the same with the shadows. Meld with them. It's easy, like humming a tune you already know."

Maladox, she decided, was a horrible teacher. Even so, she tried again. She focused on the trees that blurred by, the bridgebough they slipped under, the bed of the forest, and the world lost its color once more. Even Tallow, the glittering village below Glaeyand, seemed more like a charcoal rendering than a real place.

As they descended toward the village, she tried to draw more darkness around her, to hide Maladox and Ircundus as well, but Maladox reached back and grabbed her wrist.

"Don't. It's too much. You'll be thrown from the shadows." They dropped below the inner canopy and landed in an elm grove. Maladox helped her slip down from the saddle. "That way," he said, pointing.

Rhiannon nodded but didn't speak for fear of losing concentration.

"Quickly, now. You haven't much time." He drew Ircundus's reins over, and the onyx spread her wings and launched into the air, the *whoomph* of her wings a quiet thump under the roar in her ears.

As she headed through the forest, Rhiannon grew nervous. The task ahead seemed too big for her. She wanted to let the shadows go, spit out the lucerta from her mouth, and run away. But what her mother was doing was wrong, and Rhiannon had the power to stop it. She had to try.

She didn't know precisely where the vyrd was, but she didn't need to; she could sense her mother ahead and to the left. She clutched the knife Maladox had given her, the one he'd used to pluck Ircundus's lucerta, and crept through the forest quietly, beyond the elm grove then across a deer path and finally to the foot of a towering citadel. She kept the shadows near. The roaring in her ears rose and fell, making her worry she was making too much noise and that whoever was guarding Morraine would hear her. The garlic taste on her tongue grew so bitter her nose wrinkled and her lips drew back.

She could just make out the twinkling burrows of Glaeyand in the citadels above her and, beyond them, a flickering gray glow. A fire, she realized, leeched of color.

When she reached the next citadel, she peered over a tall root and saw three dragons lying in wait. Ruby-eyed Gwilyn was there and another two dragonriders she didn't recognize. Both the dragons and the riders stared up as a warning horn sounded. Then, the rumbling roar of a bronze broke the relative quiet. Flames burst between the trunks and branches of the citadels, but the umbrals didn't move.

An arrow streaked through the air and *thunked* into the trunk of a citadel near Gwilyn. Gwilyn ran toward his auburn dragon as another clattered from a trunk next to him. "There!" he called and pointed as Maladox and Ircundus swept past.

Gwilyn vaulted onto his auburn and flew after them. The other dragons followed, leaving the way ahead unguarded. Rhiannon opened her locket, sniffed a healthy pinch of auris, and felt the power of aura infuse her. She left her hiding place and rushed through the forest. Overhead, a battle was spreading around Glaeyand's eyrie. Dozens of dragons, both radiant and umbral, swept through the air. But the shouting and the clash of blades dwindled as she reached the vyrd's clearing. Morraine was kneeling on the stones. Rhiannon could sense her reaching toward Ancris. Rhiannon gripped the knife in both hands and crept between two standing stones.

"Throw off the shadows, child."

Rhiannon stopped. Her mother's voice was as clear as if she had whispered into Rhiannon's ear. Morraine didn't move. Knowing she couldn't keep it up much longer anyway, Rhiannon let the shadows go and felt unencumbered, *lifted* by the aura within her. The roaring fell away, and the clamor and cry of fighting dragons filled the air. Colors rushed in; the forest come alive around her, especially the ferns, which glowed pale purple in Nox's anemic light.

Morraine stood and turned to face Rhiannon. The shard of the Heartstone glittered like a fallen piece of the firmament on her chest. She looked down at Rhiannon's knife and laughed. "Do you think to stab me with it?"

Rhiannon shook her head. "I've come to give you one last chance. Give up before it's too late."

Morraine grinned, her face grisly and blue in the glow of her eyes. "Or you'll what?"

"Please, Mother, this has gone too far. You don't know what you're doing."

"Tell me, child, what am I doing?"

"You're going to destroy Ancris, and you're going to awaken Strages. But you don't know what will happen after that. No one does. So stop!"

"No. We've come too far. We will have justice."

"This isn't justice. It's revenge."

"You keep making the same mistake, child. I don't do this for me, but for everyone who's been wronged by the empire, and for all those who *would* have been wronged had I done nothing." She stalked toward Rhiannon. "When the Holt is ours again, you'll see I was right."

Rhiannon had thought about this moment, agonized over it, ever since the she faltered at the ritual. Morraine's life was an illusion. She'd died a decade ago—she was merely clinging to life like a parasite. All Rhiannon had to do was cut the ties that bound her to flesh and bone, and Morraine would become a wisp again.

Rhiannon concentrated on the knife, used it as a focus to guide the aura within her. She swiped the knife through the air and an arc of golden light sped through the air toward her mother, severing one of the ties that kept her alive.

Morraine stumbled backward. Her eyes widened. "What are you doing?"

"What I should have done weeks ago." She swiped again, and another arc swept through her mother's frail form like a scythe.

"Stop it." Morraine staggered to a standing stone, leaned against it, and blinked hard. The glow in her eyes was dimmer than only moments ago. "Stop it!"

Rhiannon felt the emptiness in her gut yawn wide. Her mother was trying to feed from her again, and it happened so fast, she went weak in the knees from it. Her chest felt like it was on fire. She slashed the knife, and another line scythed through the air.

Morraine collapsed to her knees. "Rhiannon," she grumbled, "they deserve so much more. You *know* they do."

Rhiannon stepped forward and slashed again. Another golden arc. Rhiannon could feel her mother's life slipping from her living corpse. "The dead should stay dead."

Morraine raised the shard. "We have so much yet to do."

To Rhiannon, the shard was the root of the problem. Her father had died because of it. Her mother wanted to destroy the world with it. It had turned Rhiannon's life upside down. Rhiannon stepped closer to Morraine, reached down and yanked it from her mother's neck, snapping the cord. She shook it before Morraine's glowing blue eyes. "You should have left this in Gonsalond!"

She was about to cut the last of the ties when a dragon screeched overhead. Fraoch was soaring down toward her, wings spread, mouth open. Llorn stood in the stirrups. Two auburns were behind them.

Rhiannon stumbled back, tripped, and the shard flew from her hand. She scrabbled in the grass on her hands and knees. *Found it!* Then she ran from the vyrd and hid behind a citadel. Fraoch landed near Morraine and roared.

Morraine, still on her knees, looked up at Llorn. "The vyrd—"

Llorn bent down and helped her up.

"—get in the vyrd."

Rhiannon raised her knife, but Fraoch swung her head at her and charged. Rhiannon sprinted into the forest and dove over a citadel root, certain Fraoch was right behind her. But when she poked her head above the root, Fraoch was beside Llorn in the circle the standing stones.

One of the dragonriders whistled and everyone look up. Dragons were swooping down toward the vyrd—Lorelei on Bothymus, Rylan on Vedron, the two other men on a big silver.

A golden dragon was in the lead. *"Aduro!"* the big man on its back roared, and the dragon's wings lit up and flashed so dazzlingly and bright Rhiannon shielded her eyes and spun away from it. She'd heard that Quintarch Lucran rode a gold dragon, but she wasn't sure.

When she opened her eyes again, Morraine was gone. "No!" Her sense of Morraine dwindled then vanished altogether. She felt a hollowness inside her, like part of her was missing. She fell to the ground and groaned.

Then the golden thudded down in the vyrd, and Rhiannon looked up. Lorelei followed on her great indurium, then Rylan on his viridian and the two other men on their silver. Bothymus spread his wings and lit them in a swirl of flashing blue-and-silver circles, and the two auburns launched into the air and flew away.

Somewhere, a high-pitched horn sounded. In ones and twos in the air high above, Rhiannon saw the Red Knives guiding their dragons toward the deeper forest.

Lorelei ran over to Rhiannon. "Are you okay?"

"Yes, but . . . but she got away!"

"It's all right," Lorelei told her. "You've done great. Quintarch Lucran is here with us and the other two men, who I failed to introduce to you when we met in Lodrik's Vale, are Creed and Ash. They have a—"

"Which one's the real cute one?" Rhiannon asked, then felt silly.

"That would be Ash," Lorelei said with a smile. "C'mon. I'll take you to them."

Quintarch Lucran was standing in the vyrd, shaking his head. Rylan, Ash, and Creed were standing next to him. Lorelei brought Rhiannon over.

Ash carried a case to the vyrd and began unpacking some weird-looking tools. He put them on the ground hastily and then picked one up and held it in front of his face. Then he shook his head and swore.

"Well?" Lucran asked.

"They've gone to Ancris."

"And the bridge?"

"It isn't as strong as the others, but it's there and . . . it's finished."

Lucran swayed slightly. "Can it be undone?"

"If so, I've no idea how." Ash began packing up his tools. "I'm sorry, Your Majesty. We're too late."

Lucran stared at the vyrd, then at the sky. Soft golden light drifted through the clouds. Reckoning had come and gone, the rainclouds thick enough to have hidden it. "There must be something we can do."

"There is," Ash stood and latched his case. "We fly back to Ancris and save everyone we can."

"But how?"

"By evacuating the city."

Lucran clenched his teeth. "How much time do we have?"

"The power shift has likely already started. A couple of hours, maybe less. It will start slow and then accelerate. When it does—" Ash paused and looked away from the quintarch. "When it does, Ancris goes *boom*."

NINETY-TWO: AZARIAH

Azariah had just changed into a fresh robe when the maze blossomed in his mind. A vision of Faedryn, trapped in a snarl of roots, came to him. The god stared at Azariah intensely, a demand for him to hurry so the final pages in the story of Strages' awakening could be written.

Azariah finished dressing and ordered Vattuo readied. Then he headed toward the temple's eyrie. Japheth joined him in the halls.

"I've news, Your Holiness."

A pair of young acolytes bowed as Azariah and Japheth passed them by.

"Go on," Azariah said.

"As you predicted, Llorn and Morraine appeared on Henge Hill a short while ago. A full squad of the quintarch's legionaries tried to capture them, but a host of Red Knives helped them escape."

"Where are they now?"

"In the city. We don't know where. Praefectus Damika has ordered dragons to search from the sky while soldiers go door to door."

When they reached the eyrie courtyard, an acolyte in a black habit was standing beside Vattuo, holding the old iron's crop. The dragons Azariah had ordered to fly above the temple circled in the sky overhead.

Azariah took the crop and climbed into the saddle. "Very well."

Japheth still looked confused. "Shall we search for them, Your Radiance?"

Llorn's claim that he'd raised Morraine only to assist in the bridging had always been laughable. He was planning to assault the shrine and take Strages, but he surely hadn't counted on the quintarch's forces waging a siege. And even if they somehow defeated the empire's hundreds of hardened soldiers, they'd still have to defeat the Church.

Azariah waited for the acolyte to leave, then said to Japheth, "Everything is well in hand. We still control of the temple and the shrine, and that's all that matters. I don't want it known we're worried about Llorn being in the city."

Japheth paused, then bowed. "Yes, Your Holiness."

Azariah snapped the reins and urged Vattuo to fly to the shrine. The old iron beat his wings and launched them into the air. Soon they were soaring over Mount Evalarus. As they angled toward the shrine plaza, Azariah gazed down at Henge Hill. The stones fairly glowed with power in his second sight. Even now, power was spilling into the palisade from the crucible. The earth below the city would soon erupt. All that was left was to tend to Strages and the Heartstone shard as the spell confining them was ripped apart.

They landed in the plaza. The clergy on the walls bowed, and a shepherd of the first order—an aging, bald fellow with a gray beard—rushed forward and held Vattuo's reins. "Your Radiance," he said.

Azariah dismounted, passed through the shrine doors into the antechamber. The room was empty and eerily silent—the alchemysts and laborers had all been expelled when Damika brought soldiers to the gates. Azariah walked down the tunnel to the shrine and wended his way up the causeway. At the top, Strages floated close enough to touch. The shard, bright in Azariah's second sight, floated above the ancient paragon. The thin tendrils of power snaking from the cavern walls to Strages had never been so bright. Their light cascaded along Strages' bandages, licked the desiccated skin of his face, entered the slits where his nose had once been, illuminating, ever so briefly, the inside of his head.

Azariah felt positively giddy. He spread his arms and shouted for joy. The shout echoed off the shrine walls, and Azariah smiled. Before the day was done, Strages would be freed. Azariah would learn how to control him through the shard; then he and the other illustrae could begin the next phase of their plan. They would wreak vengeance upon the quintarchs, the Holt, the world.

He'd thought surely Faedryn would feel the same as he did, that the two of them would rejoice together, but he couldn't feel his Lord within him. He felt Vattuo becoming restless out in the plaza and squeezed the crop, urging the cantankerous dragon to calm, but if anything, he became more agitated. Vattuo's annoyance likely stemmed from being watched by so many guards on the walls, but Azariah decided not to chance it—today of all days he had to take the utmost care.

He wound back down the causeway, considering all he must do in the coming days. If the histories about Yeriel's resurrection were accurate, Strages would need time to recover. It might take months, even years. In that time, the Church might be implicated in Ancris's destruction. It was why Azariah had arranged things so carefully. The predominating narrative must be that the Red Knives had orchestrated the attack. The meddlesome inquisitor, Lorelei, and her newfound ally, Rylan, had actually helped them by exposing Tyrinia's link to Marstan and, through him, Aarik Bloodhaven. If Azariah played his cards right, he might be able to shift some of the blame on them as well.

Which would help him install himself as the new quintarch. The Heartstone shard was the weapon Alra's Chosen needed to break Quintarch Lucran's hold over them. Then, when the time was right, Azariah would declare holy war on the Kin. He'd free the other paragons, wage a campaign deep into the Holt. It would give the Church all the reason it needed to assault the veil and Gonsalond itself. With Strages at his command, Azariah could tear down the veil, defeat Yeriel, and clear the path to Faedryn's prison below the Umbral Tree.

The Hissing Man was suddenly limping beside him. "Don't get ahead of yourself," he hissed, "not when victory is finally within our grasp."

Azariah felt he should be concerned about the sudden appearance of the Hissing Man, but he wasn't. The man was a scourge, but he was also Azariah's ally in the Chosen. Azariah outstripped him into the antechamber and then out to the plaza.

Vattuo shook his head, rattling his bridle. The iron dragon's wattle swayed as he uttered a low, threatening gurgle.

"What's happened?" Azariah asked a shepherd standing in the plaza.

The shepherd pointed up toward the mountain. "Four dragons with riders just landed in the temple."

"Who were they?"

"The other illustrae, Your Radiance."

Azariah paused. "You're certain?"

"Nearly so. They were wearing masks."

Azariah lapsed into silence. Their sudden arrival, he understood now, was why Vattuo was uneasy. But why would all of them have come? To witness the end, perhaps? To help defend the shrine? But if that was so, why wouldn't they have warned him?

The Hissing Man stood, bent and crooked, behind the shepherd. He looked angry enough to spit. "You spoke to them only yesterday."

"I know," Azariah said.

"They made no mention of it."

"I *know* . . ."

The shepherd's brows pinched in confusion. He looked around, then back at Azariah. "I'm sorry, Your Radiance. Were you talking to me?"

Azariah ignored him and mounted Vattuo. "Keep the gates locked while I'm gone. No one leaves. No one enters."

"Of course, Your Holiness." The shepherd bowed low and walked toward the gate.

Azariah gazed up at the shining white temple on the mountain. *Guide me, Faedryn, I beg of you.* He'd felt so certain he would be able to rely on the god's wisdom when the end was near, but the god remained silent.

The Hissing Man stared up at Azariah. "I don't like it."

"Nor do I"—Azariah snapped the reins—"but what is there to do?"

Vattuo roared and soared into the air. As they flew up over the wall, Azariah glanced back at the plaza. The Hissing Man was gone.

As they rose over the shoulder of the mountain, Azariah opened his locket for his umbris. Some of the black powder was carried away by the wind, but he didn't care. He took a healthy pinch and sniffed it. He flipped the locket and took some auris. By the time he neared the temple, he was brimming with energy. The aura was making him lightheaded, and his muscles burned from the umbra. He knew it was dangerous to mix the two, but he needed all the power he could get.

They glided over the temple walls to the eyrie courtyard, where, as the shepherd had said, four dragons hunkered with their riders: Camadaea, resplendent in a white robe and a golden mask; Ignatius in his mask of bone; Bahrian, wearing his iron mask and plain linen that, for Azariah, anyway, projected false humility; and Moryndra, who'd painted her eyes in black ointment and her lips in gold. Ignatius,

Bahrian, and Moryndra scintillated in Azariah's second sight—they'd all taken auris. Camadaea showed no signs of power, dark or bright. Azariah wondered why.

They landed near the temple steps, and the illustrae approached. Azariah dismounted and said, "I thought I made myself clear when we spoke yesterday. You are not needed here."

Camadaea's mask hid her eyes, but she seemed to take note of the missing chunk of ivory from Azariah's mask. He'd broken it the day before but could no longer recall how. "We need but a moment of your time," she said.

"I have none to spare, I'm afraid."

"It will take but a moment . . ."

Her self-assurance was unsettling. And Faedryn's silence haunted him. Had they spoken with their Lord? Had he given them some instruction? "Very well," he replied, "say what you've come to say."

"Not here," Ignatius said. "In your office."

Just then Azariah wished the ruthless little Hissing Man was with him. He would know how to get rid of these nuisances. He wasn't, though. Azariah was on his own. "This way . . ." He led them into the temple and up to his office. He was headed around his desk when, in his second sight, he saw Camadaea place a lucerta on her tongue.

Her voice purred in his mind. *Don't tell me you're surprised, Azariah.*

Azariah called on the aura within him. His fist burst into flames. He thrust his open palm toward Camadaea, but Ignatius, hands glowing as well, grabbed Azariah's wrist and yanked his arm up toward the ceiling. The flames crackled on the ceiling's thick wooden beams.

Moryndra grabbed his other hand. Azariah tried to kick her but she slipped aside, and Bahrian rushed up behind Azariah and slipped his arm around Azariah's neck. Azariah jerked free from Moryndra's grip and punched Ignatius in the face so hard his mask fell off. Ignatius bent over, clutching his face. Azariah could kick him in the head, but suddenly he didn't want to fight.

That's right, Azariah, Camadaea whispered in his head. *Relax.*

"But the cobalt lucerta," Azariah said, "how did you—?" But then he understood. "Llorn gave it to you."

Smart as a whip.

Learning the use of a lucerta, *any* lucerta, was no easy thing. Camadaea would have needed guidance. "He *taught* you how to use it as well."

Camadaea laughed bitingly. *Two marks for you! I went to him in the Holt, Azariah. I made him see that working with the four of us, as opposed to you and your twisted little friend, was in the Red Knives' best interests.*

Azariah felt Vattuo's distress, heard the sound of his trumpet through the balcony doors, heard another, louder challenge, then the *whoosh* and crackle of a bronze breathing flames. Azariah managed a single directive through the crop—*flee!*—before the will simply left him.

Camadaea strode toward Azariah, took the crop from his hand, and tossed it on the carpet.

"You would betray me for *them*?" Azariah spat.

Camadaea walked to his desk and rummaged through the drawers. *It's for a greater cause, Azariah. It's what needs to be done.*

A warning bell clanged outside. And then another and another until the city rang.

Camadaea took out a piece of fine vellum and placed it on his desk.

"But why would you help them?" Azariah asked. He was feeling desperate, helpless. "It weakens us!"

Camadaea merely smiled. *Sacrifices are sometimes necessary for the greater good.* She stepped away from the desk. *Now sit.*

Azariah obeyed through no will of his own.

Pick up the pen.

Azariah clenched his teeth, balled his fists, but soon enough his right hand picked up the pen and began to write.

> *Alra, goddess of light, how I've failed you. In my weakness, I became convinced that the path to glory—yours, not mine; never mine—lie in seeing our order rise to its rightful place. I sought out the sinful, I clasped hands with my enemies, hoping the Church would rise above the quintarchy.*
>
> *The empire was and always has been yours, but the quintarchs and their empire have blinded themselves to this truth. I still believe this to be true—the Church should rule the empire—yet by conspiring with our enemy, I have soiled your good name. I have given the quintarchs reason to doubt the illustrae—worse, to doubt the Church itself—and for this I beg your forgiveness.*
>
> *I make this confession not to absolve my sins, but so the Church may live on and spread your gospel to all corners of the earth. Through the choices I've made, many innocents will die. May you grant them peace through your light and your wisdom.*
>
> *Your most humble servant, now and always,*
> *Azariah Andrinus III*

Azariah stared at what he had written and shook his head. Outside, the warning bells continued to ring, and dragons roared. "Ancris will be destroyed. Who do you suppose will find this letter? Who do you think will care?"

"Quintarch Lucran will care very much," Ignatius said.

"So will Praefectus Damika," added Bahrian.

Moryndra nodded. "She suspects you already. We will tell them of your death when we meet with them shortly."

"And then you'll what? Hand the temple over to them?"

Before I answer that, Camadaea's voice hummed, *I need to know: Do you remember our talk after you met Llorn in the Wayward Oxen?*

Azariah frowned. "The Hissing Man met with Llorn. You know this."

She smiled again. *I thought so. Your affliction serves us well, Azariah. We'll tell*

Quintarch Lucran of the illustra who succumbed to Faedryn's lure, who plotted with the Red Knives, who killed his own son. We'll tell Lucran the man's mind, already weak, broke in that moment, that his ambitions only surged after that unforgivable act. We'll tell him you hoped to use the Red Knives to overthrow the quintarchy, that you fashioned yourself an emperor and would rule the empire alone. We'll tell him we confronted you, and that, when we said Alra would forgive you for your sins if you only confessed them, you requested time to do so. We granted that request, but sadly, when we returned to your office we found you dead, a knife through your heart and the note on your desk.

Four words echoed in Azariah's mind. *Killed his own son, killed his own son, killed his own son* . . . It was a lie. "You can't possibly think Lucran will be appeased."

Perhaps not, but it hardly matters what a ruler who let his own capital be destroyed thinks. More important is what Zabrienne thinks, what Marle thinks, what Drynon and Yarina think.

Azariah finally understood. He'd intended to sacrifice Ancris and use Strages to usurp power. Then they would attack the Red Knives and cement Azariah's claim to the throne. He would be quintarch and illustra, a ruler in the mold the Church had envisioned for centuries. If Camadaea had resorted to killing a fellow illustra on the very cusp of their success, it meant she was convinced their original plan would not work.

"You've learned something," he said. "You fear the quintarchs will unite against us."

I'm certain they will. We need a common enemy, Azariah, a powerful enemy. We need a threat that will allow us to raise the other paragons, and we won't have that unless the Red Knives control Strages.

"You can't. They'll use him to destroy cities. They'll kill thousands!"

If that is the cost of mobilizing the quintarchs against the Holt, then so be it. What matters is that the paragons are raised. All of them. That is Faedryn's vision.

With those words, Azariah felt Faedryn within him, and he was pleased. *Pleased!*

Azariah struggled to understand what might have changed. They'd hidden nothing from their Lord. He'd given his consent every step along the way. It made no sense . . .

. . . until Azariah recalled the wave of terror he'd felt coming from Faedryn, the way he'd forced him away from the Umbral Tree and back to Ancris. His best guess, never confirmed, was that Yeriel had discovered something dangerous.

Now you see, Azariah, Camadaea said. *We never accounted for Yeriel. We thought she'd stay behind the veil until we were ready. But Morraine upended all of that when she used Yeriel's shard in an attempt to master it, to master Yeriel herself.*

Without meaning to, Azariah gripped the hilt of the knife at his belt and drew it.

We need time to prepare for her. Your death buys us that. It buys us influence with the other quintarchs as well. So you see, you're still playing your part in freeing Our Lord.

Azariah gripped the knife in both hands and pressed the tip against his chest, just below his sternum.

Your death is crucial to all that follows. So rejoice!

He tried to drop the knife, but Camadaea smiled and he pulled it in, pierced his white robe, punctured his skin. He drove the knife deeper, blood coursed over his fingers, made the handle slick, and still he pushed the hilt toward his chest. He grew light-headed. Slumped from the chair. Fell onto the carpet. Thumped his head on the floor.

Camadaea stood over him and removed the blue scale from her mouth. "You're lucky, really. You will have an honored place at his side." She turned toward the doorway. "Farewell, Azariah."

Without another word, Moryndra and Bahrian trailed after her. Ignatius picked up his bone mask and put it on. Then he stared down at Azariah and sucked his teeth. Then he too was gone.

At the edge of the carpet, Vattuo's golden crop glittered. Azariah reached out and grabbed it. *Save me, Vattuo.* He felt nothing. He wasn't sure if it was because he was so weak or Vattuo was dead.

As his second sight dimmed, Azariah heard a soft crackling, like hot glass being plunged into cold water. It got louder. He felt it through the floor. The eruption had begun. The spell holding Strages was being torn apart.

Please, My Lord, I've worked so hard for this. Won't you at least let me witness it?

But Faedryn wasn't listening, or if he was, didn't care. A rumble of tumbling stone shook the temple, everything around Azariah darkened, whites and grays deepening to black. The last thing he saw was the ceiling splitting above him.

NINETY-THREE: LORELEI

Lorelei flew Bothymus toward Ancris. Quintarch Lucran rode Andrilor to her right. Rylan flew Vedron on her left. They had to get to Ancris in time to stop Morraine. At the very least, they needed to warn the people to evacuate. If they were very lucky, they might also be able to stop Llorn from stealing Strages and the Heartstone shard.

Lorelei glanced over her shoulder toward the trailing dragons, and Rylan called to her, "We haven't lost yet."

"I know, it's just . . ." She could hardly think. "Ancris is my home."

"There's still time to get everyone out of the city," he said, "and Ash said the last bridge isn't as strong as the others. Rhiannon succeeded in that much, at least."

"Yes, but that won't stop the geoflare."

They'd left Glaeyand with forty-three dragons, a force cobbled together from the dragons Quintarch Lucran had flown to Glaeyand, some from Glaeyand's eyrie, and some from the other quintarchs. More imperial mounts would be waiting in Ancris. Lucran had sent their fastest silver ahead to Ancris with orders for Damika to begin evacuating the city. Other dragons had been sent to neighboring cities and forts with orders to fly all available dragons to Ancris. They should have over a hundred radiants if they got there in time. Then they'd have to assemble and organize. And some of them would already be tired, especially the cohort they were flying back to Ancris. They'd left Ancris only the day before, fought, and were now flying back to Ancris with almost no rest.

They'd lost four dragons since they left Glaeyand. Ruko had been wounded in the shoulder in the battle for the eyrie. He'd seemed well enough when they'd departed, but when he began to flag, Lucran had ordered Ash and Creed to return to Glaeyand. Three more dragons had to drop to the citadels to rest, and several more looked like they would soon do the same.

Llorn might have twice their number, maybe three times, ready to fight. And their dragons would likely be fresh. Nearly as important as evacuating the city was preventing Llorn—or the Church—from taking Strages. Lorelei wished they'd hadn't been forced to leave Rhiannon in Glaeyand. She might have helped them with Morraine, but she was extremely weak after the attack, and Lucran reckoned it was better to keep her safe.

At last, Lorelei spotted Mount Blackthorn, then the palace, the imperial eyrie, and the barracks on its shoulders. When she was close enough to see Ancris, it was just as it was when she left. Rylan was right—they could still try to evacuate.

At the eyrie, most of the dragons were flying toward the training paddock and the meadow. Andrilor, Bothymus, and Vedron landed in front of the eyrie. Prae-fectus Damika and Skylar ran toward them. Damika was holding a sheet of vel-lum. She handed it to Lucran.

Lucran unfurled the vellum, wincing from the wound to his arm. "What of the evacuation?"

"It's underway," Damika said.

As Lucran asked about the numbers of evacuees, Lorelei stepped toward Sky-lar. "Where's my mother?"

She pointed toward Highreach. "In a shelter below the palace."

"Thank Alra. And thank you." She pointed to the vellum. "What's the scroll?"

"A confession from Azariah. He wrote it and took his own life, then Illustra Camadaea—"

"Wait, Azariah's dead?"

"According to Camadaea," Skylar said with a skeptical tone. "She and the other illustrae are all here in Ancris. Camadaea delivered the scroll to Damika person-ally, said she and the others came to clear the Church's good name."

"What of the shrine? We need access to it."

"That will be difficult. Camadaea insists that the Church guard it." Skylar glanced toward her father. "But now that you're all back, perhaps that will change."

A horn sounded—one low note followed by a high. The dracorae scanned the horizon. Several had already climbed back into their saddles. The eyrie master, Stromm, burst from the eyrie and ran toward them, waving his arms. "The Knives!" he bellowed. "The bloody Knives are here! Fly!"

Lorelei looked up. Dozens of dragons were headed toward the eyrie.

"Make for the shrine!" Lucran bellowed as he mounted Andrilor. "Secure the shrine!"

"Father, your arm!" Skylar called.

Lucran stared down at her. "Go back to the palace, now." He snapped the reins, and Andrilor lumbered forward, spread his golden wings, and launched into the sky.

Lorelei waved to Skylar. "I'll see you when it's over."

Skylar nodded and backed away. "Alra shine her light upon you."

Lorelei felt something in her gut, a giddy sensation, a restlessness. She leaned over toward Rylan. "I feel . . . funny."

He gaped at her. "Funny?"

"Not funny, but . . . look at Bothymus and Vedron." Bothymus was whipping his head back and forth. Vedron was lying on her side.

"It's the aura," Rylan shouted. "The geoflare is starting. We have to hurry!"

They heard a loud rumble. Lorelei thought it was thunder at first. Then she saw a tumble of rocks rolling from the shoulder Mount Blackthorn. "Look!"

"Alra save us," Skylar said. "Fly!"

"Lorelei, let's *go*!"

"Take care of my mother," she said to Skylar.

Skylar nodded and ran toward the palace.

Lorelei turned to Rylan. "To the shrine."

"Agreed," Rylan said, "but we need to skirt the battle."

"Right! Let's head south around Blackthorn, then cut back toward Evalarus."

Rylan nodded and snapped Vedron's reins.

They flew along the far side of the palace, and rounded Blackthorn's southern slopes, hugging tight to the rocky slope, dipping and rising with the landscape to avoid being seen by the Red Knives.

When they came around the mountain and could see Ancris again, the circle of earth inside the palisade was rising, breaking, splitting. Streets cracked. Whole neighborhoods rose into the air. Bridges across the Wend crumbled and fell, splashing into the water. The arch Skylar had helped build, and later dedicated for the victory in Syrdia, cracked in two. Half remained standing, the other half crumbled and scattered. The dome of the Curia Ancrata collapsed inward, sending a great plume of dust into the air. The hill where the Crag stood crumbled and came tumbling down. Up on Evalarus, the temple's flying buttresses fell into pieces, and the temple facade toppled forward and shattered. Above the temple, a dozen radiant dragons circled—the illustrae and shepherds guarding the shrine against the Red Knives.

The bedrock of the city continued to rise and split, but everything else, everything not imbued with aura, tumbled away. Tables and chairs tipped from homes. Crates of goods spilled from warehouse doors. Barrels and tuns toppled and spun, end over end from the door of a warehouse. Some struck a floating chunk of cobbled street and burst, spilling red wine over the edge like a waterfall.

The people of Ancris who hadn't escaped—too sick to move or refused to, to slow get out—tumbled into crevices from broken sections of streets, fell from splintered homes, plummeted down in ones and twos, and sometimes great groups. Some landed on other pieces of the city and miraculously lived, only to fall again when that island, too, broke apart. Many plunged into the dark crater of newly exposed earth that had once been below the city.

As Bothymus and Vedron flew toward the edge of the geoflare, Lorelei spotted a man and a woman hanging from the threshold of a house leaning over the edge of a piece of floating island. Rylan edged Vedron closer and was just a few feet away when the door frame cracked and the woman slid off into open air. The man tried to grab her hand, but he fell too, spinning and screaming down into the crater.

"No!" Lorelei roared as she watched them plummet. Her heart was in her throat, and it was getting harder to breathe.

"Lorelei!" Rylan shouted, pointing toward crumbling Evalarus. "Look!"

The Church's dragons, the ones that weren't guarding the temple, were leaving, flying north, away from the battle. The mystery of it brought Lorelei back from the edge of panic. "Why?" she hollered.

"I don't know," he said, "but it leaves us an opening."

Evalarus was a hundred big floating islands and thousands of smaller ones. Below it, broken pieces of the shrine were split on several smaller islands—parts of the quartzite floor on some, parts of its flame-designed quartzite walls on others. The causeway that had once led to Strages split over two pieces of earth. Lorelei swooped down for a closer look. Floating between two hunks of causeway, she saw Strages and his shimmering shard on a small slab of shrine floor.

Alra's ever-shining grace.

She soared back up and looked toward the dragon battle, radiants and umbrals of all colors in a tangle teeth, fire, and claw. She couldn't tell who was winning, but she could tell that Lucran and his dracorae were no closer to the shrine than the Red Knives or the Church's dragons.

"We have to get Strages!" she shouted.

"I know"—Rylan pointed—"but look."

Through a wide gap in the broken remnants of Evalarus, Lorelei spotted Fraoch and a large auburn flying hard toward the shrine. Fraoch had two riders: Llorn in dragonscale armor and Morraine behind him, gripping his waist. The Red Knife on the auburn was armored as well.

"Bothymus and I can distract them," Lorelei said.

Rylan nodded. "Vedron and I will go for Strages. Hold them off as long as you can!" He swept down, wove around a hunk of earth with the shattered remains of a blacksmith's forge still burning, and disappeared.

Lorelei grabbed her crossbow from behind her, cocked it, then took a bolt from the quiver, and lay it in the channel. Holding the crossbow in her right hand, she snapped the reins with her left and dug her heels into Bothymus's neck. She felt foolish for not having put Bothymus's fetter back into his bridle. She was just about to shout a command when the big indurium blared a single, high note and circled over the shrine.

"Thank you, Bothymus!" she bellowed.

Llorn and his dragonrider soared below her to the shrine and landed on the piece of quartzite floor where Strages and the shard lay. As Llorn and Morraine dismounted, the knife spotted Bothymus and pointed. Llorn took a longbow from the saddle and nocked an arrow. The auburn looked up at Bothymus, spread its frills, and roared.

Bothymus hurtled toward the shrine, snapped his wings out, and lit them up. It was like nothing Lorelei had ever seen. Raw energy blazed in expanding blue-and-white circles, teardrops, lemniscates. Fraoch stared up, utterly transfixed. Morraine looked up and her mouth fell open.

The auburn averted its gaze. The thick infusion of aura in the air seemed to have stolen its noxious breath away. Nevertheless, when its rider snapped its rains, it beat its wings and launched itself toward Bothymus, jaws snapping. Bothymus listed almost completely sideways, dodging the auburn's bite. Lorelei slid in the saddle but hung on to the saddle horn with one hand, the crossbow with the other, as Bothymus came back around and clamped his teeth on the auburn's neck, twisted his head and pulled the auburn's head from its neck in a spray of red gore. Its rider spilled from the saddle, struck the edge of the floor, and tumbled down toward the crater below. The last Lorelei saw of him was him gaping up at her with ruby-red eyes.

Morraine was still slumped in Fraoch's saddle, but the fight had left Lorelei dangerously close to Llorn, and she would have sworn she saw Strages move his head at Llorn's feet. When she looked at Llorn again, he had his bowstring to his cheek, a knocked arrow aimed at her. Lorelei raised her crossbow and fired. The bolt grazed Llorn's chin. Llorn grunted. Blood dripping down his neck, he pulled the string back again. As he aimed his arrow at Bothymus's chest, Vedron swung around the bottom of the broken causeway above them, knocked Llorn down on the quartzite floor and landed on Strages. Rylan jumped from the saddle, rolled across the floor, and snatched up the shard. Then he leapt up and sprung onto Vedron again. Vedron beat her wings, and with Strages writhing in her claws, took to the air. All he had to do was reach the edge and he could drop down, out of sight.

Llorn was back on his feet, bowstring at his cheek, sighting Vedron. He let fly. The arrow streaked through the air and sunk into Vedron's shoulder, just above the wing. Vedron shrieked and thudded down on the stone floor. Rylan tumbled from the saddle and slammed his head on the floor. The shard flew from his hand, clattering and tinging, skipped over the edge of the floor and was gone.

"No!" Llorn bellowed. He stared at the jagged edge of the floor, then he stomped toward Rylan.

Rylan lay still. Lorelei figured he was unconscious. She dropped the crossbow, leapt from Bothymus, drew her rapier, and sprinted at Llorn. She swung her rapier for his face. In one motion Llorn drew his sword, raised it and blocked the blow, their swords ringing like a warning bell. Llorn swung low, nicked her right leg, then up across her shoulder leaving a shallow cut. She slipped his guard and thrust at his neck, but he leaned away and her blade clacked off his dragonscale pauldron.

A dragon roared overhead. Llorn and Lorelei both glanced up at the sky. Five imperial radiants were diving toward them. Even if Llorn killed her, Lucran would get Llorn and Morraine, and Strages, too.

Morraine stared at the approaching dragons. Her eyes burned brightly, the color of wisps. She raised a skeletal hand toward Bothymus and screamed. A bolt of black lightning arced from her palm toward and pierced Bothymus in the chest. His silver scales smoked and burned. His skin turned black. Bothymus threw his head back and beat his wings backward, and his dazzling light show ceased.

"Strages!" Llorn bellowed. "Get Strages!"

Fraoch lumbered toward Strages. Lorelei tried to reach the squirming paragon first, but Llorn blocked her with his sword. She swung her rapier down at his neck, he blocked it, twisted his sword, and her rapier clattered to the floor.

Fraoch clamped her jaws around Strages, and Strages bared his teeth and groaned. As the cobalt dragon swept past Llorn, Llorn leapt, grabbed the saddle horn, and swung himself up in front of Morraine. Lorelei ran after them but dove to the floor as Fraoch whipped her tail and black barbs clacked against the white stones around her. As Lorelei pushed herself to a stand, Fraoch waddled to the edge of the shrine and dropped out of sight.

Lorelei ran limping to her crossbow, snatched it up, and darted to her quiver on Bothymus's saddle, but Bothymus was lying on it, writhing in pain.

She prayed Lucran's radiants would catch Llorn and Morraine, but her hopes were dashed when one of the Red Knives blew a horn and a host of umbral dragons flew to meet them. Even weakened by the aura, they were simply too many to overcome, and Lucran's exhausted radiants were barely beating their wings to keep themselves in the air.

As she watched them, she heard Rylan stir. He raised his head and looked around.

"What happened?"

"We lost him. We lost Strages."

NINETY-FOUR: AZARIAH

Azariah heard a dragon gurgling.

He coughed, and pain flared in his chest. He lay on his back on the hard tile floor of his office. His acid-ruined eyes still closed, he saw open sky above him. That seemed odd. He sat up and yanked the knife from his chest, screamed in pain, and used the umbra and aura still inside him to seal the wound and stop the bleeding. It still hurt but such is life; he could take the healing no further. Then he looked around. The entire wall behind his desk and most of the ceiling and roof were missing. Some broken beams were hanging down and chips of ceramic roof tile were scattered on the desk and the floor. Beyond that, hundreds of small chunks of land, many with buildings, or at least parts of buildings, on them, were floating in the air. Grunting from the pain, he pushed himself up, walked to the edge of the floor, and looked down. A crater of earth and rock, dark and gray in his second sight, spread far below him.

He heard the gurgling again, closer, and recognized it as Vattuo's. The dragon was flying under the temple somewhere.

He sensed the maze, but not Faedryn. A weight on his mind and his soul for so long, the god was simply gone. And Azariah himself felt different. He felt unencumbered, like he remembered himself again. But he also remembered what'd he'd done. He'd manipulated, he'd maimed, he'd murdered, and he found no solace in knowing the trickster god had forced his hand.

He also remembered what the Hissing Man had done—had made *him* do—to his son. He remembered it all now—straddling his son and driving his knife into his chest. Just when he thought he would go mad from it, there came a memory of another sort. He saw the Hissing Man standing alone on a floating hunk of rock. He was digging the earth with a shovel, then kneeling and placing a grave marker. Azariah recognized that place as Tortoise Peak. He knew the very islet the Hissing Man stood upon.

Vattuo groaned and popped his spear-shaped head up from below. *Hang on, Vattuo.* Azariah walked back across the floor to where he'd fallen. In his second sight, Vattuo's crop glittered on the carpet like an ember in ashes. He picked it up and clutched it tight. He sensed Vattuo's fear of being attacked again, his desire to leave this place, as he hobbled to the edge of the floor.

Azariah felt the dragon's hot breath on him. Gripping the edge of the floor with his wings talons, Vattuo stretched his head and neck over the floor. Azariah got down on his knees, climbed onto Vattuo's neck, and slipped backward, gingerly moving into the dragon's saddle. He grabbed the reins, snapped them, and

Vattuo dropped, spread his wings, and caught the evening air. Azariah groaned at the pain the sudden movements brought on, and when the old iron finally leveled out, he slumped forward.

They flew through the floating, fragmented remains of Ancris, flat-topped chunks of dirt floating silently in the sky, some as small as houses, others as big as the shrine and its plaza, some with ruined buildings on them, others with lawns and decorative trees, many with roots hanging down like tentacles. A horn blew—a warning that a dragon had been spotted—but he didn't see anyone chasing them, and they soared onward.

Hours later, under Nox's purple sky, he spotted the Tortoise Peak geoflare. It was quite a bit less impressive than the one in Ancris. Azariah urged Vattuo toward a particular floating isle and bid Vattuo land on it. Vattuo grumbled but eventually set down on a flat stretch of rock near its edge. As Azariah dismounted, his chest wound stretched, and he groaned and tumbled off the side of the saddle onto the rock. He pushed himself to his feet and staggered to a spade-shaped rock standing straight up from the ground.

He knelt before it. Though Nox's light was dim, his second sight allowed him to read the words etched into the rock's surface:

Here lies Cassian, beloved of Azariah

The Hissing Man had etched the grave marker after bringing Cassian's body to the isle and burying him. Staring at it, he remembered chasing Cassian through an apple orchard in the temple district. Eating crunchy green apples while he told Cassian about his mother. He remember Cassian standing as—

Footsteps approached—*thump scrape, thump scrape.*

"We're free," the Hissing Man rasped.

"I know. But why?"

The Hissing Man chuckled, then wheezed and coughed. "The question isn't *why,* but what to do about it."

Azariah's first instinct was to fly west as far as he could go and never come back. But he'd been a man of Alra once. A holy man. As had his son. He touched the grave marker. Felt the rough, cold stone. Trailed his fingers over his son's name, and a new purpose was born inside him.

"We'll find a place to hide," he said.

"We'll find a place to heal," the Hissing Man added.

"Then we'll go to the Holt and bring Faedryn's plans tumbling down around his ears."

The Hissing Man was silent for a time, then he laughed and laughed and laughed.

NINETY-FIVE: RYLAN

R ylan flew Vedron west over the foothills. A thick layer of clouds occluded
Nox's light, casting the landscape in murky darkness, but he could still
make out the dark outline of Mount Blackthorn and the glittering lanterns
of Highreach. The eyrie glimmered as well, though with far fewer lights. He
tugged on Vedron's reins and skirted well wide of both, to avoid being seen by a
nightglass.

The arrow in Vedron's shoulder hadn't damaged any tendons or blood vessels.
Rylan had managed to pull it out and dress the wound with the supplies he always
kept in Vedron's saddlebags, and she'd been able to glide down from the shrine.
The following morning, she was able to fly, albeit slowly.

More than a week had passed since the geoflare in Ancris. He'd left Ancris two
days after it. Though Lucran had guaranteed his safety, Rylan hadn't been convinced it would do much good. He, or anyone that even looked like Kin, was
likely to be shot on sight, so he'd left and made camp near Thervindal's Tor beside
the Diamondflow.

When they parted, Lorelei had held Rylan's hand. "I understand why you're
leaving, but I want you to know not everyone looks at you that way."

"Do you?"

He'd meant it as a joke, but Lorelei stared into his eyes and said, "You did as
much as anyone. I'll never forget that."

He found himself uncomfortable, showered by her kindness, but he thanked her.

"Skylar wants to talk to you as well."

"She does?"

The way Lorelei had glanced at Rylan's leather satchel made him nervous, but
she nodded and squeezed his hand. "I do, too. There's just been so much to do,
trying to cobble a working set of inquisitors together. Can you come back in a
week, after things have settled a bit?"

"I don't know, Lorelei."

"Please. It's important. We'll know more about how Lucran wants to respond
by then."

They both knew the attack and the theft of Strages was only the beginning of
the troubles for the empire and the Holt. "Where will I meet you?"

"Come at night. Look for a lantern among the islands."

"There'll be only one?"

She shrugged. "I imagine so."

Rylan peered at her. "Why so cryptic?"

"It's a surprise. Just come."

When the time came for their meeting, Rylan had mounted and Vedron soared over the forest toward Ancris. Golden lights glimmered in the valley ahead. Some were from parts of the city that hadn't been destroyed. Others were from refugee camps. In the center of it all was a dark hole in the earth. The land around the crucible had apparently lifted, enough to send the River Wend on a new course entirely, south around the crater.

He looked for a light among the floating islands but saw none. Perhaps Lorelei had been delayed, forgotten, or changed her mind. He was just thinking he might try another day when he saw a lone flickering light, high in the broken fragments of Ancris.

He flew toward it, over the largest of the refugee camps, where people were dancing around a fire, and a violin was playing a lively tune often played in the Holt to celebrate the end of harvest. The island ahead was so wide that several intact buildings and the broken remains of several more were on it. As he neared the light, he realized it was a brazier set in the center of what had been a city street. Three dragons hunkered near it: a silver, a brass, and a magnificent indurium—Bothymus of course. The silver was Ruko. Rylan didn't recognize the brass.

As he got closer, he saw that brazier lit up the door to a tavern behind it. Seeing its sign had the bright yellow flower of The Bent Tulip on it, Rylan laughed. "A surprise, indeed."

He landed and slipped down from the saddle. Vedron lashed her tail excitedly and gamboled toward Bothymus, cooing. Rylan was about to tell Vedron to be careful, but Bothymus lowered his head and touched his snout to her neck, and they rubbed their heads together gently.

Rylan smiled.

He heard conversation as he approached the tavern door. He realized he was a little nervous. He exhaled a long breath and opened the door. A candle in a brass sconce lit the entryway. In the dark tavern beyond, a lone table was lit by a dozen candles. Sitting around the table were Lorelei, Creed, Ash, and Skylar.

Lorelei, sitting closest to the door, beckoned to him.

Rylan stepped inside and closed the door. Only then did he see who was sitting at their table behind a thick wooden beam—Kellen bloody Vesarius. His face was still burned and blistered, and his left shoulder still bandaged, but he smiled and nodded.

Lorelei waved at the empty chair beside her. "Join us, Rylan."

"Yes!" Ash said, perhaps a bit more loudly than necessary. "Come join us, Rylan!"

Rylan looked at all the mugs and glasses filled with beer and other drinks, and asked, "Where's Eladora?"

"She told us to make ourselves at home," Lorelei said.

"She *ordered* us," Creed said, standing. He walked over behind the bar and filled a goblet with a dark brew. Then he brought it to the table and set it in front of the empty chair. "So sit. Drink."

Rylan sat, took the glass, and raised it around. "To better days."

The others, even Kellen, raised their drinks. "To better days."

Rylan sipped his a sweet, heady stout. It had notes of raisins, cinnamon, and, interestingly, a hint of rosewater. He licked the froth from his lips and set it down. "This is from the abbey in Thicket."

Creed winked. "I know."

Skylar looked around, seeming to check if anyone else wanted to speak. When no one did, she put both hands on the table, and said, "Thank you for coming, Rylan. We have a lot to discuss before we're too deep in our cups, the most pressing of which is Strages. We need to find out where Llorn has taken him and what he plans to do."

Rylan had barely taken a sip of his beer, but he quickly realized this was why they'd invited him. "And you think I can help with that?"

"You've done so once already."

"Yes, when Llorn had no idea what I was doing. If I so much as show my face in the Holt, he'll have me killed."

"I'm aware of the danger," Skylar said evenly, "but you have contacts in the Holt and in the Knives. We need to find out what they plan to do before it's too late . . . again."

"Start with Glaeyand," Lorelei said. "Learn what you can from your family."

"They might tell *you* what you want to know," Rylan said to her. "They might tell Skylar or Lucran, but they won't tell me. My father is *dead*."

"Yes, but you tried to save him. You were the only one who tried to save him."

Rylan stared at the thin layer of froth on his beer. "Perhaps I could speak to Willow, but the more I know, the more it'll help. When news of Marstan's attempt to make peace spreads, she might not be safe. Her whole family might not be safe."

"*Your* family," Kellen said.

"They were never my family."

"There's a lot to talk about," Skylar interjected, "but let's start with this. It appears the Church has disavowed all knowledge of Azariah and his—in their words—*unspeakable* betrayal of their faith. They've promised to make amends and help Ancris rebuild."

Lorelei stared at her, then said, "But . . ."

"But," Skylar continued, "a delegation from the other capitals arrived yesterday. The other quintarchs pledged their support, but I still think they blame us, blame *Father*, for everything that's happened."

"Meaning . . . ?" Rylan prompted.

Skylar shrugged. "It's too soon to tell if anything will come of it. A formal council will take place soon. Until then, we'll do our best to make clear who's at fault."

"You mean the Red Knives," Rylan said.

"Of course she means the Red Knives," Kellen said.

Rylan shook his head and stared at Skylar. "The quintarchs will hear *the Knives*, but they'll blame the Kin."

Skylar straightened in her chair. "Don't think the realities of the situation are lost on me. They aren't. I've asked for and been granted a seat at the upcoming council. Please believe me when I say I'll do my best to differentiate between the two."

Rylan was far from relieved, but he was also well aware there was only so much she could do. "I'll try, of course."

Skylar seemed to relax again. "Thank you."

Creed took a long swig of beer and set the glass down with a thump. "It's clear enough what the Red Knives want to do with Strages. The question I have is what Azariah had hoped to do with him."

Ash spun his glass in his hand and stared at it. Then he shrugged. "No one can do anything without the shard."

"The shard hasn't been found?" Rylan asked.

"The search continues," replied Lorelei, "but we're starting to think one of Llorn's riders found it."

"My point is," Creed said, squeezing Ash's good shoulder affectionately, "I'm not sure Azariah is not in league with the other illustrae. What would *they* have done if they nabbed Strages?"

"I've been giving that a lot of thought," Lorelei said, "and one thing keeps coming up. What if the shrines are actually prisons?"

"Prisons?" Creed reeled. "You can't be serious."

"I'm perfectly serious. What if they were prisons, like Faedryn's in Gonsalond?" She turned to Rylan. "Remember the inscription on Yeriel's shrine? *Here lies Yeriel Darksinger, Umbral Witch, betrayer of Faedryn and all his fell servants. May she atone for her sins when Alra rises again.*"

"So?" Rylan asked.

"What sins? And which fell servants? Could it be the paragons were not, in fact, Alra's allies? Maybe they were her enemies, and the shards were supposed to keep them, and Faedryn, in check?"

Rylan's mind spun. He had no idea what the truth of it might be, but he knew one thing: "That's blasphemy."

"In the eyes of the Church, yes, and I can see why. If gives lie to their most closely held beliefs. The Church and the Chosen would kill to keep it secret. Which might be why Azariah was willing to murder to get the chalice."

"The truth is buried in the past," Kellen said, "which is why I've brought this." He tugged open a canvas bag next to his chair, pulled out a twine-bound book with a wood cover, and set it on the table. "Nearly forty years ago now, Rygmora, mother of Llorn, Morraine, and Aarik, hid in the Holt after the empire learned she was resurrecting the ancient ways of the Kin. She was communing with the citadel trees in a ritual everyone had thought was lost during the Talon Wars. This"— he pressed his fingers of on the cover—"is a copy of an excerpt from the book of their ancient rituals, the Book of the Holt."

Lorelei's eyes widened as Kellen slid the book toward her. "Where did you get this?"

"I found it"—he glanced at Rylan—"during a raid in Andalingr while I was stationed there. For a long time, I thought it was nonsense. I nearly burned it for heresy but never had the heart to. Even if it is heretical nonsense, it's still a part of history."

Lorelei opened the cover. The first page contained several passages of flowing script in purple ink. "What's in it?"

"Mostly Rygmora's visions in her rituals that, as far as I'm aware, have been lost to other histories—the arrival of the Kin in the Holt, the bonding of the first dragon, the formation of the Alran Church."

"She might have made them up," Creed said.

"It's possible, but we know it was Rygmora who revived several lost techniques. The use of onyx lucertae, for example, and, later, of cobalts'. If you read it, it's hard not to believe her visions were accurate."

Lorelei flipped to the next page, apparently oblivious to the conversation, but Rylan knew her well enough to know she could read and listen intently at the same time.

"A passage in the original," Kellen went on, "describes the very ritual Rygmora used to commune with the trees and learn their buried knowledge."

"That ritual isn't in this book?" Rylan asked.

"Right. This one is a copy of a copy—it's incomplete."

"We need to find the original," Lorelei said, looking up from the book. "It could unlock everything."

"I'm not sure about *everything*," Kellen said, "but yes, I think we could learn about histories now lost to us and tell us a lot about what Azariah had planned and what the other illustrae may still be planning."

They talked more after that. They drank and told stories of the Sundering, as Ancris's destruction was now being called. Ash slowly cheered up and even laughed a couple of times. Kellen did too eventually. After a while, the candles started guttering out, and the conversation wound down.

"I really should head back to the palace," Skylar said. "I have an early meeting tomorrow. Kellen, would you mind flying me back?"

Kellen stared at Skylar, then Lorelei. "As you wish."

They headed toward the front door, but Skylar stopped beside Lorelei and touched her shoulder. "Arrange a time for us to speak again, okay?" Before Lorelei could respond, she left.

Creed tugged on Ash's sleeve. "We should be going, too."

Ash hugged Lorelei. "See you tomorrow." He kissed her cheek; then he nodded politely to Rylan. "Another day, hopefully soon."

Rylan nodded back. "Hopefully."

They left, the door thudded closed, and Rylan found himself alone with Lorelei.

"That was considerably more awkward than I'd expected." When Rylan, confused, shook his head, Lorelei said, "I asked them to give us some time together."

Rylan tried to force a smile.

Lorelei returned the smile, but it was there and gone in a moment. They blew out the candles and went to the entryway, where the room's remaining lit candle flickered in its sconce. "You risked a lot for this city, Rylan. For the empire."

"I didn't do it for the empire."

"I know, but you helped us just the same." She opened her mouth, closed it again. "You've been a friend. A real friend."

"So have you." Lorelei's gratitude was misplaced, but the words Rylan had spoken were pure, unalloyed truth.

Tears welled in her eyes, and she blinked them away. Then she leaned in and kissed his cheek. "Thank you. For everything."

Then she headed out the door, book under her arm. Rylan held the door open and waited for her to walk away. Vedron warbled, Bothymus snorted, and Lorelei flew away.

As he watched them go, Rylan touched his cheek where Lorelei had kissed him, noting the traces of jasmine perfume that still laced the air. Then he shook his head and banished the notion that she could have feelings for him. Surely, it was only gratitude and nothing more. He looked around the darkened room, picturing it alive with revelers, conversation, and song, then he blew out the candle and left.

As he mounted Vedron, he realized Lorelei hadn't offered to meet again. Perhaps she was just nervous. He decided it was for the best. She probably wouldn't want to speak to him when she learned what he'd done.

He flew east for several hours. Reckoning arrived as he neared Thervindal's Tor. By then, the sky had cleared, and the bright sun had risen. He landed and went to the dry hollow in the rock where he'd hidden his satchel, took it out and unwrapped the cloth bundle, and stared at the Heartstone shard.

He'd separated from the others the night of the Sundering, flown Vedron around the many floating islands near the broken shrine, and found the shard in the rubble of the shrine wall on a small island floating below the shrine floor. Then he'd flown away quickly, before Damika's search parties arrived.

It shone brightly in the early morning sun. The power he held in his hands . . . Llorn, the Church, the empire—they all would kill for it. He didn't know what to do with it, but he knew, as he'd known the moment he'd found it, that he couldn't trust anyone else with it. Not Lucran, not Skylar, not even Lorelei.

He folded the cloth back around it, put it back in the satchel, and slung the satchel over his shoulder. He felt terrible for not telling the truth of it to Lorelei.

"I'm sorry," he whispered, and touched his cheek.

He returned to Vedron. As he climbed into the saddle, he felt her desire to fly along the Diamondflow, to splash the water with her wings and slap it with her tail.

"That sounds wonderful," he said, and snapped the reins.

NINETY-SIX: RHIANNON

Rhiannon walked with Maladox along a deer path deep in the forest with their onyx dragon, Ircundus, lumbering behind them. The air was cool and humid. A fog rose off the damp ground after the nightlong rain. The clouds above the forest's canopy were still heavy and roiling.

The deer path led them to a shallow rise and then a gently sloping wood. Maladox wore a woodsman's cloak, Rhiannon her aspirant's robes. Both had their hoods pulled up to ward off the rain still falling from the trees. Birdsong filled the chill air. When a flying lynx yowled, Ircundus arched her neck and made a surprisingly similar call.

Rhiannon held Yeriel's shard, still wrapped in leather, in both hands and felt for the veil, for Gonsalond, for Yeriel herself, but as had been true for the past four days, she felt little besides a vague sense that Yeriel was *somewhere* ahead, which put Maladox in a temper.

"I want to stop traipsing about these bloody fucking woods, girl," he said, whacking the wet ferns with his walking stick.

"We will," Rhiannon replied.

"I want to sleep under a roof." The lynx yowled again, and he pointed up at it. "I'd even take a bloody lynx burrow at this point."

"I'm pretty sure they have dry places to sleep in Gonsalond."

"That remains to be seen. And we're about as close to Gonsalond as we are to Lux."

"You're being dramatic."

Maladox guffawed. "You said yourself the veil is impenetrable!"

"I found it once, remember?"

"Yes, but you said that was when the veil opened for the wardens. You found fuck all before that. Not surprisingly, that's the precise amount you've found since we left Glaeyand as well!"

Rhiannon spun around, and Maladox to come to a sudden, lurching halt behind her. "You whine as much as Irik, you know that?"

He stared down at her. "Not wrong, though, am I?"

What could she say? He was mostly right—not completely, but mostly. Searching for Yeriel felt like trying to thread a needle—no matter how careful she was with the thread, it seemed to avoid the hole at the last moment. The veil was preventing her from finding Yeriel. She turned and continued along the path.

"How do you even know we're anywhere near the veil?" Maladox called after her.

"Because I feel it."

"That's what you said yesterday." He whacked another fern. "And the day before that."

"I told you. The shard is tricky. So is the veil."

"Then how do you know you'll ever find it? We might walk these woods 'til the end of time, always thinking it's around the next bend."

Rhiannon had thought the exact same thing many times since she'd slunk away from the infirmary in Glaeyand. But she couldn't give up. It was too important. Yeriel was powerful. She knew secrets about Strages and the other paragons. Rhiannon had to find her.

Plus, the idea of going back to Thicket terrified her. She'd defied her mother. She'd tried to send her back to her grave. Morraine would never forgive her, and even if she did, Llorn certainly wouldn't.

Rain started hissing on the canopy again, dripping down onto the hood of her robe.

"Bloody fucking hell," Maladox said. "Let's go north and find the Diamond-flow. Skjalgard can't be far. We'll rest. Eat. Warm up. Then we can come back and try again."

Rhiannon stopped, turned, and looked at Maladox, then at lumbering Ircundus behind him. They were both exhausted and sopping wet.

"Fine. We'll go to Skjalgard, but only for—"

She stopped, for she'd felt something behind her, like clouds parting to reveal the sun.

"What is it, girl?" Maladox asked.

Rhiannon turned left and shivered. Yeriel was standing beside a citadel tree ten paces away. She wore a wool dress, blue and green, and dry. Her thick black hair writhed. Her skin was deathly pale, her lips lilac purple. Behind her, seven warrior women and seven ivory dragons, Yeriel's personal guard and their mounts, stood amidst the trees. They were the same women who'd attacked Llorn and Morraine at the vyrd in the Torchlands.

Ircundus spread her wings, pounded her tail on the damp ground. Maladox had promised to control the angry onyx if and when they found Yeriel. He seemed to be preventing her from attacking, but Rhiannon wasn't sure how long it would last.

"You would give up so soon?" Yeriel approached Rhiannon, barely glancing at Ircundus and Maladox. "Many people have searched for Gonsalond for years, and you're ready to give up after four days?"

"I wasn't going to stop."

Yeriel smiled. "Is that so?"

"I needed to find you."

"And why is that?"

"Because I need help. Because I think I can help *you*."

"How so, dear girl?"

"I might be able to stop Llorn. Stop my mother. Strages is free. You're going to need all the help you can get."

Yeriel did not reply, but the her snake-like hair began twisting frenetically.

Rhiannon unwrapped the shard and held it out. "I offer you this, as a show of good faith."

Yeriel's hair calmed. Her eyes widened and she took the shard. "You ask for nothing in return?"

"Just consider helping us and letting us help you."

Yeriel stared at Rhiannon for a time, her eyes glowing softly. "Come to Gonsalond, and we'll talk?"

"Very well." Rhiannon said. They were finally on their way. "Come on, Maladox."

"I'm afraid that's impossible."

"Maladox comes, or I'm not coming."

"Why should I care?"—she waved the shard in the air—"I have *this*."

"Because you said you saw something in me, remember? You offered to bring me to Gonsalond then."

"Because you were a threat."

"No, that was only part of it. You saw power in me. You said I was a true child of the Holt. That's why you wanted me to come. And that's why you're going to let Maladox and Ircundus come, too."

She felt a little foolish, blithering like a child, yet Yeriel's smile faded. She stared hard at Maladox, then at Ircundus. Ircundus roared.

Yeriel turned and headed back toward the Seven. "Very well, Rhiannon of House Bloodhaven. They may come."

Maladox was still stiff as stone. Rhiannon went to him and took his hand.

"You don't have to come," she said.

He looked at the ivories, at the hard-eyed women, at Yeriel. Then he squeezed her hand. "And who'd keep you out of trouble if I didn't, hmm?"

Rhiannon smiled. Still holding his hand, they followed Yeriel through the woods Behind them, Ircundus beat her tail on the ground, cooed, and stomped after them.